MADELEINE L'ENGLE'S

Received On

DEC 2 8 2022

Magnolia Library

A Wrinkle in Time

THE GRAPHIC NOVEL

NO LONGER PROPERTY OF
SEATTLE PUBLIC LIBRARY

ADAPTED AND ILLUSTRATED BY
HOPE LARSON

SQUARE
FISH

FARRAR STRAUS GIROUX • NEW YORK

SQUARE
FISH

An imprint of Macmillan Publishing Group, LLC
175 Fifth Avenue
New York, NY 10010
mackids.com

A WRINKLE IN TIME: THE GRAPHIC NOVEL.
Text copyright © 1962 by Crosswicks, Ltd.
Pictures copyright © 2012 by Hope Larson.
All rights reserved. Printed in the United States of America by
LSC Communications, Harrisonburg, Virginia.

Square Fish and the Square Fish logo are trademarks of Macmillan and
are used by Farrar Straus Giroux under license from Macmillan.

Square Fish books may be purchased for business or promotional use.
For information on bulk purchases, please contact
the Macmillan Corporate and Premium Sales Department at
(800) 221-7945 x5442 or by e-mail at specialmarkets@macmillan.com.

Library of Congress Cataloging-in-Publication Data
Larson, Hope.
    A wrinkle in time / Madeleine L'Engle ; adapted and illustrated by Hope Larson.
        p. cm.
    Summary: A graphic novel adaptation of the classic tale in which Meg Murry and her
friends become involved with unearthly strangers and a search for Meg's father, who
has disappeared while engaged in secret work for the government.
    ISBN 978-1-250-05694-8
    1. Graphic novels. [1. Graphic novels. 2. Science fiction. 3. L'Engle, Madeleine.
Wrinkle in time—Adaptations.] I. L'Engle, Madeleine. Wrinkle in time. II. Title.
PZ7.7.L37Wr 2012   741.5'973—dc22   2010044120

Originally published in the United States by Farrar Straus Giroux
First Square Fish Edition: 2015
Book designed by Hope Larson and Andrew Arnold
Colored by Jenn Manley Lee
Square Fish logo designed by Filomena Tuosto

15   17   19   20   18   16

AR: 2.7 / LEXILE: 740L

For Charles Wadsworth Cano and Wallace Collin Franklin
—M.L.

To Mom and Dad
—H.L.

Table of Contents

A Wrinkle in Time

1
Mrs Whatsit

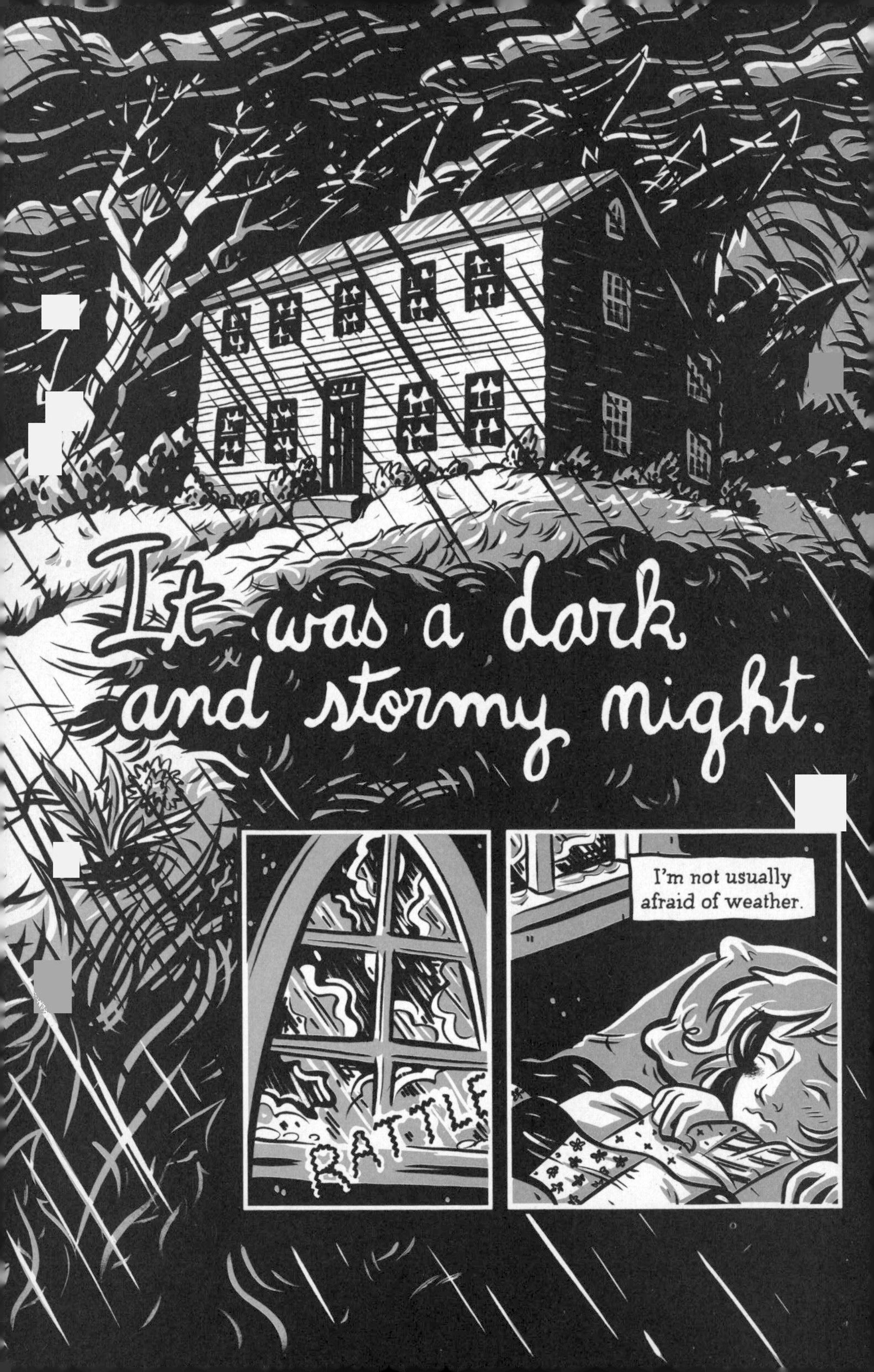
It was a dark and stormy night.
RATTLE
I'm not usually afraid of weather.

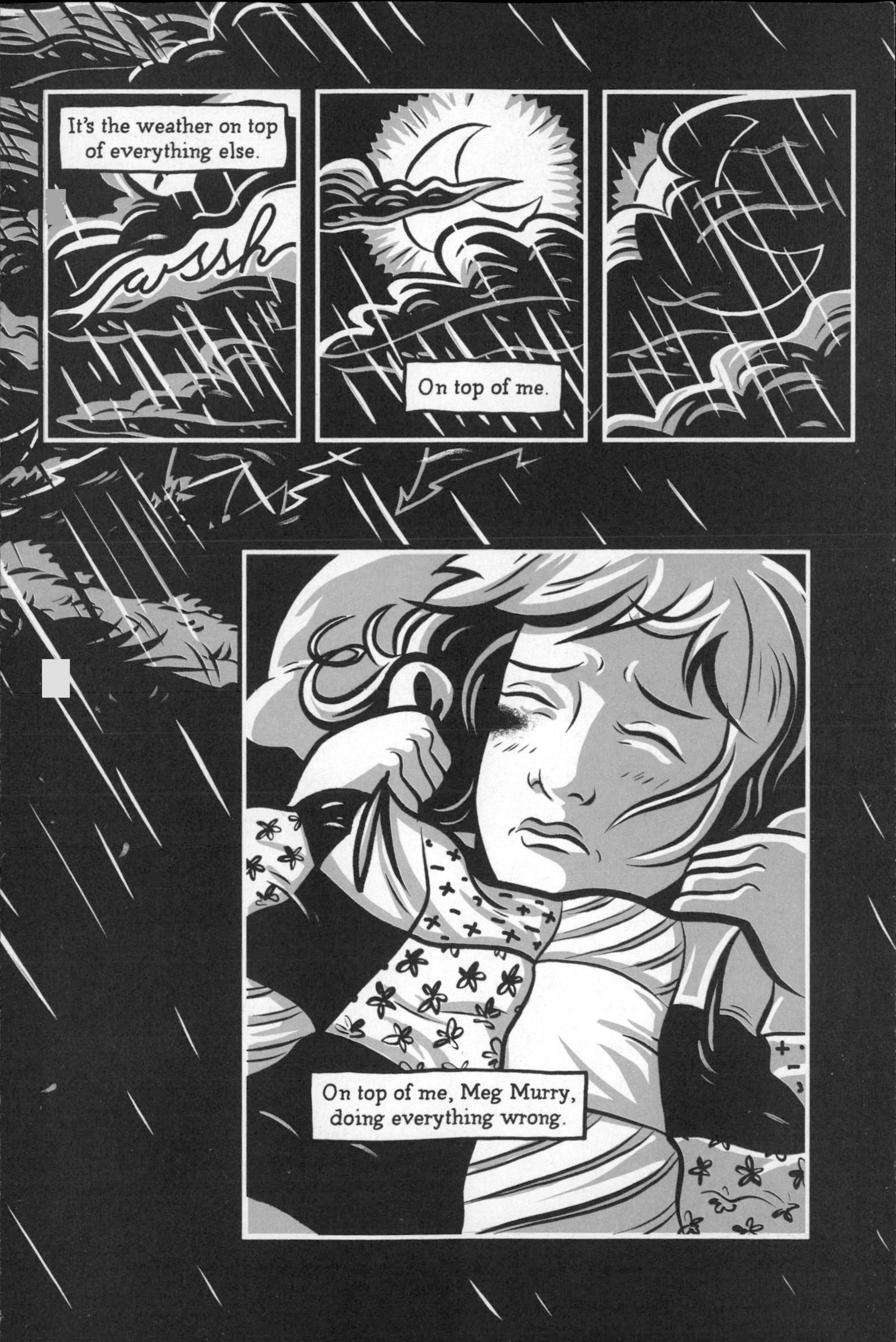
It's the weather on top of everything else.
wssh
On top of me.
On top of me, Meg Murry, doing everything wrong.

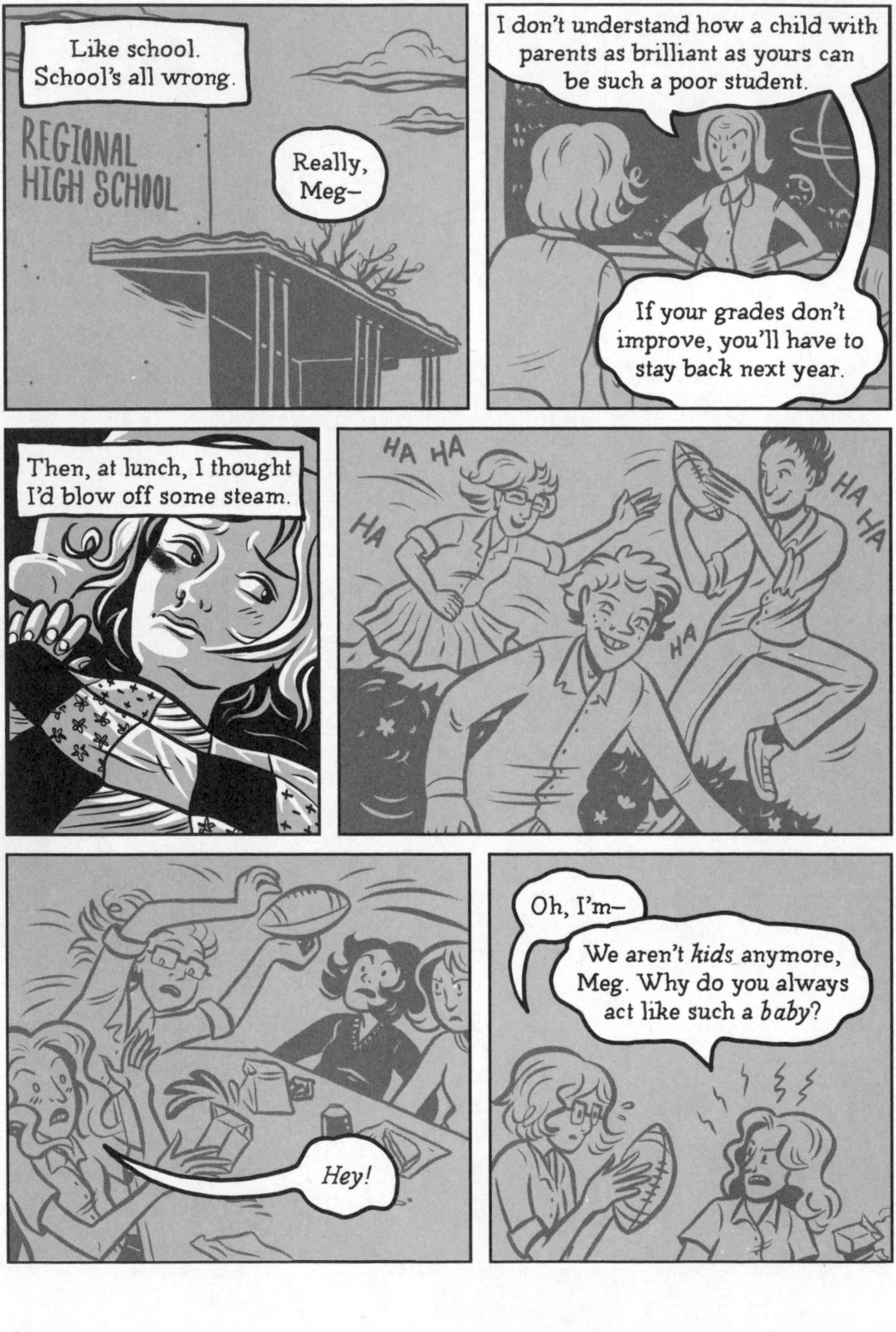

Like school. School's all wrong.
REGIONAL HIGH SCHOOL
Really, Meg—
I don't understand how a child with parents as brilliant as yours can be such a poor student.
If your grades don't improve, you'll have to stay back next year.
Then, at lunch, I thought I'd blow off some steam.
HA HA
HA
HA HA
HA
Hey!
Oh, I'm—
We aren't *kids* anymore, Meg. Why do you always act like such a *baby*?

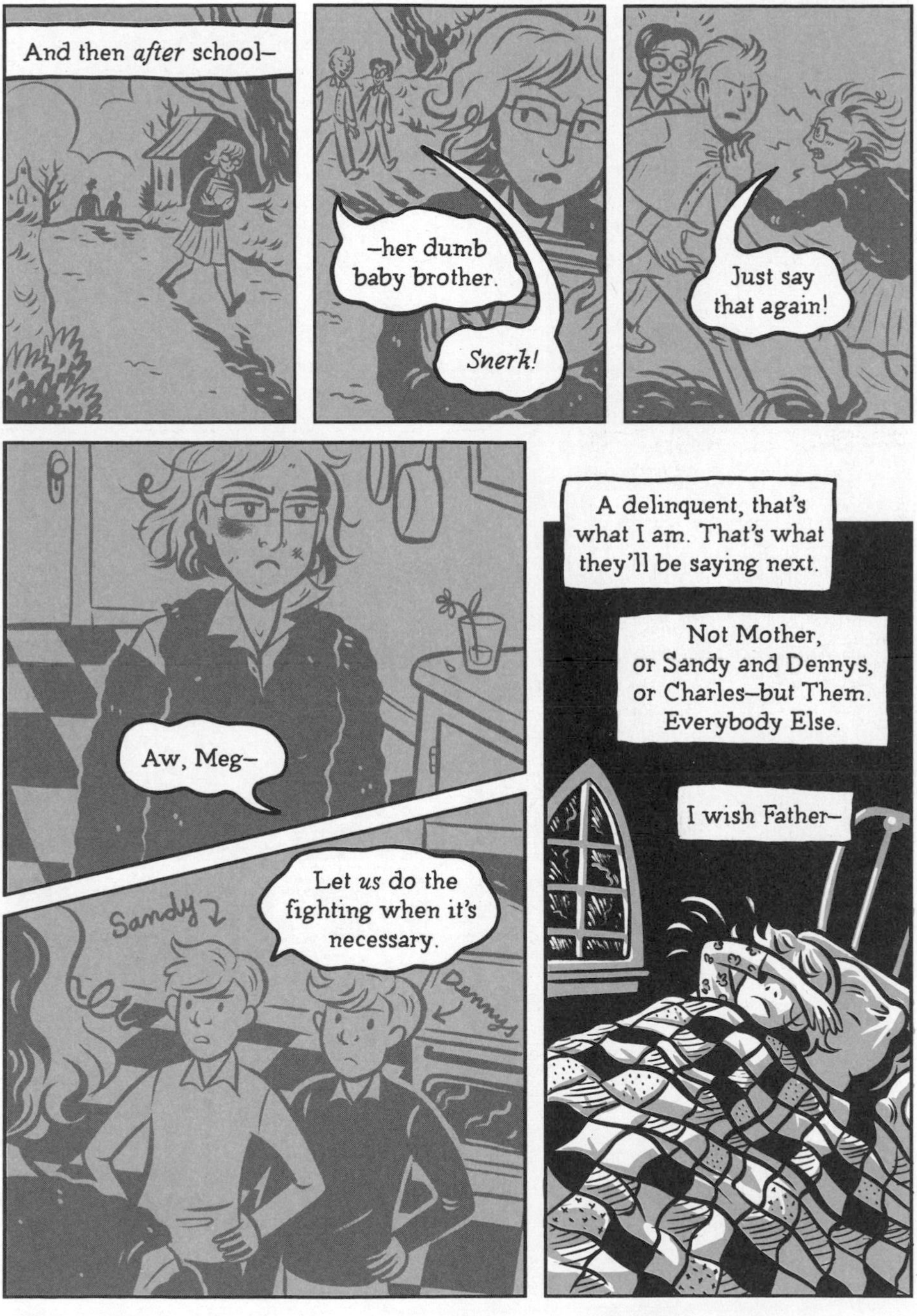
And then *after* school—
—her dumb baby brother.
Snerk!
Just say that again!
Aw, Meg—
Let *us* do the fighting when it's necessary.
Sandy
Dennys
A delinquent, that's what I am. That's what they'll be saying next.
Not Mother, or Sandy and Dennys, or Charles—but Them. Everybody Else.
I wish Father—

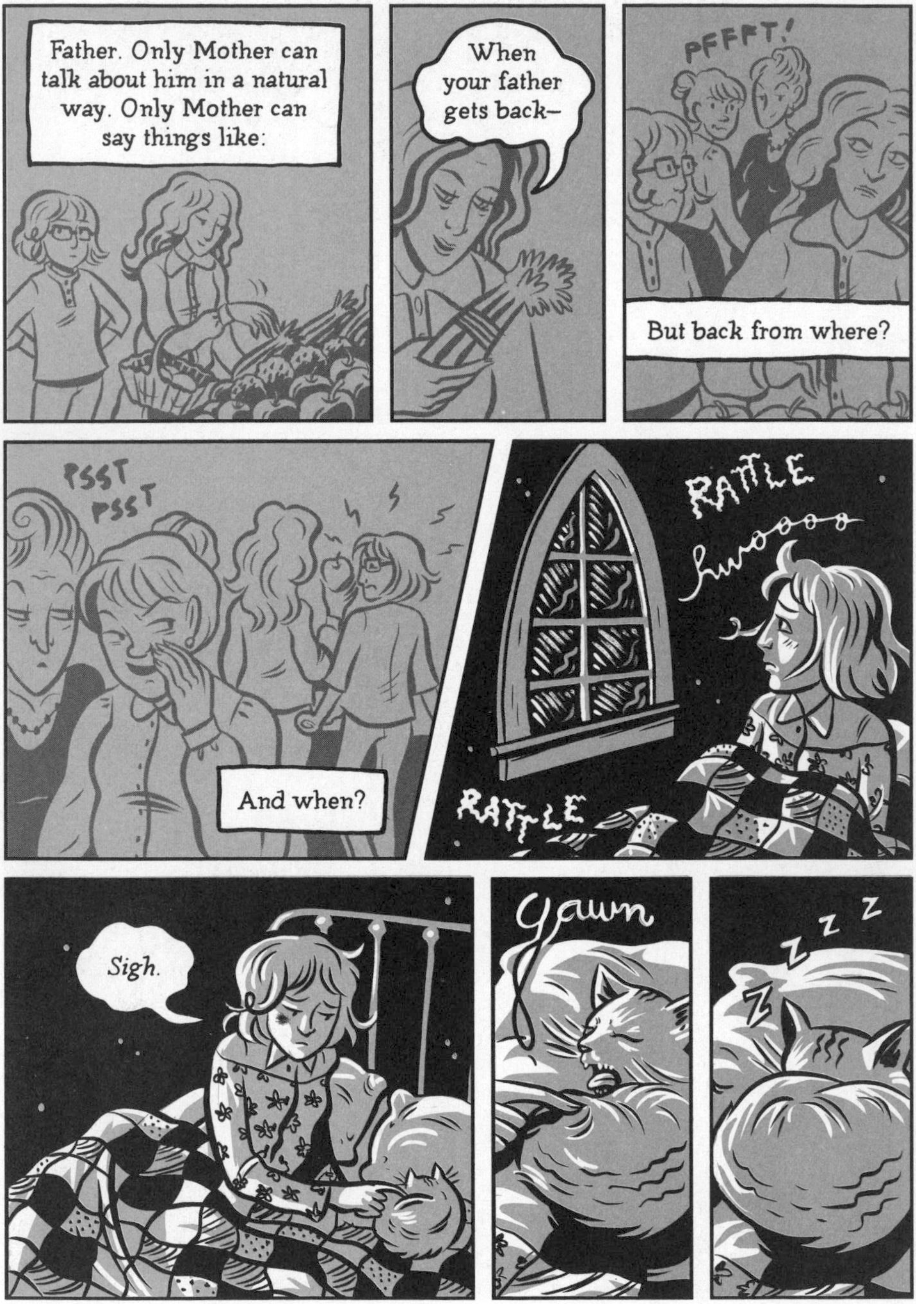
Father. Only Mother can talk about him in a natural way. Only Mother can say things like:
When your father gets back—
PFFFT!
But back from where?
PSST PSST
And when?
RATTLE
hwoooo
RATTLE
Sigh.
yawn
Z Z Z
Z

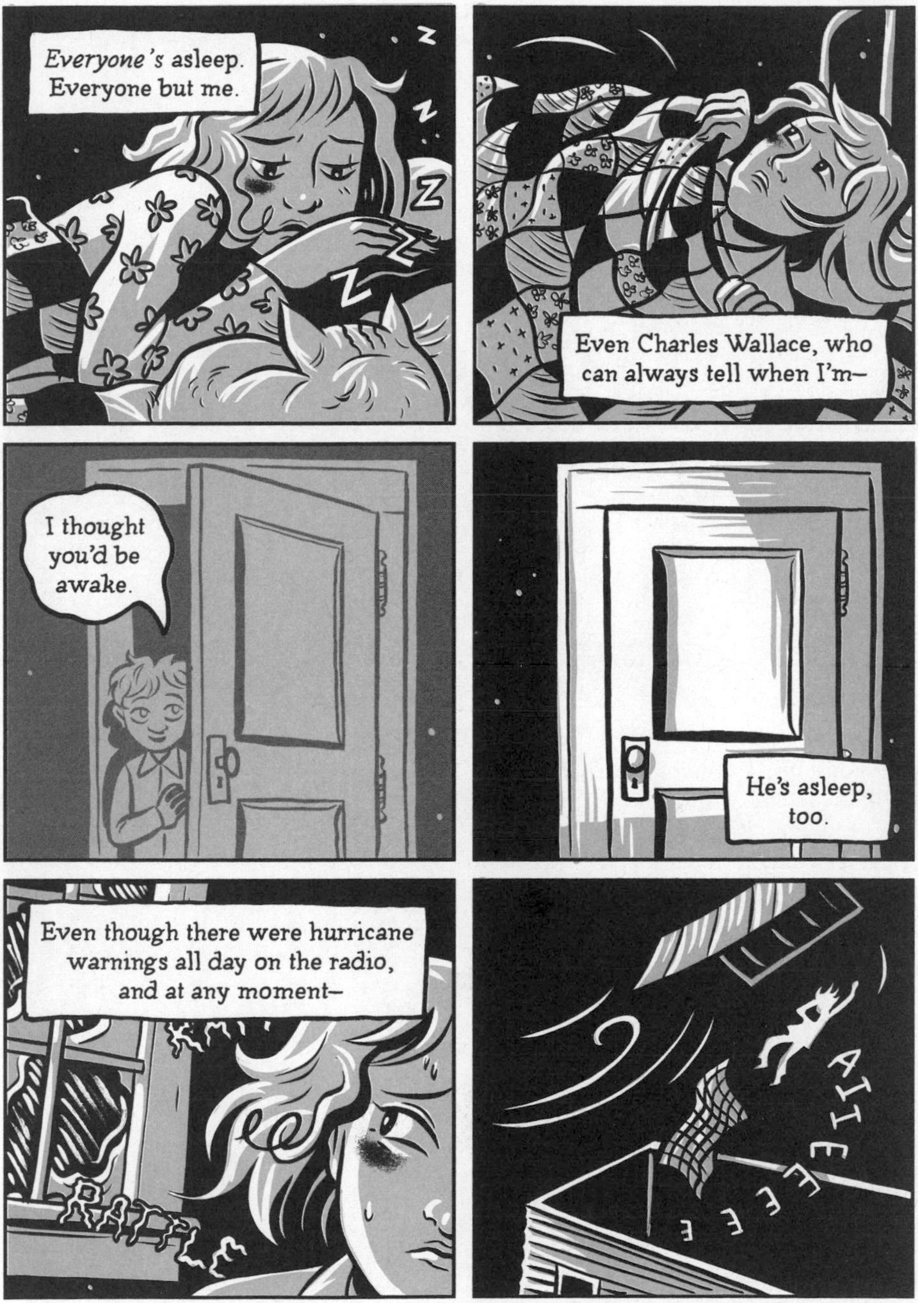
Everyone's asleep. Everyone but me.
Z
Z
Z
Z
Z
Even Charles Wallace, who can always tell when I'm—
I thought you'd be awake.
He's asleep, too.
Even though there were hurricane warnings all day on the radio, and at any moment—
RATTLE
AIIEEEEE

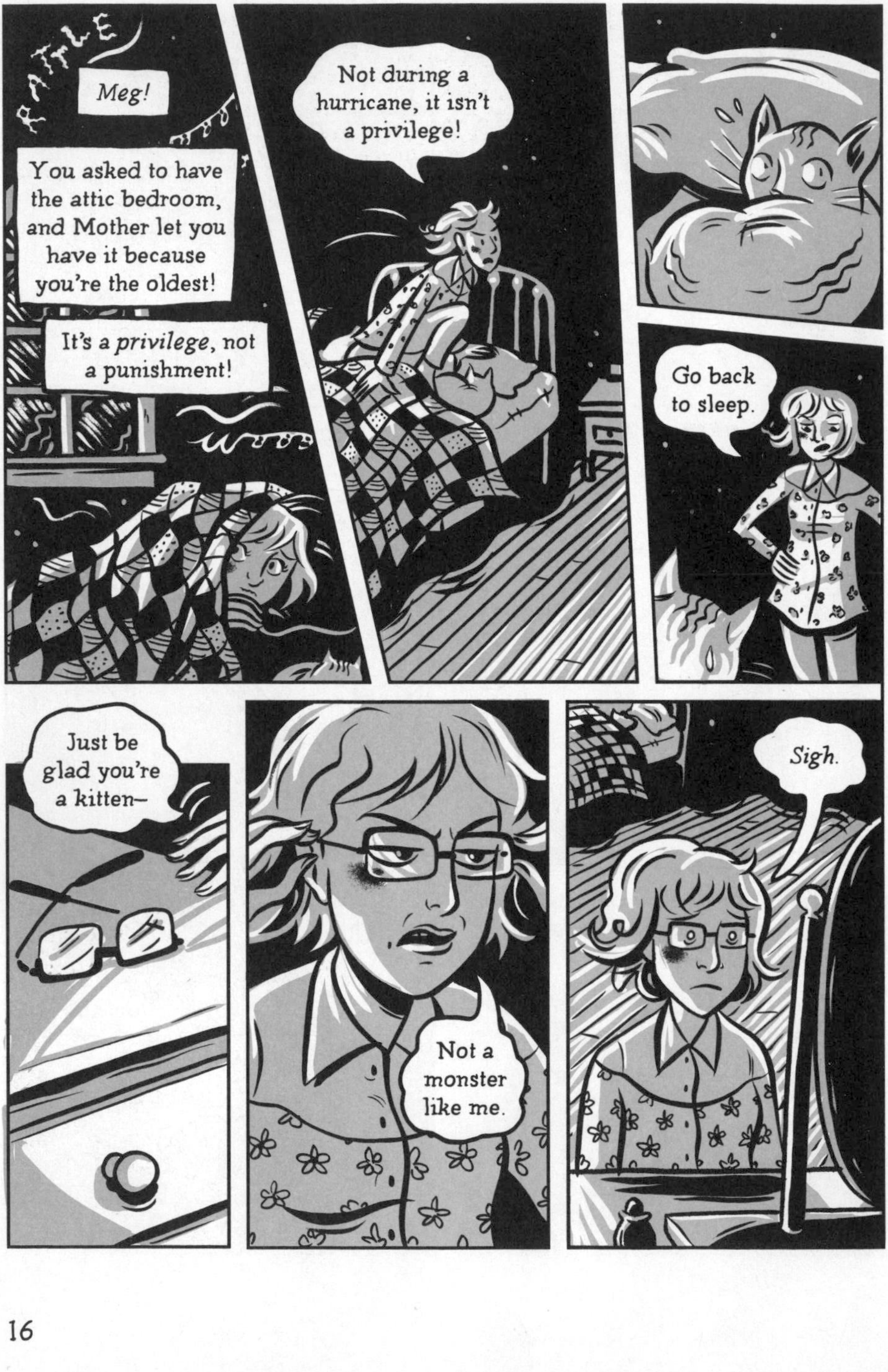
RATTLE
Meg!
You asked to have the attic bedroom, and Mother let you have it because you're the oldest!
It's a *privilege*, not a punishment!
Not during a hurricane, it isn't a privilege!
Go back to sleep.
Just be glad you're a kitten–
Not a monster like me.
Sigh.

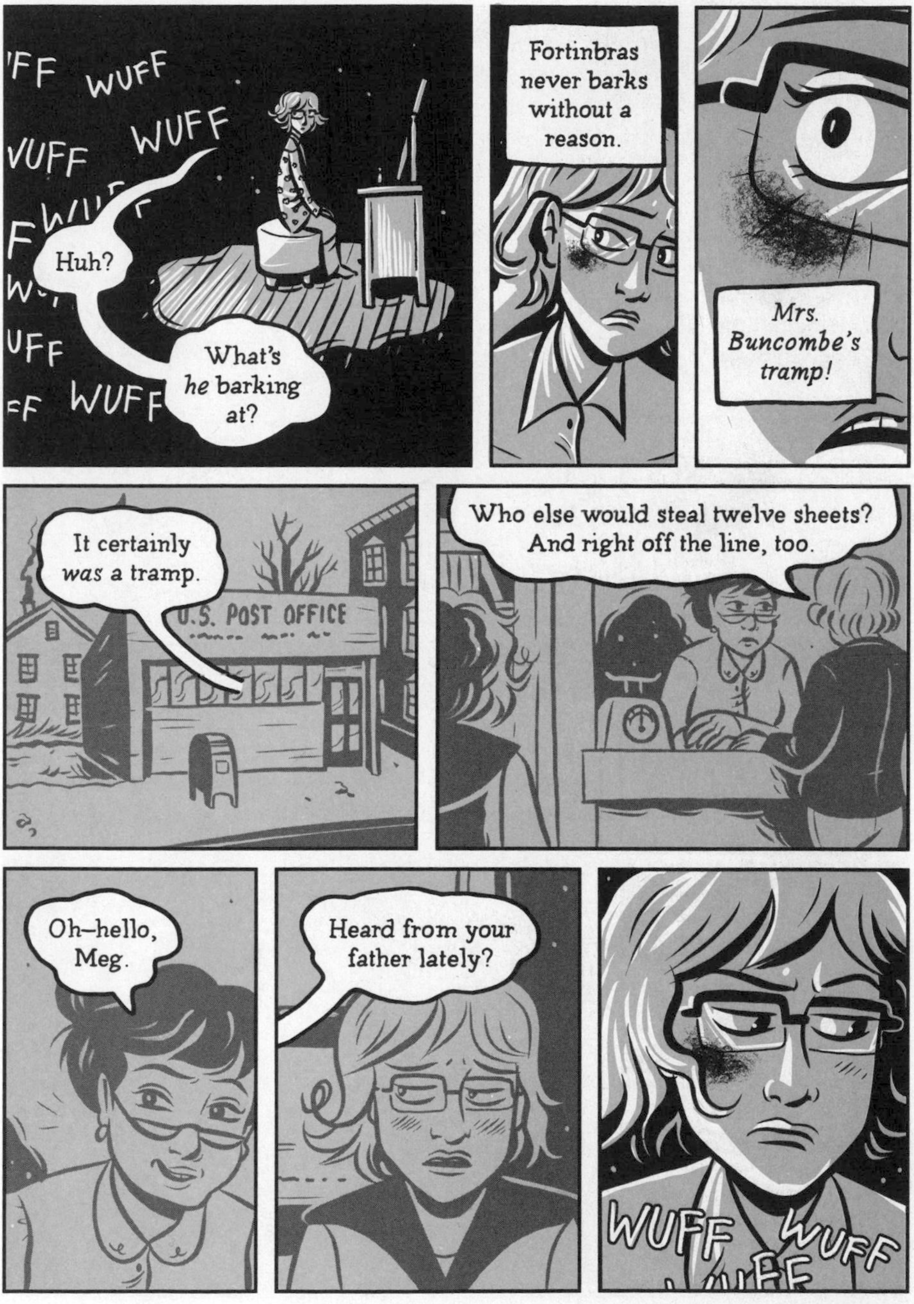
WUFF
WUFF
WUFF
Huh?
What's *he* barking at?
WUFF
Fortinbras never barks without a reason.
Mrs. Buncombe's tramp!
It certainly *was* a tramp.
U.S. POST OFFICE
Who else would steal twelve sheets? And right off the line, too.
Oh–hello, Meg.
Heard from your father lately?
WUFF
WUFF

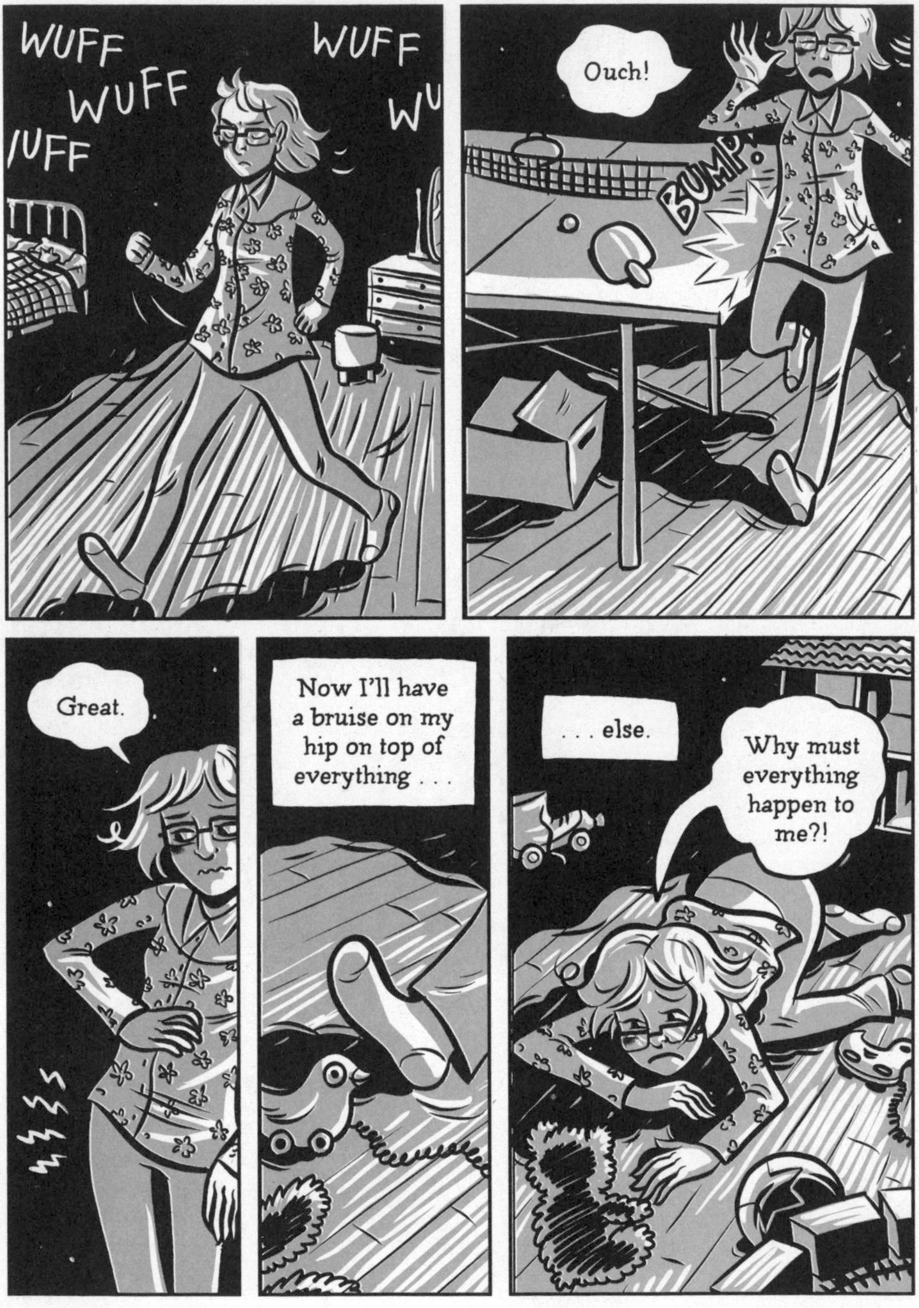
WUFF
WUFF
WUFF
WUFF
WU
/UFF
Ouch!
BUMP!
Great.
Now I'll have a bruise on my hip on top of everything . . .
. . . else.
Why must everything happen to me?!

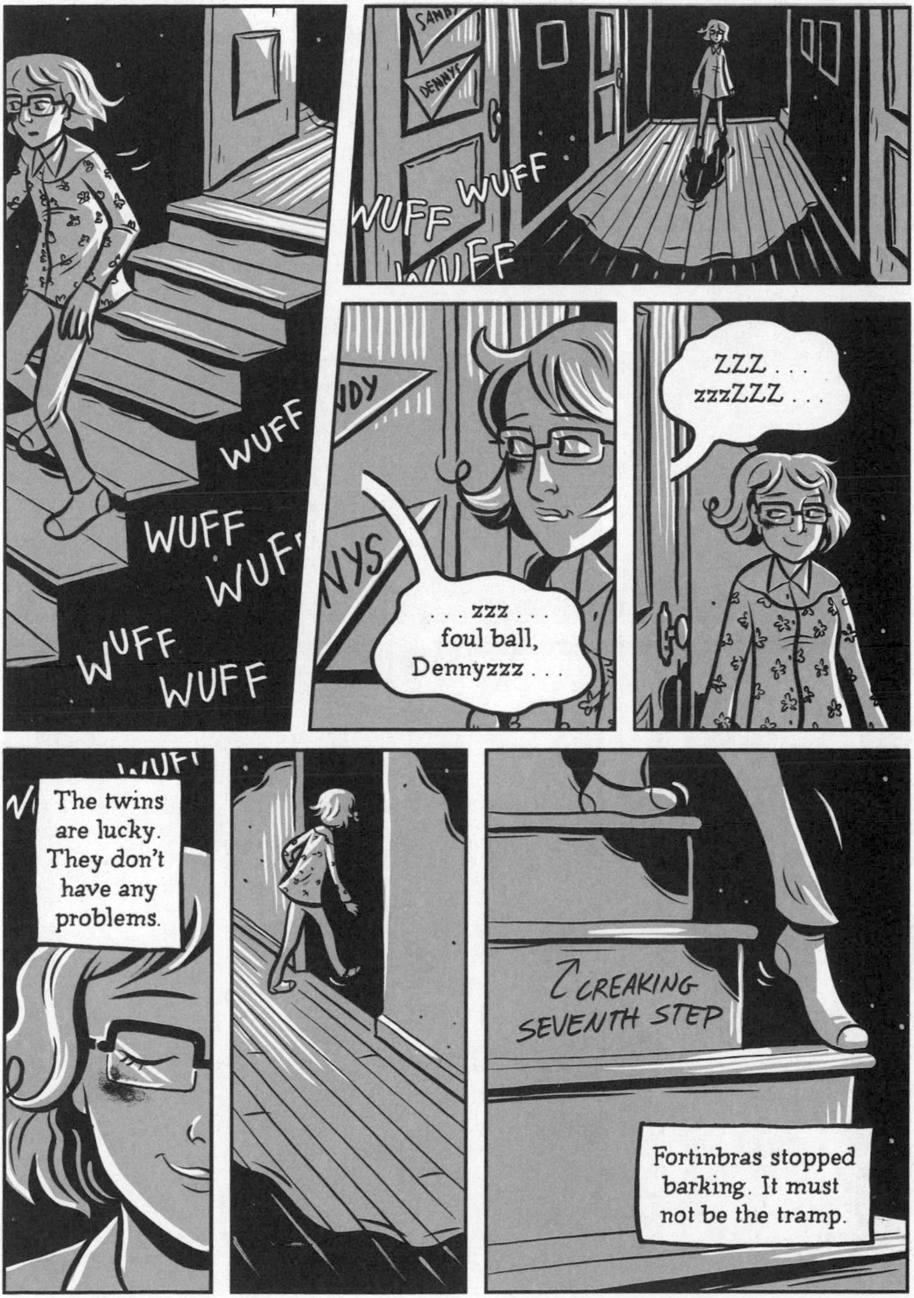
WUFF
WUFF
WUFF
WUFF
WUFF
SANDY
DENNYS
WUFF WUFF
WUFF
. . . zzz . . .
foul ball,
Dennyzzz . . .
ZZZ . . .
zzzZZZ . . .
The twins are lucky. They don't have any problems.
CREAKING SEVENTH STEP
Fortinbras stopped barking. It must not be the tramp.

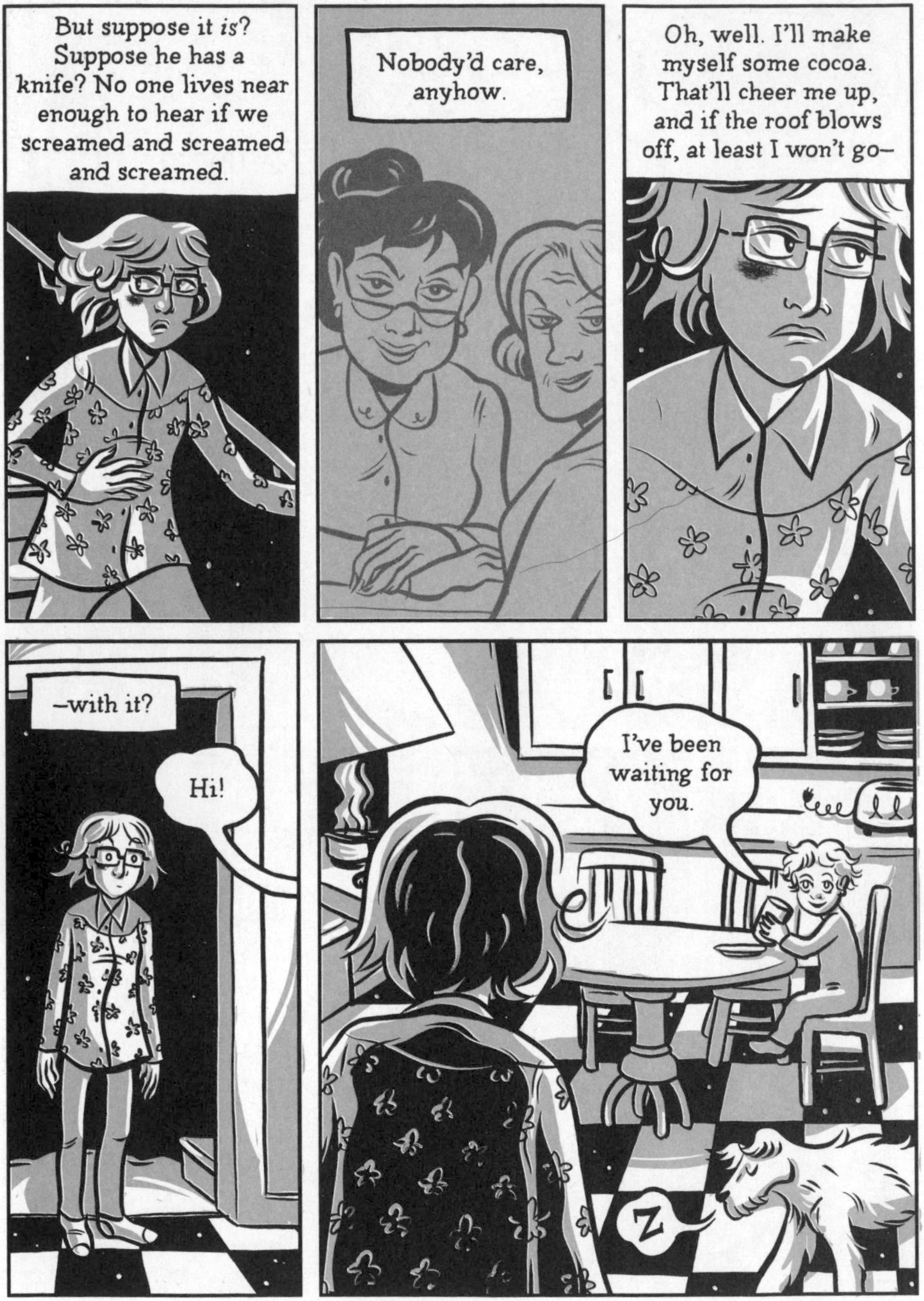
But suppose it *is*? Suppose he has a knife? No one lives near enough to hear if we screamed and screamed and screamed.
Nobody'd care, anyhow.
Oh, well. I'll make myself some cocoa. That'll cheer me up, and if the roof blows off, at least I won't go–
–with it?
Hi!
I've been waiting for you.
Z

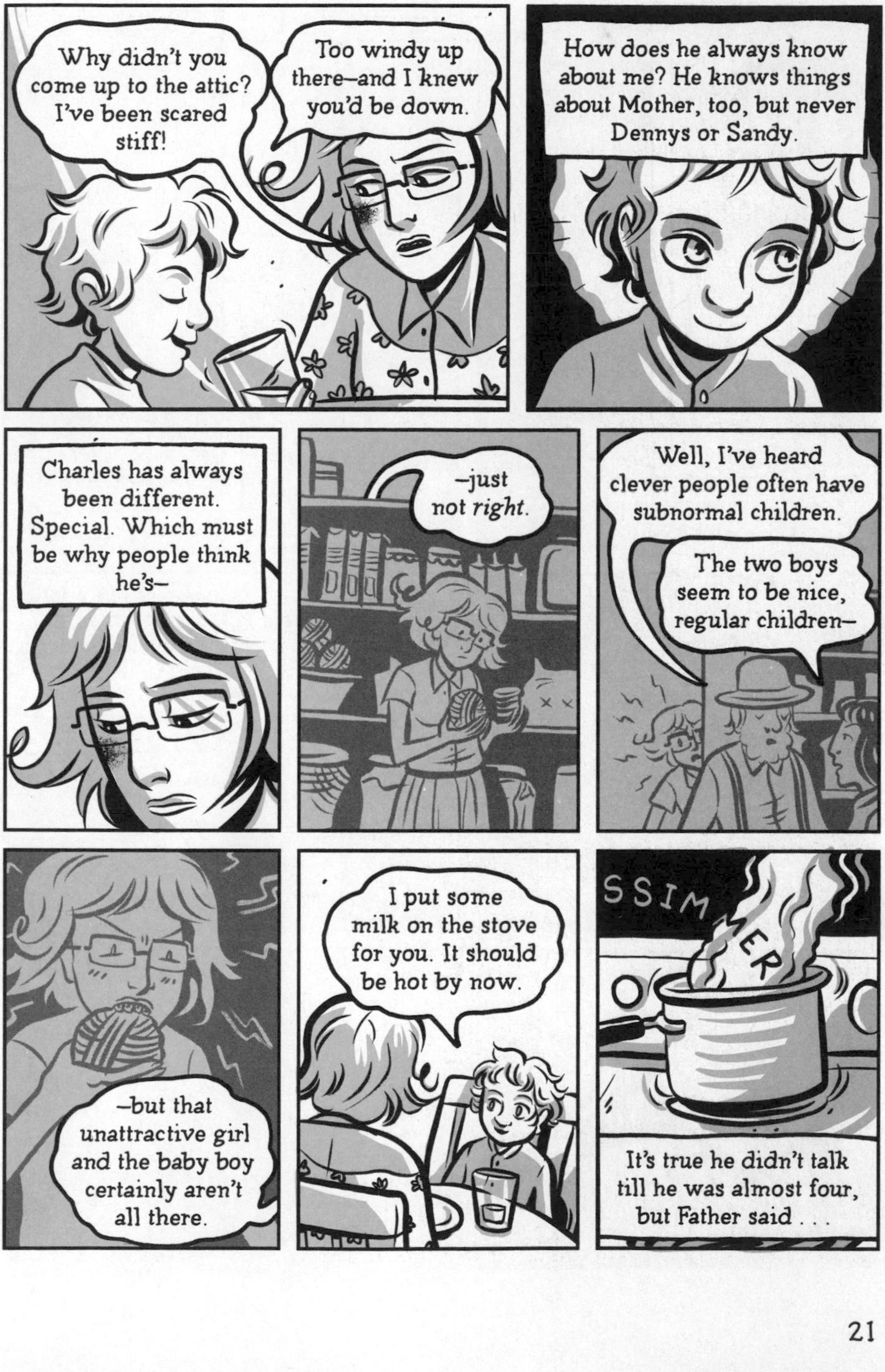
Why didn't you come up to the attic? I've been scared stiff!
Too windy up there—and I knew you'd be down.
How does he always know about me? He knows things about Mother, too, but never Dennys or Sandy.
Charles has always been different. Special. Which must be why people think he's—
—just not *right*.
Well, I've heard clever people often have subnormal children.
The two boys seem to be nice, regular children—
—but that unattractive girl and the baby boy certainly aren't all there.
I put some milk on the stove for you. It should be hot by now.
SSIMMER
It's true he didn't talk till he was almost four, but Father said . . .

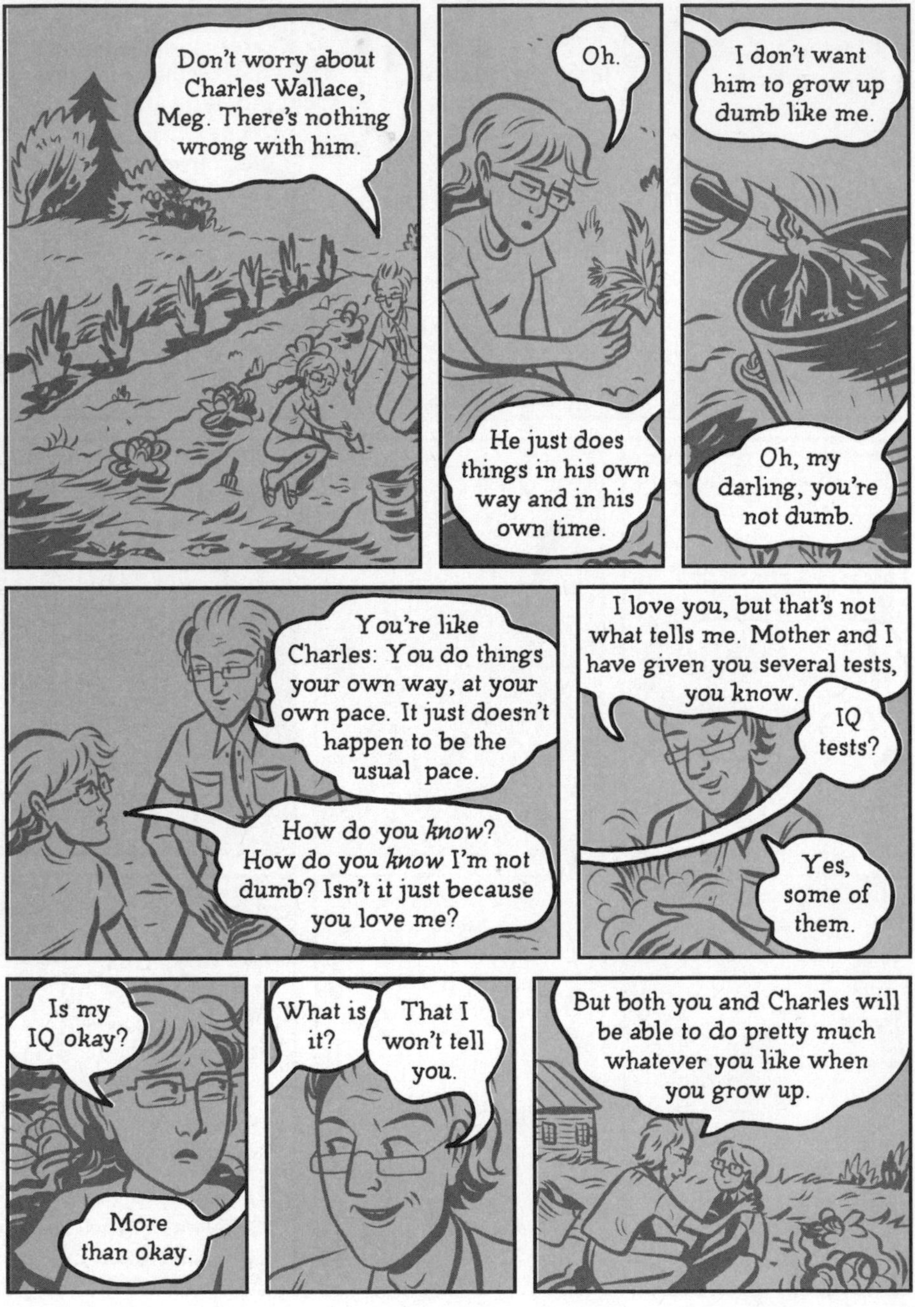
Don't worry about Charles Wallace, Meg. There's nothing wrong with him.
Oh.
He just does things in his own way and in his own time.
I don't want him to grow up dumb like me.
Oh, my darling, you're not dumb.
You're like Charles: You do things your own way, at your own pace. It just doesn't happen to be the usual pace.
How do you *know*? How do you *know* I'm not dumb? Isn't it just because you love me?
I love you, but that's not what tells me. Mother and I have given you several tests, you know.
IQ tests?
Yes, some of them.
Is my IQ okay?
More than okay.
What is it?
That I won't tell you.
But both you and Charles will be able to do pretty much whatever you like when you grow up.

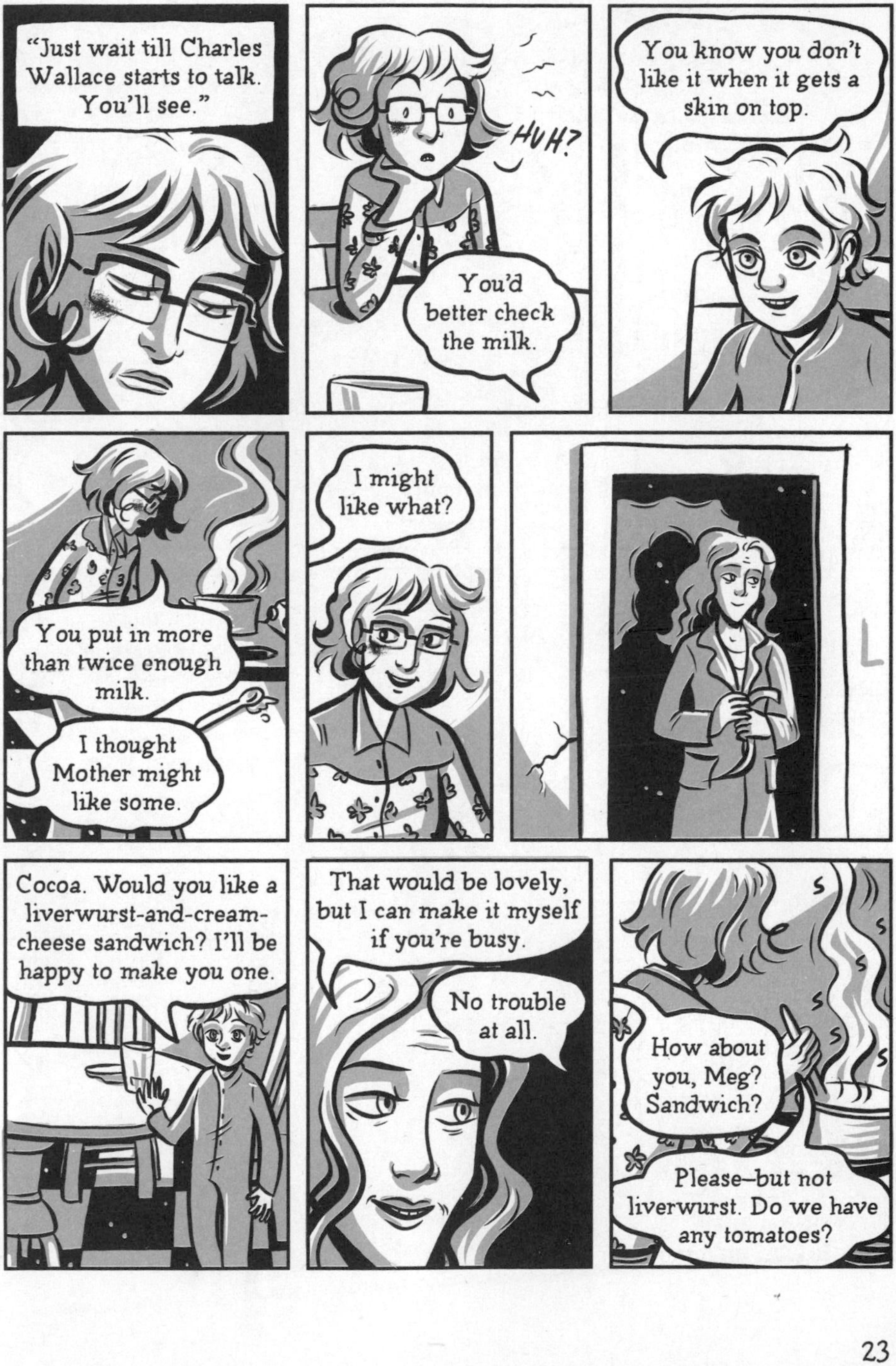
"Just wait till Charles Wallace starts to talk. You'll see."
HUH?
You'd better check the milk.
You know you don't like it when it gets a skin on top.
You put in more than twice enough milk.
I thought Mother might like some.
I might like what?
Cocoa. Would you like a liverwurst-and-cream-cheese sandwich? I'll be happy to make you one.
That would be lovely, but I can make it myself if you're busy.
No trouble at all.
How about you, Meg? Sandwich?
Please—but not liverwurst. Do we have any tomatoes?

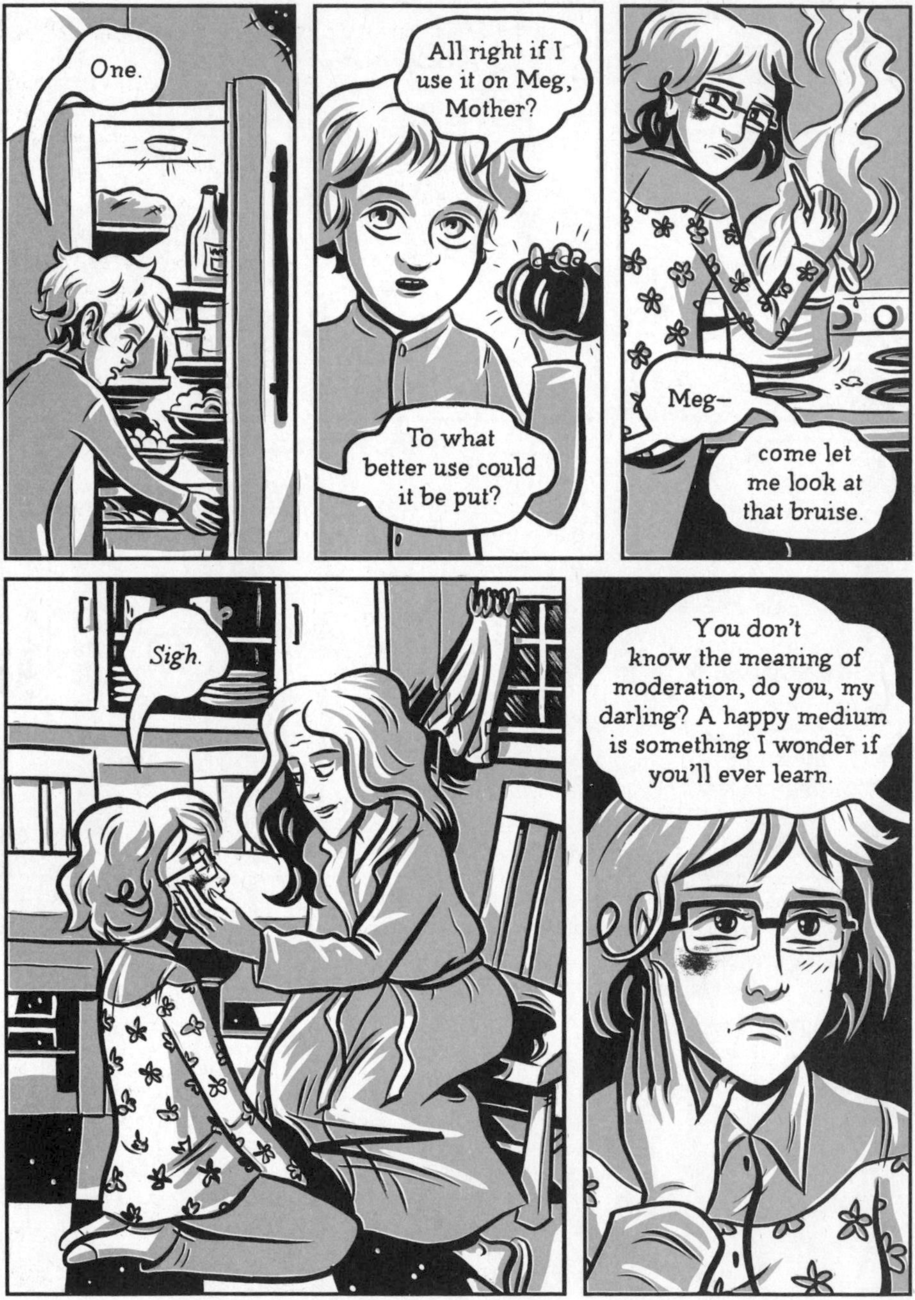
One.
All right if I use it on Meg, Mother?
To what better use could it be put?
Meg–
come let me look at that bruise.
Sigh.
You don't know the meaning of moderation, do you, my darling? A happy medium is something I wonder if you'll ever learn.

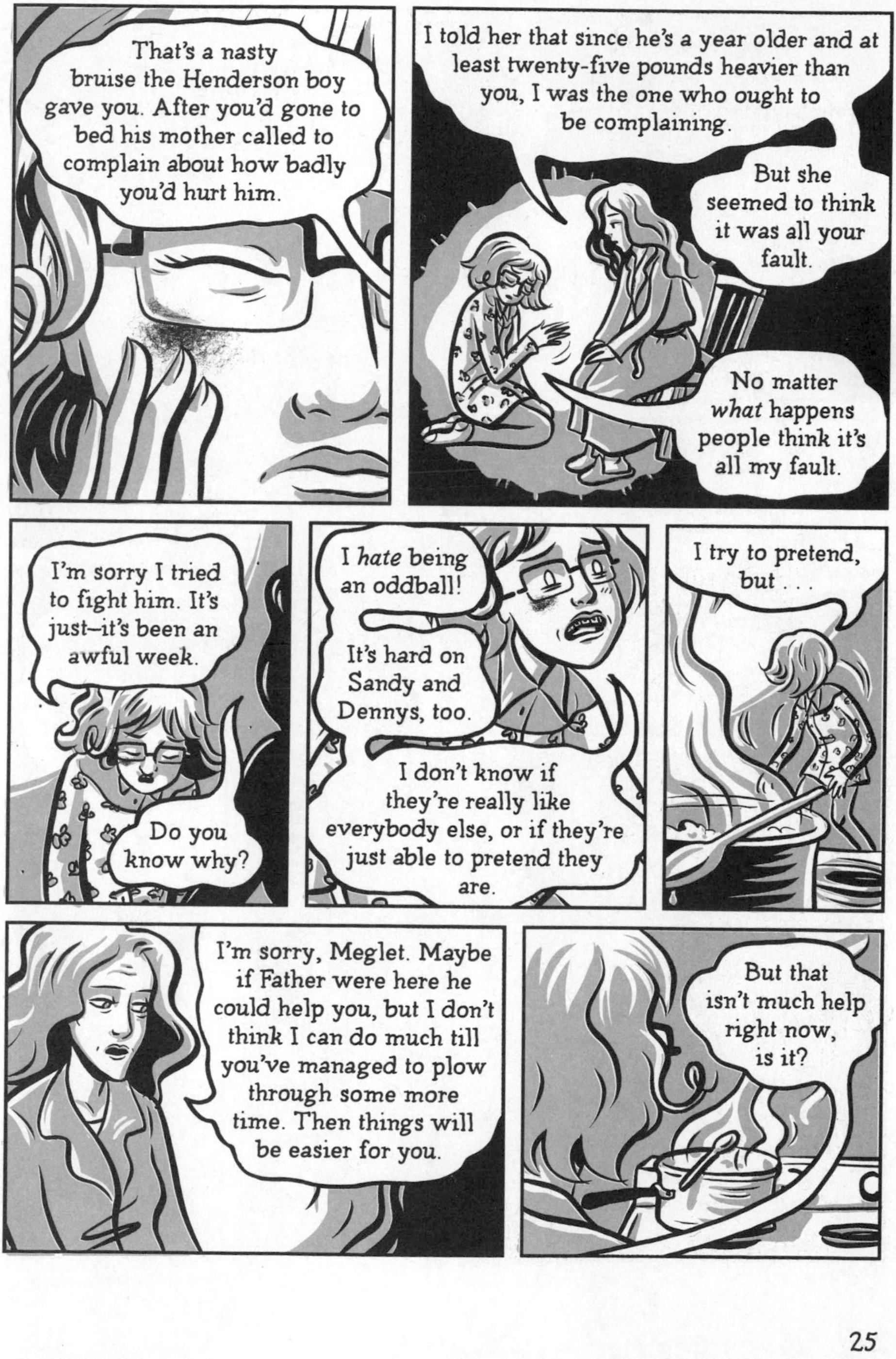
That's a nasty bruise the Henderson boy gave you. After you'd gone to bed his mother called to complain about how badly you'd hurt him.
I told her that since he's a year older and at least twenty-five pounds heavier than you, I was the one who ought to be complaining.
But she seemed to think it was all your fault.
No matter *what* happens people think it's all my fault.
I'm sorry I tried to fight him. It's just—it's been an awful week.
Do you know why?
I *hate* being an oddball!
It's hard on Sandy and Dennys, too.
I don't know if they're really like everybody else, or if they're just able to pretend they are.
I try to pretend, but . . .
I'm sorry, Meglet. Maybe if Father were here he could help you, but I don't think I can do much till you've managed to plow through some more time. Then things will be easier for you.
But that isn't much help right now, is it?

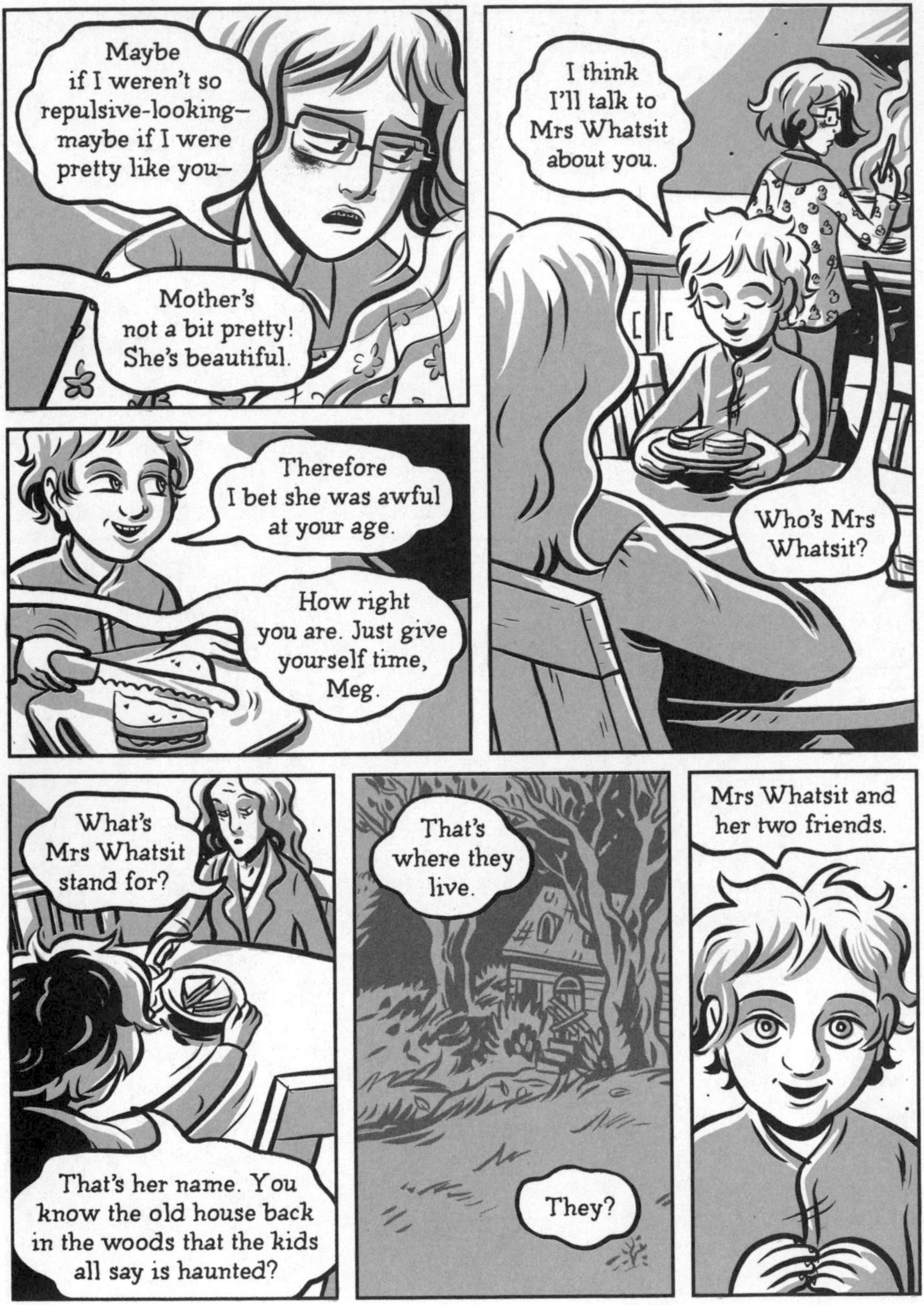

Maybe if I weren't so repulsive-looking— maybe if I were pretty like you—
Mother's not a bit pretty! She's beautiful.
I think I'll talk to Mrs Whatsit about you.
Therefore I bet she was awful at your age.
How right you are. Just give yourself time, Meg.
Who's Mrs Whatsit?
What's Mrs Whatsit stand for?
That's her name. You know the old house back in the woods that the kids all say is haunted?
That's where they live.
They?
Mrs Whatsit and her two friends.

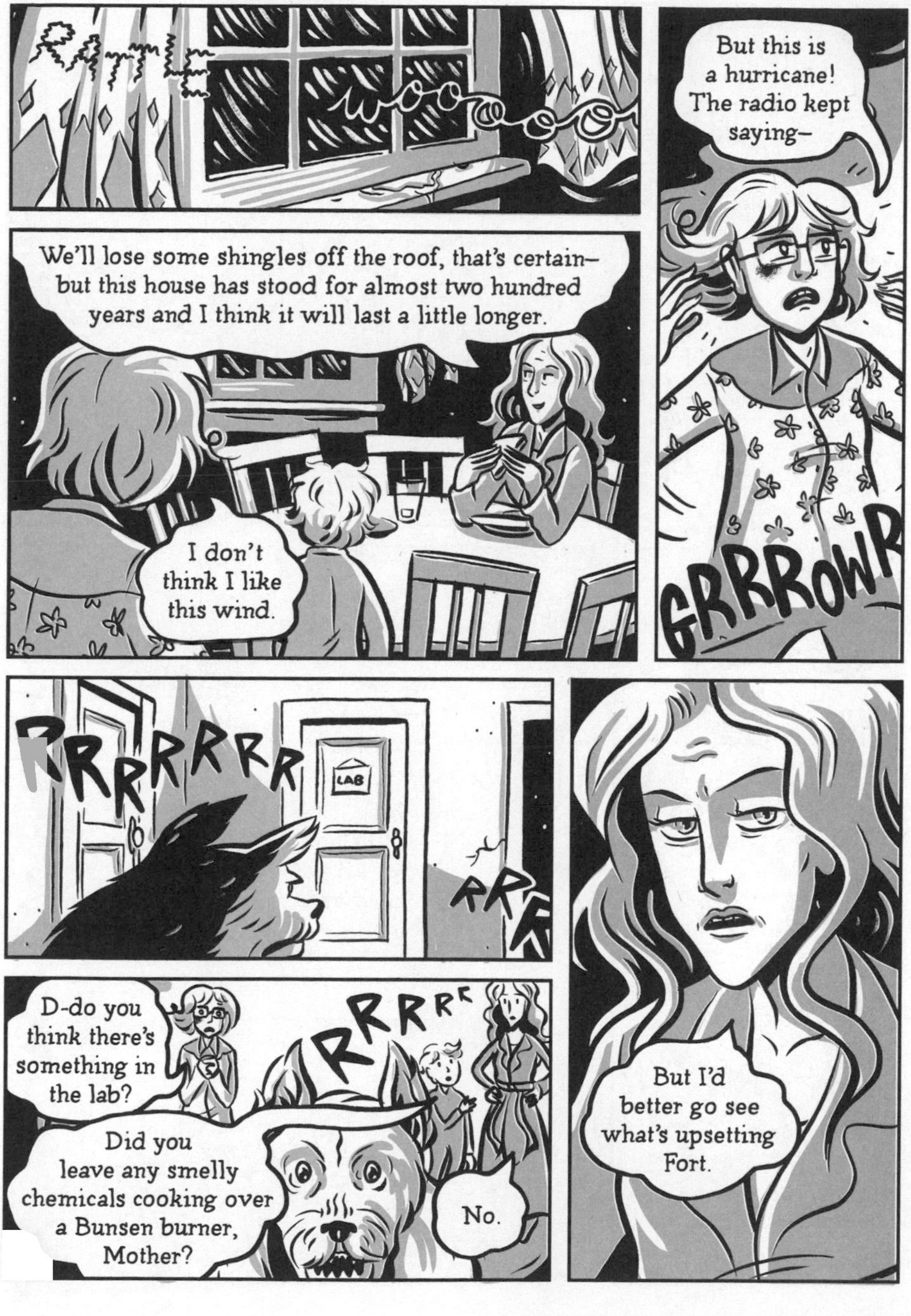
RATTLE
WOOOooooo
But this is a hurricane! The radio kept saying–
We'll lose some shingles off the roof, that's certain–but this house has stood for almost two hundred years and I think it will last a little longer.
I don't think I like this wind.
GRRROWR
RRRRRRR
LAB
RRR
D-do you think there's something in the lab?
RRRRR
Did you leave any smelly chemicals cooking over a Bunsen burner, Mother?
No.
But I'd better go see what's upsetting Fort.

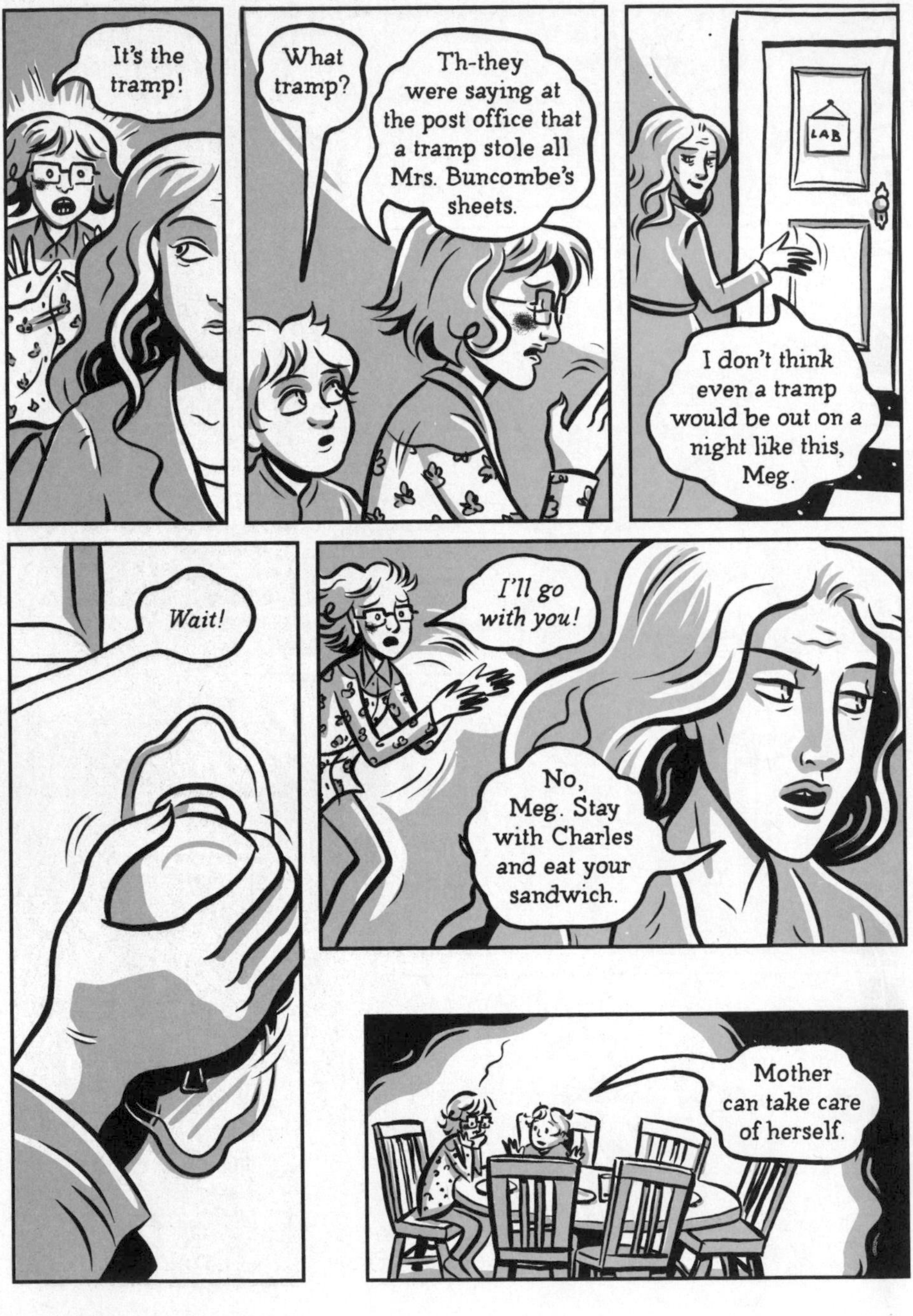
It's the tramp!
What tramp?
Th-they were saying at the post office that a tramp stole all Mrs. Buncombe's sheets.
LAB
I don't think even a tramp would be out on a night like this, Meg.
Wait!
I'll go with you!
No, Meg. Stay with Charles and eat your sandwich.
Mother can take care of herself.

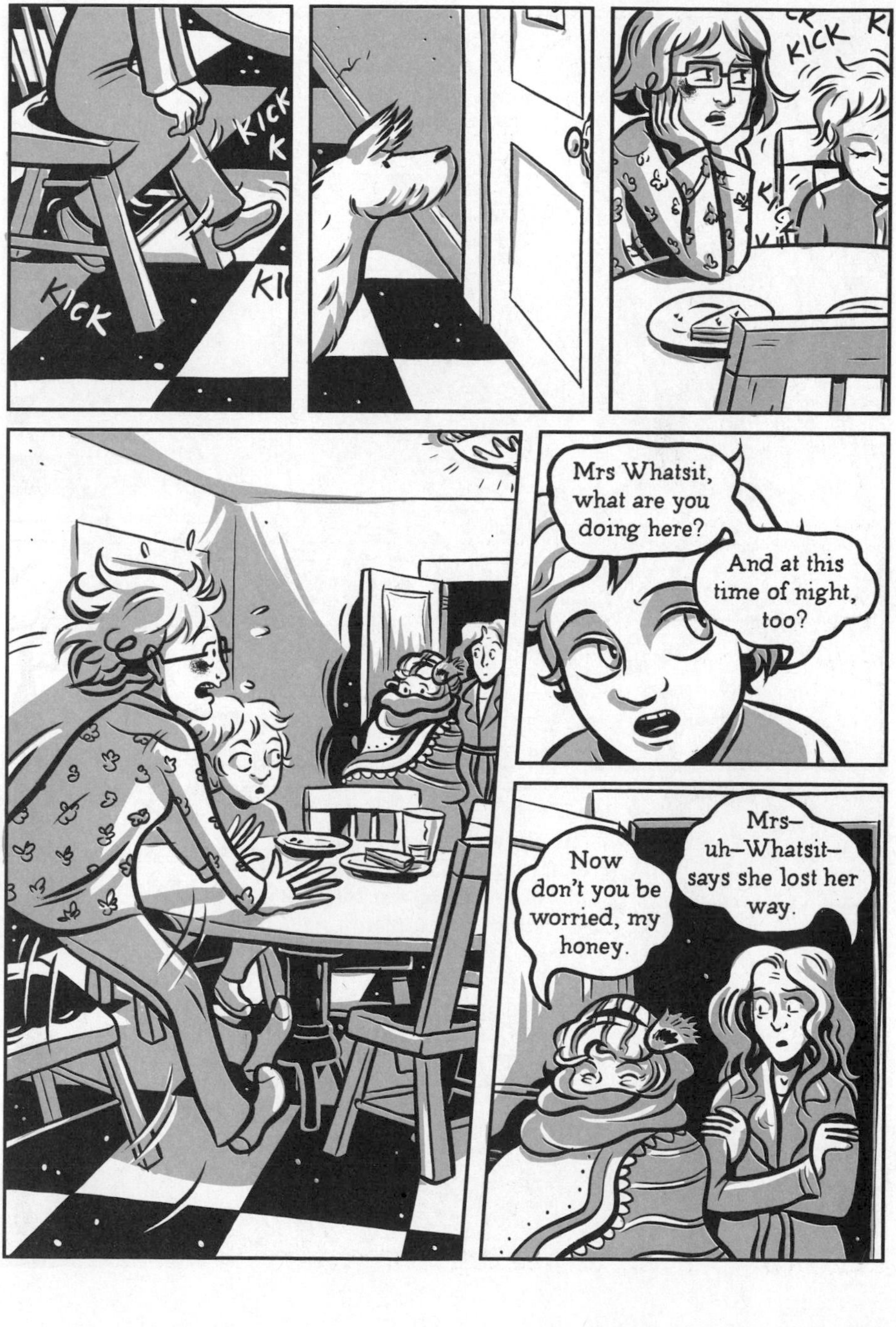
KICK
K
KICK
KI
CK
KICK
KI
KIC
Mrs Whatsit, what are you doing here?
And at this time of night, too?
Mrs— uh—Whatsit— says she lost her way.
Now don't you be worried, my honey.

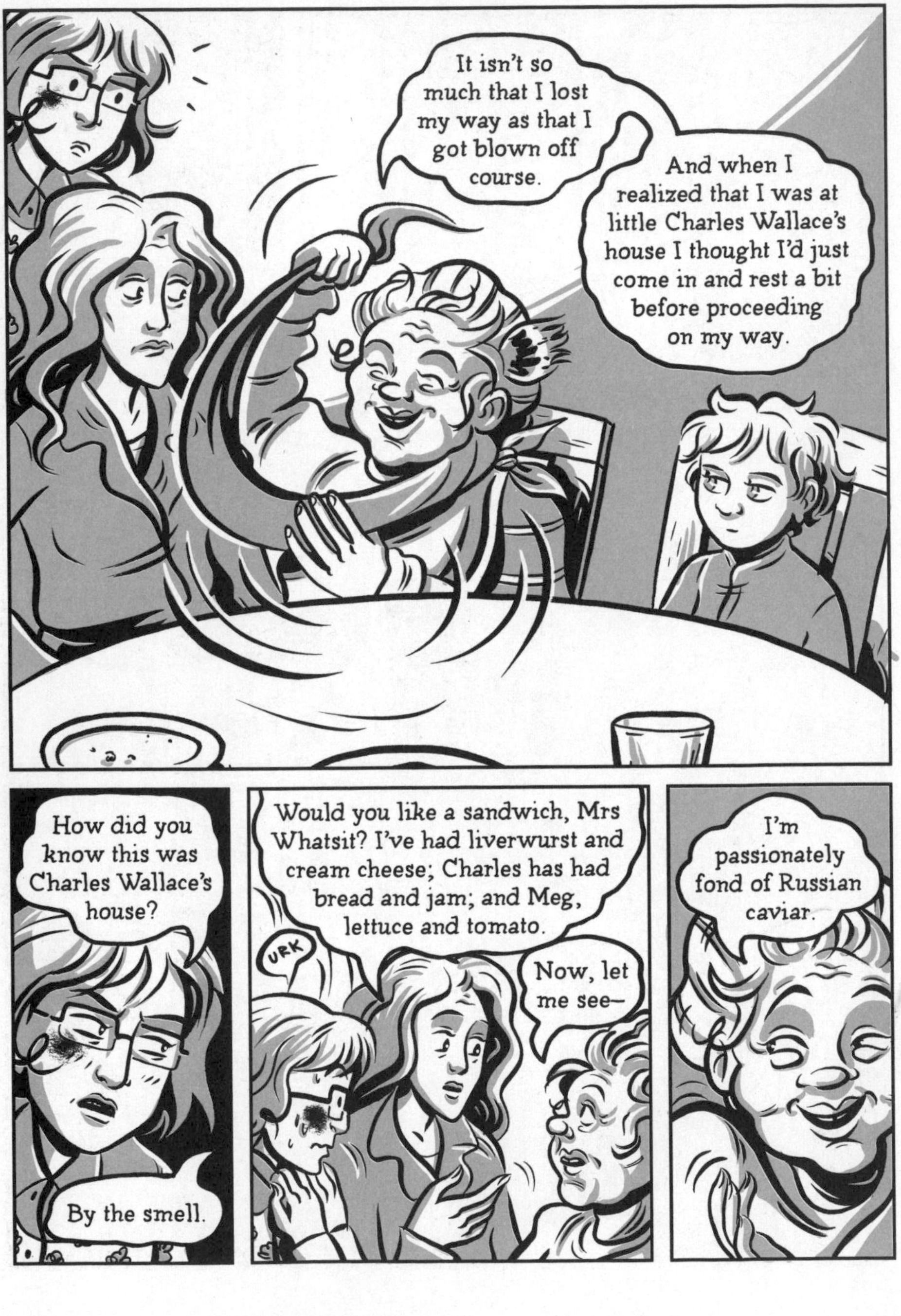
It isn't so much that I lost my way as that I got blown off course.
And when I realized that I was at little Charles Wallace's house I thought I'd just come in and rest a bit before proceeding on my way.
How did you know this was Charles Wallace's house?
By the smell.
Would you like a sandwich, Mrs Whatsit? I've had liverwurst and cream cheese; Charles has had bread and jam; and Meg, lettuce and tomato.
URK
Now, let me see—
I'm passionately fond of Russian caviar.

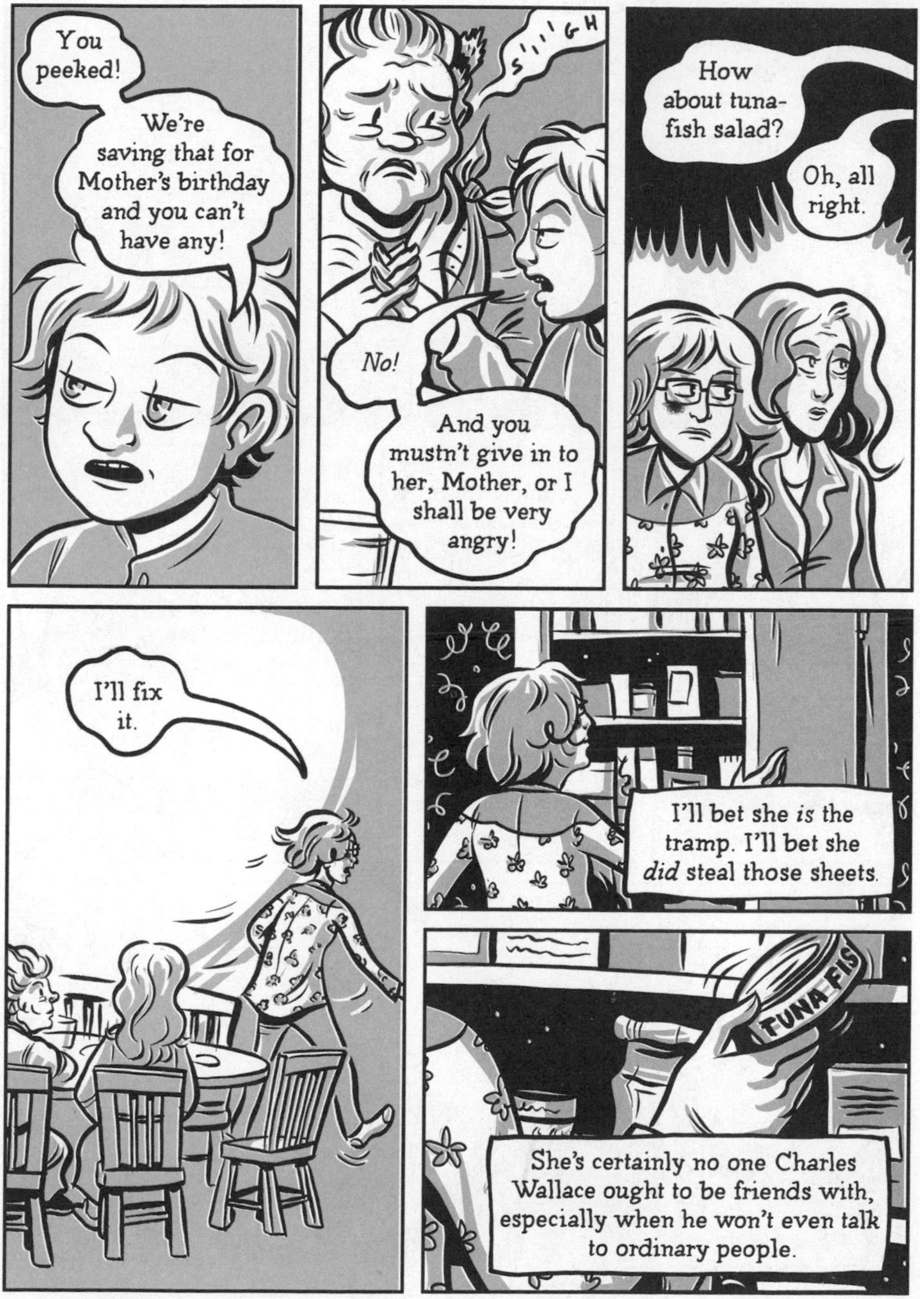

You peeked!
We're saving that for Mother's birthday and you can't have any!
S'''IGH
No!
And you mustn't give in to her, Mother, or I shall be very angry!
How about tuna-fish salad?
Oh, all right.
I'll fix it.
I'll bet she *is* the tramp. I'll bet she *did* steal those sheets.
TUNA FIS
She's certainly no one Charles Wallace ought to be friends with, especially when he won't even talk to ordinary people.

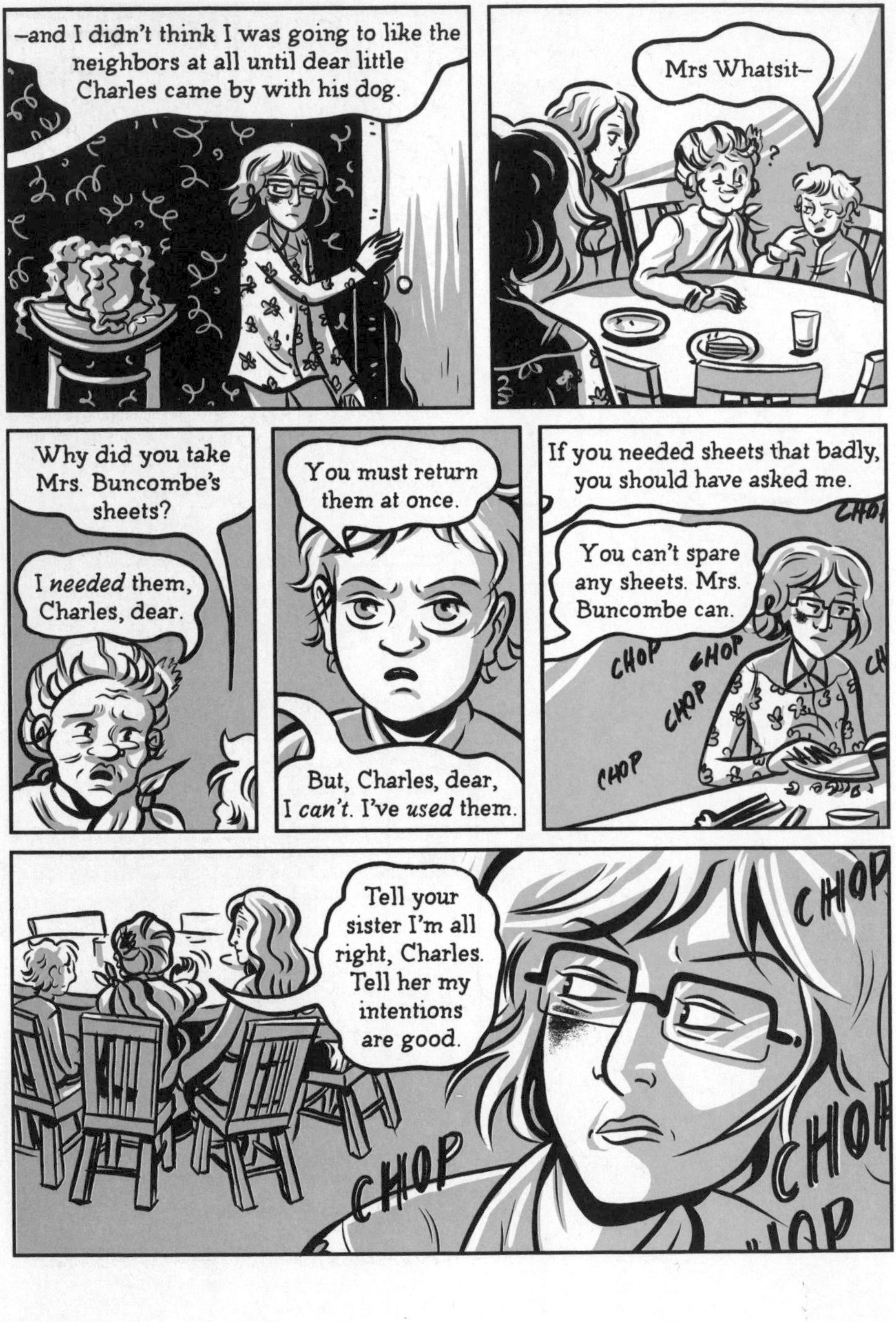
–and I didn't think I was going to like the neighbors at all until dear little Charles came by with his dog.
Mrs Whatsit–
Why did you take Mrs. Buncombe's sheets?
I *needed* them, Charles, dear.
You must return them at once.
But, Charles, dear, I *can't*. I've *used* them.
If you needed sheets that badly, you should have asked me.
You can't spare any sheets. Mrs. Buncombe can.
CHOP
CHOP
CHOP
CHOP
Tell your sister I'm all right, Charles. Tell her my intentions are good.
CHOP
CHOP
CHOP

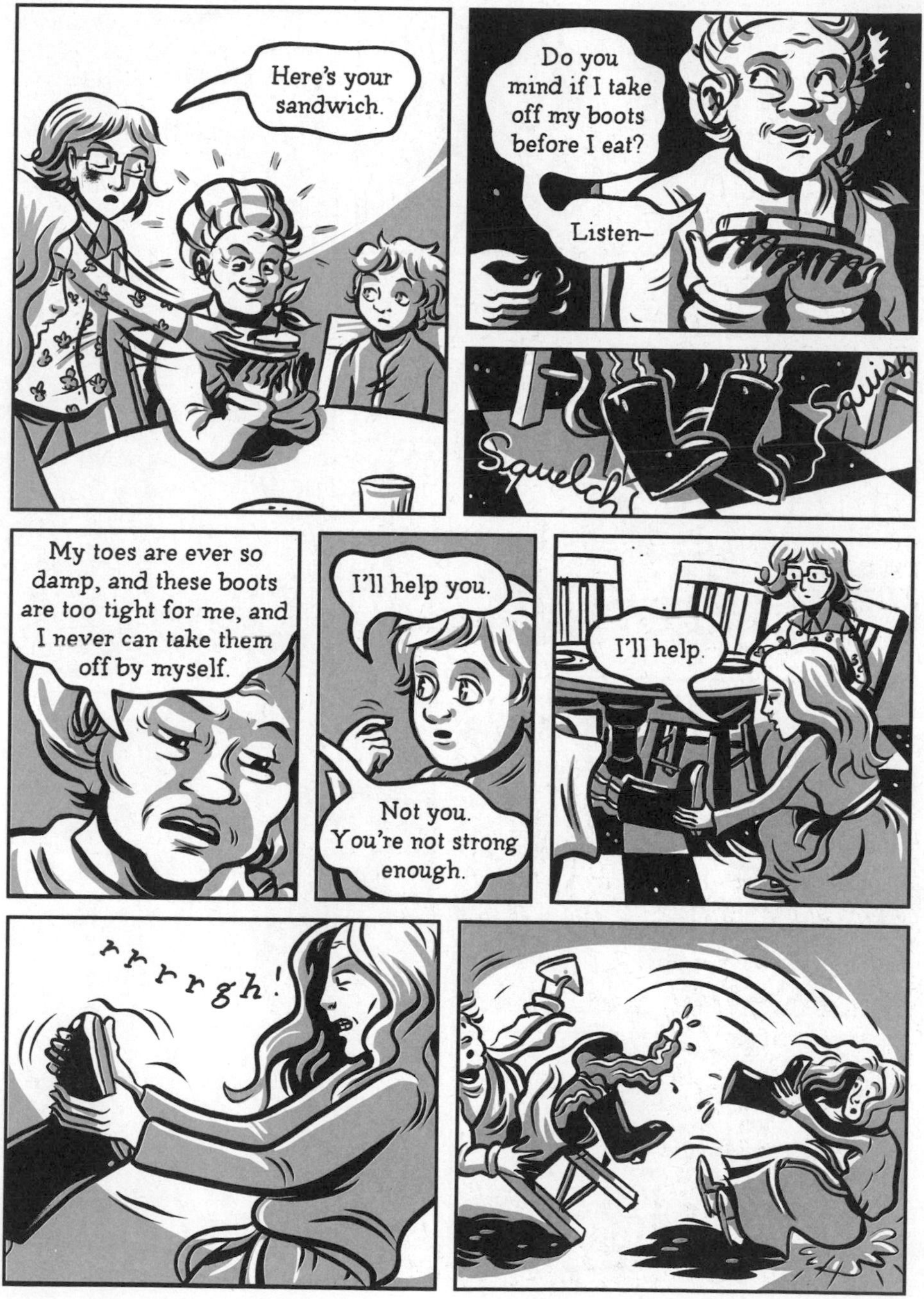

Here's your sandwich.
Do you mind if I take off my boots before I eat?
Listen–
Squelch
squish
My toes are ever so damp, and these boots are too tight for me, and I never can take them off by myself.
I'll help you.
Not you. You're not strong enough.
I'll help.
rrrrgh!

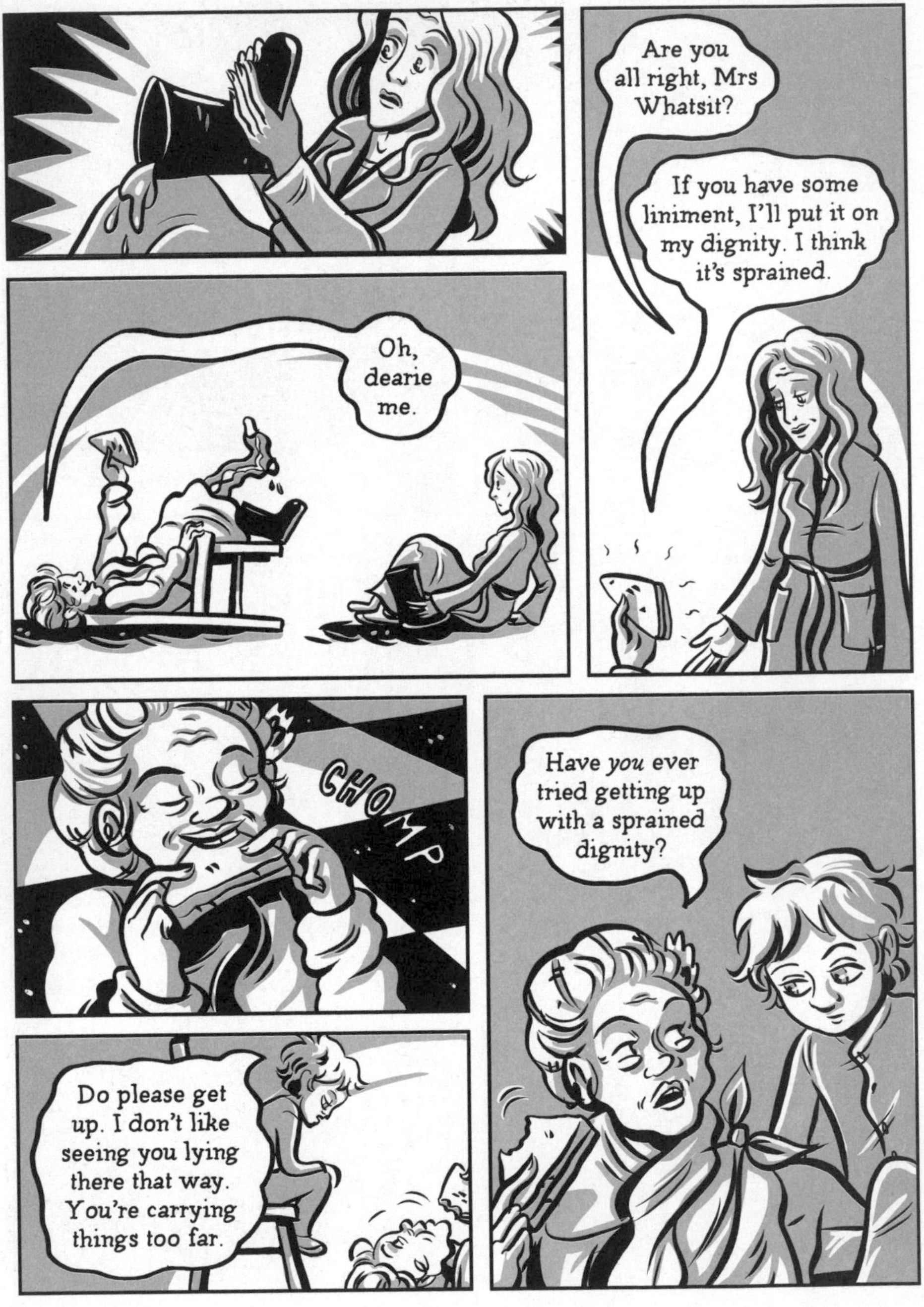
Are you all right, Mrs Whatsit?
If you have some liniment, I'll put it on my dignity. I think it's sprained.
Oh, dearie me.
CHOMP
Do please get up. I don't like seeing you lying there that way. You're carrying things too far.
Have *you* ever tried getting up with a sprained dignity?

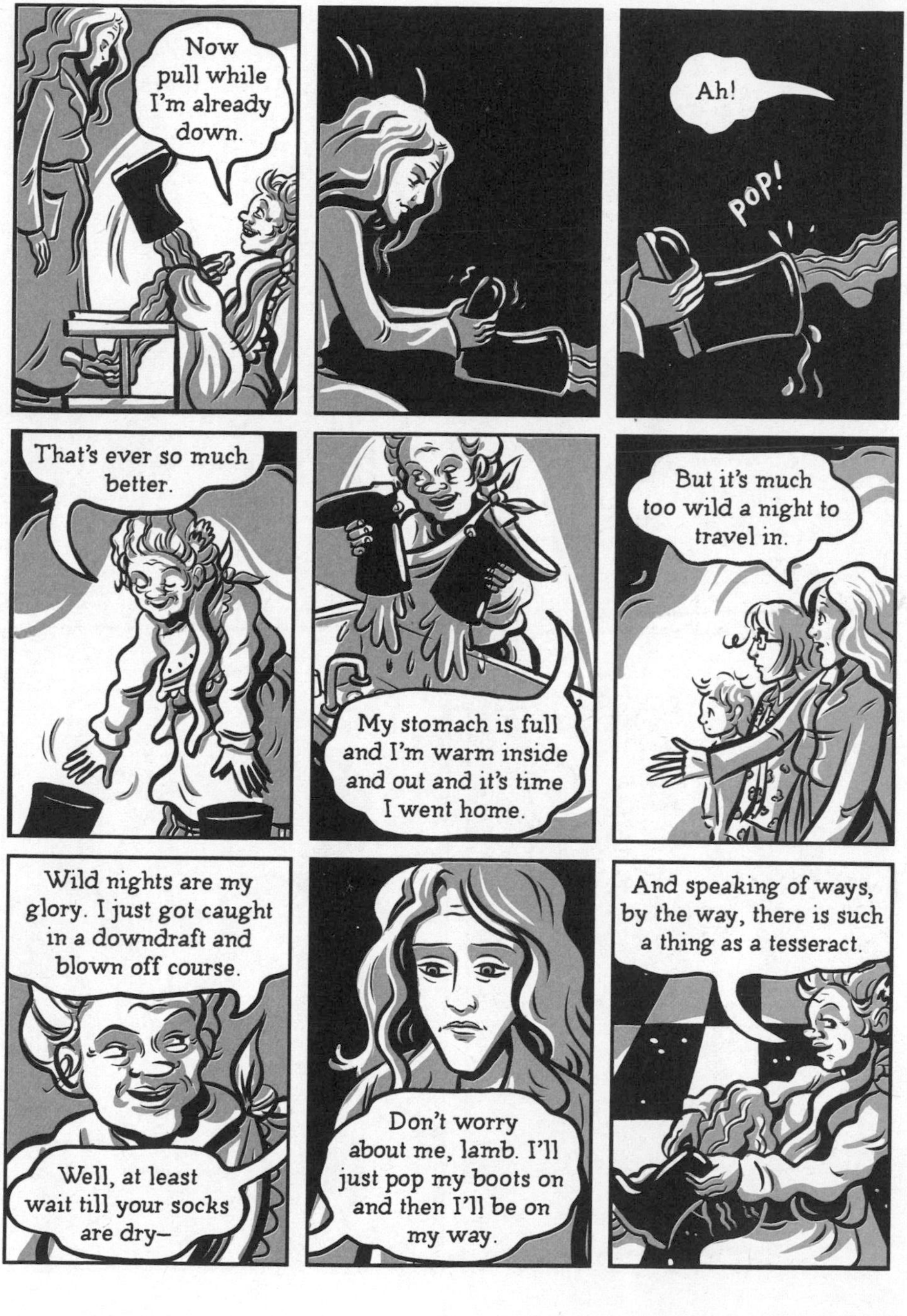
Now pull while I'm already down.
Ah!
POP!
That's ever so much better.
My stomach is full and I'm warm inside and out and it's time I went home.
But it's much too wild a night to travel in.
Wild nights are my glory. I just got caught in a downdraft and blown off course.
Well, at least wait till your socks are dry–
Don't worry about me, lamb. I'll just pop my boots on and then I'll be on my way.
And speaking of ways, by the way, there is such a thing as a tesseract.

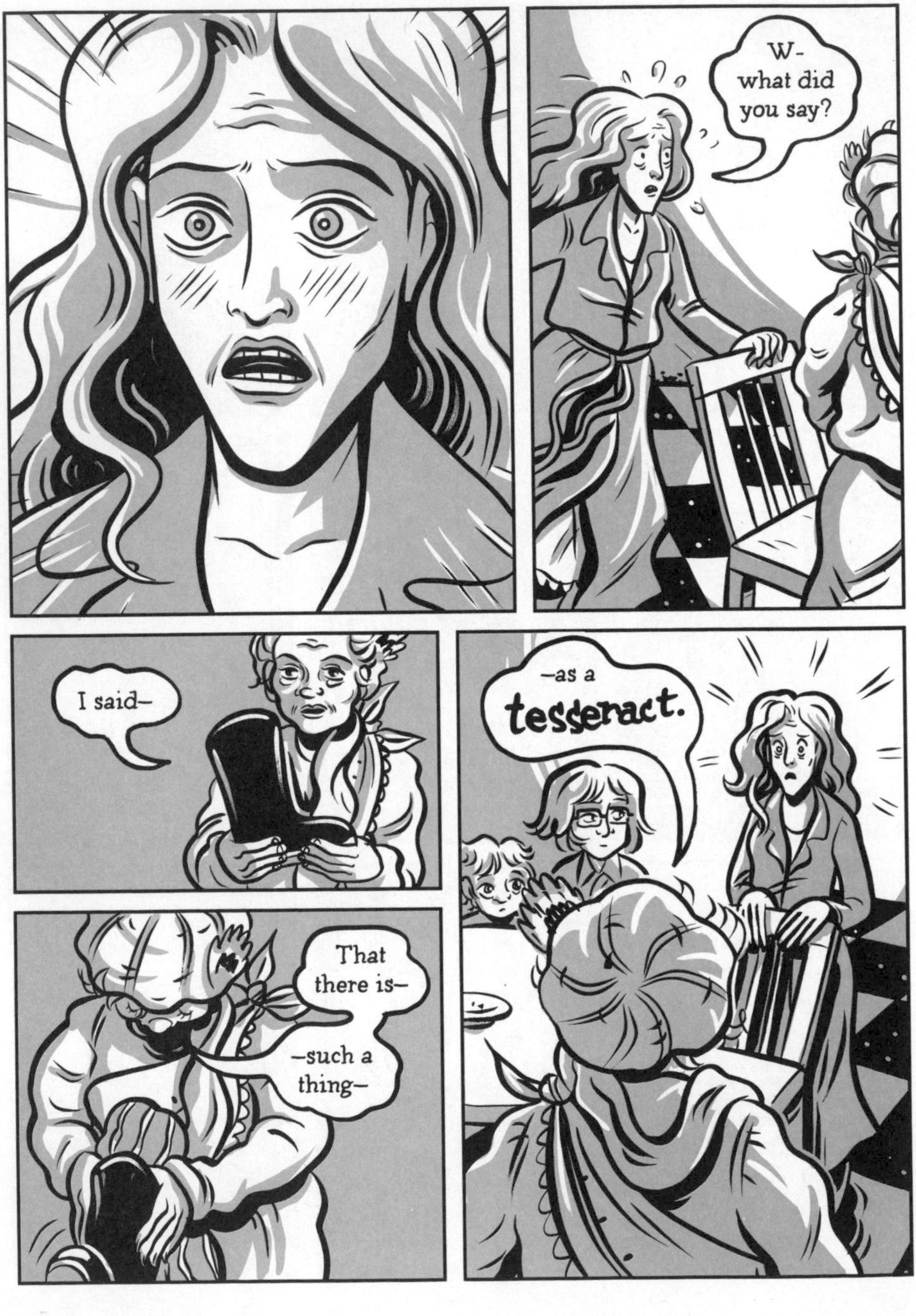
W-
what did
you say?
I said–
–as a
tesseract.
That
there is–
–such a
thing–

2
Mrs Who

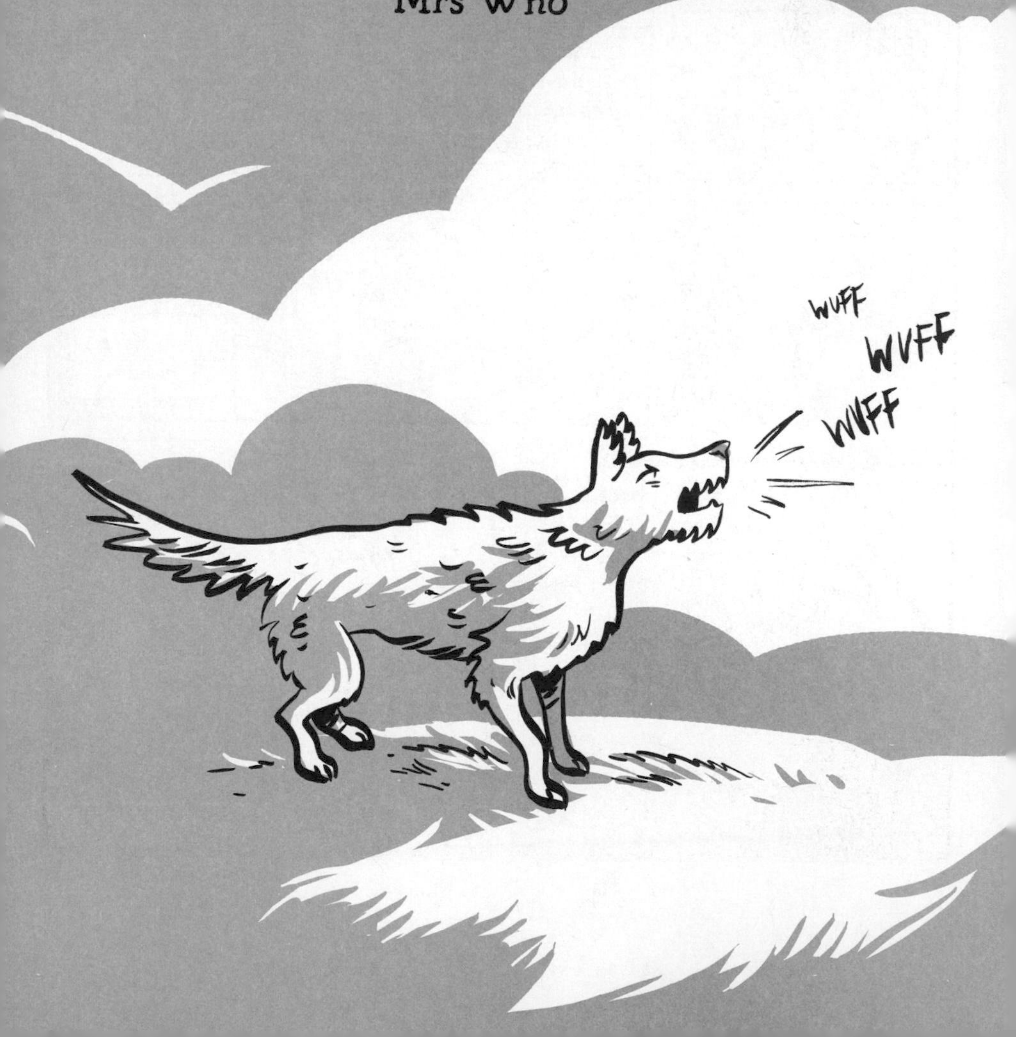
WUFF
WUFF
WUFF

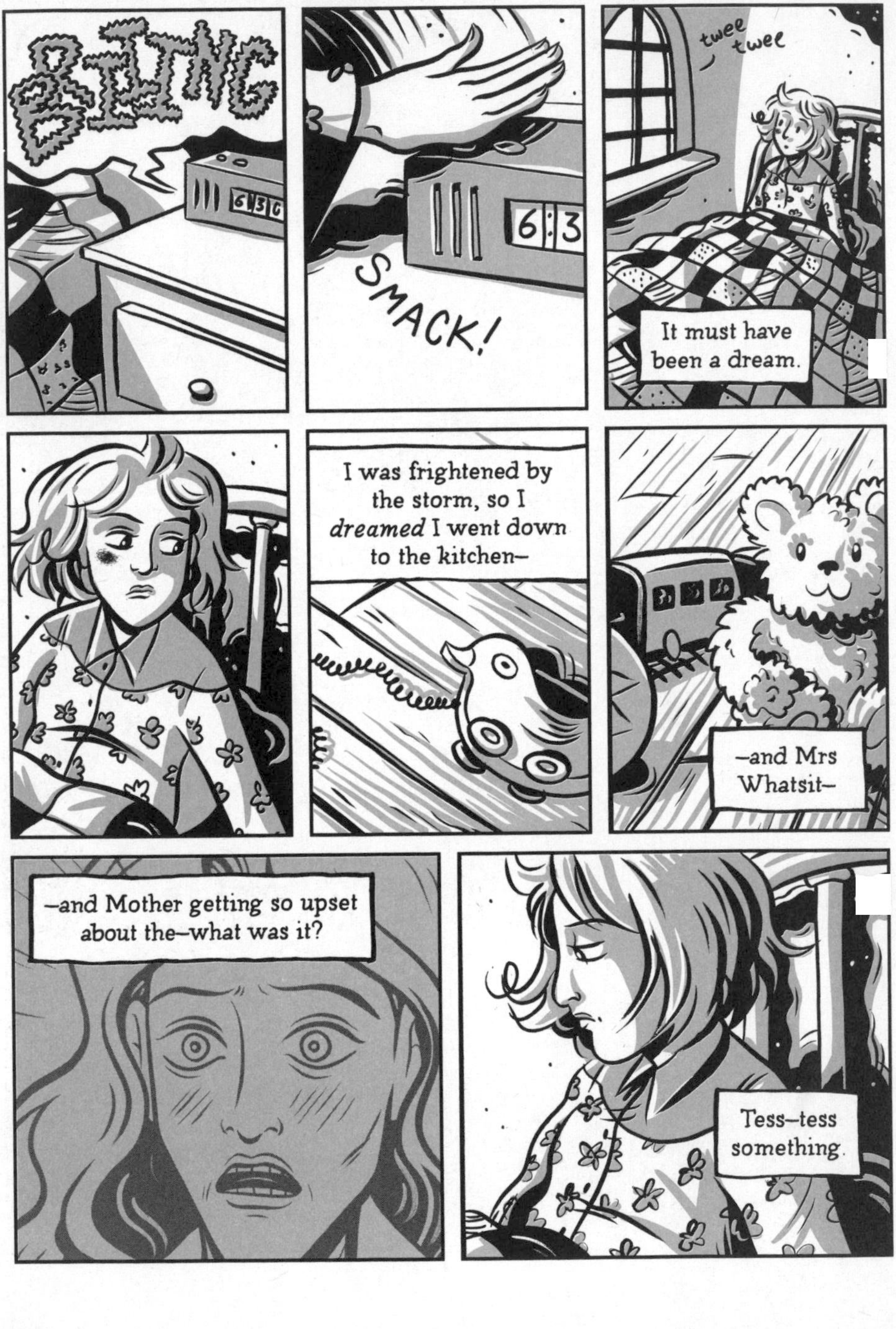

BRING
SMACK!
twee twee
It must have been a dream.
I was frightened by the storm, so I *dreamed* I went down to the kitchen–
–and Mrs Whatsit–
–and Mother getting so upset about the–what was it?
Tess–tess something.

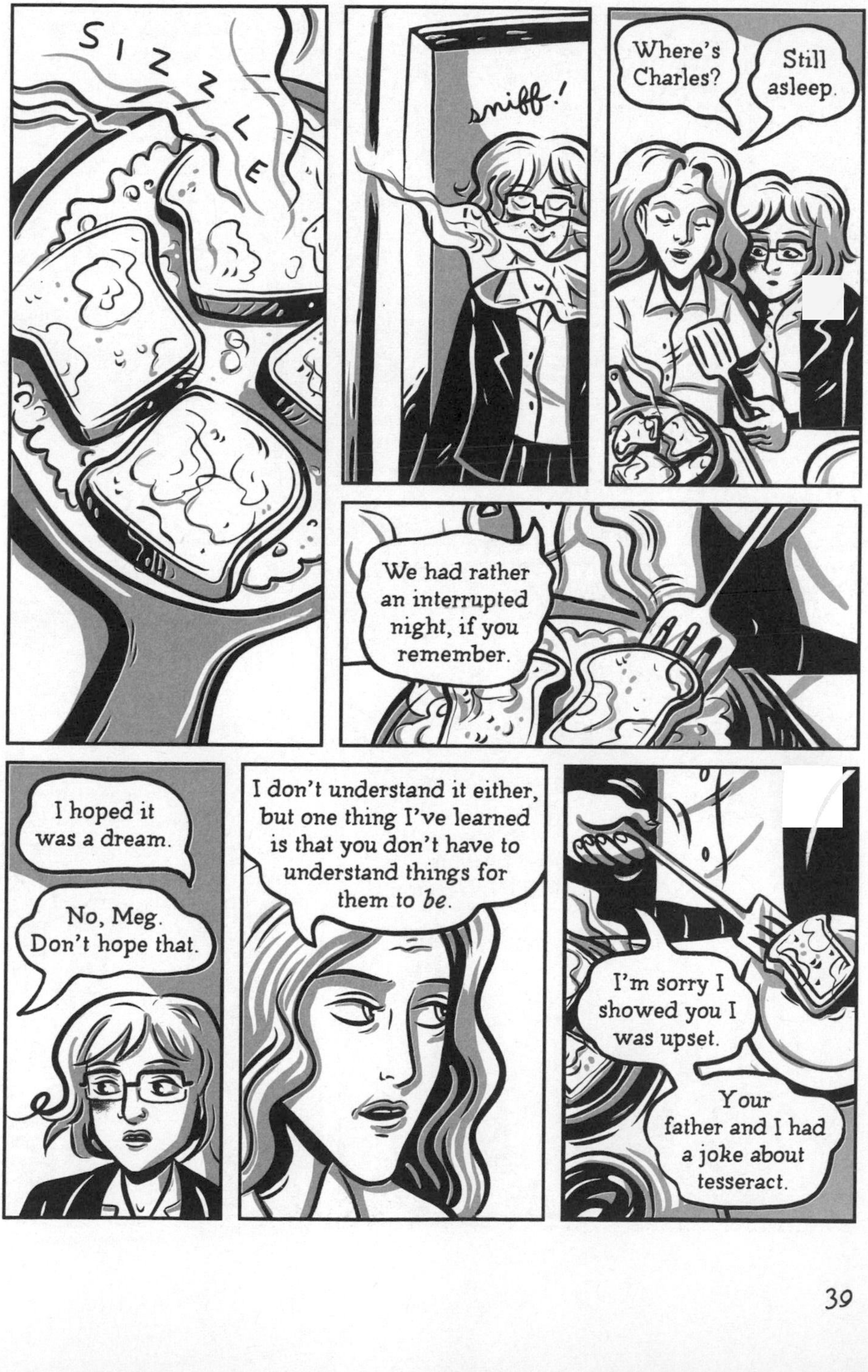
SIZZLE
sniff!
Where's Charles?
Still asleep.
We had rather an interrupted night, if you remember.
I hoped it was a dream.
No, Meg. Don't hope that.
I don't understand it either, but one thing I've learned is that you don't have to understand things for them to *be*.
I'm sorry I showed you I was upset.
Your father and I had a joke about tesseract.

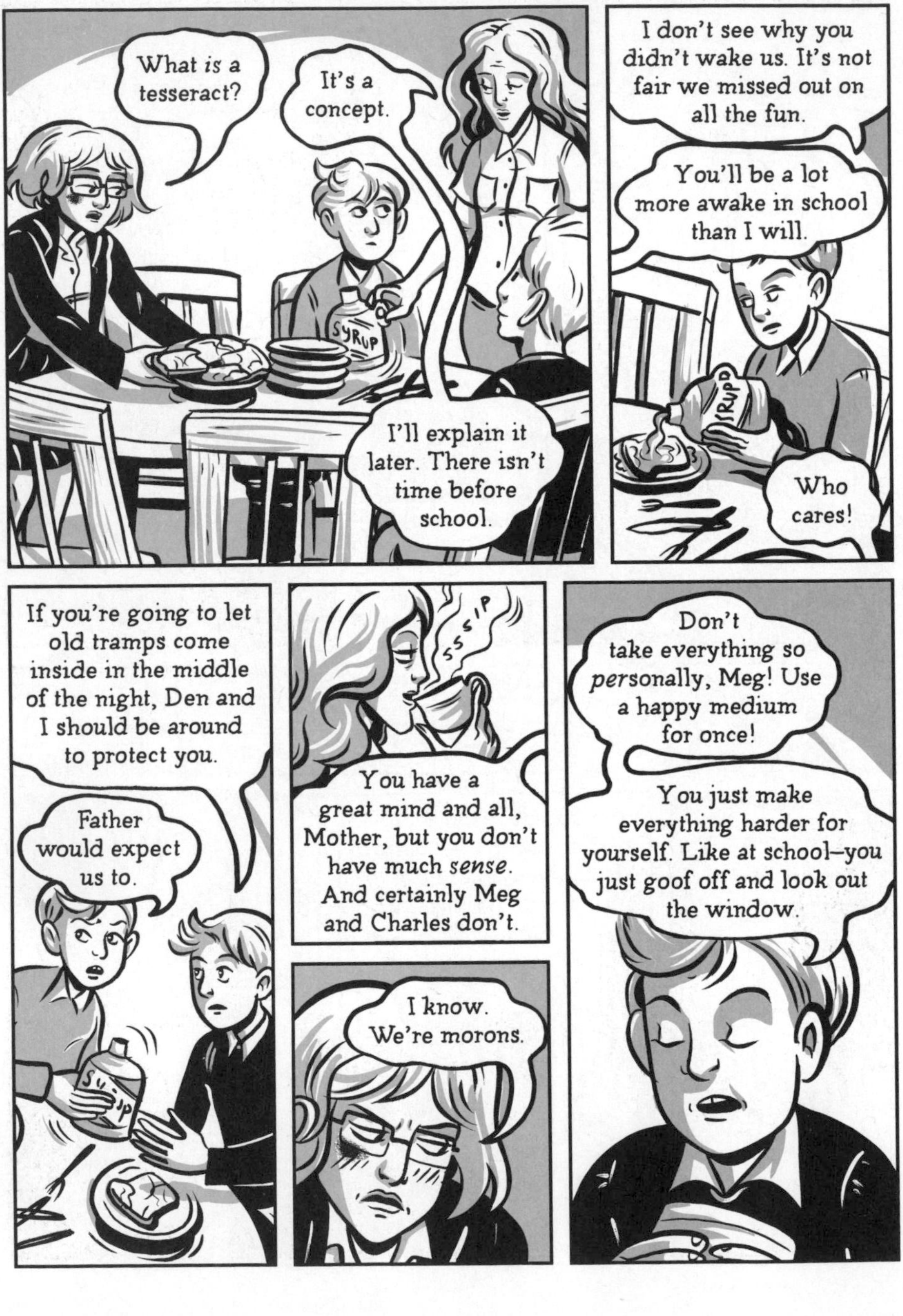
What *is* a tesseract?
It's a concept.
I'll explain it later. There isn't time before school.
I don't see why you didn't wake us. It's not fair we missed out on all the fun.
You'll be a lot more awake in school than I will.
Who cares!
SYRUP
If you're going to let old tramps come inside in the middle of the night, Den and I should be around to protect you.
Father would expect us to.
SSSIP
You have a great mind and all, Mother, but you don't have much *sense*. And certainly Meg and Charles don't.
I know. We're morons.
Don't take everything so *per*sonally, Meg! Use a happy medium for once!
You just make everything harder for yourself. Like at school—you just goof off and look out the window.

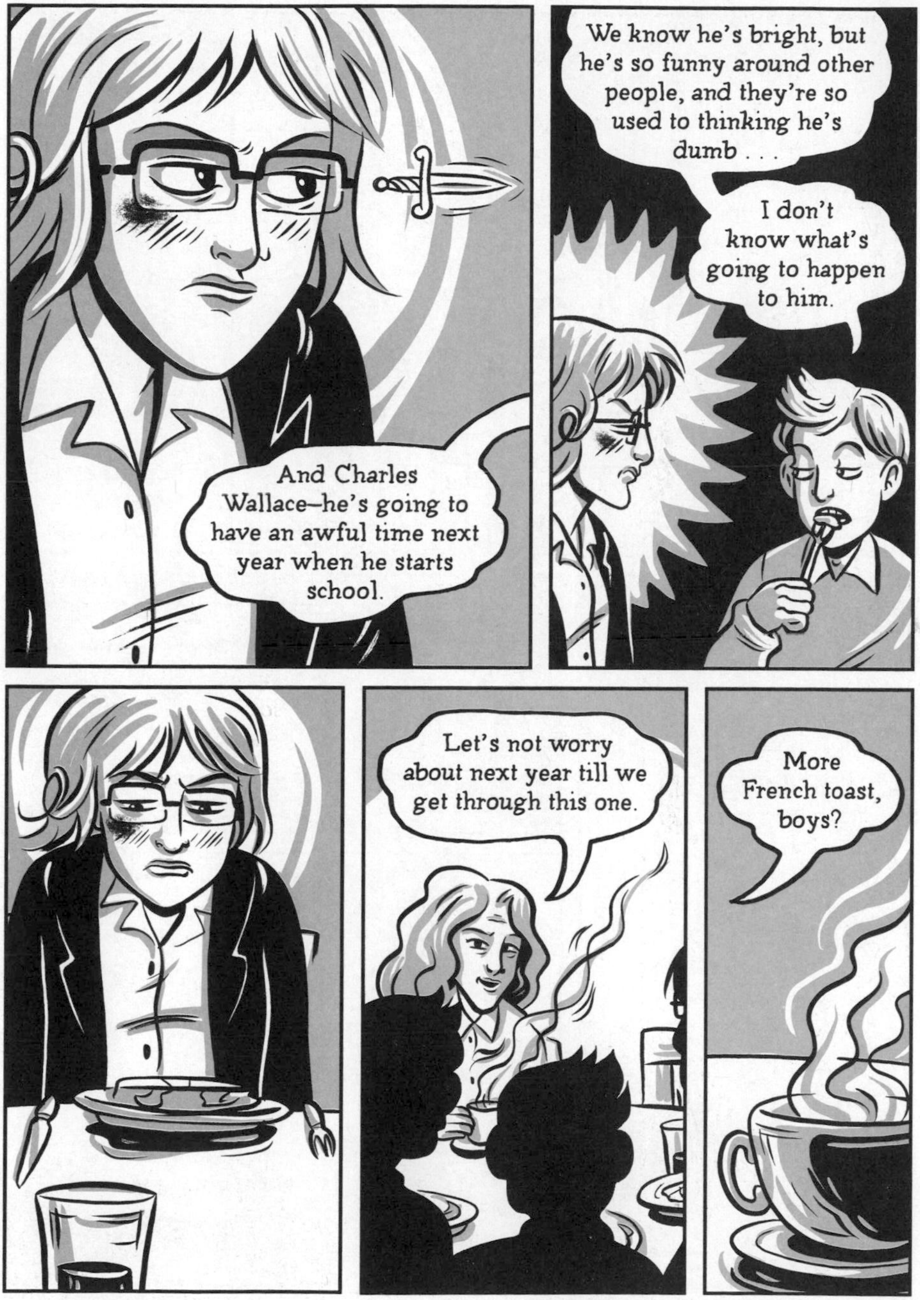
And Charles Wallace—he's going to have an awful time next year when he starts school.
We know he's bright, but he's so funny around other people, and they're so used to thinking he's dumb . . .
I don't know what's going to happen to him.
Let's not worry about next year till we get through this one.
More French toast, boys?

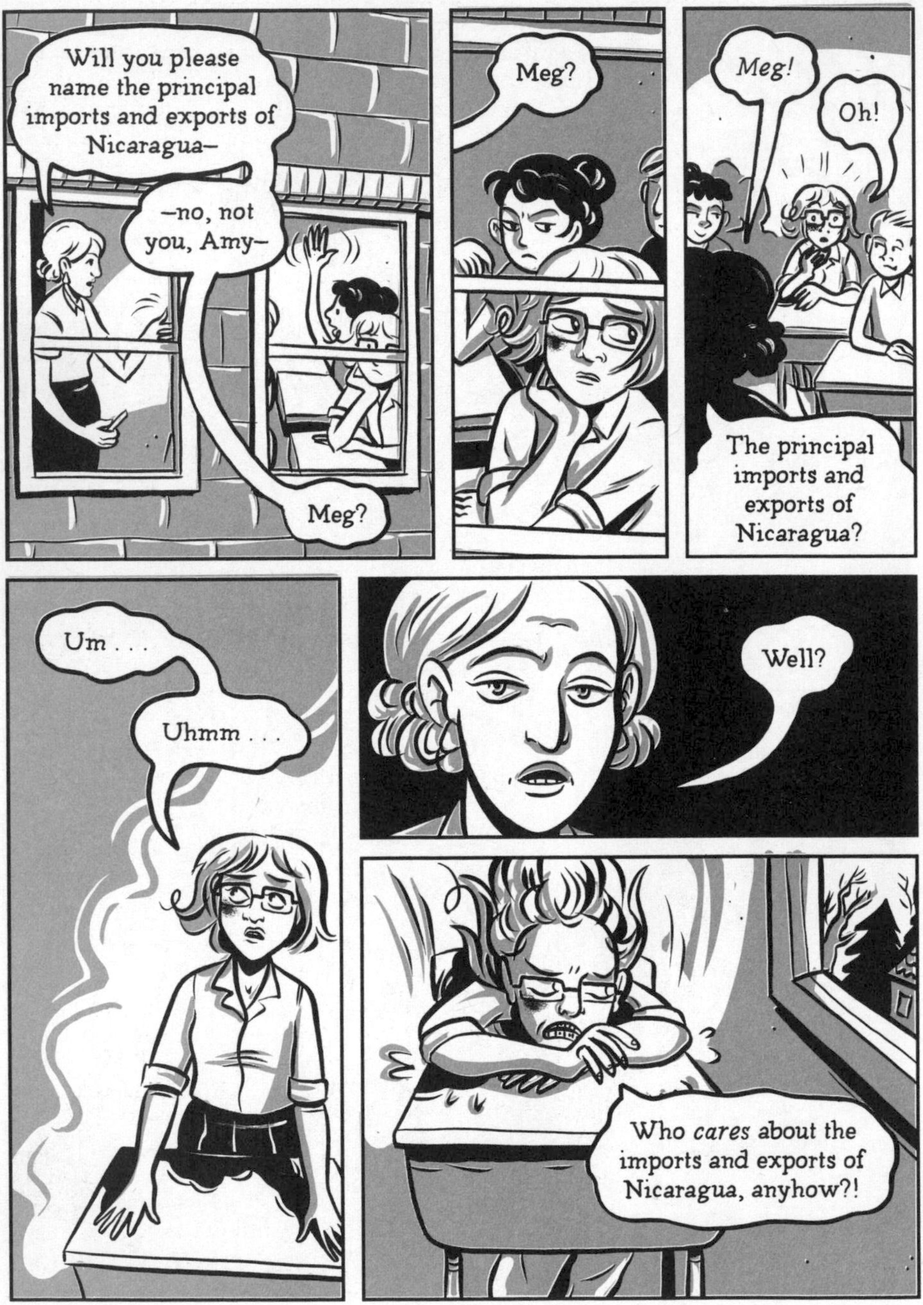
Will you please name the principal imports and exports of Nicaragua–
–no, not you, Amy–
Meg?
Meg?
Meg!
Oh!
The principal imports and exports of Nicaragua?
Um . . .
Uhmm . . .
Well?
Who *cares* about the imports and exports of Nicaragua, anyhow?!

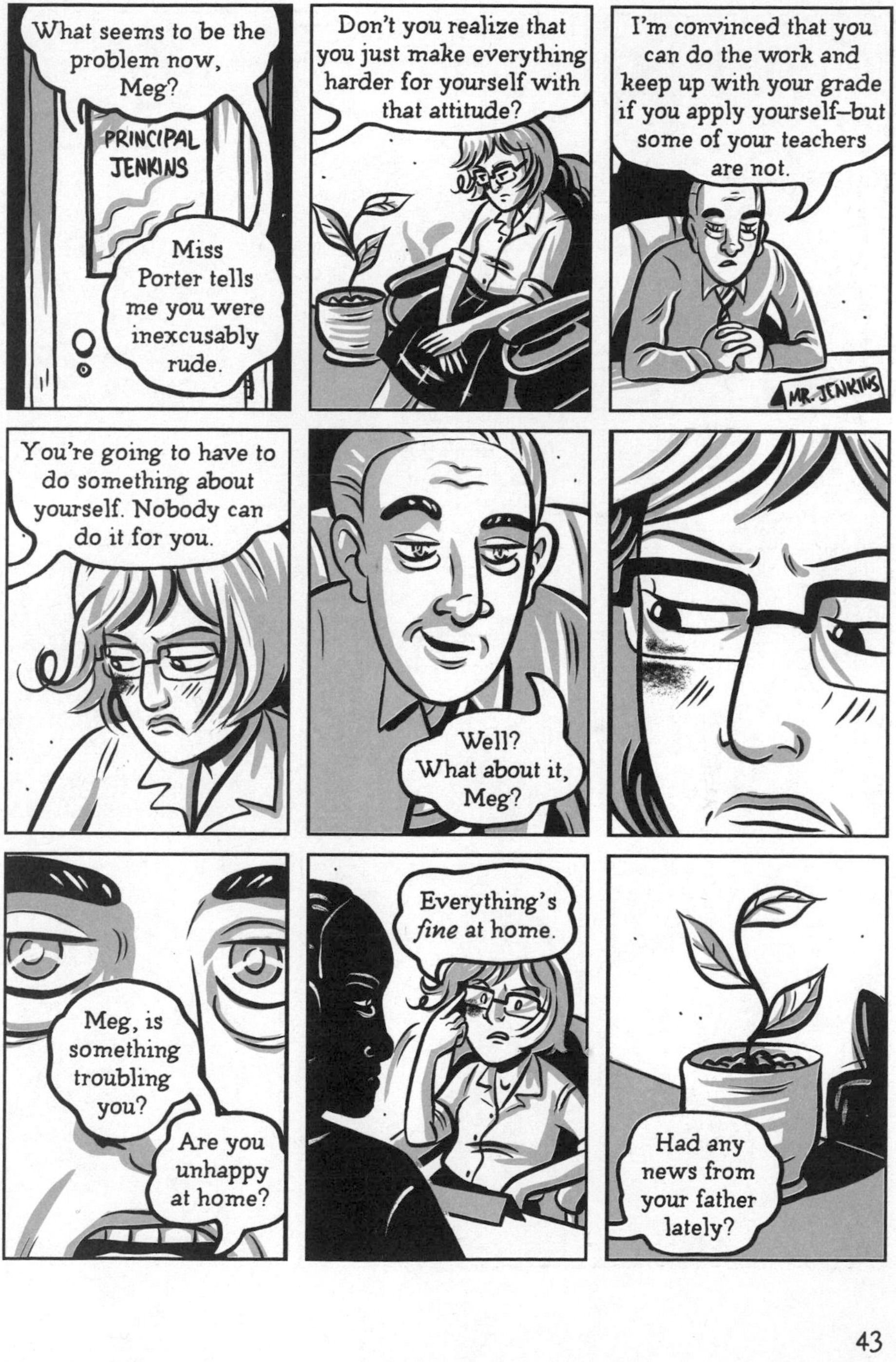
What seems to be the problem now, Meg?
PRINCIPAL JENKINS
Miss Porter tells me you were inexcusably rude.
Don't you realize that you just make everything harder for yourself with that attitude?
I'm convinced that you can do the work and keep up with your grade if you apply yourself—but some of your teachers are not.
MR. JENKINS
You're going to have to do something about yourself. Nobody can do it for you.
Well? What about it, Meg?
Meg, is something troubling you?
Are you unhappy at home?
Everything's *fine* at home.
Had any news from your father lately?

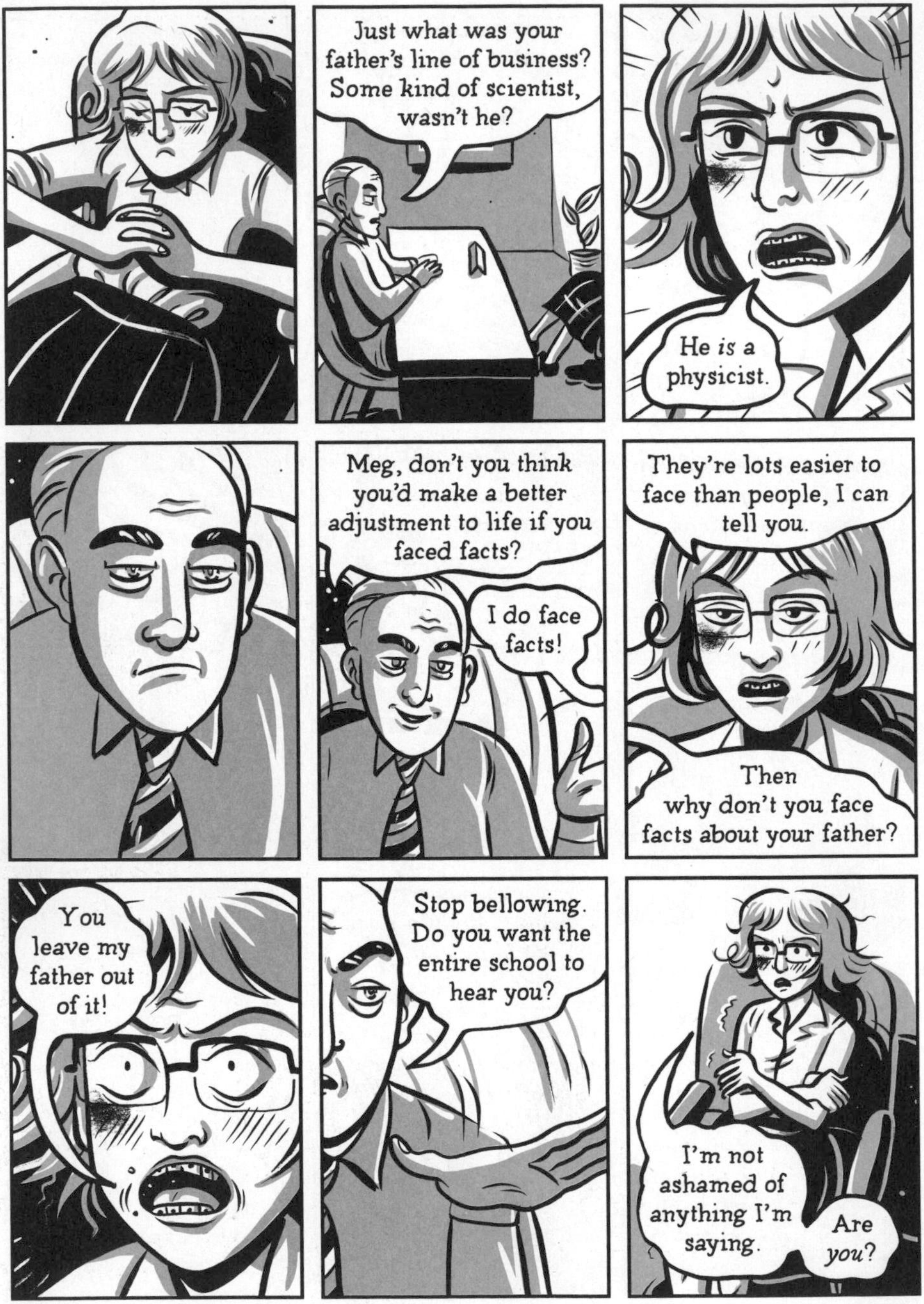
Just what was your father's line of business? Some kind of scientist, wasn't he?
He *is* a physicist.
Meg, don't you think you'd make a better adjustment to life if you faced facts?
I do face facts!
They're lots easier to face than people, I can tell you.
Then why don't you face facts about your father?
You leave my father out of it!
Stop bellowing. Do you want the entire school to hear you?
I'm not ashamed of anything I'm saying.
Are *you*?

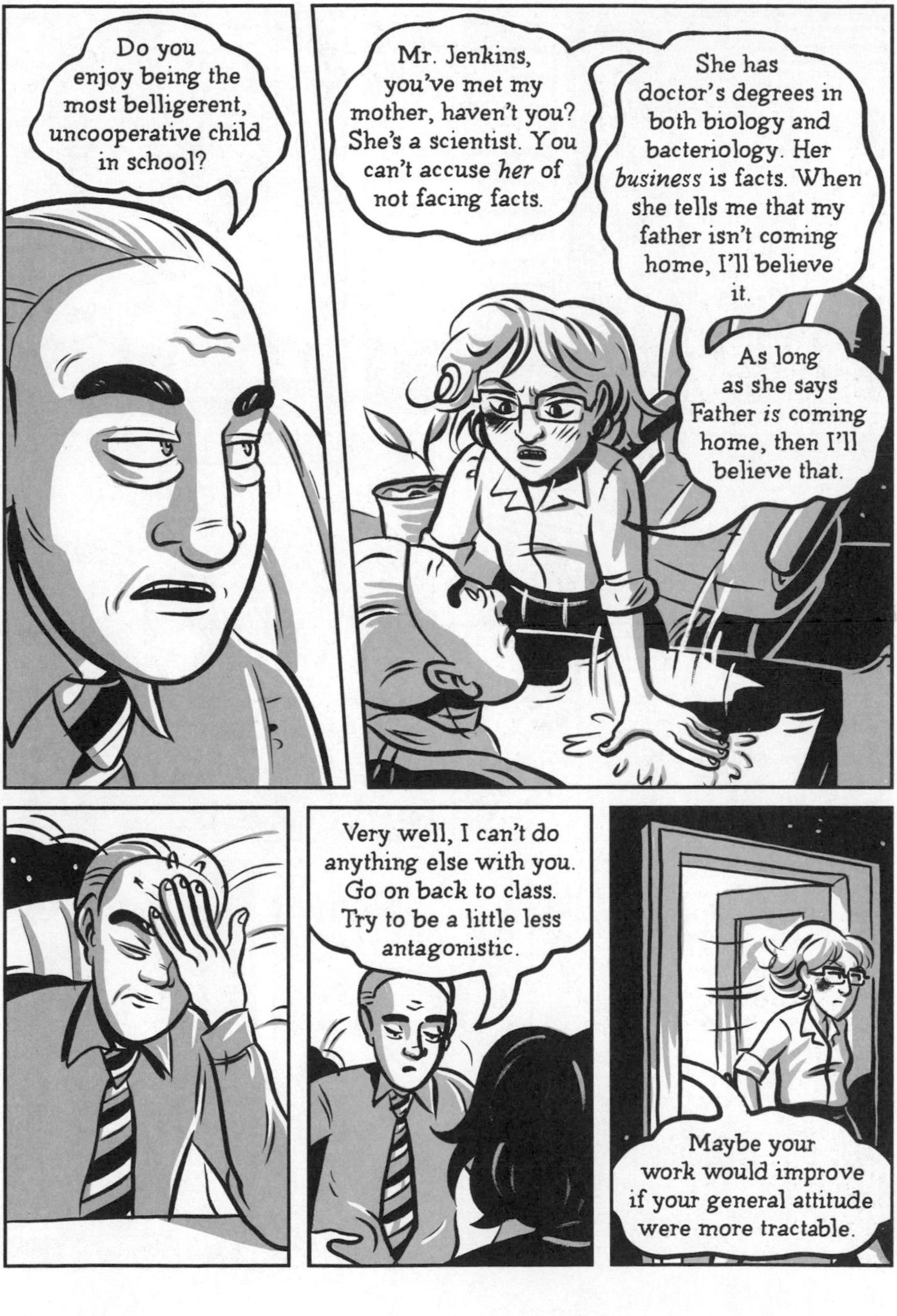
Do you enjoy being the most belligerent, uncooperative child in school?
Mr. Jenkins, you've met my mother, haven't you? She's a scientist. You can't accuse *her* of not facing facts.
She has doctor's degrees in both biology and bacteriology. Her *business* is facts. When she tells me that my father isn't coming home, I'll believe it.
As long as she says Father *is* coming home, then I'll believe that.
Very well, I can't do anything else with you. Go on back to class. Try to be a little less antagonistic.
Maybe your work would improve if your general attitude were more tractable.

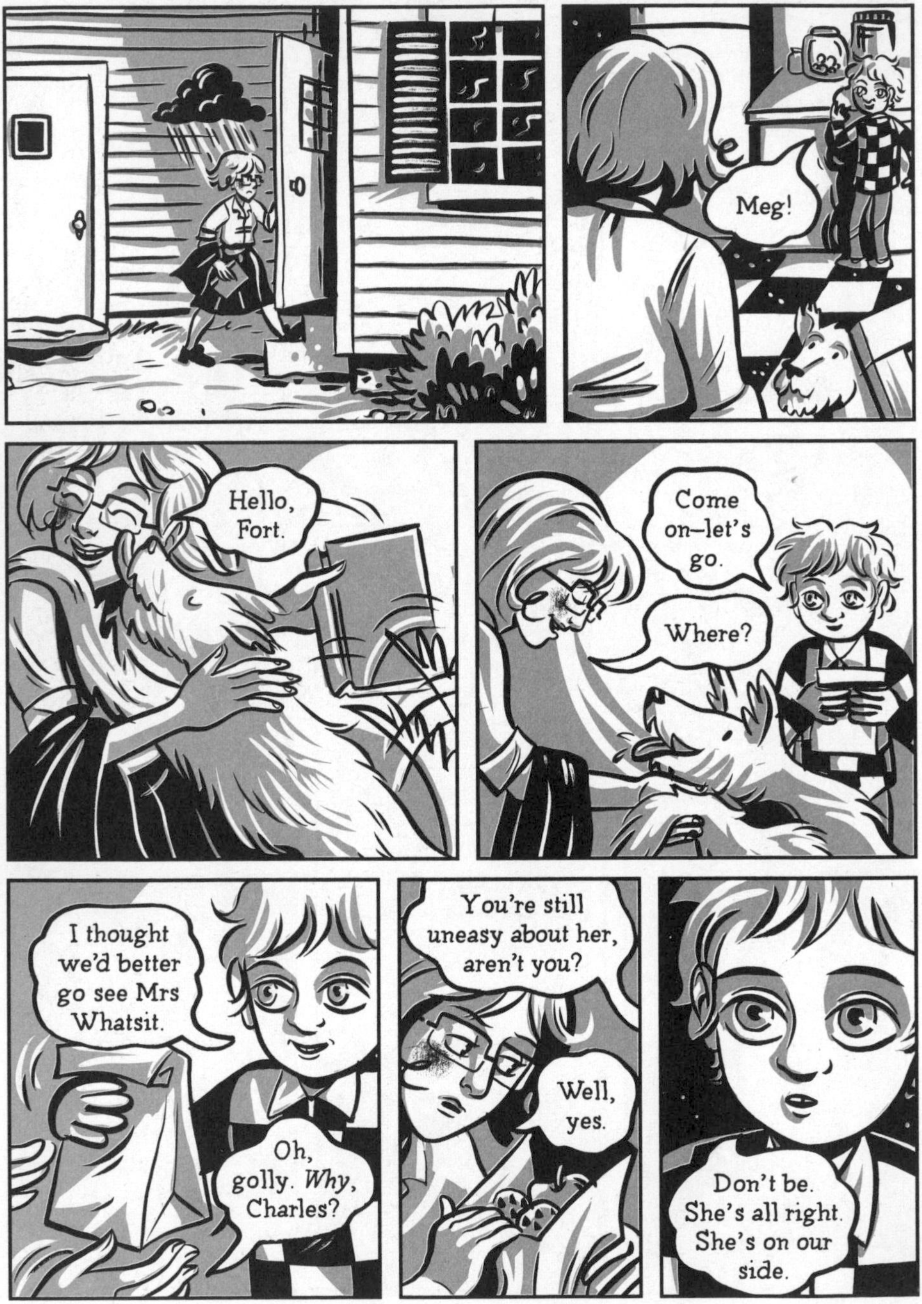

Meg!
Hello, Fort.
Come on–let's go.
Where?
I thought we'd better go see Mrs Whatsit.
Oh, golly. *Why*, Charles?
You're still uneasy about her, aren't you?
Well, yes.
Don't be. She's all right. She's on our side.

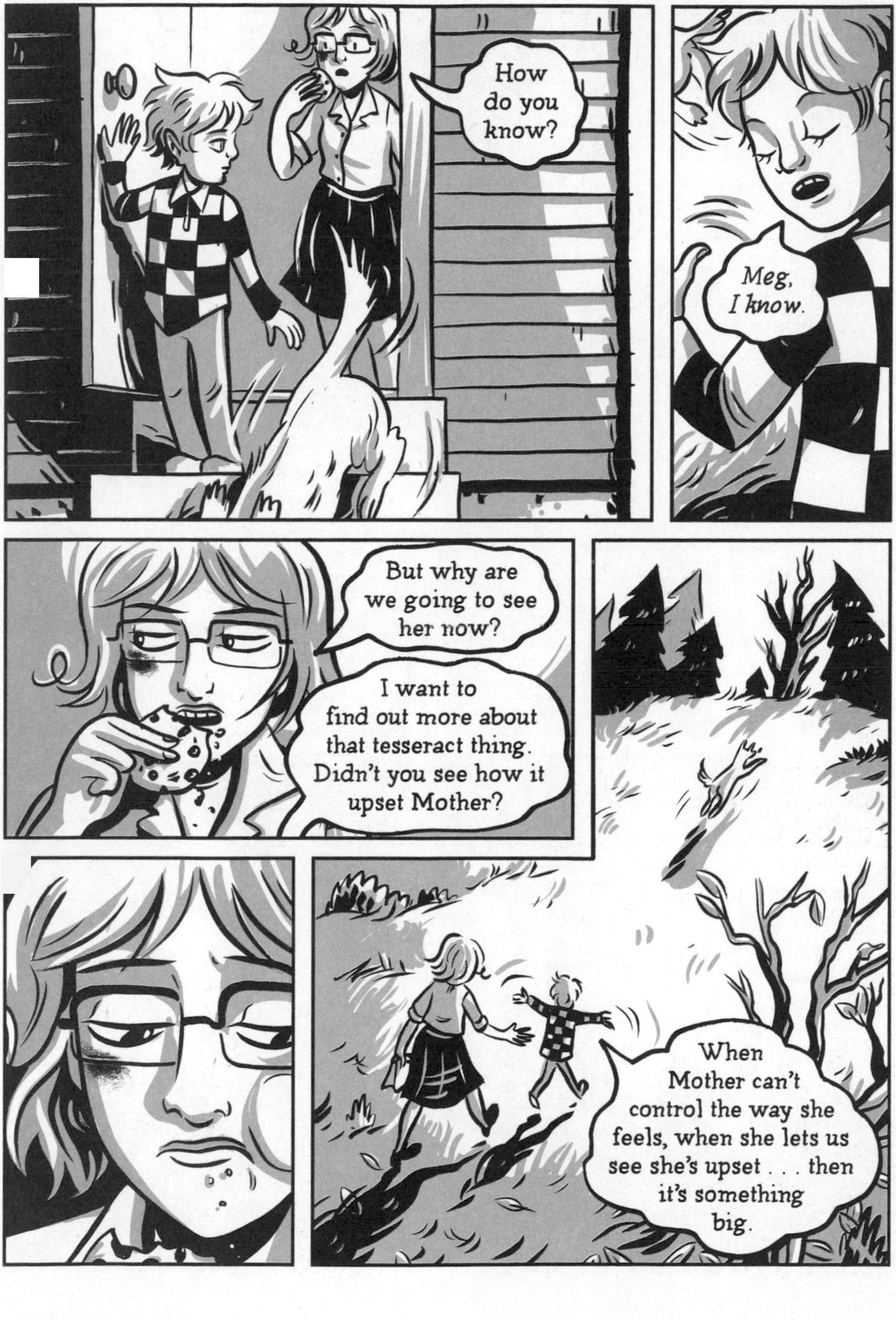
How do you know?
Meg, I know.
But why are we going to see her now?
I want to find out more about that tesseract thing. Didn't you see how it upset Mother?
When Mother can't control the way she feels, when she lets us see she's upset . . . then it's something big.

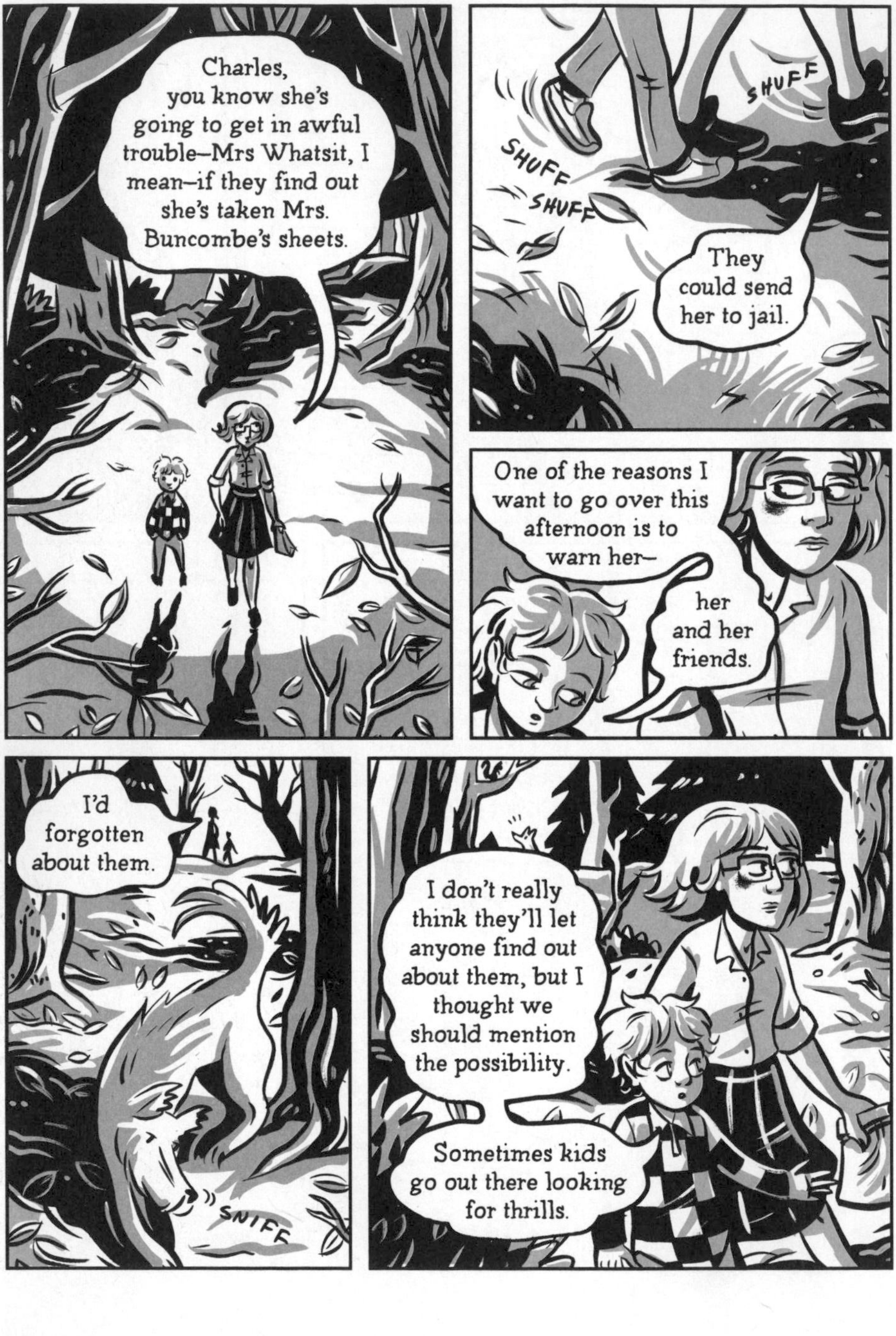
Charles, you know she's going to get in awful trouble—Mrs Whatsit, I mean—if they find out she's taken Mrs. Buncombe's sheets.
SHUFF
SHUFF
SHUFF
They could send her to jail.
One of the reasons I want to go over this afternoon is to warn her—
her and her friends.
I'd forgotten about them.
SNIFF
I don't really think they'll let anyone find out about them, but I thought we should mention the possibility.
Sometimes kids go out there looking for thrills.

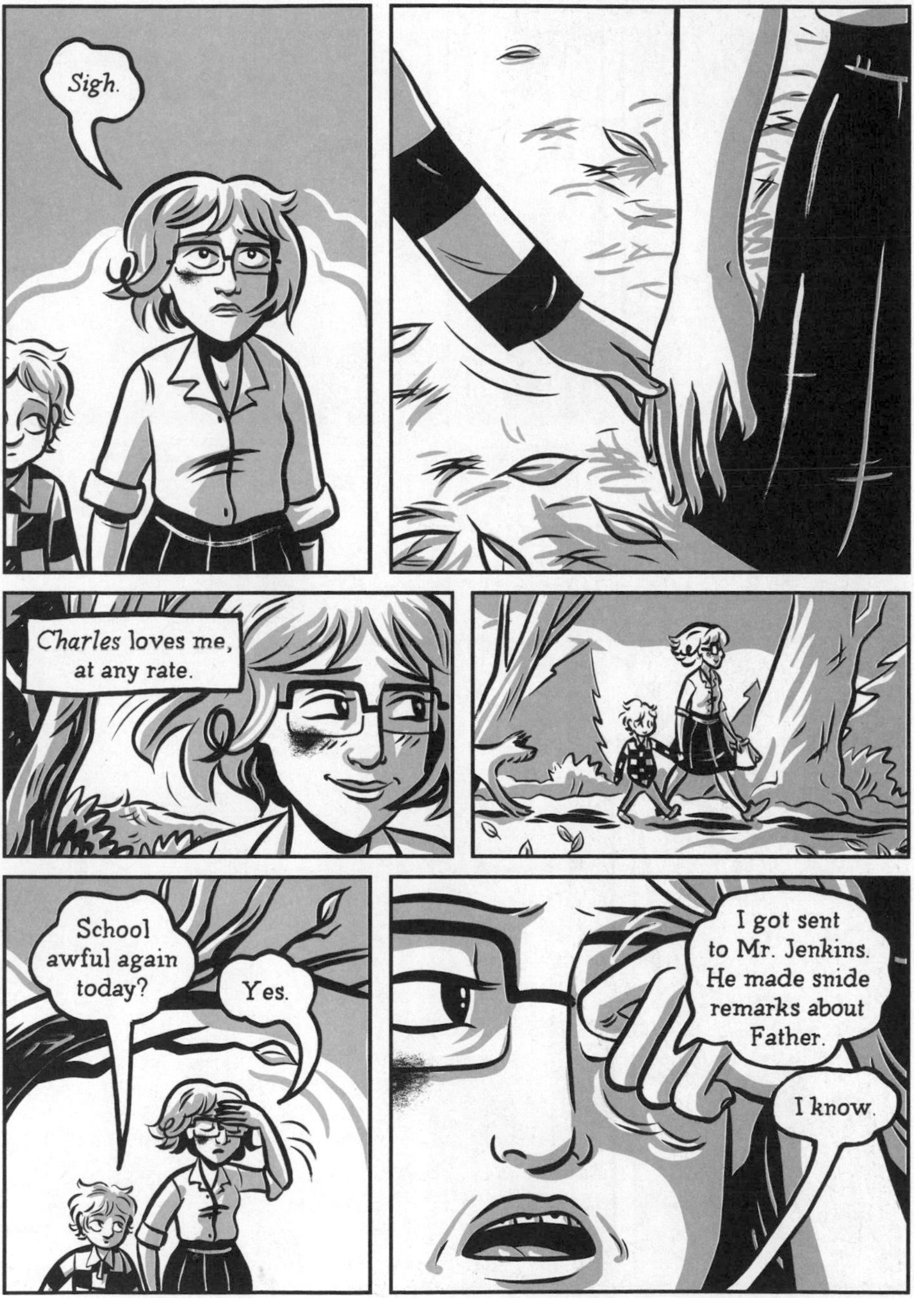
Sigh.
Charles loves me, at any rate.
School awful again today?
Yes.
I got sent to Mr. Jenkins. He made snide remarks about Father.
I know.

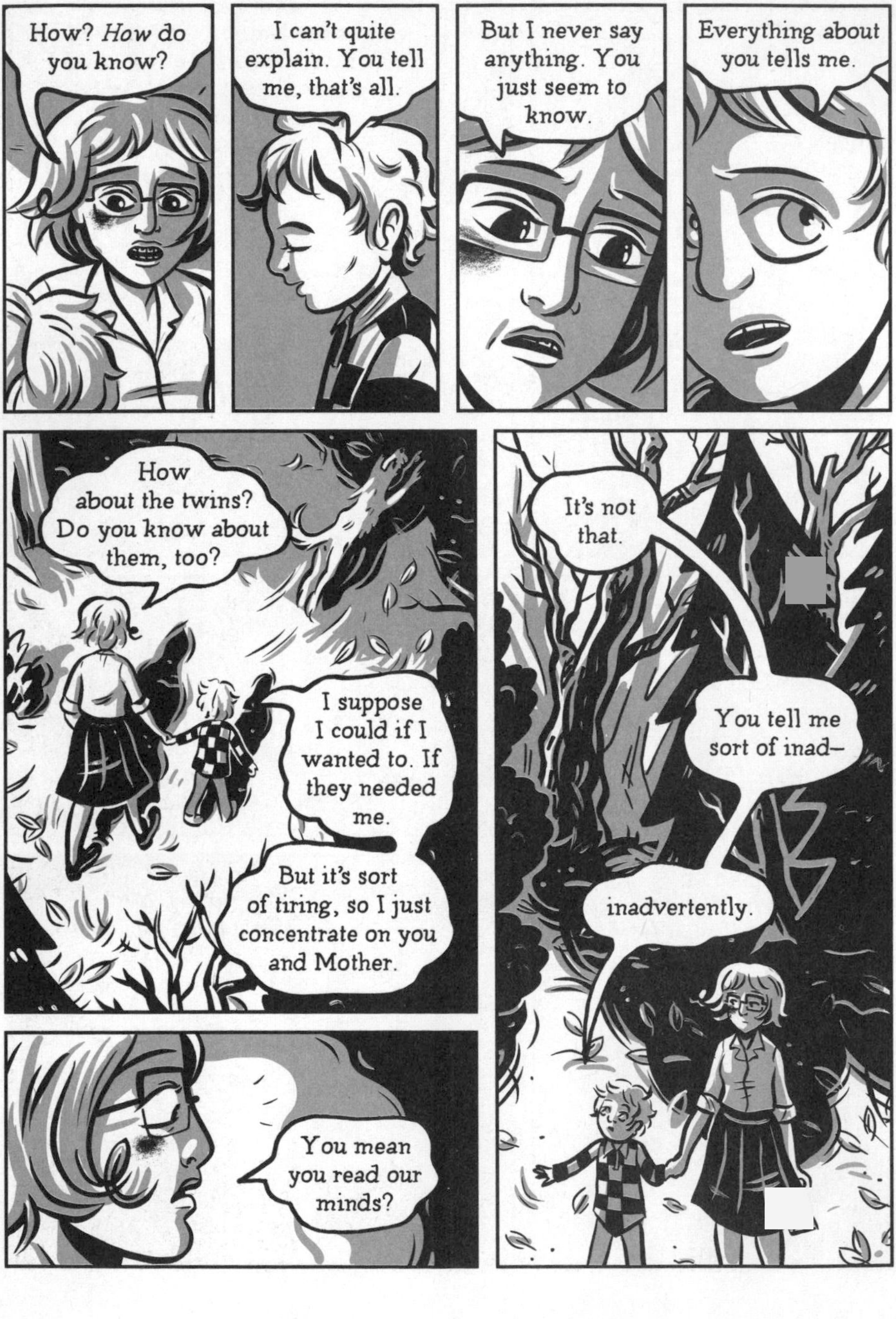

How? *How* do you know?
I can't quite explain. You tell me, that's all.
But I never say anything. You just seem to know.
Everything about you tells me.
How about the twins? Do you know about them, too?
I suppose I could if I wanted to. If they needed me.
But it's sort of tiring, so I just concentrate on you and Mother.
You mean you read our minds?
It's not that.
You tell me sort of inad–
inadvertently.

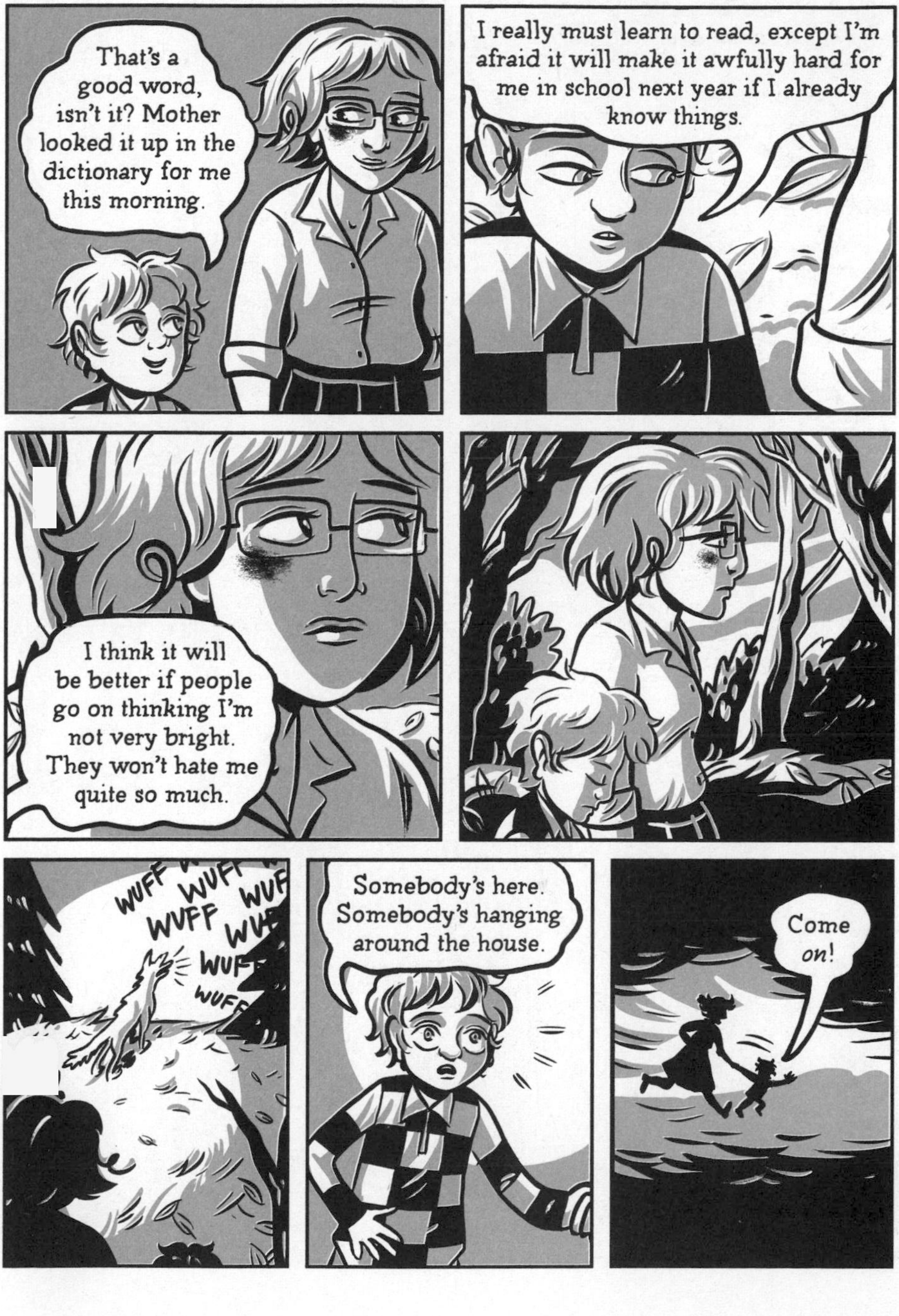
That's a good word, isn't it? Mother looked it up in the dictionary for me this morning.
I really must learn to read, except I'm afraid it will make it awfully hard for me in school next year if I already know things.
I think it will be better if people go on thinking I'm not very bright. They won't hate me quite so much.
WUFF WUFF WUFF WUFF WUFF WUFF
Somebody's here. Somebody's hanging around the house.
Come *on*!

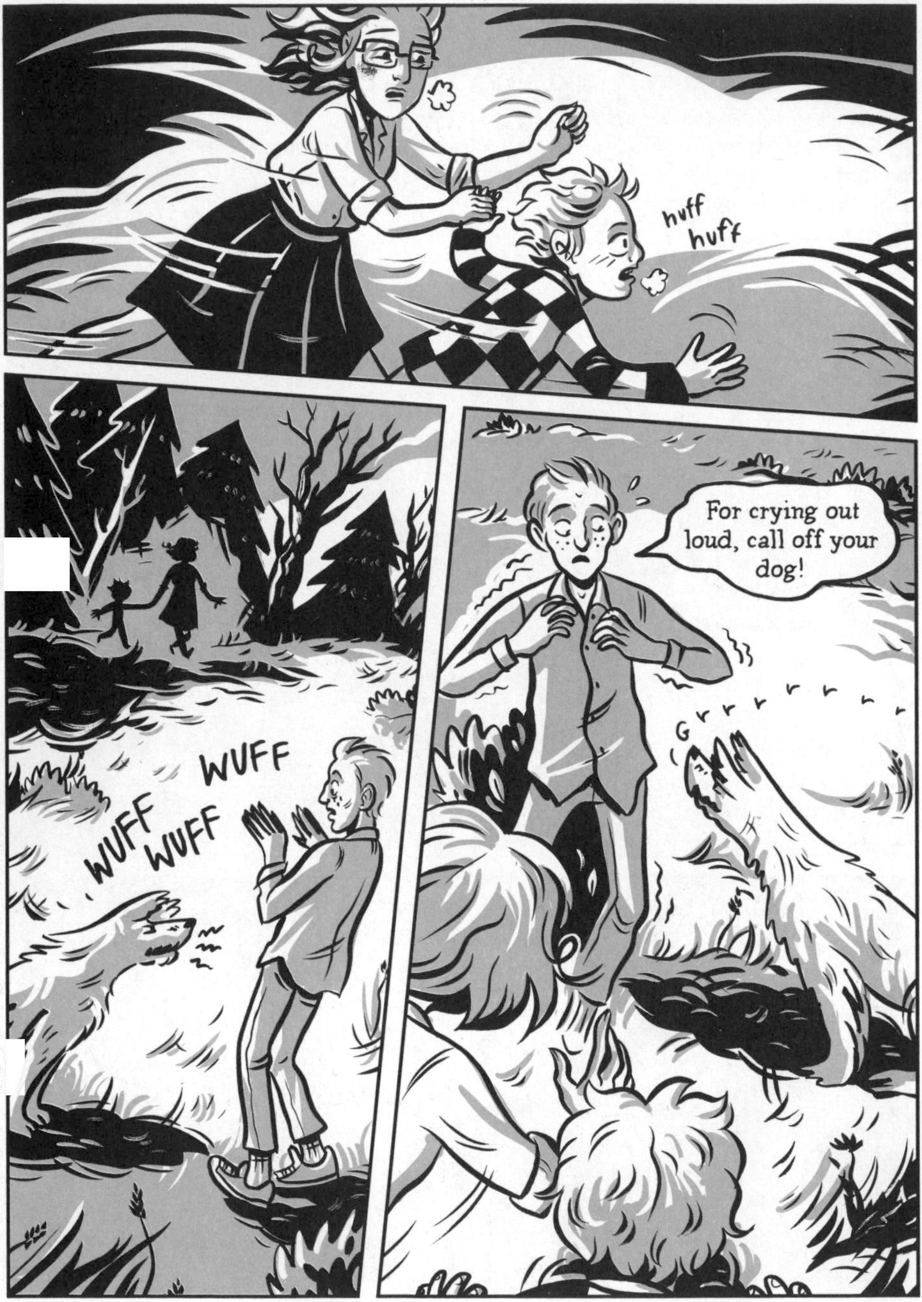
huff
huff
WUFF
WUFF
WUFF
For crying out loud, call off your dog!
Grrrrrrrr

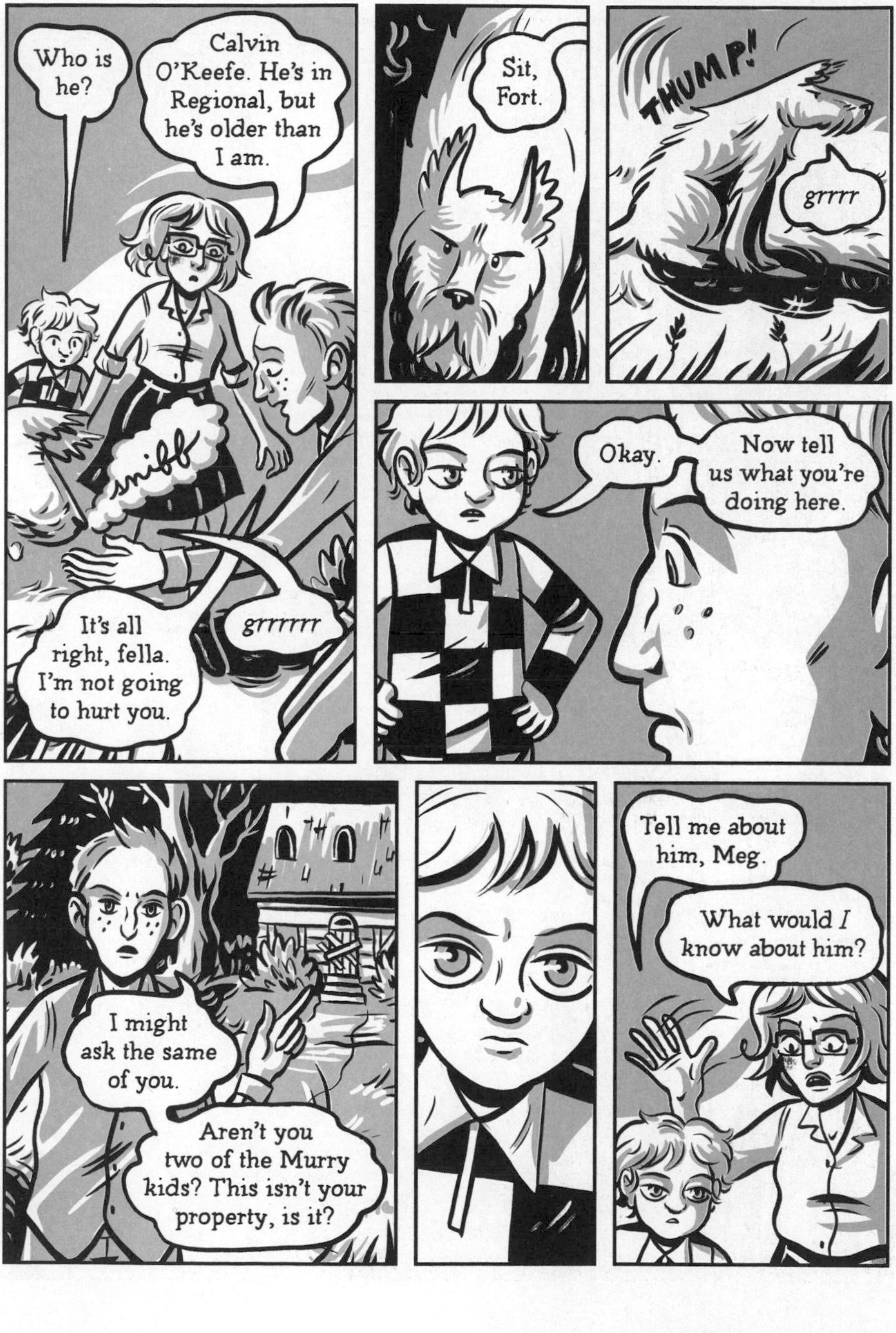
Who is he?
Calvin O'Keefe. He's in Regional, but he's older than I am.
sniff
It's all right, fella. I'm not going to hurt you.
grrrrrr
Sit, Fort.
THUMP!
grrrr
Okay.
Now tell us what you're doing here.
I might ask the same of you.
Aren't you two of the Murry kids? This isn't your property, is it?
Tell me about him, Meg.
What would *I* know about him?

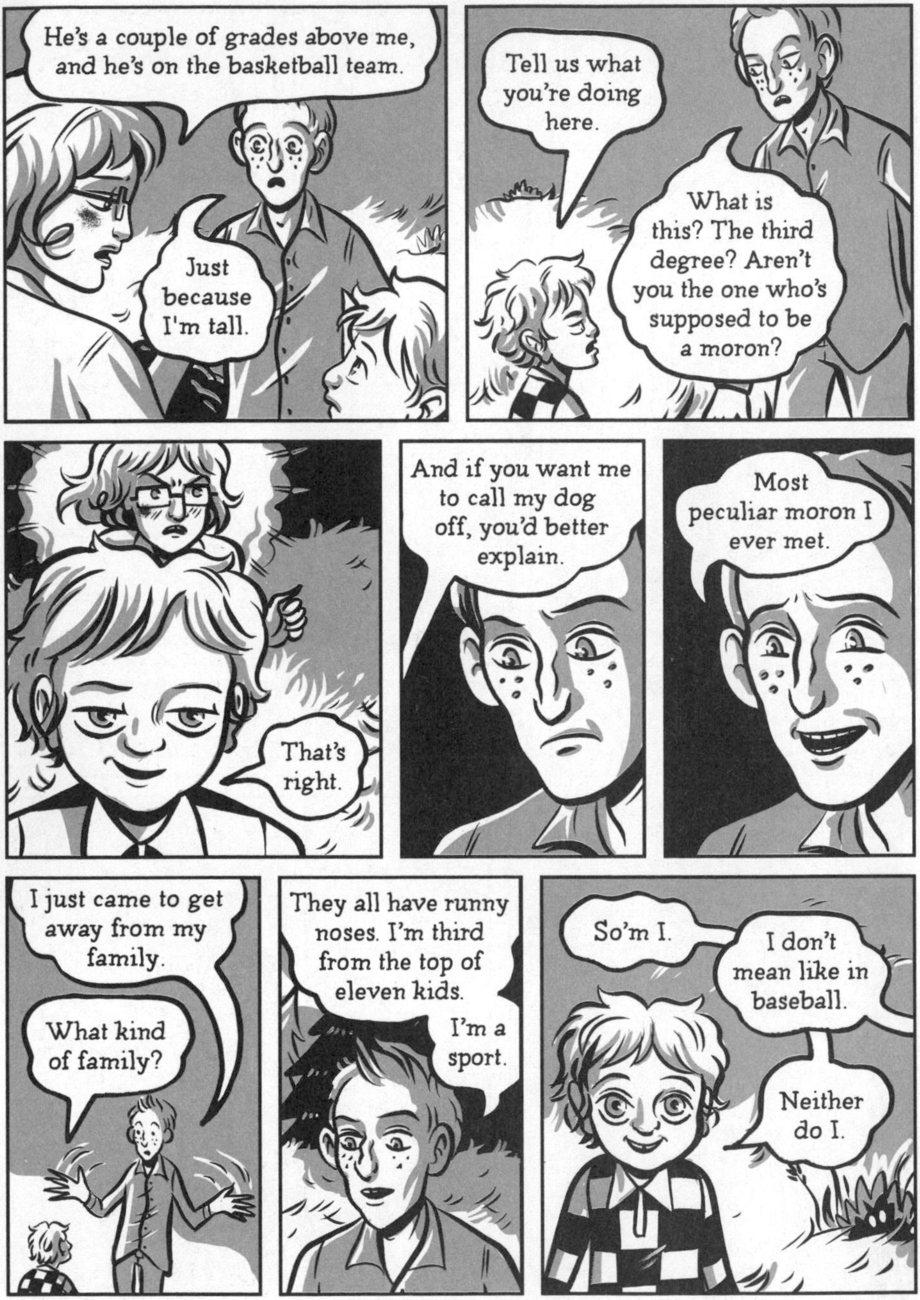
He's a couple of grades above me, and he's on the basketball team.
Just because I'm tall.
Tell us what you're doing here.
What is this? The third degree? Aren't you the one who's supposed to be a moron?
That's right.
And if you want me to call my dog off, you'd better explain.
Most peculiar moron I ever met.
I just came to get away from my family.
What kind of family?
They all have runny noses. I'm third from the top of eleven kids.
I'm a sport.
So'm I.
I don't mean like in baseball.
Neither do I.

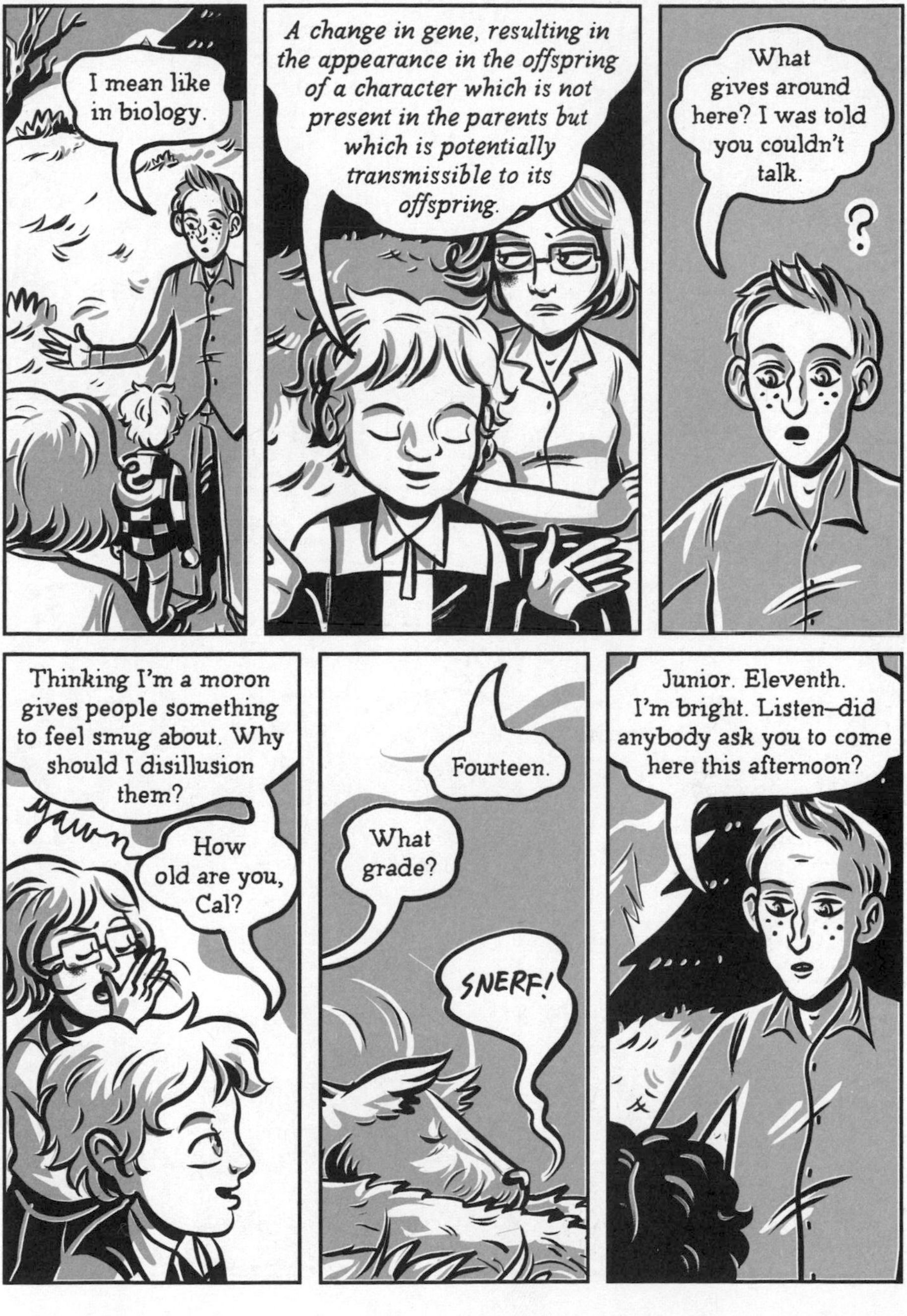

I mean like in biology.
A change in gene, resulting in the appearance in the offspring of a character which is not present in the parents but which is potentially transmissible to its offspring.
What gives around here? I was told you couldn't talk.
?
Thinking I'm a moron gives people something to feel smug about. Why should I disillusion them?
yawn
How old are you, Cal?
Fourteen.
What grade?
SNERF!
Junior. Eleventh. I'm bright. Listen—did anybody ask you to come here this afternoon?

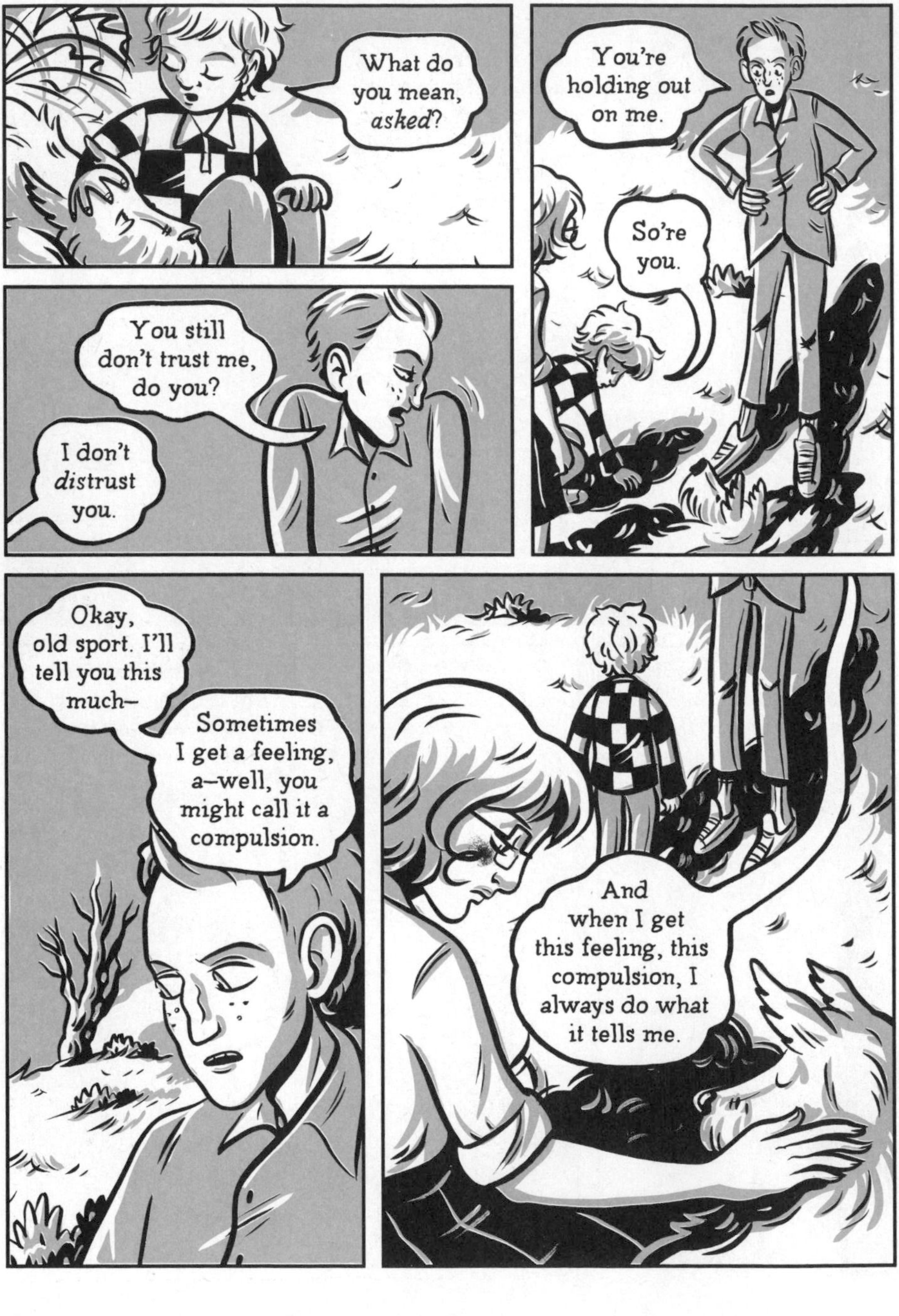
What do you mean, *asked*?
You're holding out on me.
So're you.
You still don't trust me, do you?
I don't *dis*trust you.
Okay, old sport. I'll tell you this much–
Sometimes I get a feeling, a–well, you might call it a compulsion.
And when I get this feeling, this compulsion, I always do what it tells me.

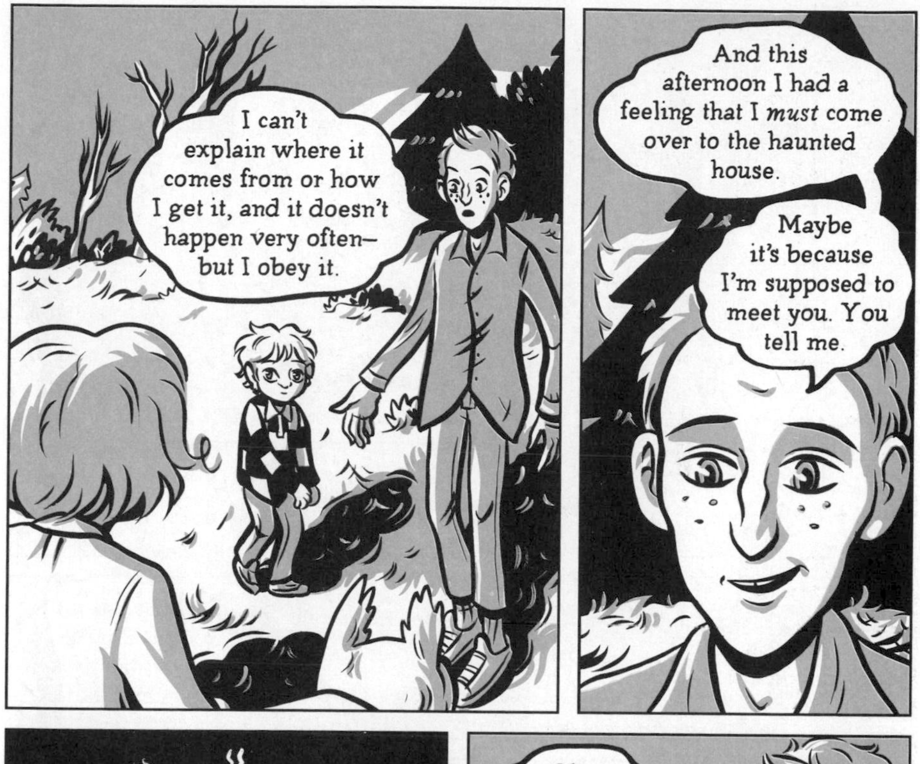
I can't explain where it comes from or how I get it, and it doesn't happen very often—but I obey it.
And this afternoon I had a feeling that I *must* come over to the haunted house.
Maybe it's because I'm supposed to meet you. You tell me.
Okay. I believe you. I think I'd like to trust you.
Maybe you'd better come home with us and have dinner.

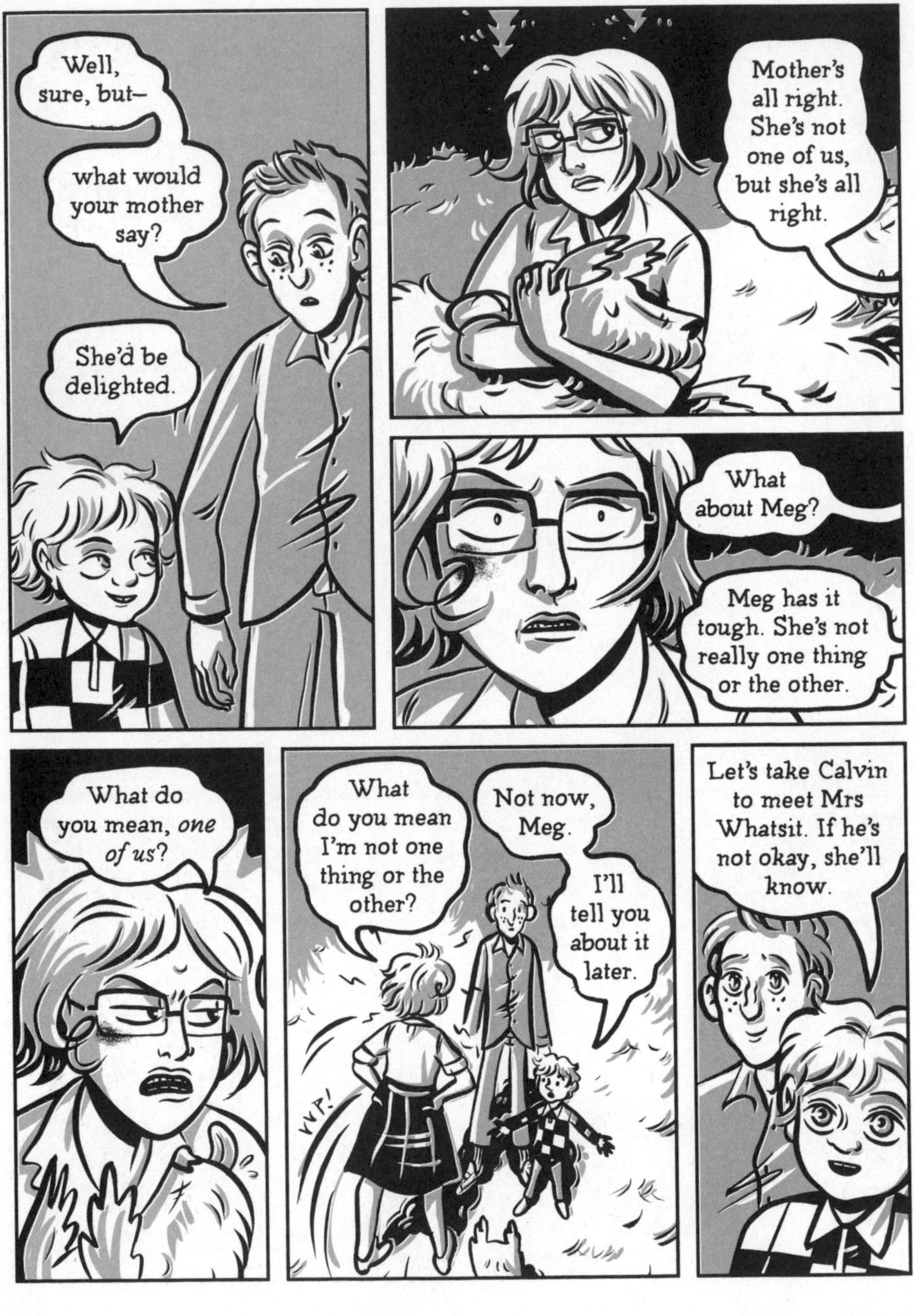
Well, sure, but–
what would your mother say?
She'd be delighted.
Mother's all right. She's not one of us, but she's all right.
What about Meg?
Meg has it tough. She's not really one thing or the other.
What do you mean, *one of us*?
What do you mean I'm not one thing or the other?
Not now, Meg.
I'll tell you about it later.
VVP!
Let's take Calvin to meet Mrs Whatsit. If he's not okay, she'll know.

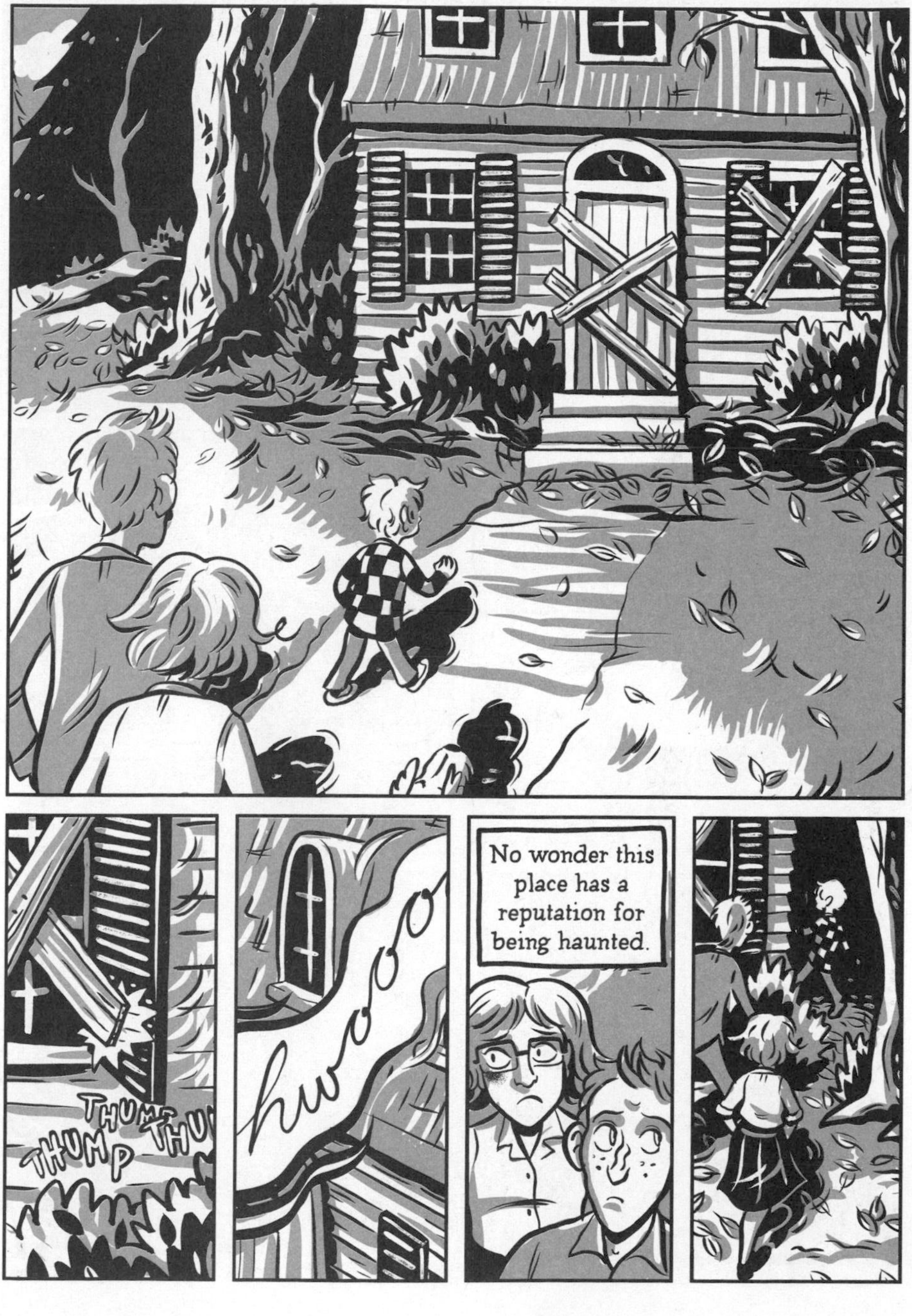
THUMP
THUMP
hwoooo
No wonder this place has a reputation for being haunted.

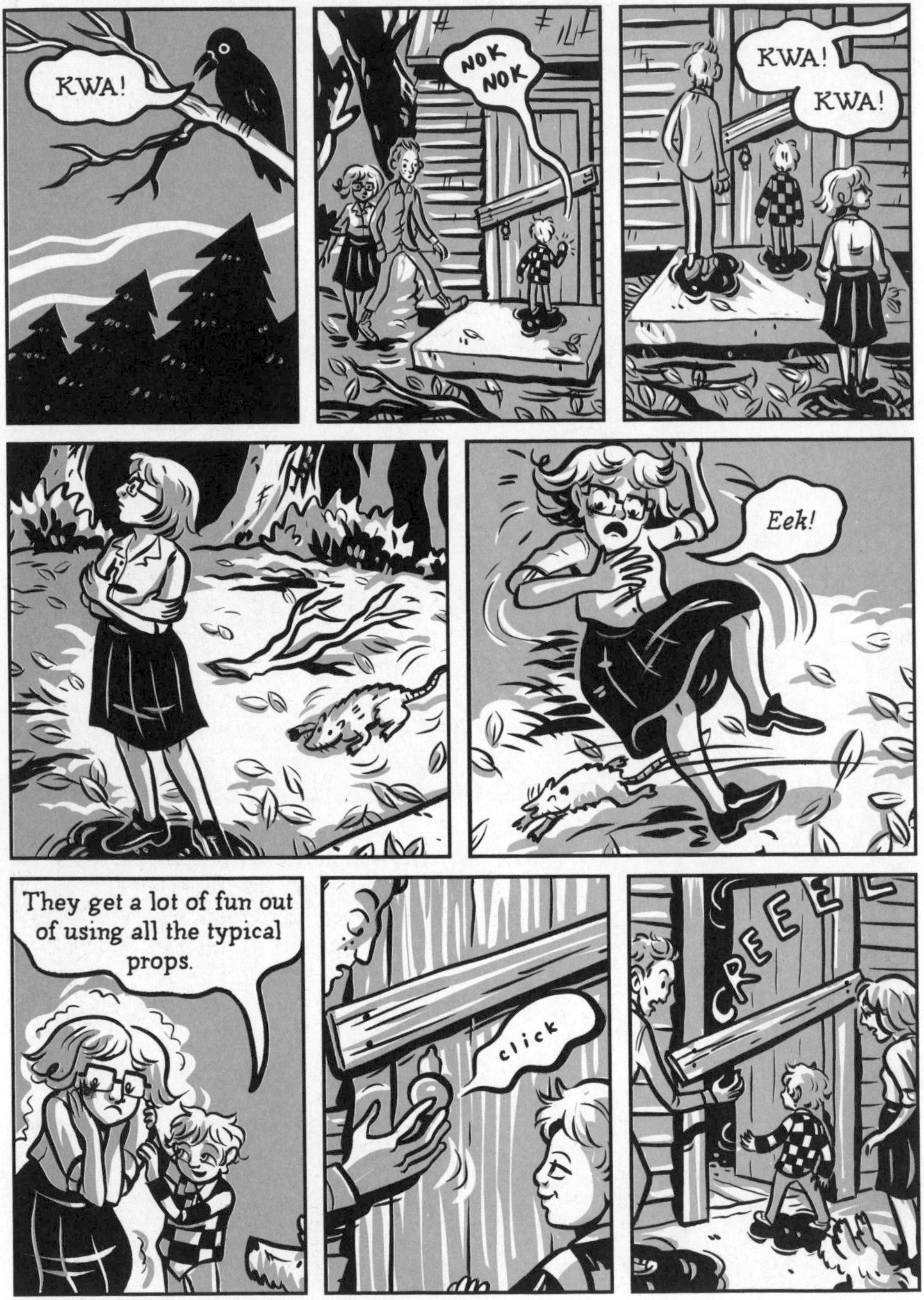
KWA!
NOK NOK
KWA!
KWA!
Eek!
They get a lot of fun out of using all the typical props.
click
CREEEL

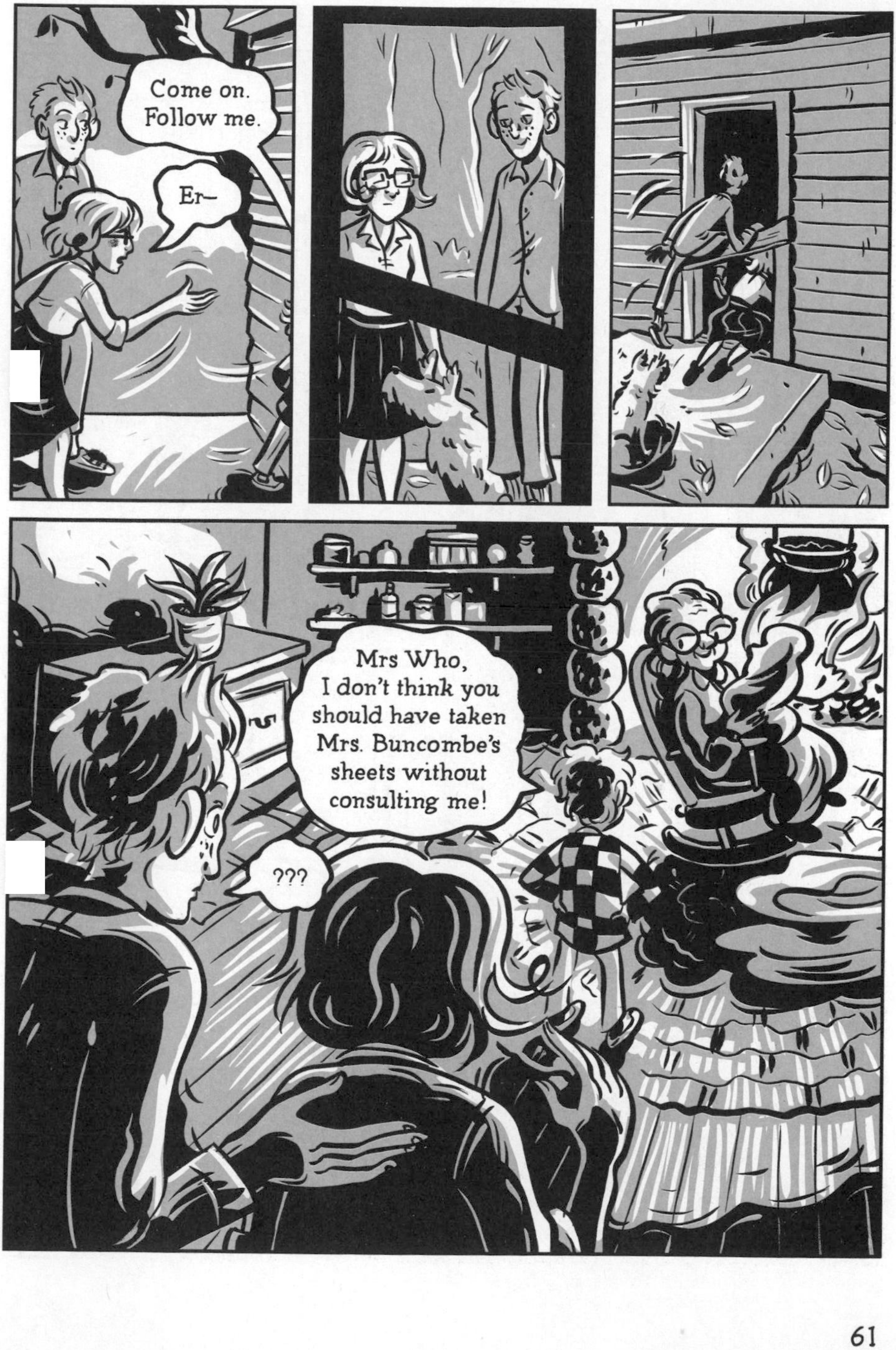
Come on. Follow me.
Er—
Mrs Who, I don't think you should have taken Mrs. Buncombe's sheets without consulting me!
???

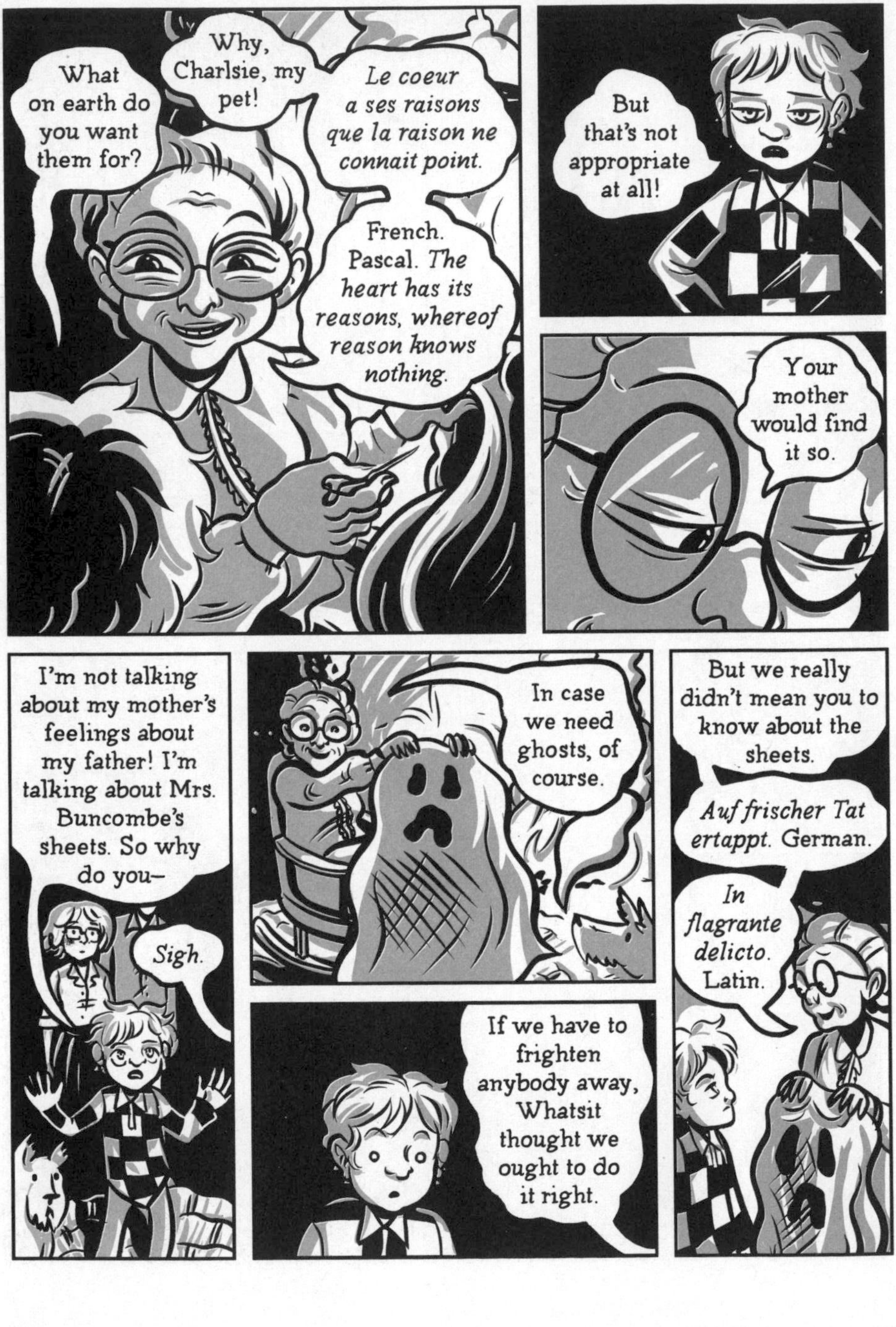

What on earth do you want them for?
Why, Charlsie, my pet!
Le coeur a ses raisons que la raison ne connait point.
French. Pascal. *The heart has its reasons, whereof reason knows nothing.*
But that's not appropriate at all!
Your mother would find it so.
I'm not talking about my mother's feelings about my father! I'm talking about Mrs. Buncombe's sheets. So why do you–
Sigh.
In case we need ghosts, of course.
If we have to frighten anybody away, Whatsit thought we ought to do it right.
But we really didn't mean you to know about the sheets.
Auf frischer Tat ertappt. German.
In flagrante delicto. Latin.

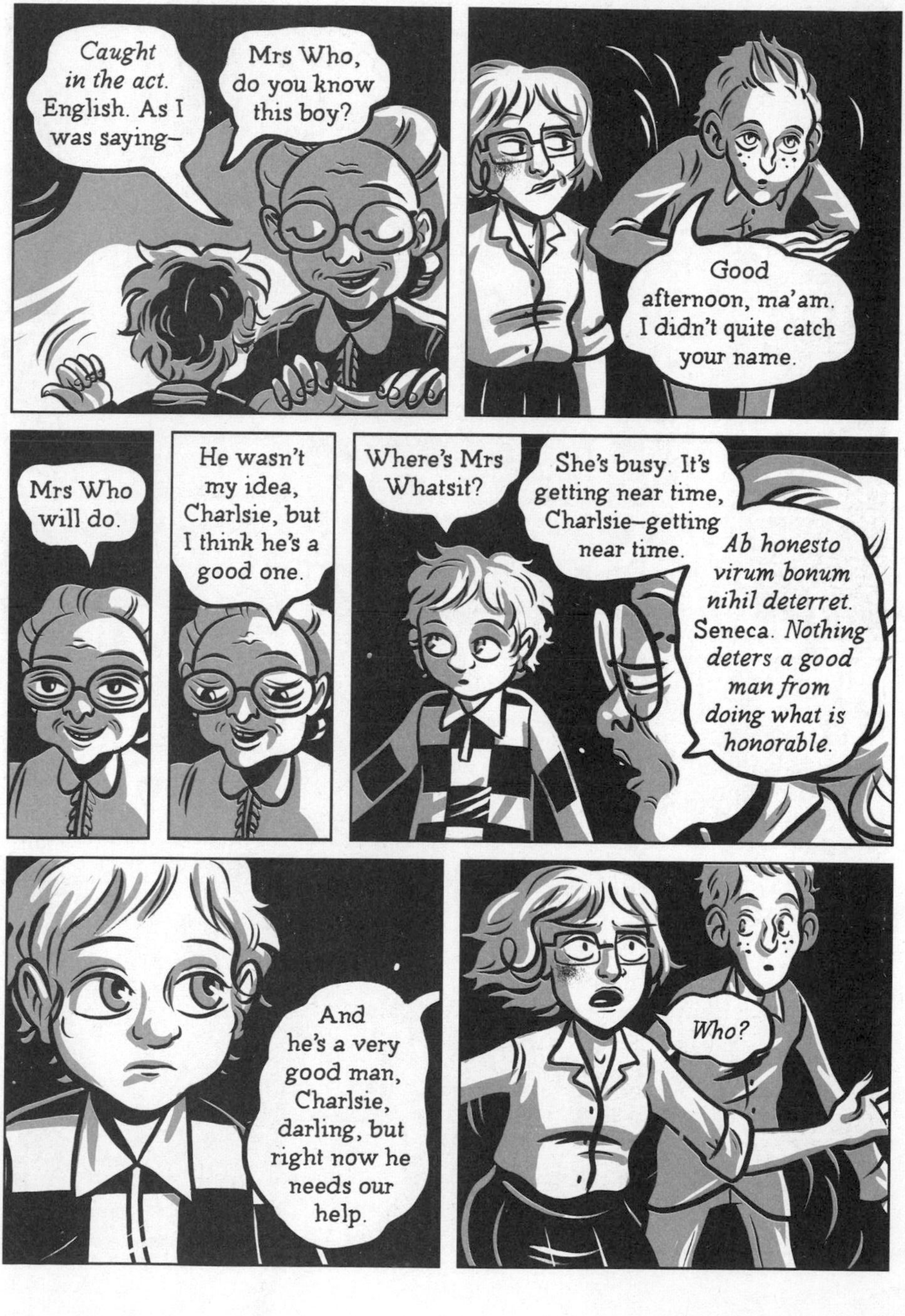
Caught in the act. English. As I was saying–
Mrs Who, do you know this boy?
Good afternoon, ma'am. I didn't quite catch your name.
Mrs Who will do.
He wasn't my idea, Charlsie, but I think he's a good one.
Where's Mrs Whatsit?
She's busy. It's getting near time, Charlsie–getting near time.
Ab honesto virum bonum nihil deterret. Seneca. *Nothing deters a good man from doing what is honorable.*
And he's a very good man, Charlsie, darling, but right now he needs our help.
Who?

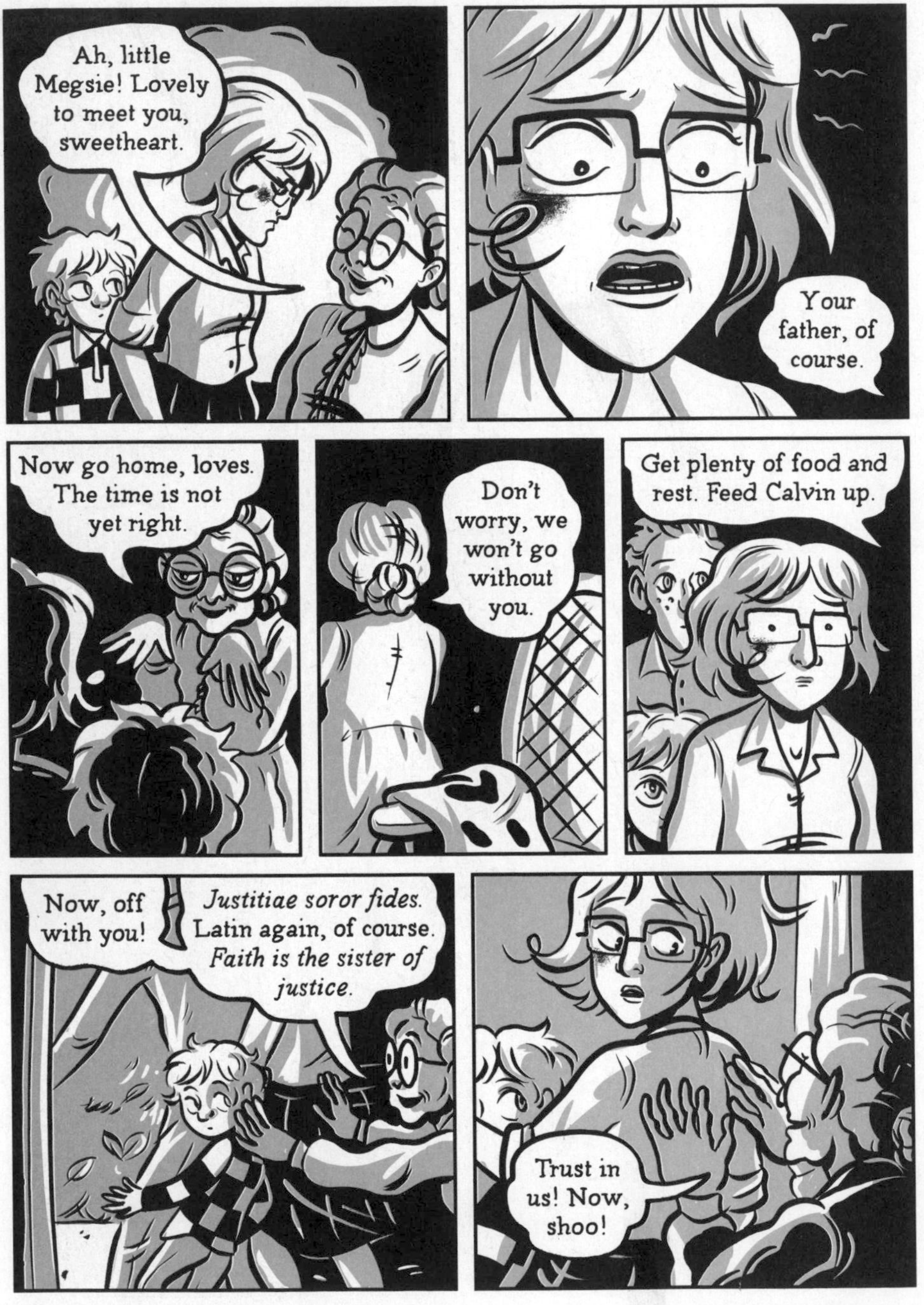

Ah, little Megsie! Lovely to meet you, sweetheart.
Your father, of course.
Now go home, loves. The time is not yet right.
Don't worry, we won't go without you.
Get plenty of food and rest. Feed Calvin up.
Now, off with you!
Justitiae soror fides. Latin again, of course. *Faith is the sister of justice.*
Trust in us! Now, shoo!

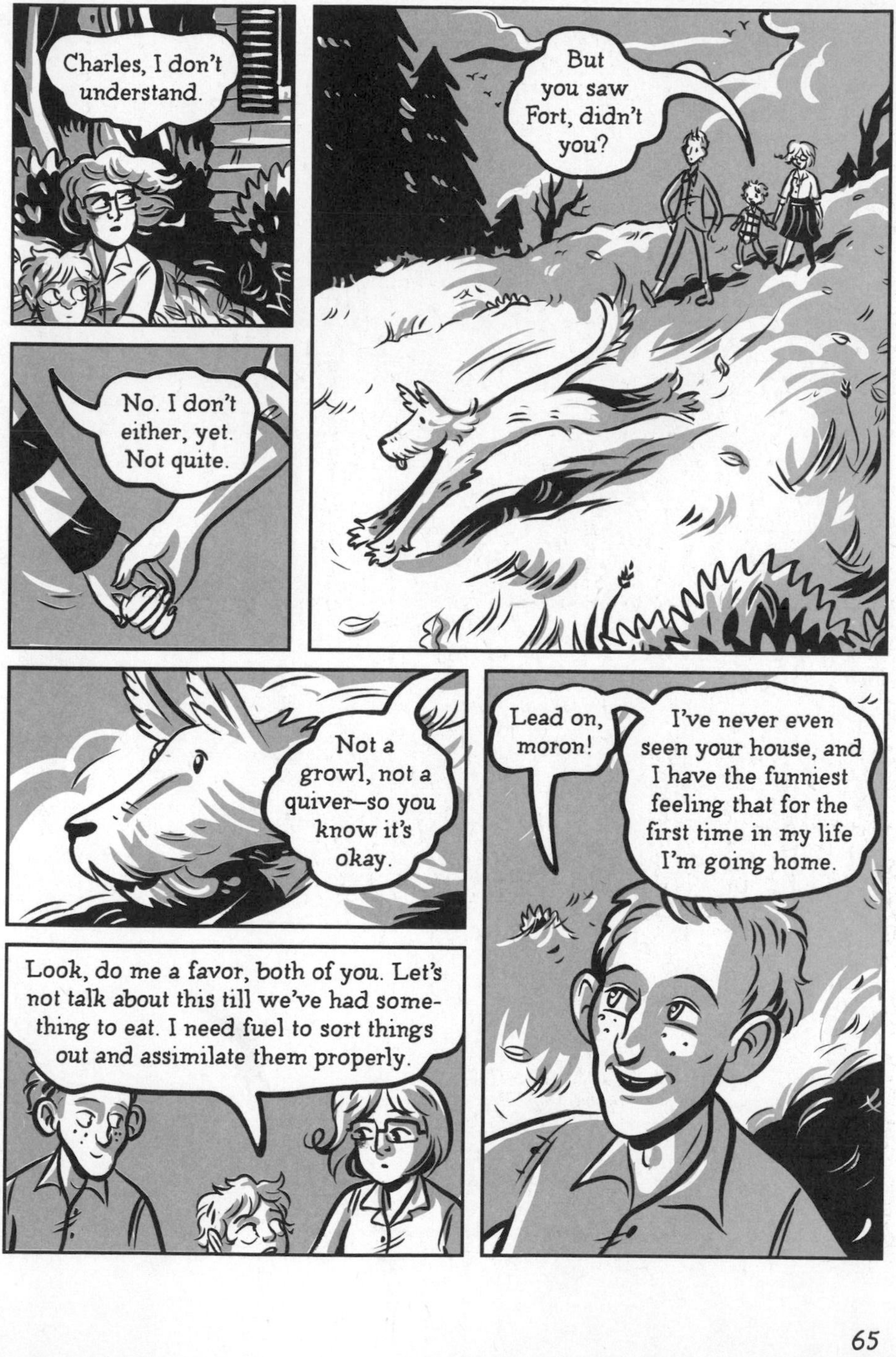
Charles, I don't understand.
But you saw Fort, didn't you?
No. I don't either, yet. Not quite.
Not a growl, not a quiver—so you know it's okay.
Lead on, moron!
I've never even seen your house, and I have the funniest feeling that for the first time in my life I'm going home.
Look, do me a favor, both of you. Let's not talk about this till we've had something to eat. I need fuel to sort things out and assimilate them properly.

3
Mrs Which

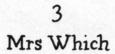

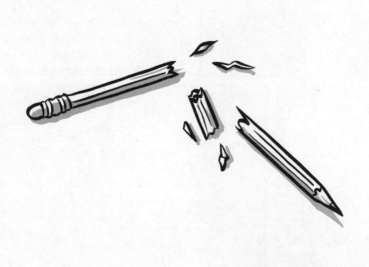

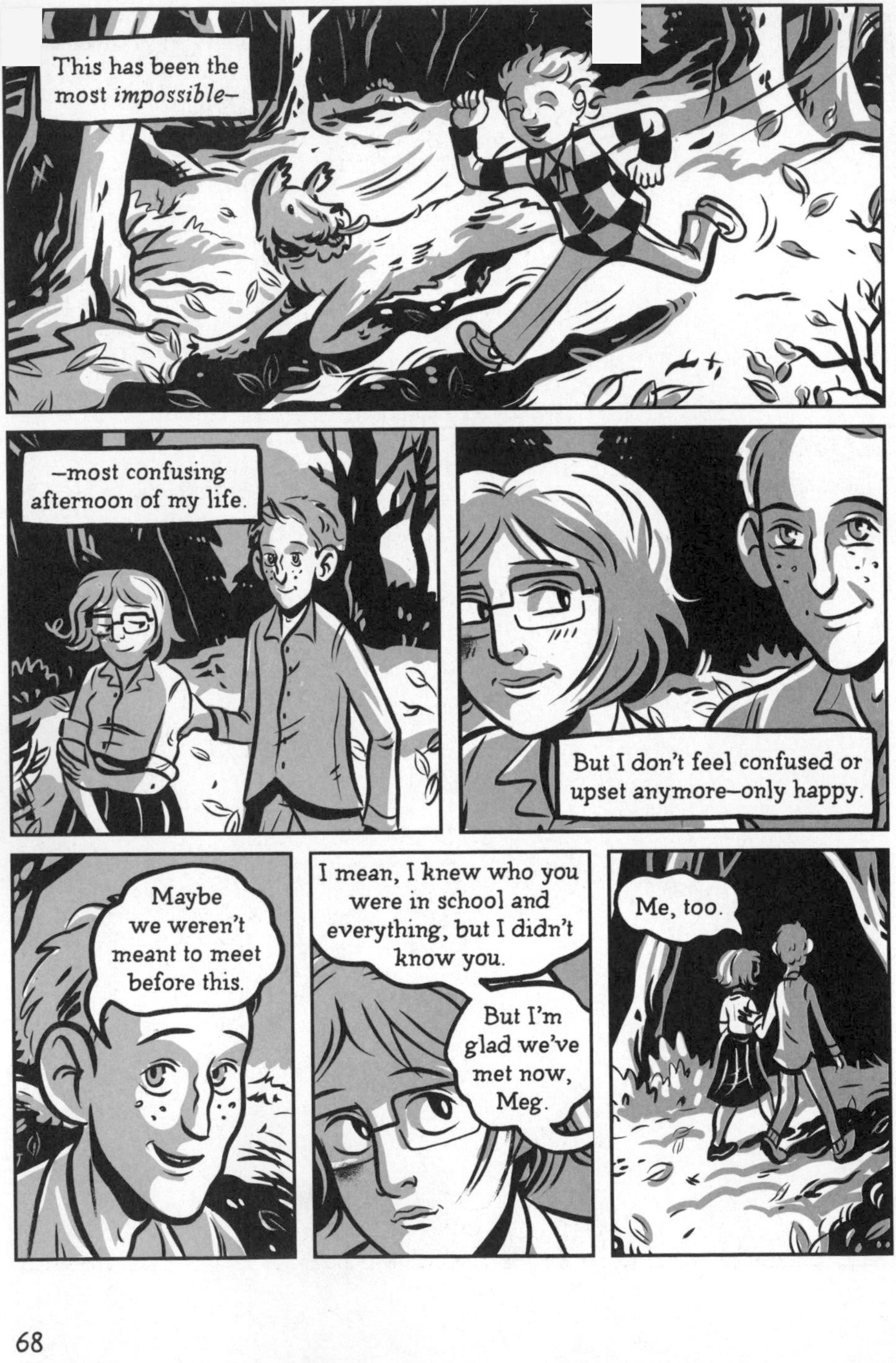
This has been the most *impossible*–
–most confusing afternoon of my life.
But I don't feel confused or upset anymore–only happy.
Maybe we weren't meant to meet before this.
I mean, I knew who you were in school and everything, but I didn't know you.
But I'm glad we've met now, Meg.
Me, too.

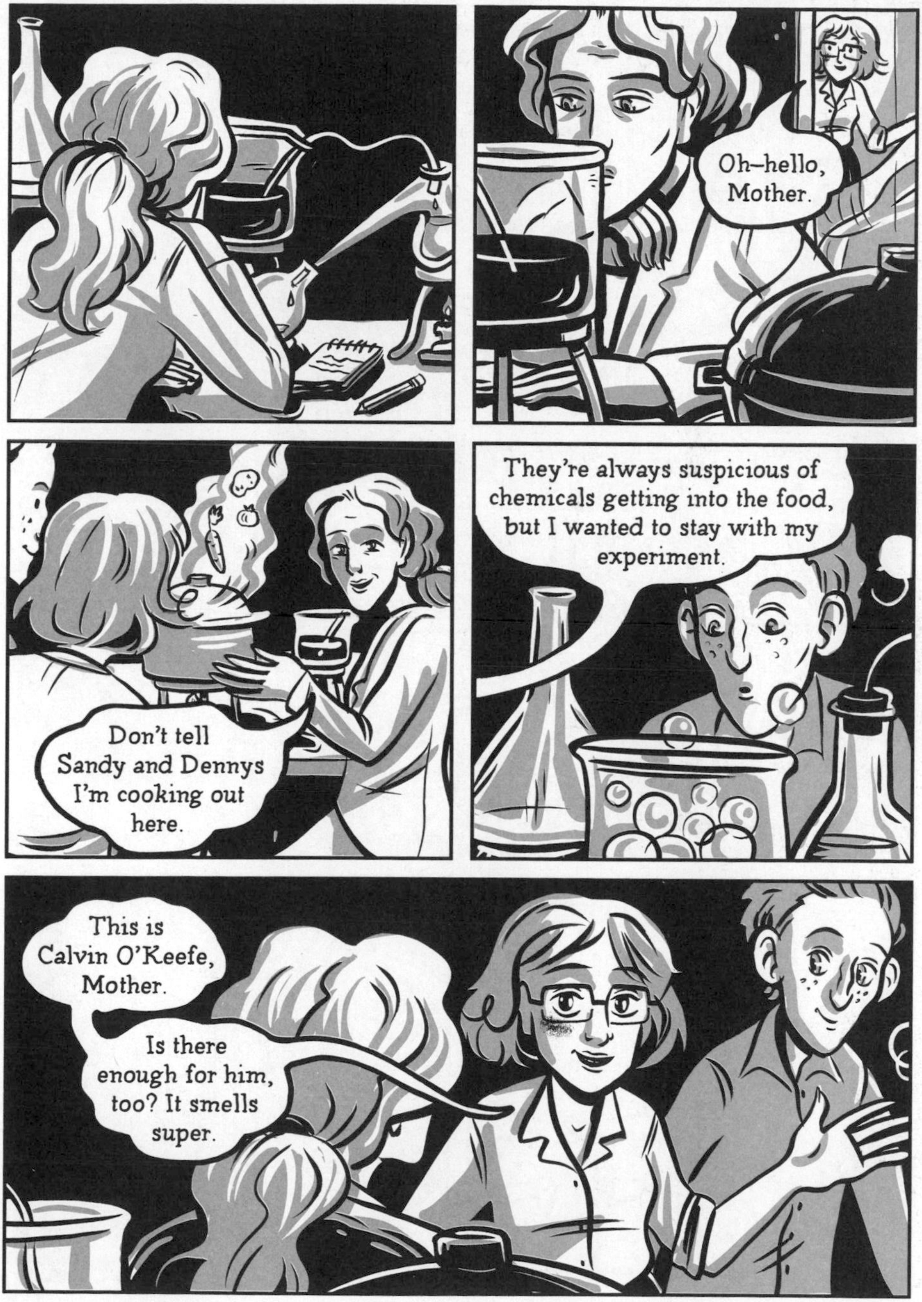

Oh–hello, Mother.
Don't tell Sandy and Dennys I'm cooking out here.
They're always suspicious of chemicals getting into the food, but I wanted to stay with my experiment.
This is Calvin O'Keefe, Mother.
Is there enough for him, too? It smells super.

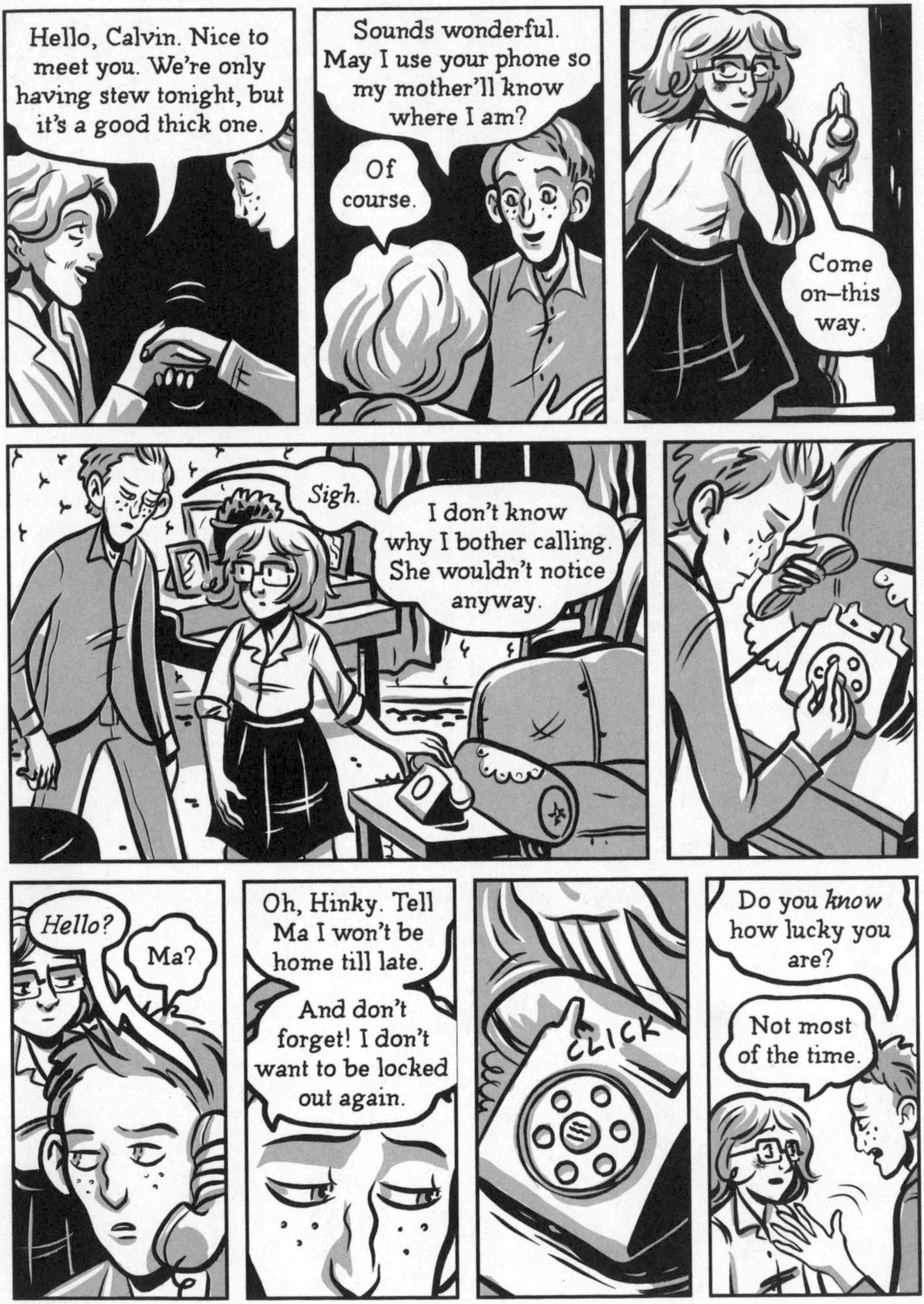
Hello, Calvin. Nice to meet you. We're only having stew tonight, but it's a good thick one.
Sounds wonderful. May I use your phone so my mother'll know where I am?
Of course.
Come on—this way.
Sigh.
I don't know why I bother calling. She wouldn't notice anyway.
Hello?
Ma?
Oh, Hinky. Tell Ma I won't be home till late.
And don't forget! I don't want to be locked out again.
CLICK
Do you *know* how lucky you are?
Not most of the time.

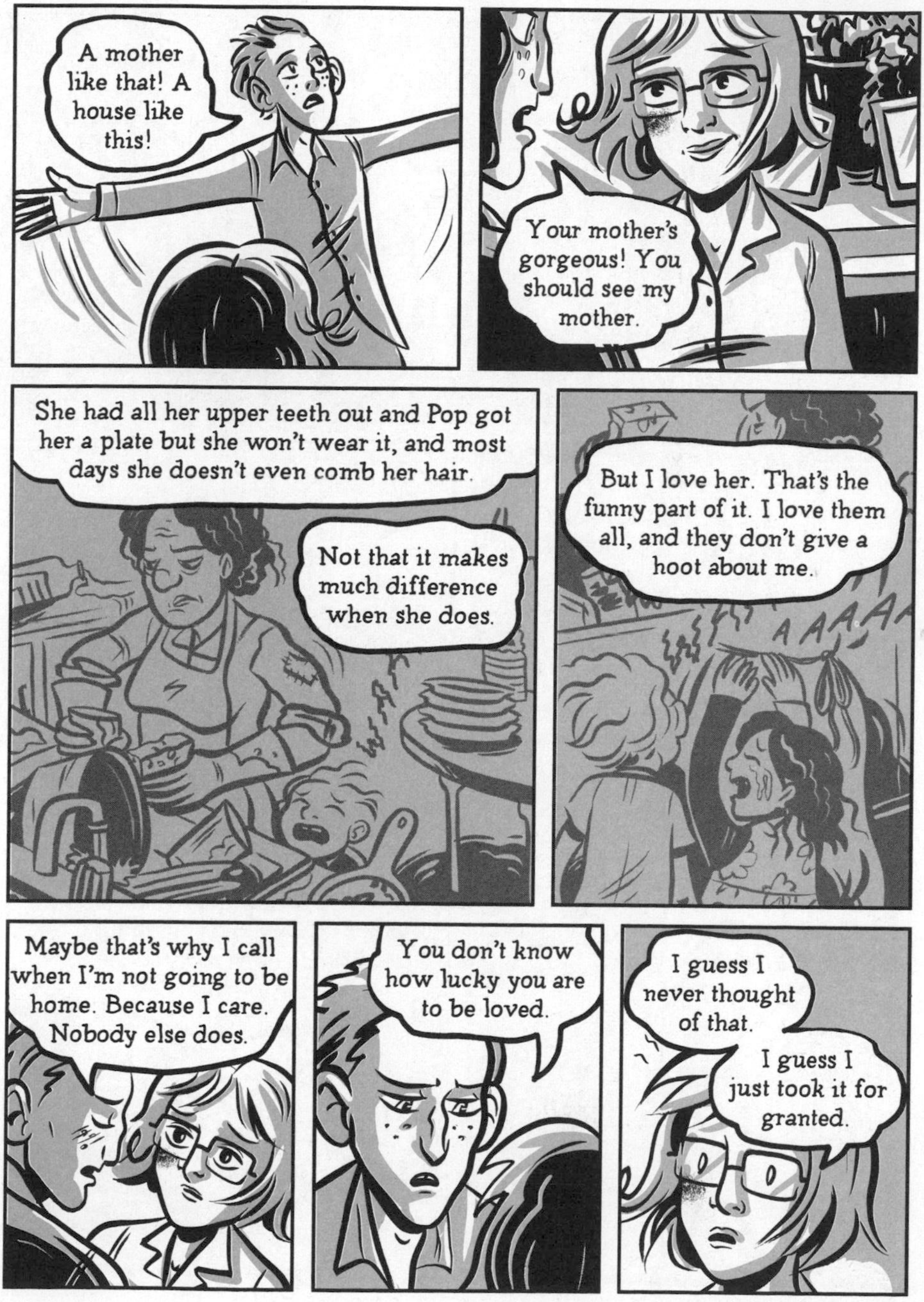

A mother like that! A house like this!
Your mother's gorgeous! You should see my mother.
She had all her upper teeth out and Pop got her a plate but she won't wear it, and most days she doesn't even comb her hair.
Not that it makes much difference when she does.
But I love her. That's the funny part of it. I love them all, and they don't give a hoot about me.
AAAAA
Maybe that's why I call when I'm not going to be home. Because I care. Nobody else does.
You don't know how lucky you are to be loved.
I guess I never thought of that.
I guess I just took it for granted.

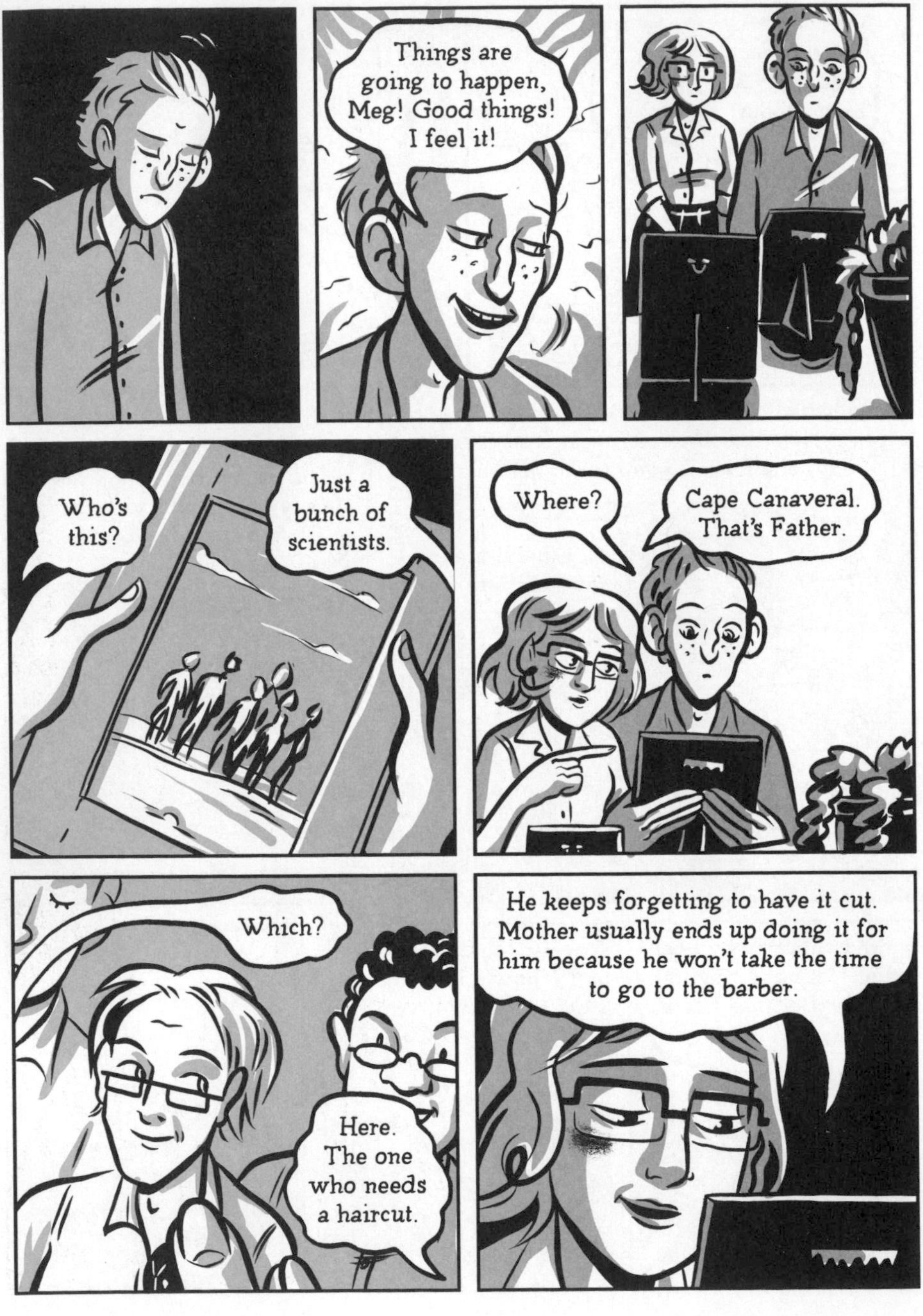
Things are going to happen, Meg! Good things! I feel it!
Who's this?
Just a bunch of scientists.
Where?
Cape Canaveral. That's Father.
Which?
Here. The one who needs a haircut.
He keeps forgetting to have it cut. Mother usually ends up doing it for him because he won't take the time to go to the barber.

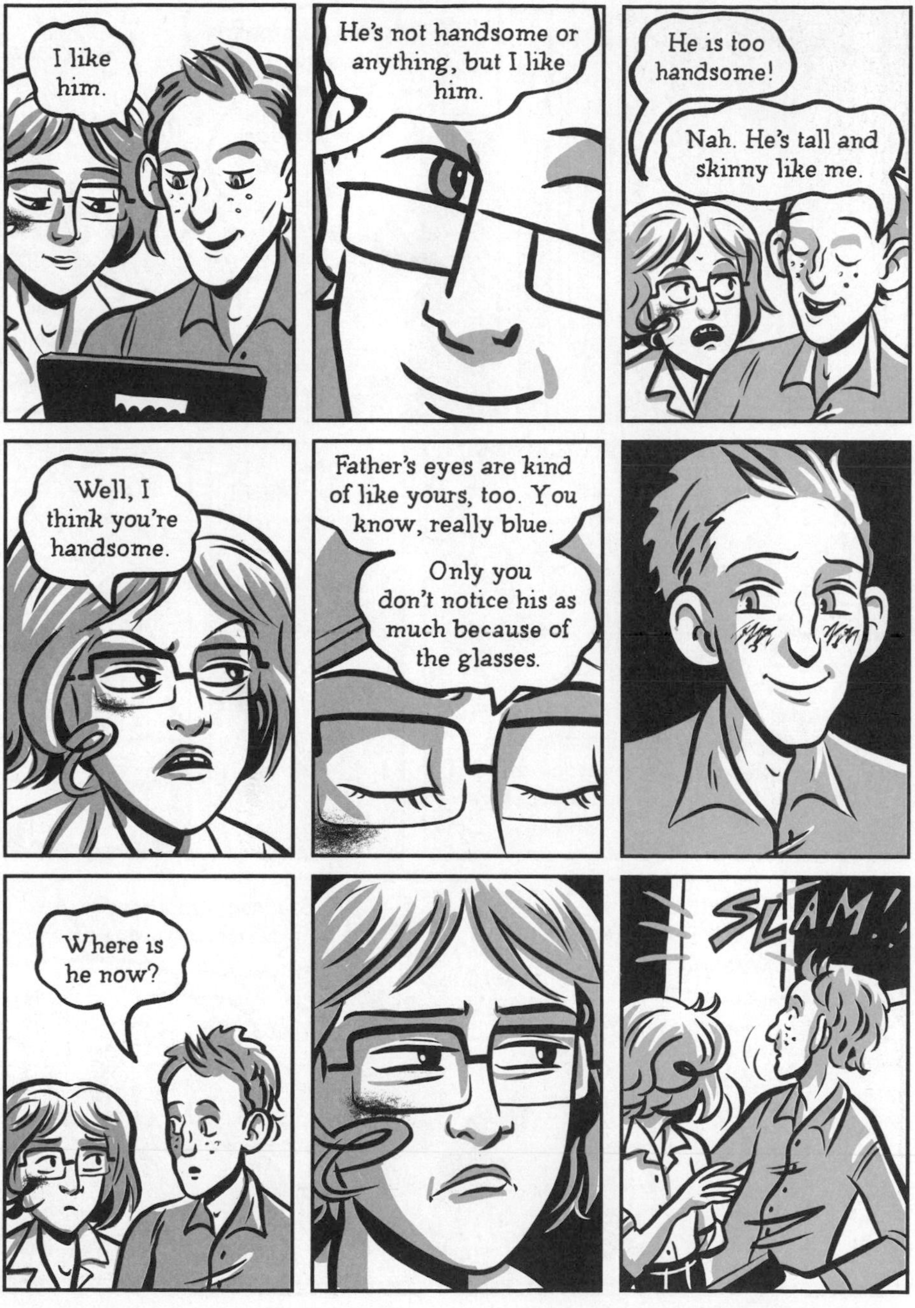
I like him.
He's not handsome or anything, but I like him.
He is too handsome!
Nah. He's tall and skinny like me.
Well, I think you're handsome.
Father's eyes are kind of like yours, too. You know, really blue.
Only you don't notice his as much because of the glasses.
Where is he now?
SLAM!

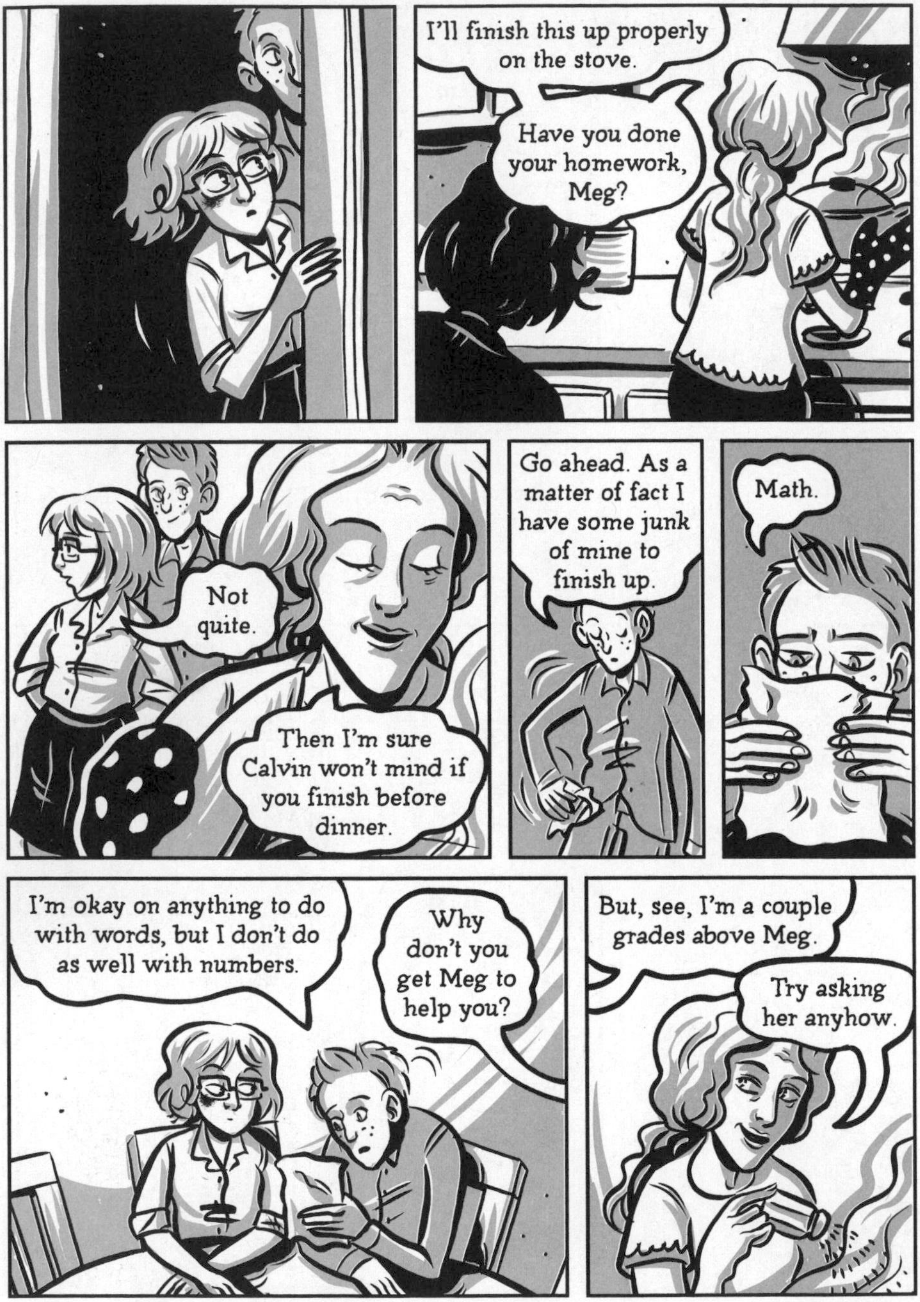
I'll finish this up properly on the stove.
Have you done your homework, Meg?
Not quite.
Then I'm sure Calvin won't mind if you finish before dinner.
Go ahead. As a matter of fact I have some junk of mine to finish up.
Math.
I'm okay on anything to do with words, but I don't do as well with numbers.
Why don't you get Meg to help you?
But, see, I'm a couple grades above Meg.
Try asking her anyhow.

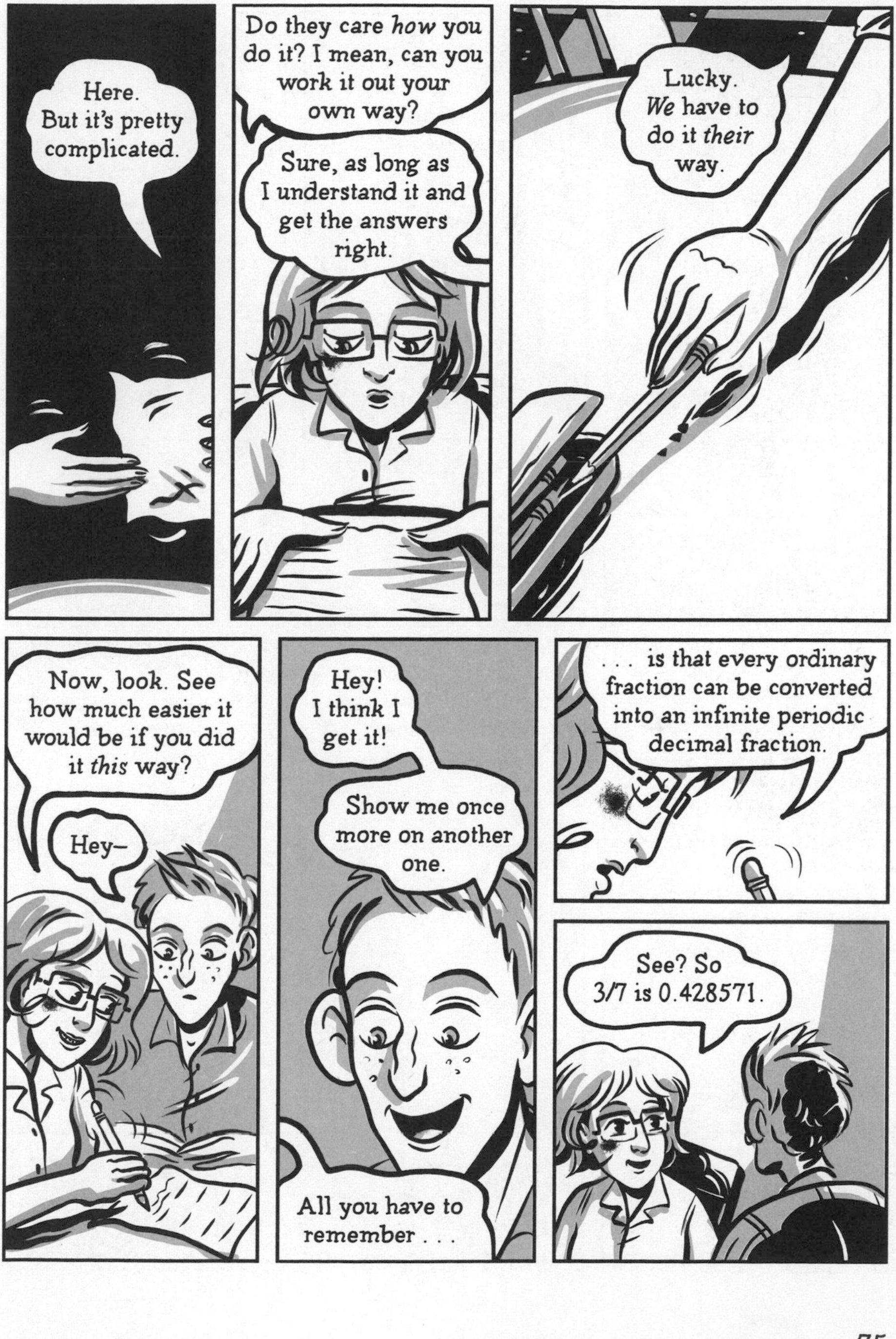
Here.
But it's pretty complicated.
Do they care *how* you do it? I mean, can you work it out your own way?
Sure, as long as I understand it and get the answers right.
Lucky. *We* have to do it *their* way.
Now, look. See how much easier it would be if you did it *this* way?
Hey–
Hey! I think I get it!
Show me once more on another one.
All you have to remember . . .
. . . is that every ordinary fraction can be converted into an infinite periodic decimal fraction.
See? So 3/7 is 0.428571.

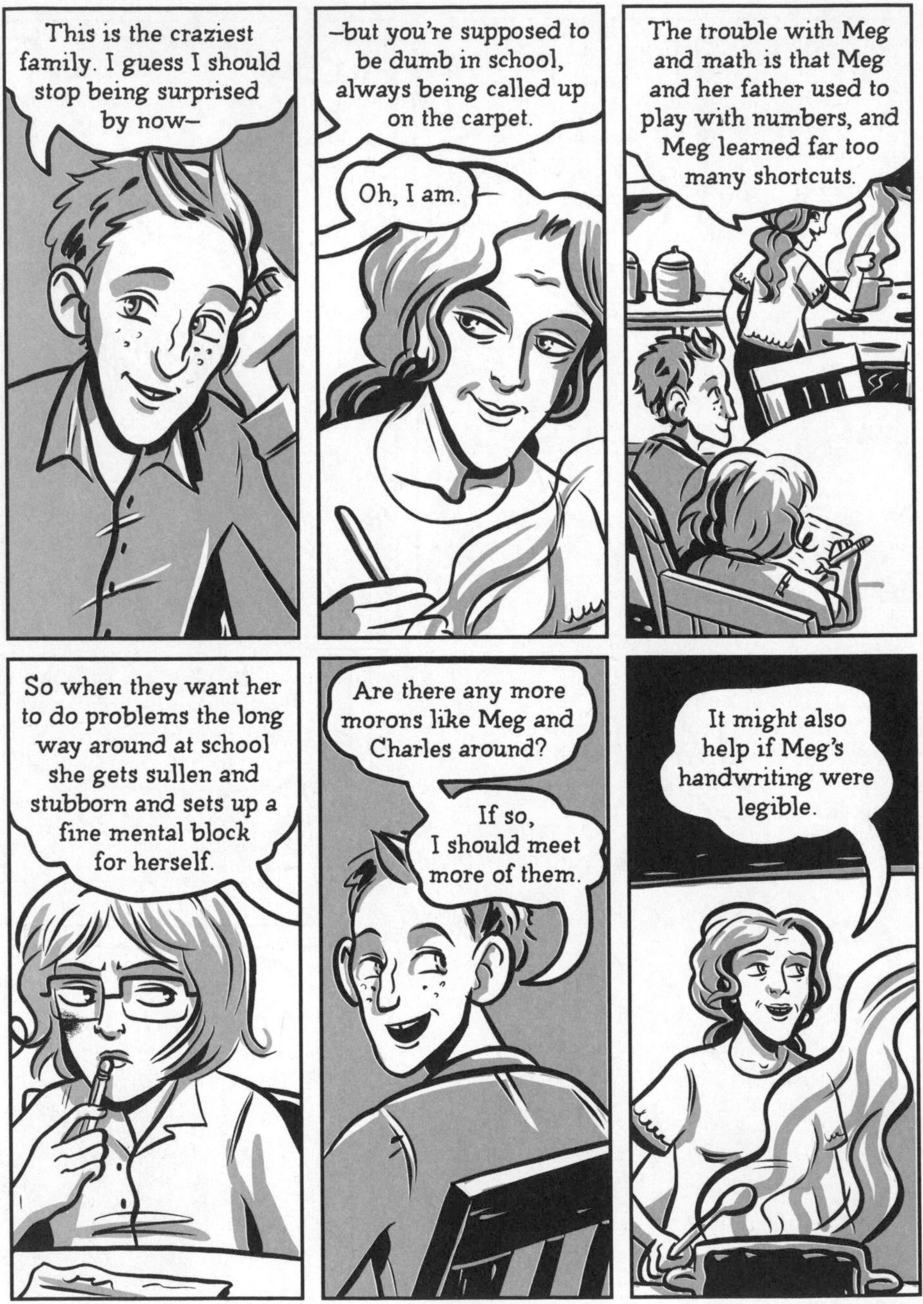
This is the craziest family. I guess I should stop being surprised by now–
–but you're supposed to be dumb in school, always being called up on the carpet.
Oh, I am.
The trouble with Meg and math is that Meg and her father used to play with numbers, and Meg learned far too many shortcuts.
So when they want her to do problems the long way around at school she gets sullen and stubborn and sets up a fine mental block for herself.
Are there any more morons like Meg and Charles around?
If so, I should meet more of them.
It might also help if Meg's handwriting were legible.

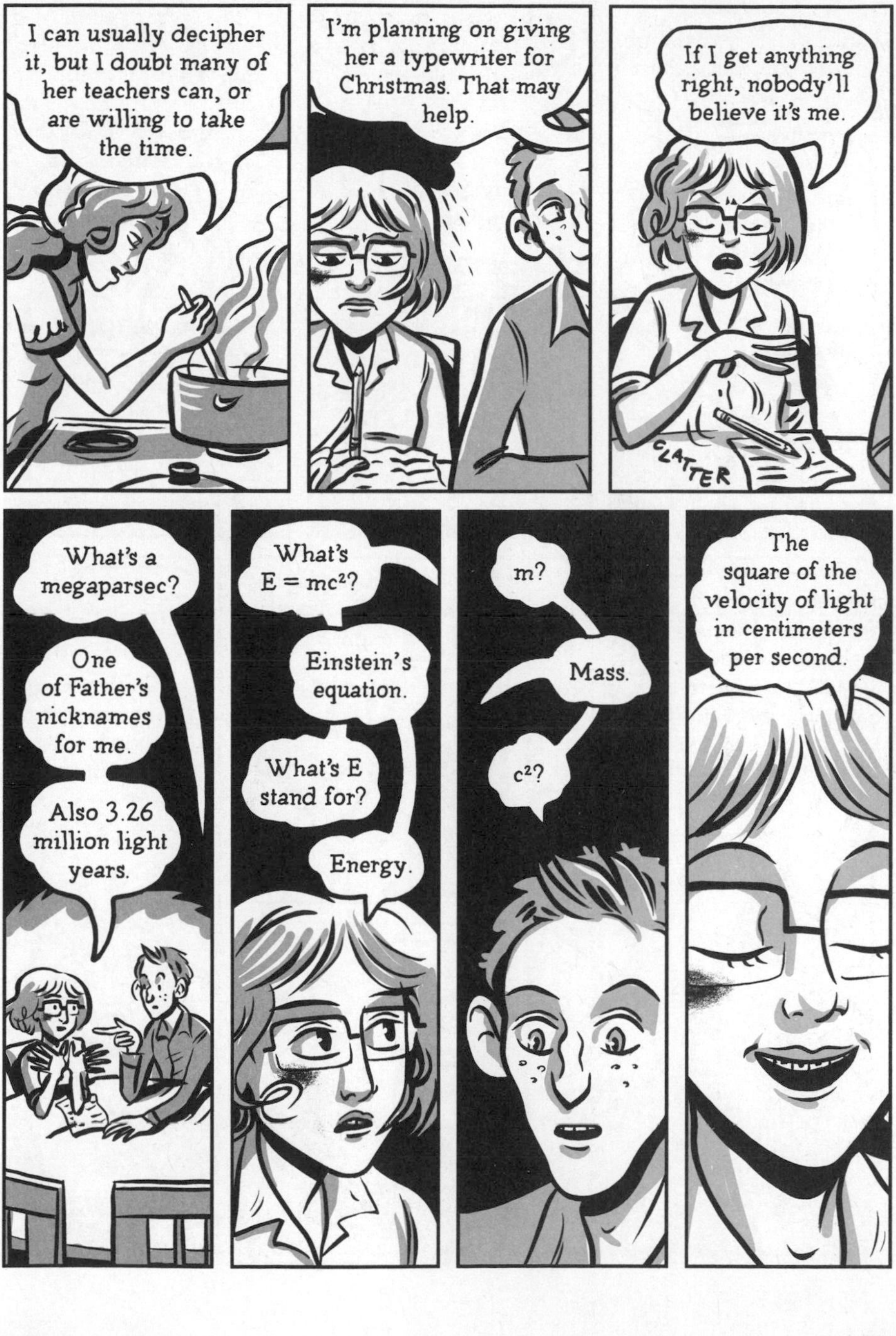
I can usually decipher it, but I doubt many of her teachers can, or are willing to take the time.
I'm planning on giving her a typewriter for Christmas. That may help.
If I get anything right, nobody'll believe it's me.
CLATTER
What's a megaparsec?
One of Father's nicknames for me.
Also 3.26 million light years.
What's E = mc²?
Einstein's equation.
What's E stand for?
Energy.
m?
Mass.
c²?
The square of the velocity of light in centimeters per second.

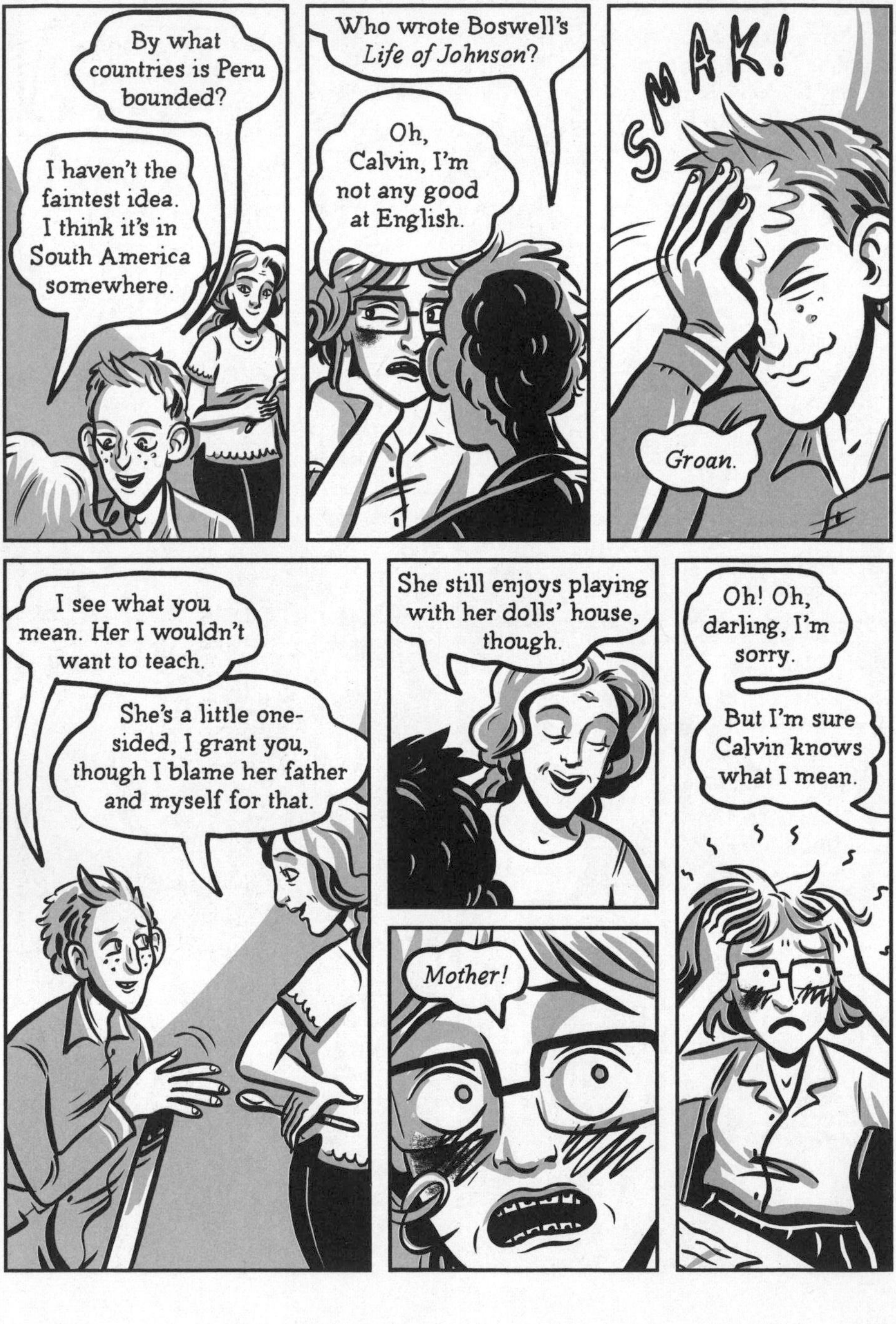
By what countries is Peru bounded?
I haven't the faintest idea. I think it's in South America somewhere.
Who wrote Boswell's *Life of Johnson*?
Oh, Calvin, I'm not any good at English.
SMAK!
Groan.
I see what you mean. Her I wouldn't want to teach.
She's a little one-sided, I grant you, though I blame her father and myself for that.
She still enjoys playing with her dolls' house, though.
Mother!
Oh! Oh, darling, I'm sorry.
But I'm sure Calvin knows what I mean.

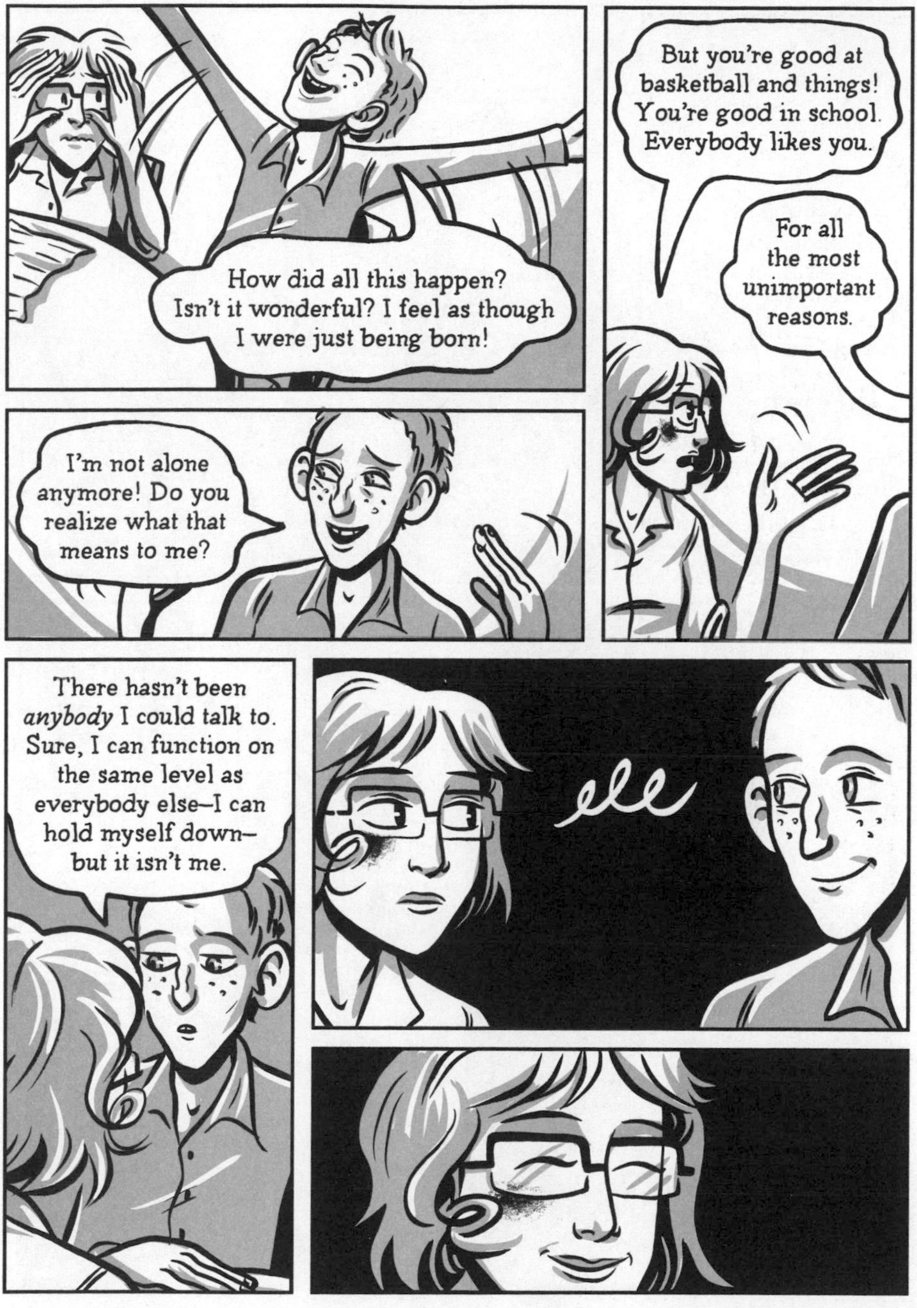
How did all this happen? Isn't it wonderful? I feel as though I were just being born!
But you're good at basketball and things! You're good in school. Everybody likes you.
For all the most unimportant reasons.
I'm not alone anymore! Do you realize what that means to me?
There hasn't been *anybody* I could talk to. Sure, I can function on the same level as everybody else–I can hold myself down–but it isn't me.

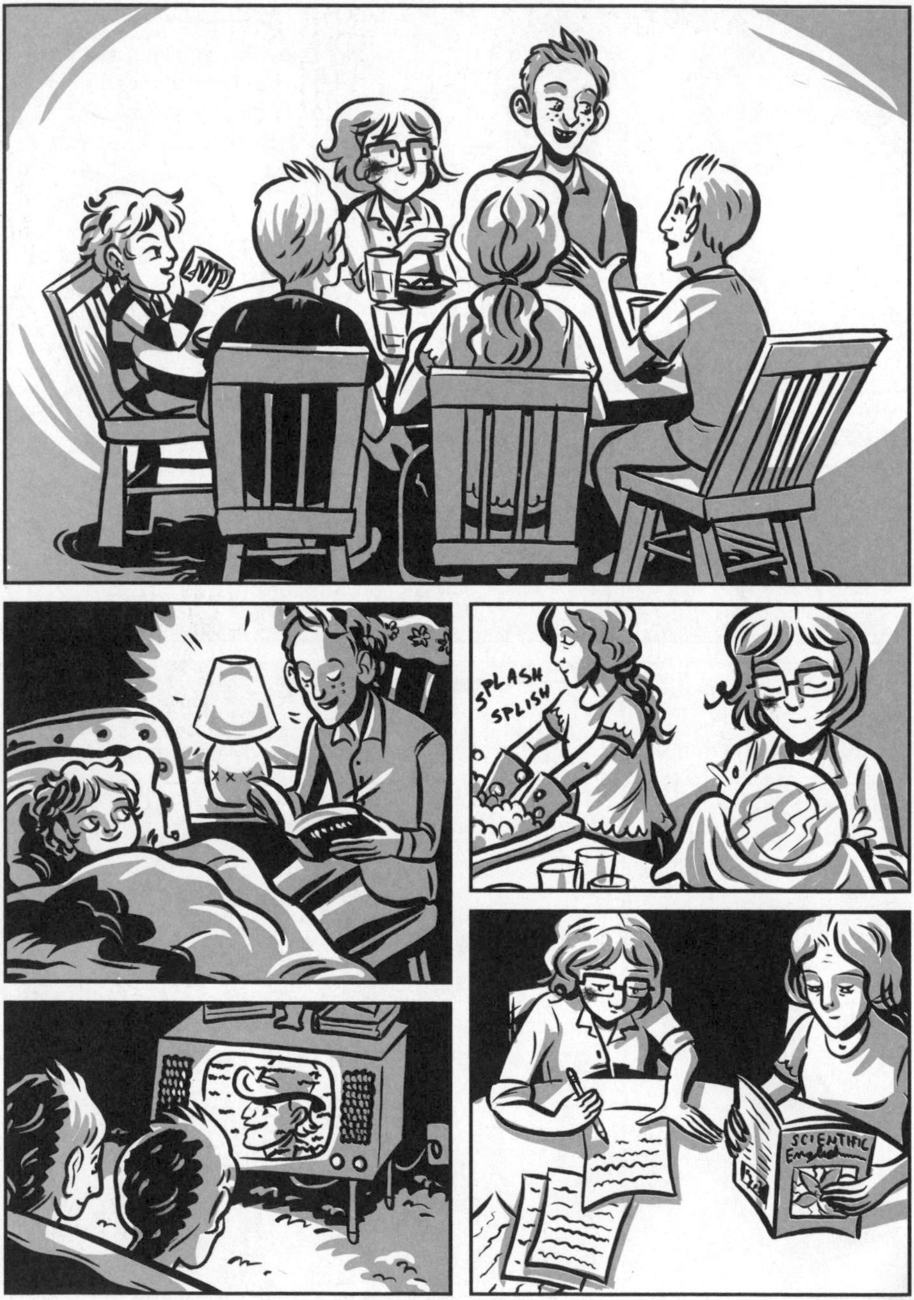
SPLASH
SPLISH
SCIENTIFIC

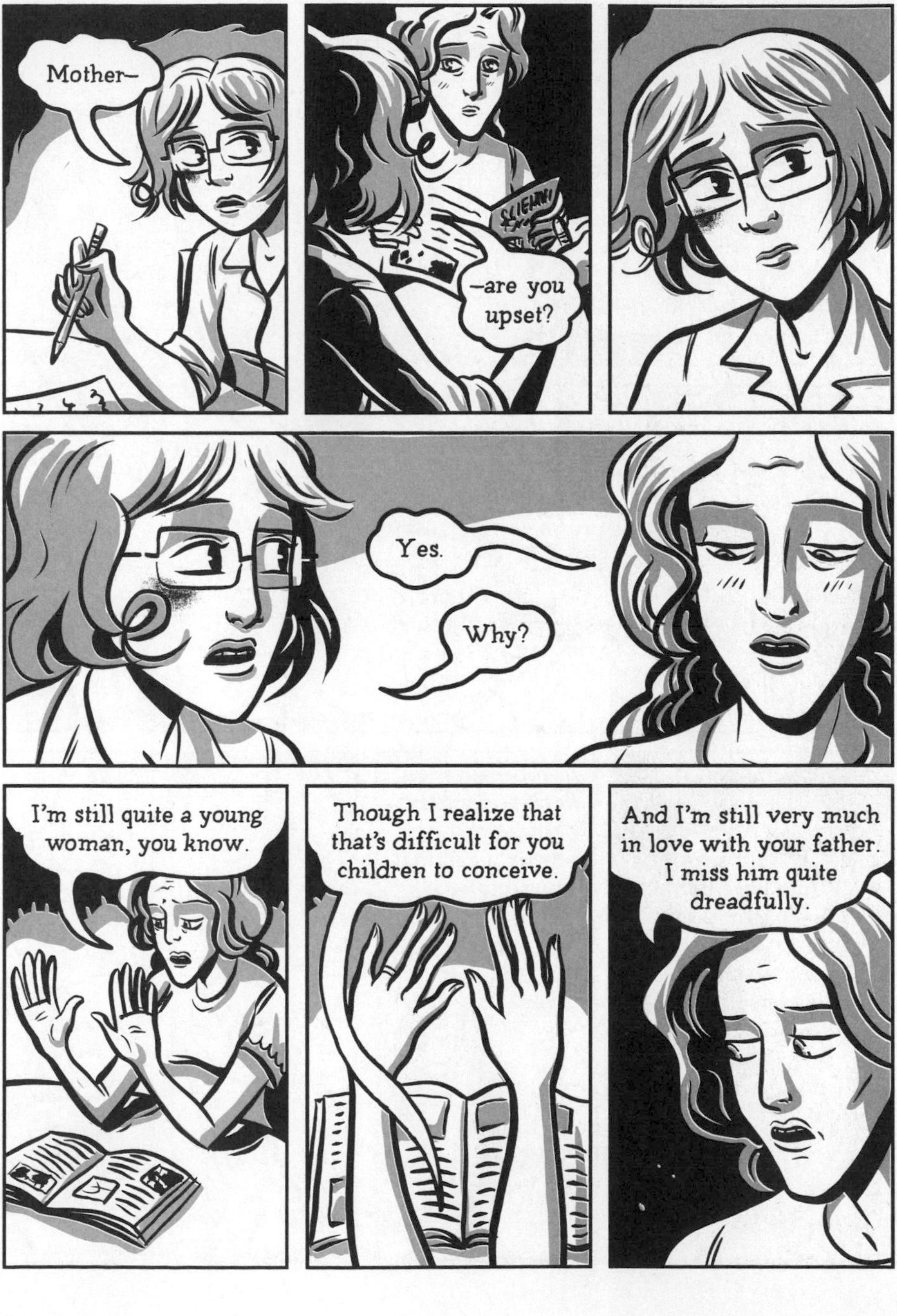
Mother–
–are you upset?
Yes.
Why?
I'm still quite a young woman, you know.
Though I realize that that's difficult for you children to conceive.
And I'm still very much in love with your father. I miss him quite dreadfully.

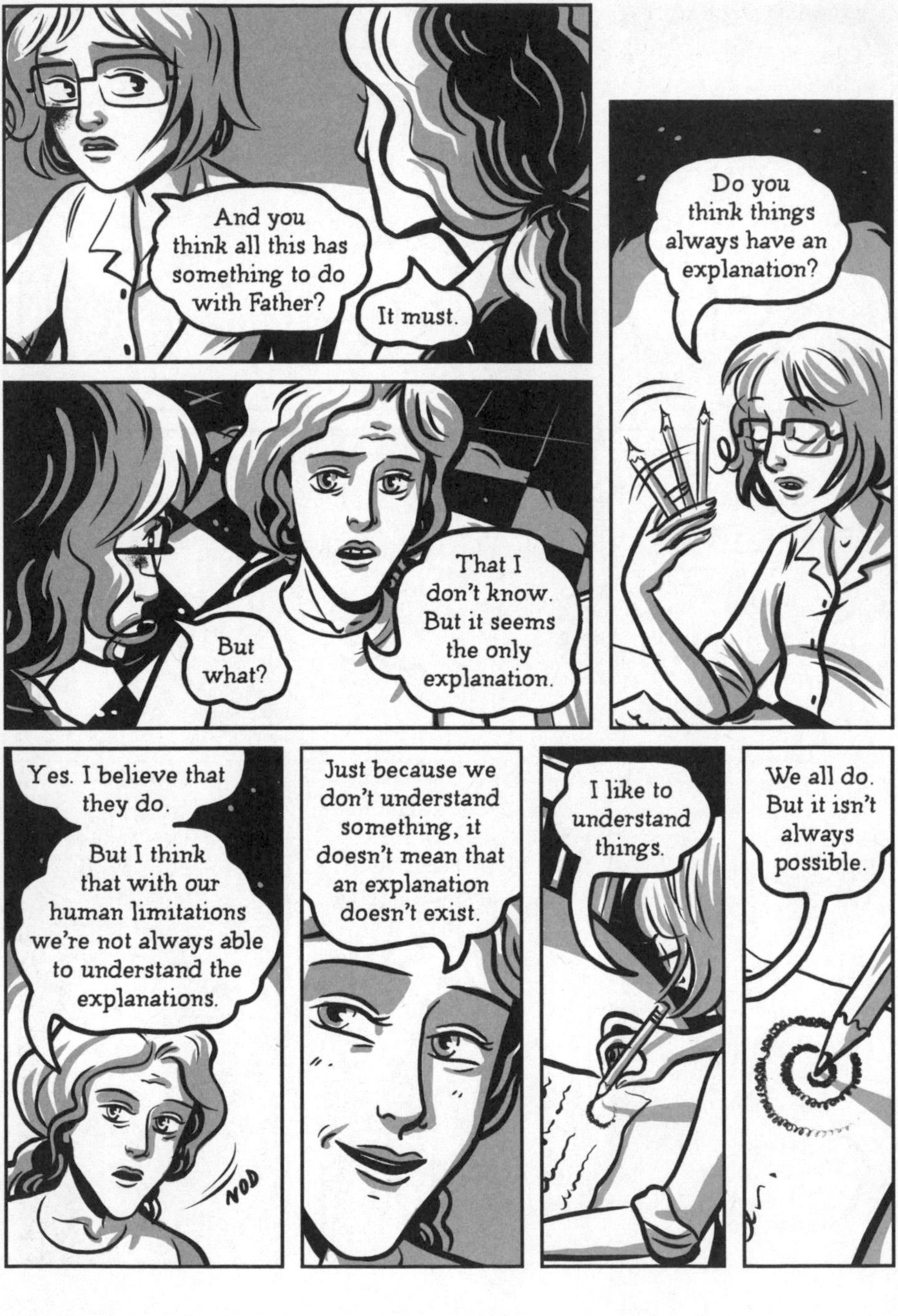
And you think all this has something to do with Father?
It must.
Do you think things always have an explanation?
But what?
That I don't know. But it seems the only explanation.
Yes. I believe that they do.
But I think that with our human limitations we're not always able to understand the explanations.
NOD
Just because we don't understand something, it doesn't mean that an explanation doesn't exist.
I like to understand things.
We all do. But it isn't always possible.

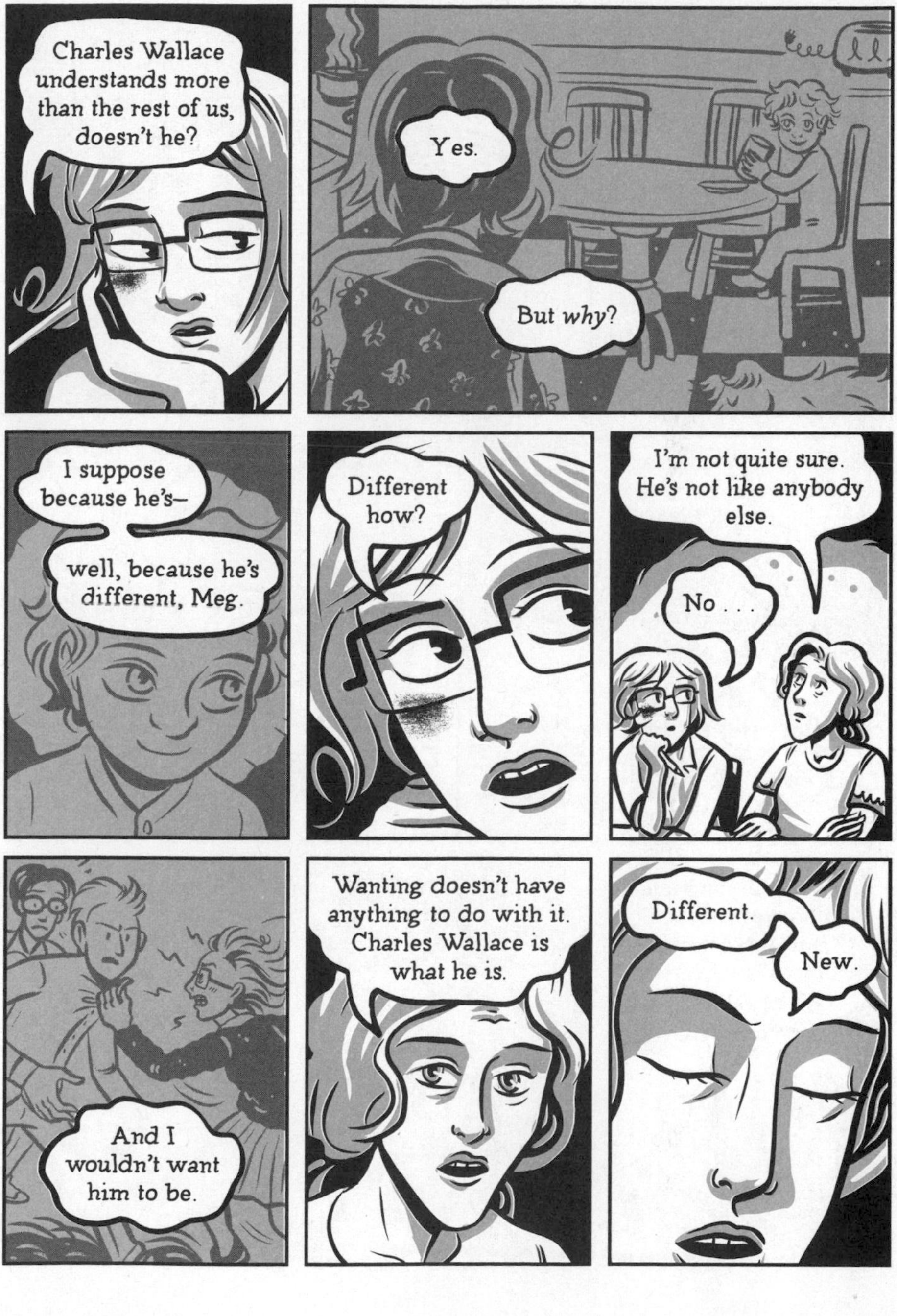
Charles Wallace understands more than the rest of us, doesn't he?
Yes.
But *why*?
I suppose because he's–
well, because he's different, Meg.
Different how?
I'm not quite sure. He's not like anybody else.
No . . .
And I wouldn't want him to be.
Wanting doesn't have anything to do with it. Charles Wallace is what he is.
Different.
New.

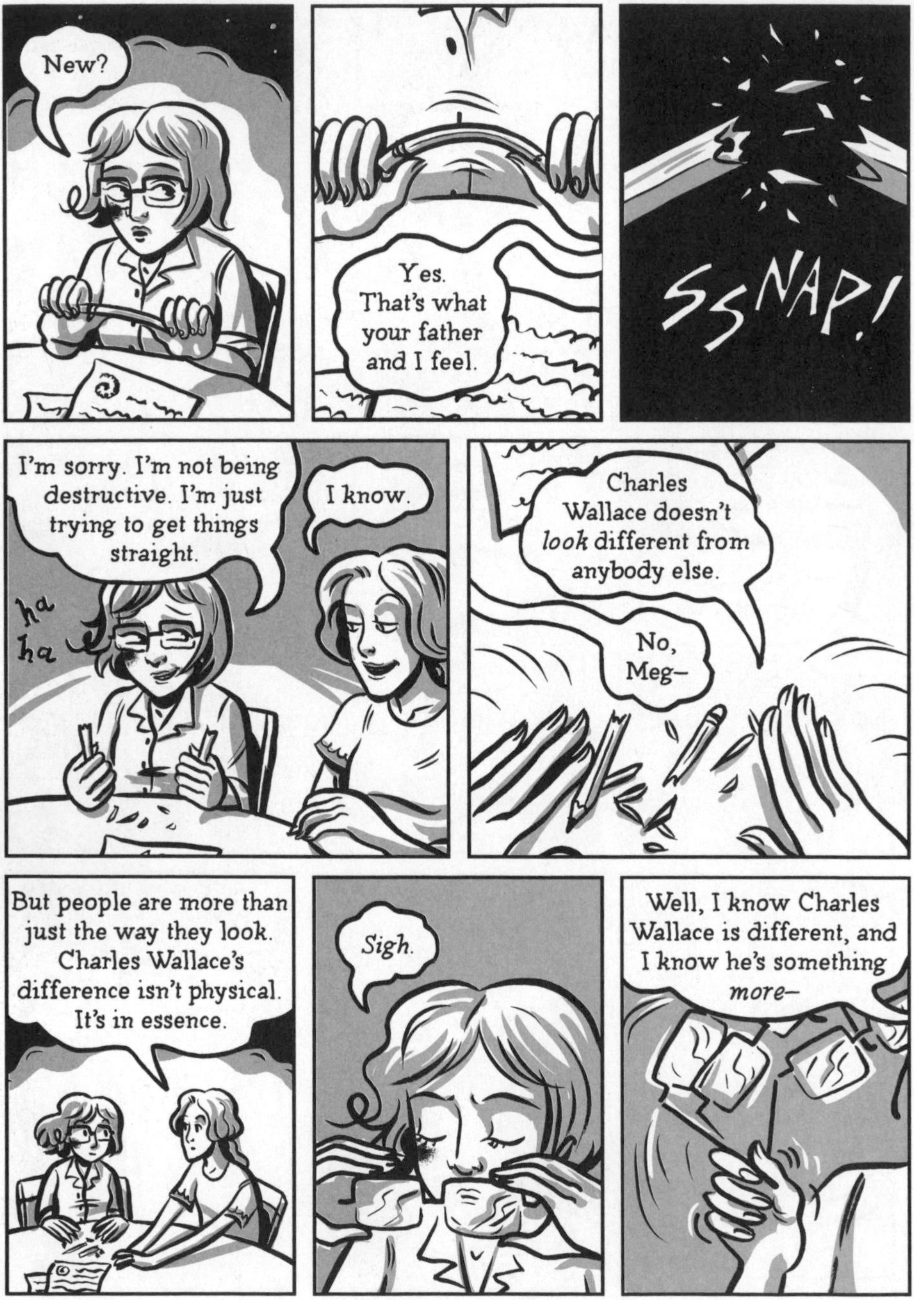
New?
Yes. That's what your father and I feel.
SSNAP!
I'm sorry. I'm not being destructive. I'm just trying to get things straight.
I know.
ha ha
Charles Wallace doesn't *look* different from anybody else.
No, Meg–
But people are more than just the way they look. Charles Wallace's difference isn't physical. It's in essence.
Sigh.
Well, I know Charles Wallace is different, and I know he's something *more*–

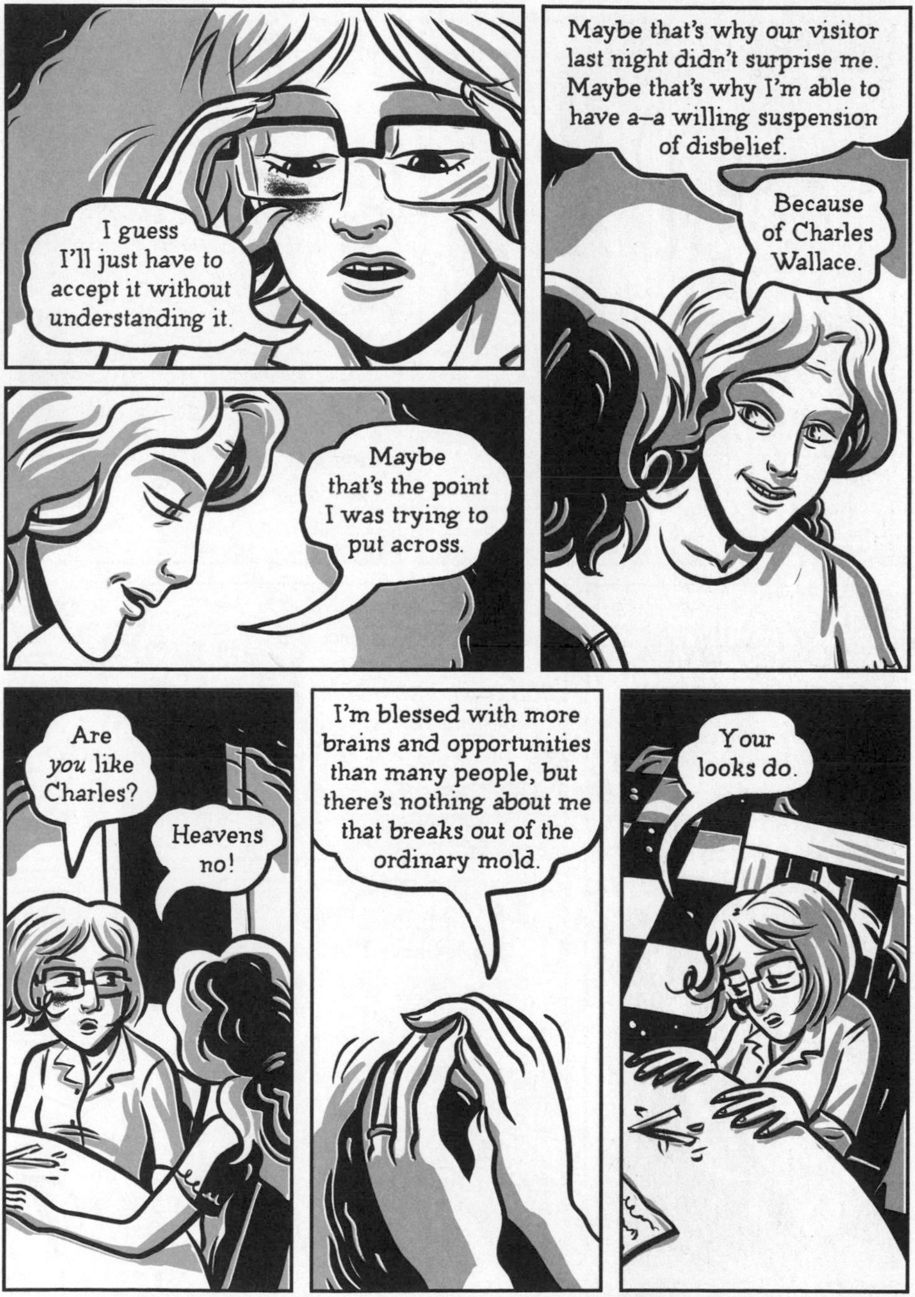
I guess I'll just have to accept it without understanding it.
Maybe that's why our visitor last night didn't surprise me. Maybe that's why I'm able to have a—a willing suspension of disbelief.
Because of Charles Wallace.
Maybe that's the point I was trying to put across.
Are *you* like Charles?
Heavens no!
I'm blessed with more brains and opportunities than many people, but there's nothing about me that breaks out of the ordinary mold.
Your looks do.

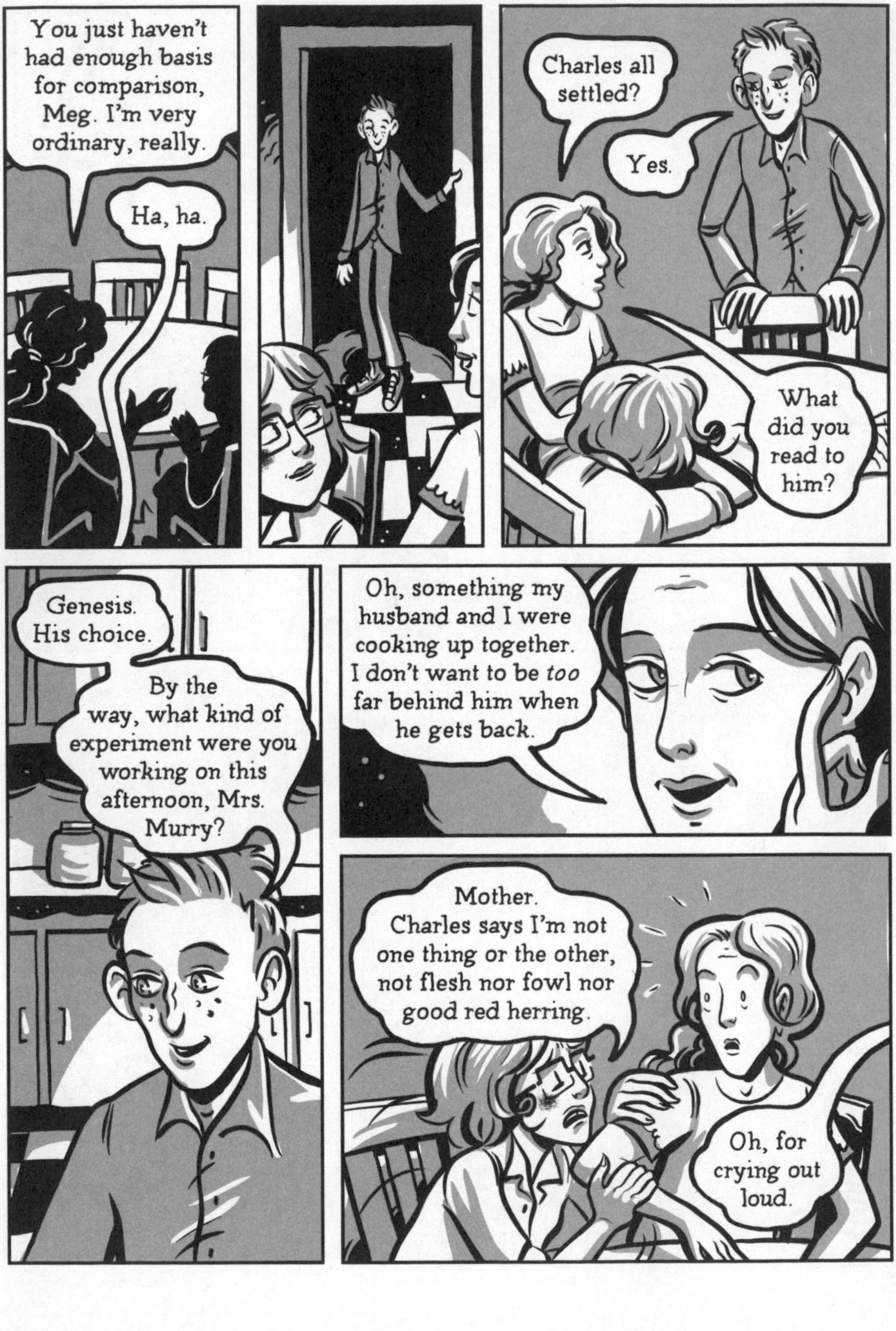

You just haven't had enough basis for comparison, Meg. I'm very ordinary, really.
Ha, ha.
Charles all settled?
Yes.
What did you read to him?
Genesis. His choice.
By the way, what kind of experiment were you working on this afternoon, Mrs. Murry?
Oh, something my husband and I were cooking up together. I don't want to be *too* far behind him when he gets back.
Mother. Charles says I'm not one thing or the other, not flesh nor fowl nor good red herring.
Oh, for crying out loud.

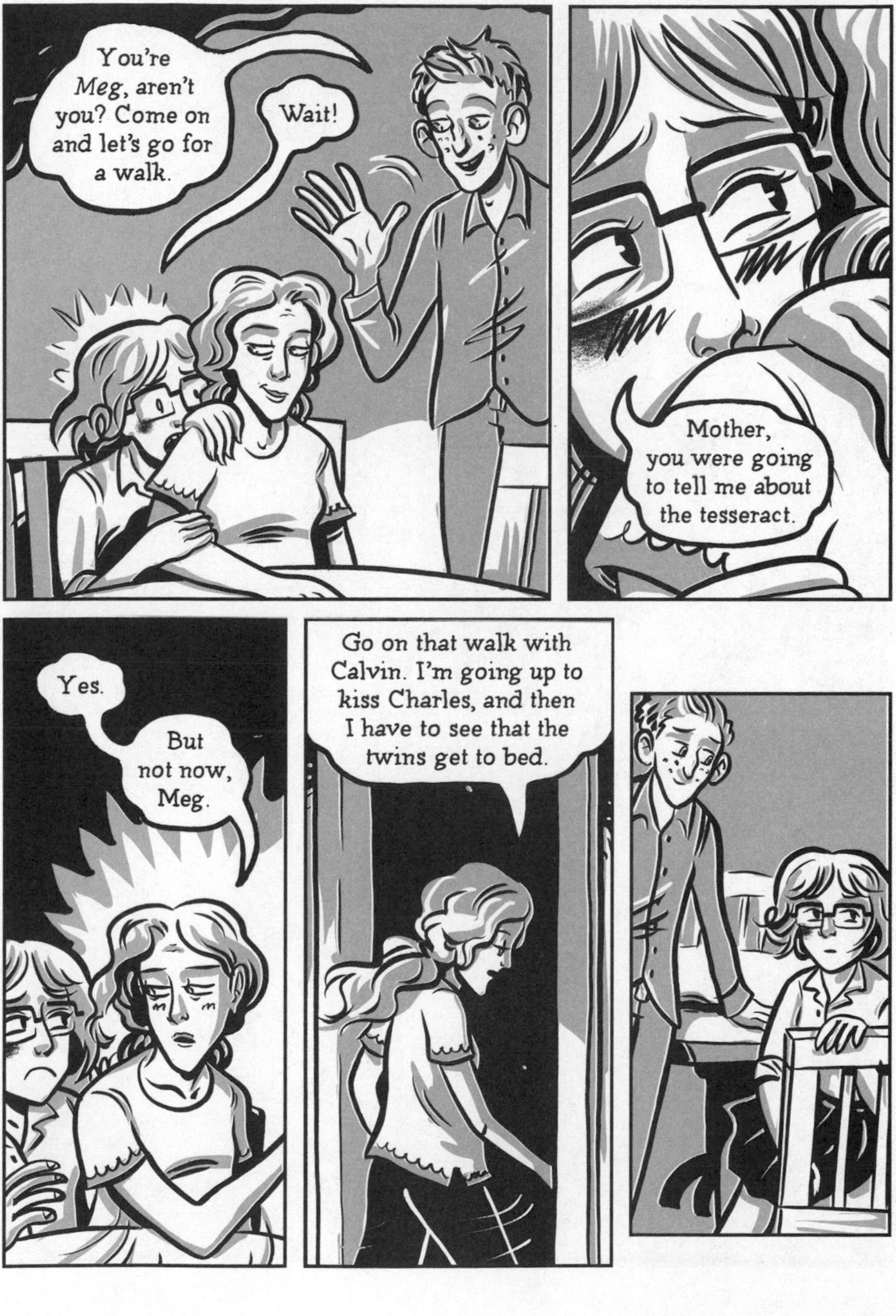
You're *Meg*, aren't you? Come on and let's go for a walk.
Wait!
Mother, you were going to tell me about the tesseract.
Yes.
But not now, Meg.
Go on that walk with Calvin. I'm going up to kiss Charles, and then I have to see that the twins get to bed.

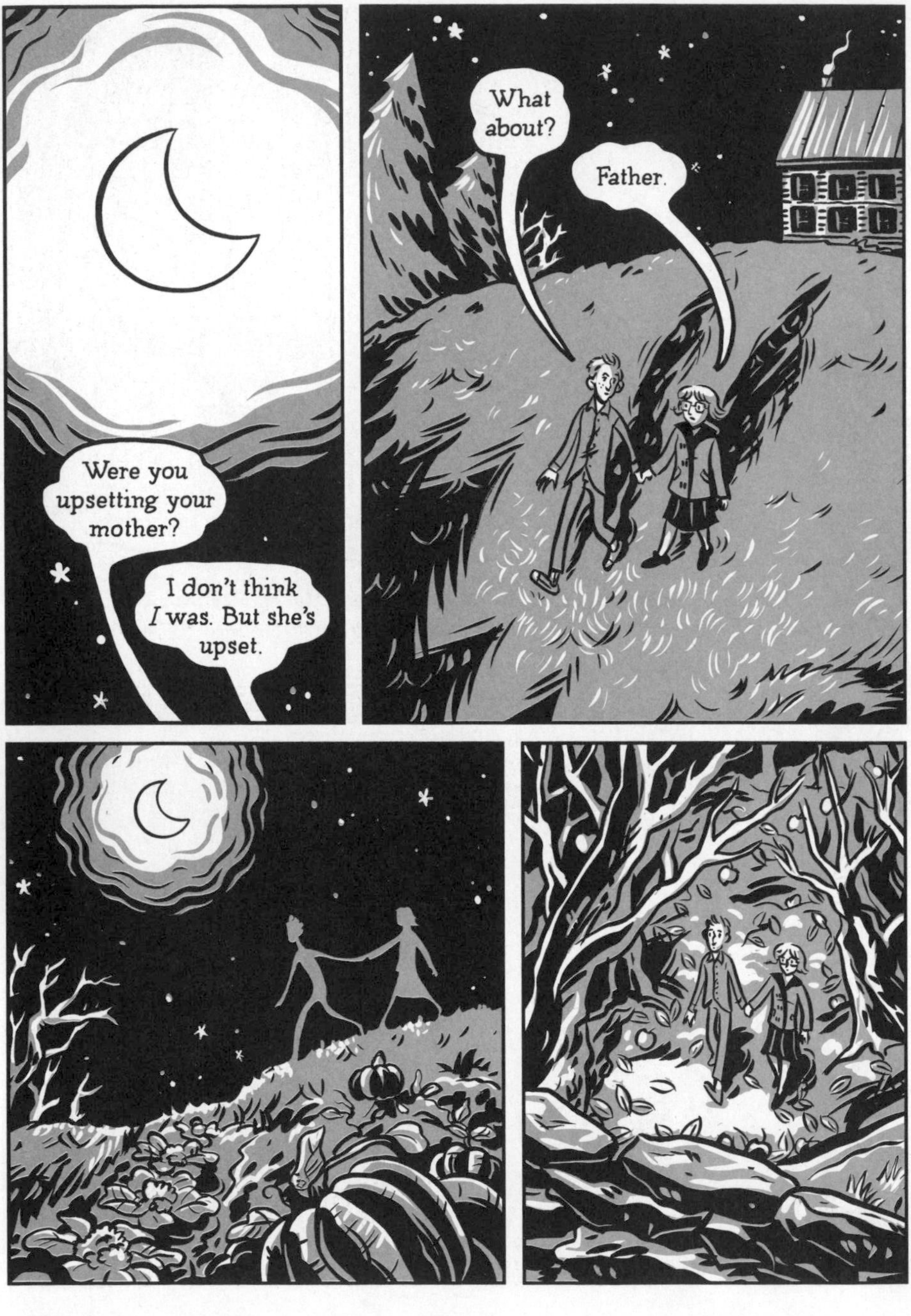
Were you upsetting your mother?
I don't think *I* was. But she's upset.
What about?
Father.

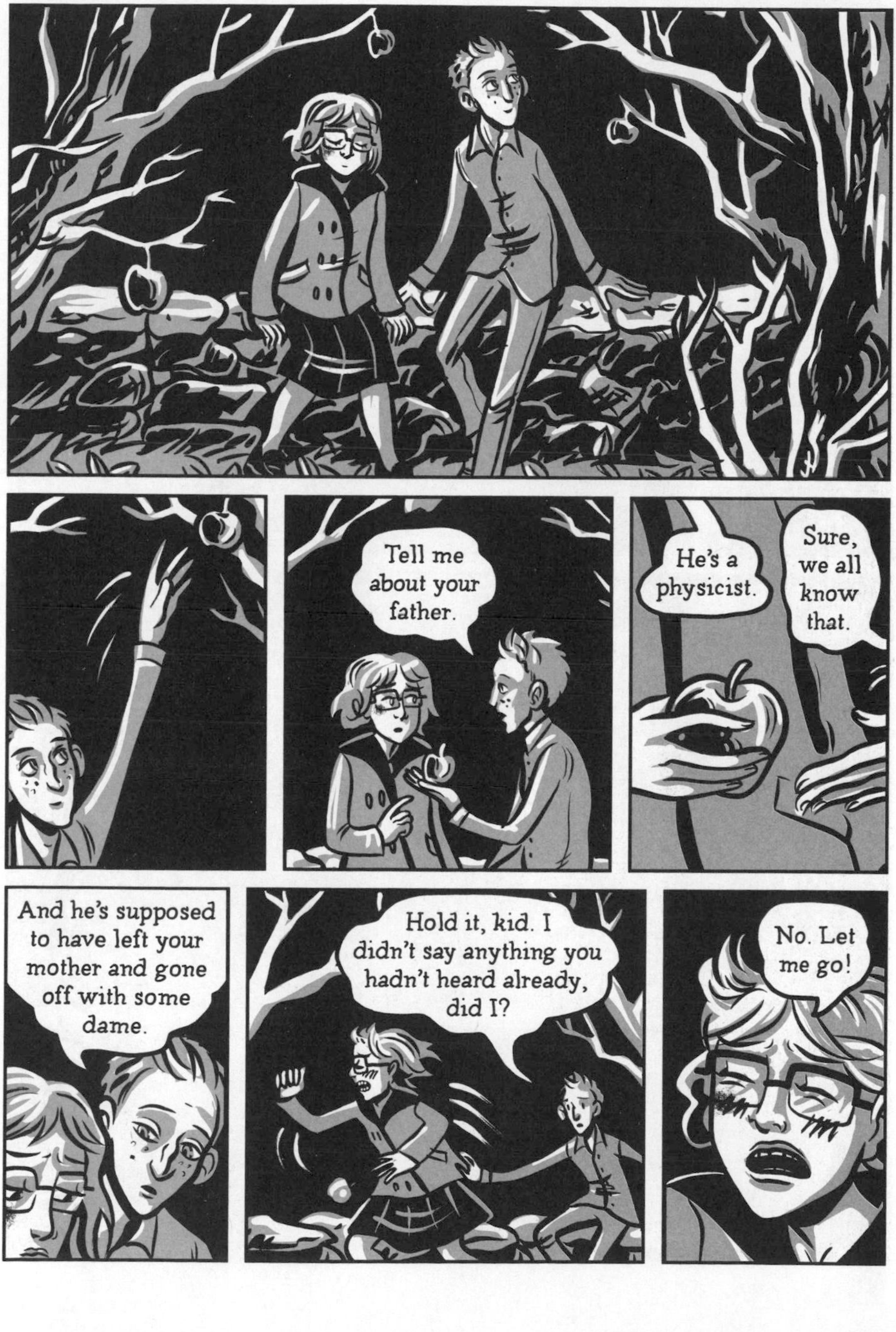
Tell me about your father.
He's a physicist.
Sure, we all know that.
And he's supposed to have left your mother and gone off with some dame.
Hold it, kid. I didn't say anything you hadn't heard already, did I?
No. Let me go!

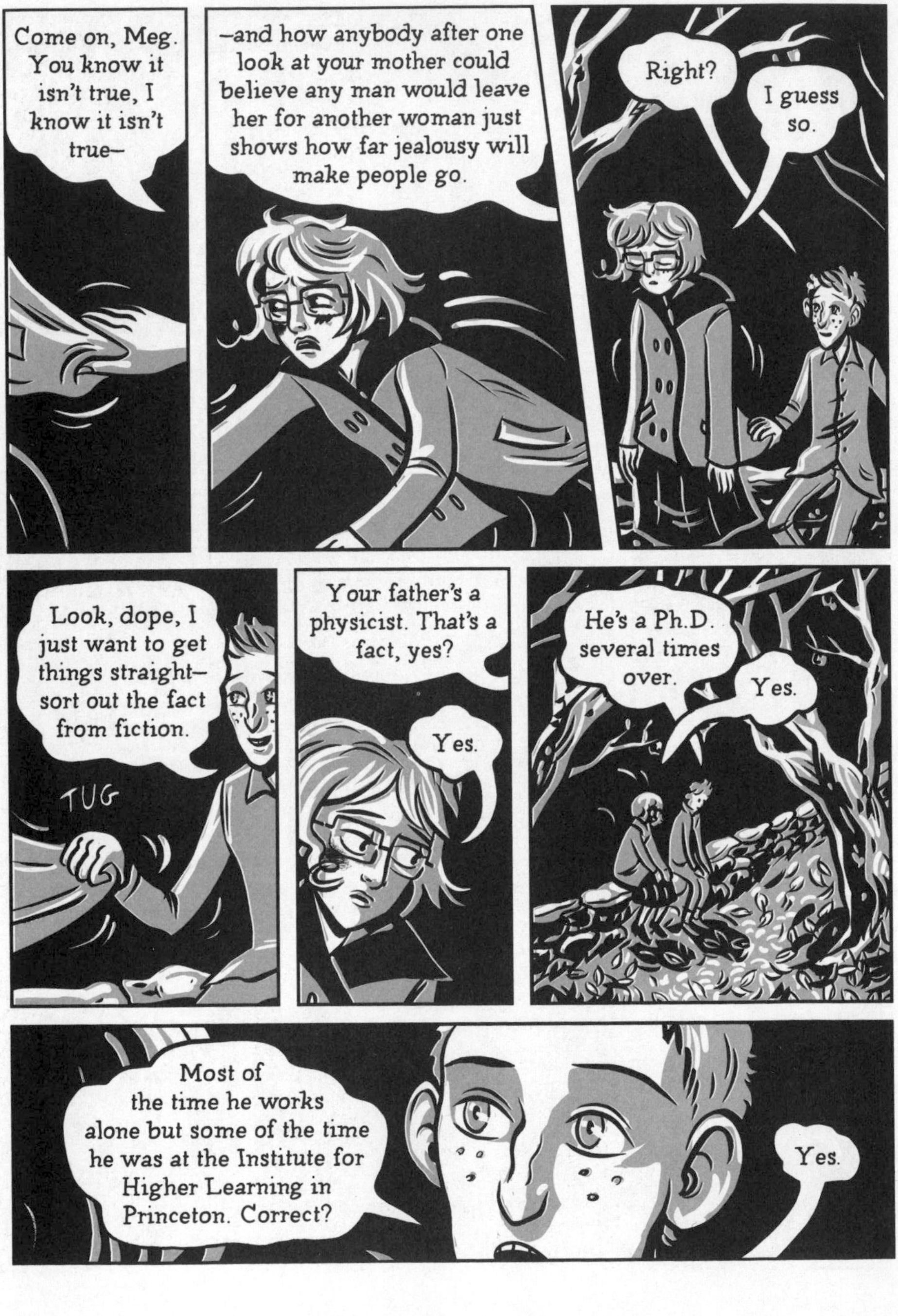
Come on, Meg. You know it isn't true, I know it isn't true—
—and how anybody after one look at your mother could believe any man would leave her for another woman just shows how far jealousy will make people go.
Right?
I guess so.
Look, dope, I just want to get things straight— sort out the fact from fiction.
TUG
Your father's a physicist. That's a fact, yes?
Yes.
He's a Ph.D. several times over.
Yes.
Most of the time he works alone but some of the time he was at the Institute for Higher Learning in Princeton. Correct?
Yes.

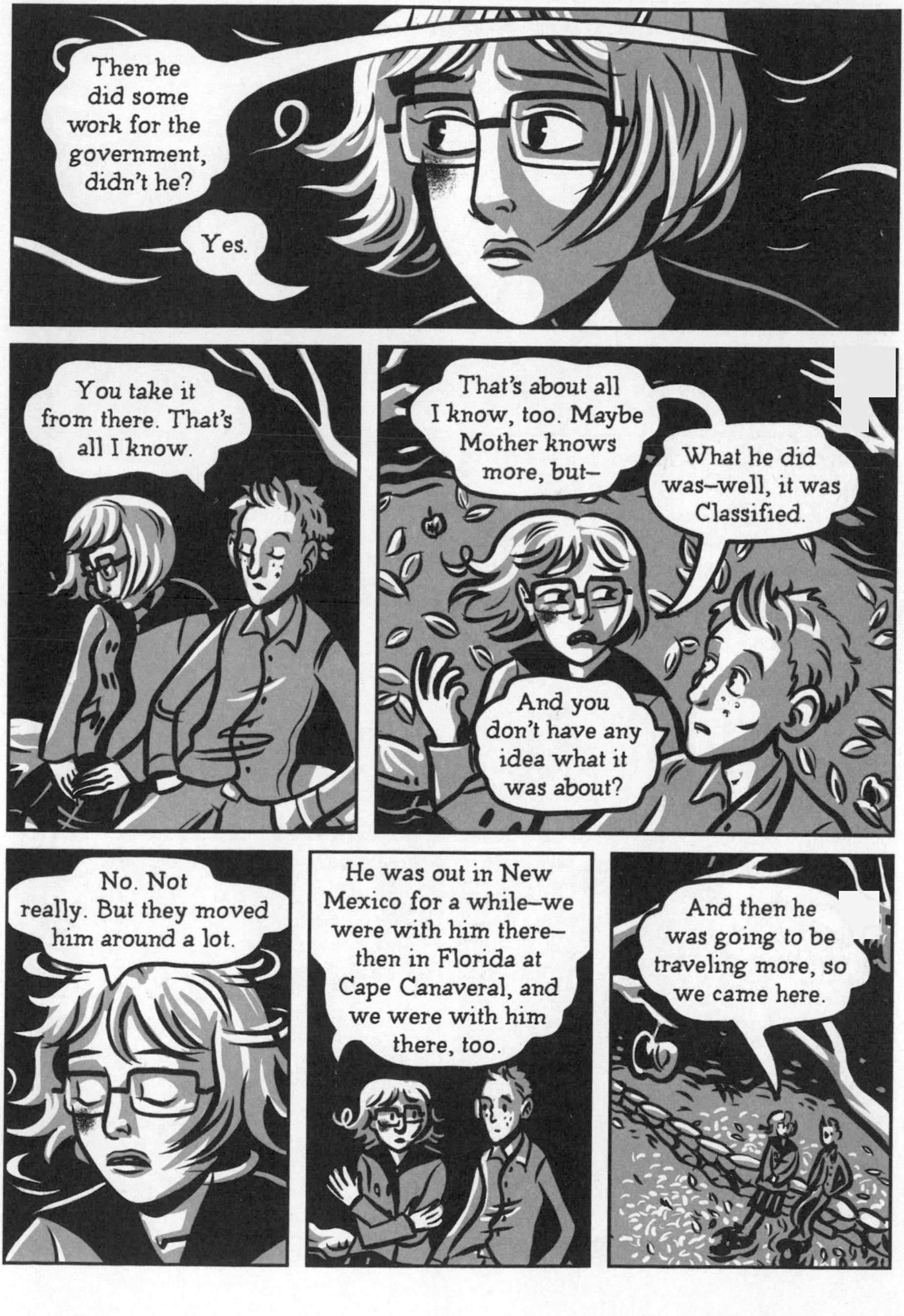

Then he did some work for the government, didn't he?
Yes.
You take it from there. That's all I know.
That's about all I know, too. Maybe Mother knows more, but–
What he did was–well, it was Classified.
And you don't have any idea what it was about?
No. Not really. But they moved him around a lot.
He was out in New Mexico for a while–we were with him there–then in Florida at Cape Canaveral, and we were with him there, too.
And then he was going to be traveling more, so we came here.

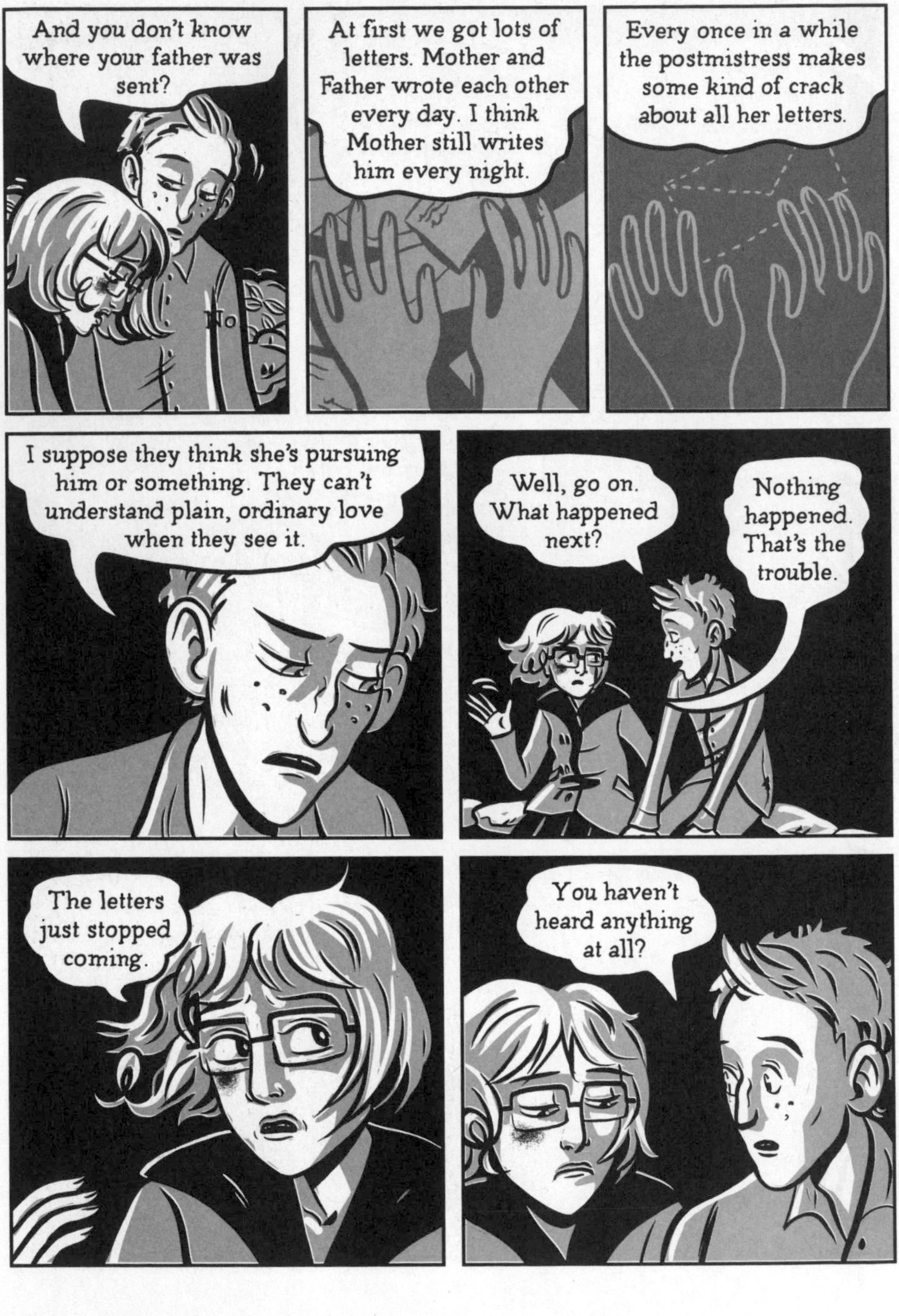
And you don't know where your father was sent?
At first we got lots of letters. Mother and Father wrote each other every day. I think Mother still writes him every night.
Every once in a while the postmistress makes some kind of crack about all her letters.
I suppose they think she's pursuing him or something. They can't understand plain, ordinary love when they see it.
Well, go on. What happened next?
Nothing happened. That's the trouble.
The letters just stopped coming.
You haven't heard anything at all?

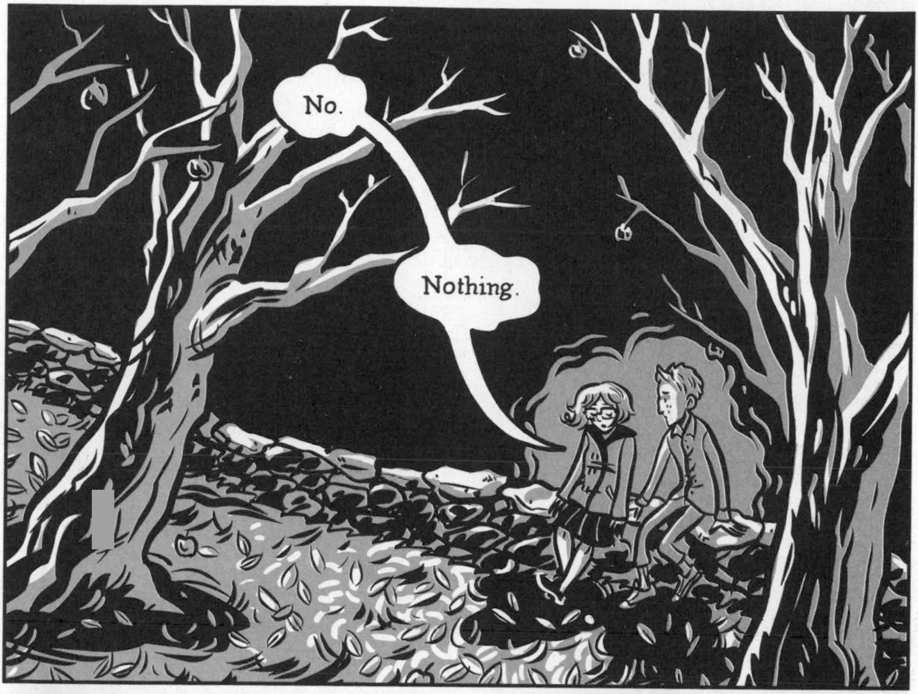
No.
Nothing.

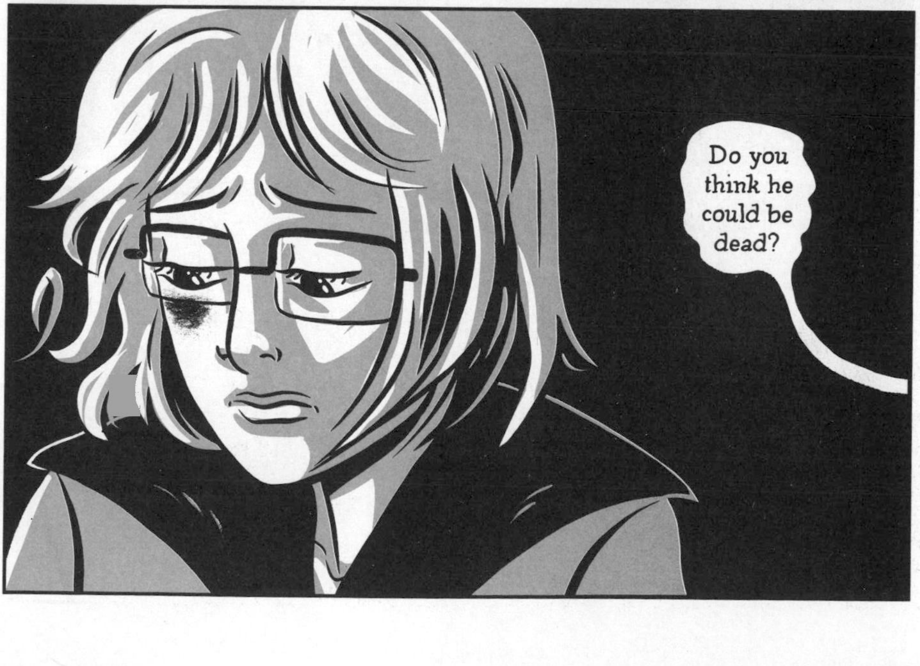
Do you think he could be dead?

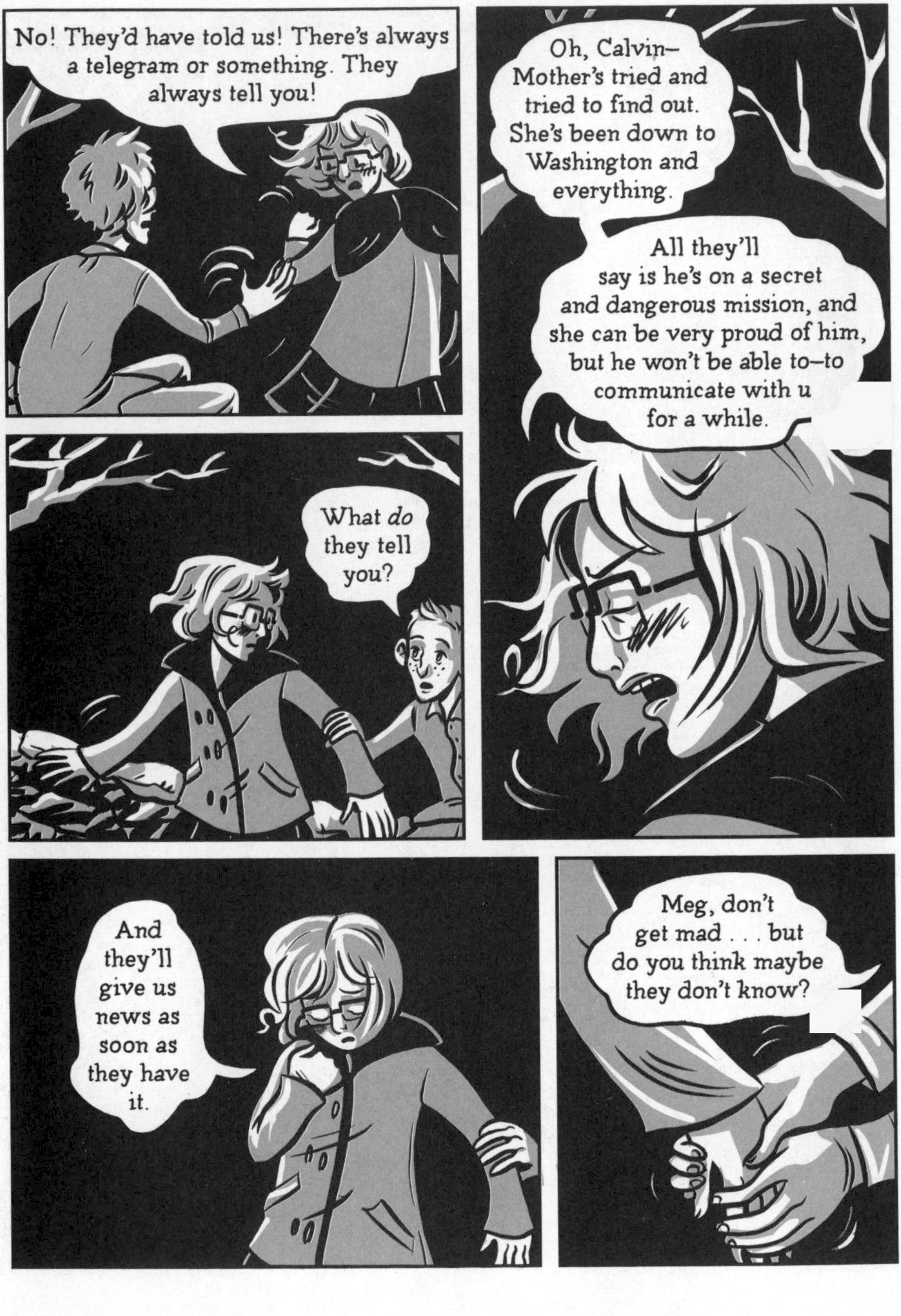
No! They'd have told us! There's always a telegram or something. They always tell you!
Oh, Calvin— Mother's tried and tried to find out. She's been down to Washington and everything.
All they'll say is he's on a secret and dangerous mission, and she can be very proud of him, but he won't be able to—to communicate with u for a while.
What *do* they tell you?
And they'll give us news as soon as they have it.
Meg, don't get mad . . . but do you think maybe they don't know?

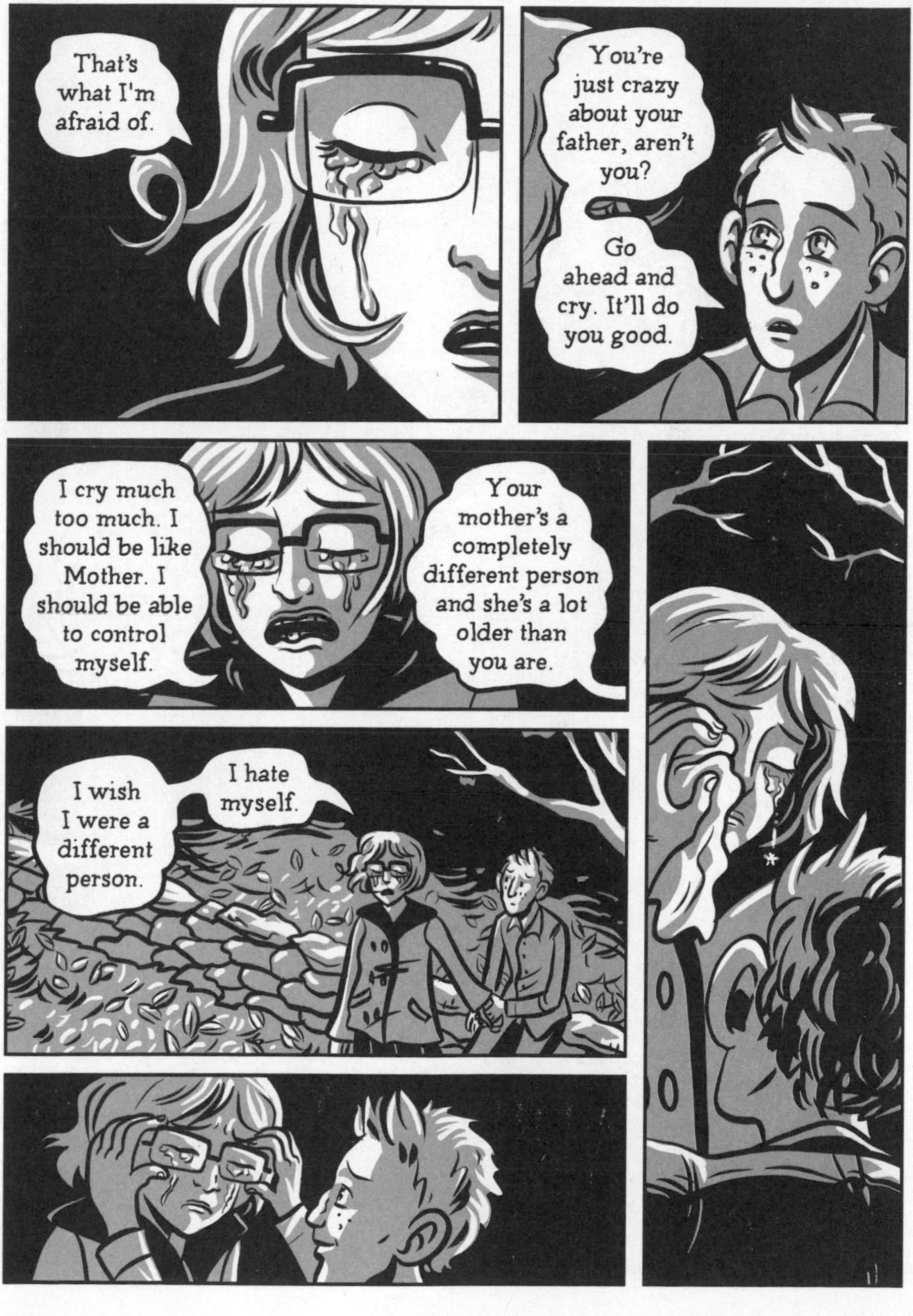

That's what I'm afraid of.
You're just crazy about your father, aren't you?
Go ahead and cry. It'll do you good.
I cry much too much. I should be like Mother. I should be able to control myself.
Your mother's a completely different person and she's a lot older than you are.
I wish I were a different person.
I hate myself.

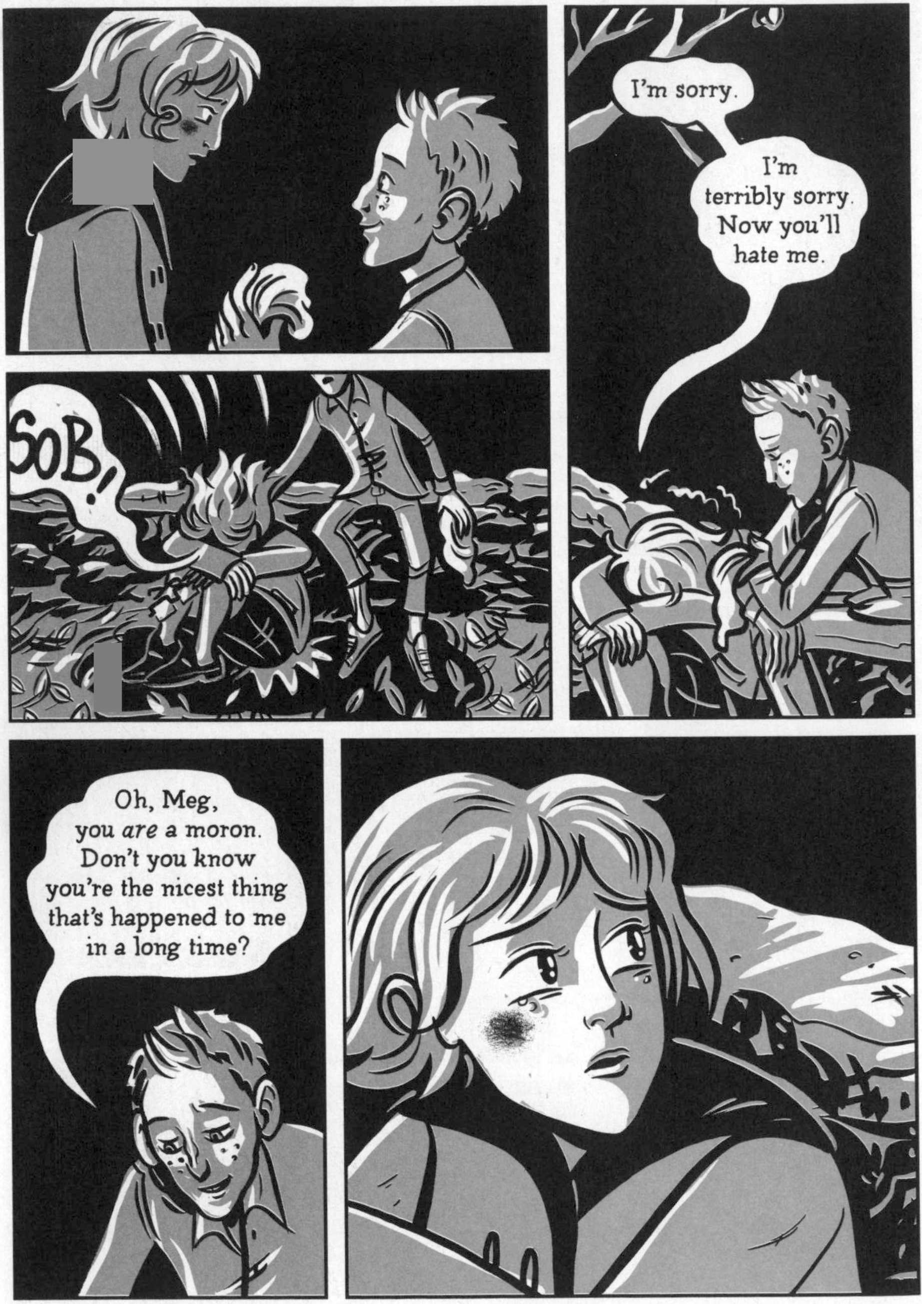
I'm sorry.
I'm terribly sorry. Now you'll hate me.
SOB!
Oh, Meg, you *are* a moron. Don't you know you're the nicest thing that's happened to me in a long time?

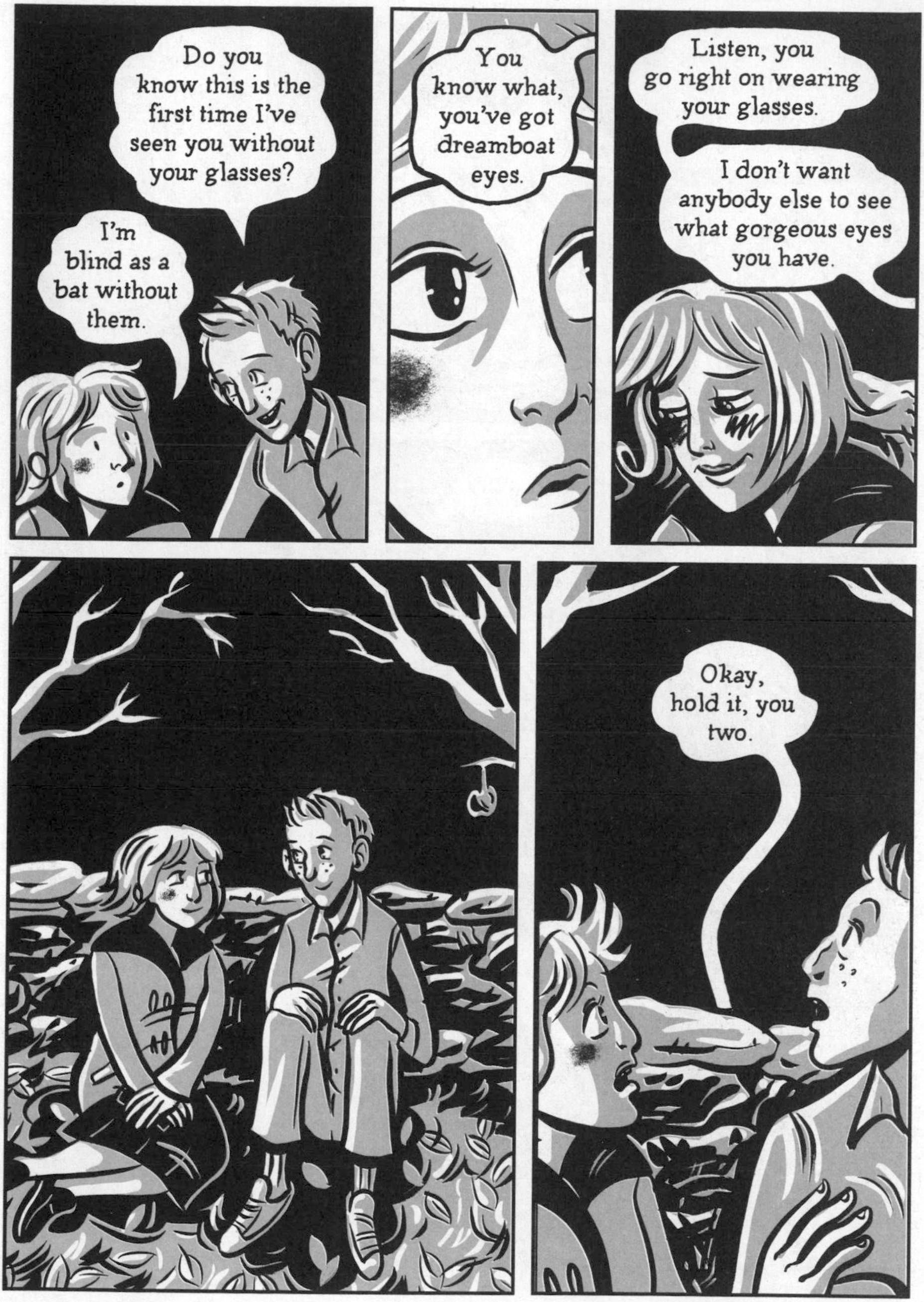
Do you know this is the first time I've seen you without your glasses?
I'm blind as a bat without them.
You know what, you've got dreamboat eyes.
Listen, you go right on wearing your glasses.
I don't want anybody else to see what gorgeous eyes you have.
Okay, hold it, you two.

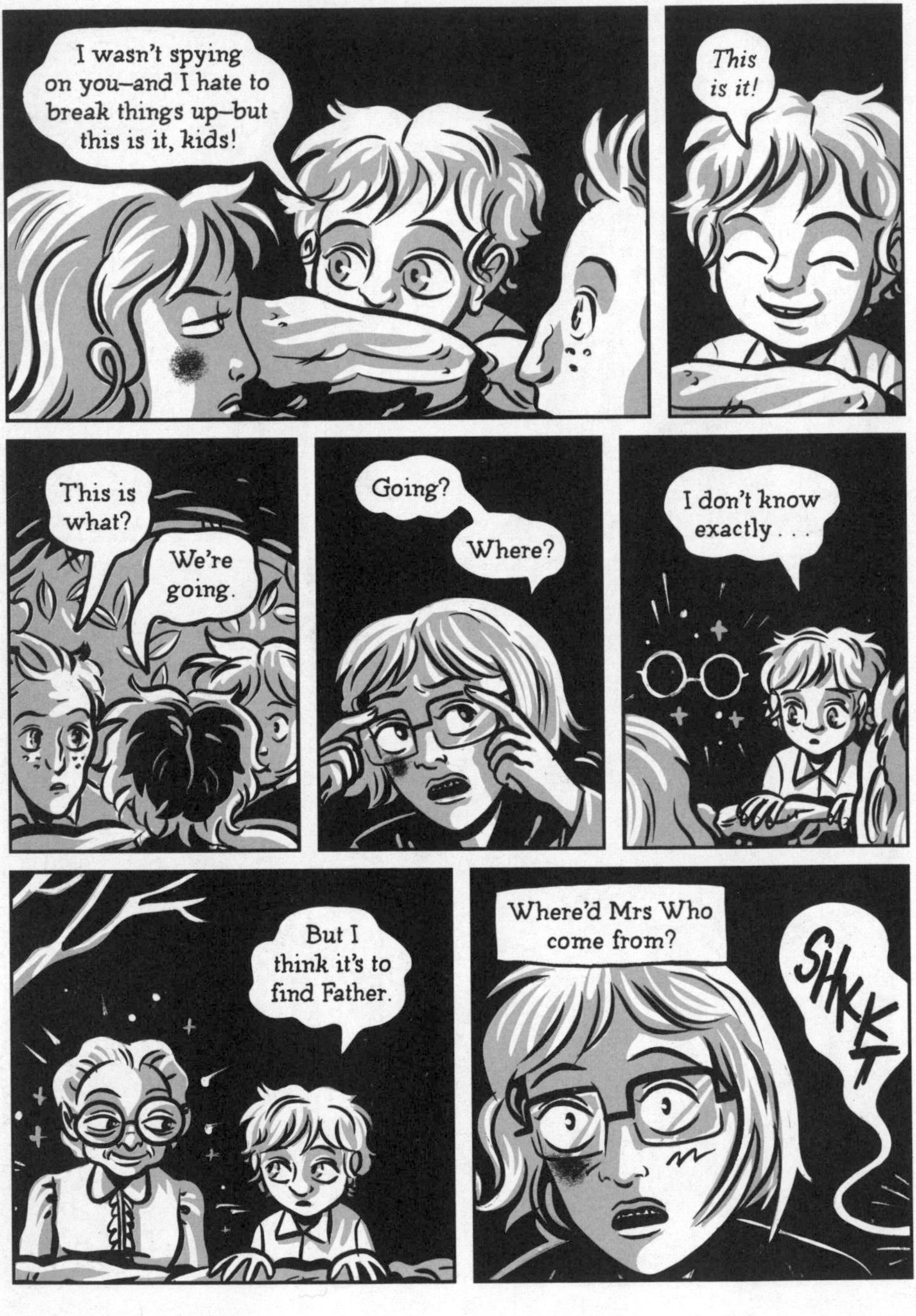
I wasn't spying on you—and I hate to break things up—but this is it, kids!
This is it!
This is what?
We're going.
Going?
Where?
I don't know exactly . . .
But I think it's to find Father.
Where'd Mrs Who come from?
SHKKT

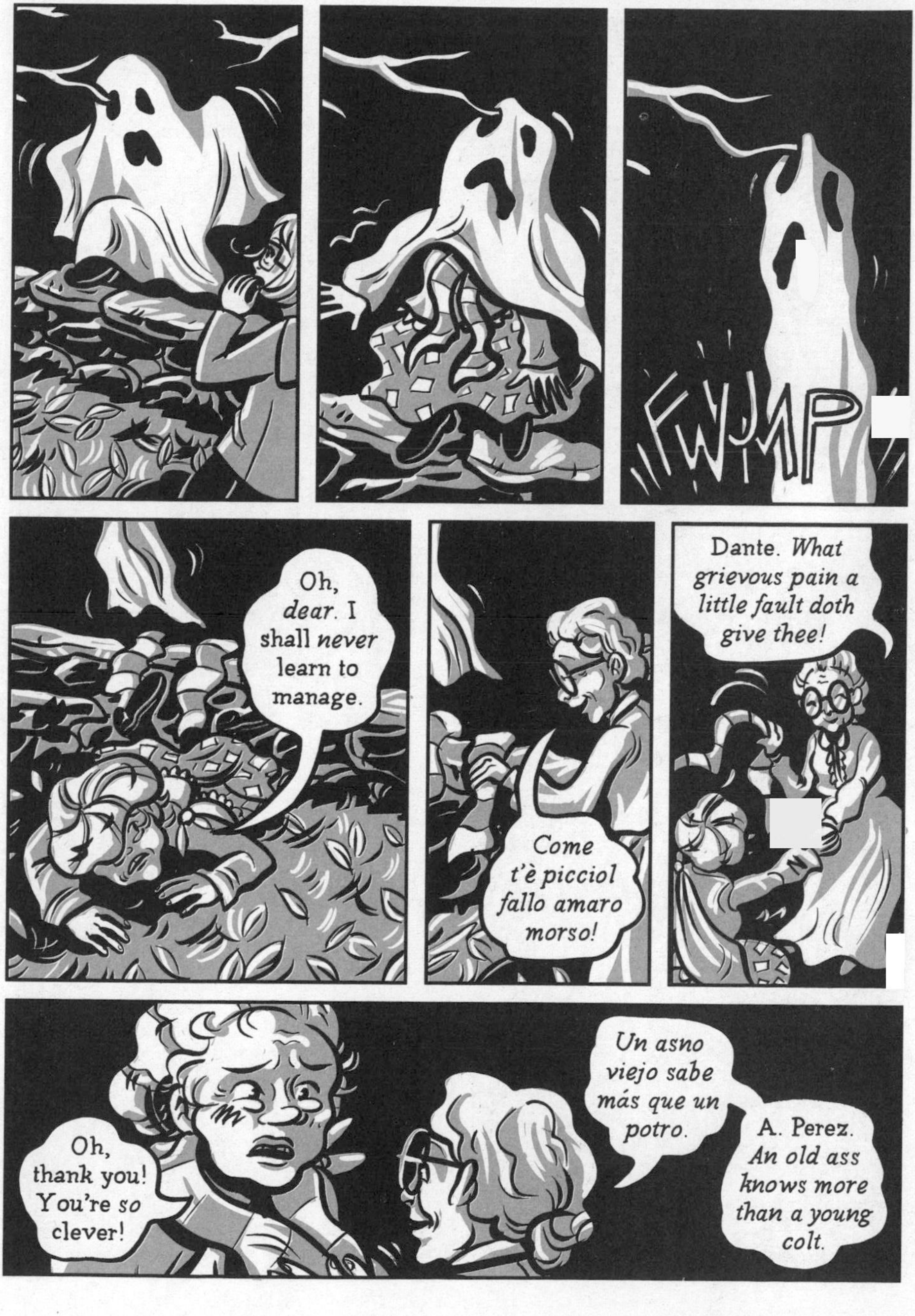
FWUMP
Oh, dear. I shall never learn to manage.
Come t'è picciol fallo amaro morso!
Dante. What grievous pain a little fault doth give thee!
Oh, thank you! You're so clever!
Un asno viejo sabe más que un potro.
A. Perez. An old ass knows more than a young colt.

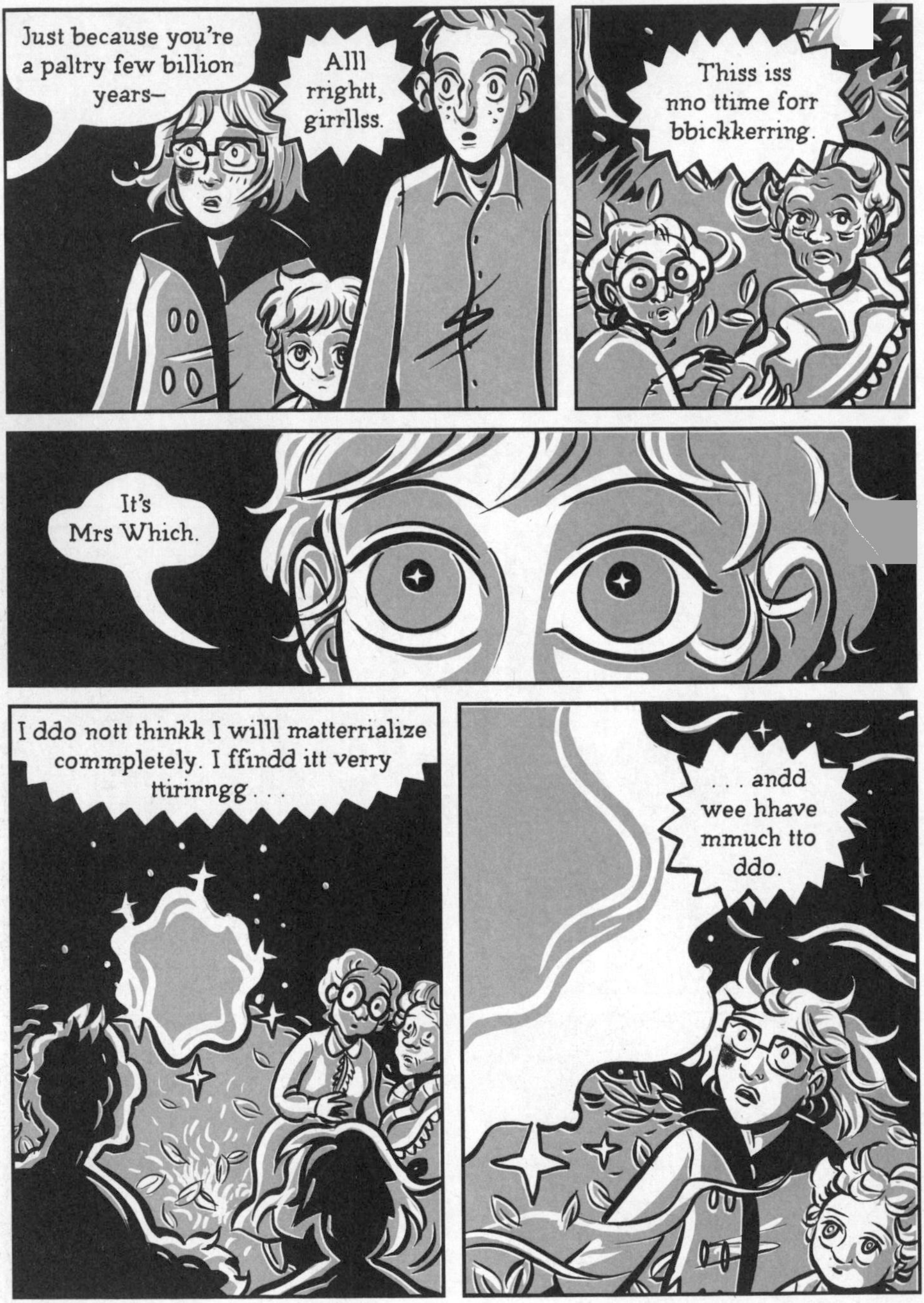
Just because you're a paltry few billion years—
Alll rrightt, girrllss.
Thiss iss nno ttime forr bbickkerring.
It's Mrs Which.
I ddo nott thinkk I willl matterrialize commpletely. I ffindd itt verry ttirinngg . . .
. . . andd wee hhave mmuch tto ddo.

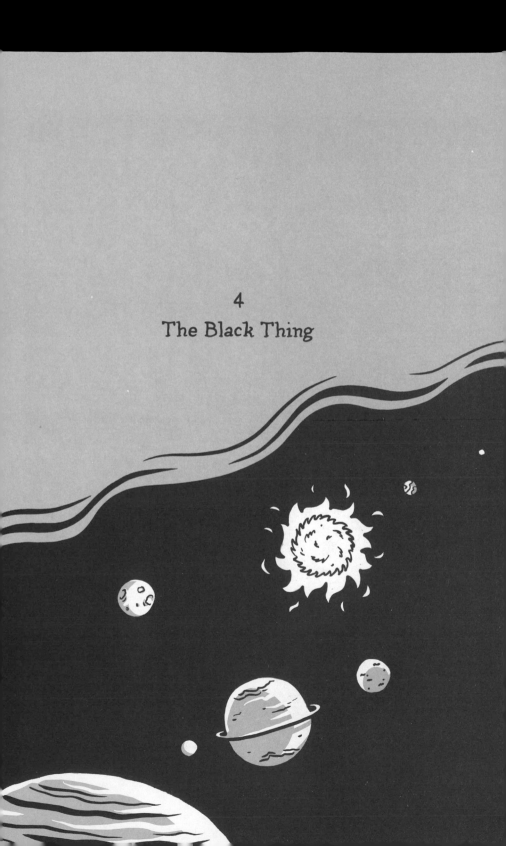

4
The Black Thing

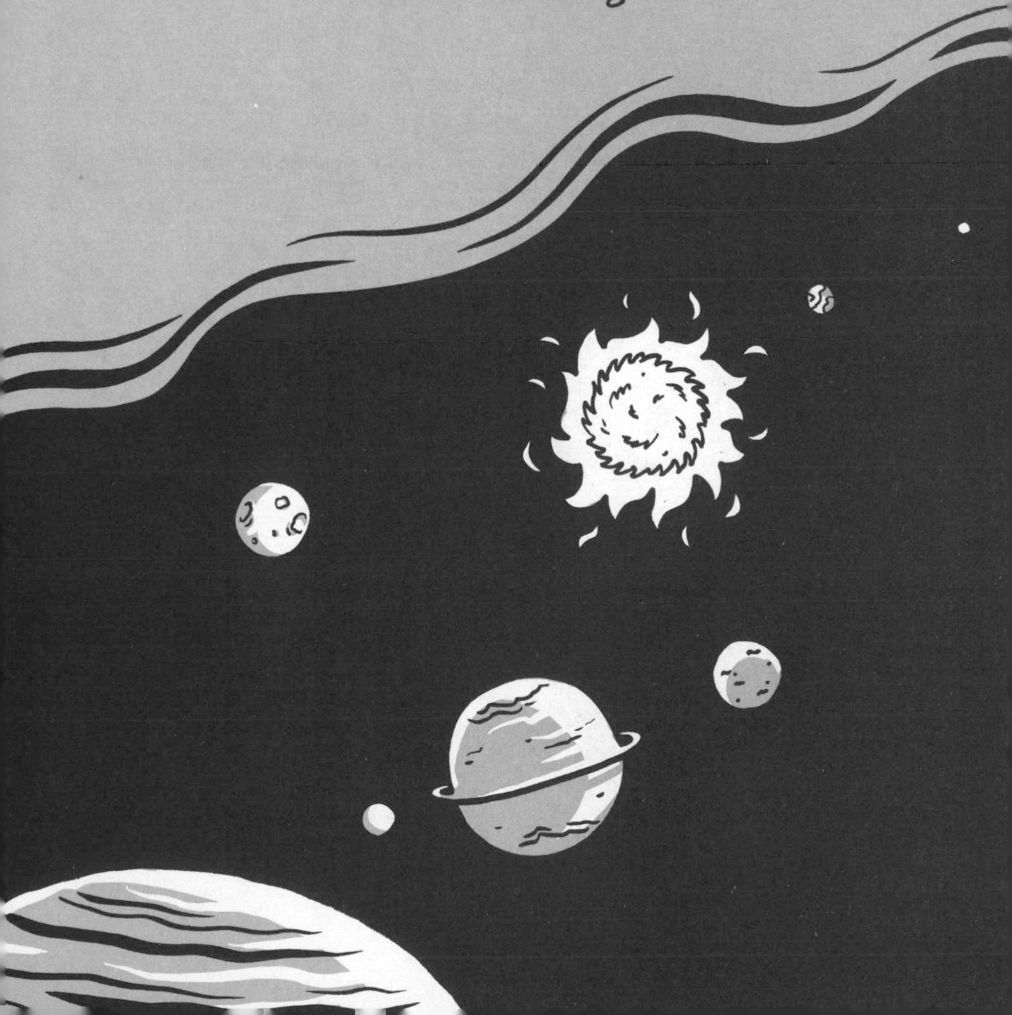

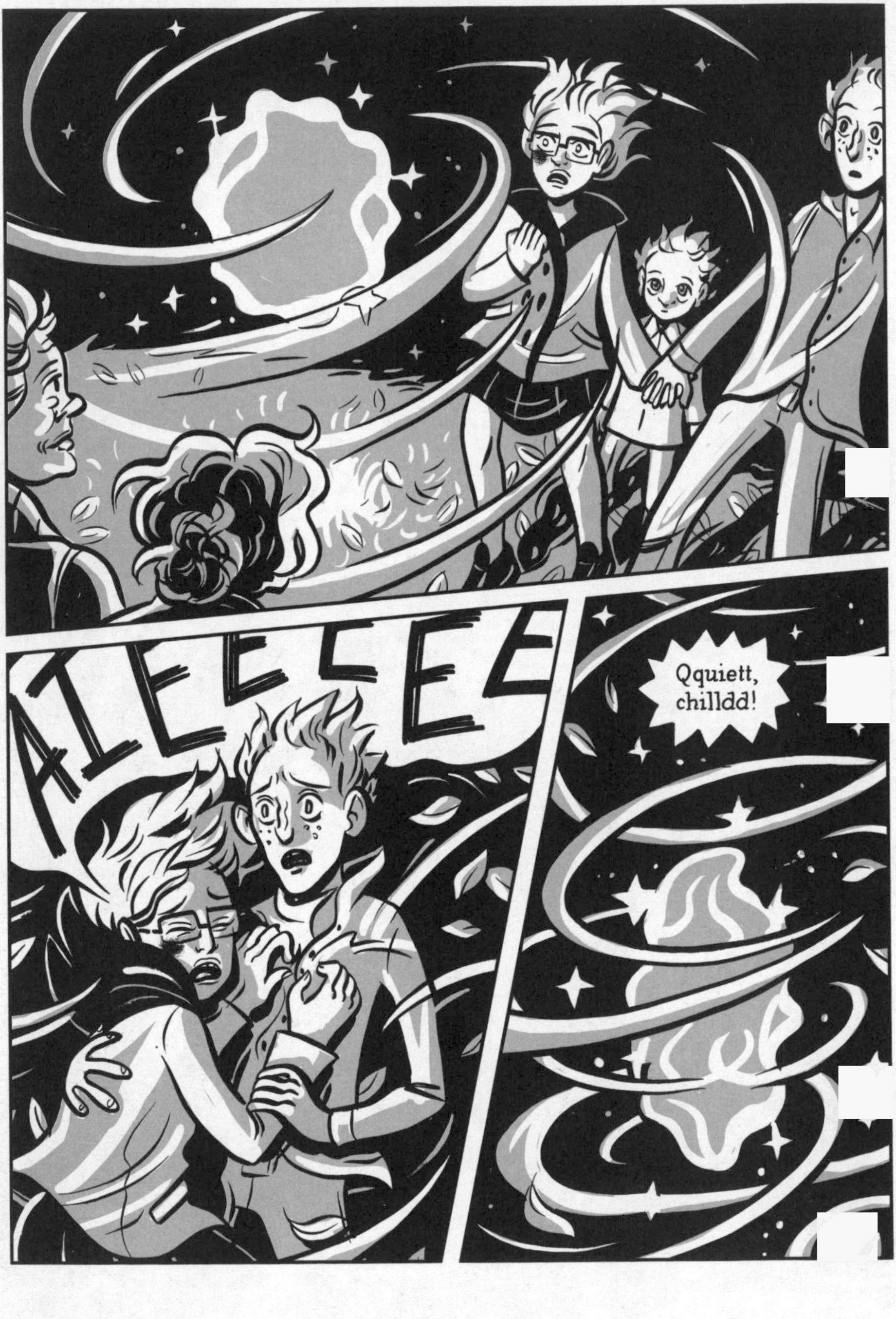
AIEEEEE
Qquiett, chillldd!

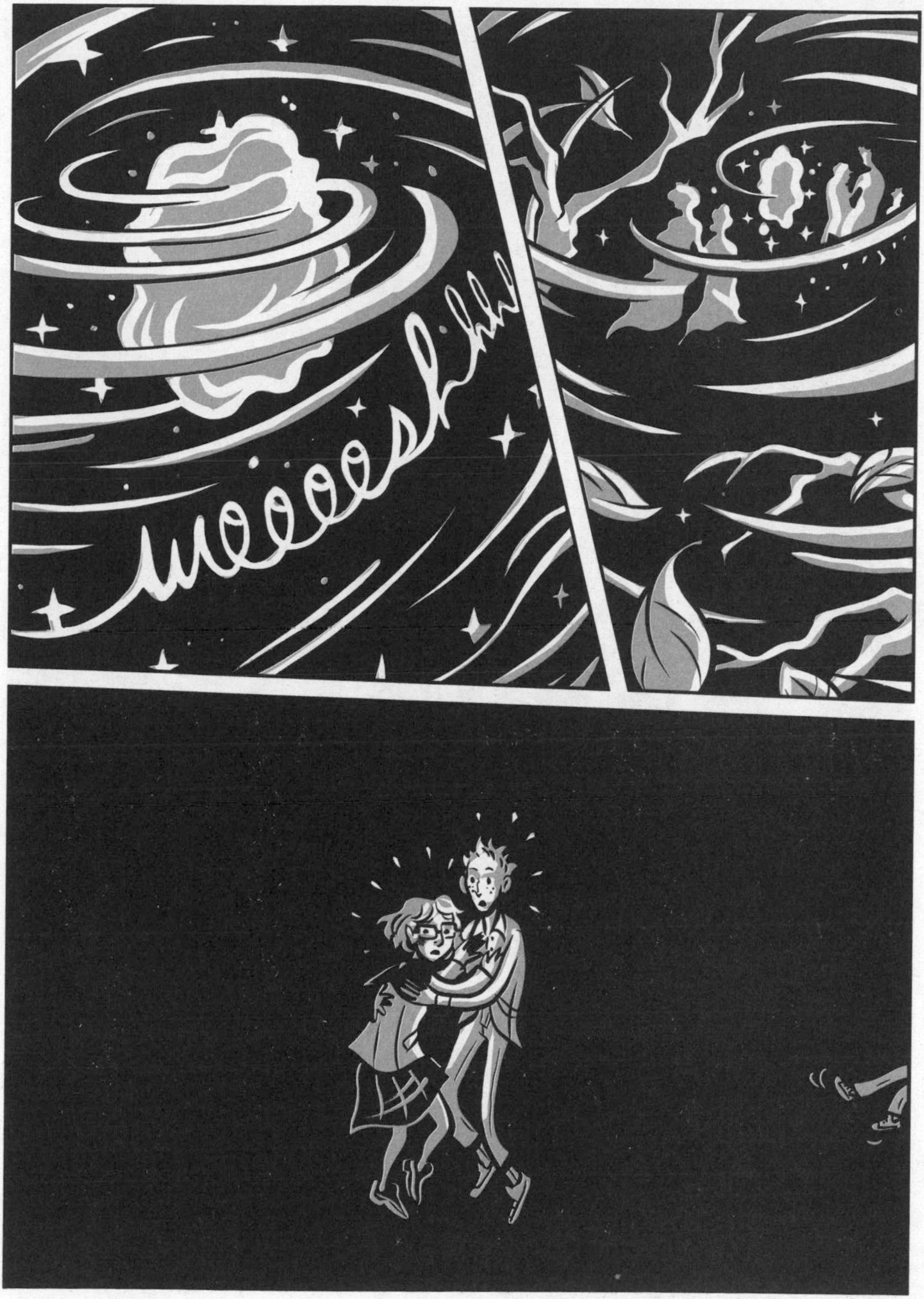
wooooshhh

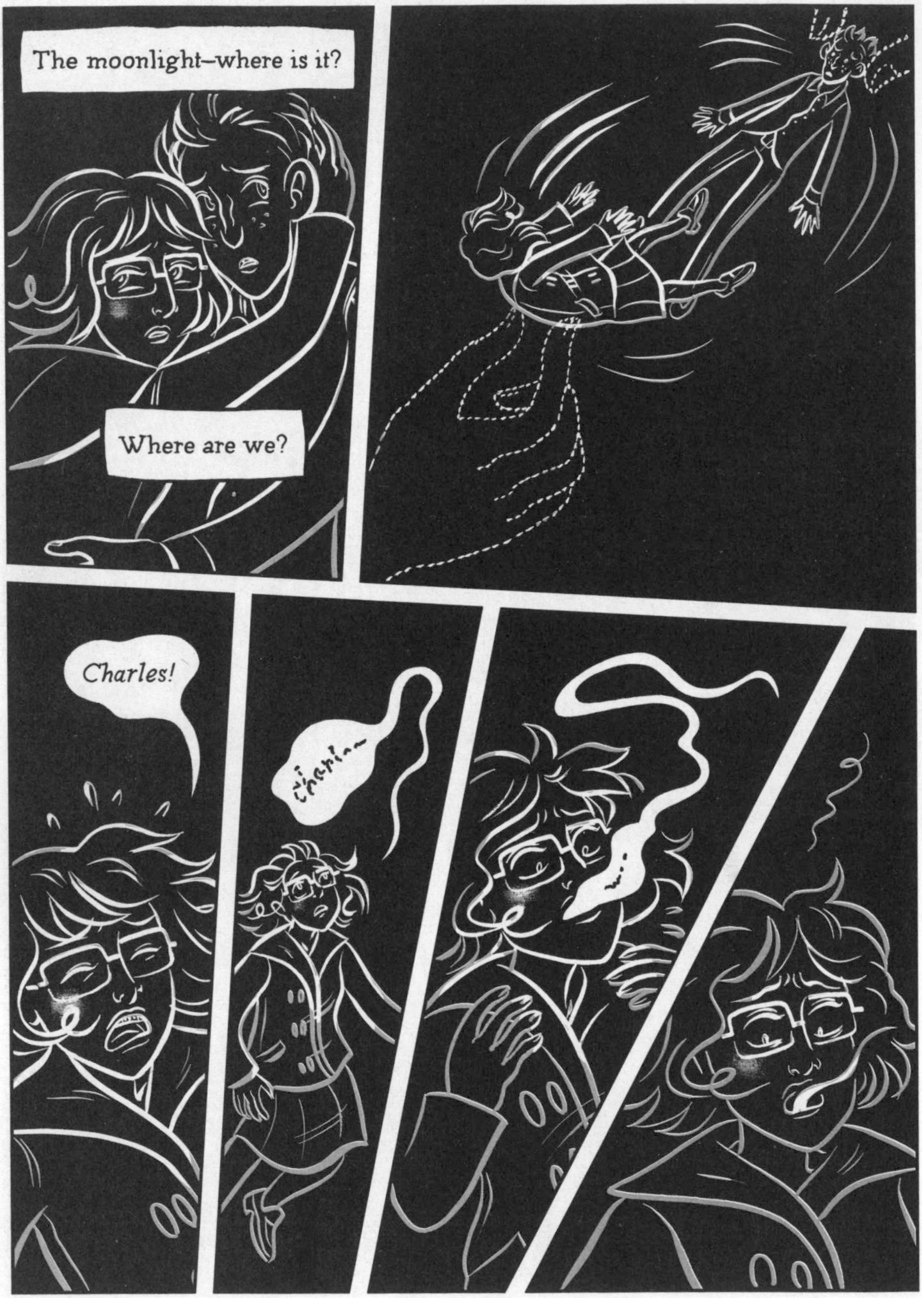

The moonlight—where is it?
Where are we?
Charles!

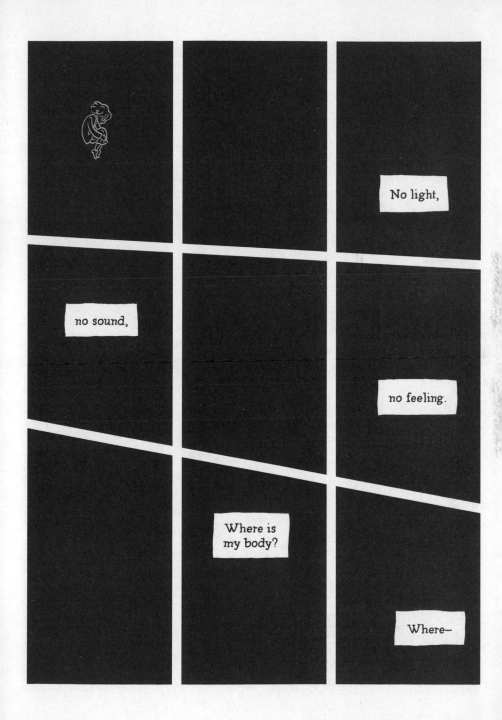

No light,

no sound,

no feeling.

Where is
my body?

Where—

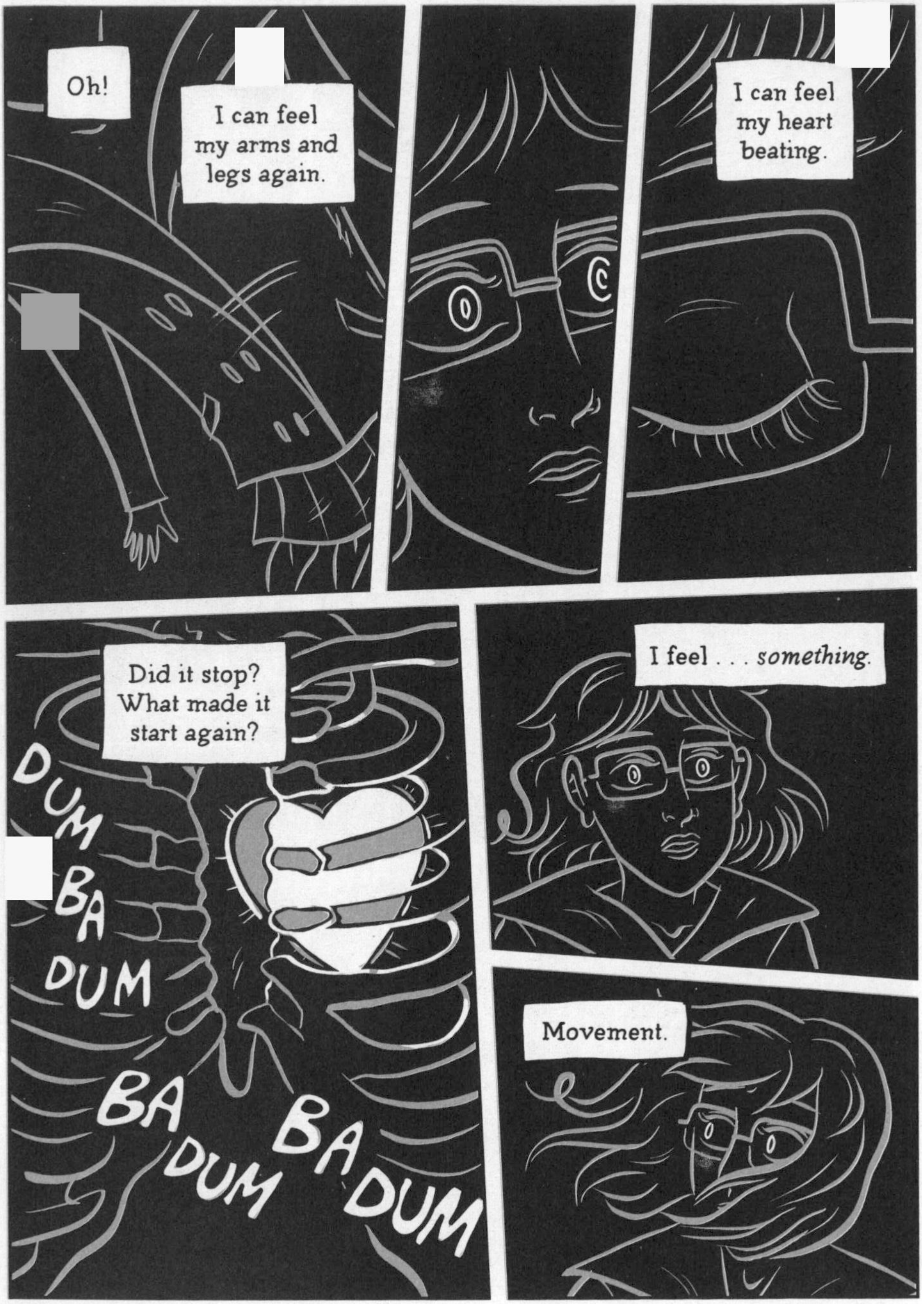
Oh!
I can feel my arms and legs again.
I can feel my heart beating.
Did it stop? What made it start again?
DUM BA DUM
BA DUM BA DUM
I feel . . . *something.*
Movement.

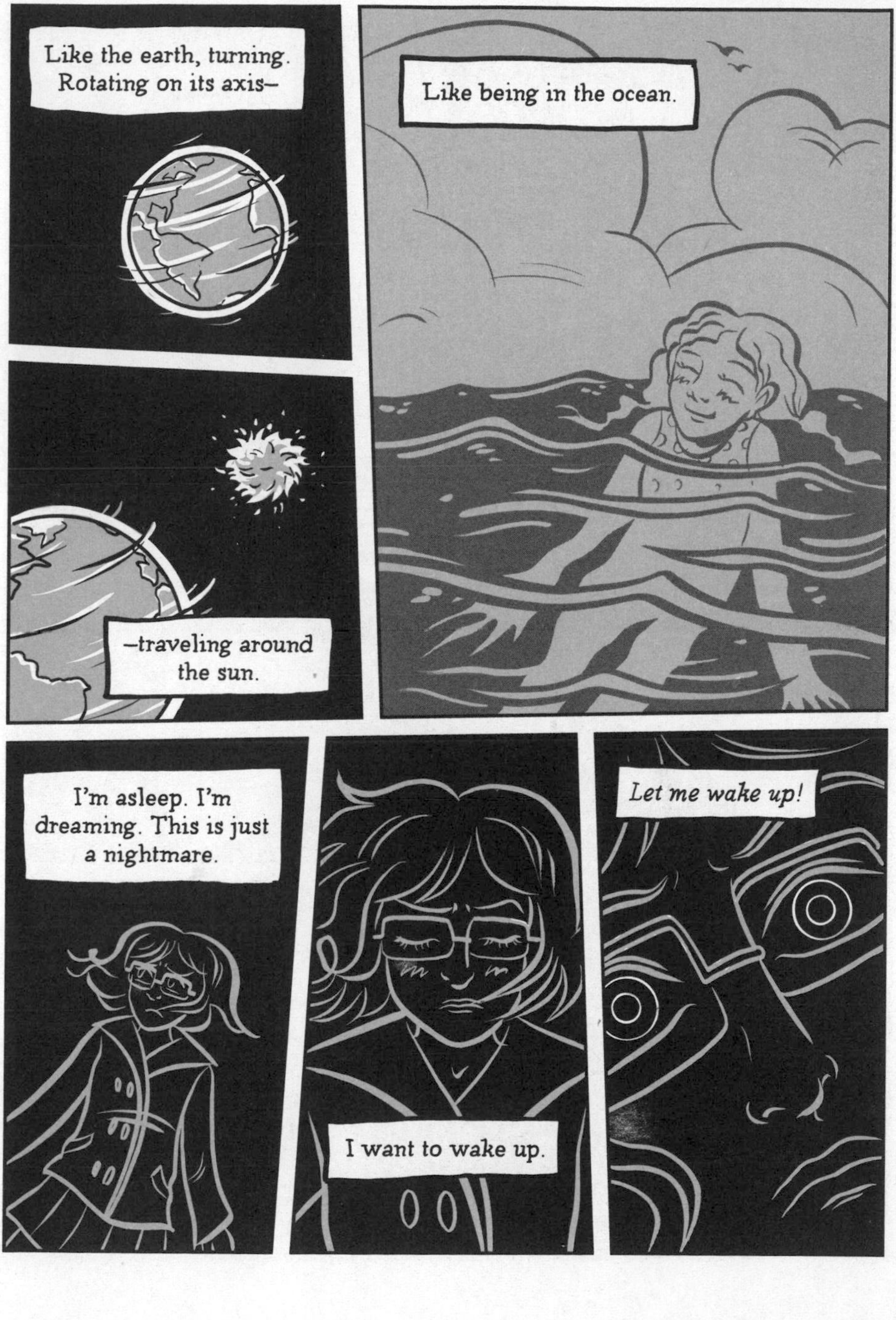
Like the earth, turning. Rotating on its axis–
–traveling around the sun.
Like being in the ocean.
I'm asleep. I'm dreaming. This is just a nightmare.
I want to wake up.
Let me wake up!

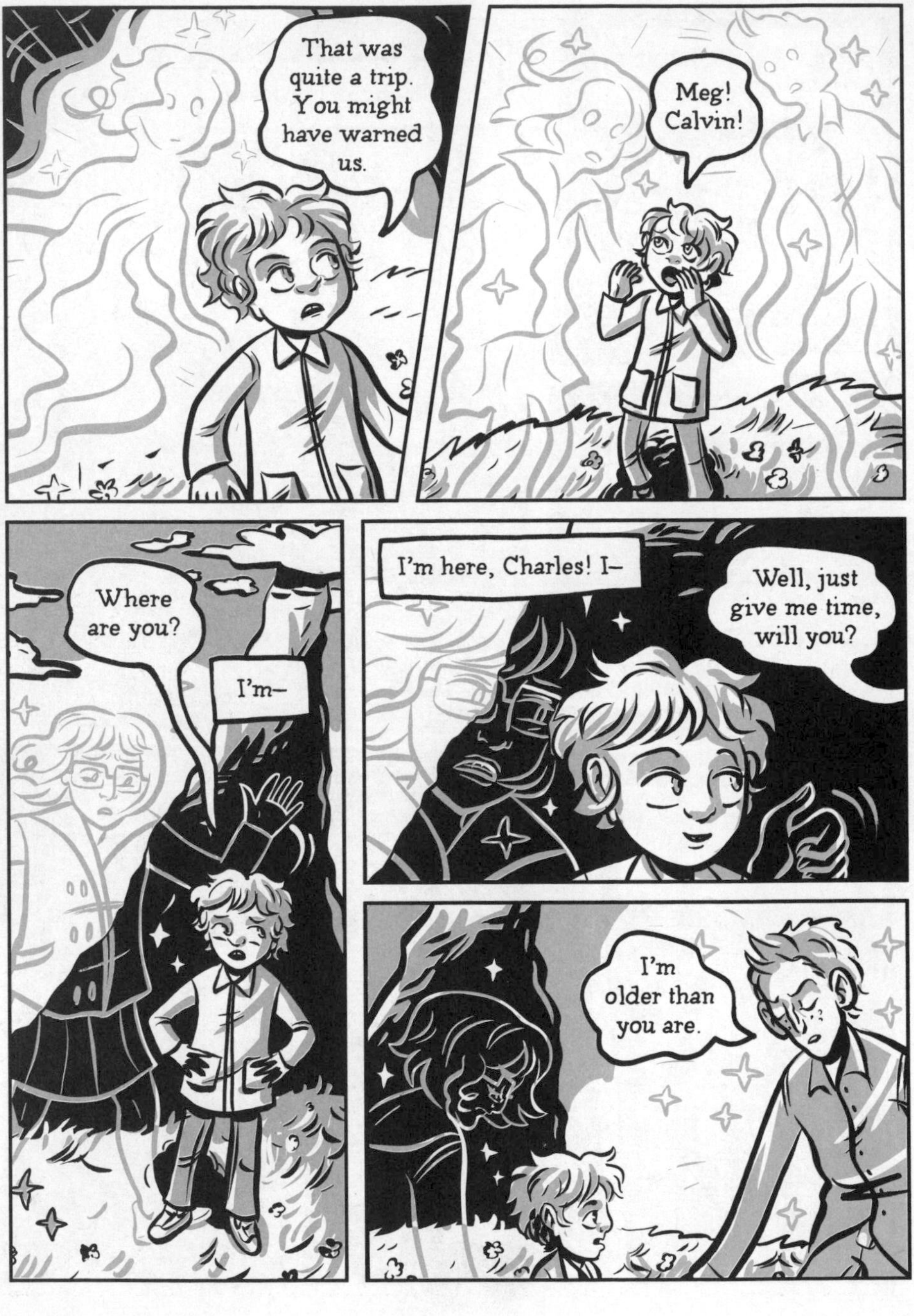
That was quite a trip. You might have warned us.
Meg! Calvin!
Where are you?
I'm–
I'm here, Charles! I–
Well, just give me time, will you?
I'm older than you are.

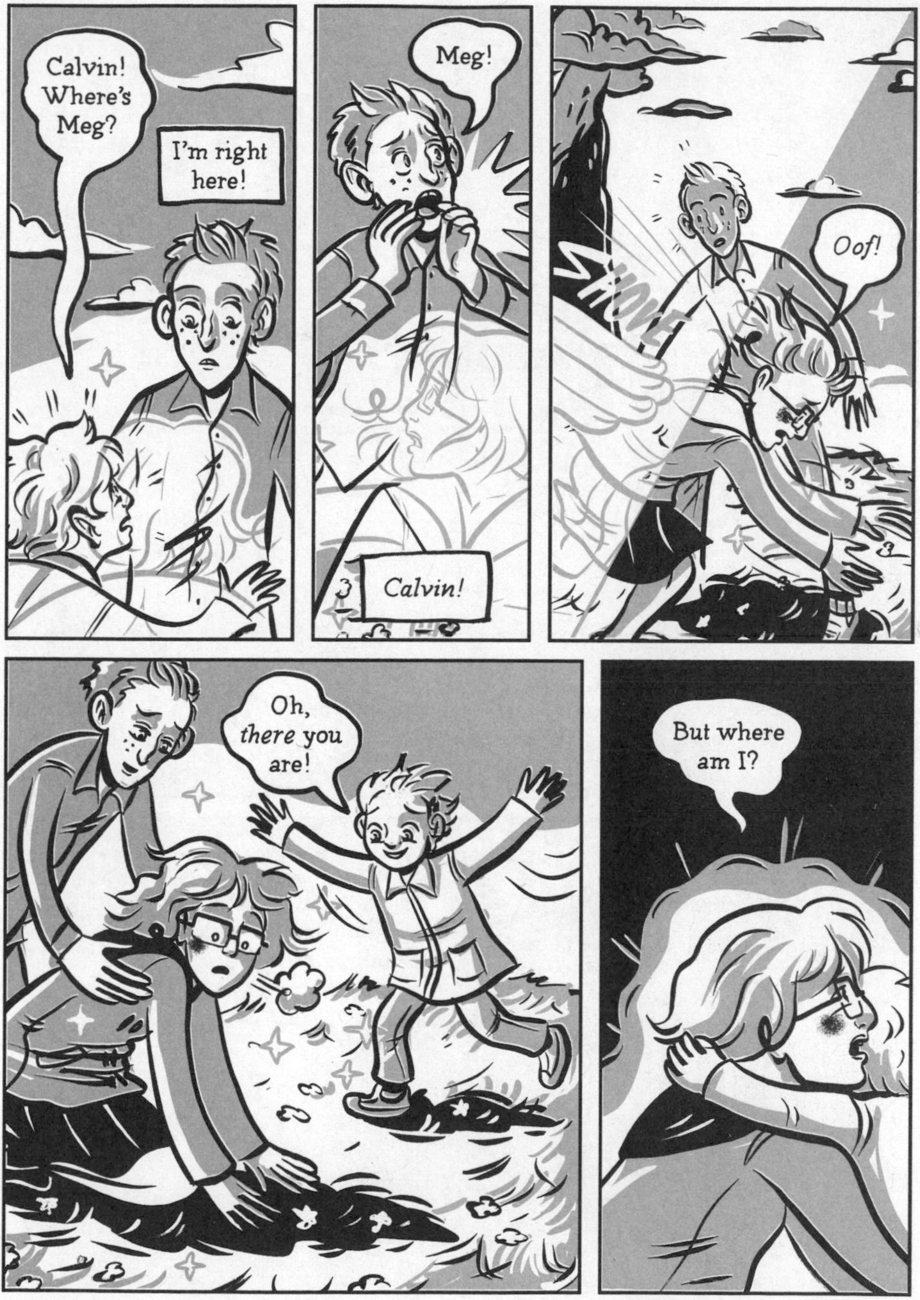
Calvin! Where's Meg?
I'm right here!
Meg!
Calvin!
SHOVE
Oof!
Oh, *there* you are!
But where am I?

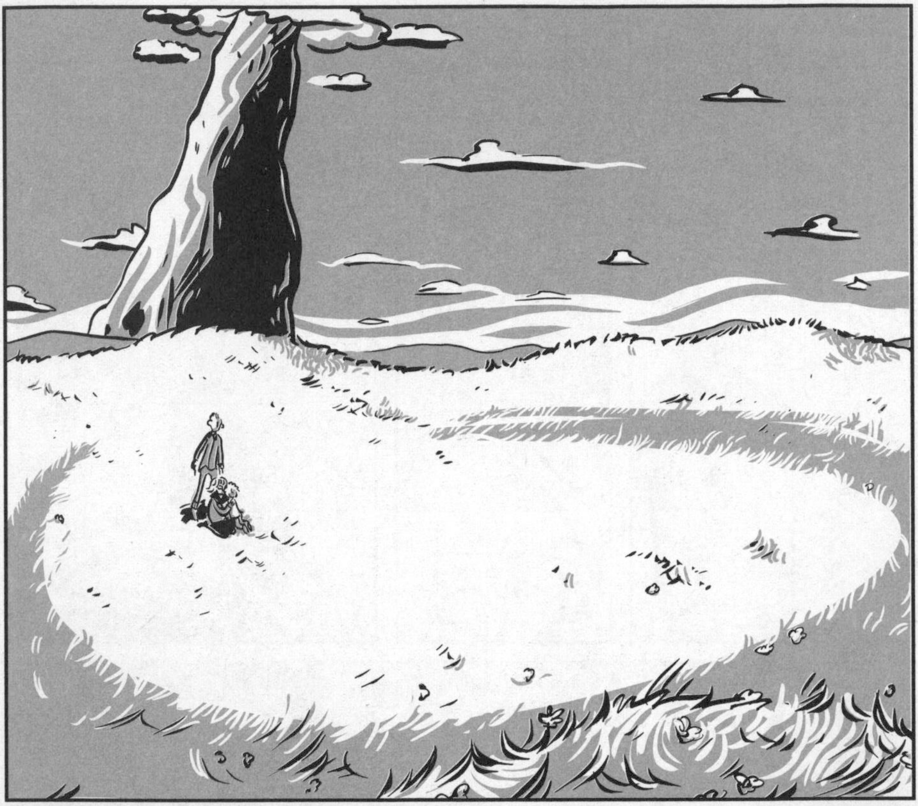

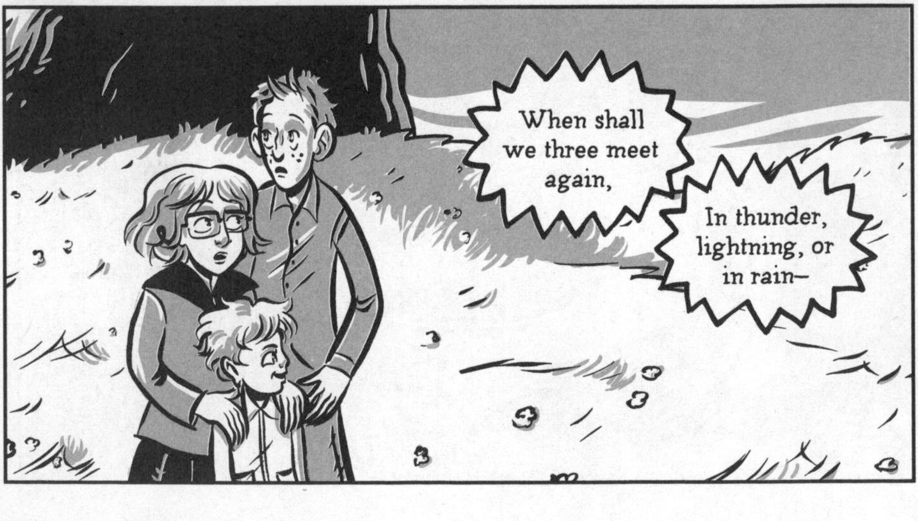
When shall we three meet again,
In thunder, lightning, or in rain–

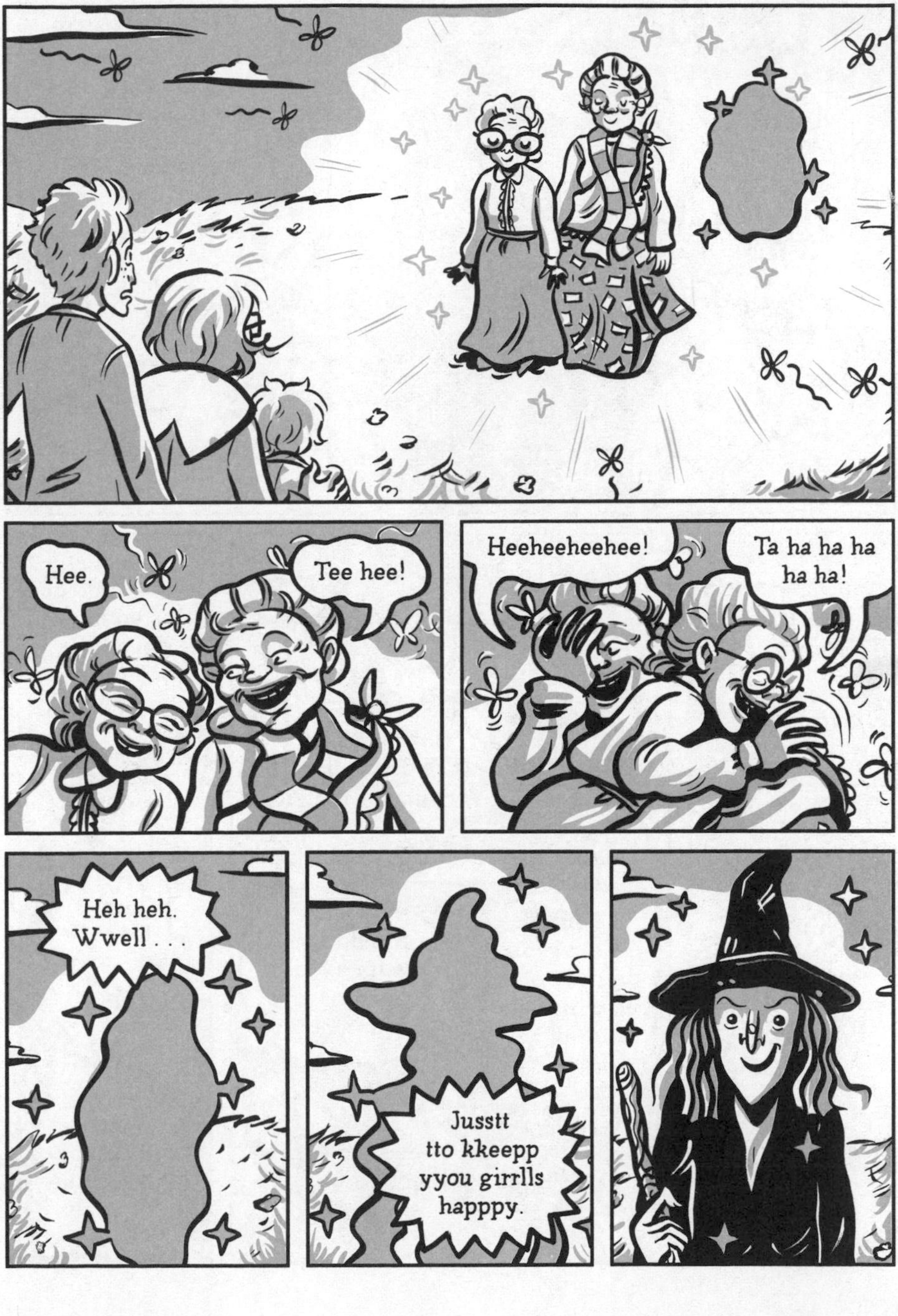
Hee.
Tee hee!
Heeheeheehee!
Ta ha ha ha ha ha!
Heh heh. Wwell . . .
Jusstt tto kkeepp yyou girrlls happpy.

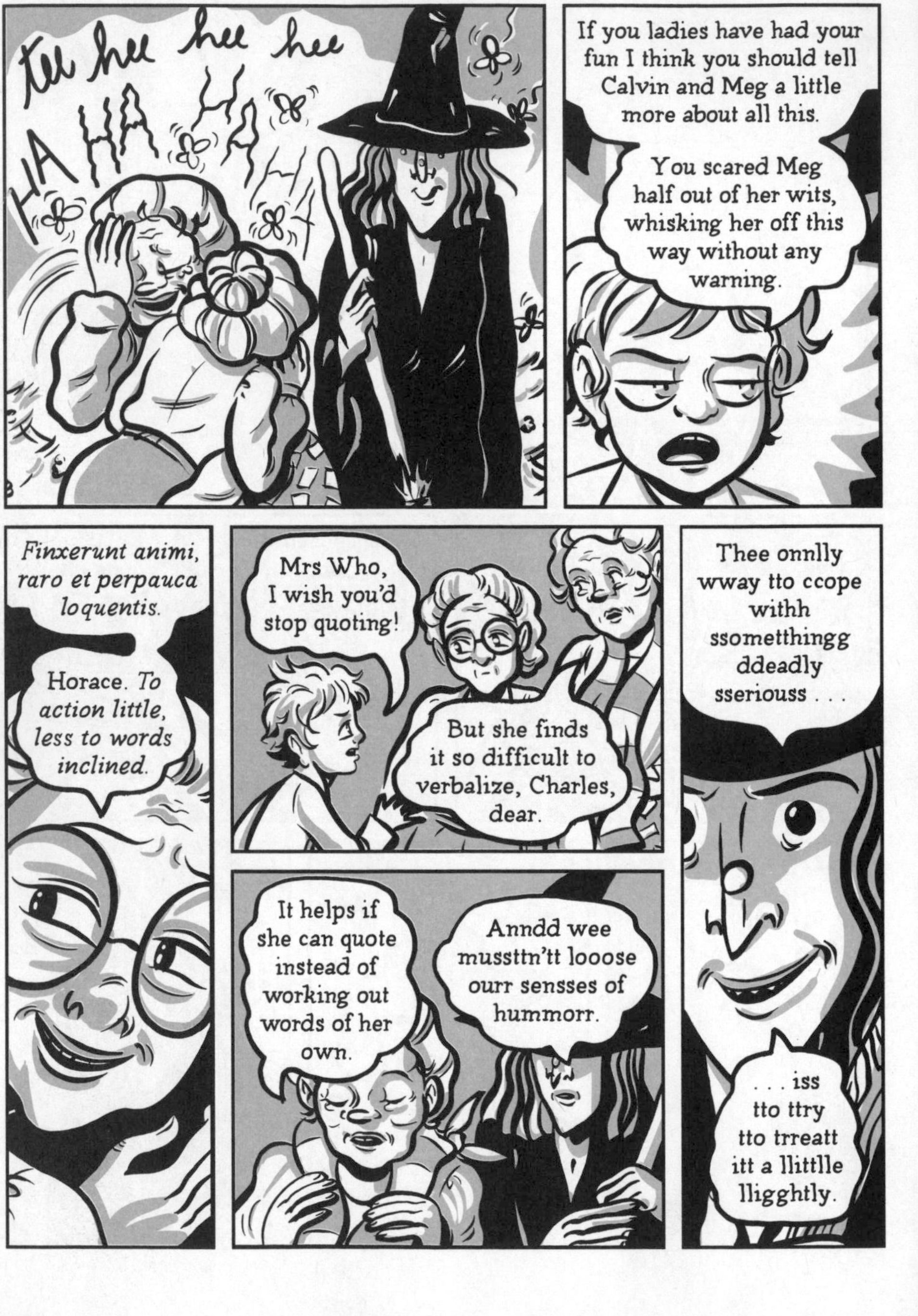

tee hee hee hee
HA HA HA HA
If you ladies have had your fun I think you should tell Calvin and Meg a little more about all this.
You scared Meg half out of her wits, whisking her off this way without any warning.
Finxerunt animi, raro et perpauca loquentis.
Horace. *To action little, less to words inclined.*
Mrs Who, I wish you'd stop quoting!
But she finds it so difficult to verbalize, Charles, dear.
It helps if she can quote instead of working out words of her own.
Anndd wee mussttn'tt looose ourr sensses of hummorr.
Thee onnlly wway tto ccope withh ssometthingg ddeadly sseriouss . . .
. . . iss tto ttry tto trreatt itt a llittlle lligghtly.

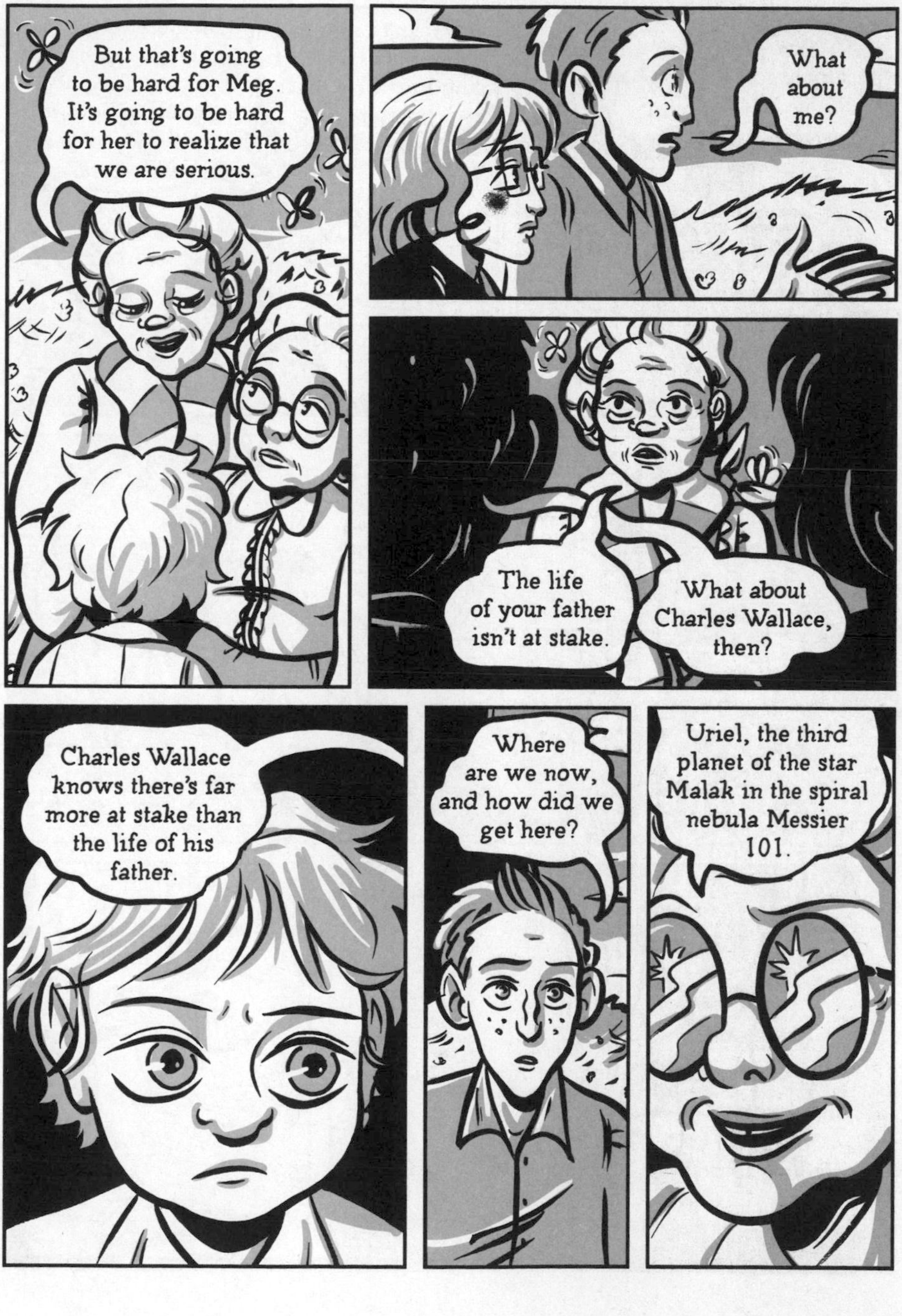
But that's going to be hard for Meg. It's going to be hard for her to realize that we are serious.
What about me?
The life of your father isn't at stake.
What about Charles Wallace, then?
Charles Wallace knows there's far more at stake than the life of his father.
Where are we now, and how did we get here?
Uriel, the third planet of the star Malak in the spiral nebula Messier 101.

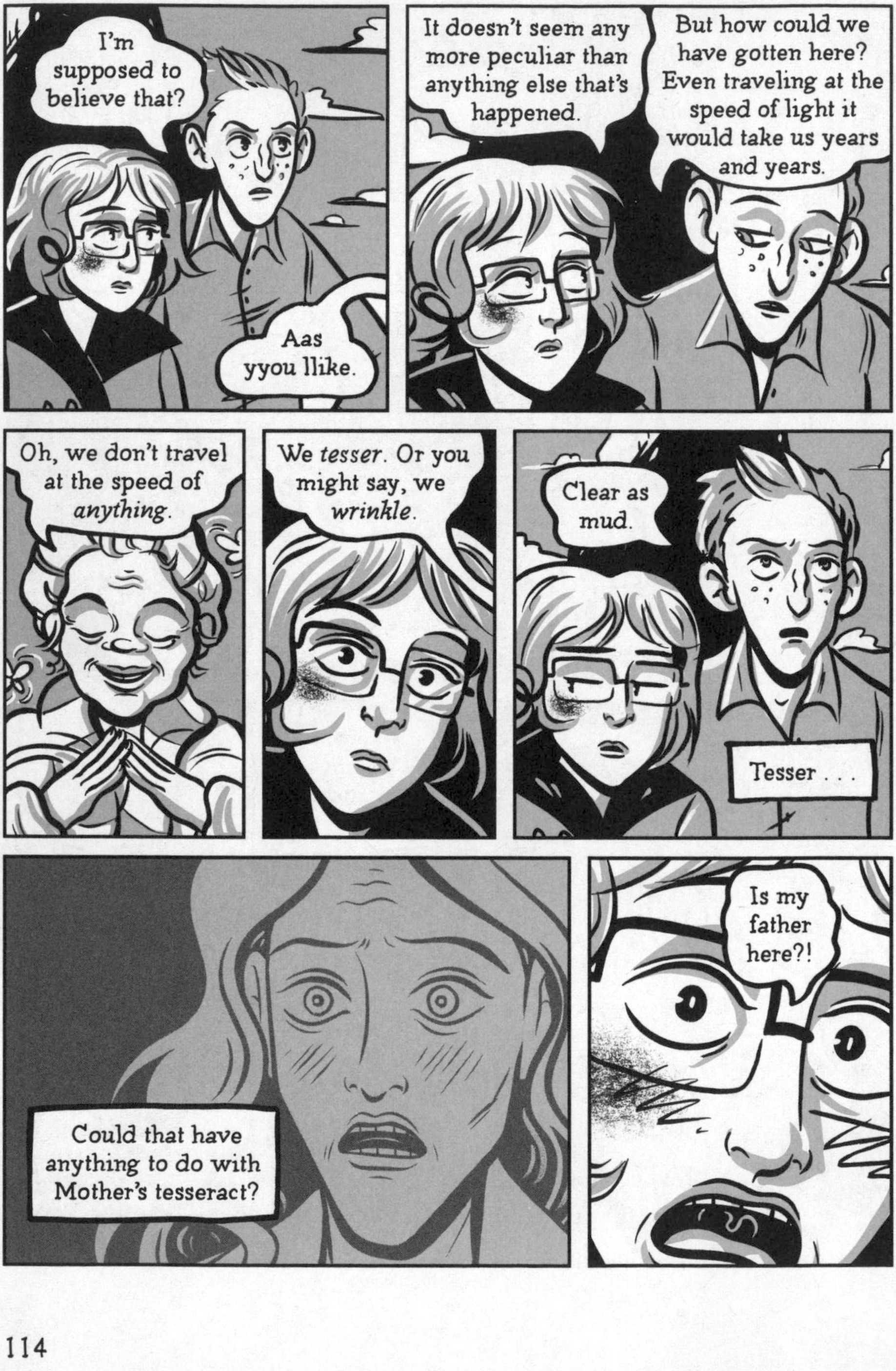
I'm supposed to believe that?
Aas yyou llike.
It doesn't seem any more peculiar than anything else that's happened.
But how could we have gotten here? Even traveling at the speed of light it would take us years and years.
Oh, we don't travel at the speed of *anything*.
We *tesser*. Or you might say, we *wrinkle*.
Clear as mud.
Tesser . . .
Could that have anything to do with Mother's tesseract?
Is my father here?!

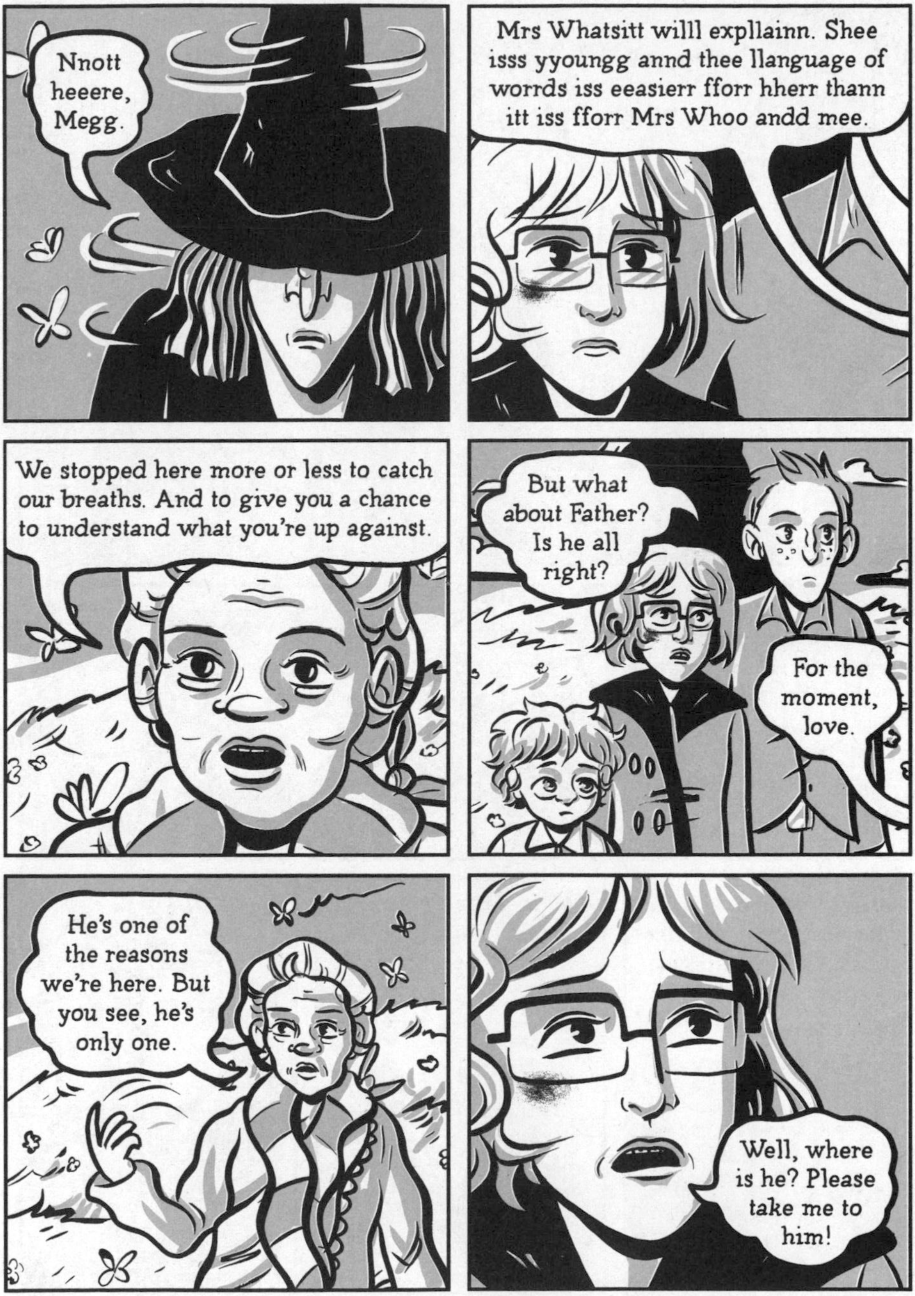
Nnott heeere, Megg.
Mrs Whatsitt willl expllainn. Shee isss yyoungg annd thee llanguage of worrds iss eeasierr fforr hherr thann itt iss fforr Mrs Whoo andd mee.
We stopped here more or less to catch our breaths. And to give you a chance to understand what you're up against.
But what about Father? Is he all right?
For the moment, love.
He's one of the reasons we're here. But you see, he's only one.
Well, where is he? Please take me to him!

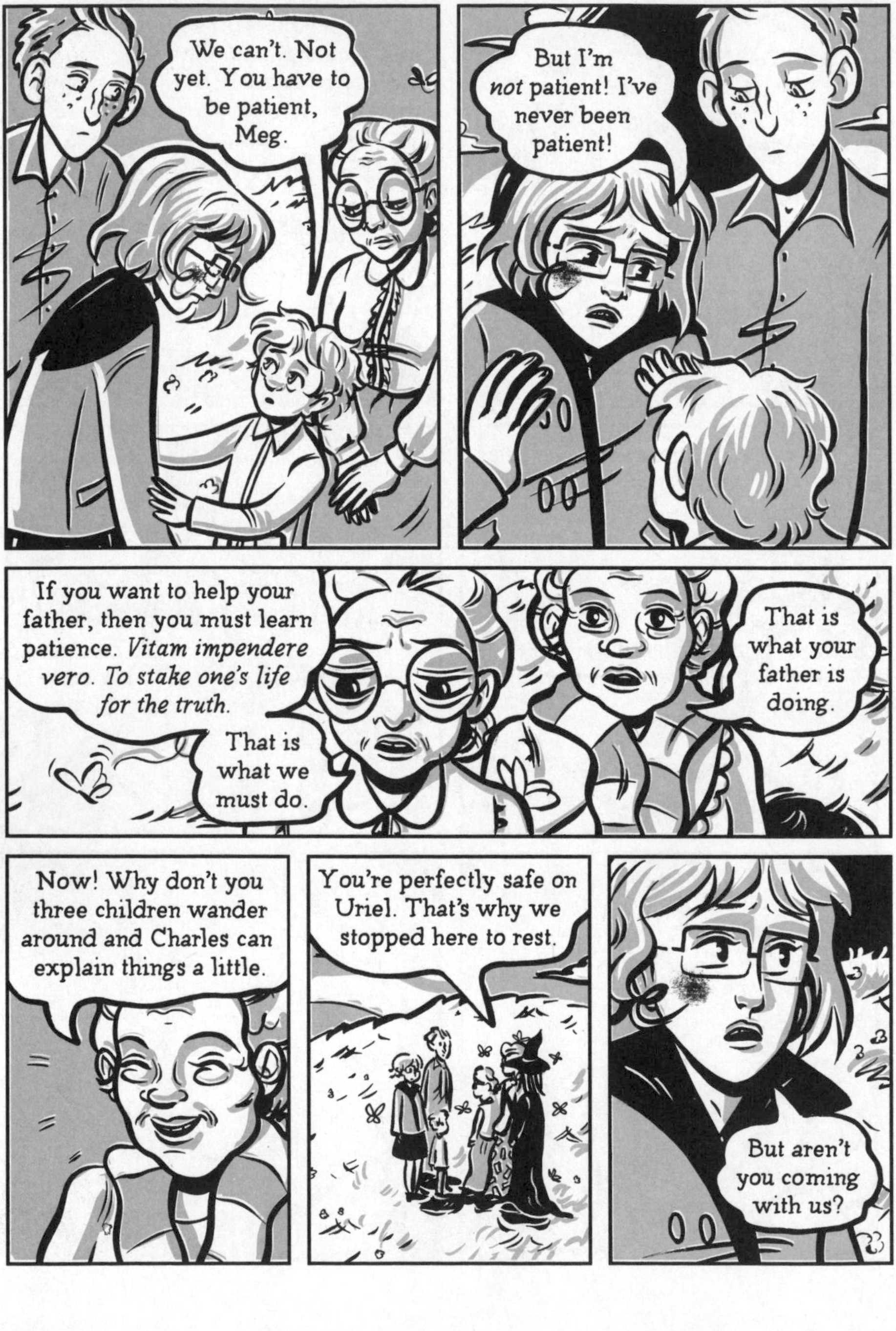
We can't. Not yet. You have to be patient, Meg.
But I'm *not* patient! I've never been patient!
If you want to help your father, then you must learn patience. *Vitam impendere vero. To stake one's life for the truth.*
That is what we must do.
That is what your father is doing.
Now! Why don't you three children wander around and Charles can explain things a little.
You're perfectly safe on Uriel. That's why we stopped here to rest.
But aren't you coming with us?

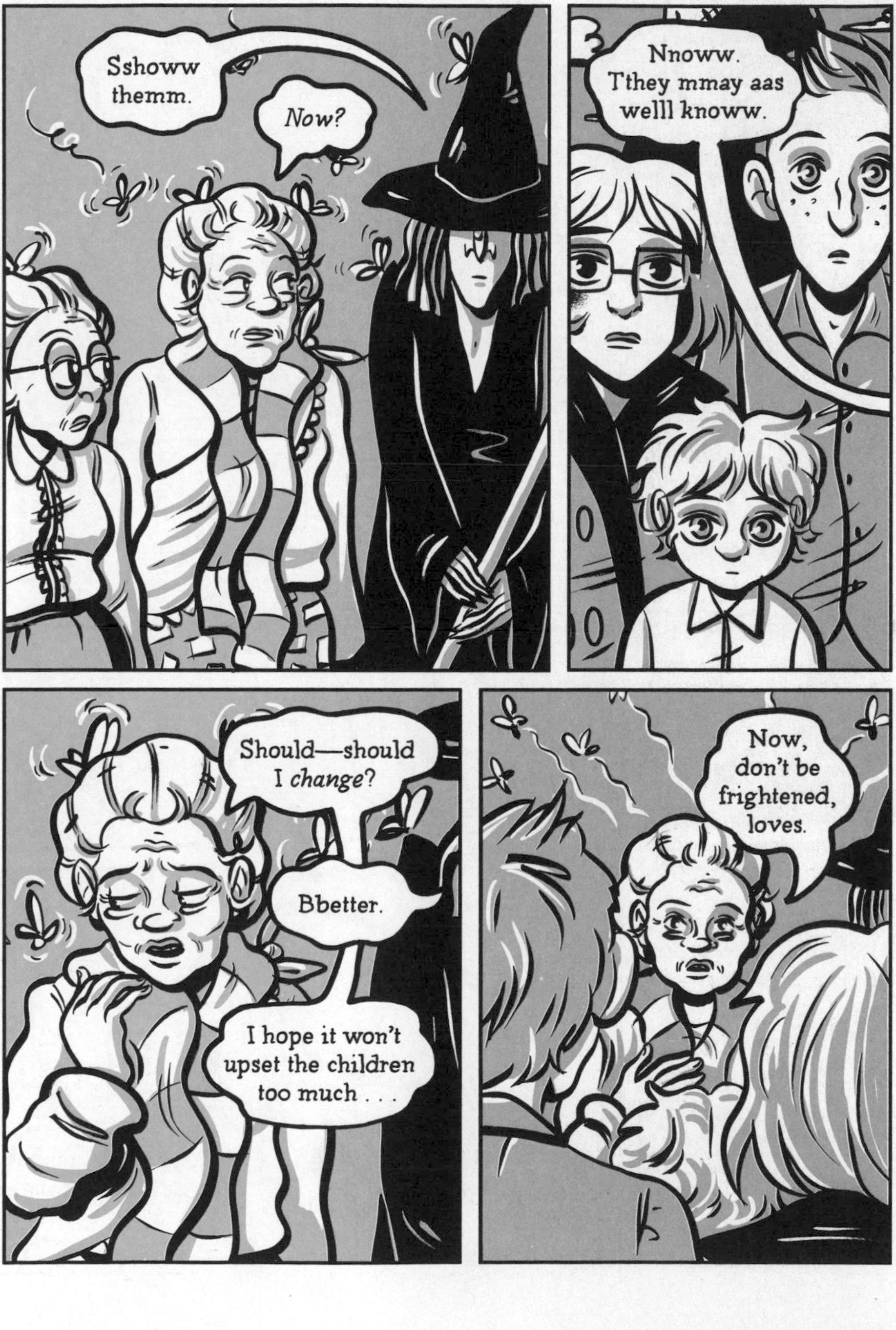
Sshoww themm.
Now?
Nnoww. Tthey mmay aas welll knoww.
Should—should I *change*?
Bbetter.
I hope it won't upset the children too much . . .
Now, don't be frightened, loves.

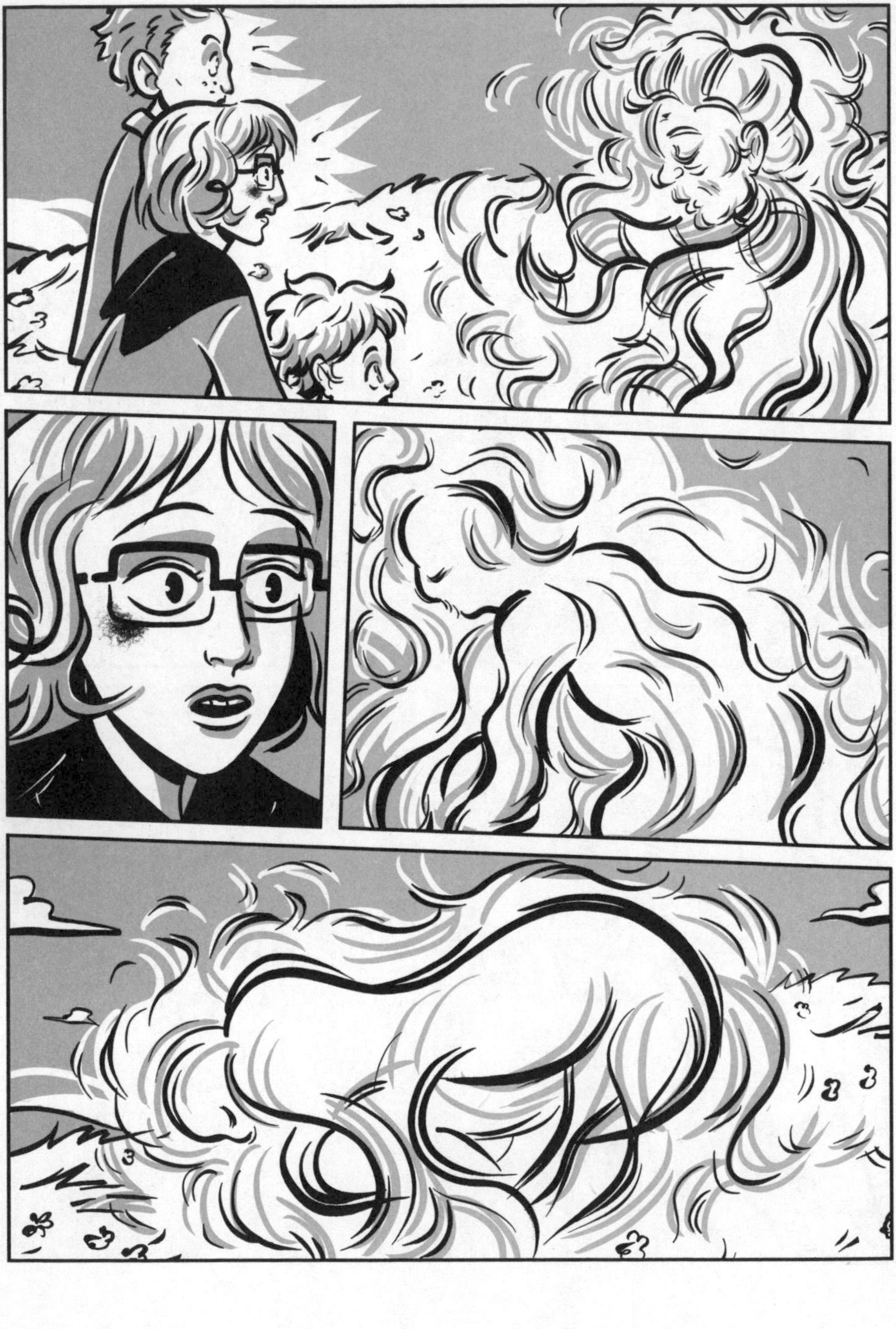

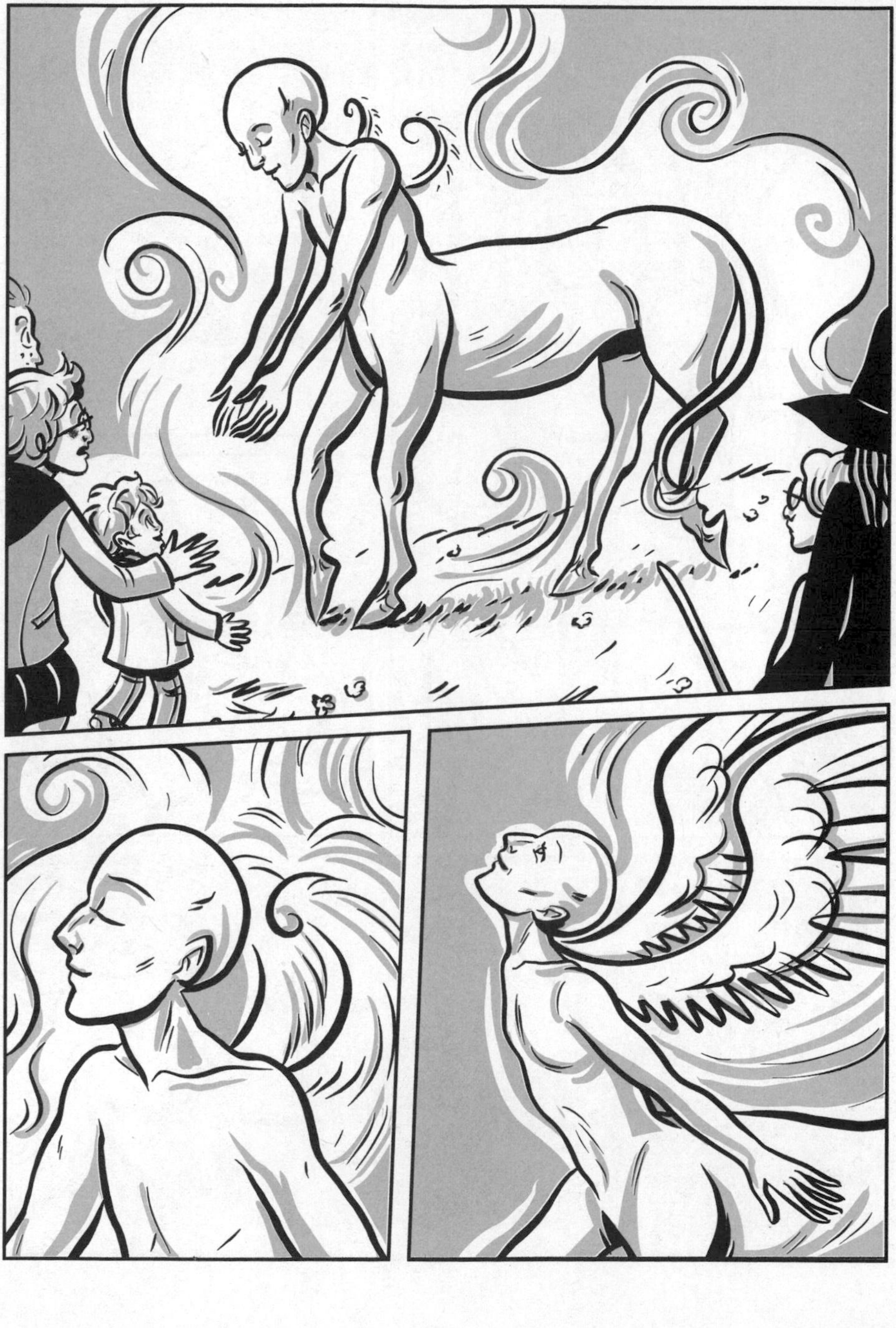

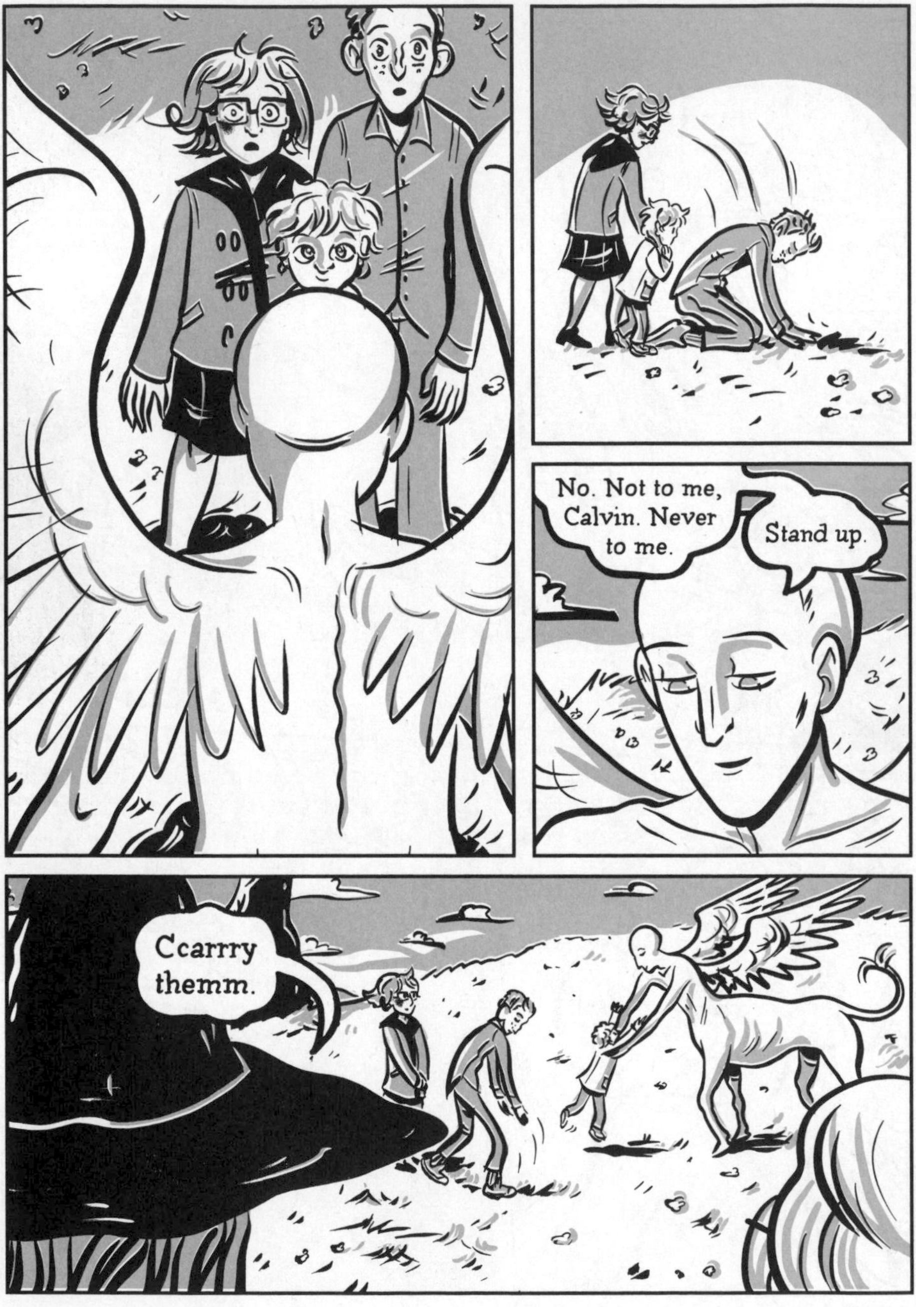
No. Not to me, Calvin. Never to me.
Stand up.
Ccarrry themm.

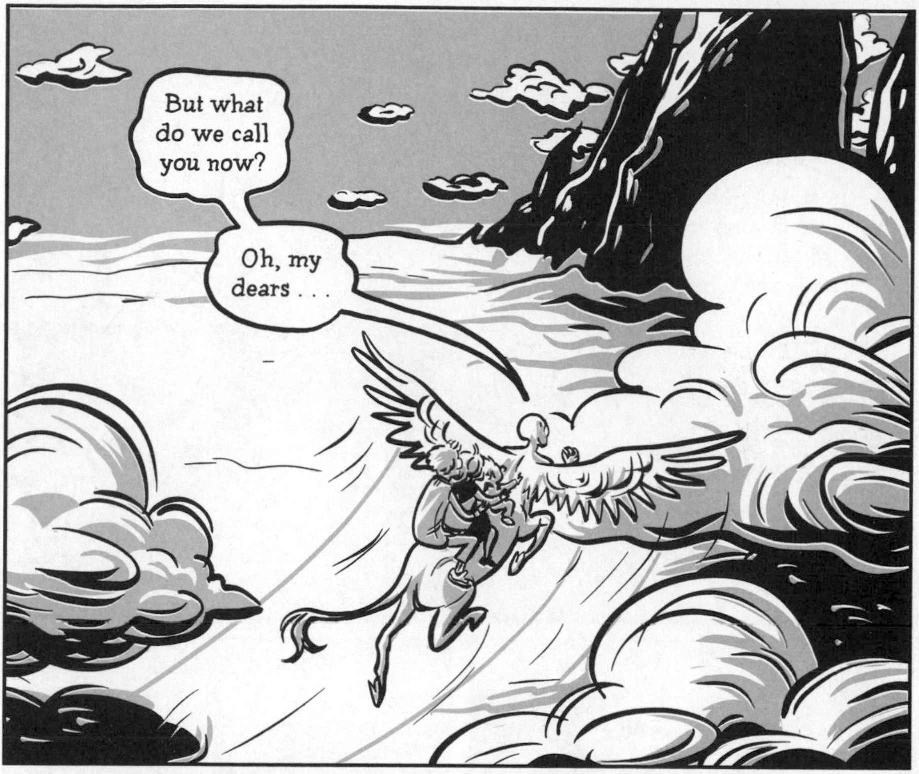
But what do we call you now?
Oh, my dears . . .

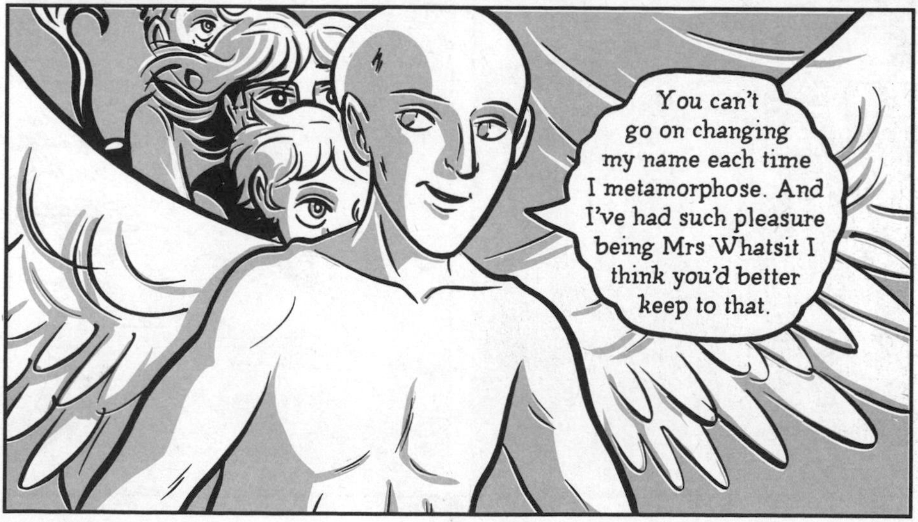
You can't go on changing my name each time I metamorphose. And I've had such pleasure being Mrs Whatsit I think you'd better keep to that.

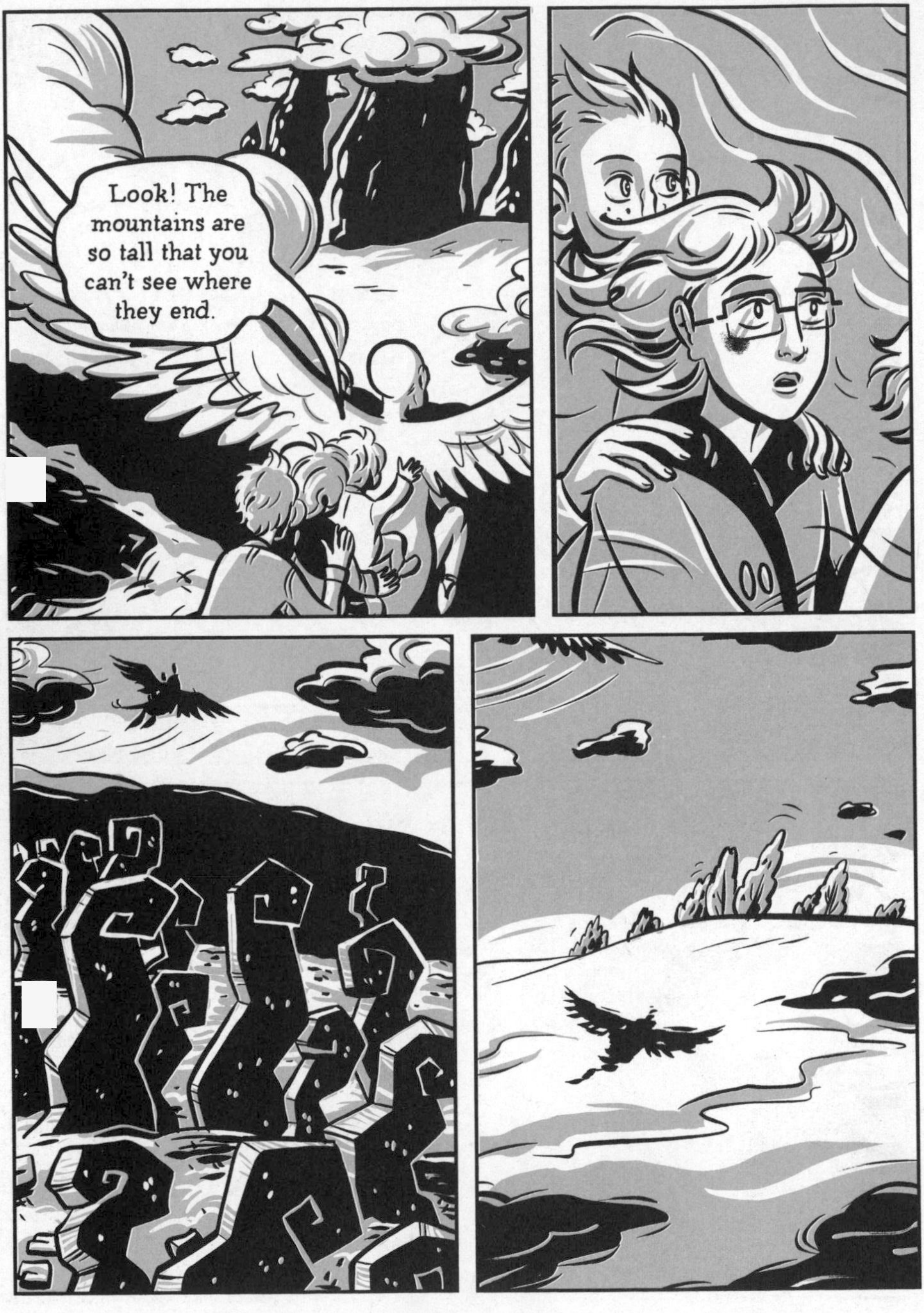
Look! The mountains are so tall that you can't see where they end.

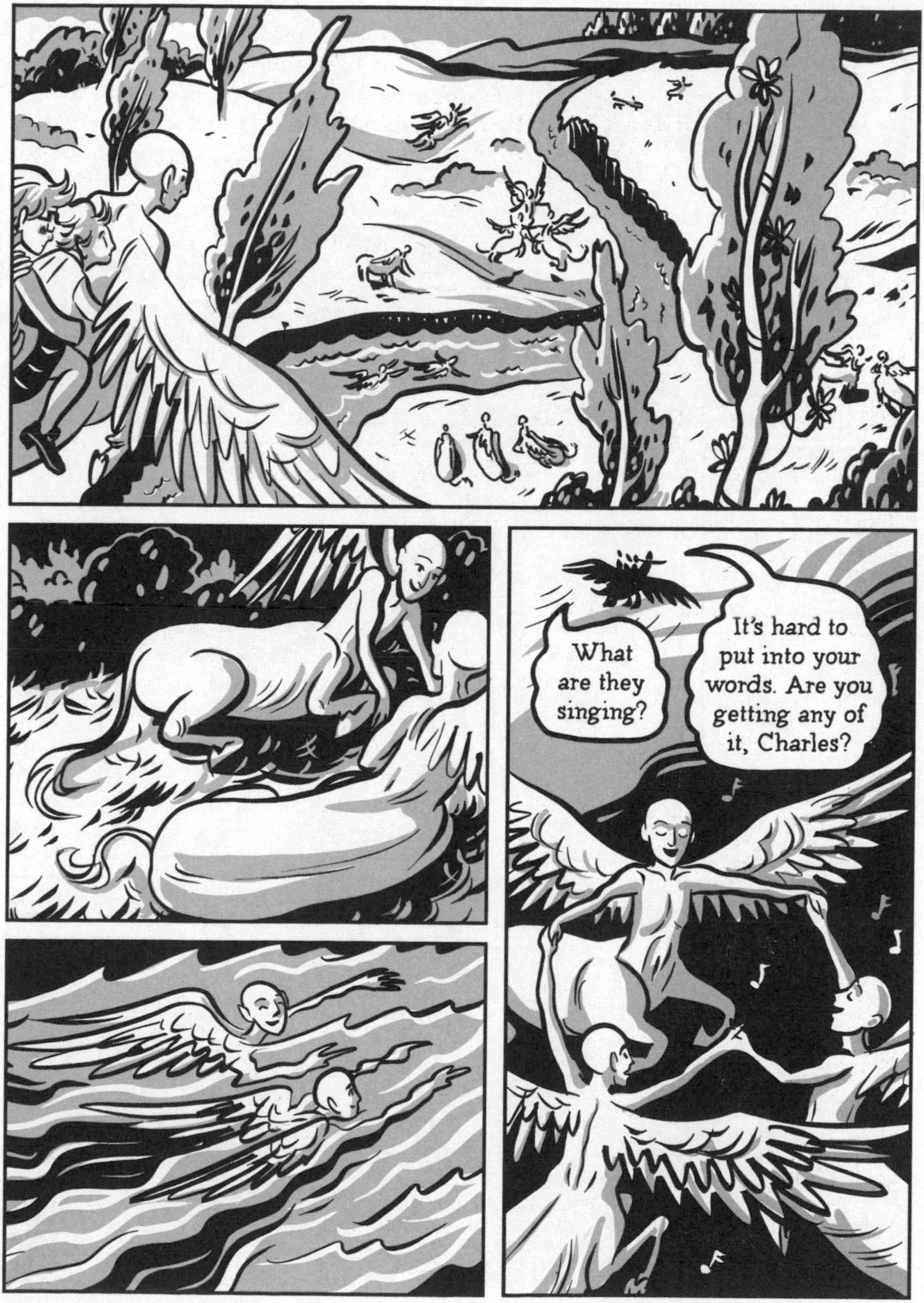
What are they singing?
It's hard to put into your words. Are you getting any of it, Charles?

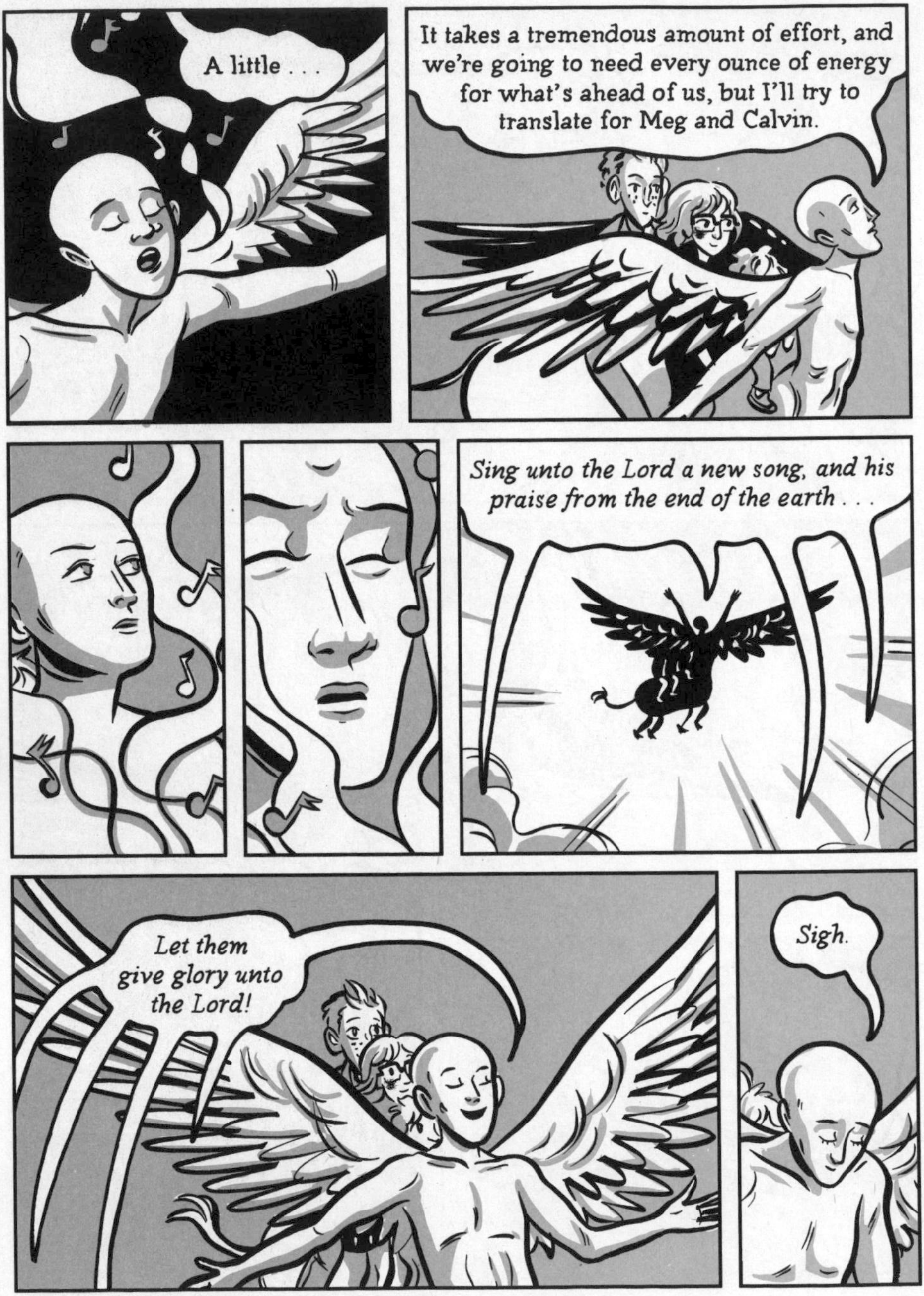
A little . . .
It takes a tremendous amount of effort, and we're going to need every ounce of energy for what's ahead of us, but I'll try to translate for Meg and Calvin.
Sing unto the Lord a new song, and his praise from the end of the earth . . .
Let them give glory unto the Lord!
Sigh.

We must go now, children. But first–
? ?
Each of you take one.

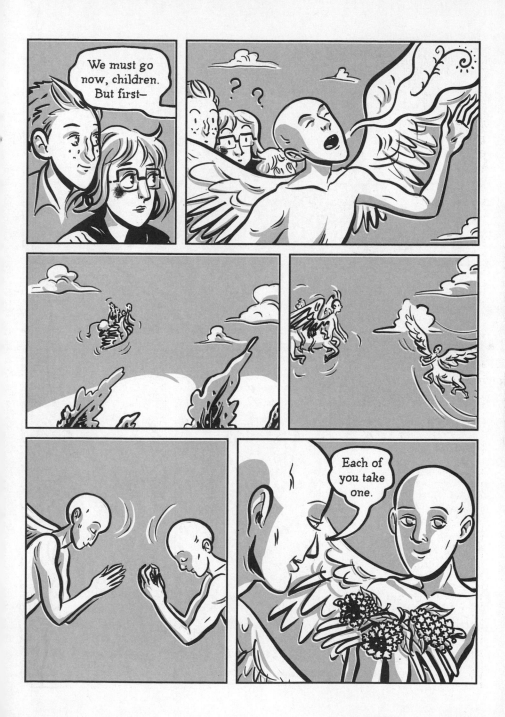

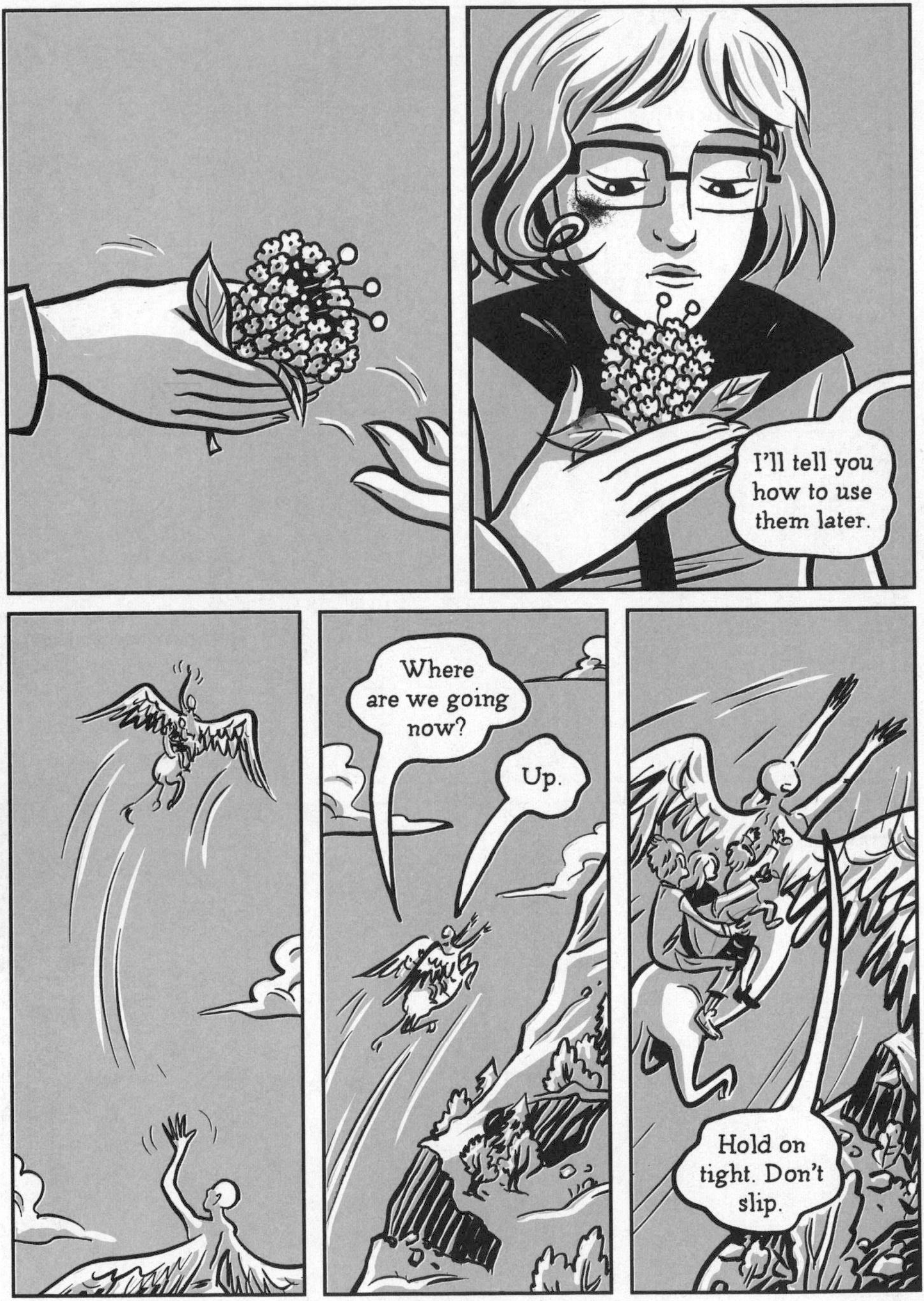
I'll tell you how to use them later.
Where are we going now?
Up.
Hold on tight. Don't slip.

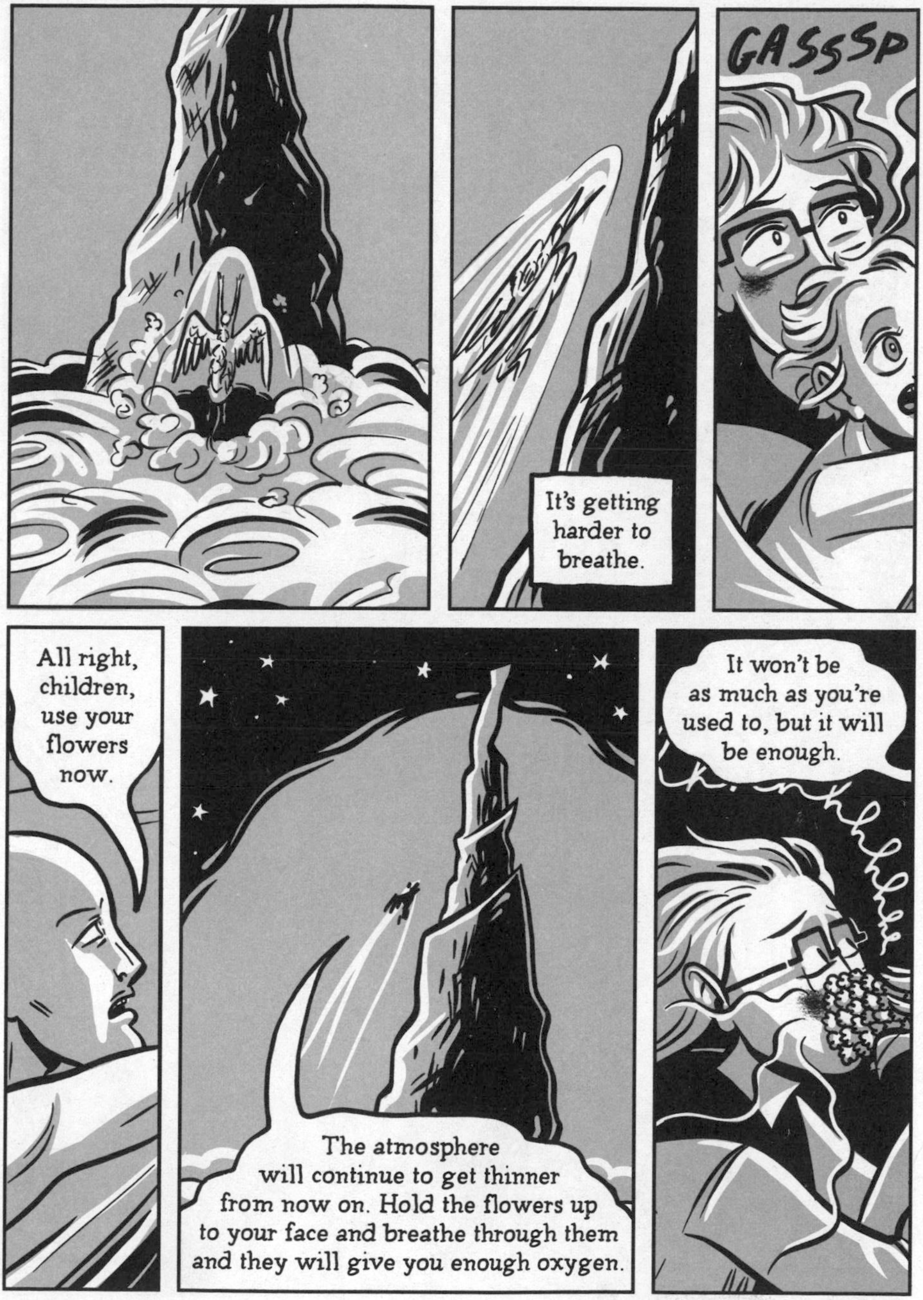
It's getting harder to breathe.
GASSSP
All right, children, use your flowers now.
The atmosphere will continue to get thinner from now on. Hold the flowers up to your face and breathe through them and they will give you enough oxygen.
It won't be as much as you're used to, but it will be enough.

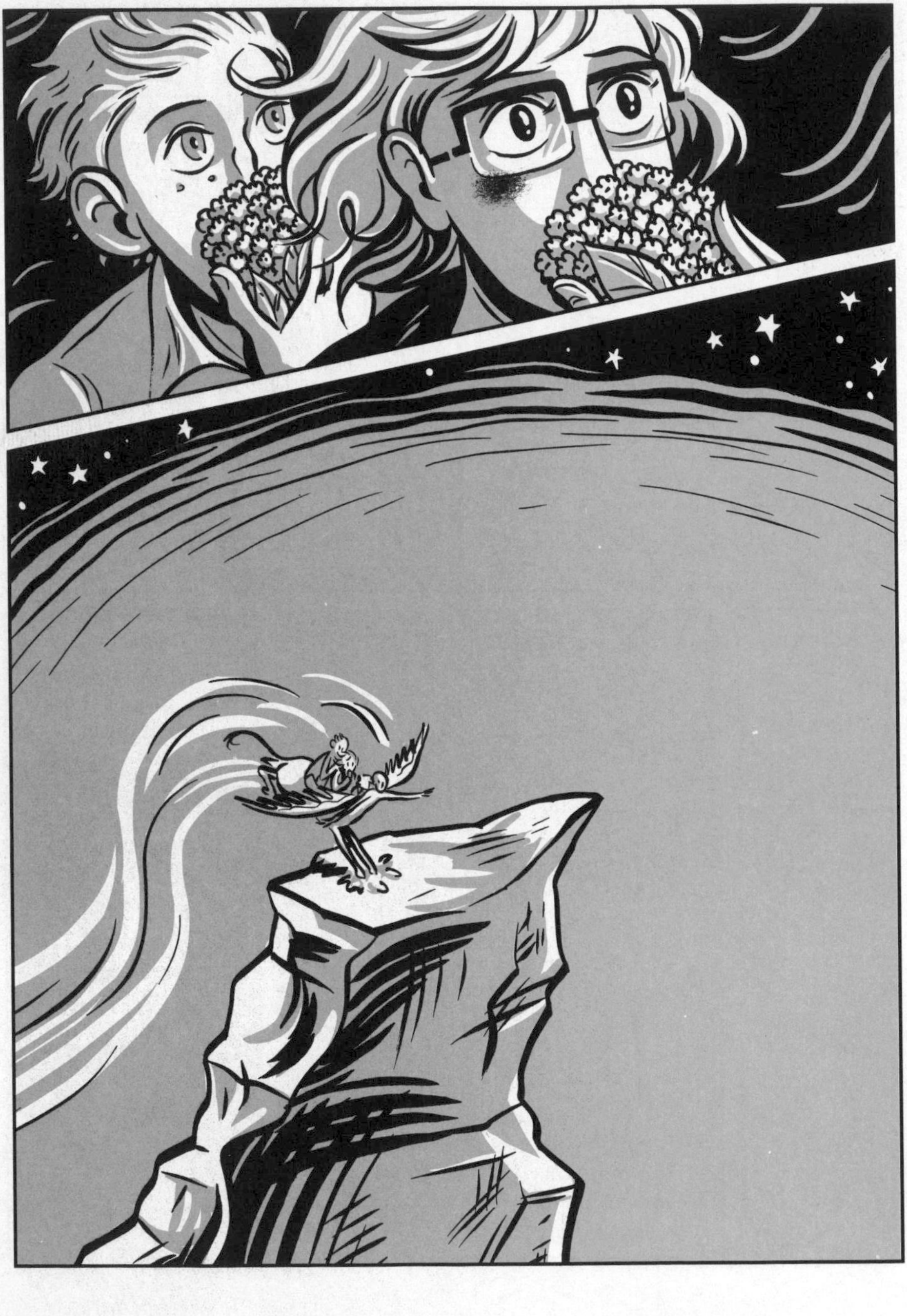

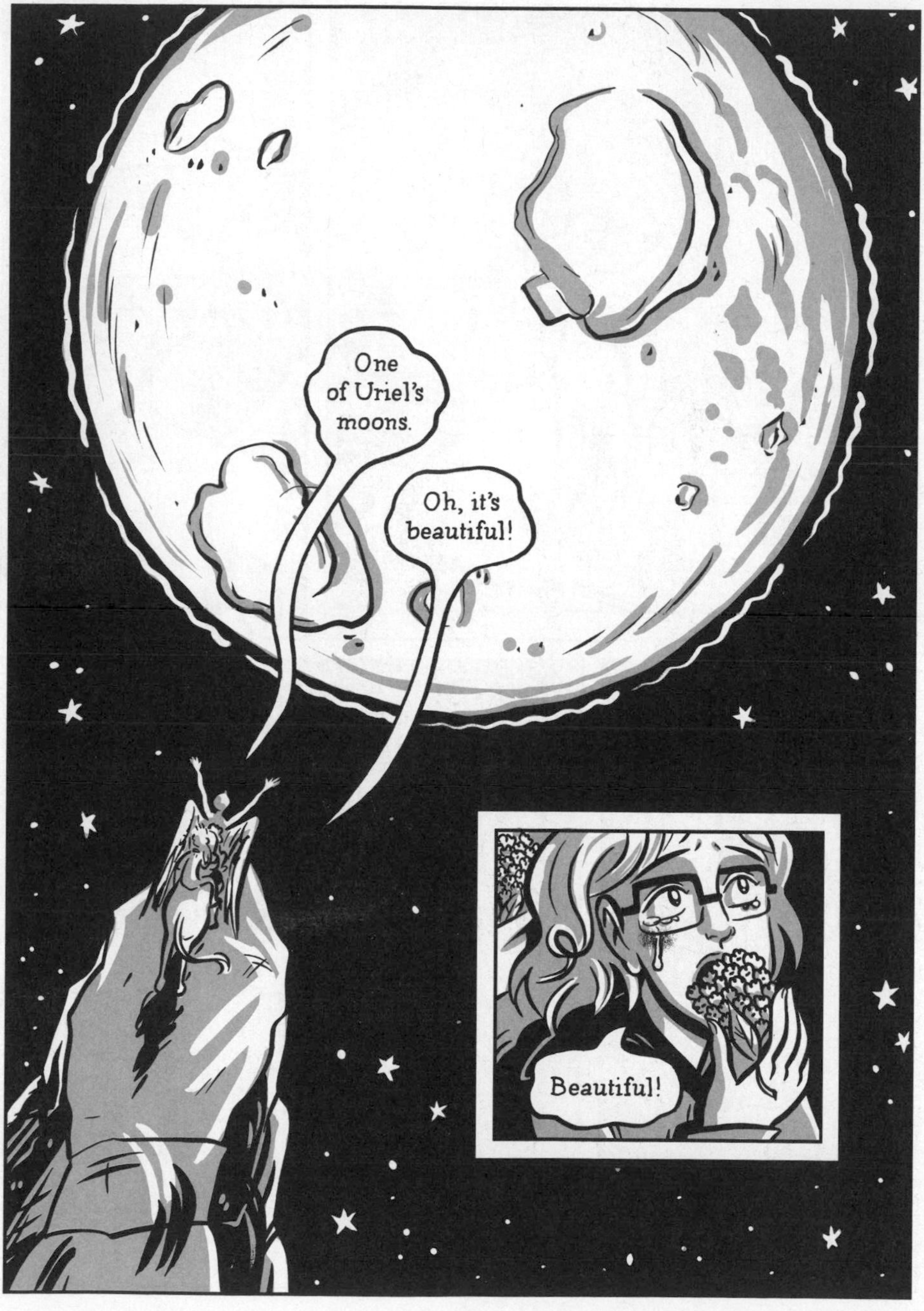
One of Uriel's moons.
Oh, it's beautiful!
Beautiful!

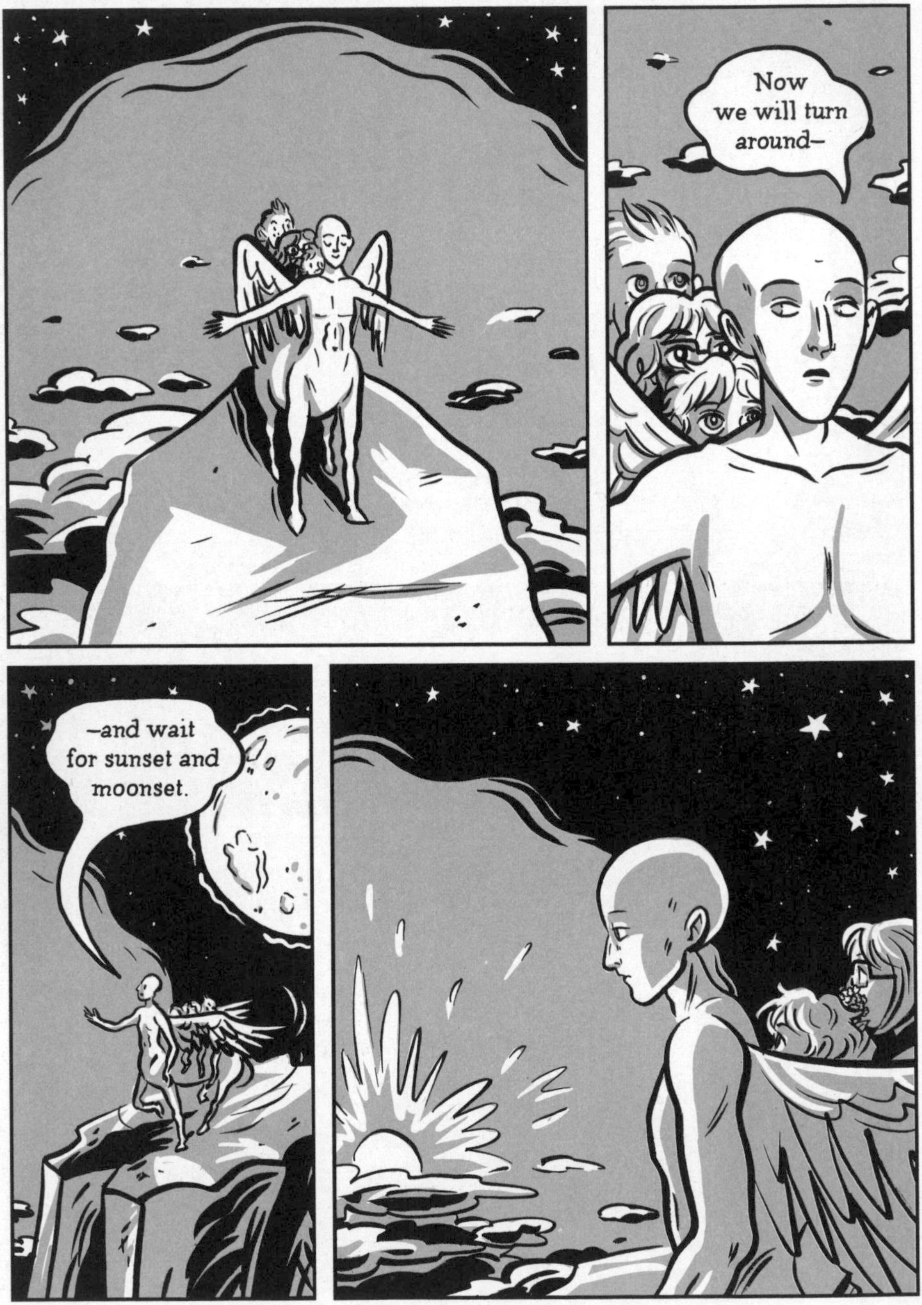
Now we will turn around–
–and wait for sunset and moonset.

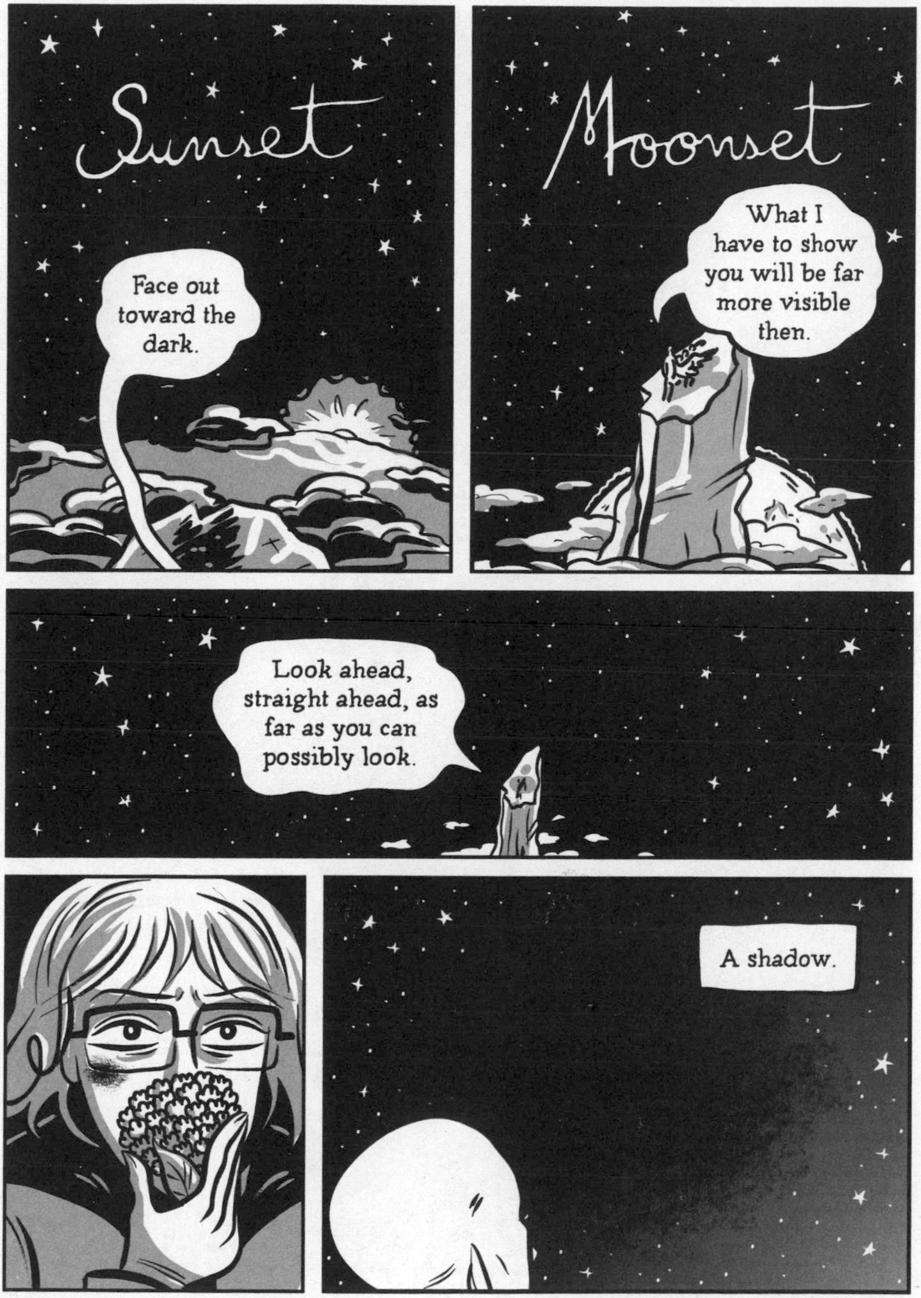
Sunset
Face out toward the dark.
Moonset
What I have to show you will be far more visible then.
Look ahead, straight ahead, as far as you can possibly look.
A shadow.

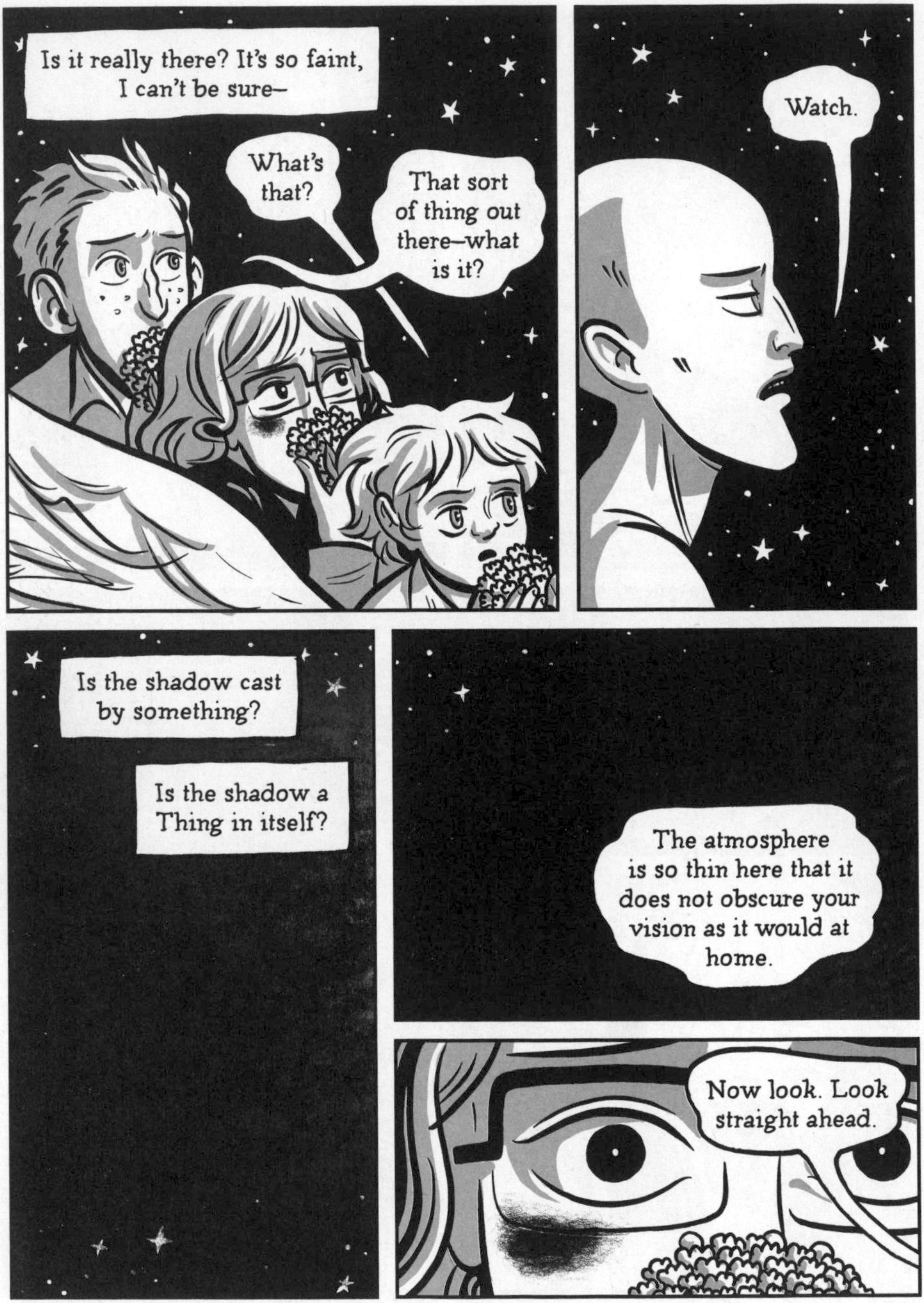

Is it really there? It's so faint, I can't be sure–
What's that?
That sort of thing out there–what is it?
Watch.
Is the shadow cast by something?
Is the shadow a Thing in itself?
The atmosphere is so thin here that it does not obscure your vision as it would at home.
Now look. Look straight ahead.

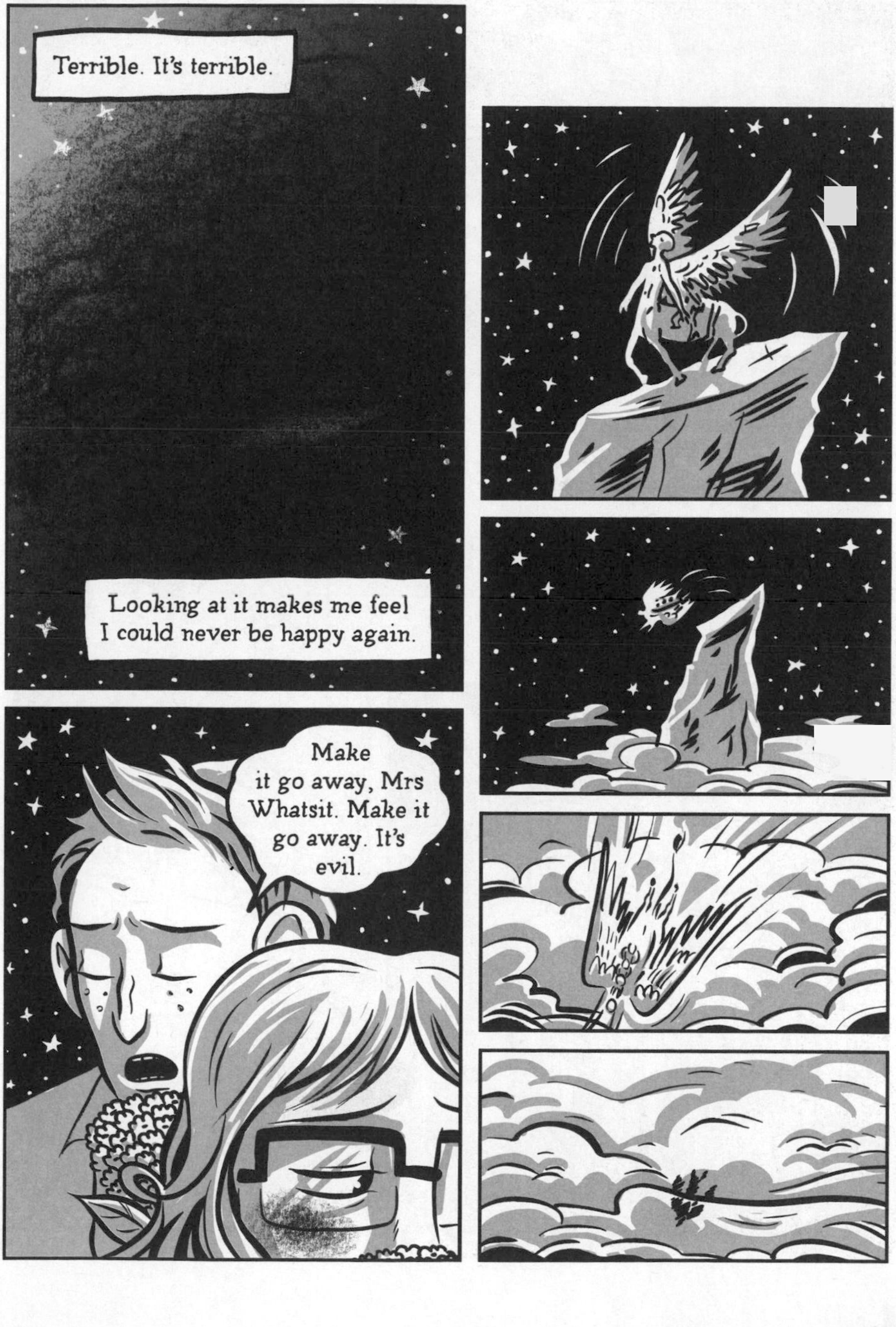
Terrible. It's terrible.
Looking at it makes me feel I could never be happy again.
Make it go away, Mrs Whatsit. Make it go away. It's evil.

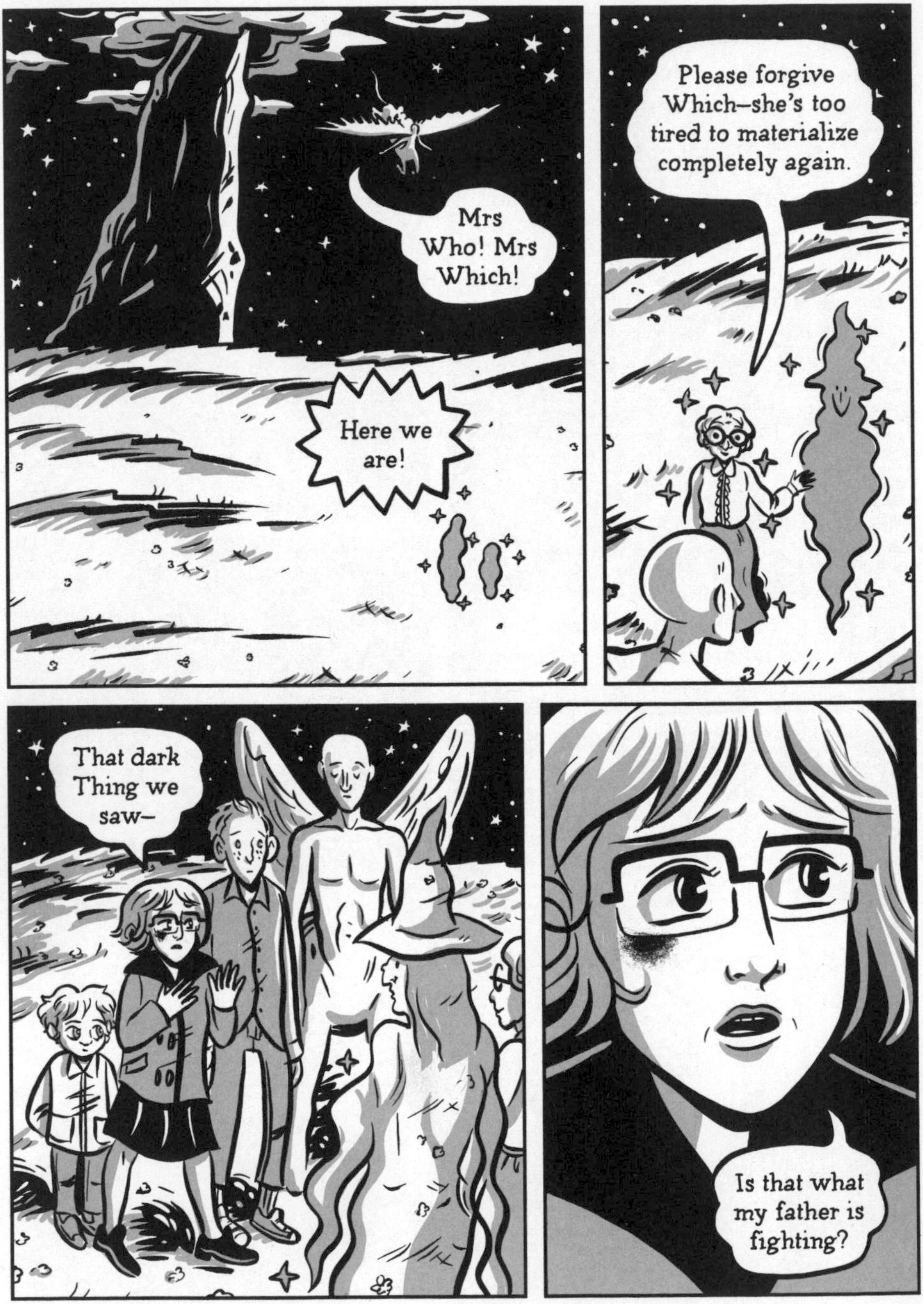
Mrs
Who! Mrs
Which!
Here we
are!
Please forgive
Which–she's too
tired to materialize
completely again.
That dark
Thing we
saw–
Is that what
my father is
fighting?

5
The Tesseract

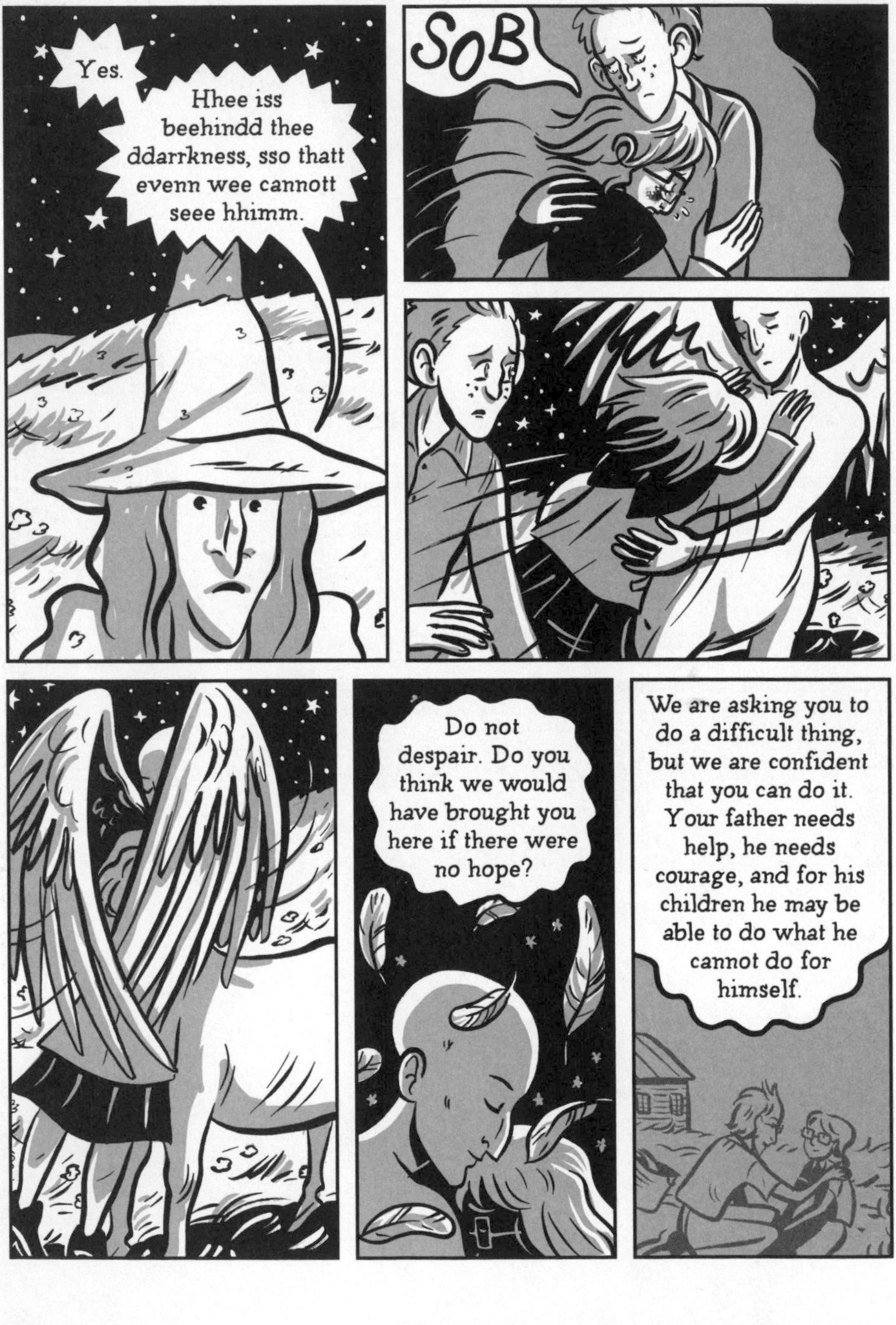
Yes.
Hhee iss beehindd thee ddarrkness, sso thatt evenn wee cannott seee hhimm.
SOB
Do not despair. Do you think we would have brought you here if there were no hope?
We are asking you to do a difficult thing, but we are confident that you can do it. Your father needs help, he needs courage, and for his children he may be able to do what he cannot do for himself.

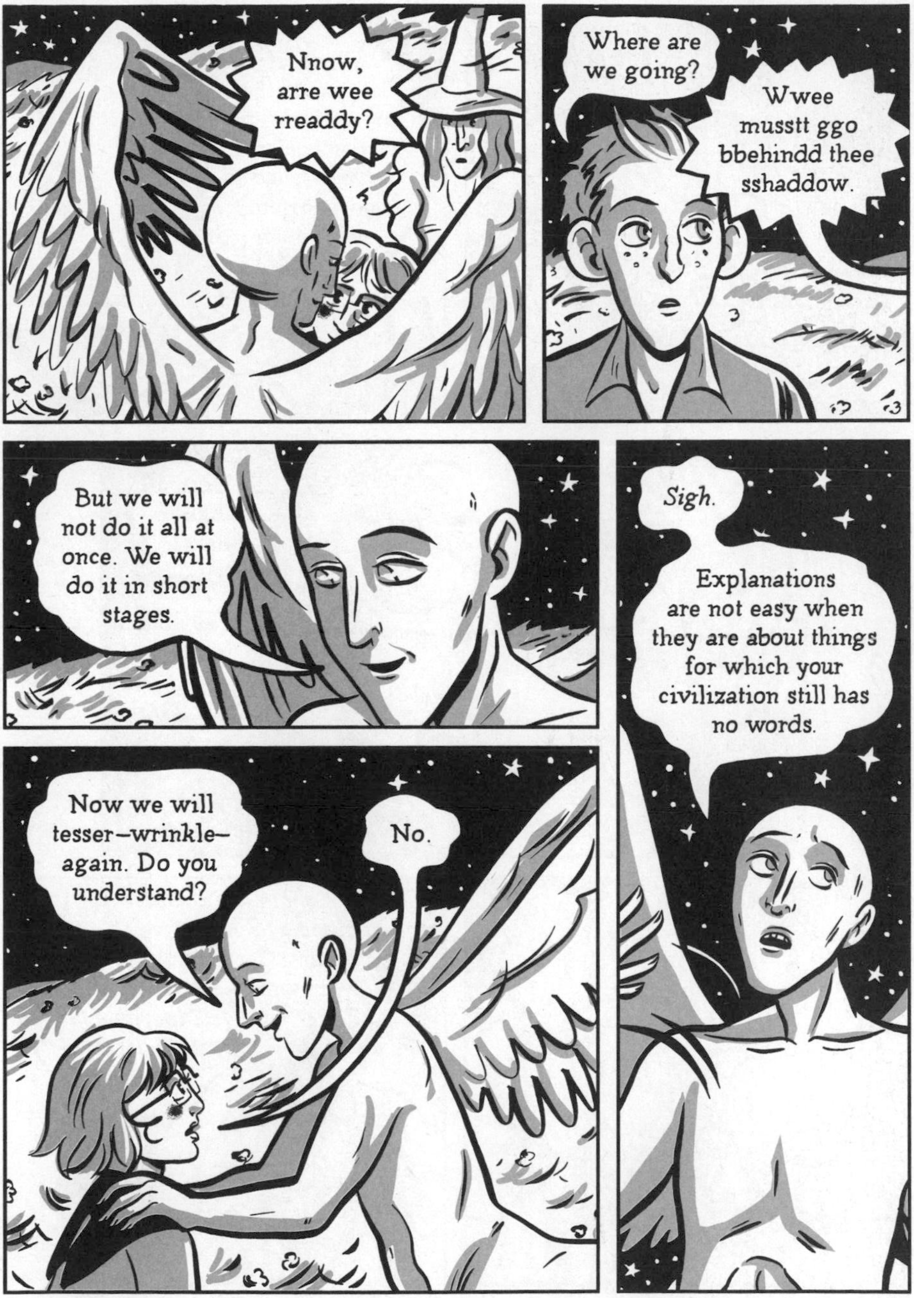
Nnow, arre wee rreaddy?
Where are we going?
Wwee musstt ggo bbehindd thee sshaddow.
But we will not do it all at once. We will do it in short stages.
Sigh.
Explanations are not easy when they are about things for which your civilization still has no words.
Now we will tesser—wrinkle—again. Do you understand?
No.

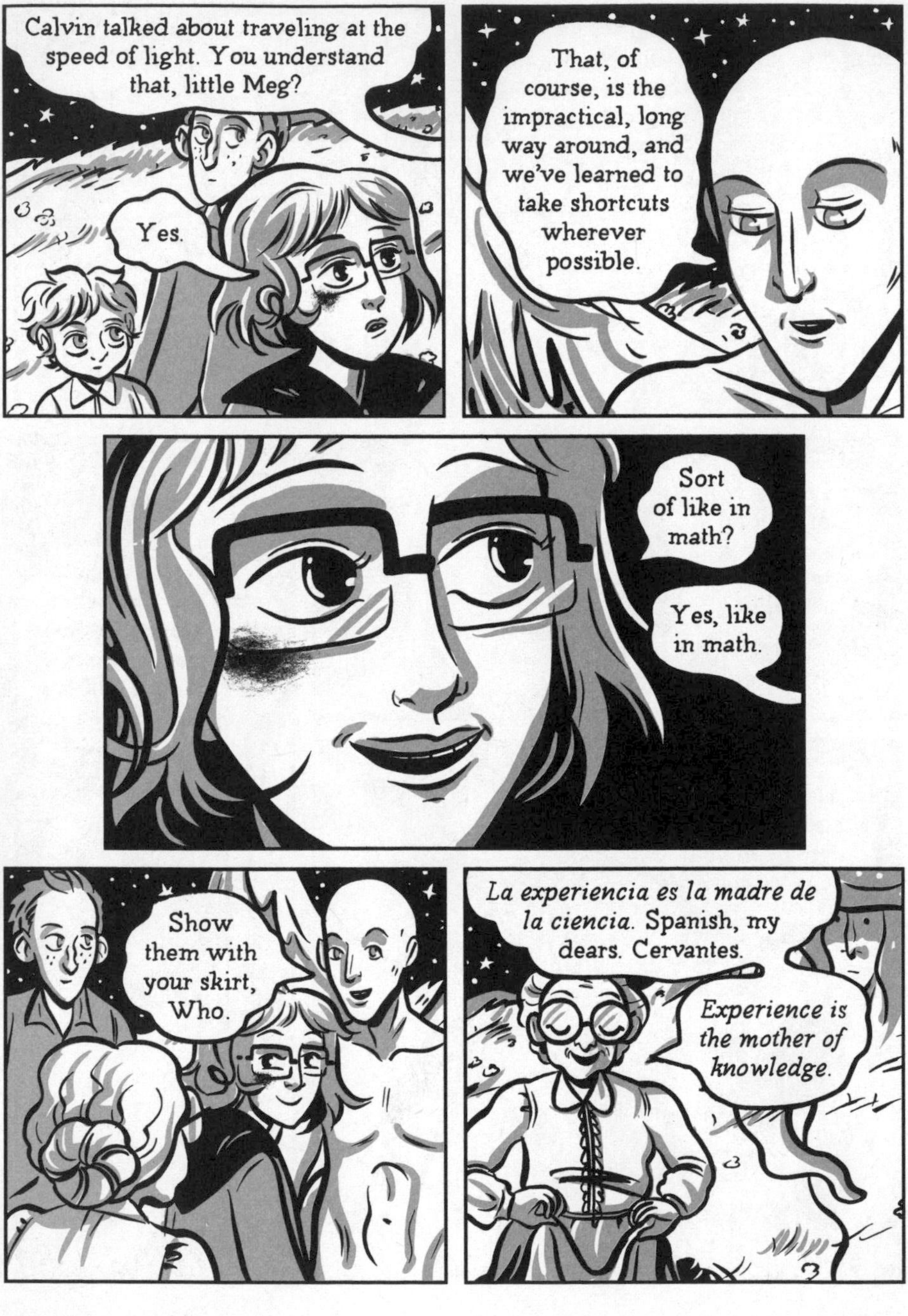

Calvin talked about traveling at the speed of light. You understand that, little Meg?
Yes.
That, of course, is the impractical, long way around, and we've learned to take shortcuts wherever possible.
Sort of like in math?
Yes, like in math.
Show them with your skirt, Who.
La experiencia es la madre de la ciencia. Spanish, my dears. Cervantes.
Experience is the mother of knowledge.

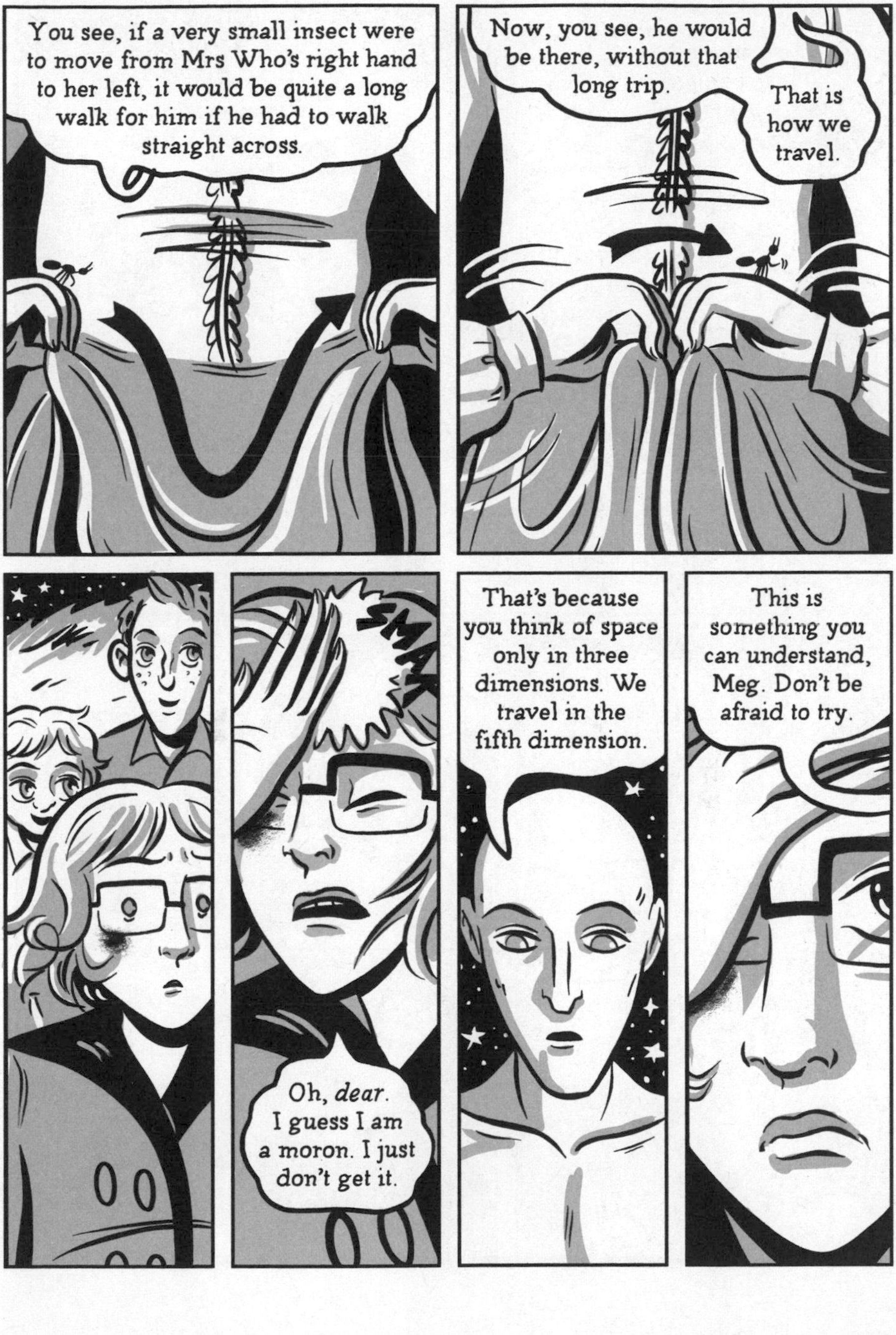
You see, if a very small insect were to move from Mrs Who's right hand to her left, it would be quite a long walk for him if he had to walk straight across.
Now, you see, he would be there, without that long trip.
That is how we travel.
Oh, *dear*. I guess I am a moron. I just don't get it.
That's because you think of space only in three dimensions. We travel in the fifth dimension.
This is something you can understand, Meg. Don't be afraid to try.

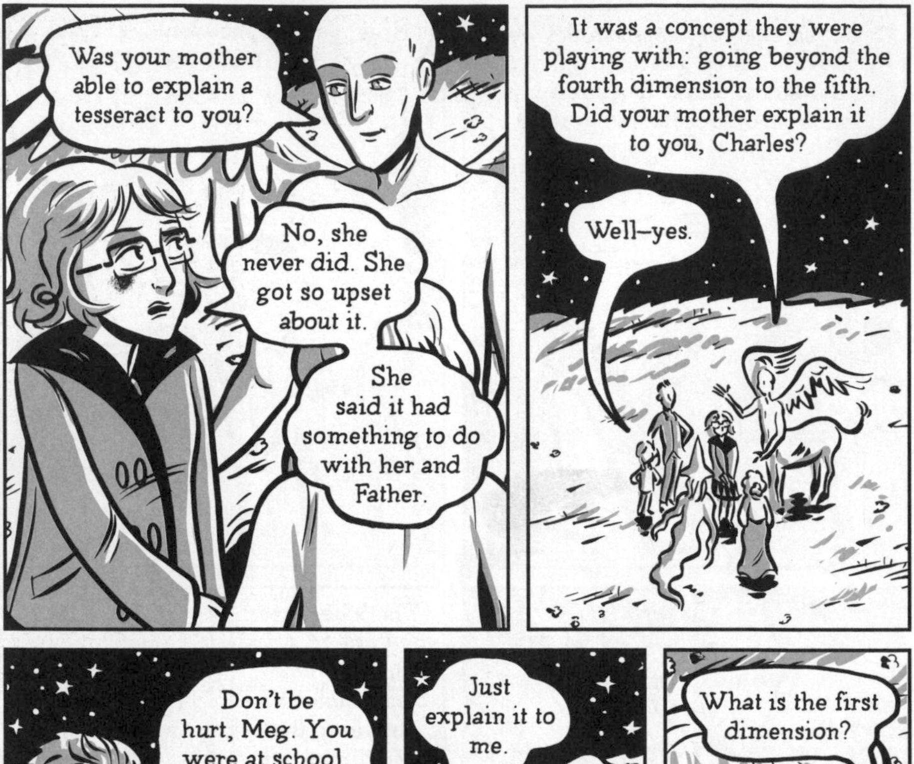
Was your mother able to explain a tesseract to you?
No, she never did. She got so upset about it.
She said it had something to do with her and Father.
It was a concept they were playing with: going beyond the fourth dimension to the fifth. Did your mother explain it to you, Charles?
Well—yes.
Don't be hurt, Meg. You were at school, and I just kept at her till I got it out of her.
Just explain it to me.
Okay.
What is the first dimension?

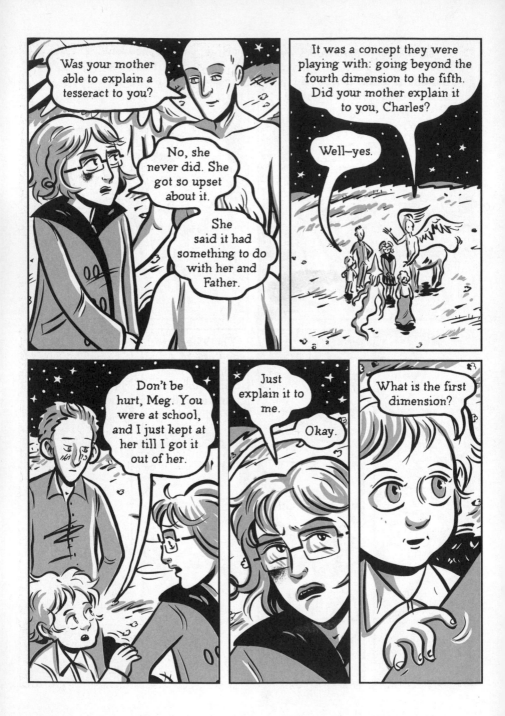

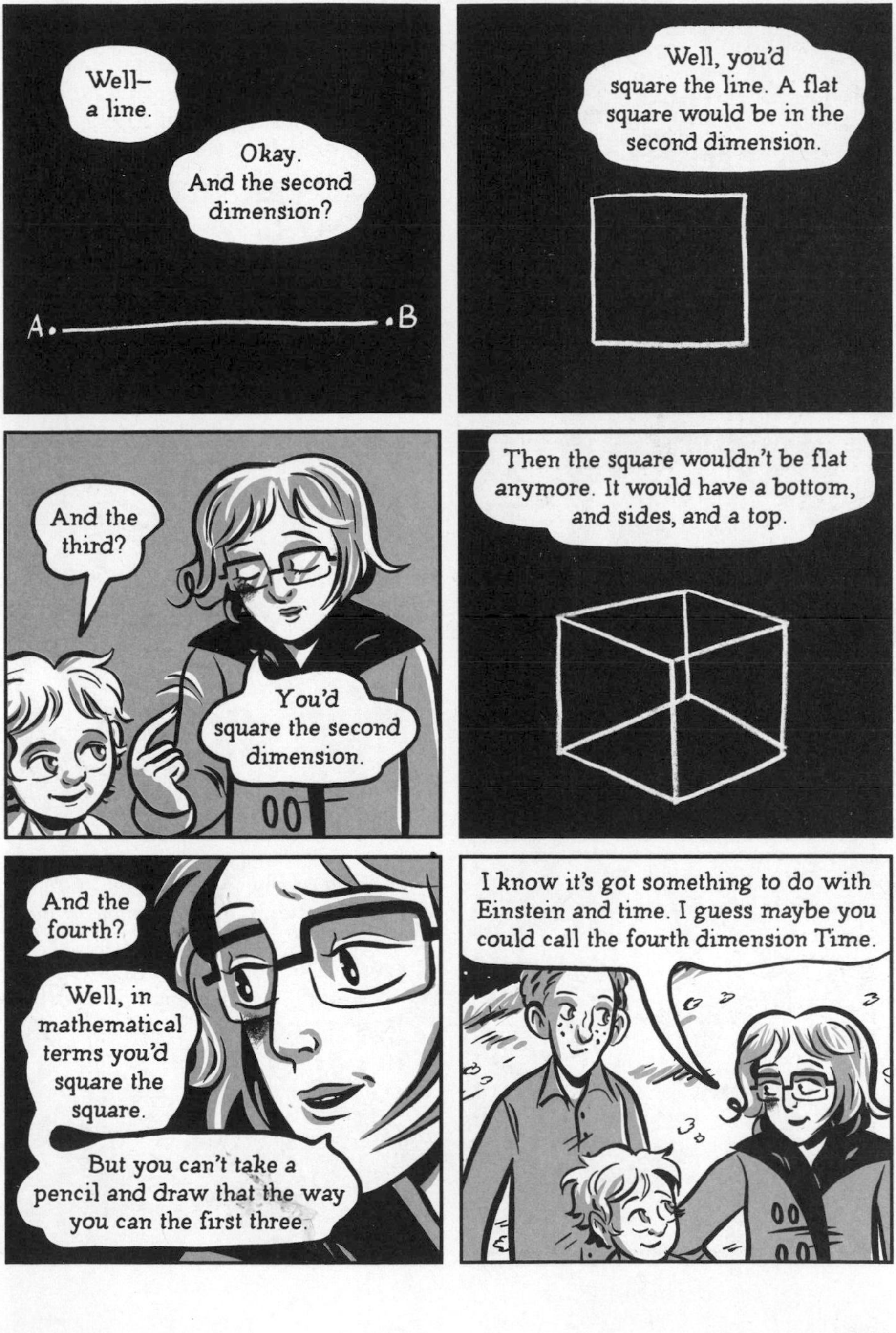
Well—
a line.
Okay.
And the second dimension?
A.
B
Well, you'd square the line. A flat square would be in the second dimension.
And the third?
You'd square the second dimension.
Then the square wouldn't be flat anymore. It would have a bottom, and sides, and a top.
And the fourth?
Well, in mathematical terms you'd square the square.
But you can't take a pencil and draw that the way you can the first three.
I know it's got something to do with Einstein and time. I guess maybe you could call the fourth dimension Time.

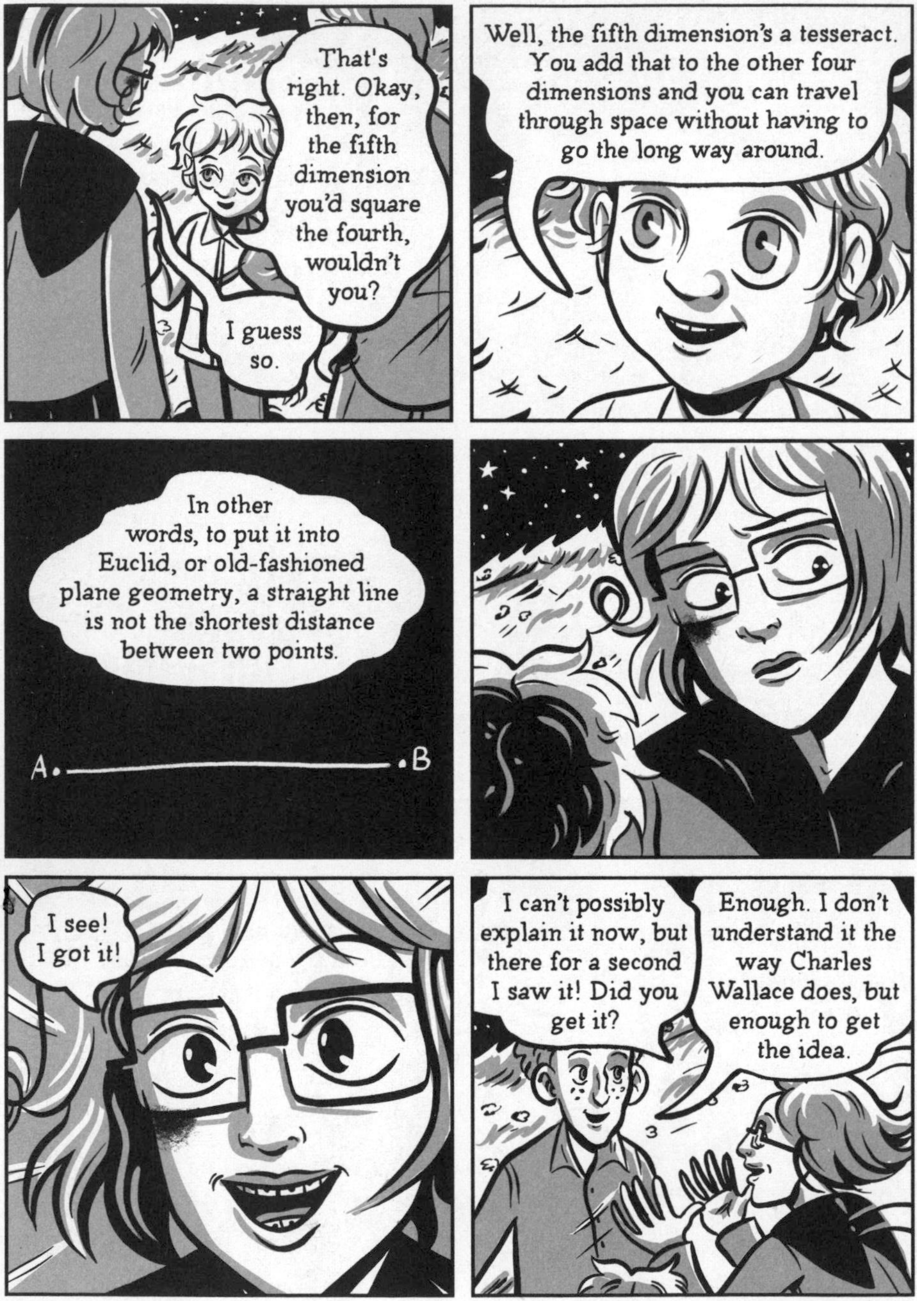
That's right. Okay, then, for the fifth dimension you'd square the fourth, wouldn't you?
I guess so.
Well, the fifth dimension's a tesseract. You add that to the other four dimensions and you can travel through space without having to go the long way around.
In other words, to put it into Euclid, or old-fashioned plane geometry, a straight line is not the shortest distance between two points.
A
B
I see! I got it!
I can't possibly explain it now, but there for a second I saw it! Did you get it?
Enough. I don't understand it the way Charles Wallace does, but enough to get the idea.

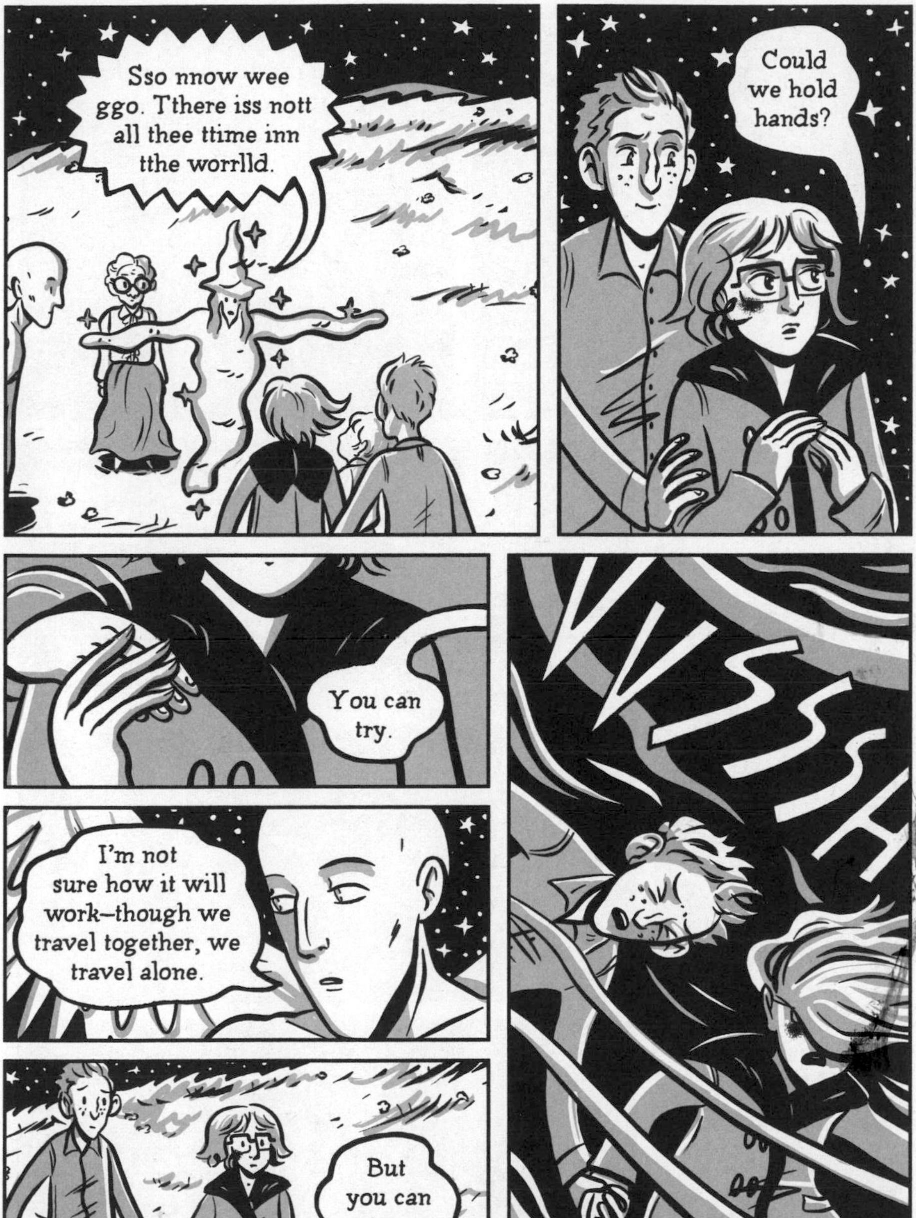
Sso nnow wee ggo. Tthere iss nott all thee ttime inn tthe worrlld.
Could we hold hands?
You can try.
I'm not sure how it will work–though we travel together, we travel alone.
But you can try.
VVSSSH

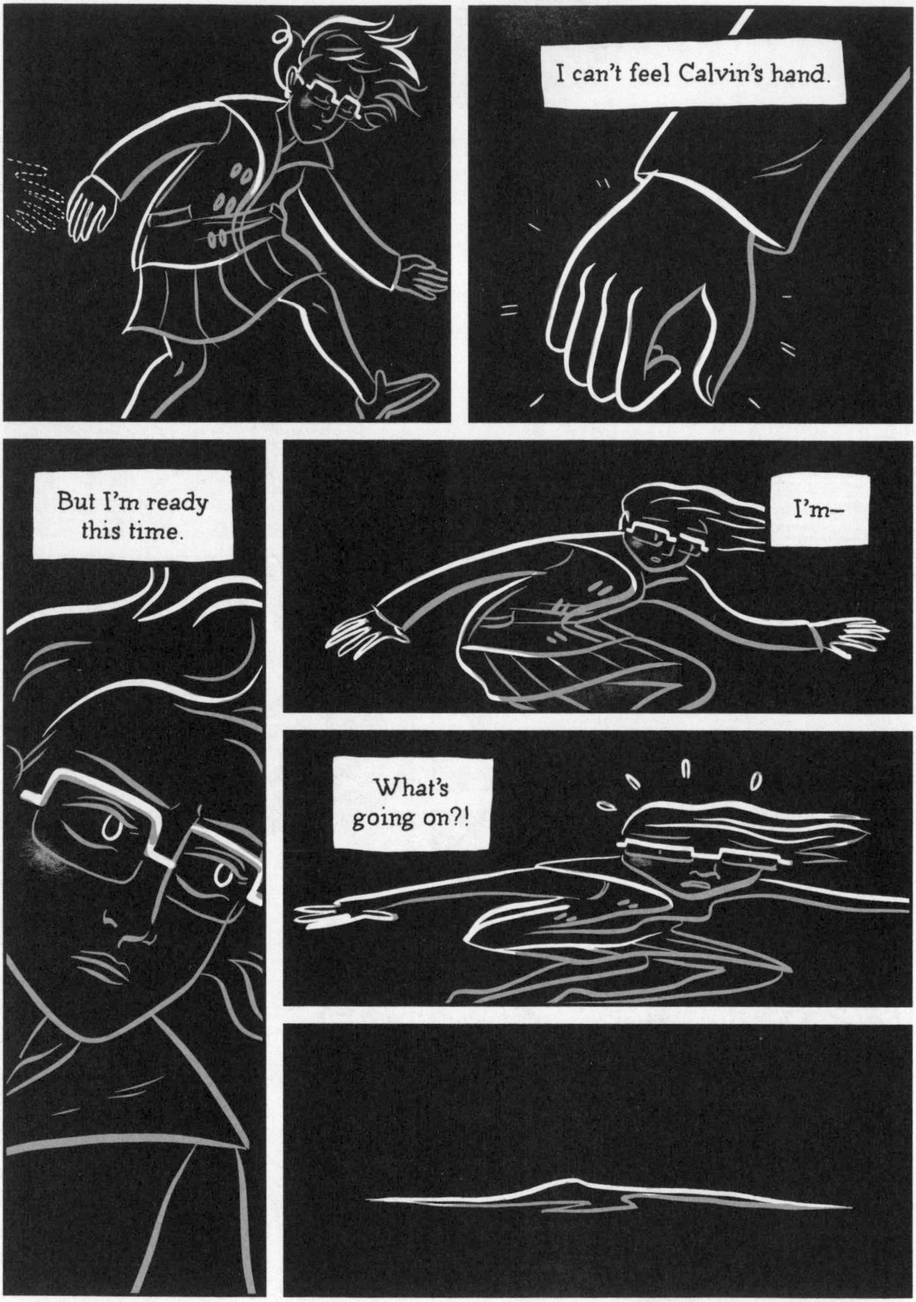
I can't feel Calvin's hand.
But I'm ready this time.
I'm–
What's going on?!

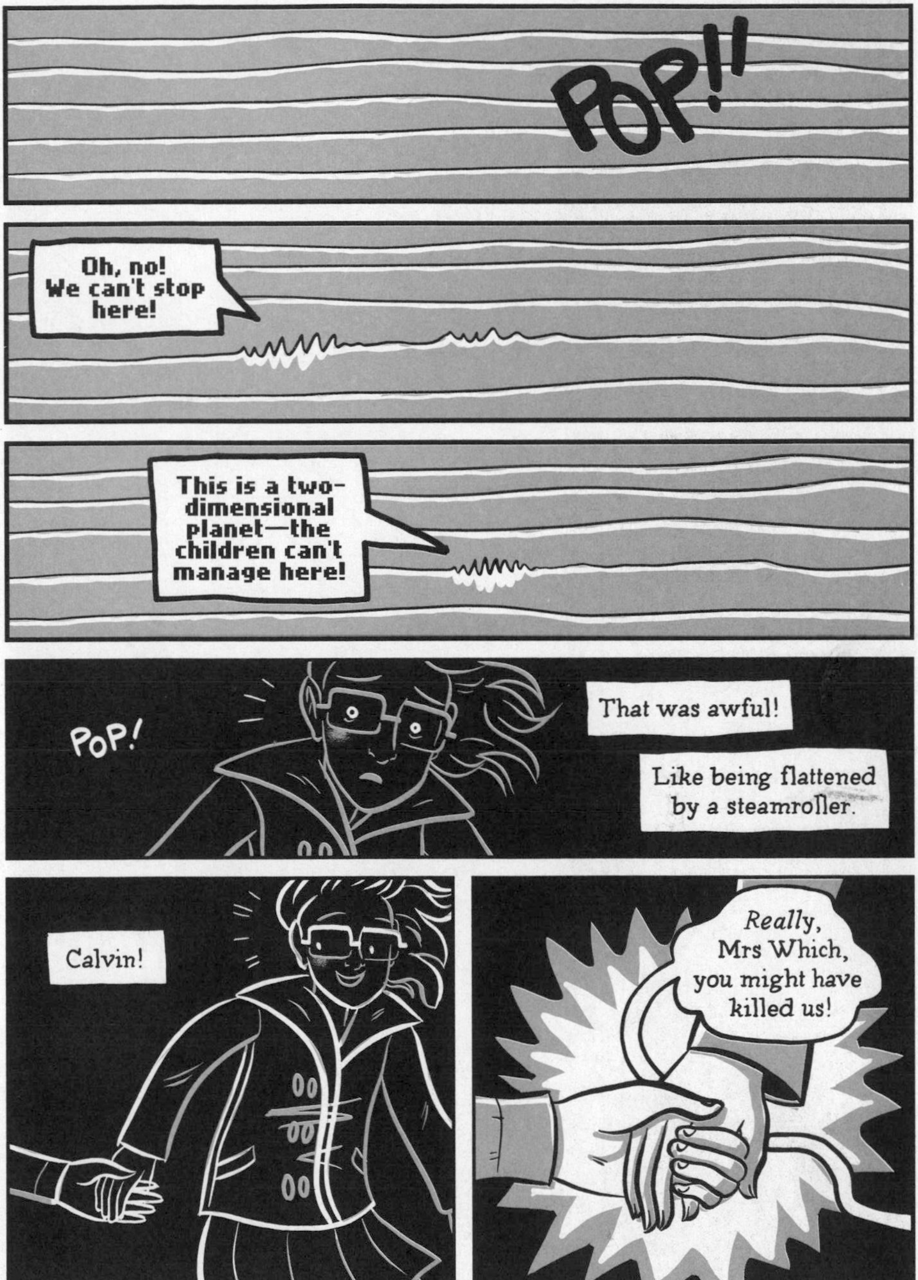
POP!!
Oh, no! We can't stop here!
This is a two-dimensional planet—the children can't manage here!
POP!
That was awful!
Like being flattened by a steamroller.
Calvin!
Really, Mrs Which, you might have killed us!

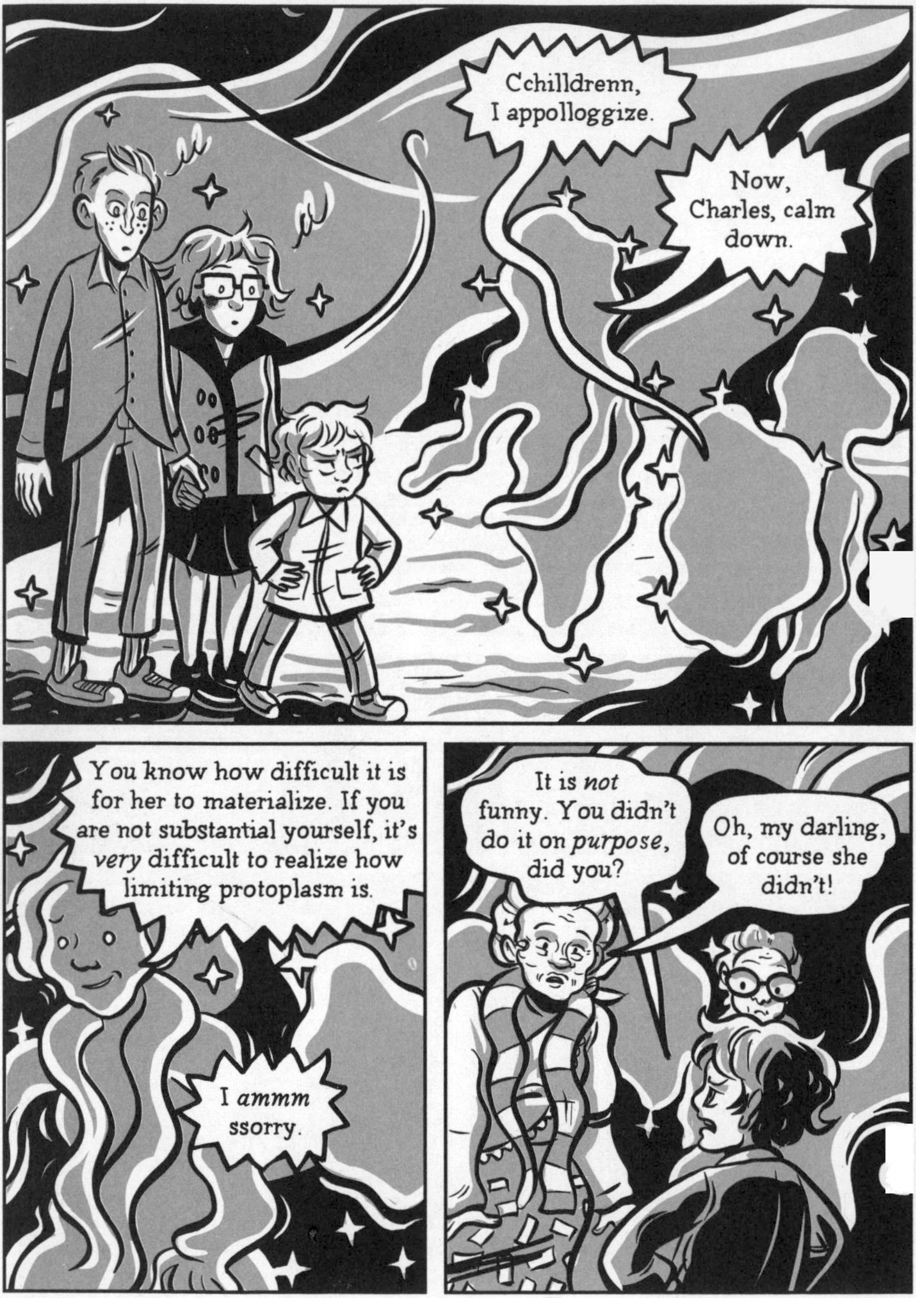
Cchilldrenn,
I appolloggize.
Now, Charles, calm down.
You know how difficult it is for her to materialize. If you are not substantial yourself, it's *very* difficult to realize how limiting protoplasm is.
I *ammm* ssorry.
It is *not* funny. You didn't do it on *purpose*, did you?
Oh, my darling, of course she didn't!

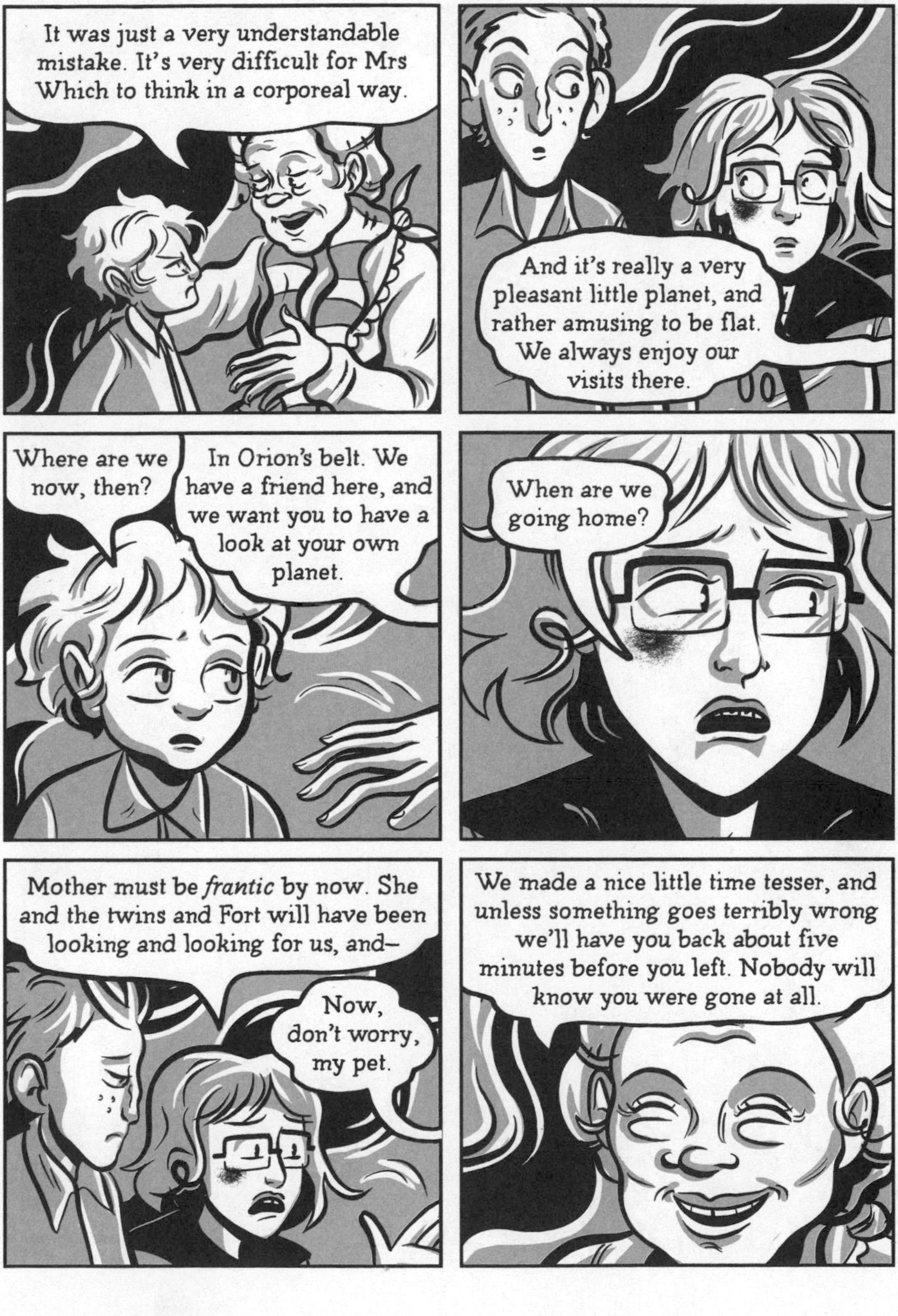

It was just a very understandable mistake. It's very difficult for Mrs Which to think in a corporeal way.
And it's really a very pleasant little planet, and rather amusing to be flat. We always enjoy our visits there.
Where are we now, then?
In Orion's belt. We have a friend here, and we want you to have a look at your own planet.
When are we going home?
Mother must be *frantic* by now. She and the twins and Fort will have been looking and looking for us, and–
Now, don't worry, my pet.
We made a nice little time tesser, and unless something goes terribly wrong we'll have you back about five minutes before you left. Nobody will know you were gone at all.

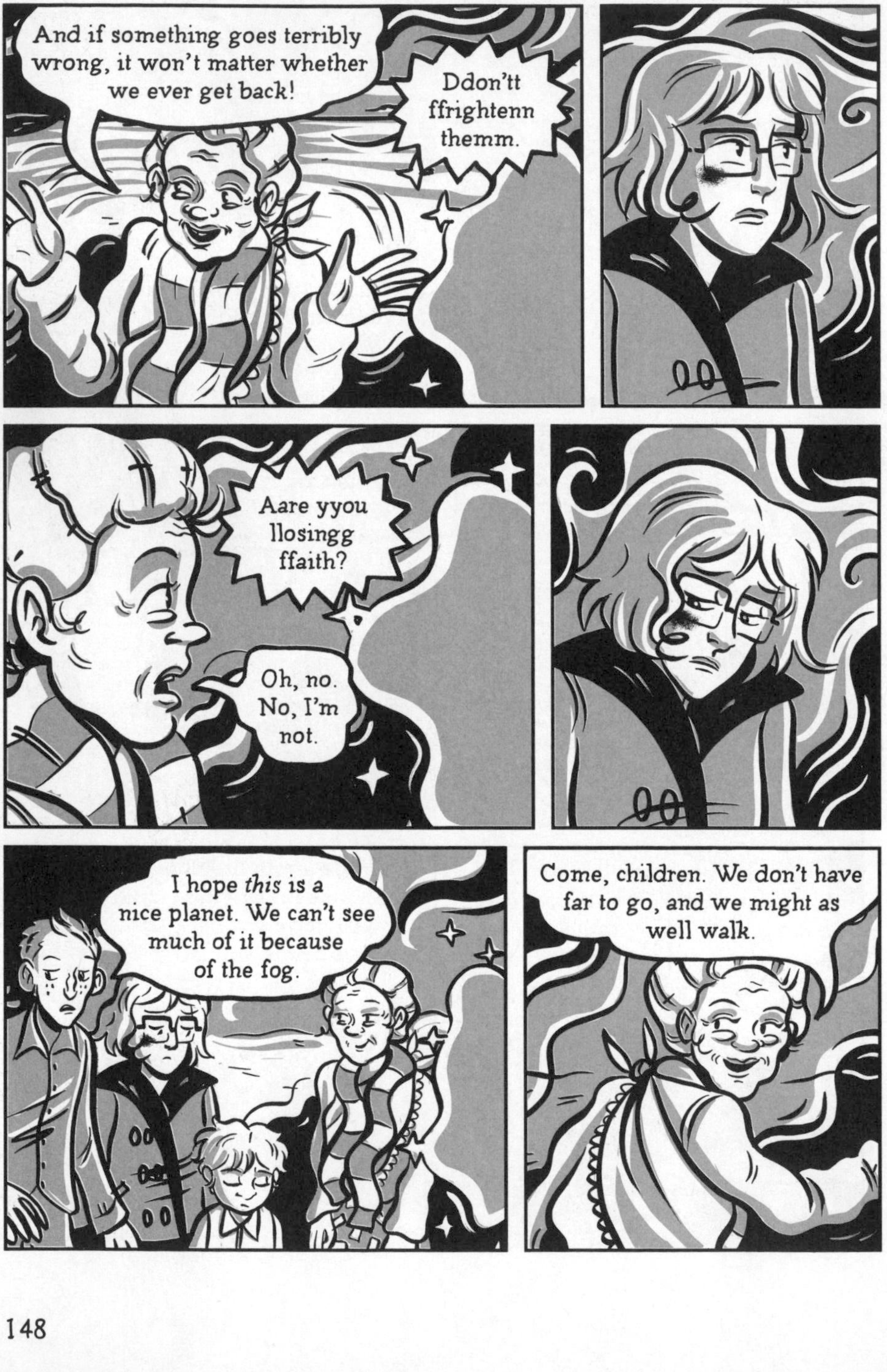
And if something goes terribly wrong, it won't matter whether we ever get back!
Ddon'tt ffrightenn themm.
Aare yyou llosingg ffaith?
Oh, no. No, I'm not.
I hope *this* is a nice planet. We can't see much of it because of the fog.
Come, children. We don't have far to go, and we might as well walk.

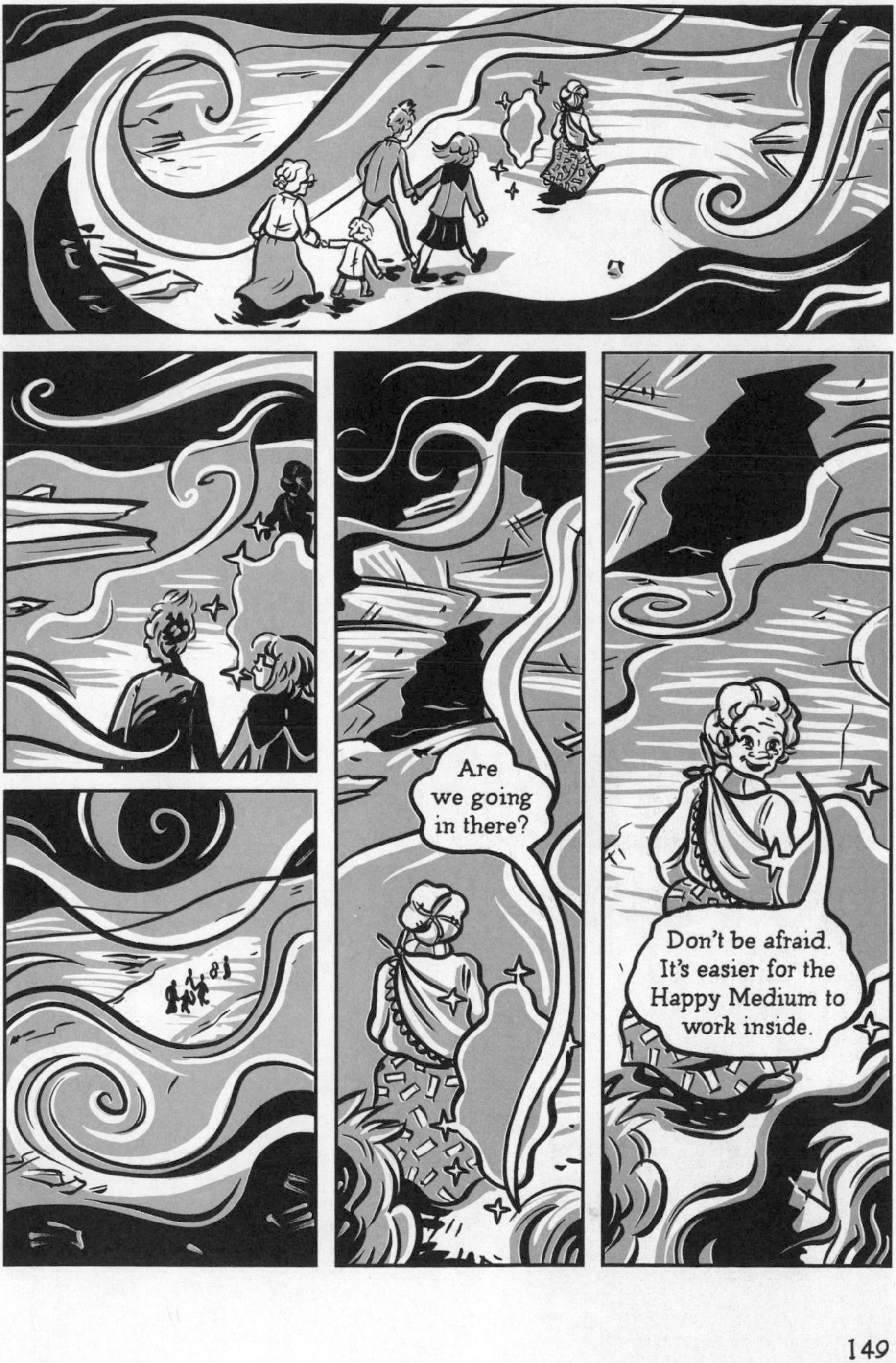
Are we going in there?
Don't be afraid. It's easier for the Happy Medium to work inside.

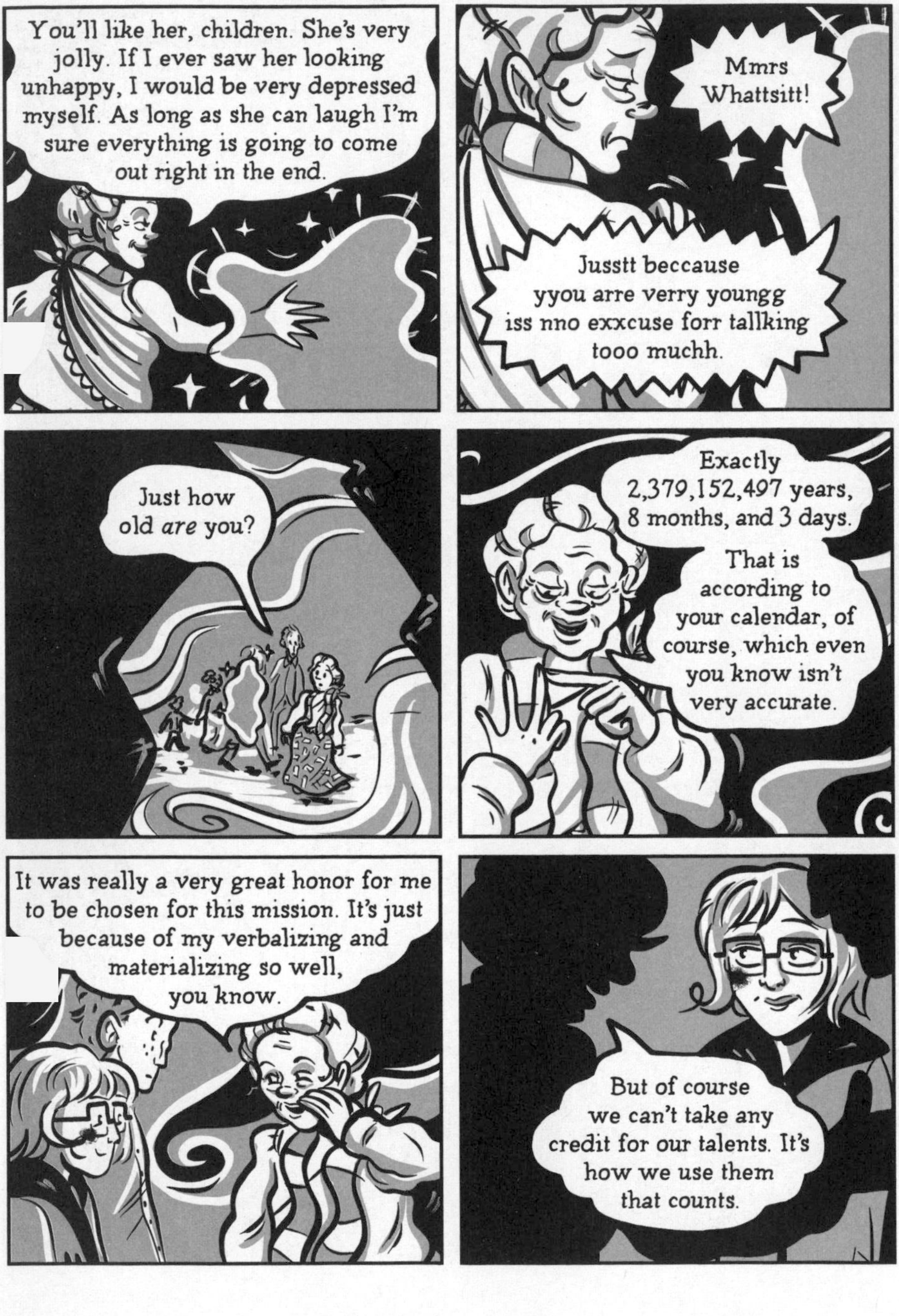
You'll like her, children. She's very jolly. If I ever saw her looking unhappy, I would be very depressed myself. As long as she can laugh I'm sure everything is going to come out right in the end.
Mmrs Whattsitt!
Jusstt beccause yyou arre verry youngg iss nno exxcuse forr tallking tooo muchh.
Just how old *are* you?
Exactly 2,379,152,497 years, 8 months, and 3 days.
That is according to your calendar, of course, which even you know isn't very accurate.
It was really a very great honor for me to be chosen for this mission. It's just because of my verbalizing and materializing so well, you know.
But of course we can't take any credit for our talents. It's how we use them that counts.

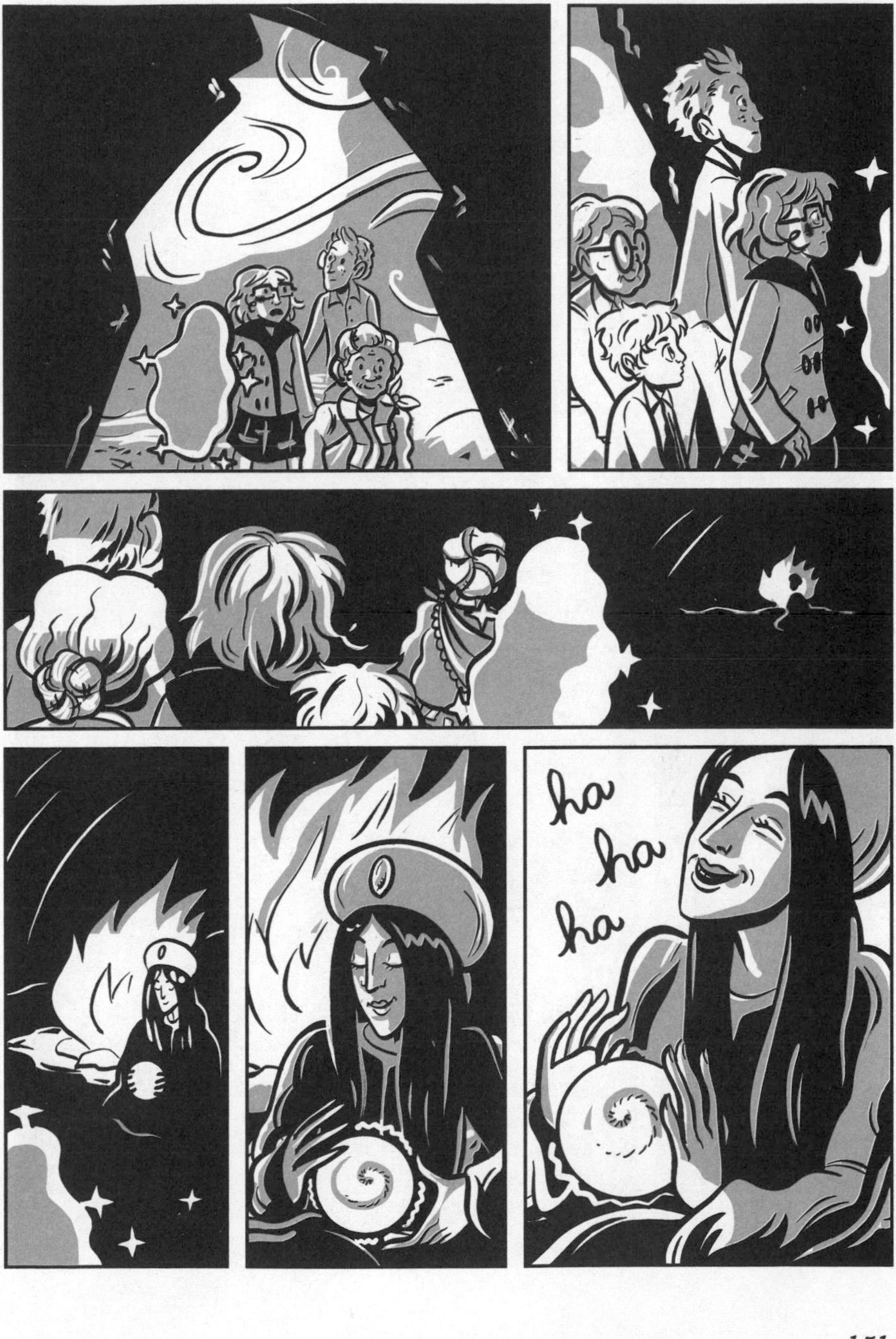
ha
ha
ha

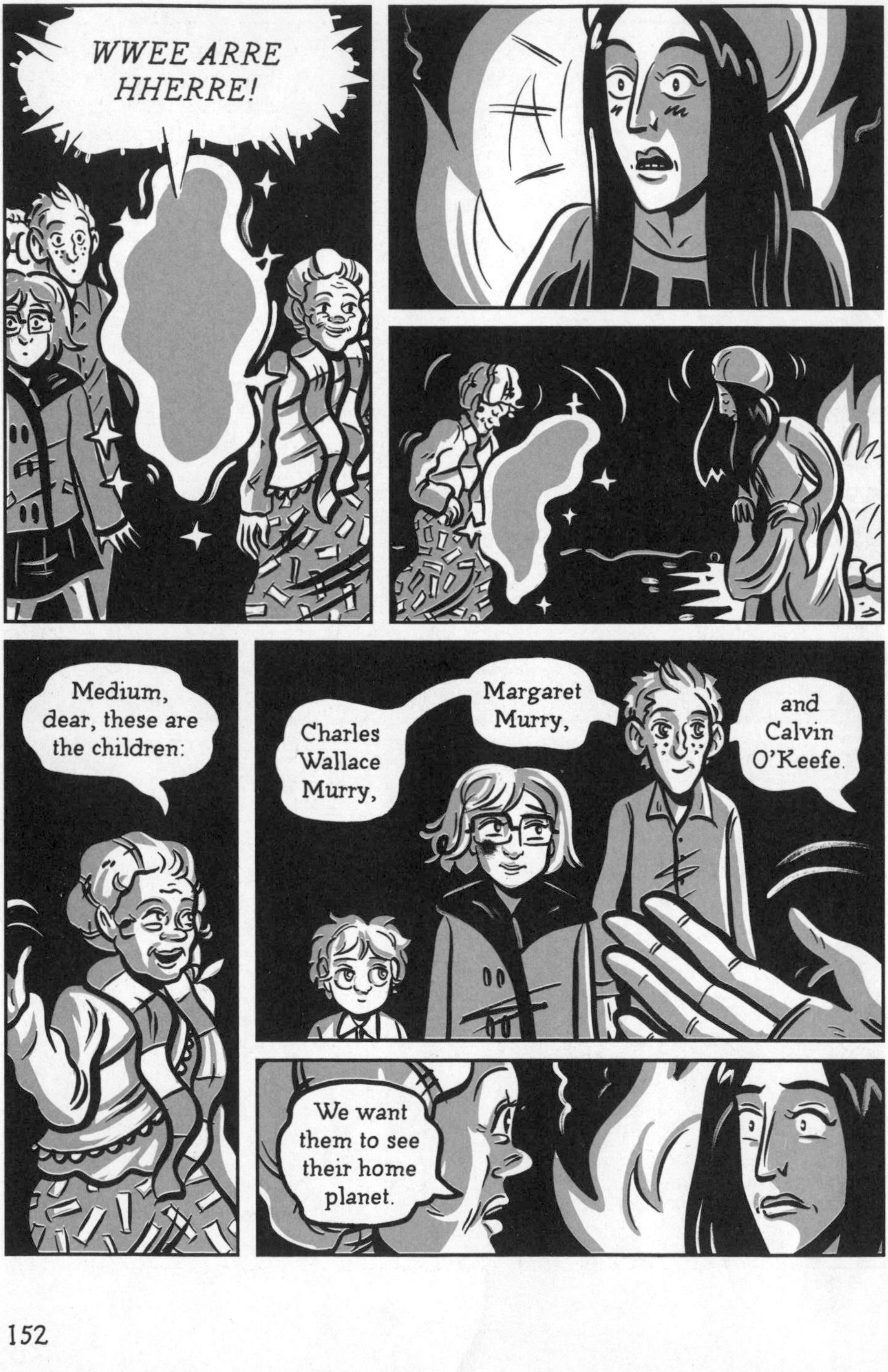
WWEE ARRE HHERRE!
Medium, dear, these are the children:
Charles Wallace Murry,
Margaret Murry,
and Calvin O'Keefe.
We want them to see their home planet.

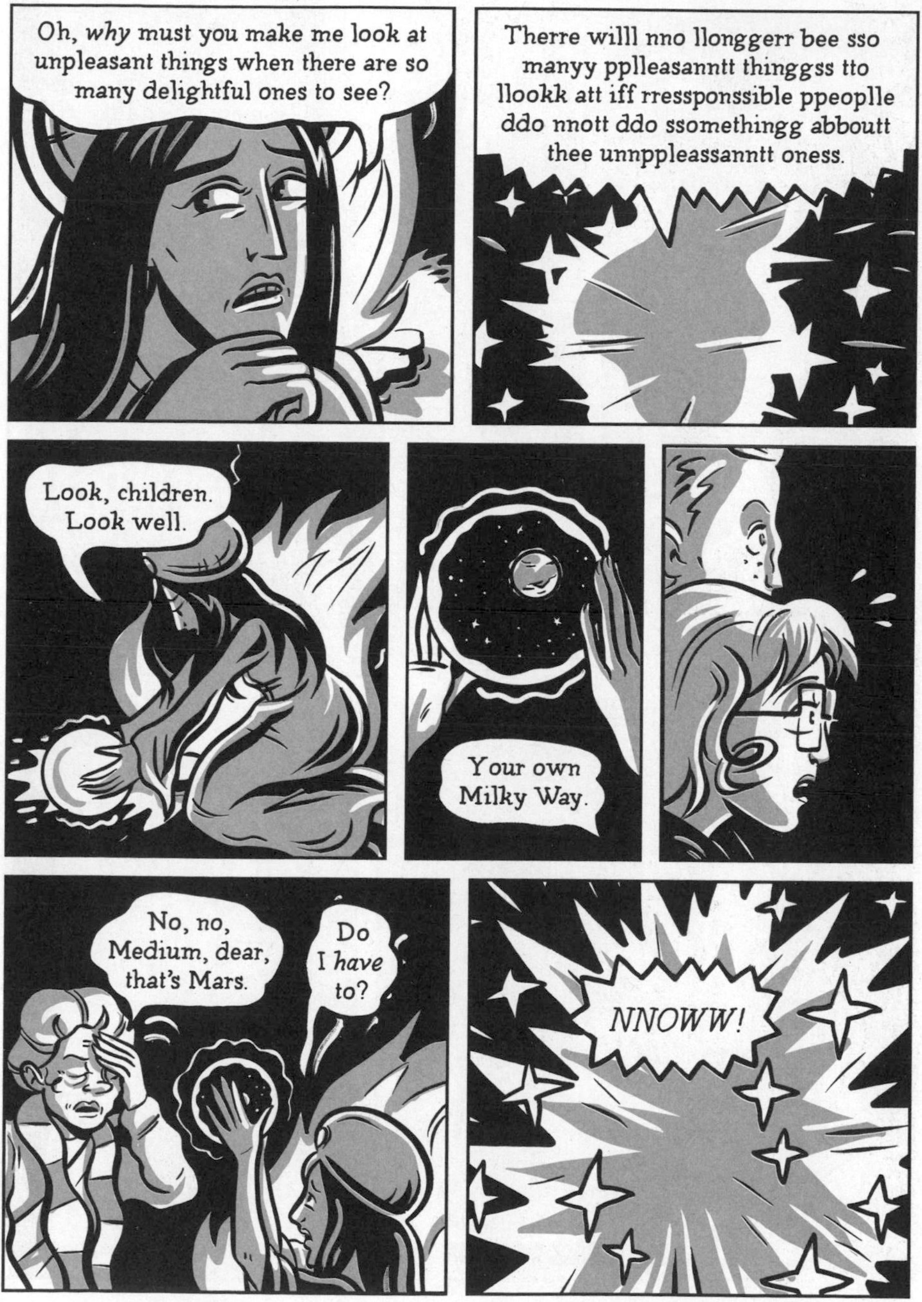

Oh, *why* must you make me look at unpleasant things when there are so many delightful ones to see?
Therre willl nno llonggerr bee sso manyy pplleasanntt thinggss tto llookk att iff rressponssible ppeopllle ddo nnott ddo ssomethingg abboutt thee unnppleassanntt oness.
Look, children. Look well.
Your own Milky Way.
No, no, Medium, dear, that's Mars.
Do I *have* to?
NNOWW!

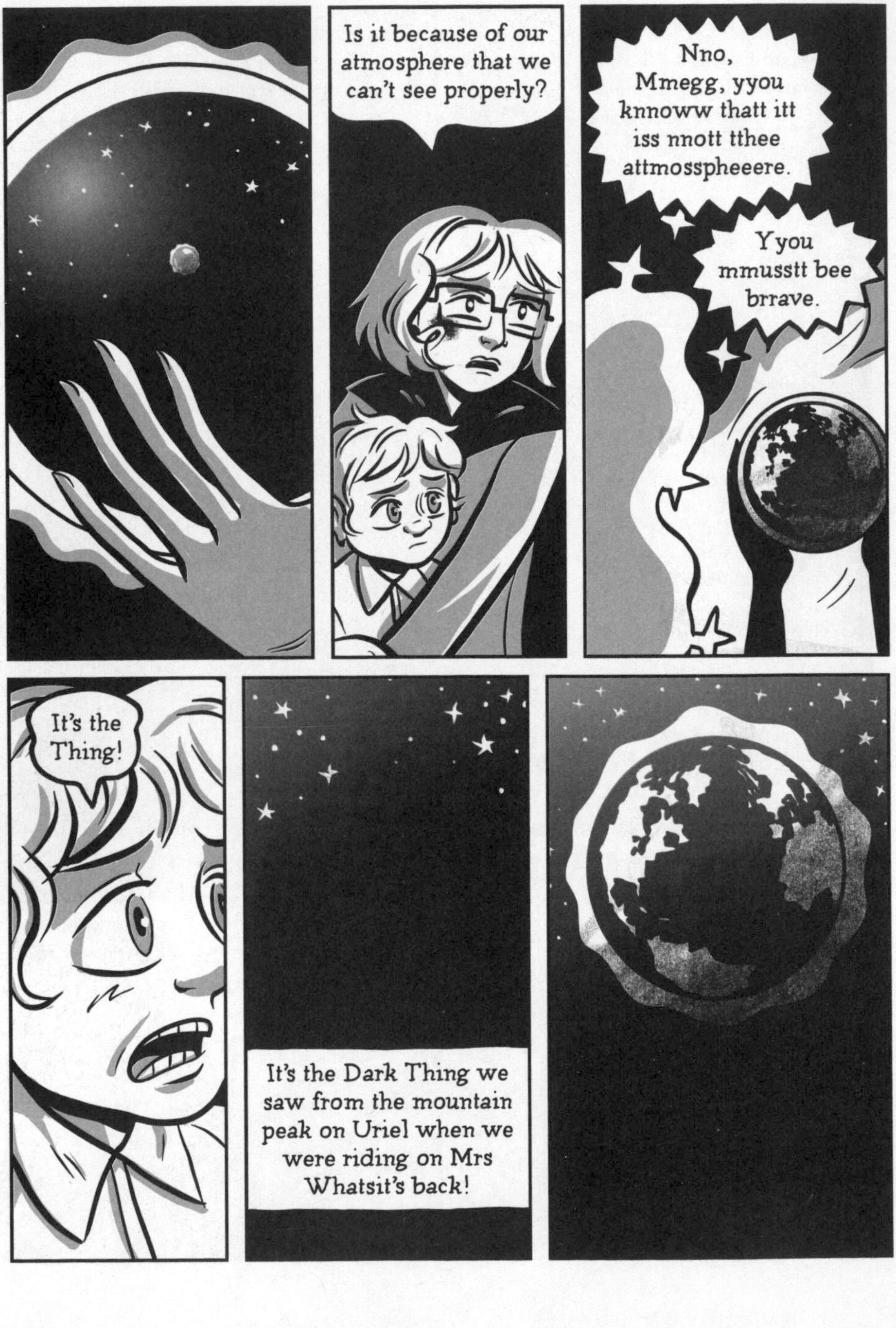
Is it because of our atmosphere that we can't see properly?
Nno, Mmegg, yyou knnoww thatt itt iss nnott tthee attmossphеeere.
Yyou mmusstt bee brrave.
It's the Thing!
It's the Dark Thing we saw from the mountain peak on Uriel when we were riding on Mrs Whatsit's back!

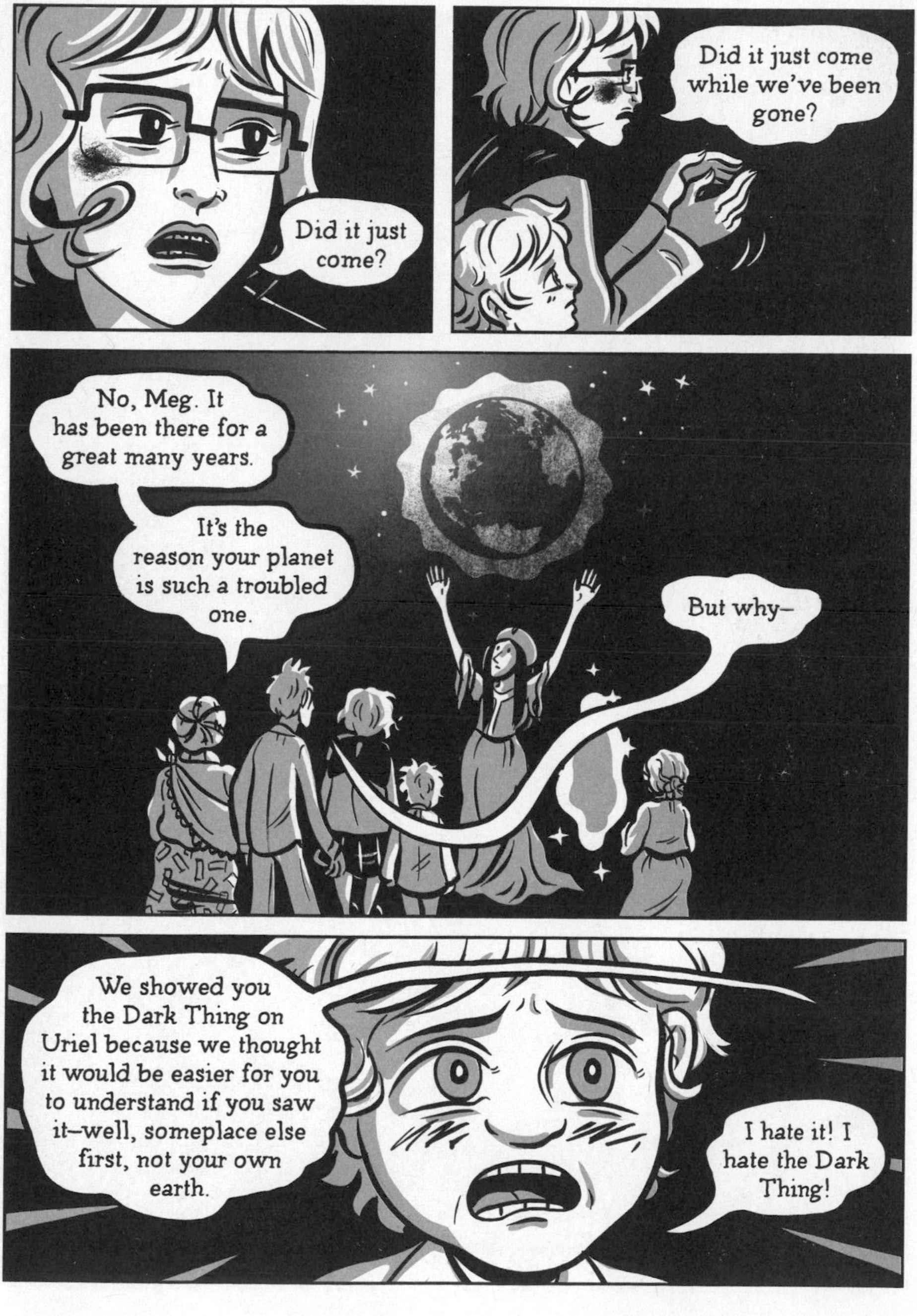
Did it just come?
Did it just come while we've been gone?
No, Meg. It has been there for a great many years.
It's the reason your planet is such a troubled one.
But why–
We showed you the Dark Thing on Uriel because we thought it would be easier for you to understand if you saw it–well, someplace else first, not your own earth.
I hate it! I hate the Dark Thing!

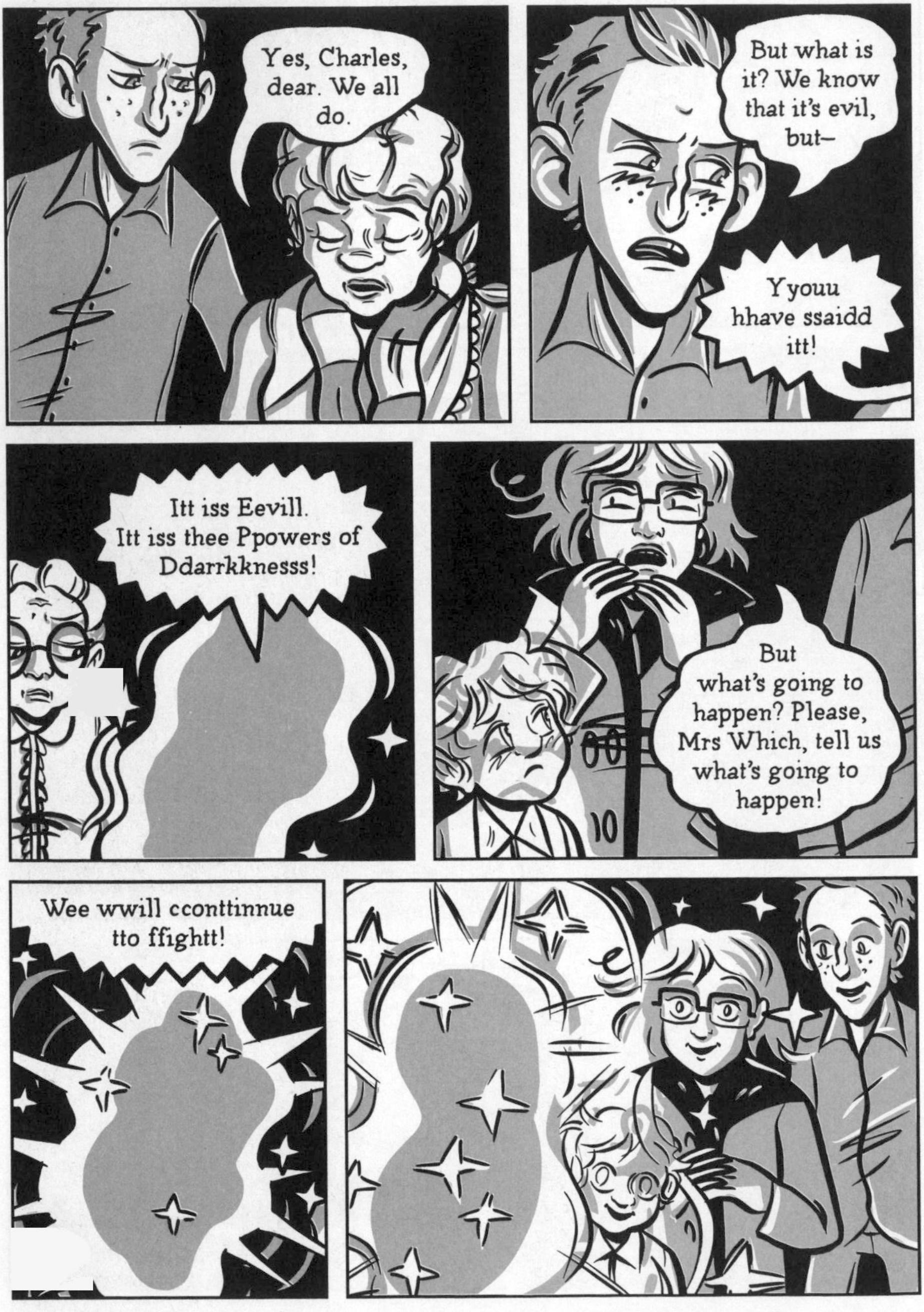
Yes, Charles, dear. We all do.
But what is it? We know that it's evil, but–
Yyouu hhave ssaidd itt!
Itt iss Eevill. Itt iss thee Ppowers of Ddarrkknesss!
But what's going to happen? Please, Mrs Which, tell us what's going to happen!
Wee wwill ccontinnue tto ffightt!

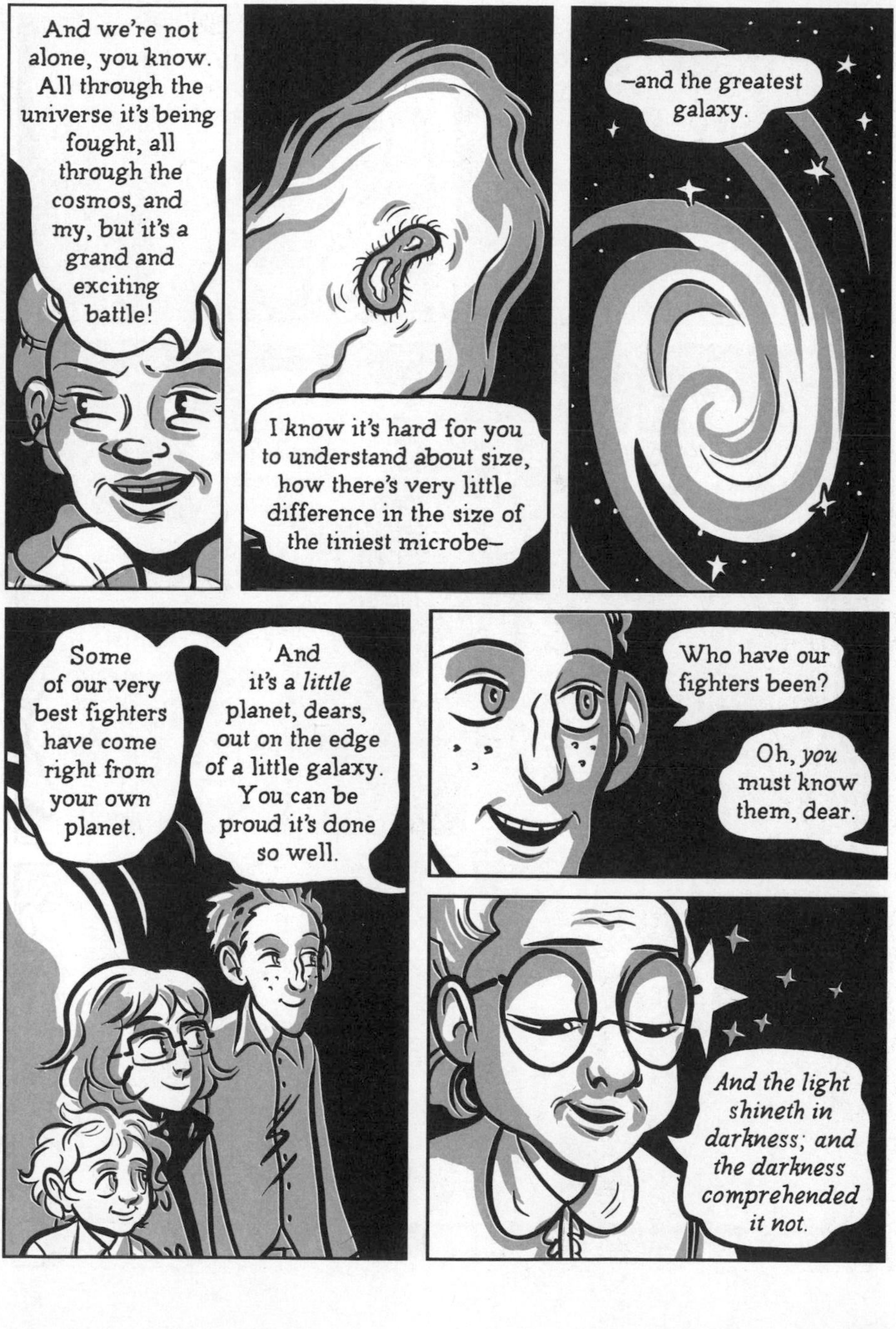
And we're not alone, you know. All through the universe it's being fought, all through the cosmos, and my, but it's a grand and exciting battle!
I know it's hard for you to understand about size, how there's very little difference in the size of the tiniest microbe—
—and the greatest galaxy.
Some of our very best fighters have come right from your own planet.
And it's a *little* planet, dears, out on the edge of a little galaxy. You can be proud it's done so well.
Who have our fighters been?
Oh, *you* must know them, dear.
And the light shineth in darkness; and the darkness comprehended it not.

158

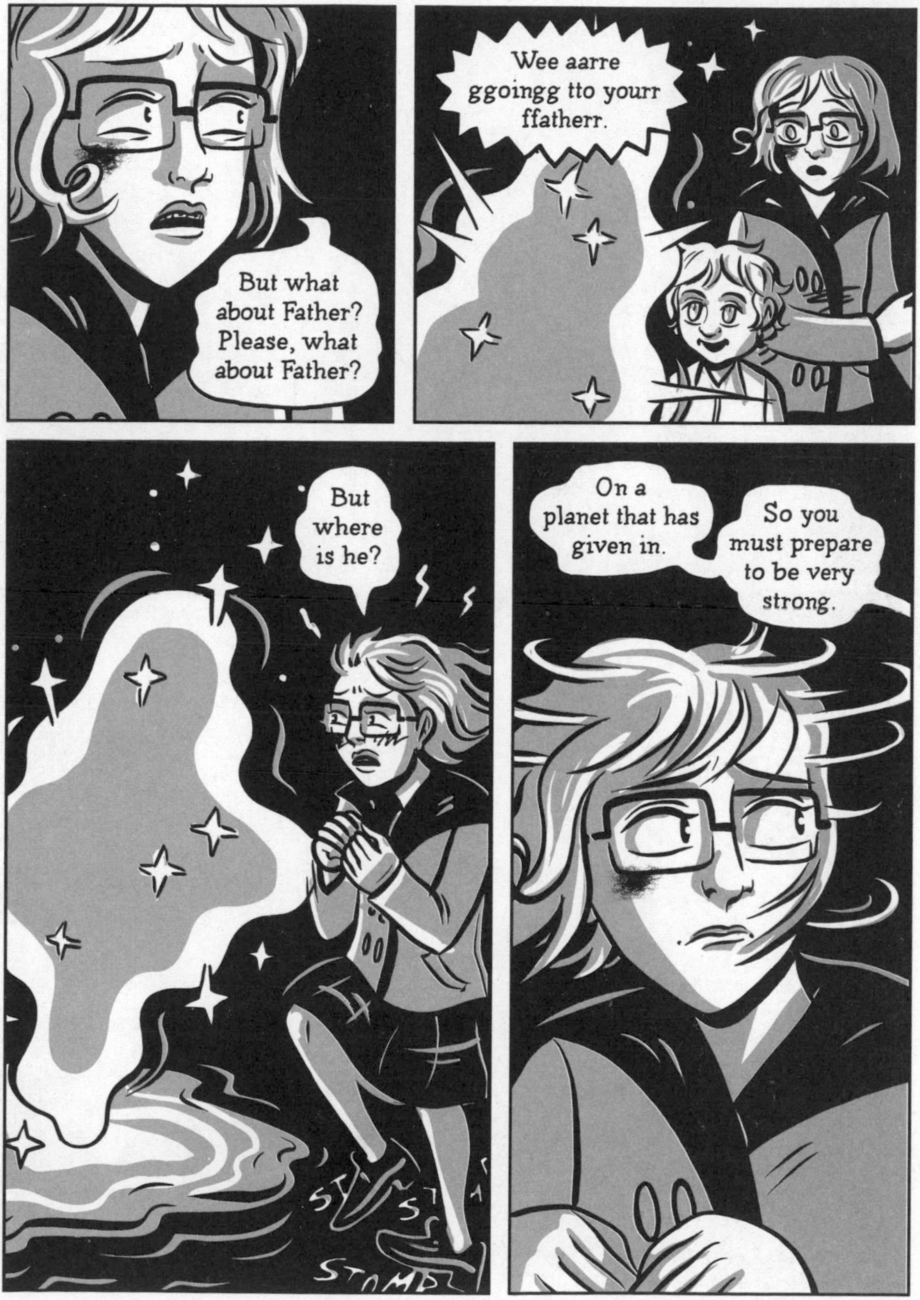
But what about Father? Please, what about Father?
Wee aarre ggoingg tto yourr ffatherr.
But where is he?
STAMP
On a planet that has given in.
So you must prepare to be very strong.

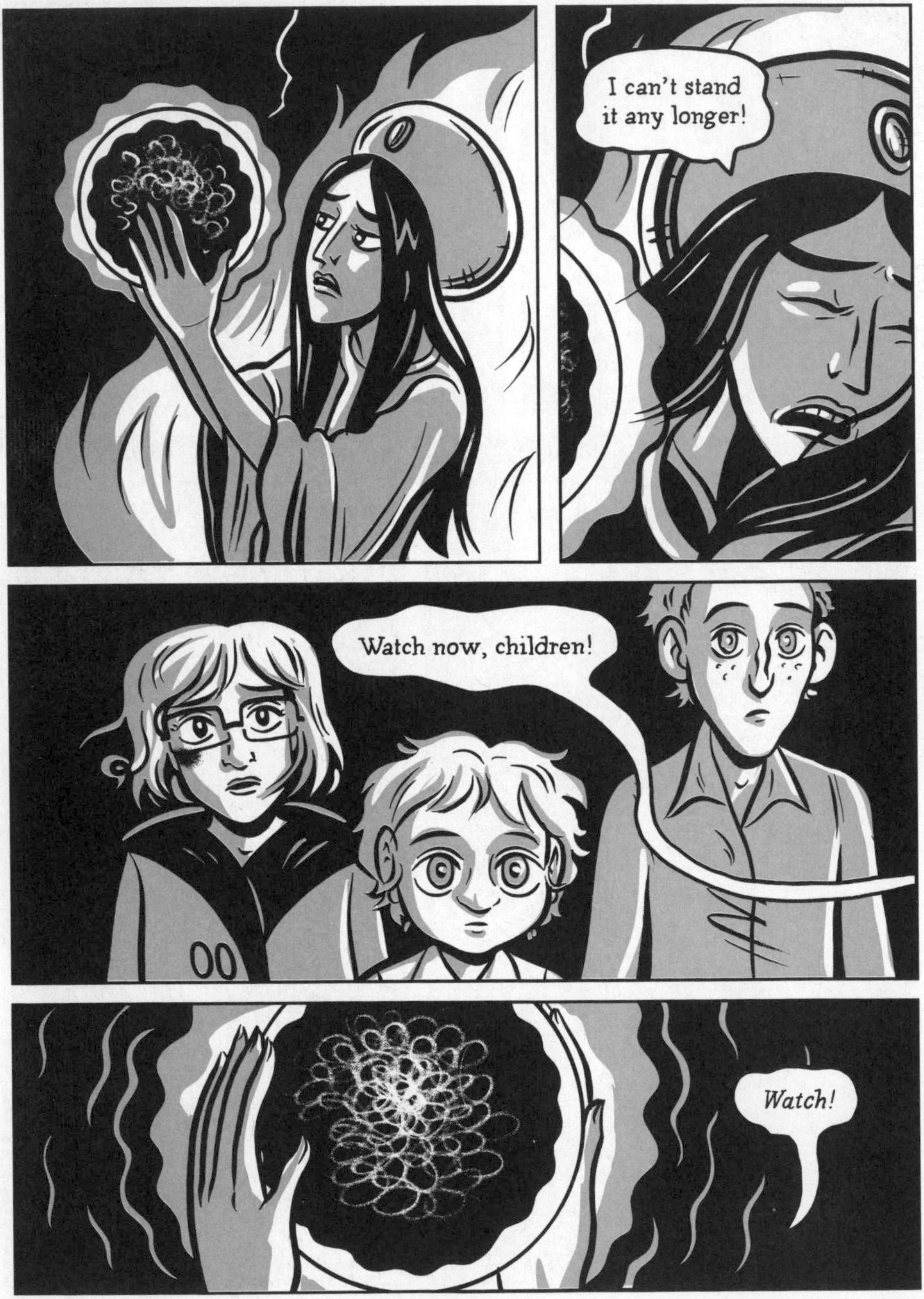
I can't stand it any longer!
Watch now, children!
Watch!

6
The Happy Medium

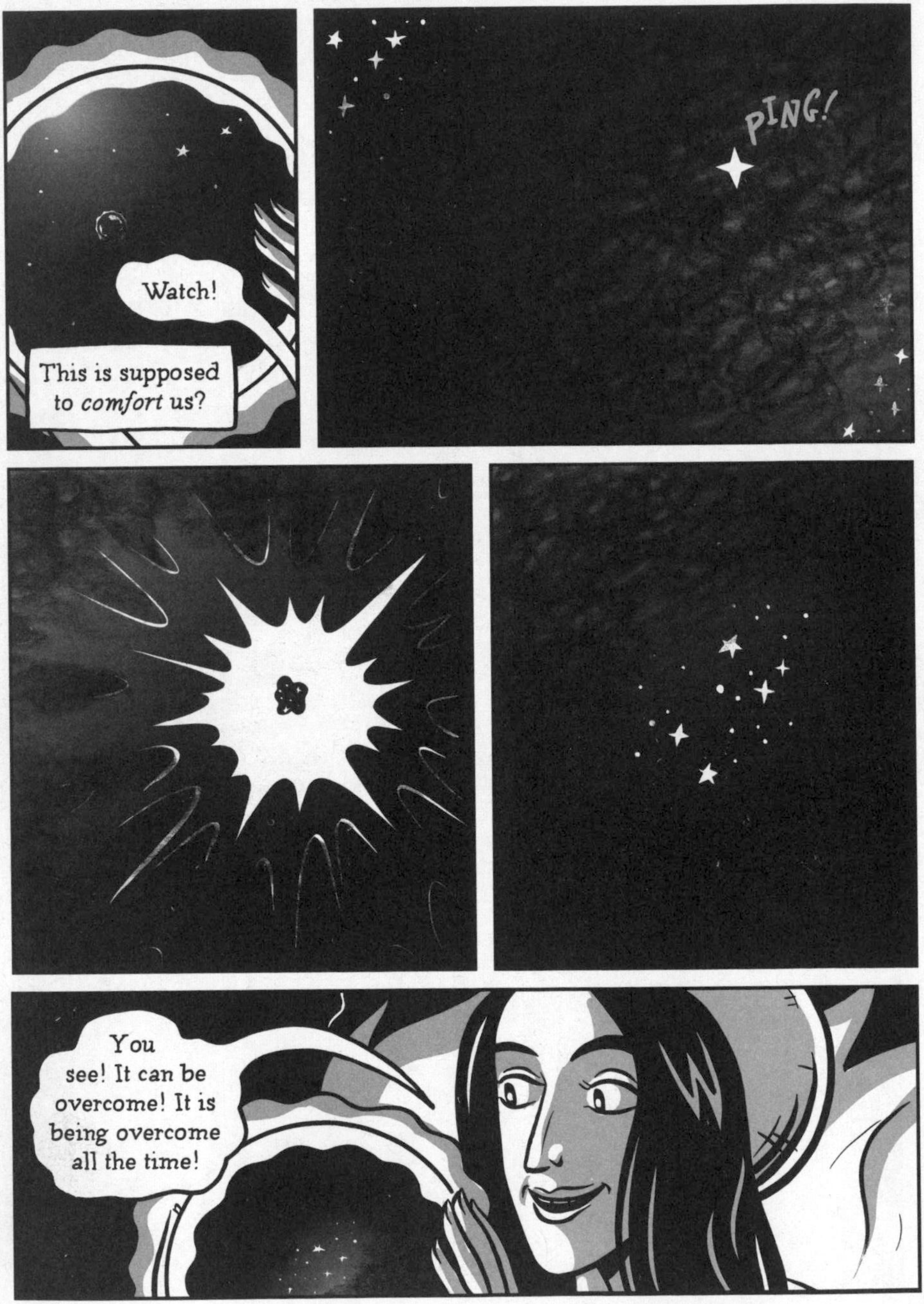
Watch!
This is supposed to *comfort* us?
PING!
You see! It can be overcome! It is being overcome all the time!

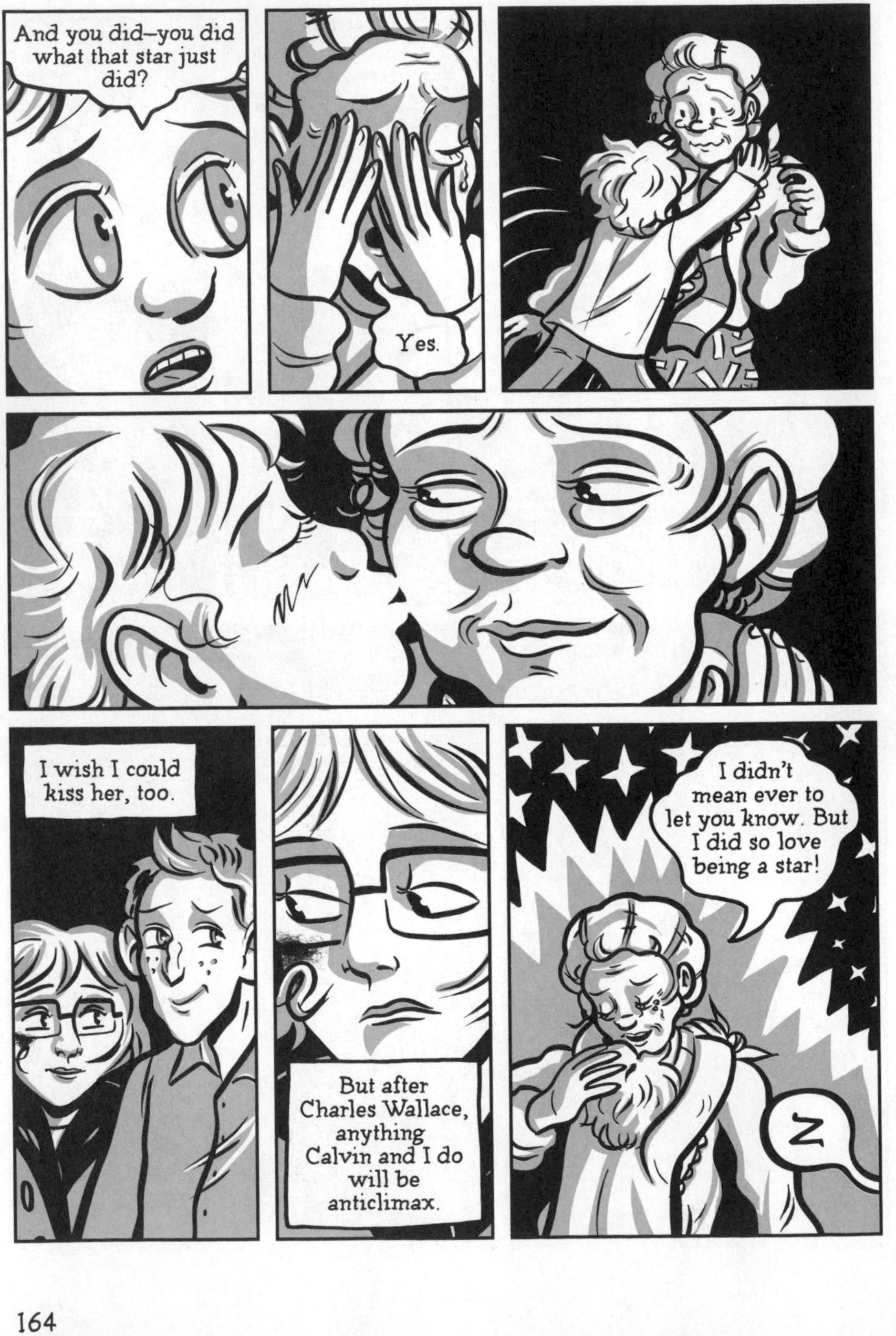
And you did—you did what that star just did?
Yes.
I wish I could kiss her, too.
But after Charles Wallace, anything Calvin and I do will be anticlimax.
I didn't mean ever to let you know. But I did so love being a star!
Z

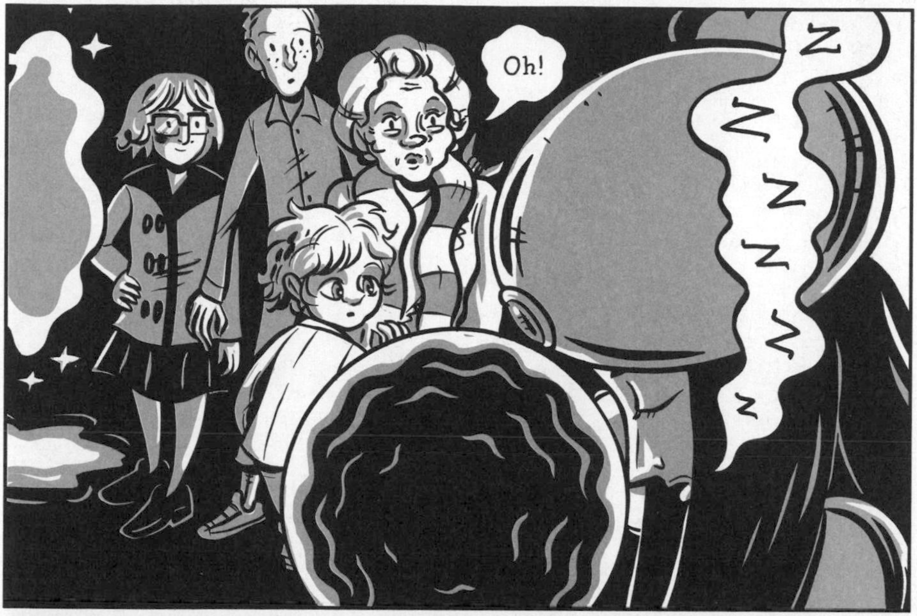
Oh!
Z Z Z Z Z Z Z

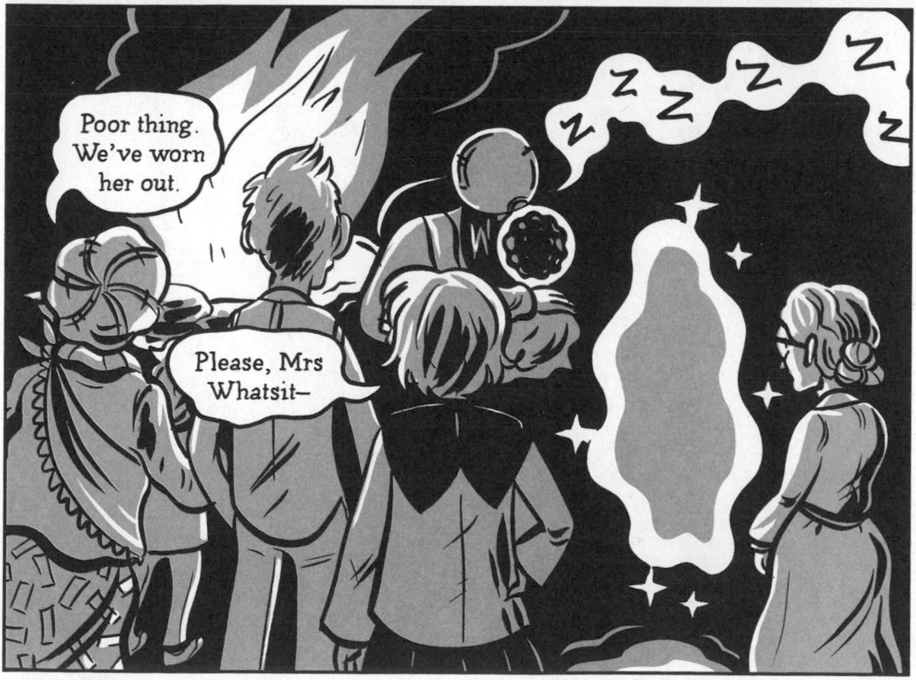
Poor thing. We've worn her out.
Z Z Z Z Z Z Z
Please, Mrs Whatsit–

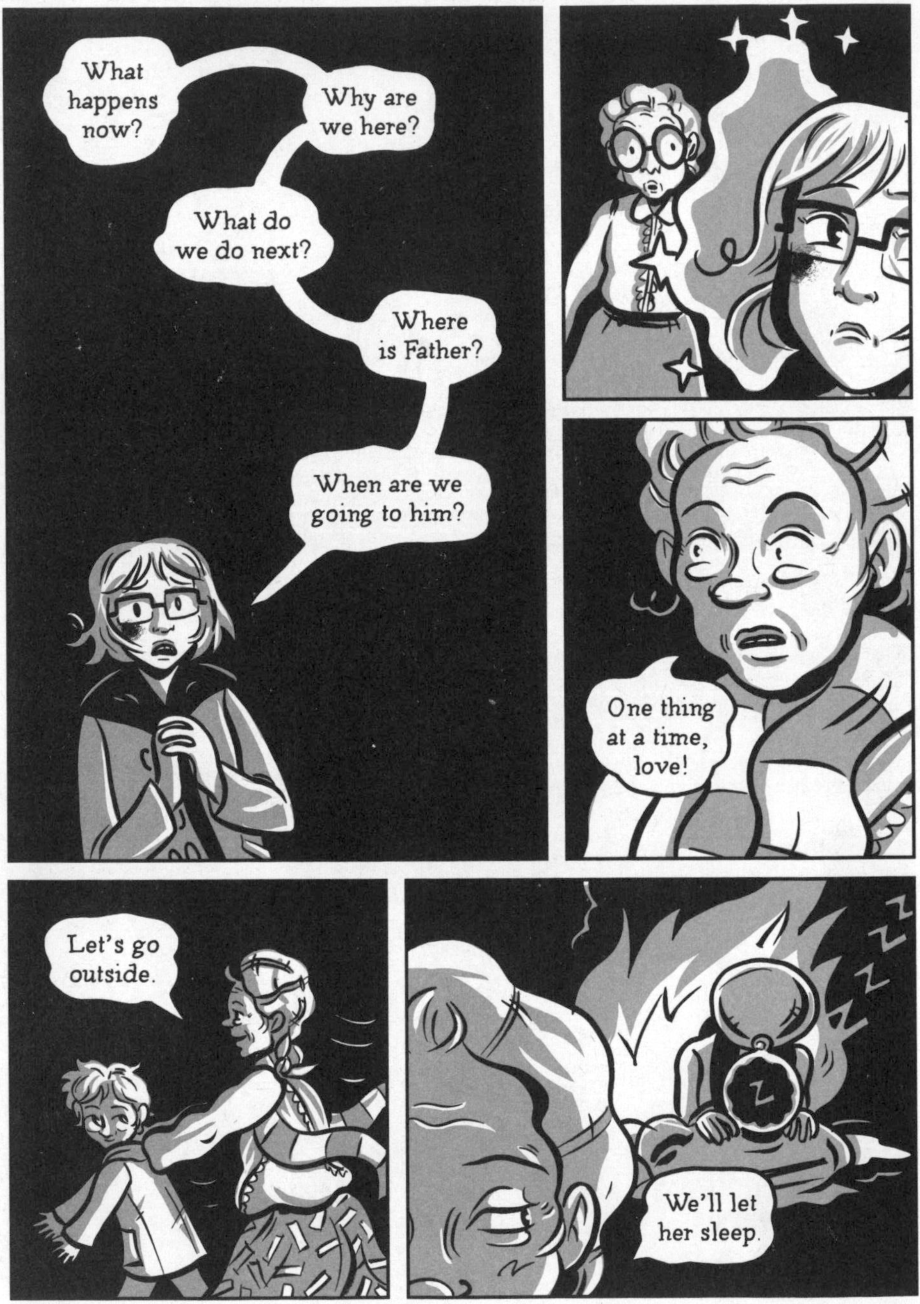
What happens now?
Why are we here?
What do we do next?
Where is Father?
When are we going to him?
One thing at a time, love!
Let's go outside.
We'll let her sleep.

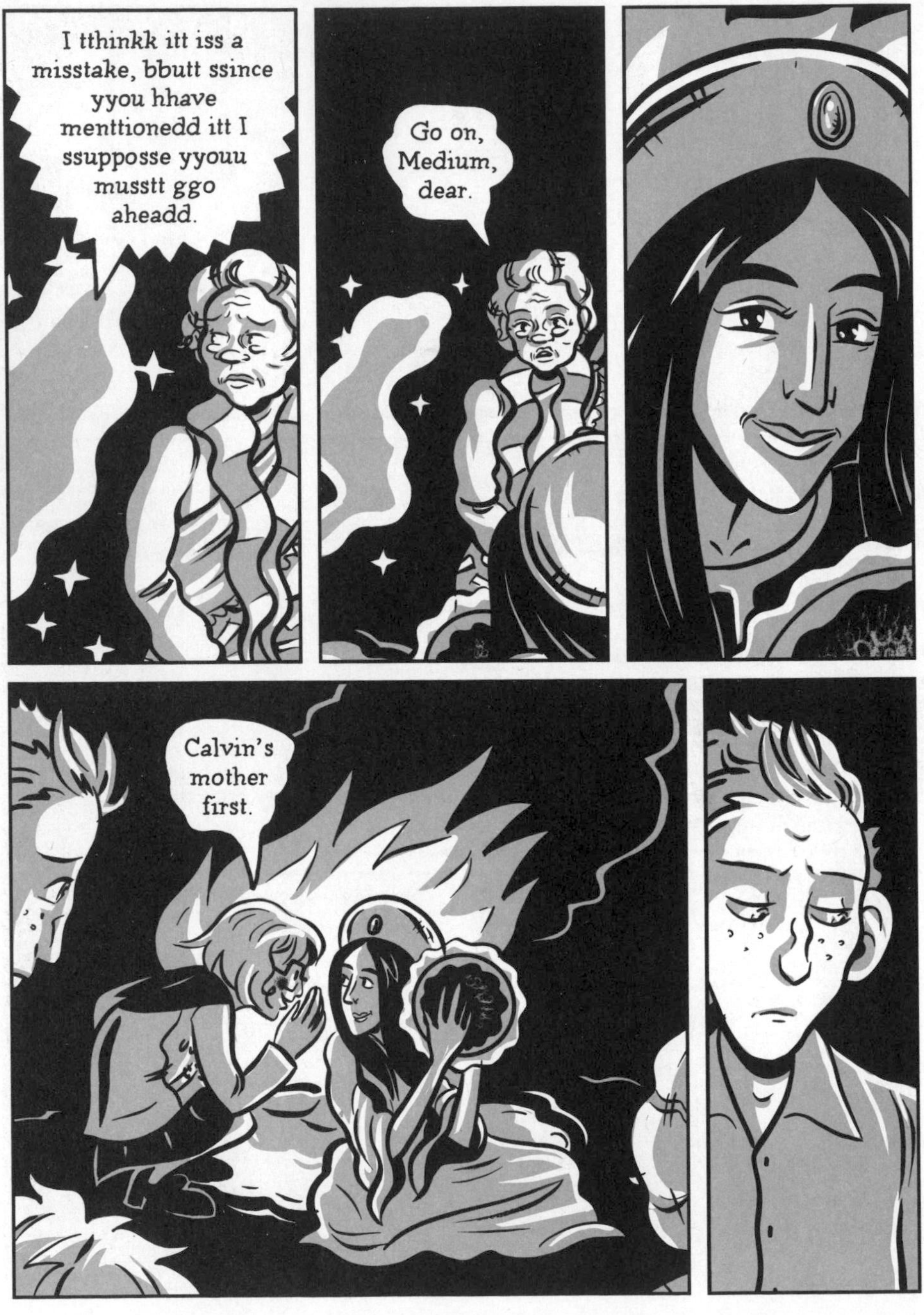
I tthinkk itt iss a misstake, bbutt ssince yyou hhave menttionedd itt I ssupposse yyouu musstt ggo aheadd.
Go on, Medium, dear.
Calvin's mother first.

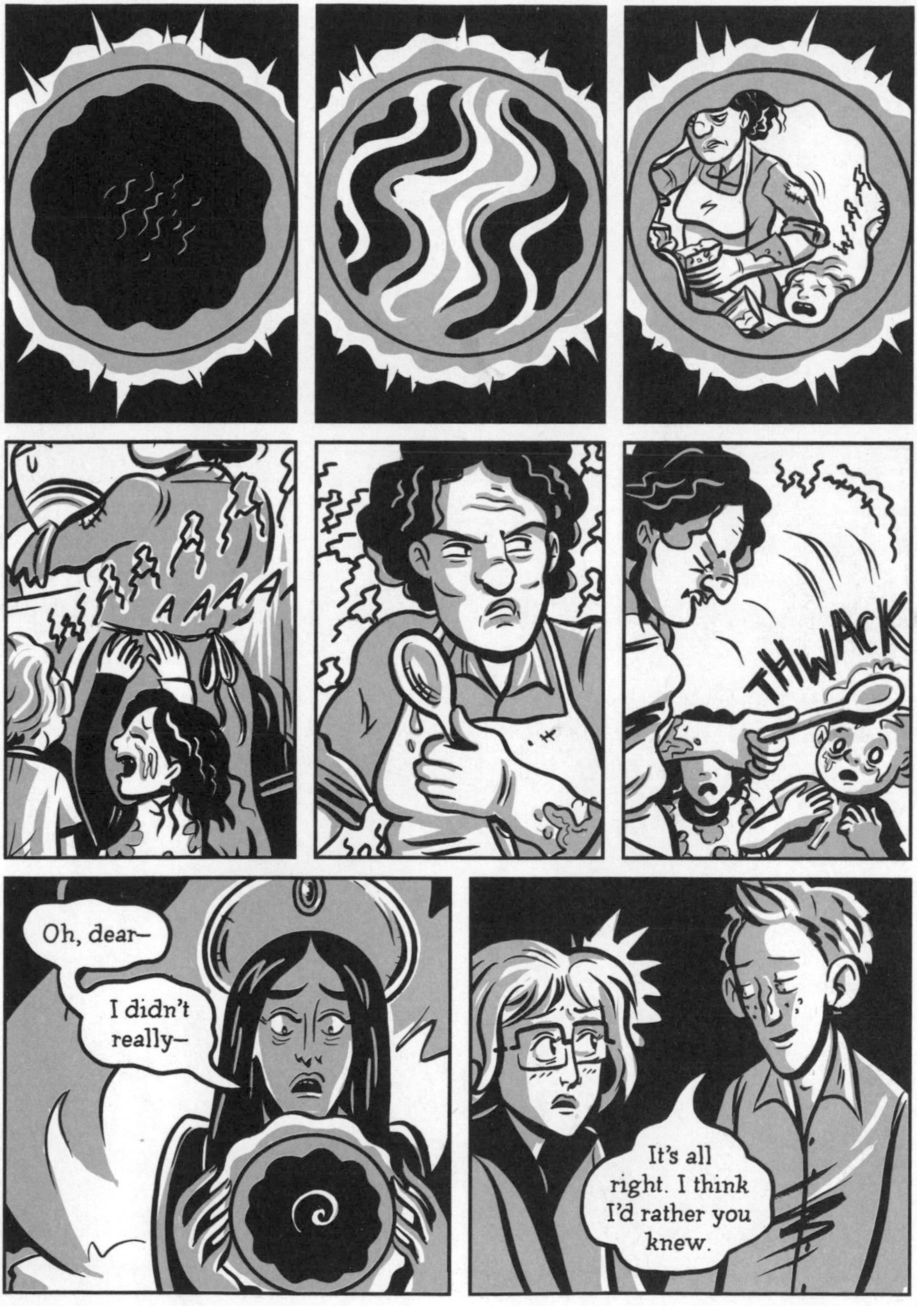
AAAAA
THWACK
Oh, dear—
I didn't really—
It's all right. I think I'd rather you knew.

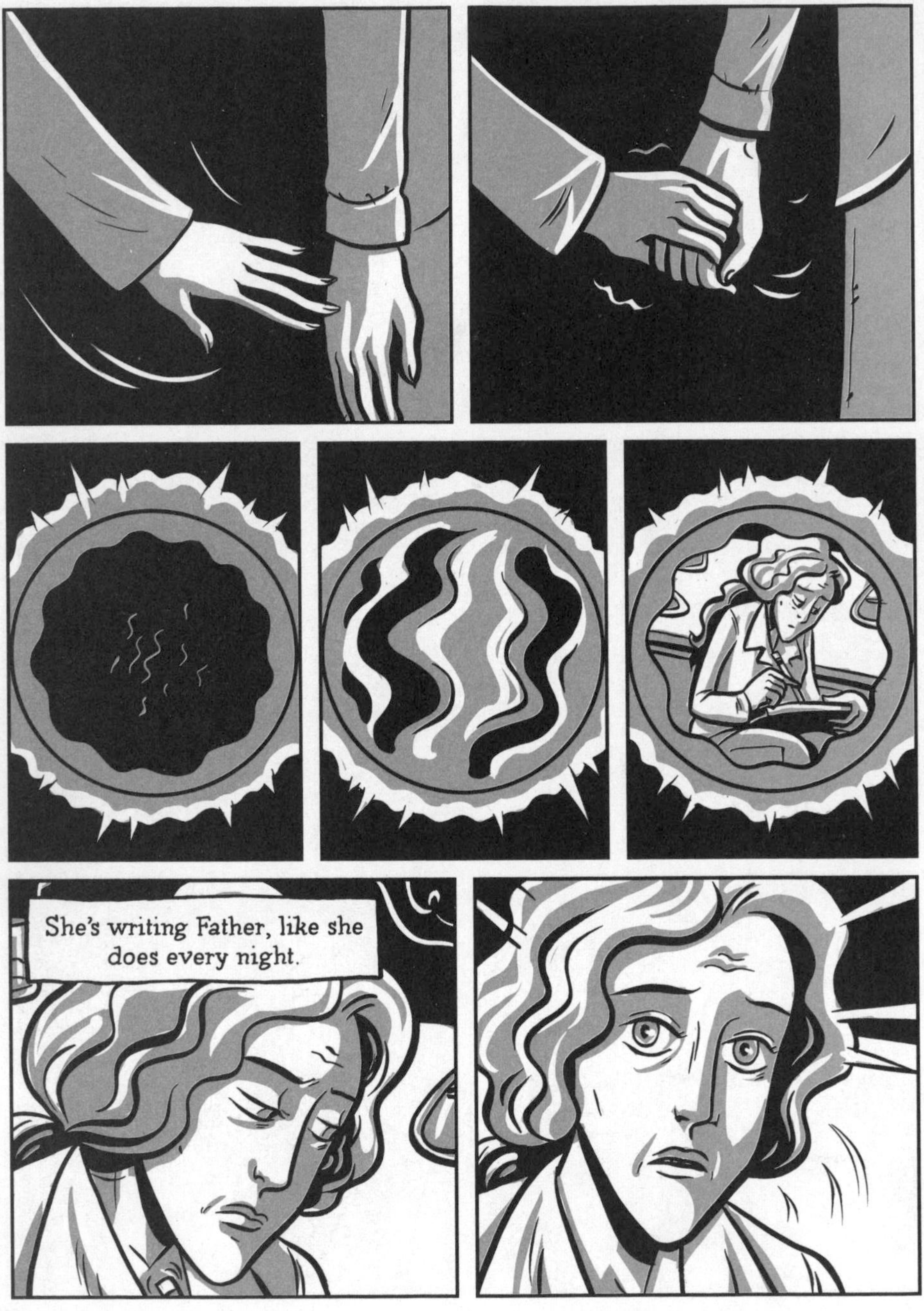
She's writing Father, like she does every night.

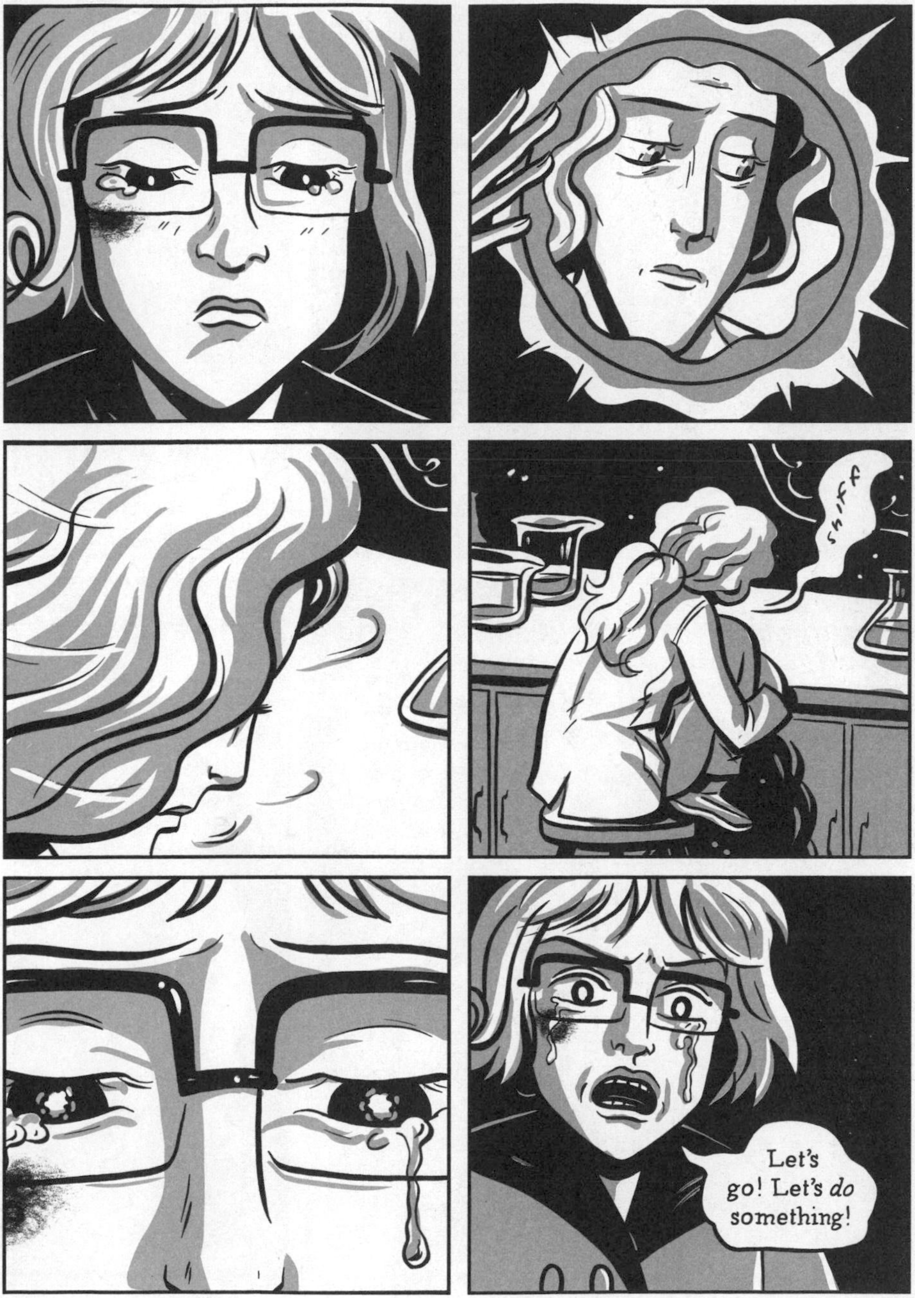
sniff
Let's go! Let's *do* something!

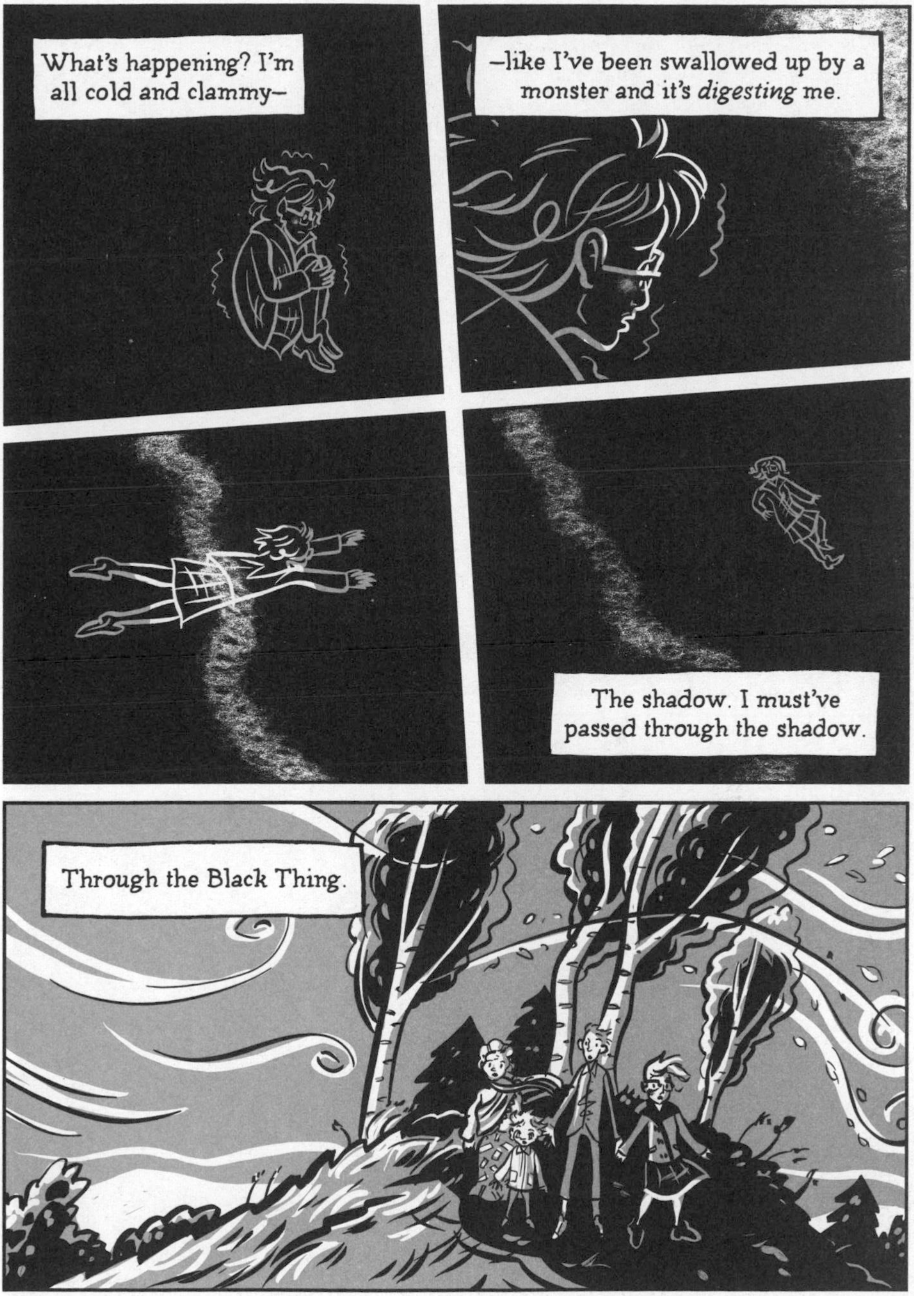
What's happening? I'm all cold and clammy–
–like I've been swallowed up by a monster and it's *digesting* me.
The shadow. I must've passed through the shadow.
Through the Black Thing.

179

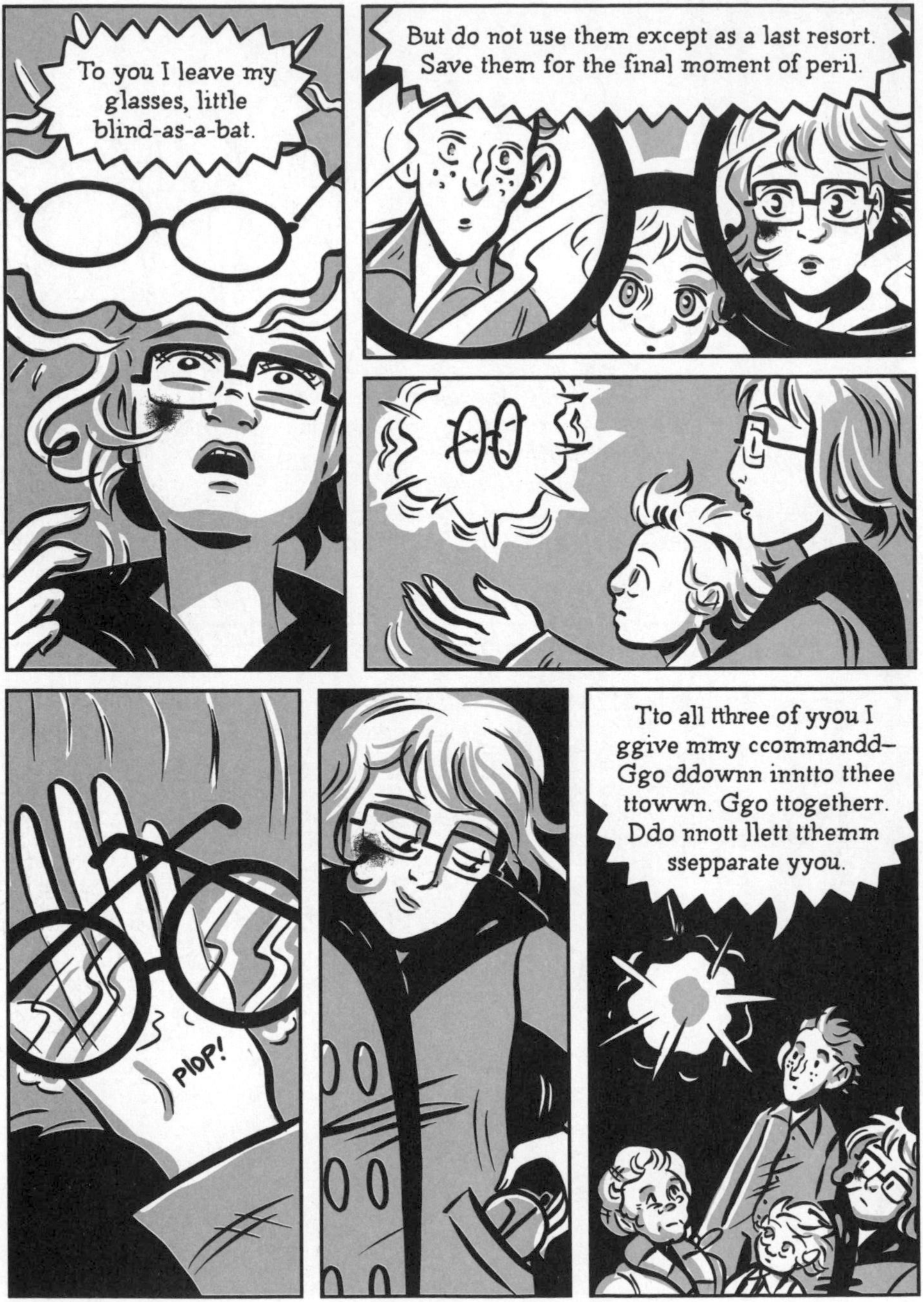

To you I leave my glasses, little blind-as-a-bat.
But do not use them except as a last resort. Save them for the final moment of peril.
PLOP!
Tto all tthree of yyou I ggive mmy ccommandd– Ggo ddownn inntto tthee ttowwn. Ggo ttogetherr. Ddo nnott llett tthemm ssepparate yyou.

181

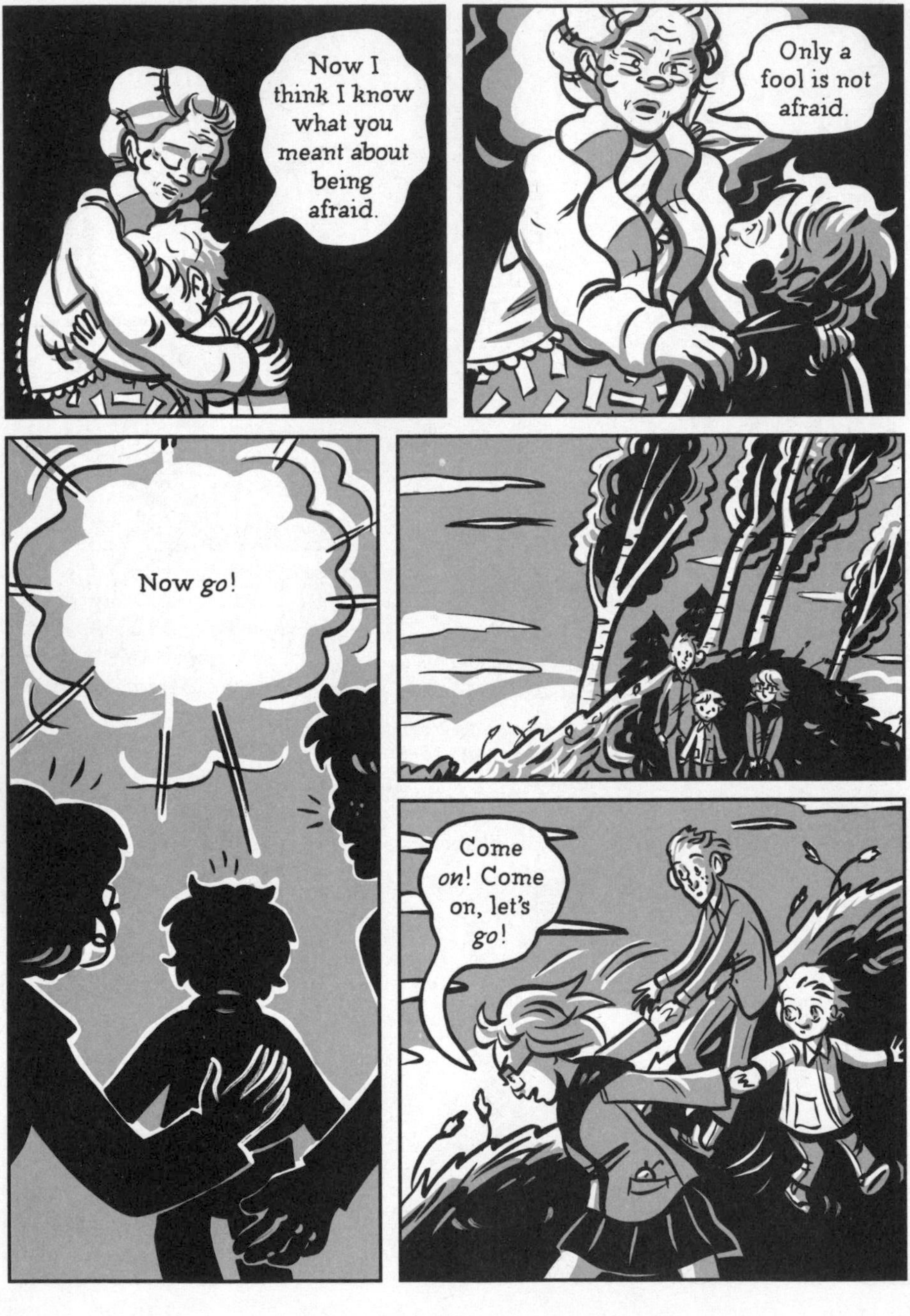
Now I think I know what you meant about being afraid.
Only a fool is not afraid.
Now *go*!
Come *on*! Come on, let's *go*!

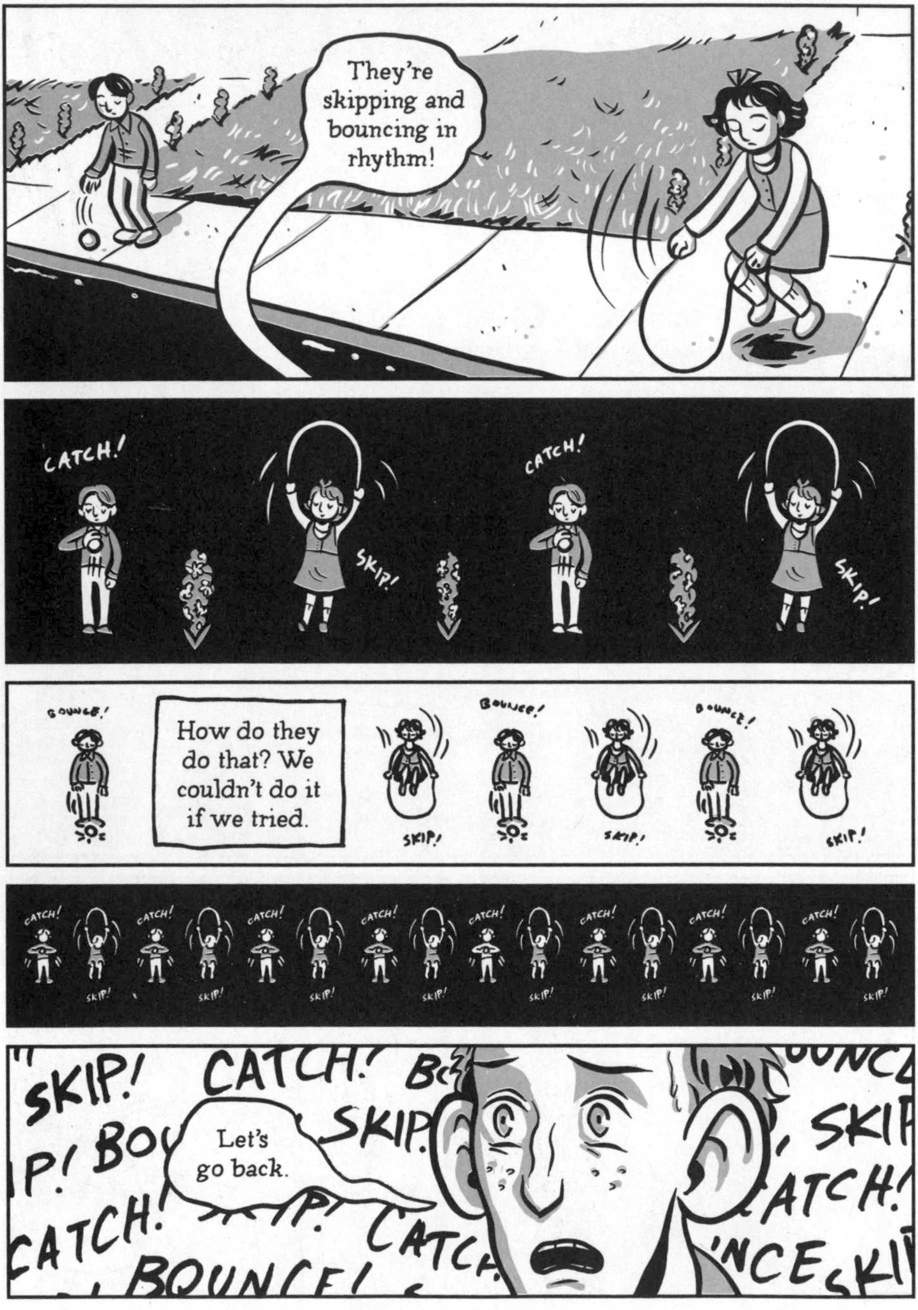

They're skipping and bouncing in rhythm!
CATCH!
SKIP!
CATCH!
SKIP!
BOUNCE!
How do they do that? We couldn't do it if we tried.
SKIP!
BOUNCE!
SKIP!
BOUNCE!
SKIP!
Let's go back.

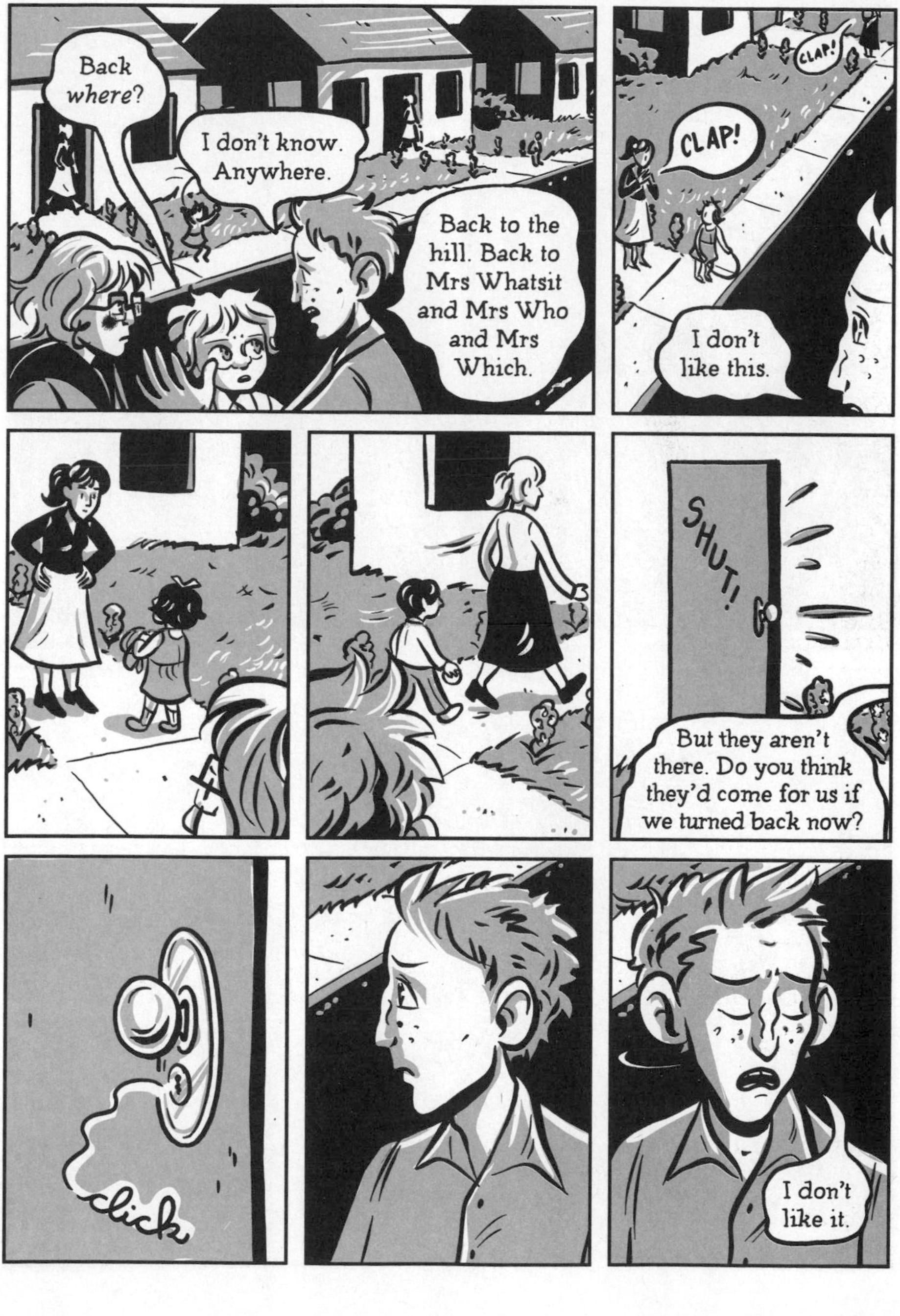
Back where?
I don't know. Anywhere.
Back to the hill. Back to Mrs Whatsit and Mrs Who and Mrs Which.
CLAP!
CLAP!
I don't like this.
SHUT!
But they aren't there. Do you think they'd come for us if we turned back now?
click
I don't like it.

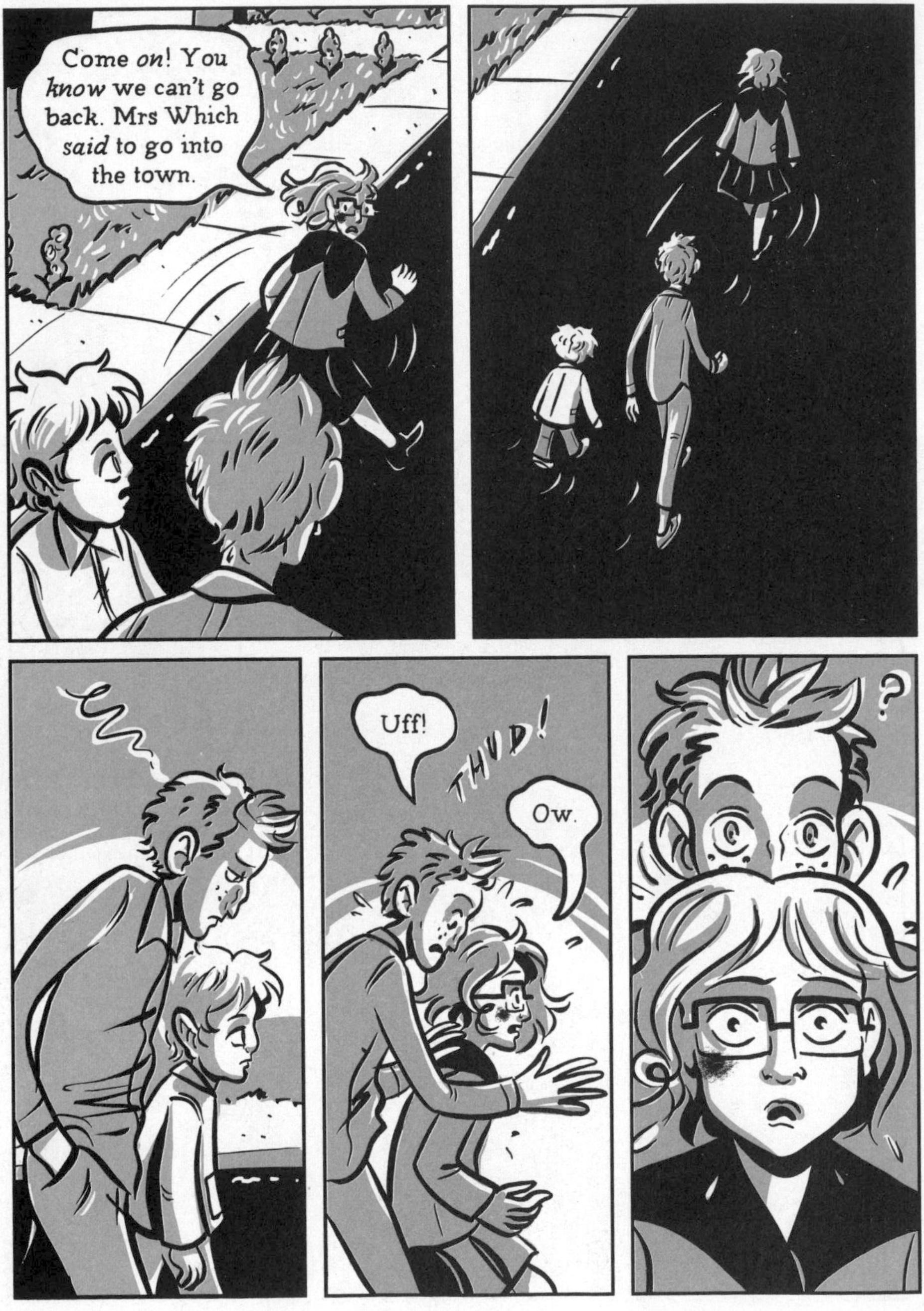

Come *on*! You *know* we can't go back. Mrs Which *said* to go into the town.
Uff!
THUD!
Ow.
?

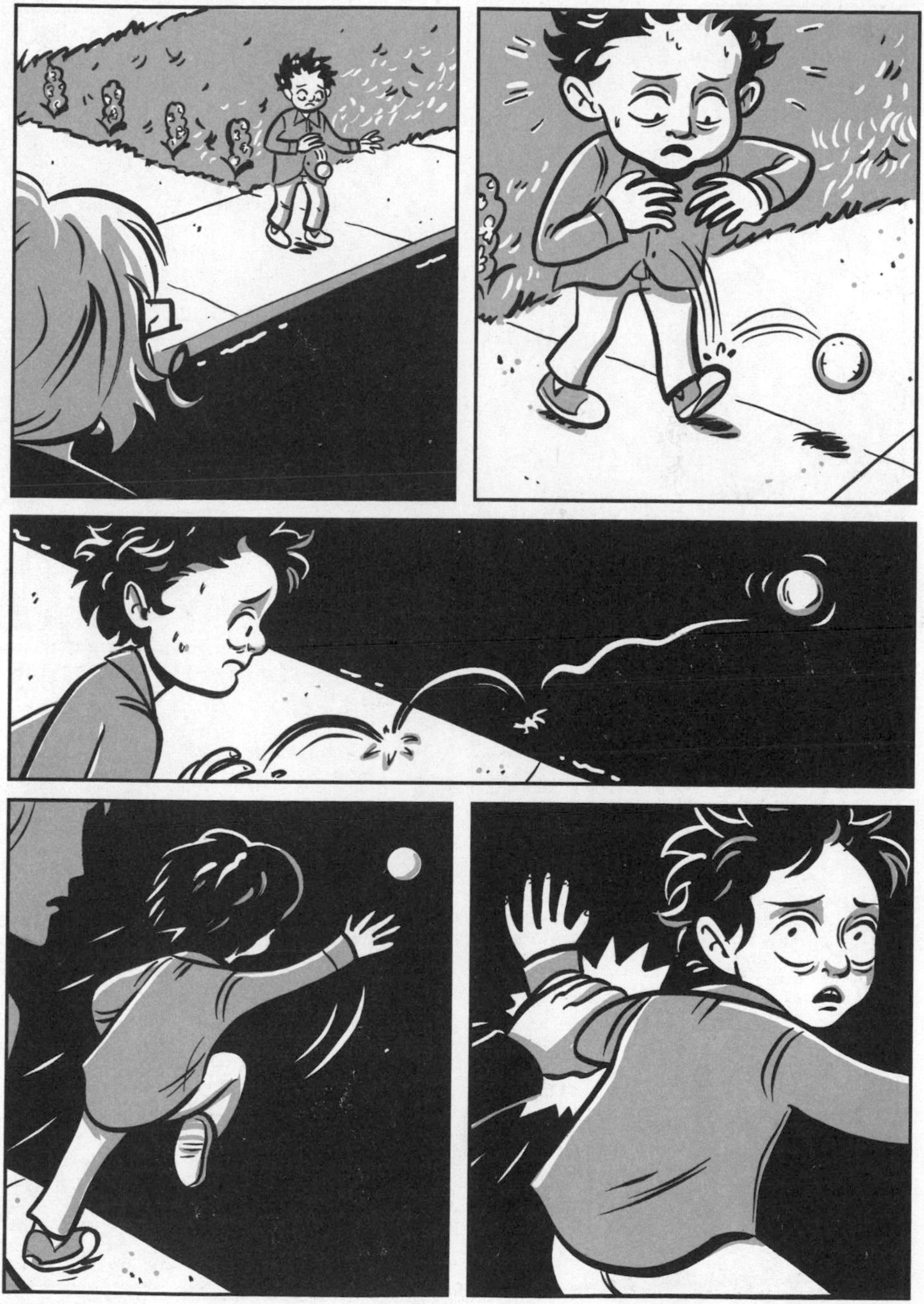

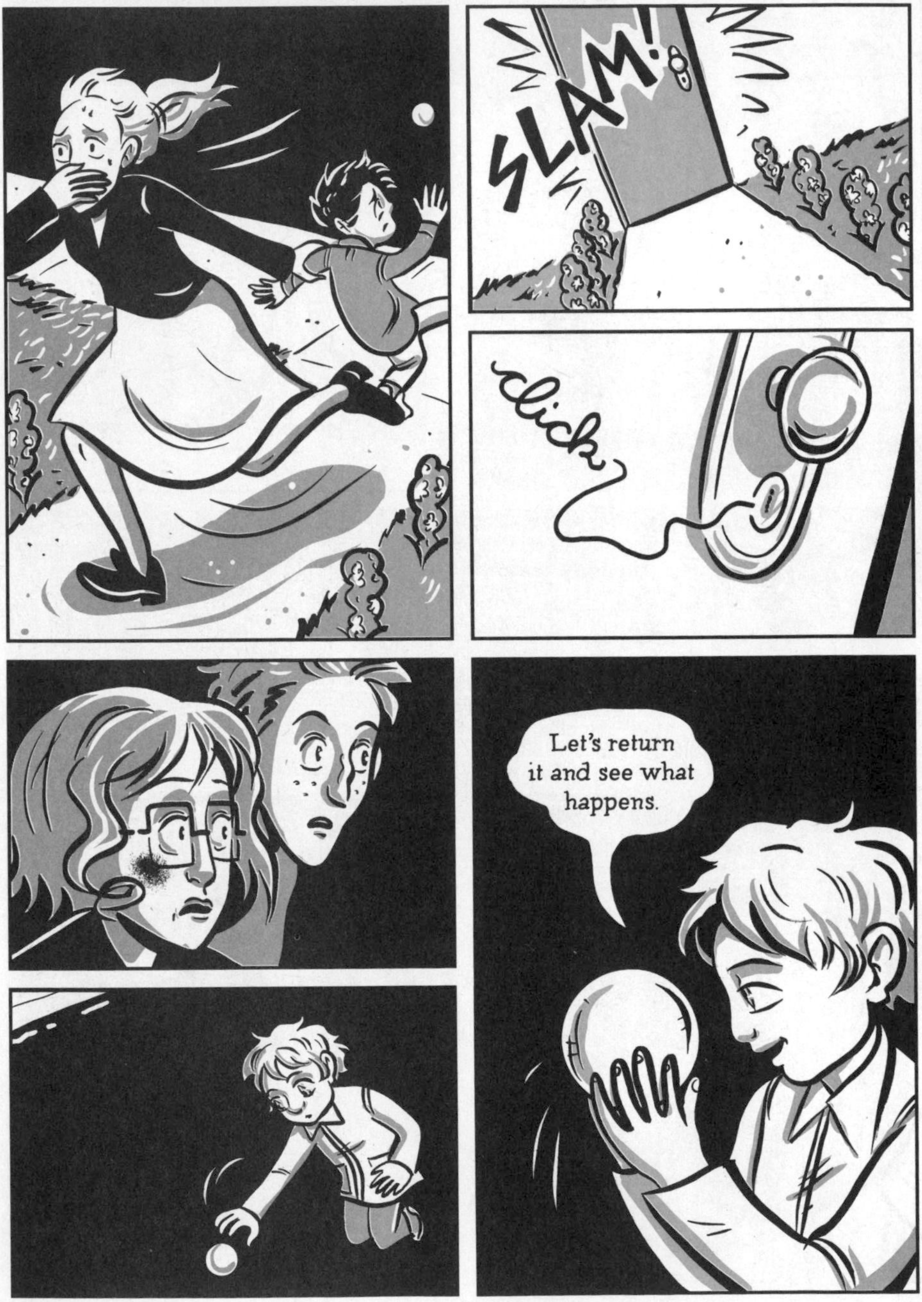
SLAM!
click
Let's return it and see what happens.

189

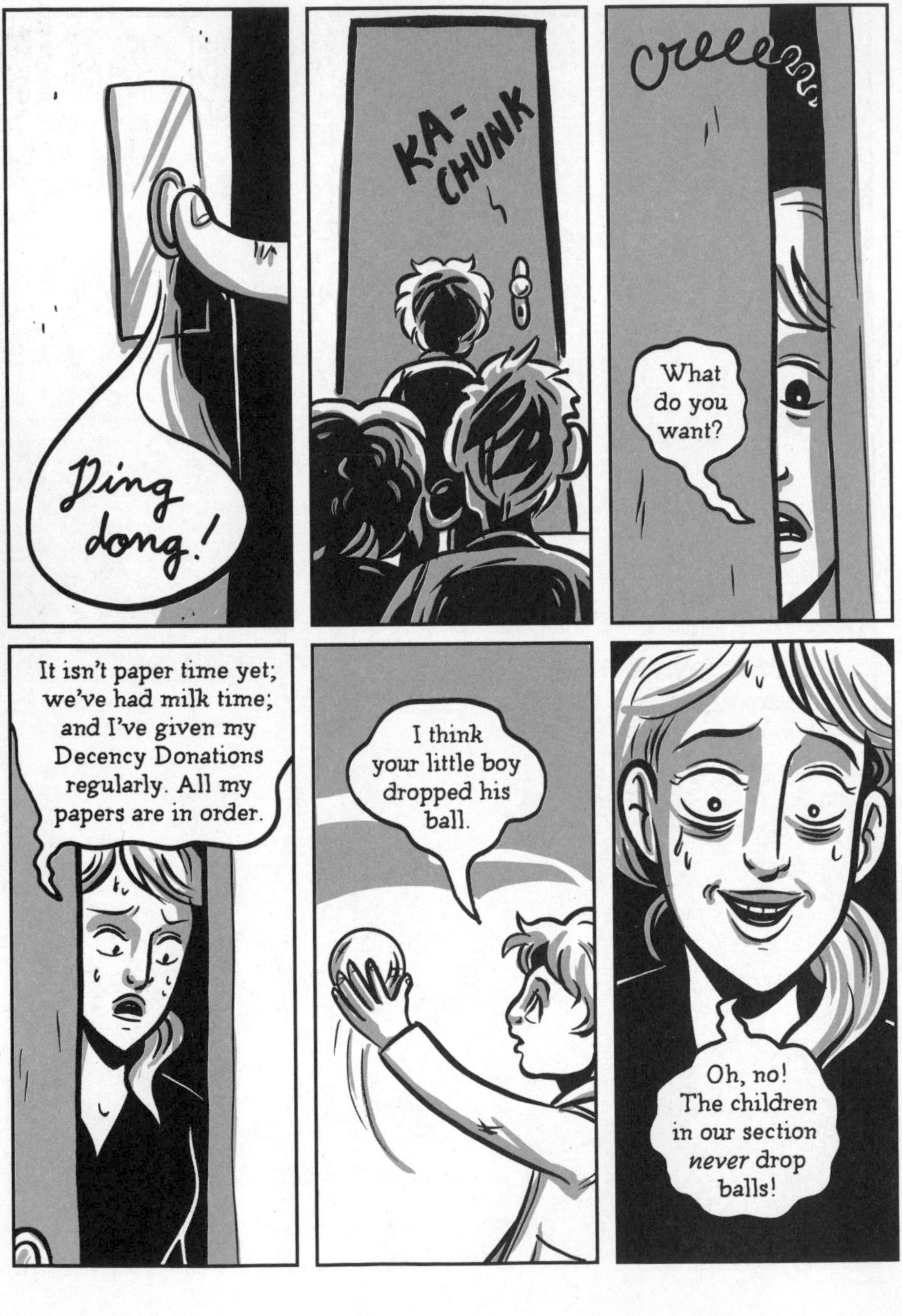
Ding dong!
KA-CHUNK
Creeeee
What do you want?
It isn't paper time yet; we've had milk time; and I've given my Decency Donations regularly. All my papers are in order.
I think your little boy dropped his ball.
Oh, no! The children in our section *never* drop balls!

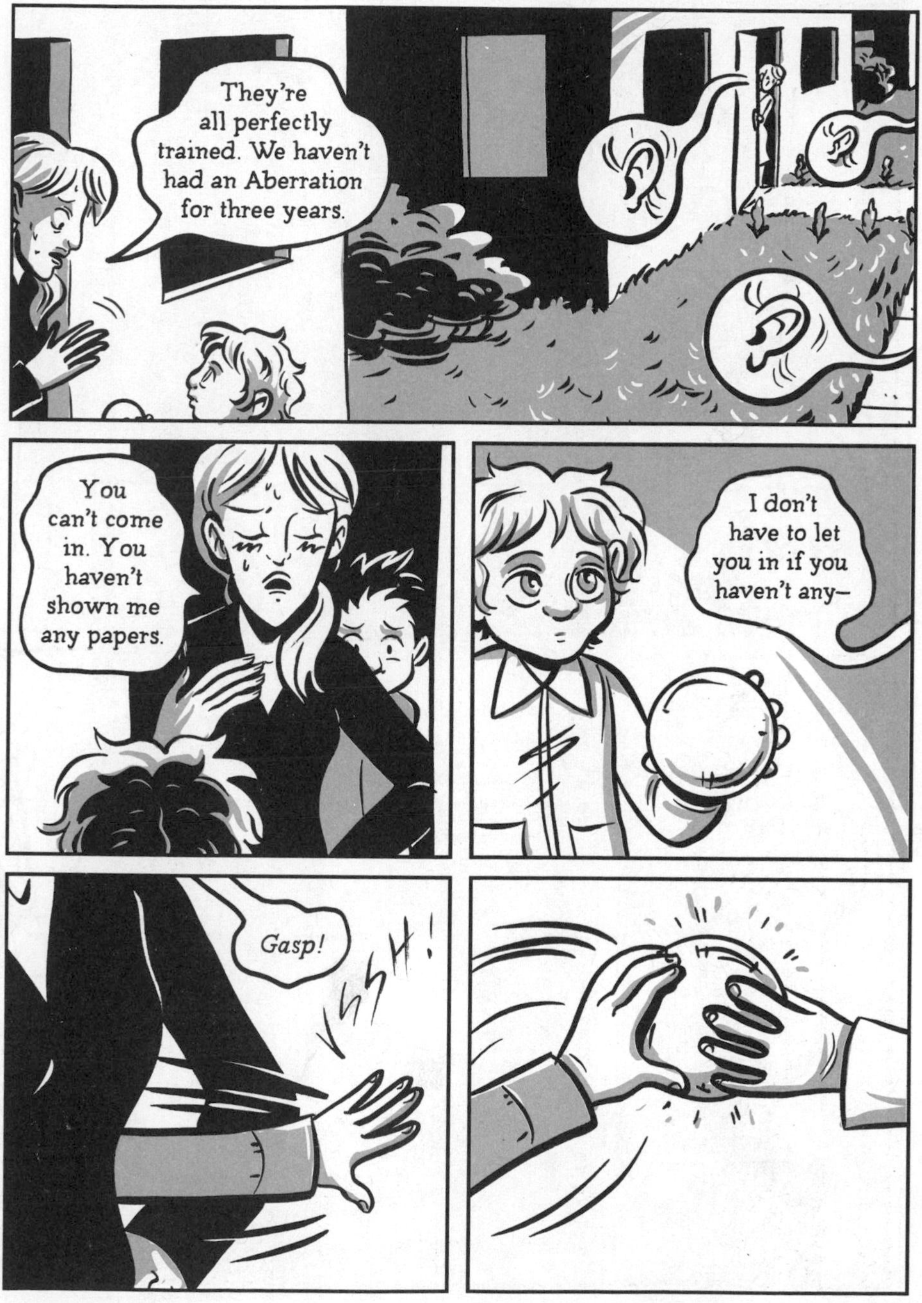
They're all perfectly trained. We haven't had an Aberration for three years.
You can't come in. You haven't shown me any papers.
I don't have to let you in if you haven't any—
Gasp!
SSH!

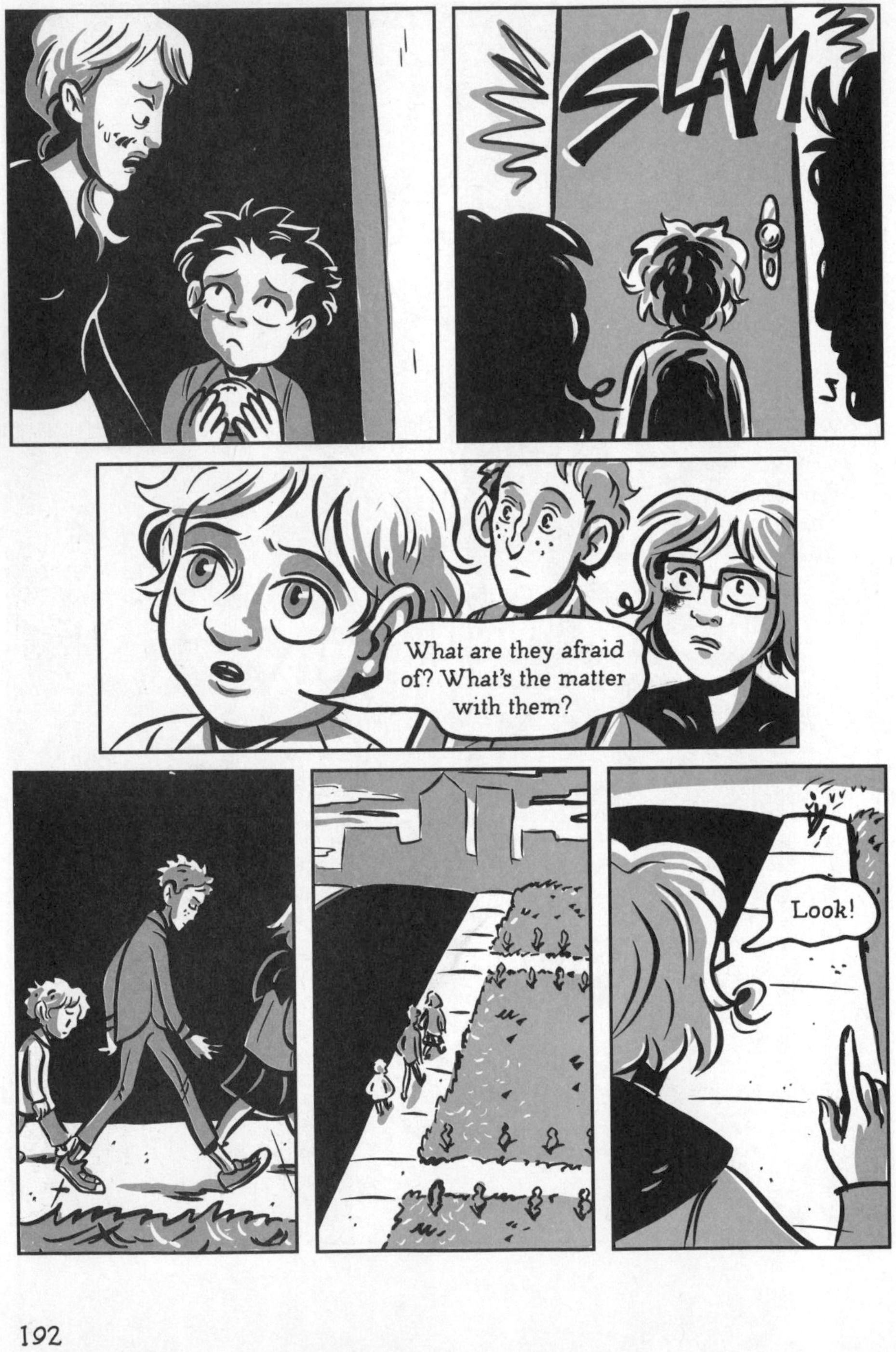
SLAM
What are they afraid of? What's the matter with them?
Look!

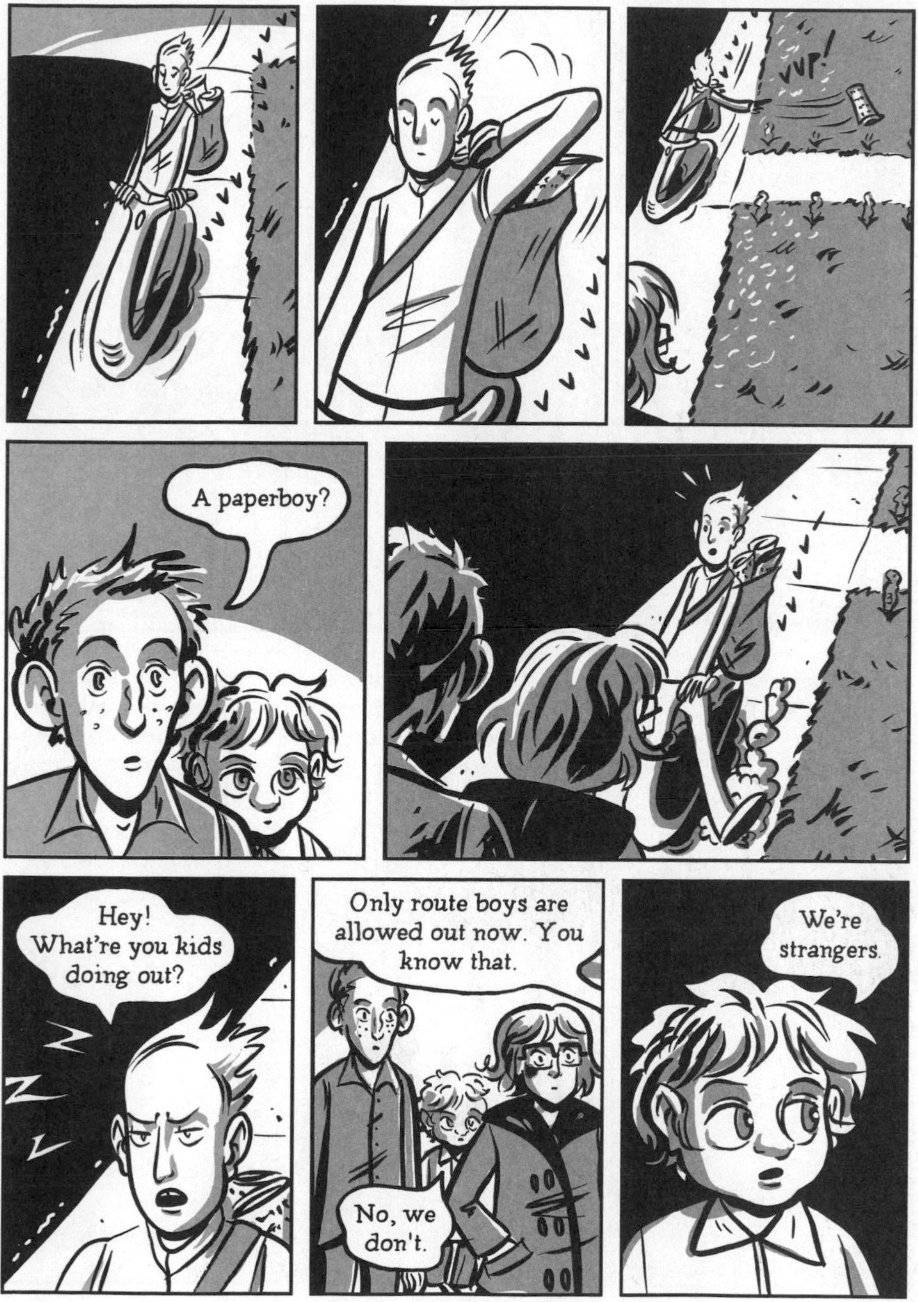
VVP!
A paperboy?
Hey!
What're you kids doing out?
Only route boys are allowed out now. You know that.
No, we don't.
We're strangers.

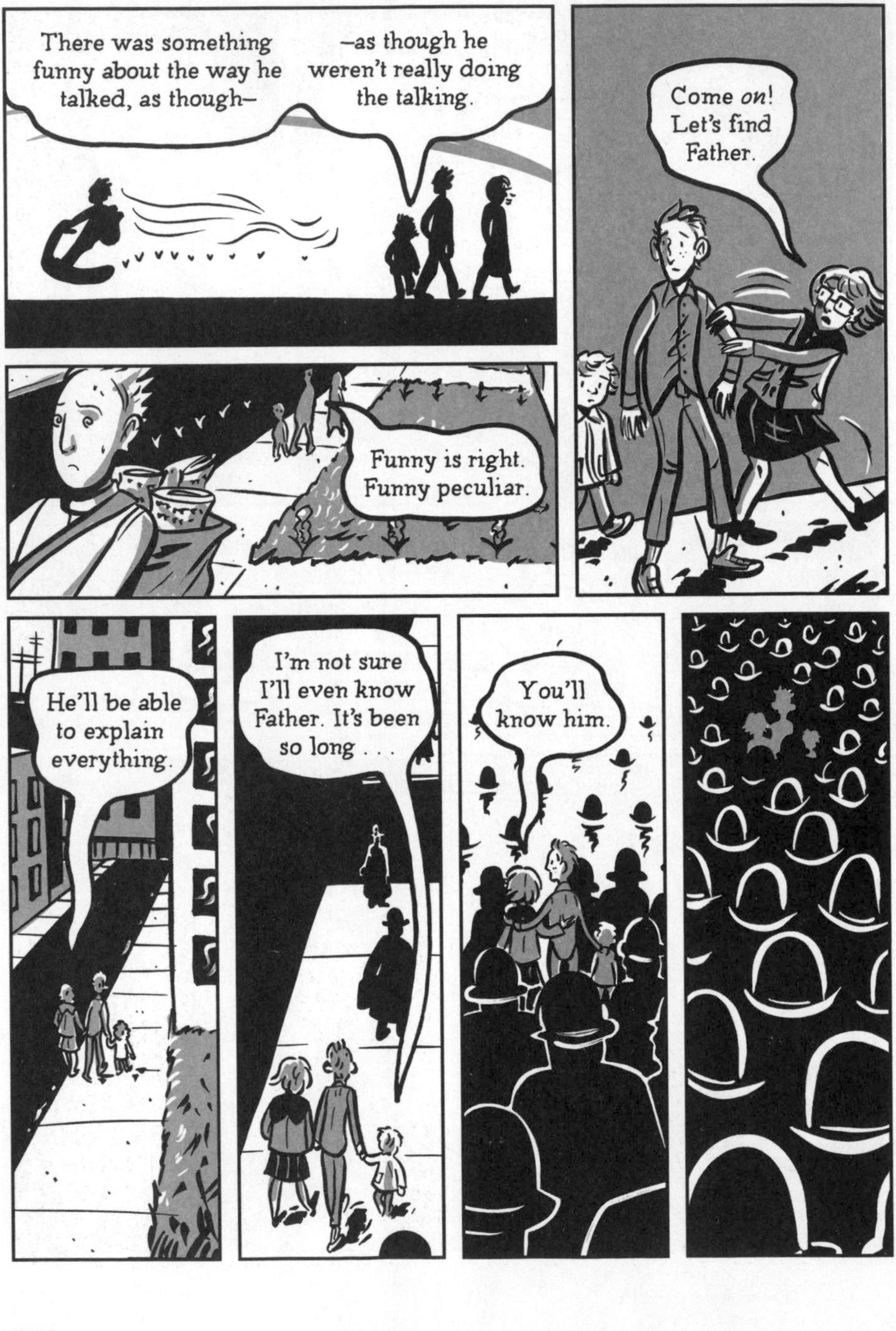
There was something funny about the way he talked, as though–
–as though he weren't really doing the talking.
Come *on*! Let's find Father.
Funny is right. Funny peculiar.
He'll be able to explain everything.
I'm not sure I'll even know Father. It's been so long . . .
You'll know him.

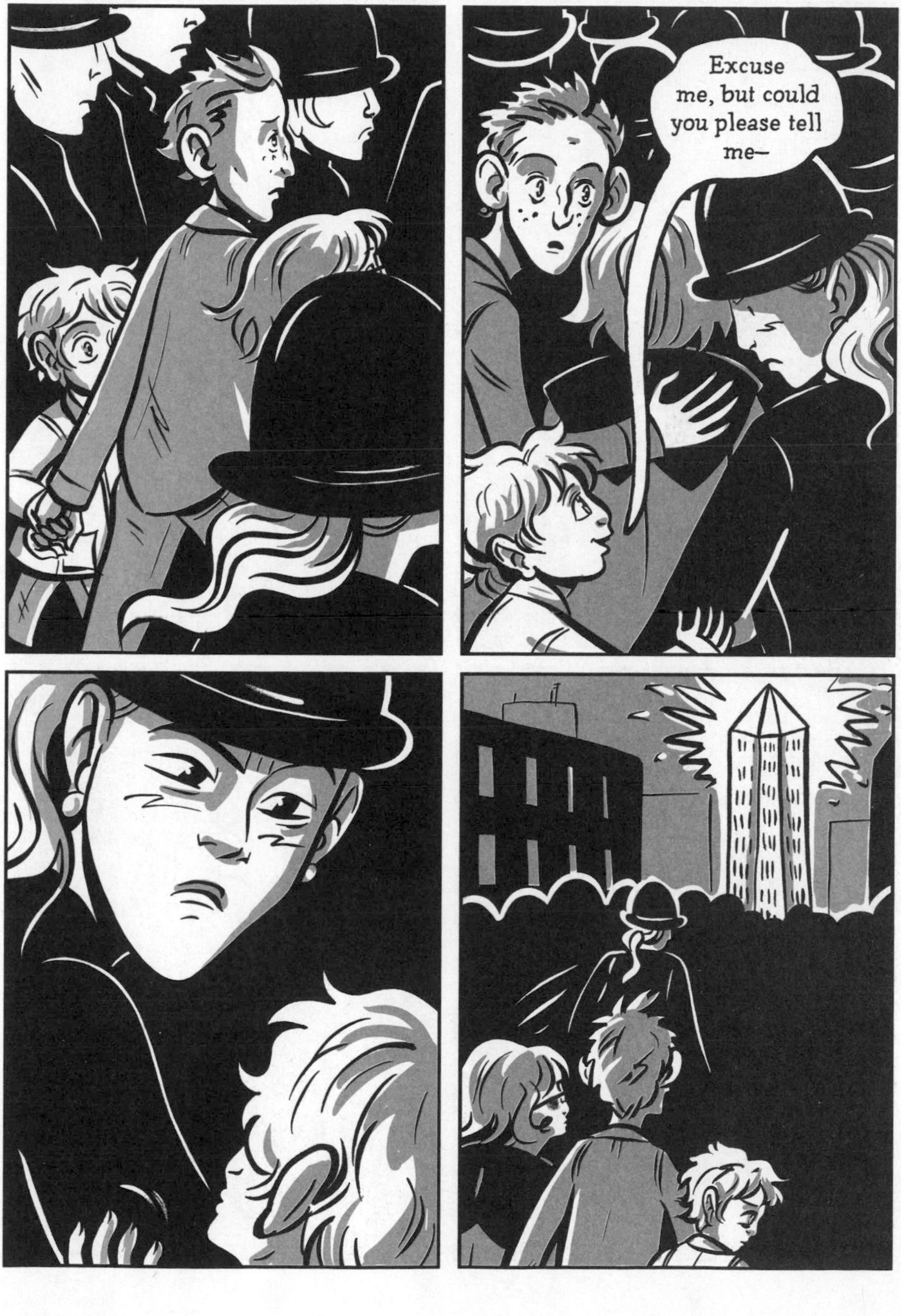
Excuse me, but could you please tell me–

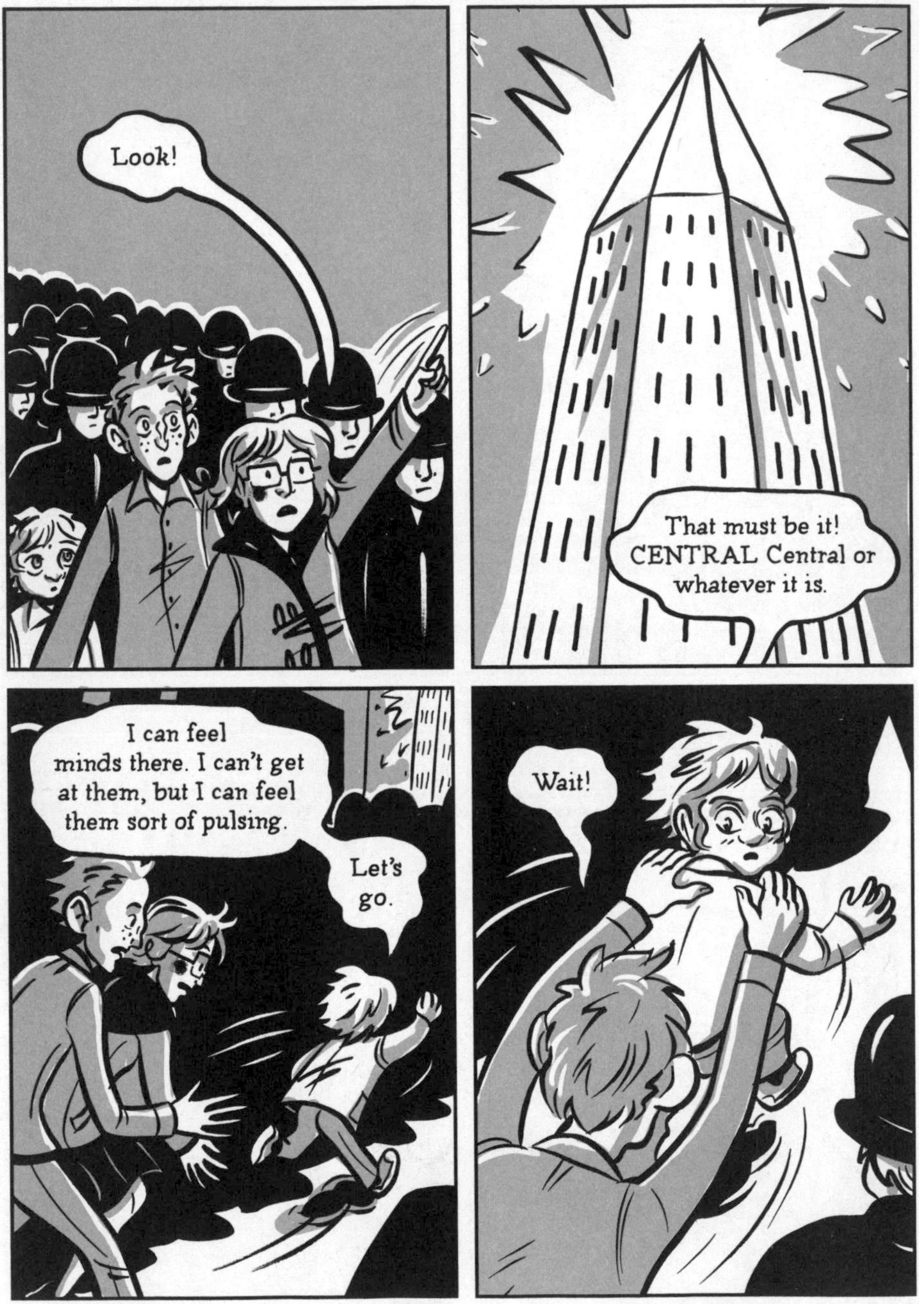
Look!
That must be it! CENTRAL Central or whatever it is.
I can feel minds there. I can't get at them, but I can feel them sort of pulsing.
Let's go.
Wait!

7
The Man with Red Eyes

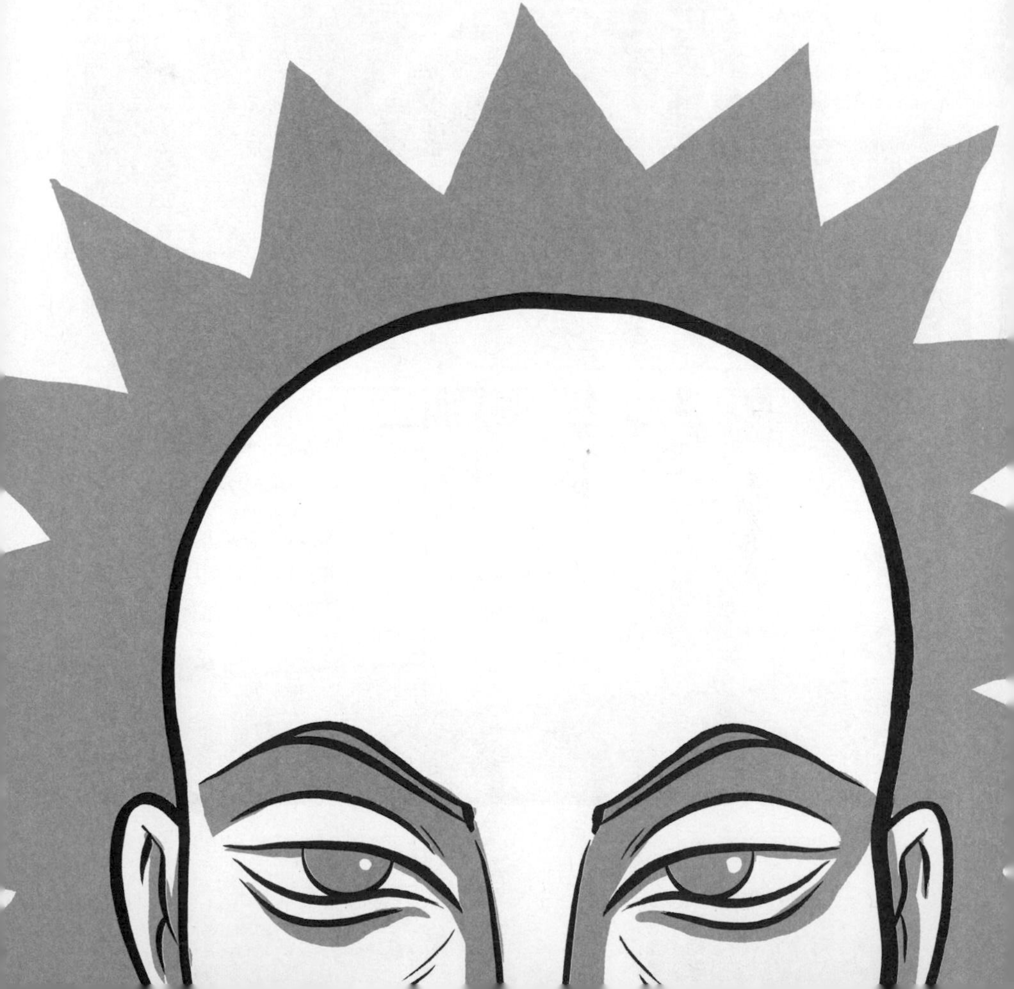

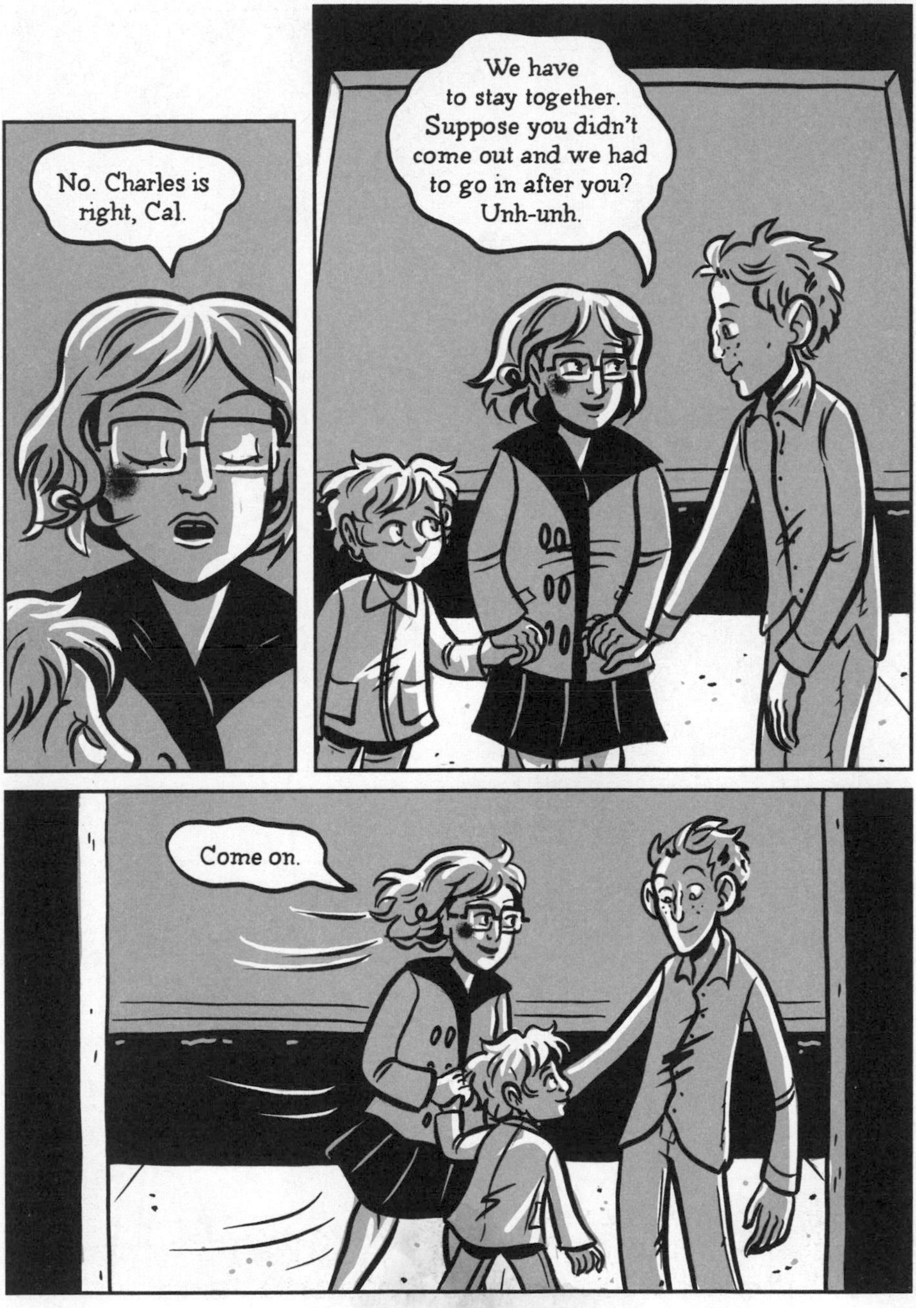
No. Charles is right, Cal.
We have to stay together. Suppose you didn't come out and we had to go in after you? Unh-unh.
Come on.

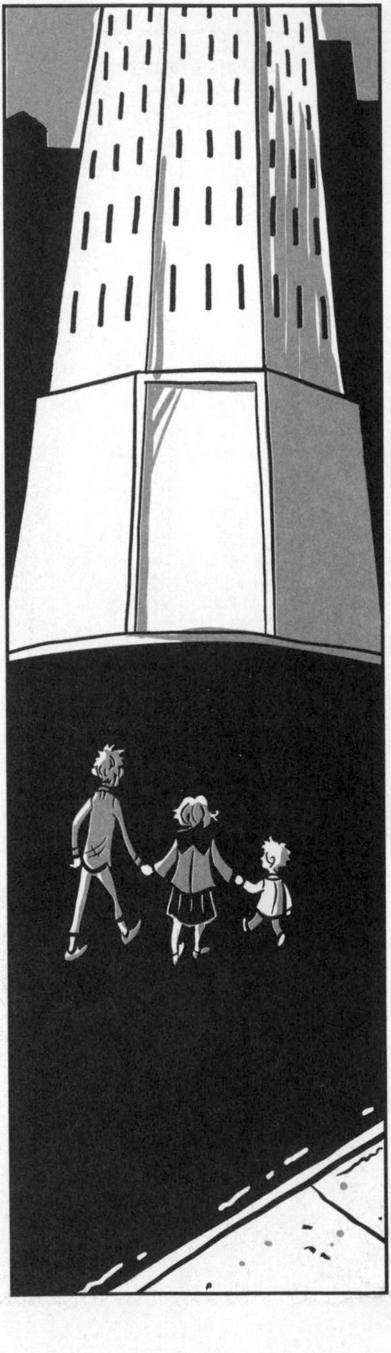

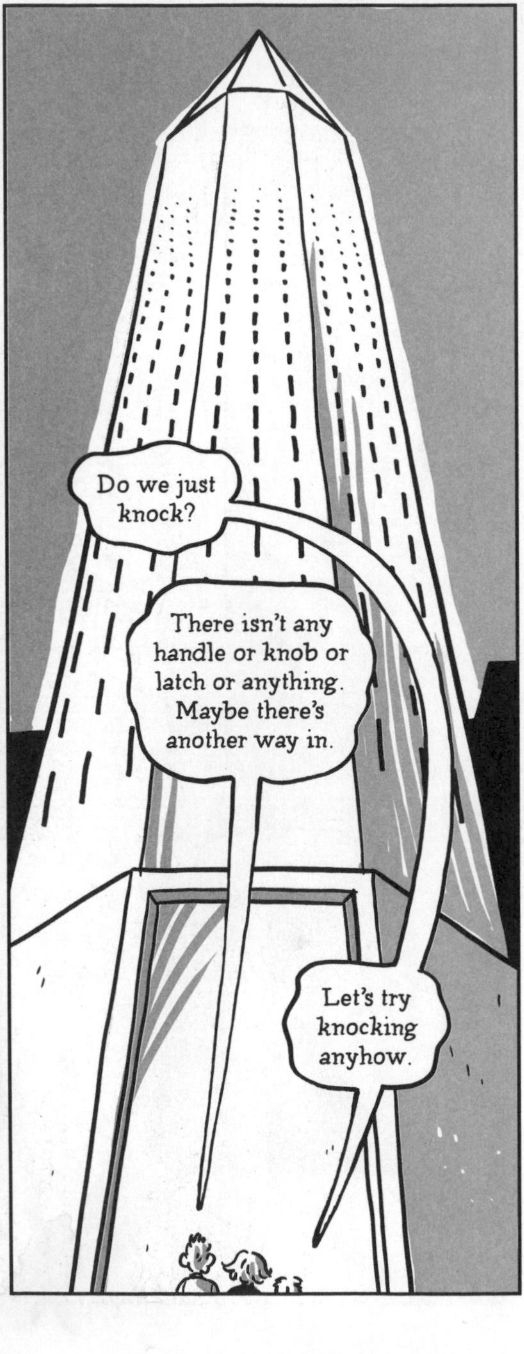
Do we just knock?
There isn't any handle or knob or latch or anything. Maybe there's another way in.
Let's try knocking anyhow.

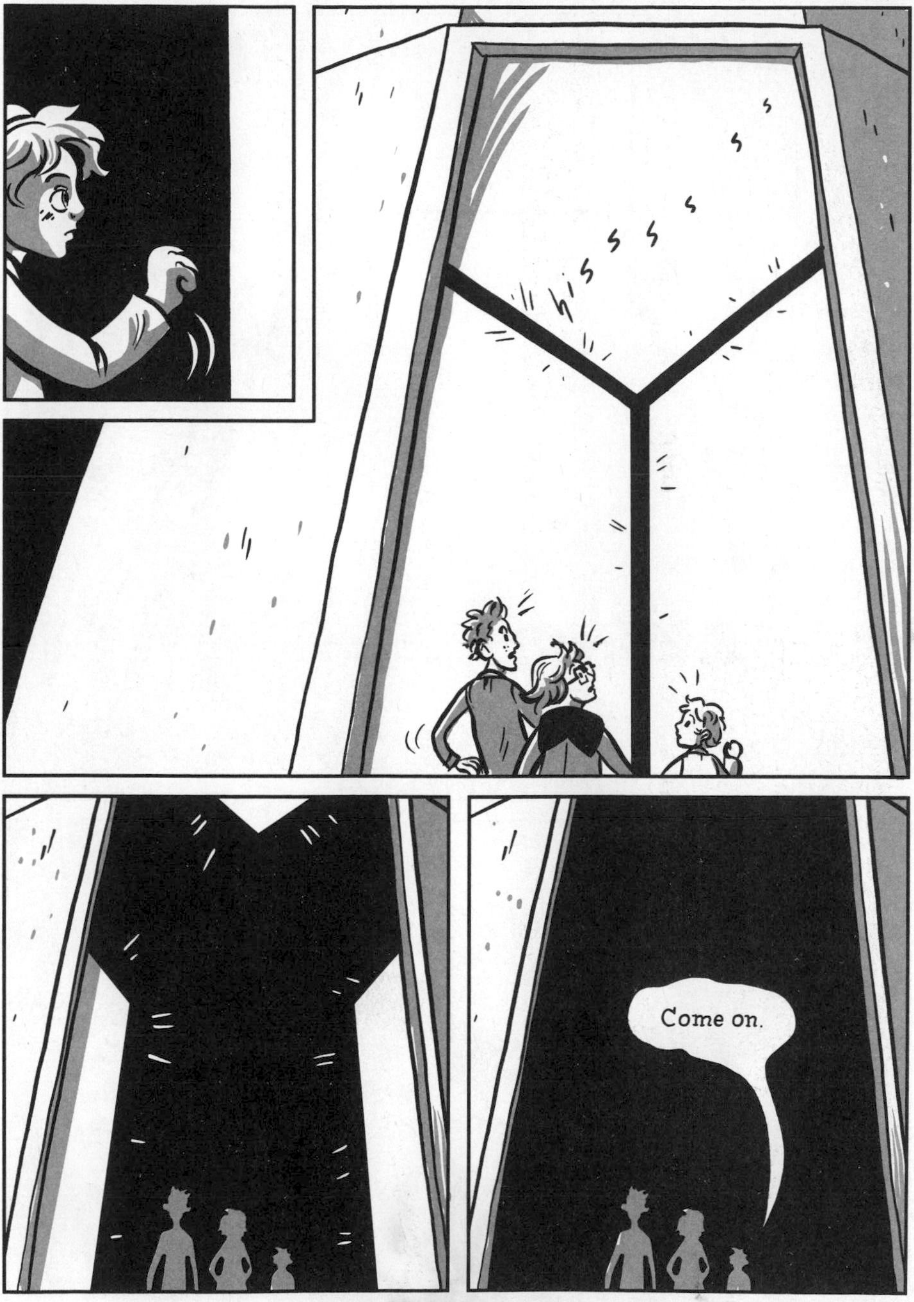
hissss
Come on.

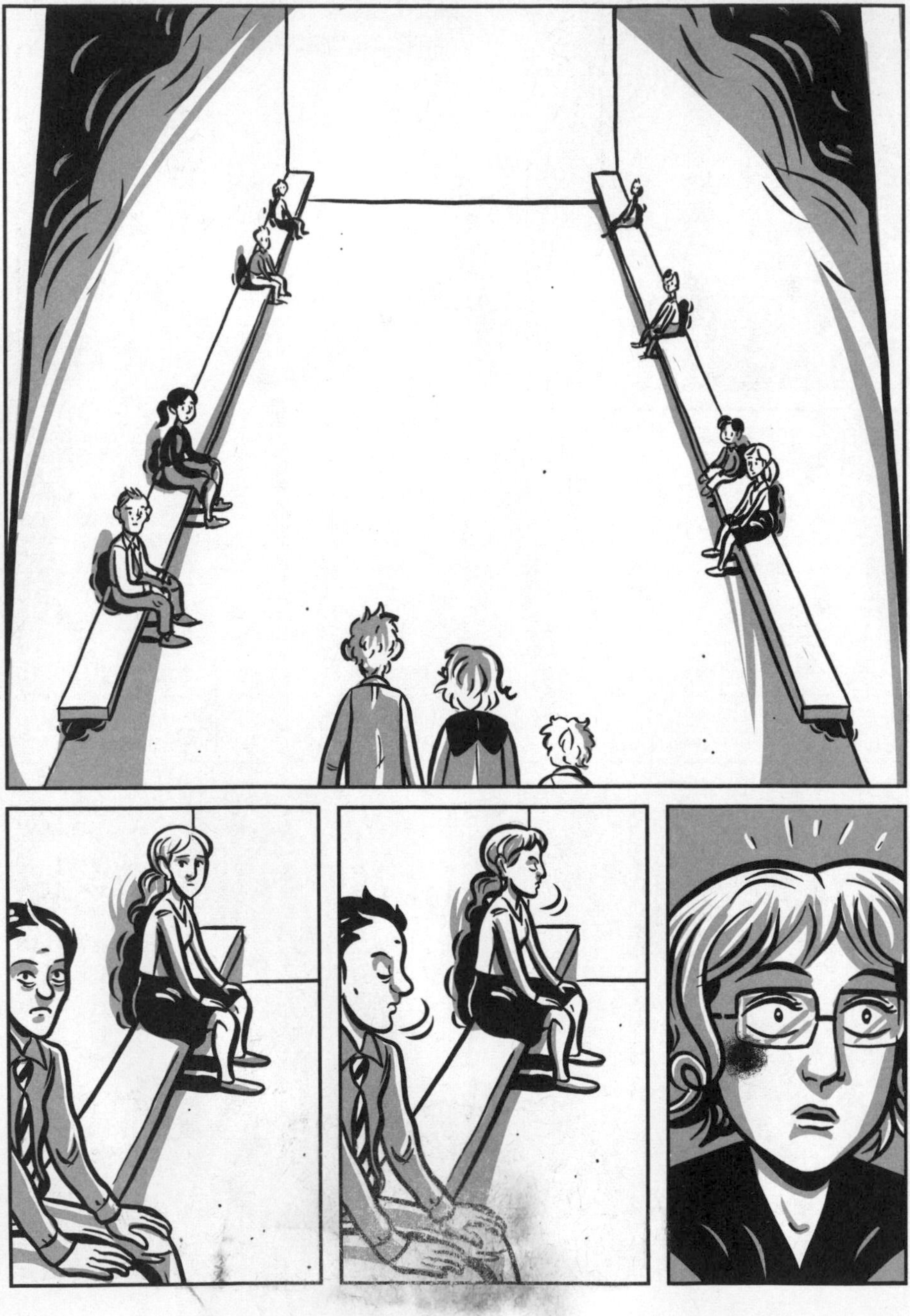

211

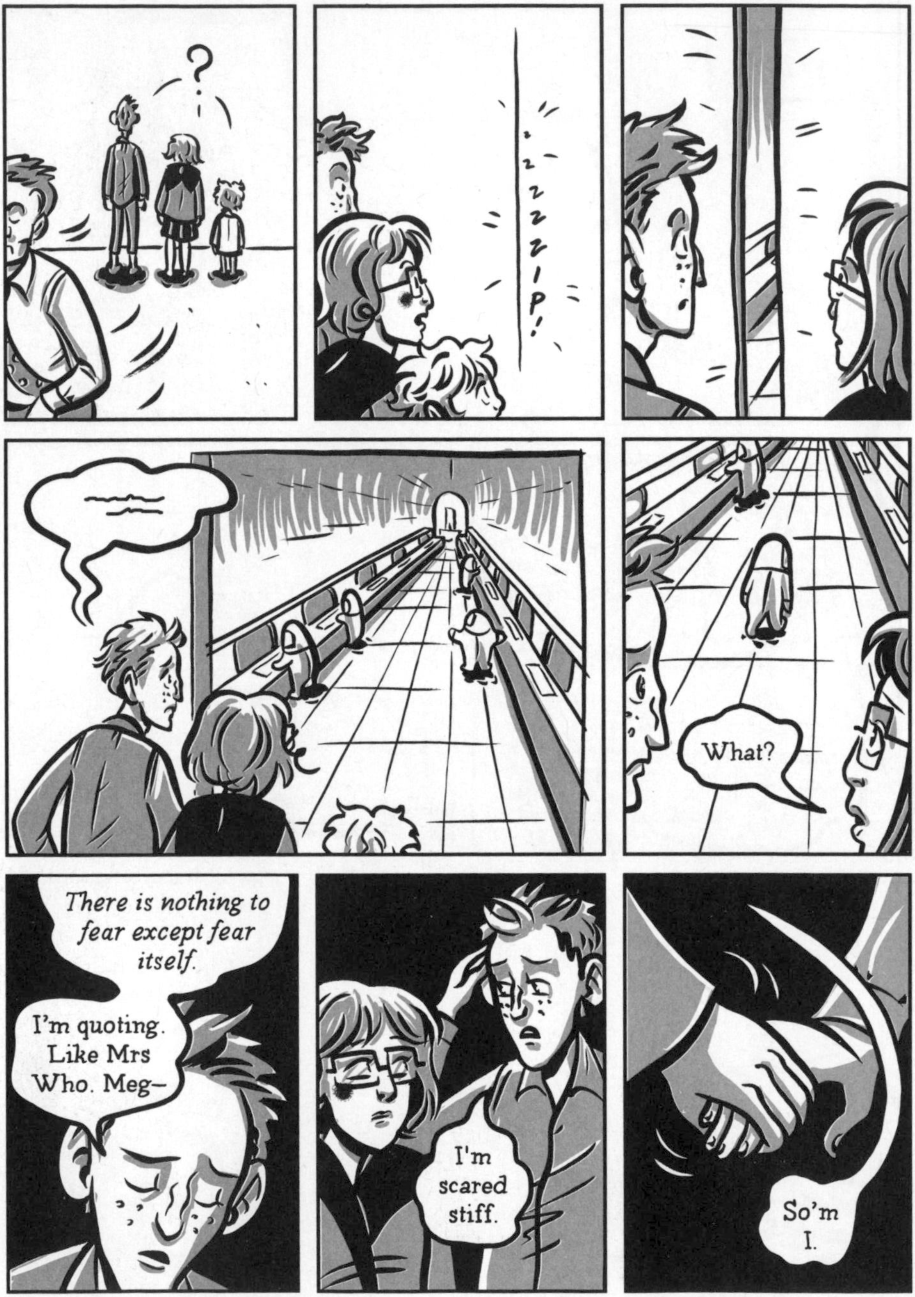
?
ZZZZIP!
What?
There is nothing to fear except fear itself.
I'm quoting. Like Mrs Who. Meg–
I'm scared stiff.
So'm I.

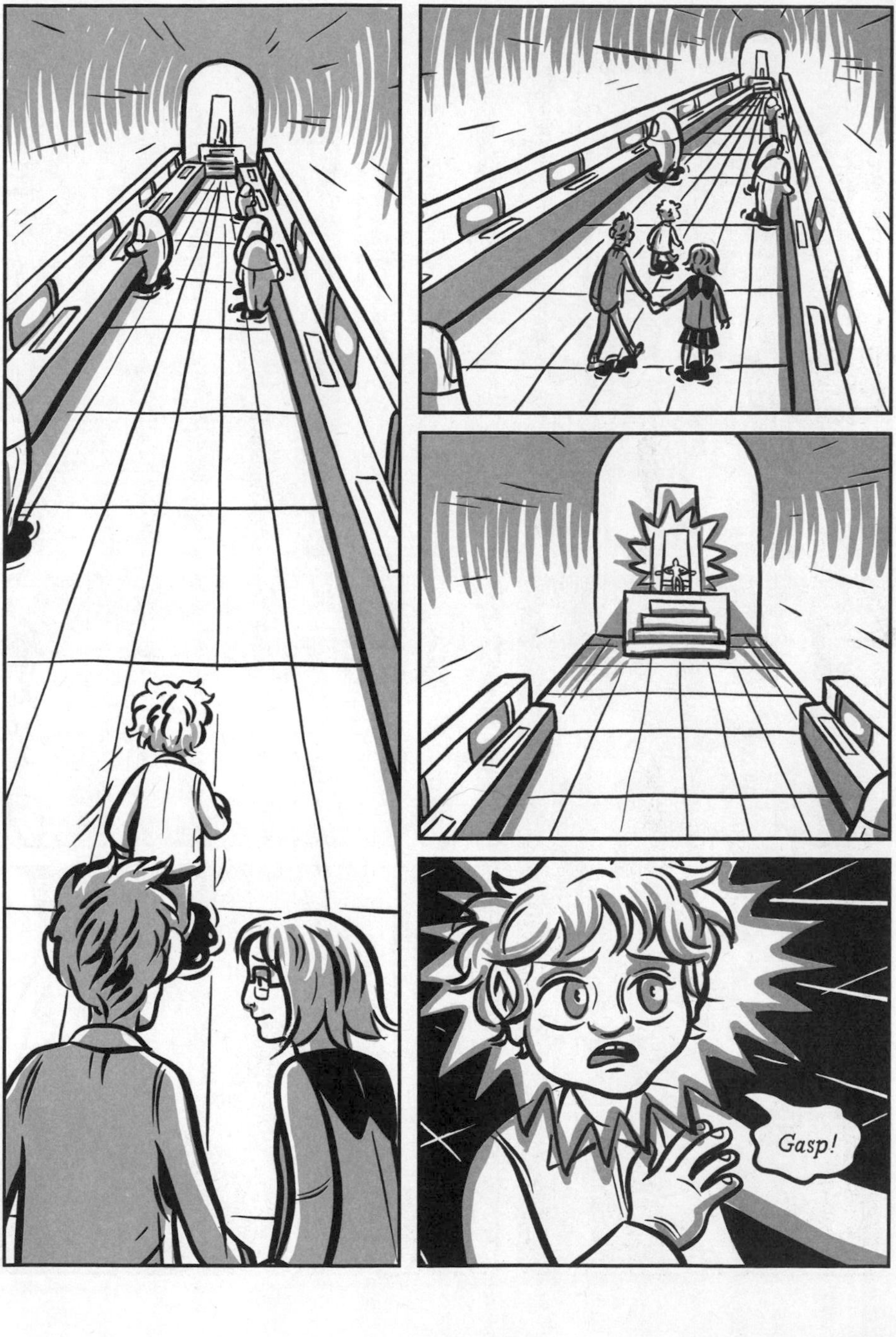
Gasp!

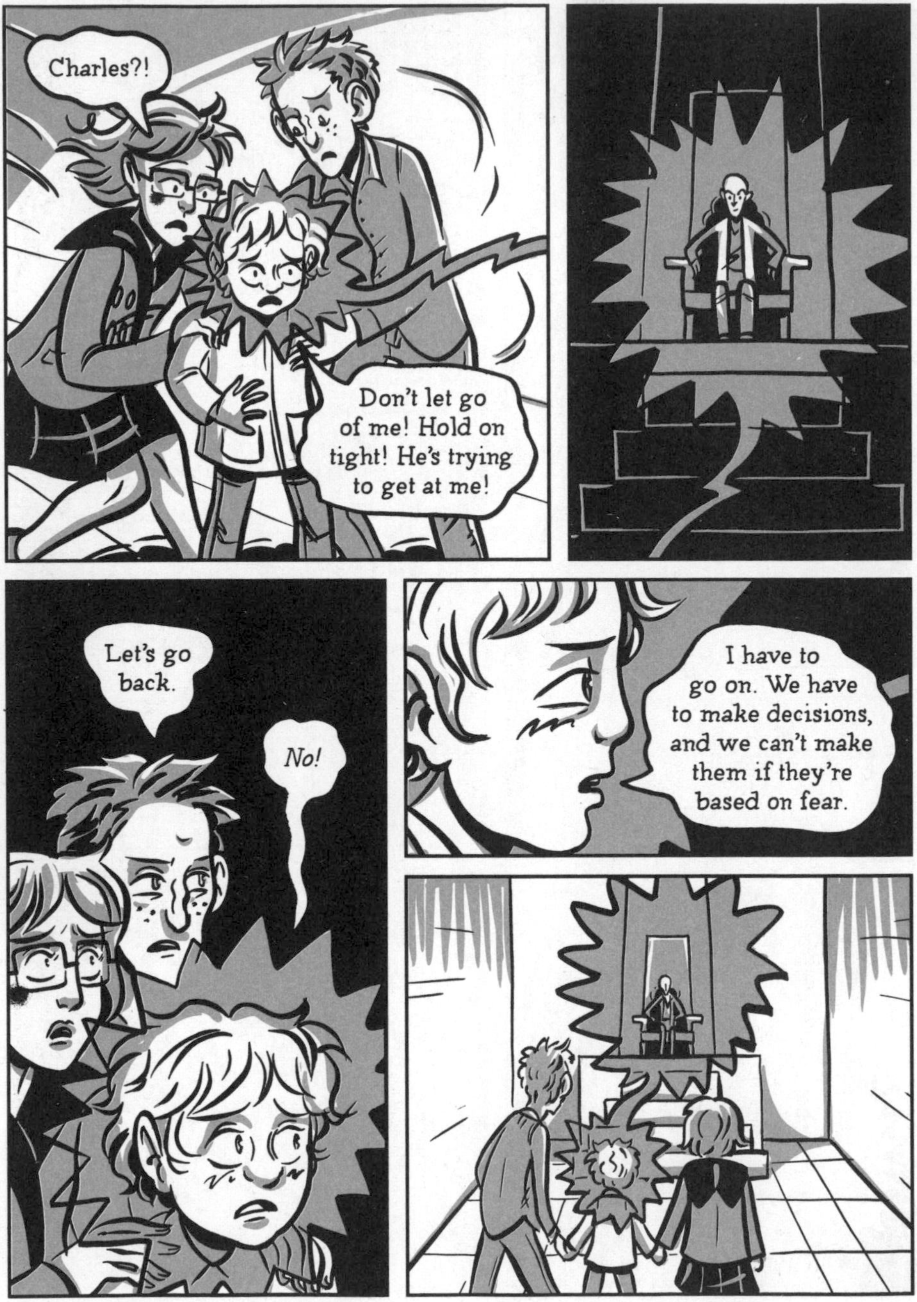
Charles?!
Don't let go of me! Hold on tight! He's trying to get at me!
Let's go back.
No!
I have to go on. We have to make decisions, and we can't make them if they're based on fear.

215

217

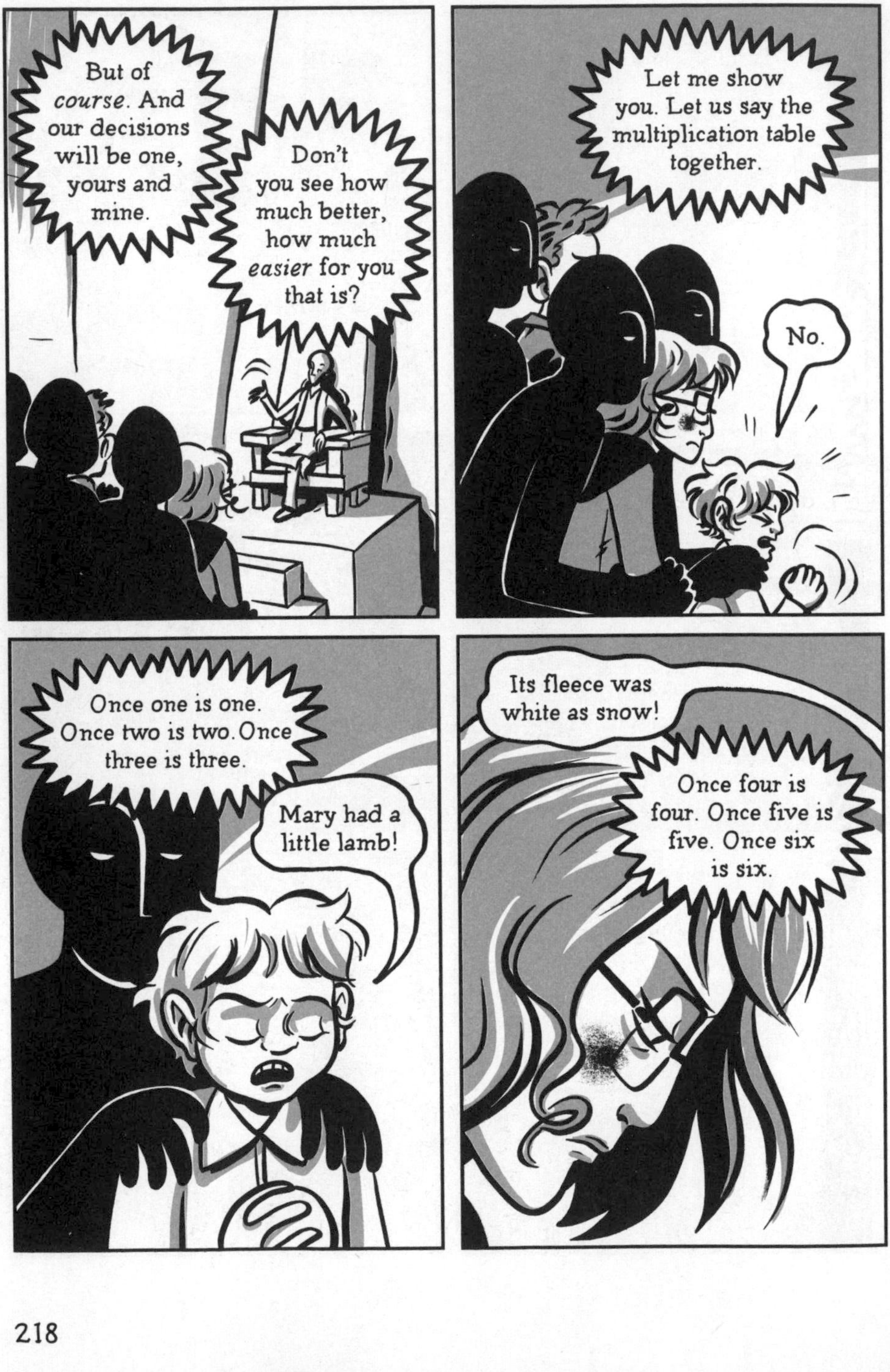
But of *course*. And our decisions will be one, yours and mine.
Don't you see how much better, how much *easier* for you that is?
Let me show you. Let us say the multiplication table together.
No.
Once one is one. Once two is two. Once three is three.
Mary had a little lamb!
Its fleece was white as snow!
Once four is four. Once five is five. Once six is six.

219

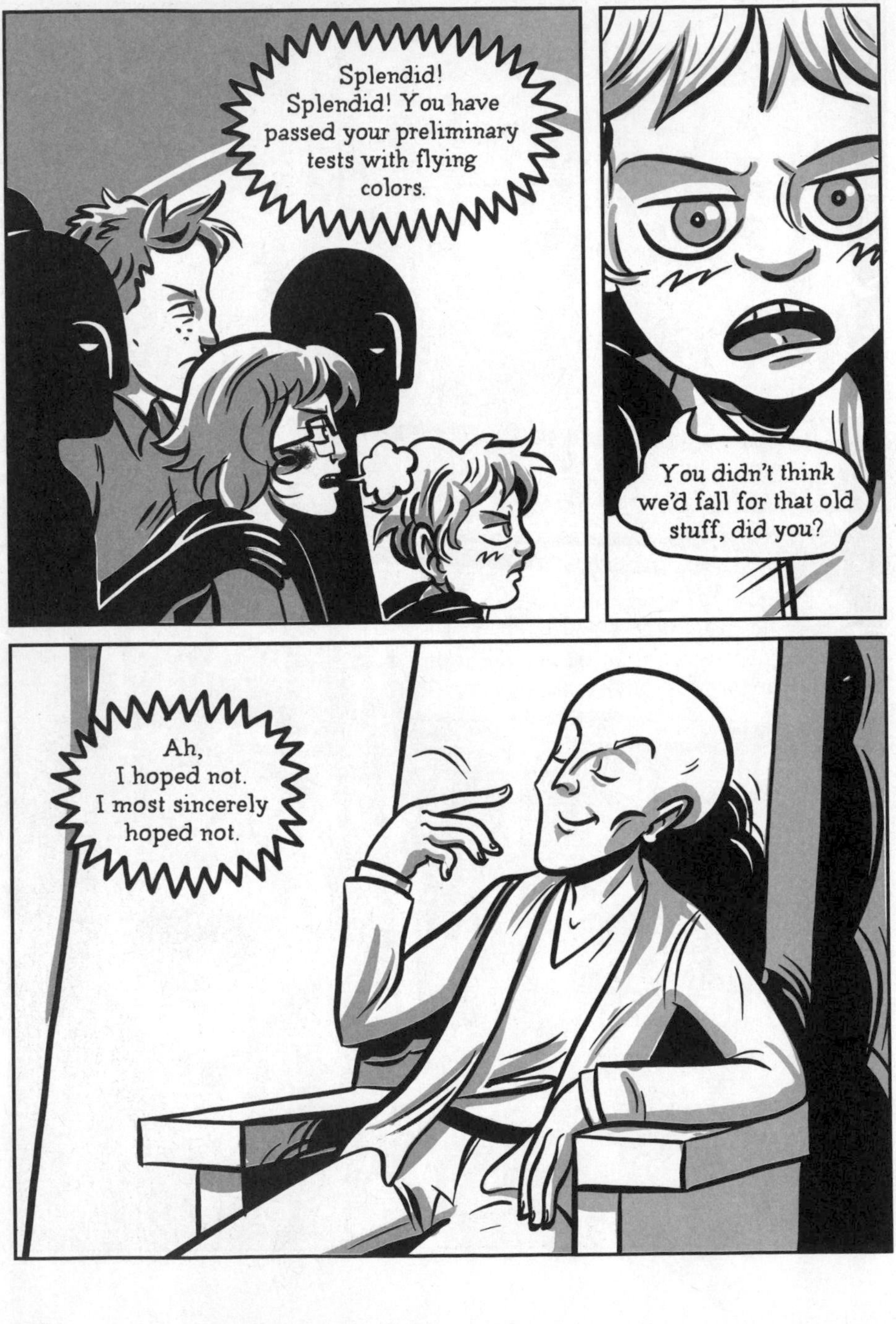
Splendid! Splendid! You have passed your preliminary tests with flying colors.
You didn't think we'd fall for that old stuff, did you?
Ah, I hoped not. I most sincerely hoped not.

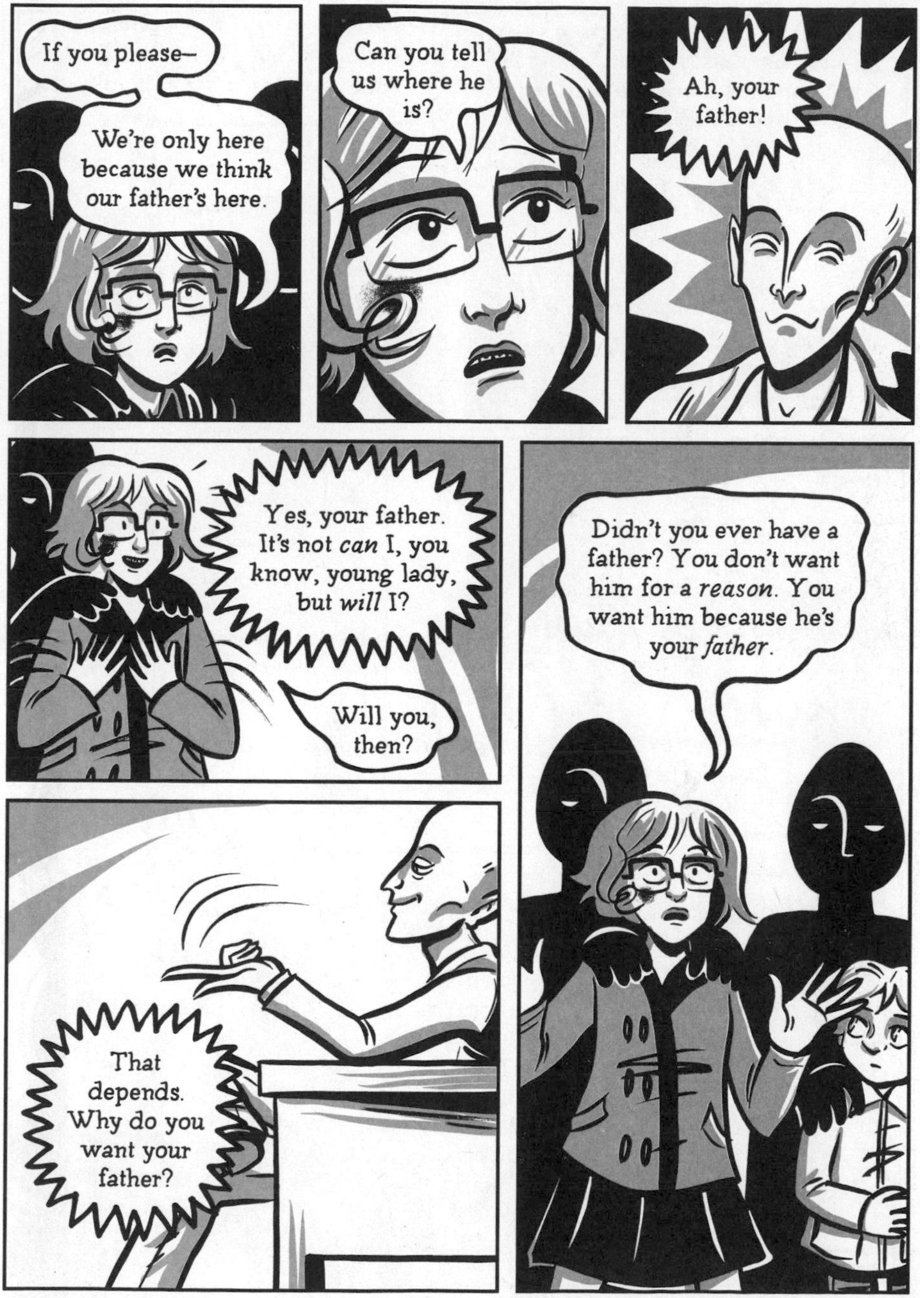

If you please—
We're only here because we think our father's here.
Can you tell us where he is?
Ah, your father!
Yes, your father. It's not *can* I, you know, young lady, but *will* I?
Will you, then?
That depends. Why do you want your father?
Didn't you ever have a father? You don't want him for a *reason*. You want him because he's your *father*.

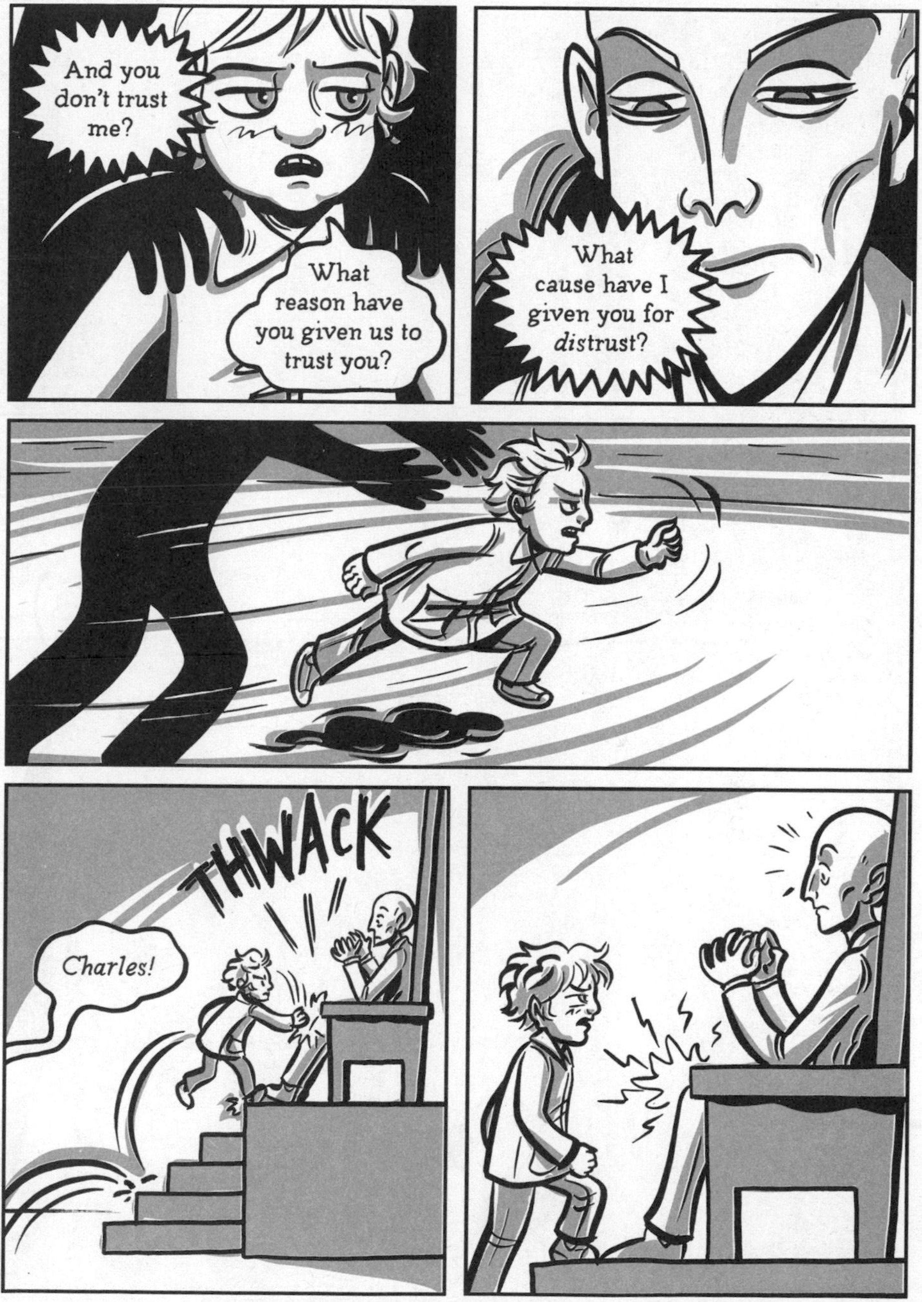
And you don't trust me?
What reason have you given us to trust you?
What cause have I given you for *dis*trust?
THWACK
Charles!

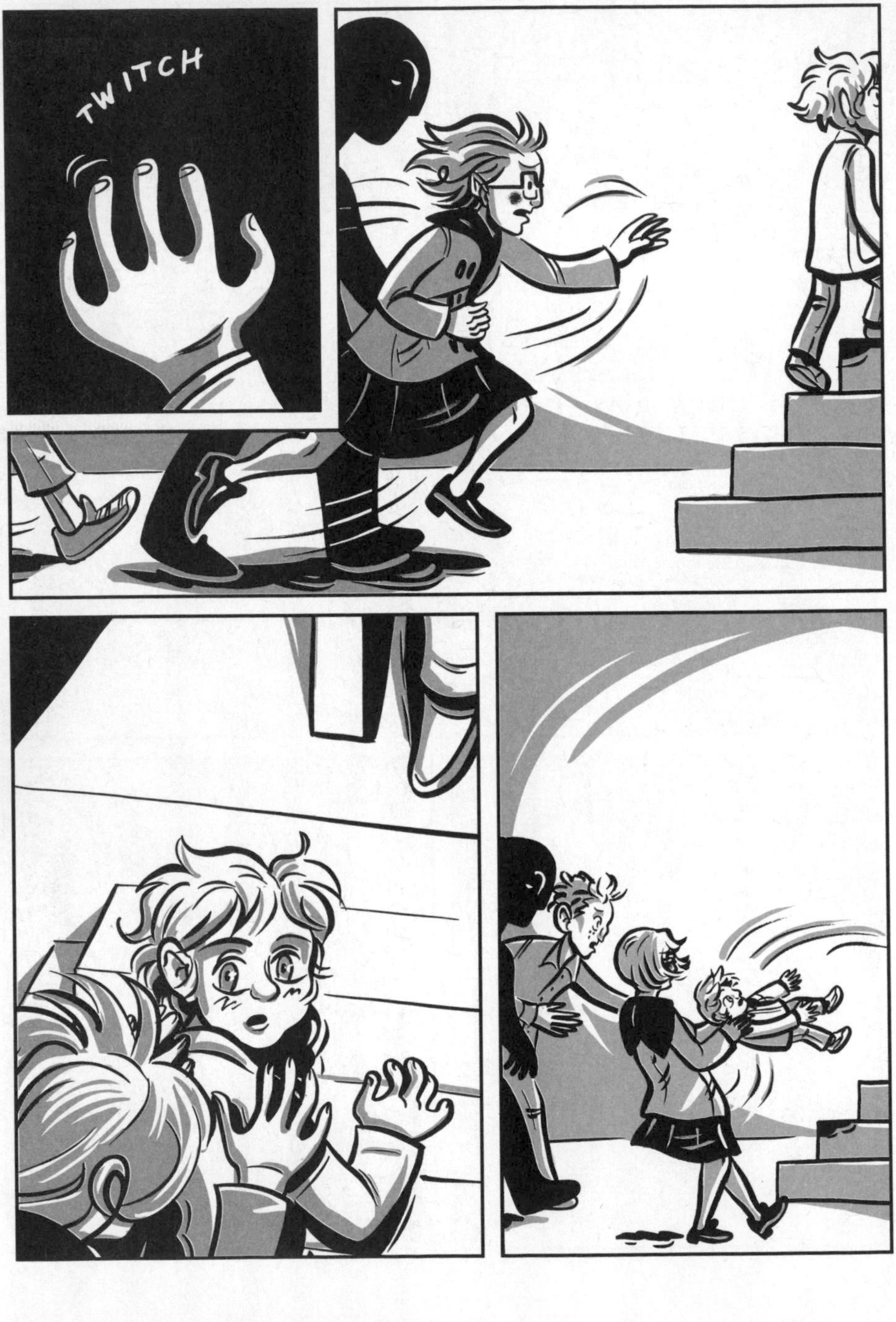
TWITCH

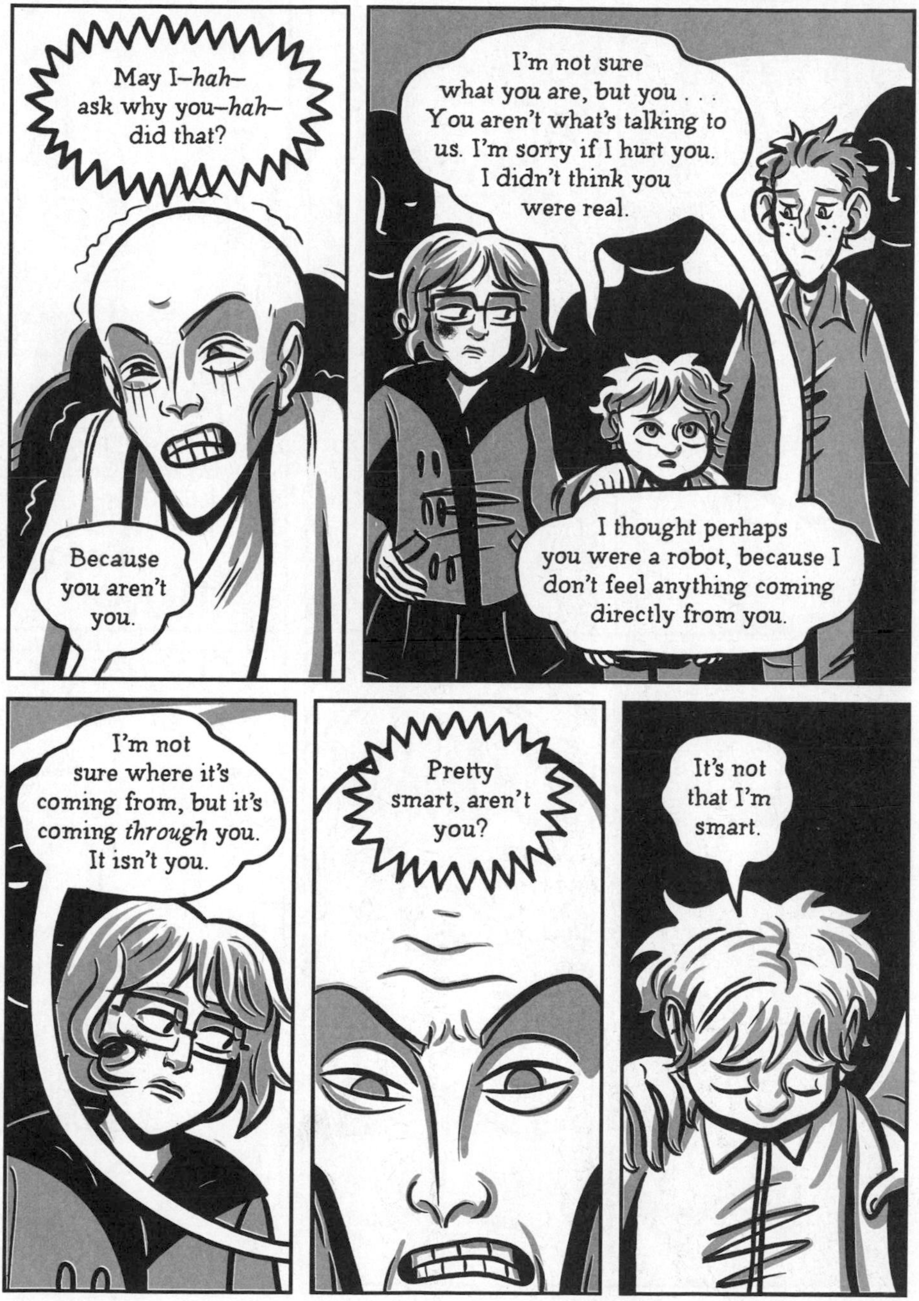
May I—*hah*—ask why you—*hah*—did that?
Because you aren't you.
I'm not sure what you are, but you . . . You aren't what's talking to us. I'm sorry if I hurt you. I didn't think you were real.
I thought perhaps you were a robot, because I don't feel anything coming directly from you.
I'm not sure where it's coming from, but it's coming *through* you. It isn't you.
Pretty smart, aren't you?
It's not that I'm smart.

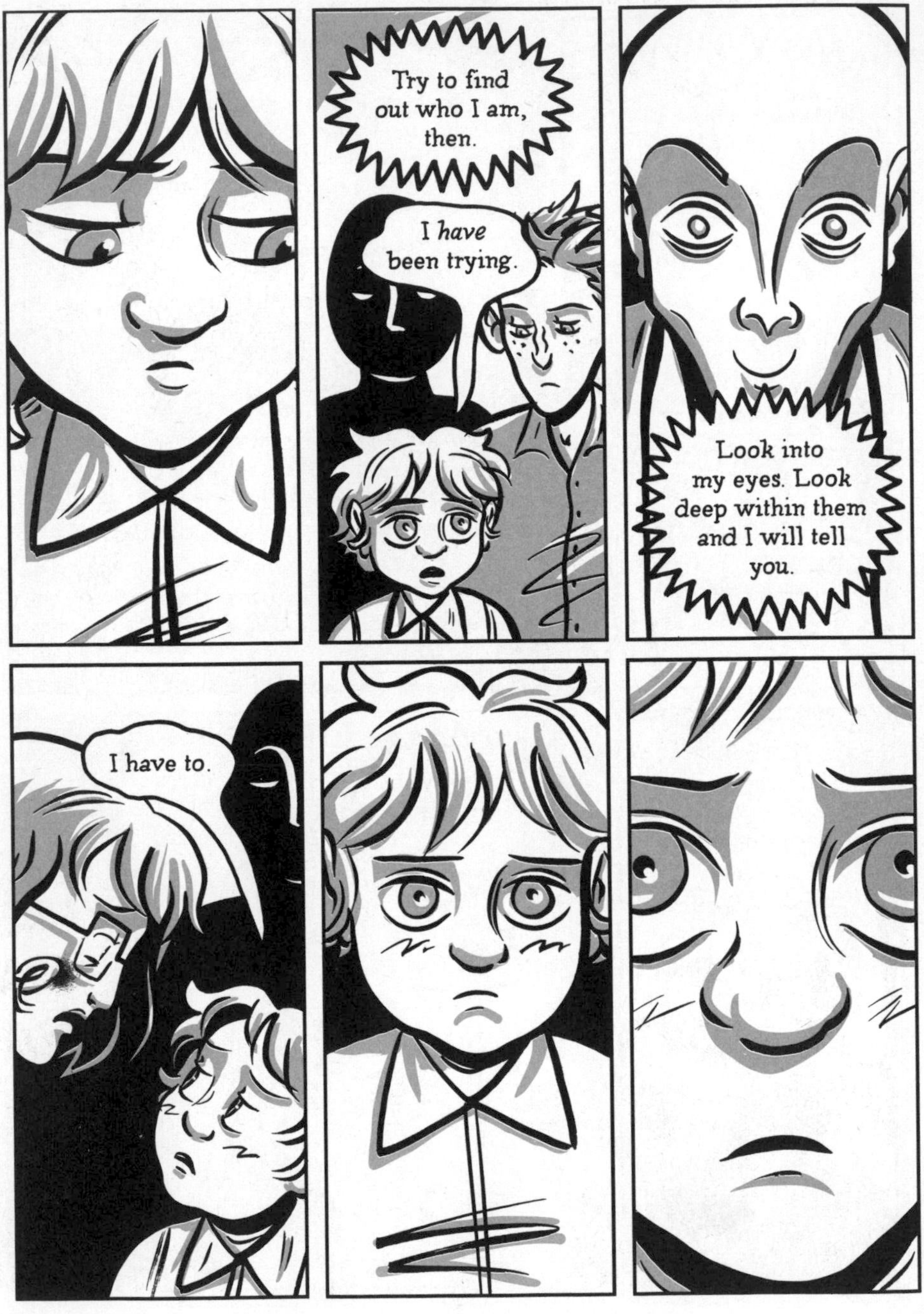
Try to find out who I am, then.
I *have* been trying.
Look into my eyes. Look deep within them and I will tell you.
I have to.

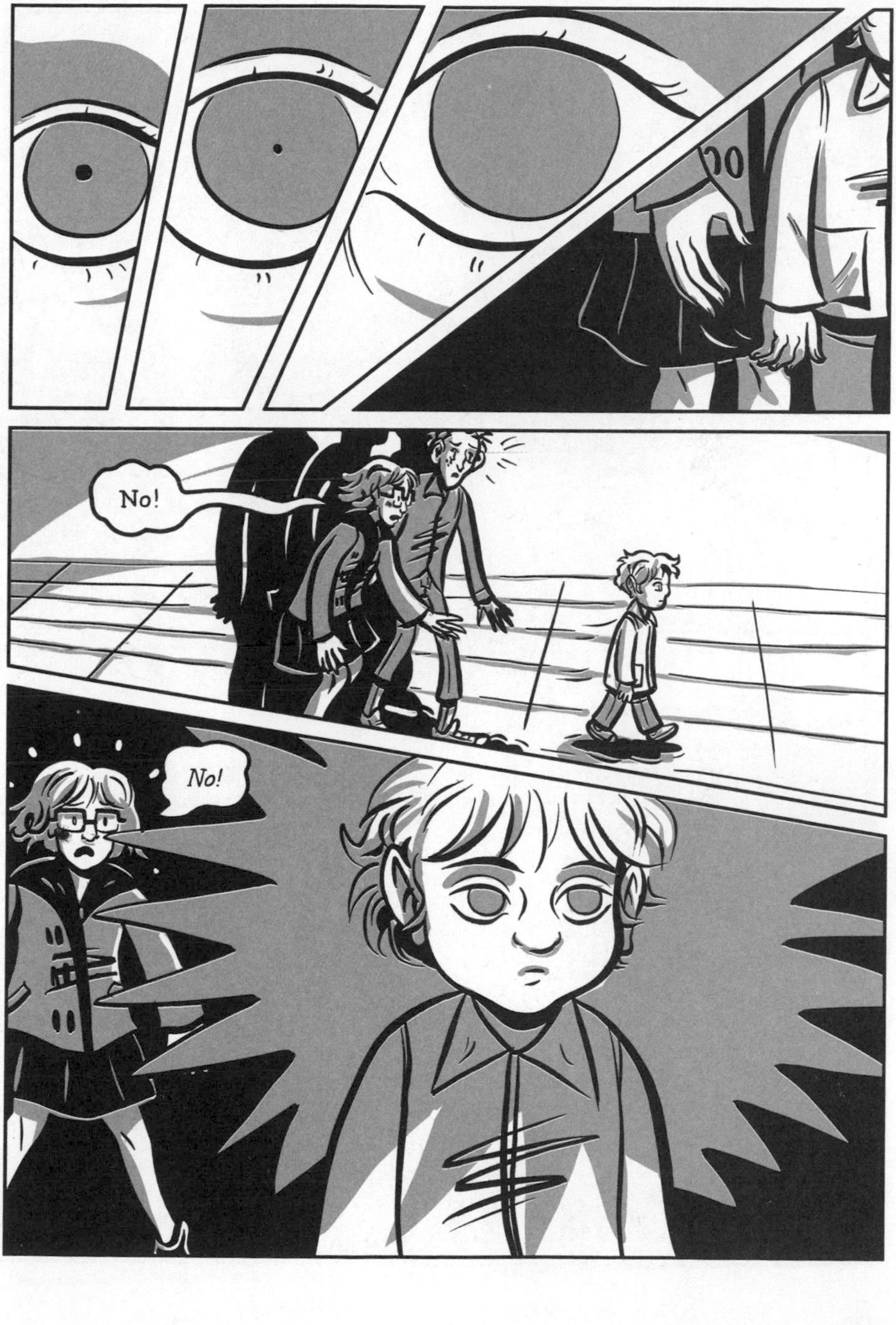
No!
No!

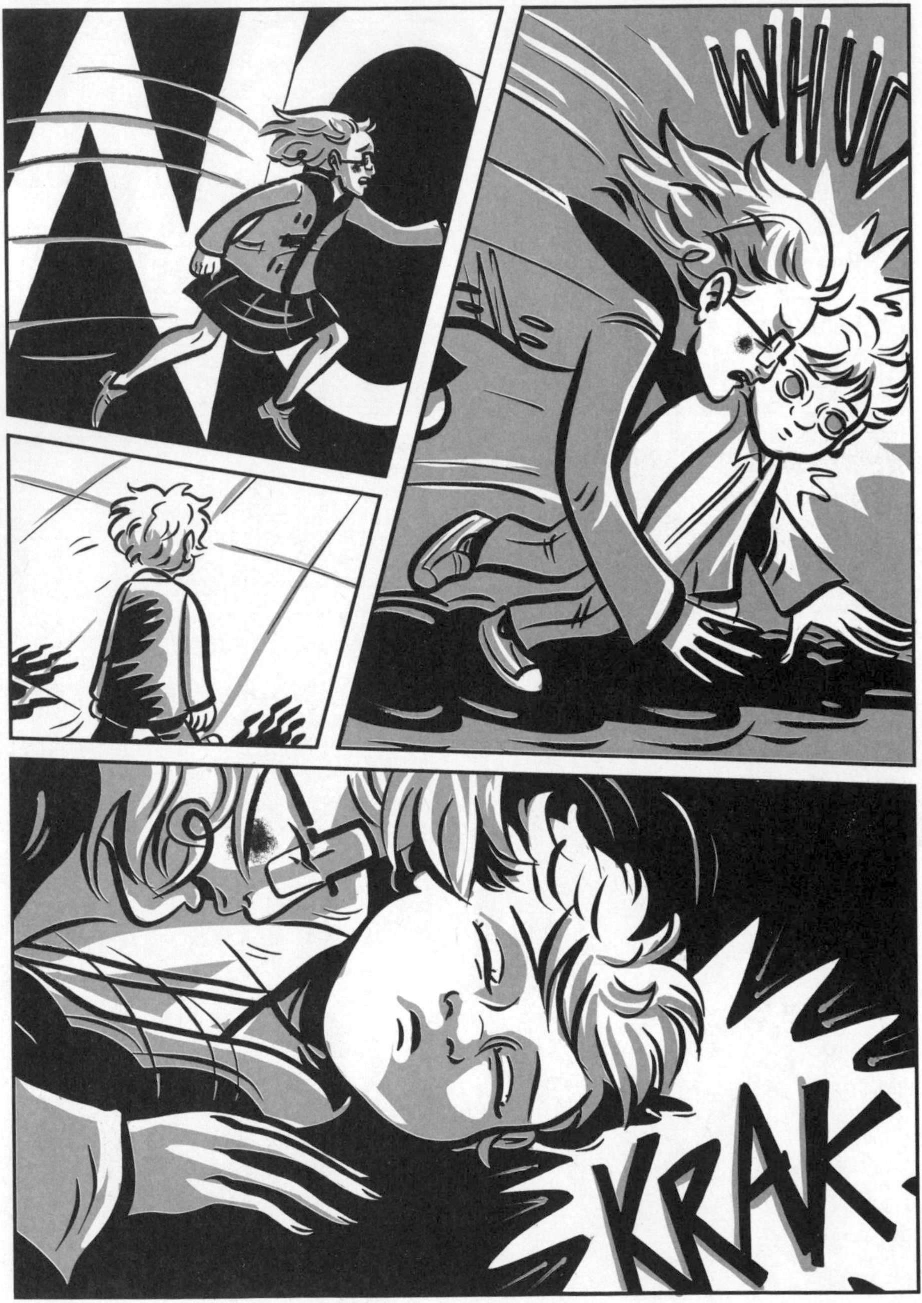
WHUD
KRAK

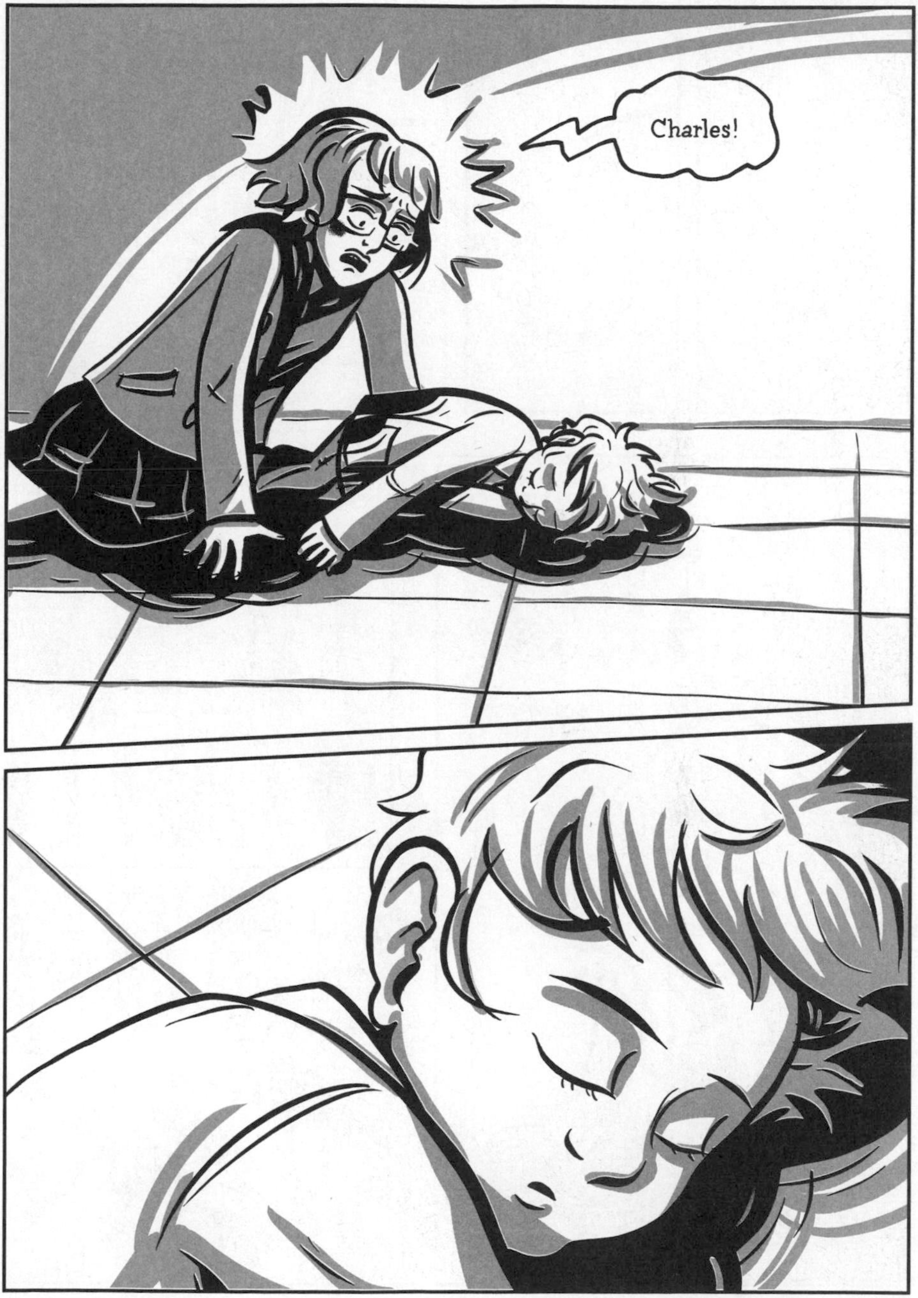
Charles!

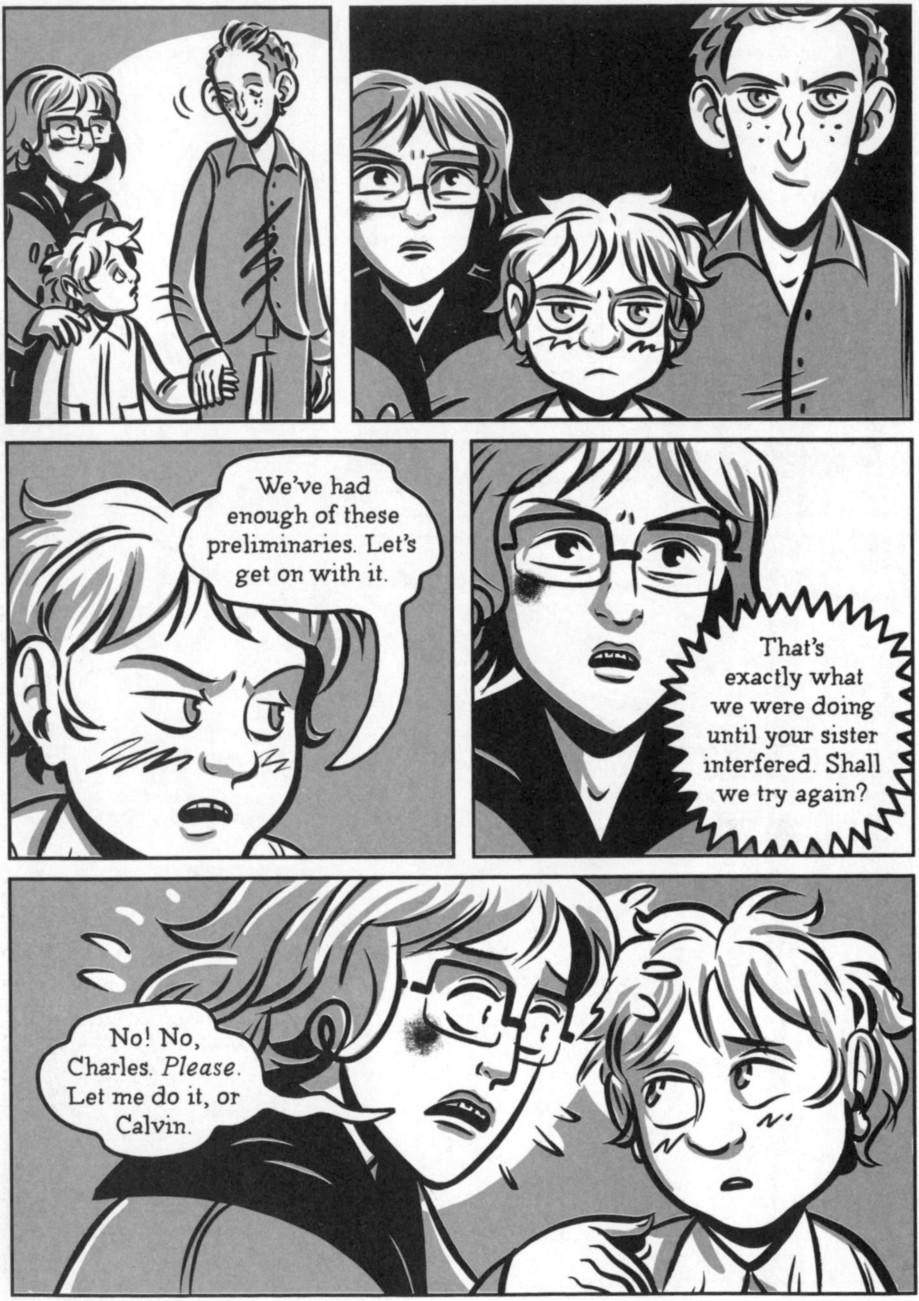

We've had enough of these preliminaries. Let's get on with it.
That's exactly what we were doing until your sister interfered. Shall we try again?
No! No, Charles. *Please*. Let me do it, or Calvin.

Panel 1: But it is only the little boy whose neurological system is complex enough. If you tried to conduct the necessary neurons, your brains would explode.

Panel 2: And Charles's wouldn't?

I think not.

Panel 3: But there's a possibility?

There's always a possibility.

Panel 4: Then he mustn't do it.

I think you will have to grant him the right to make his own decisions.

Panel 5: Ah, here we are!

233

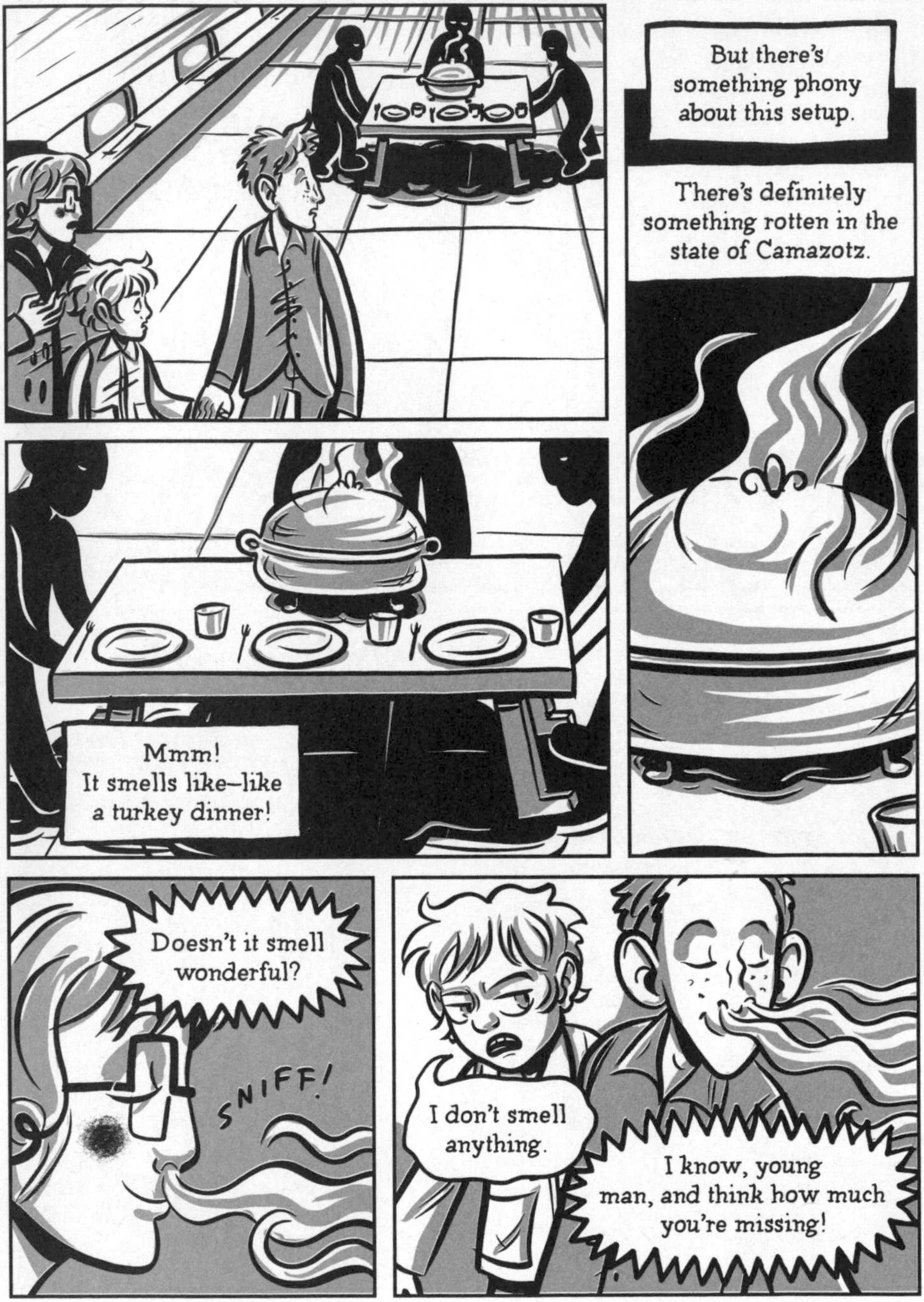
But there's something phony about this setup.
There's definitely something rotten in the state of Camazotz.
Mmm! It smells like—like a turkey dinner!
Doesn't it smell wonderful?
SNIFF!
I don't smell anything.
I know, young man, and think how much you're missing!

236

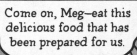

Hahahahaha! Go on, little fellow. Eat!
PTEW
Ugh! This is unfair!
I don't think we should eat this stuff, but if you're going to, I'd better, too.
It tastes all right.
Try some of mine, Charles.
Still tastes like sand.
Yes, because you've shut your mind entirely to me.
The other two can't—I can get in through the chinks.
Not all the way in, but enough to give them a turkey dinner.

Come on, Meg—eat this delicious food that has been prepared for us.

No!

No!

No!

No!

NO!

SMASH

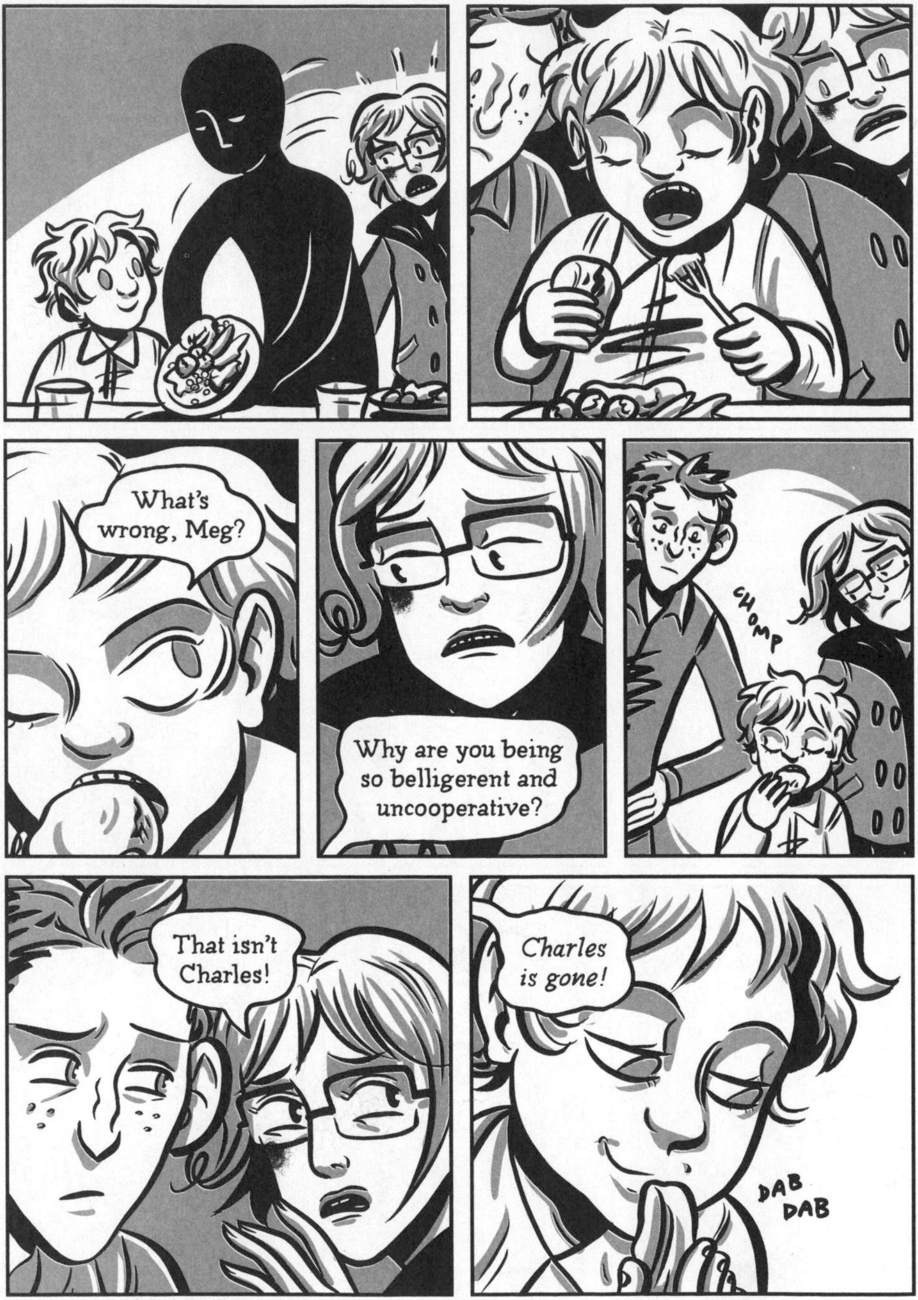
What's wrong, Meg?
Why are you being so belligerent and uncooperative?
CHOMP
That isn't Charles!
Charles is gone!
DAB DAB

8
The Transparent Column

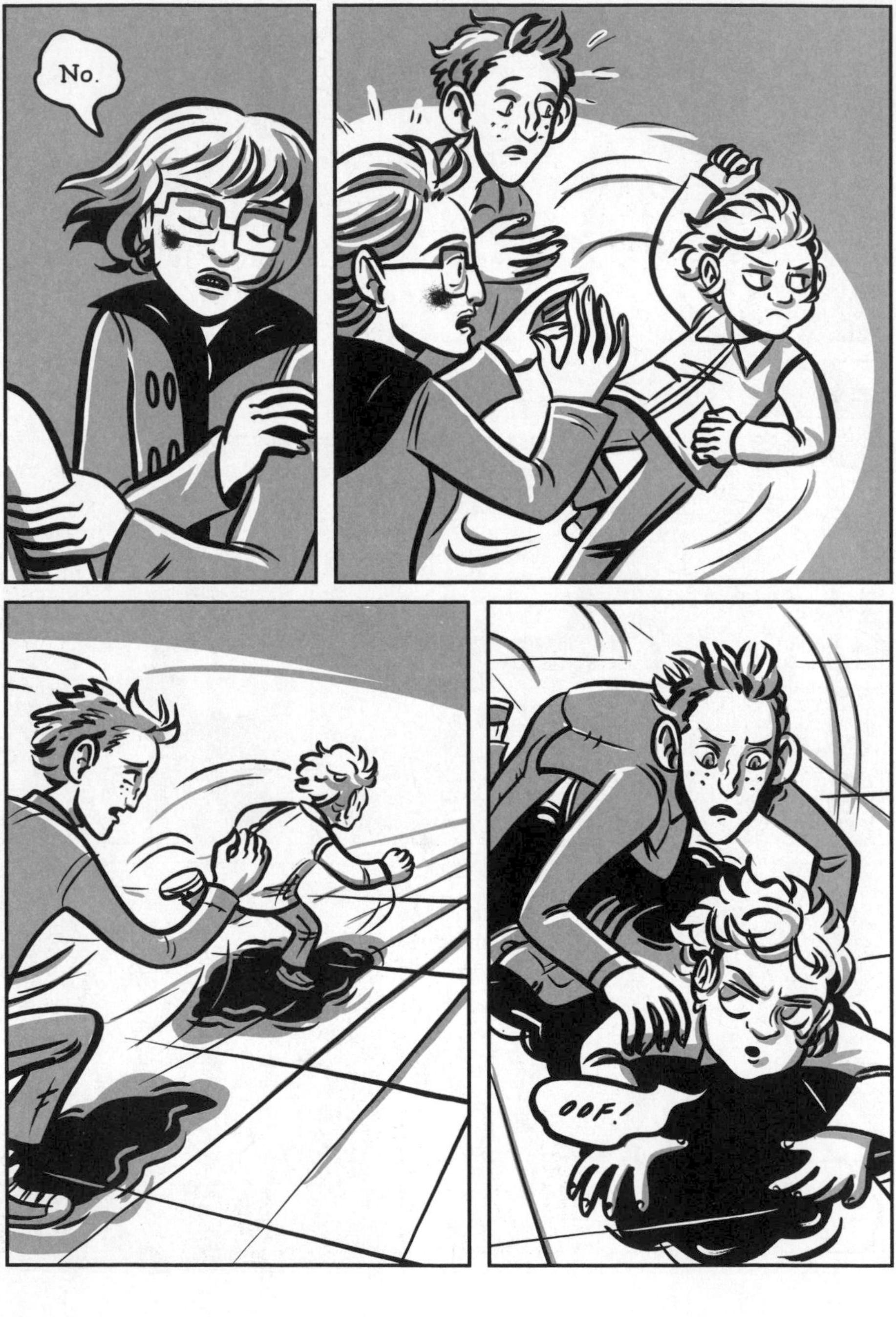
No.
OOF!

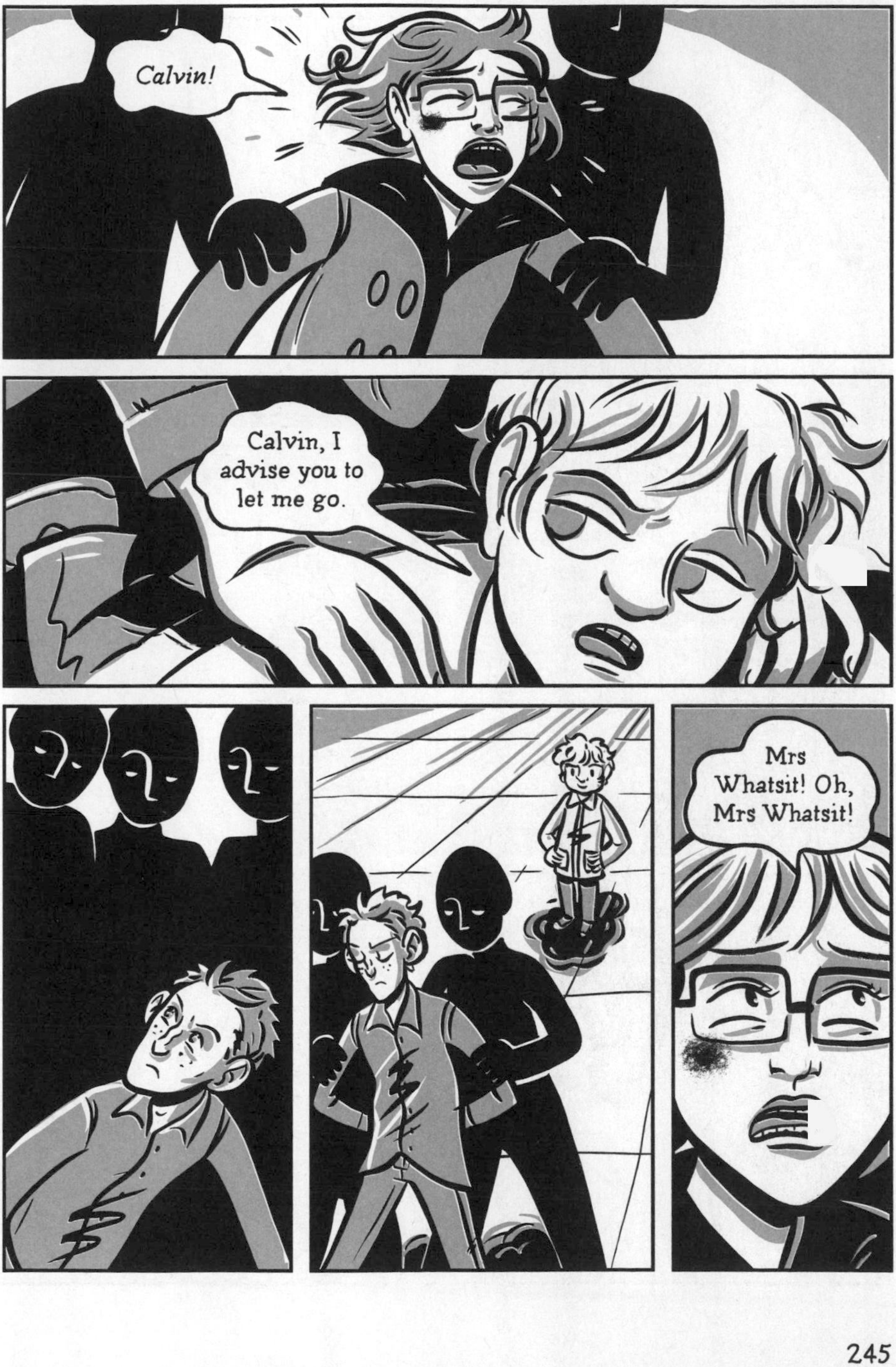
Calvin!
Calvin, I advise you to let me go.
Mrs Whatsit! Oh, Mrs Whatsit!

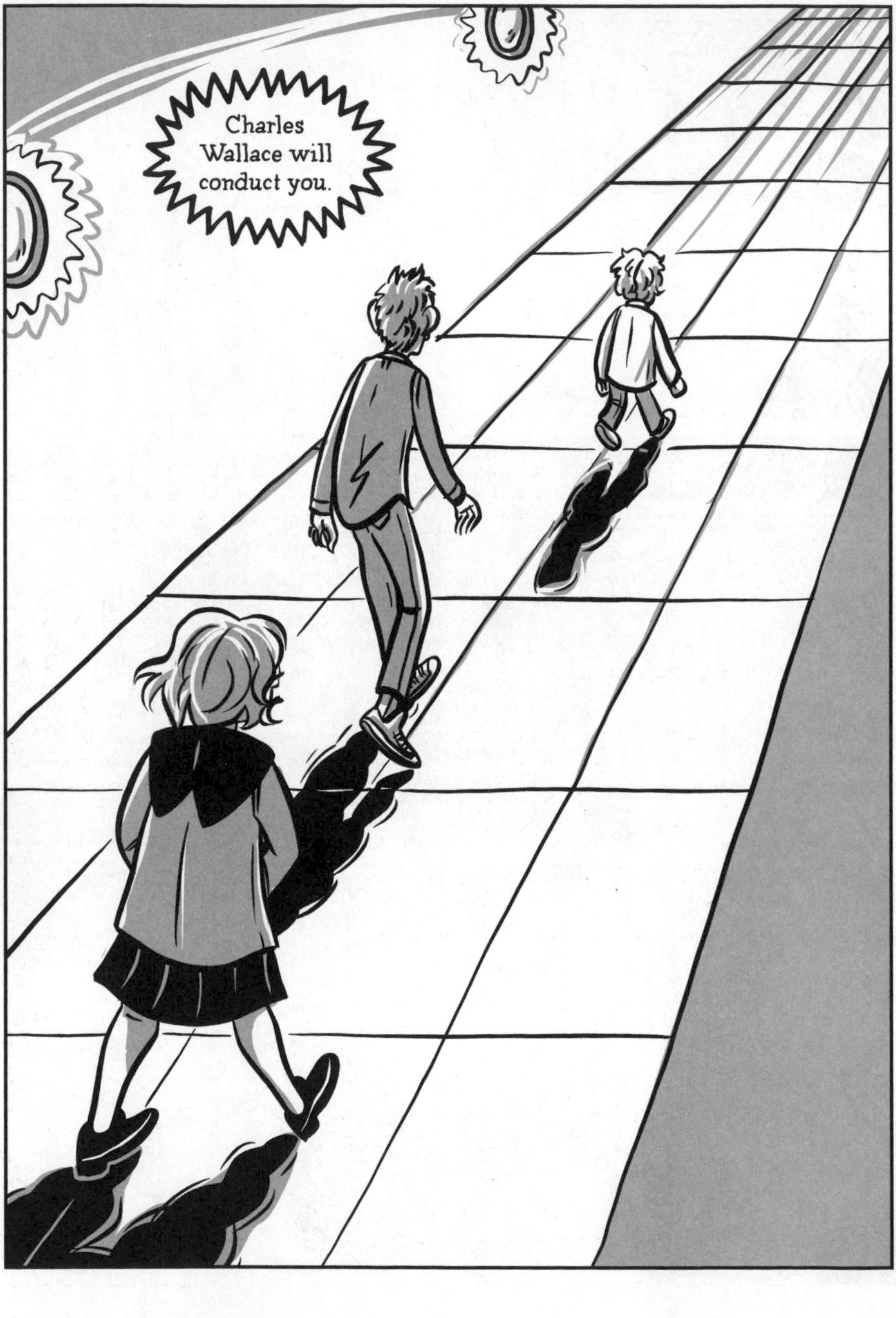
Charles Wallace will conduct you.

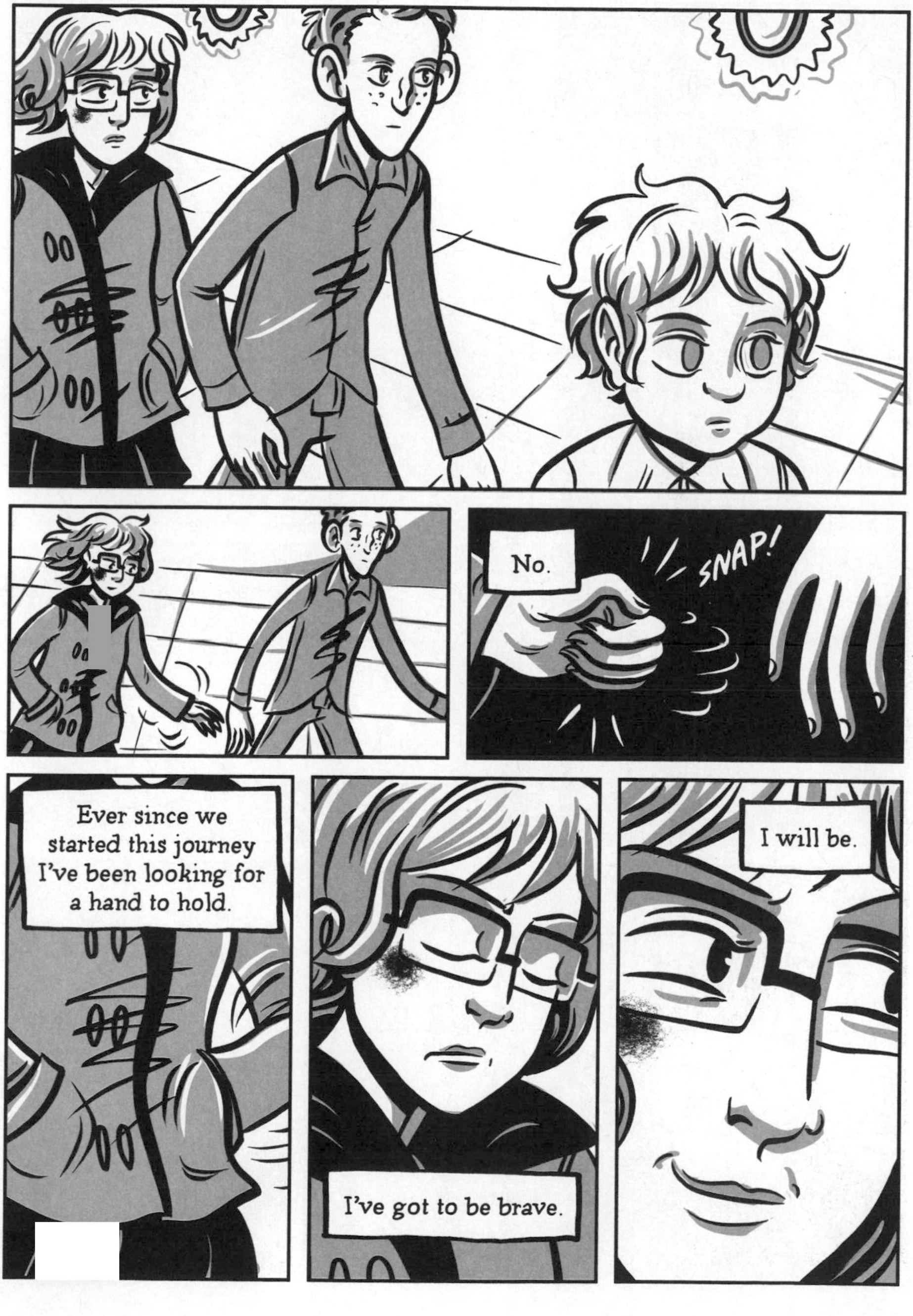
No.
SNAP!
Ever since we started this journey I've been looking for a hand to hold.
I've got to be brave.
I will be.

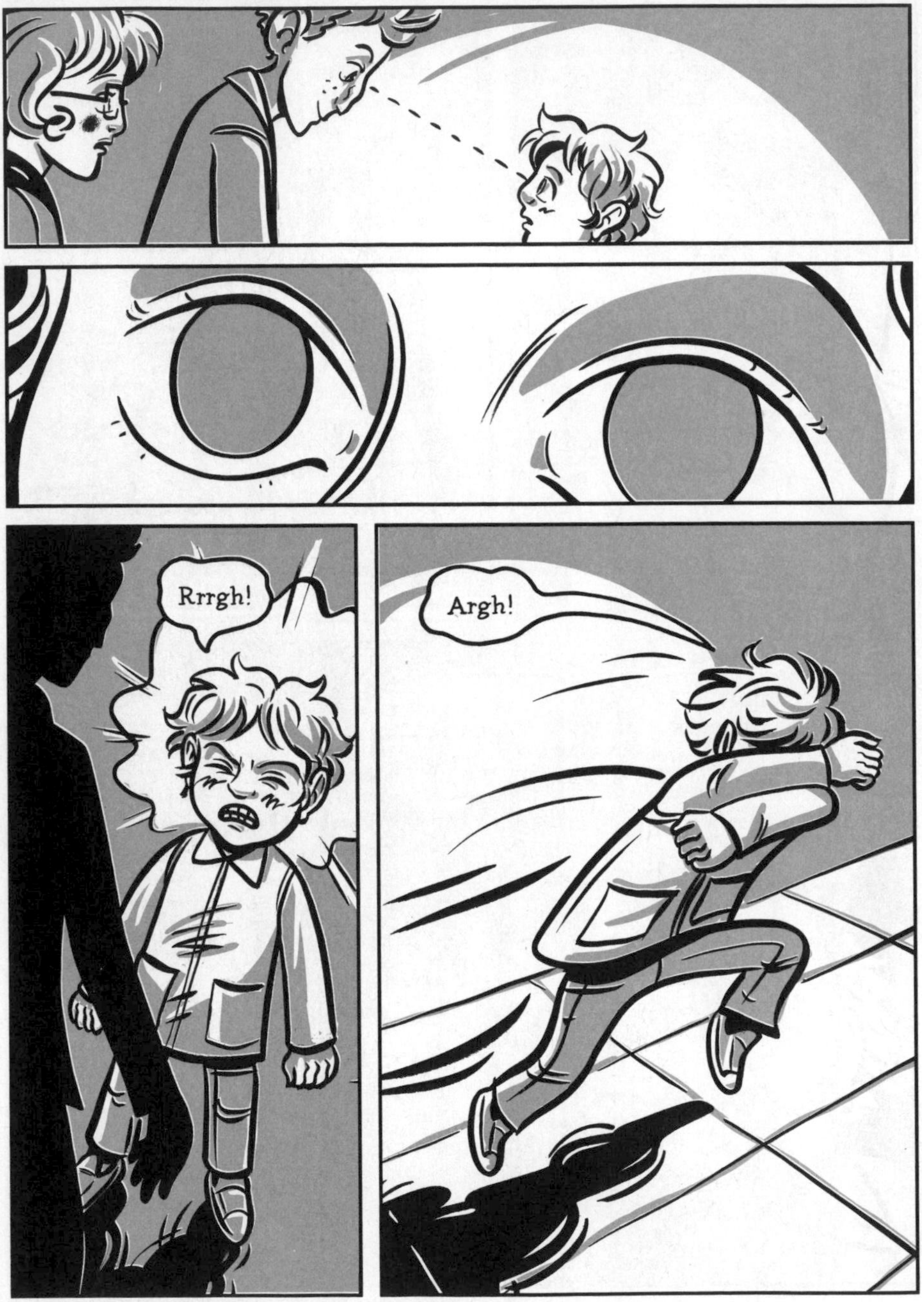
Rrrgh!
Argh!

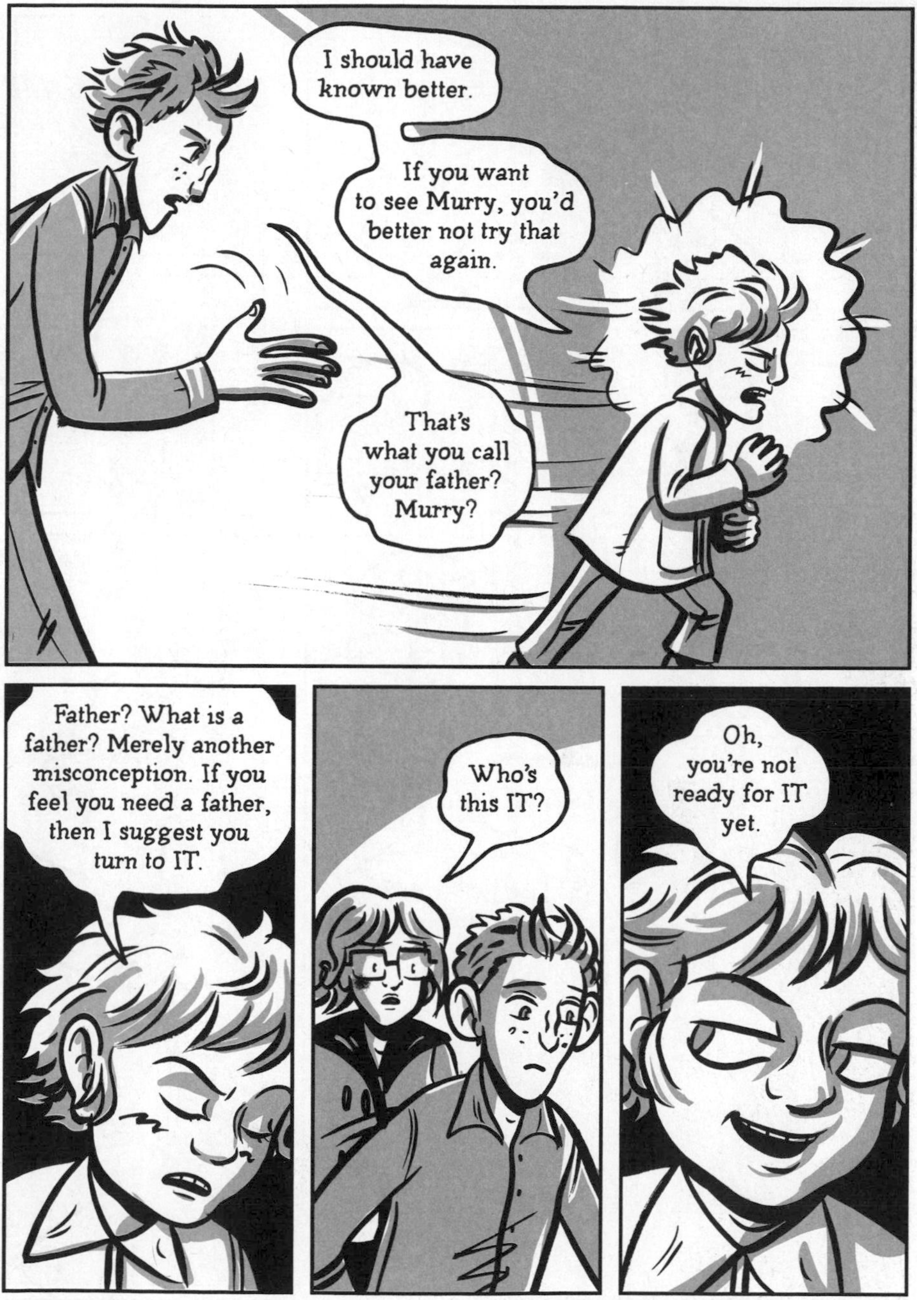
I should have known better.
If you want to see Murry, you'd better not try that again.
That's what you call your father? Murry?
Father? What is a father? Merely another misconception. If you feel you need a father, then I suggest you turn to IT.
Who's this IT?
Oh, you're not ready for IT yet.

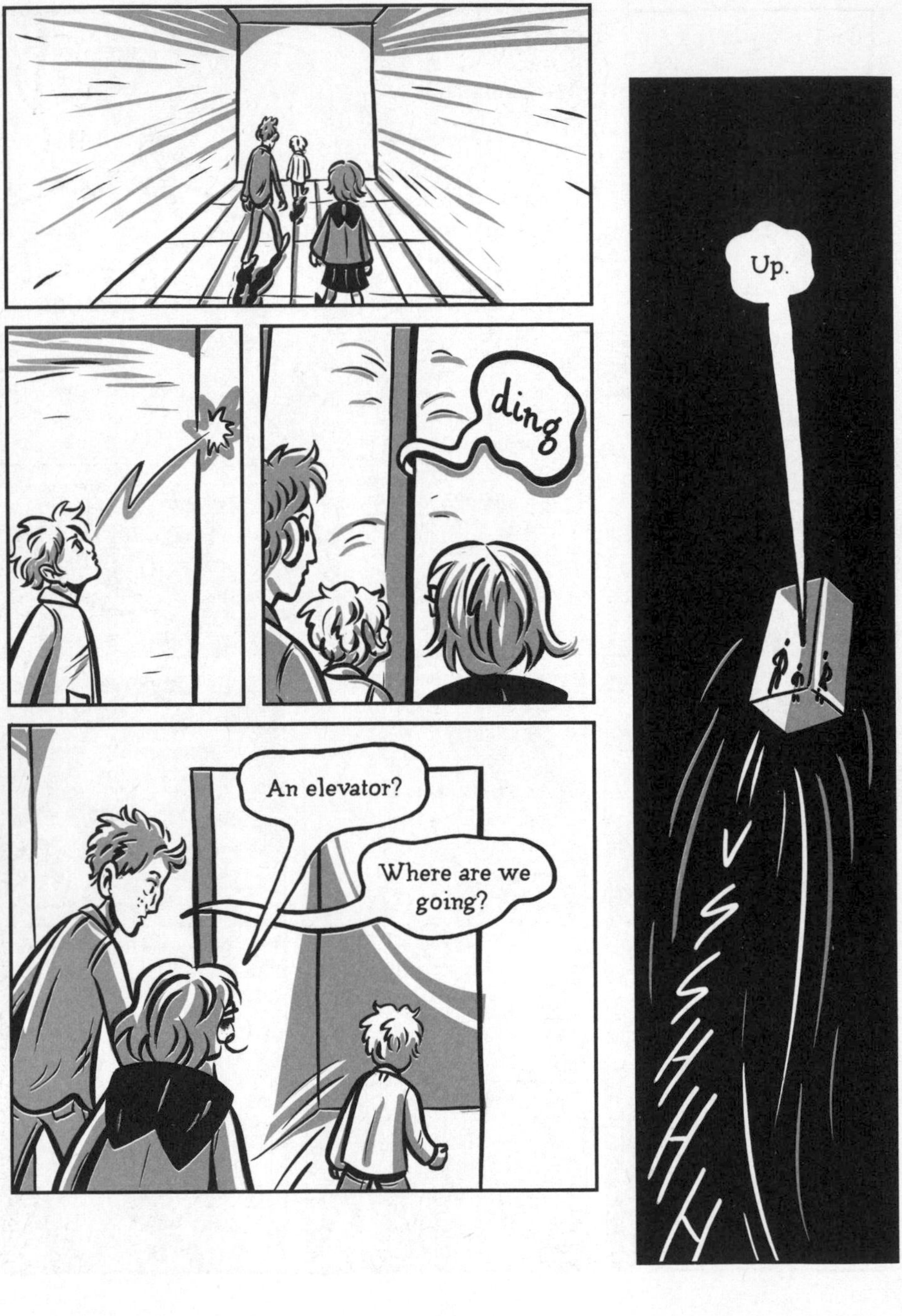
ding
An elevator?
Where are we going?
Up.
VSSHHHH

255

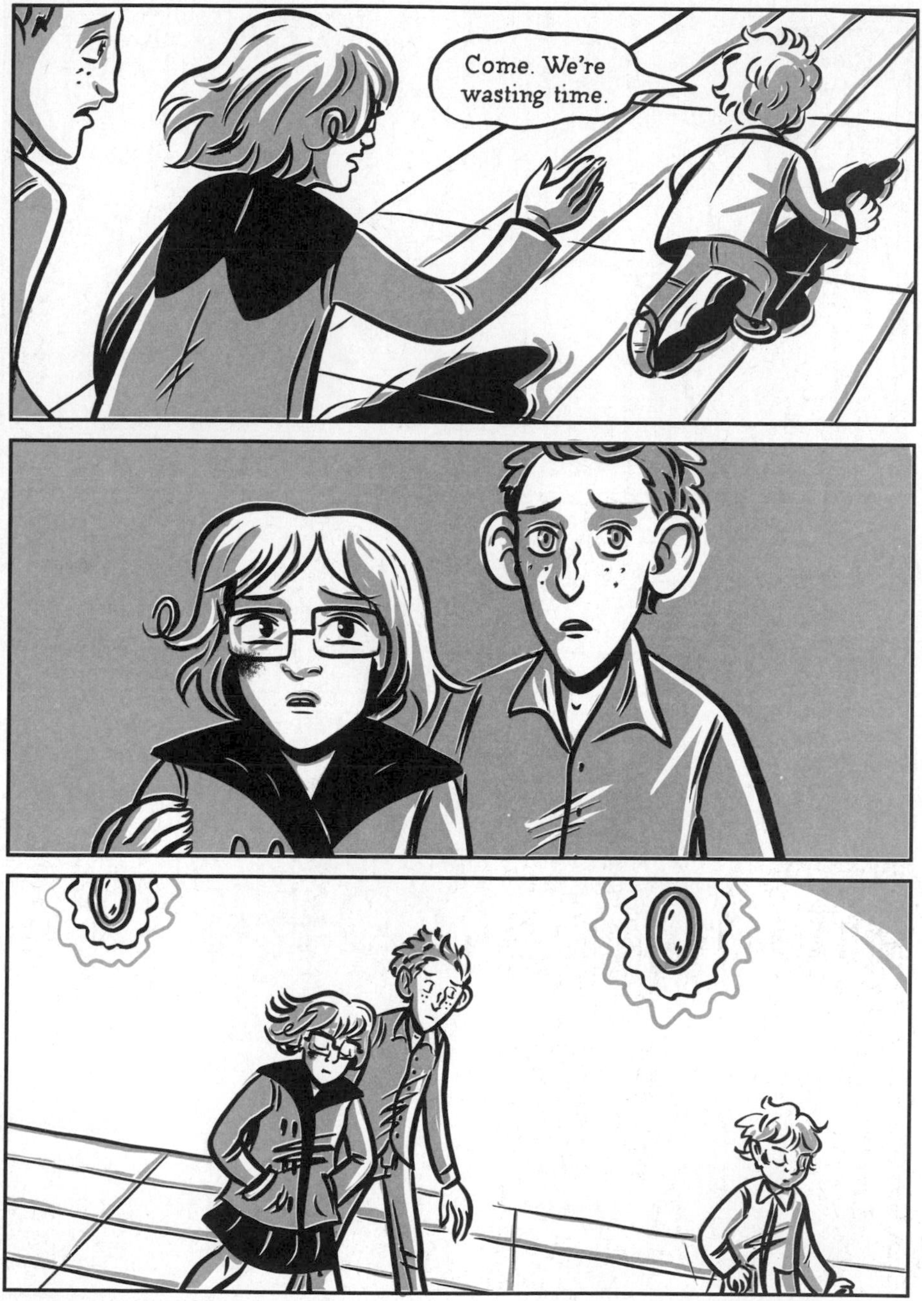
Come. We're wasting time.

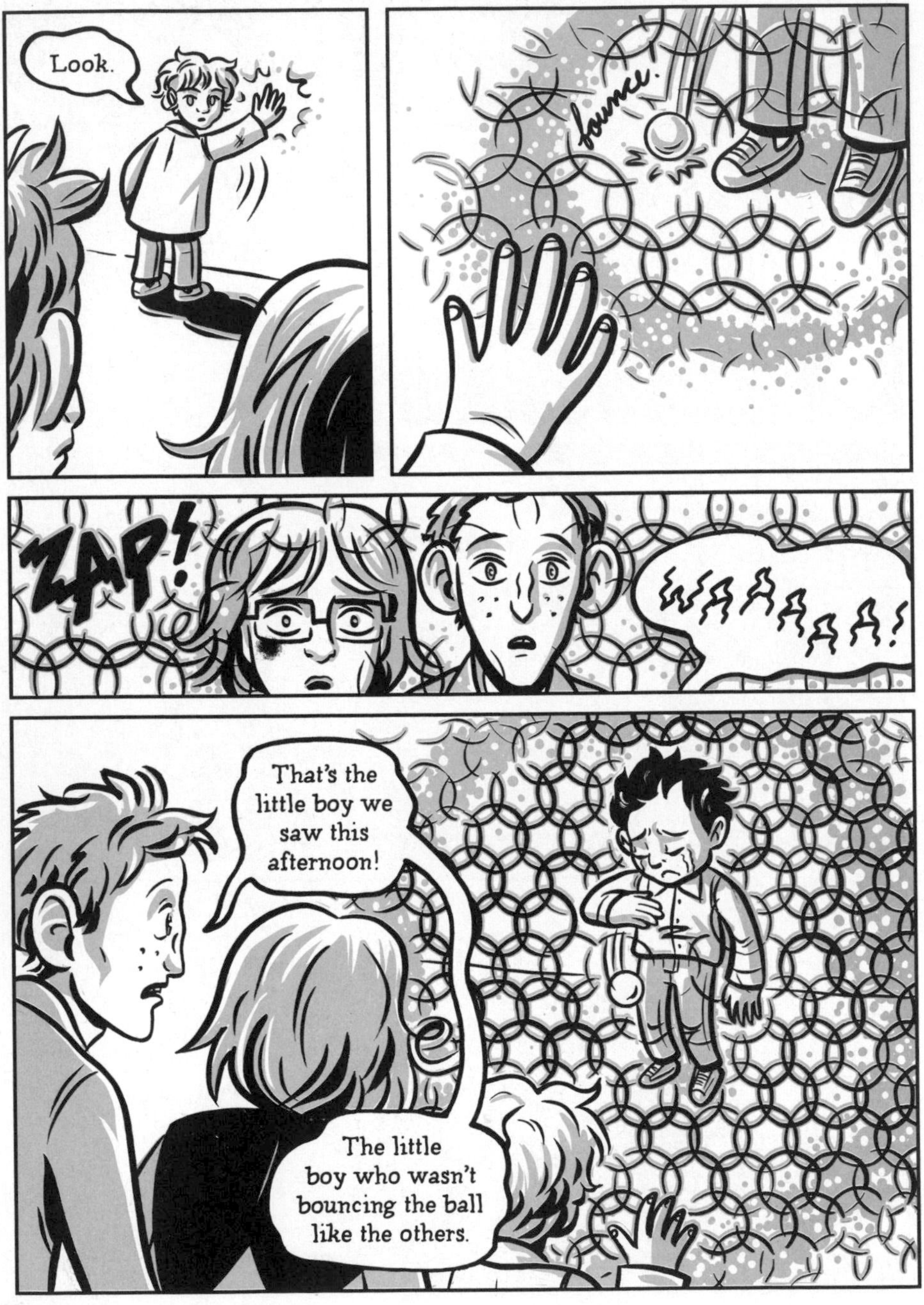
Look.
bounce!
ZAP!
WAAAAAA!
That's the little boy we saw this afternoon!
The little boy who wasn't bouncing the ball like the others.

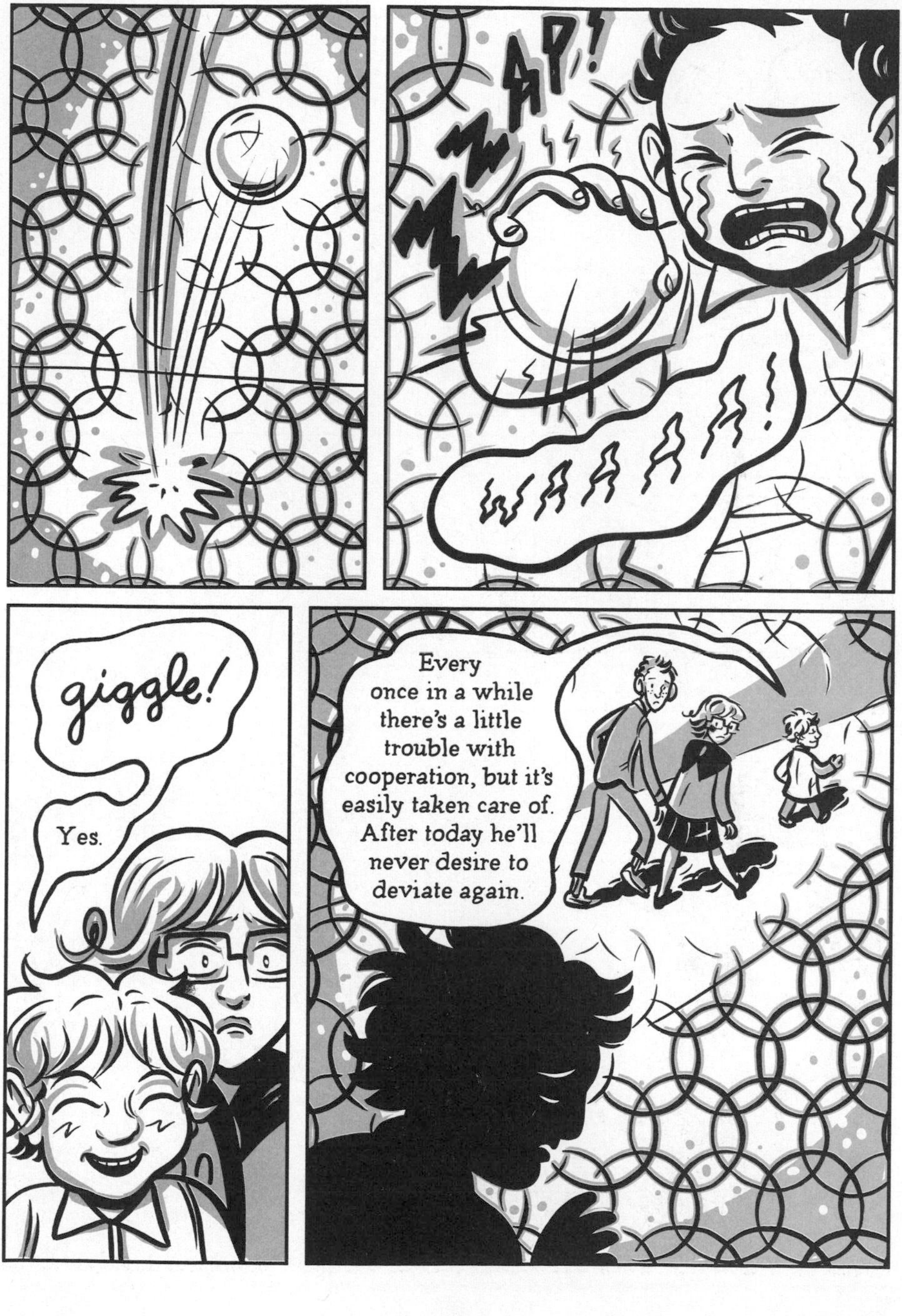
ZAP!
WAAAA!
giggle!
Yes.
Every once in a while there's a little trouble with cooperation, but it's easily taken care of. After today he'll never desire to deviate again.

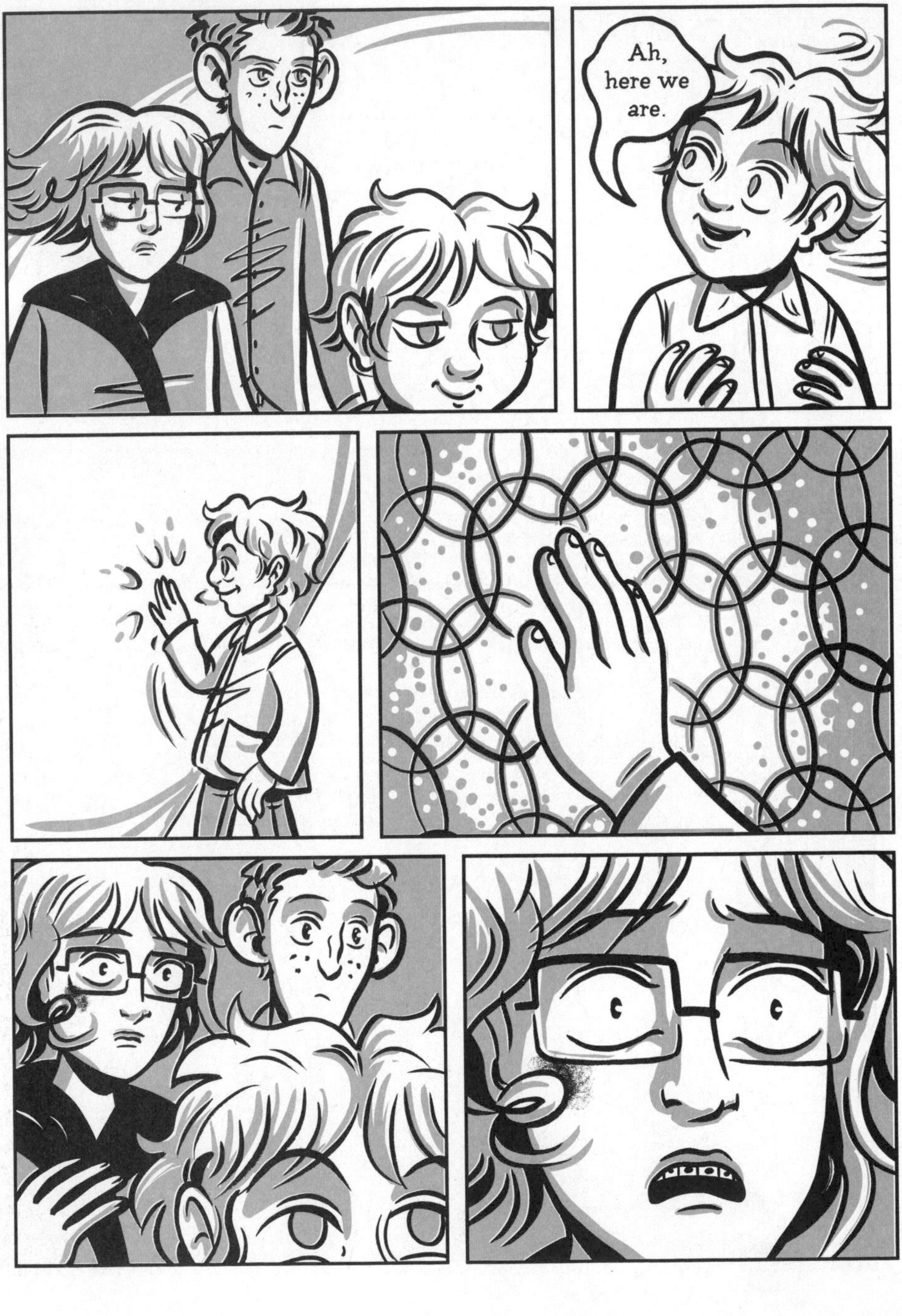
Ah, here we are.

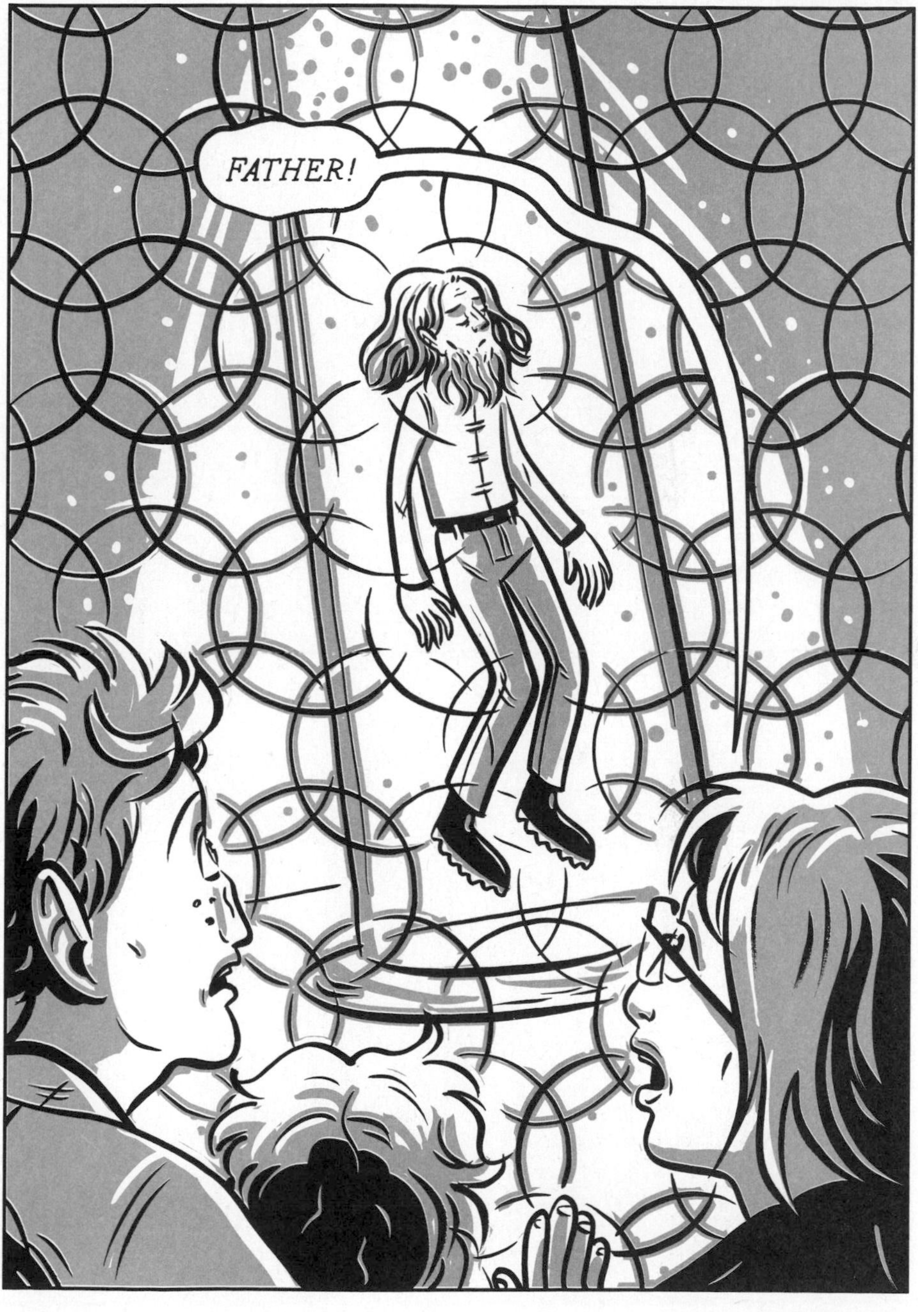
FATHER!

9

IT

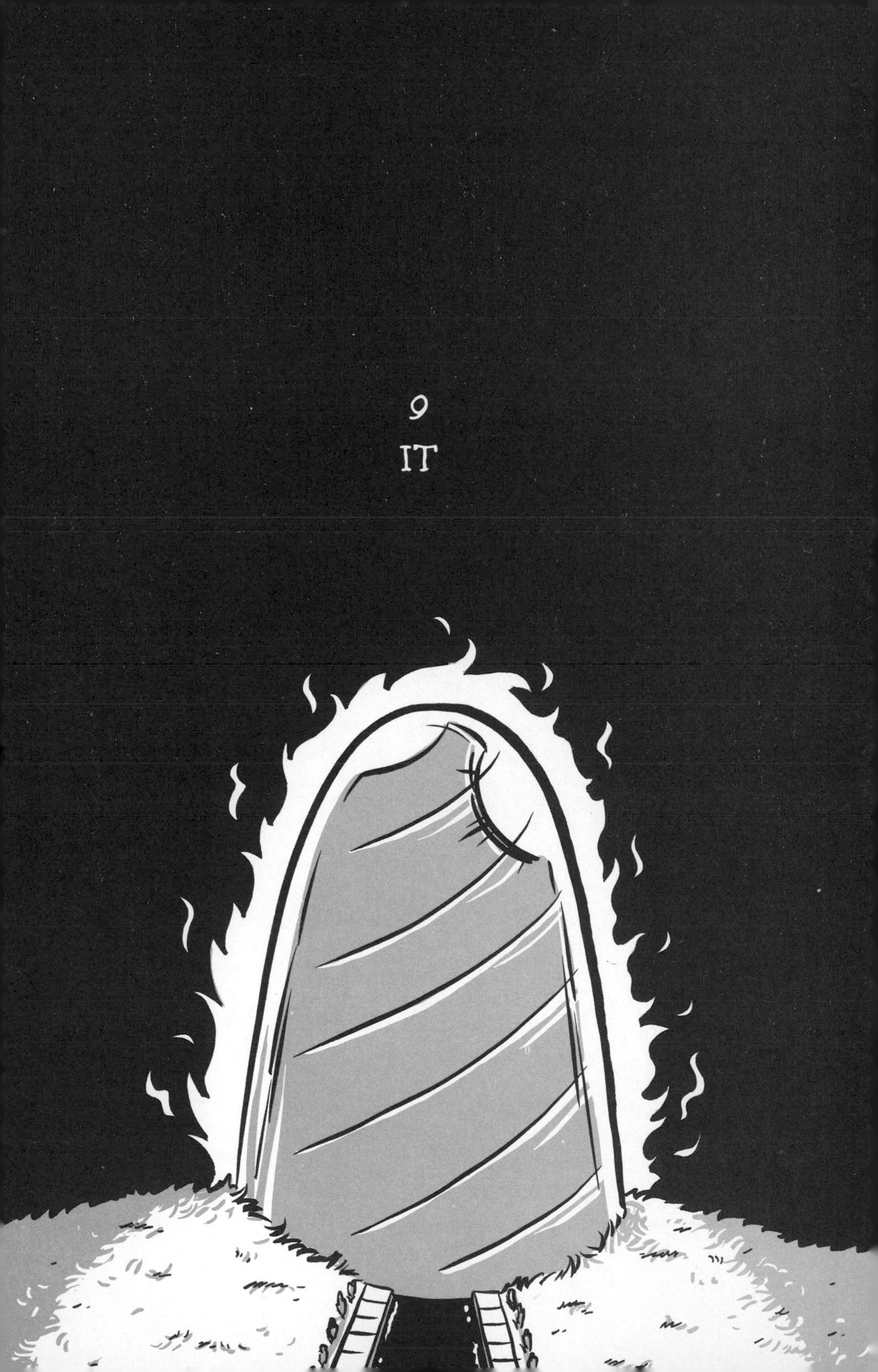

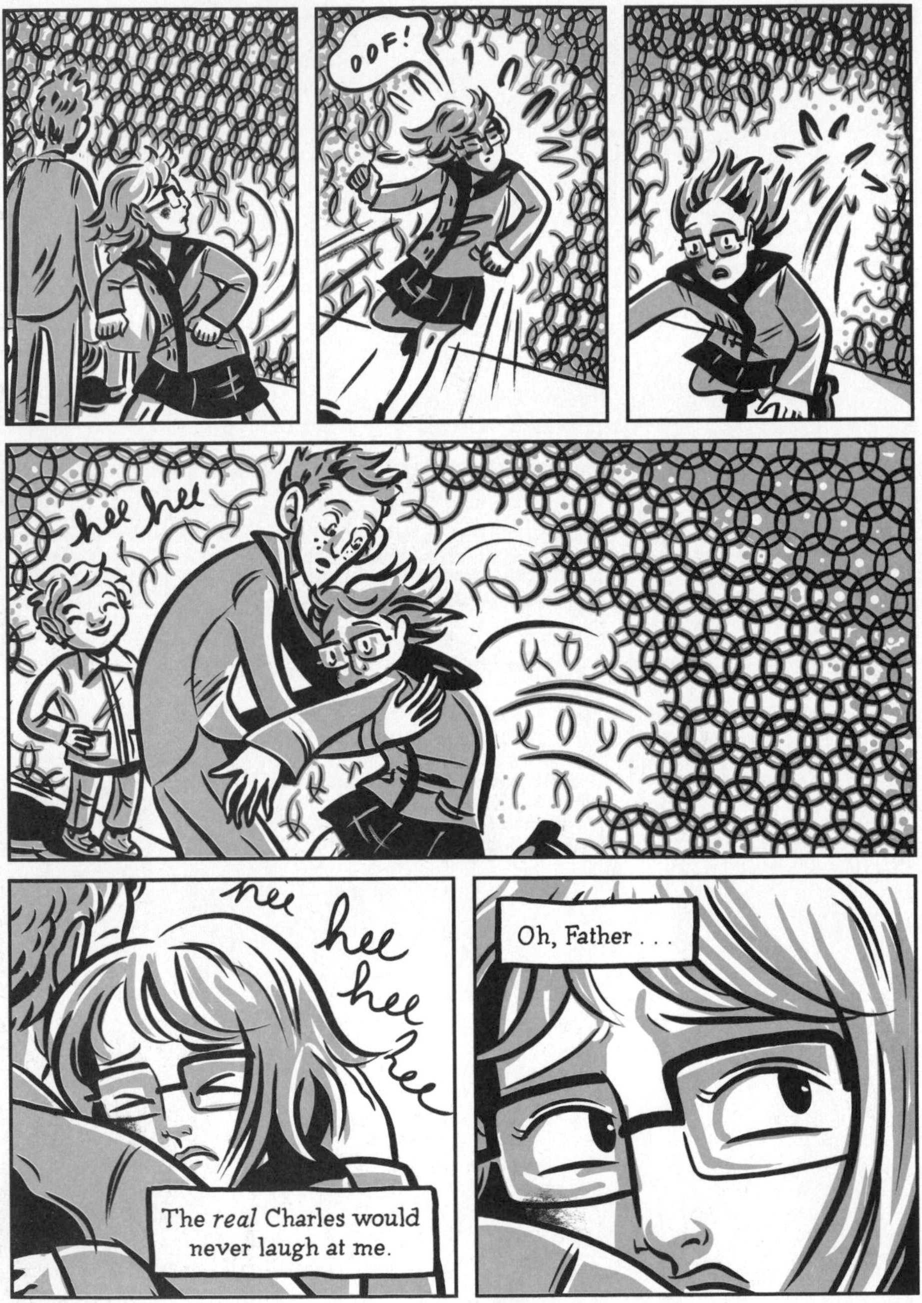
OOF!
hee hee
hee
hee
hee
hee
The *real* Charles would never laugh at me.
Oh, Father . . .

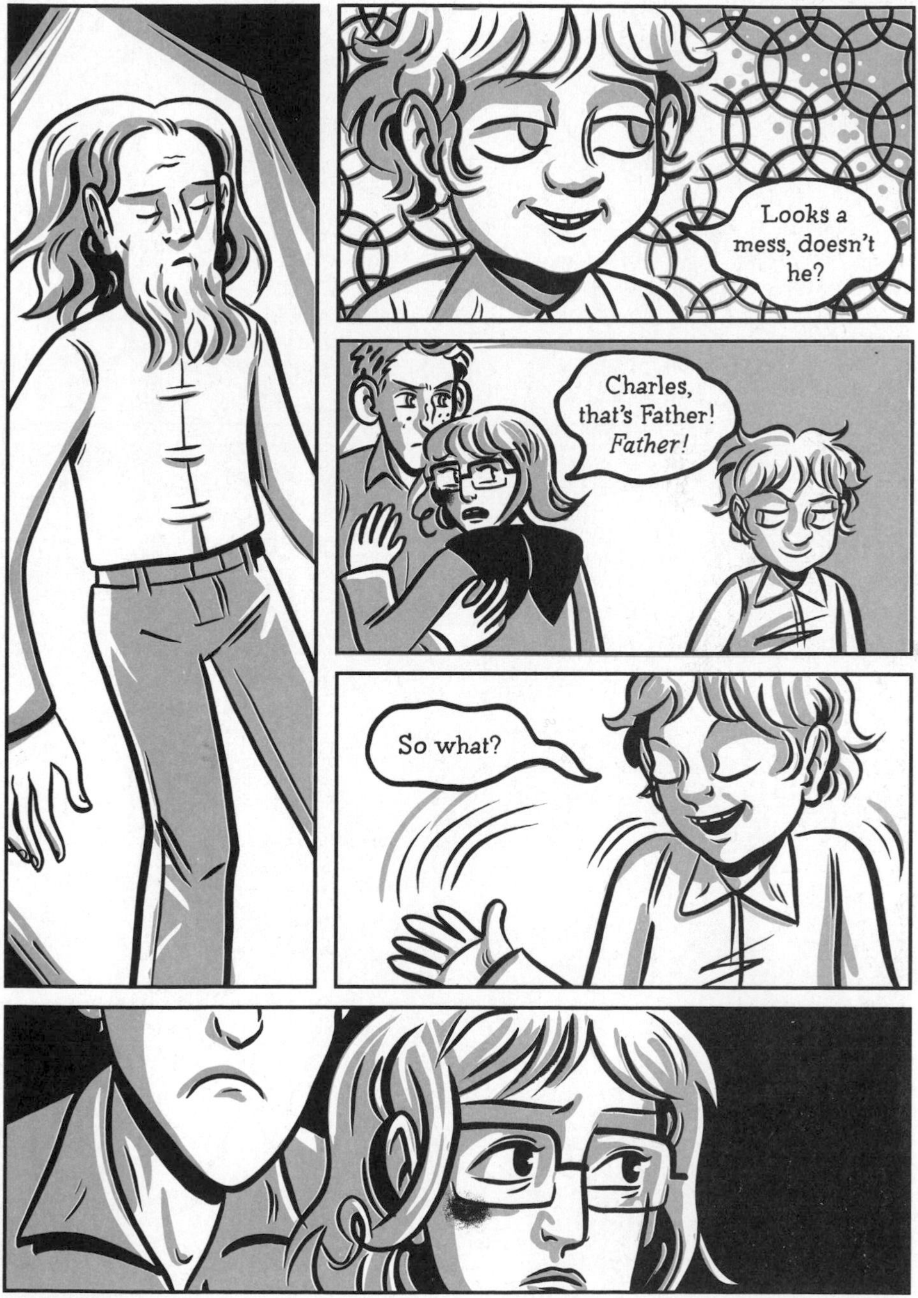
Looks a mess, doesn't he?
Charles, that's Father! *Father!*
So what?

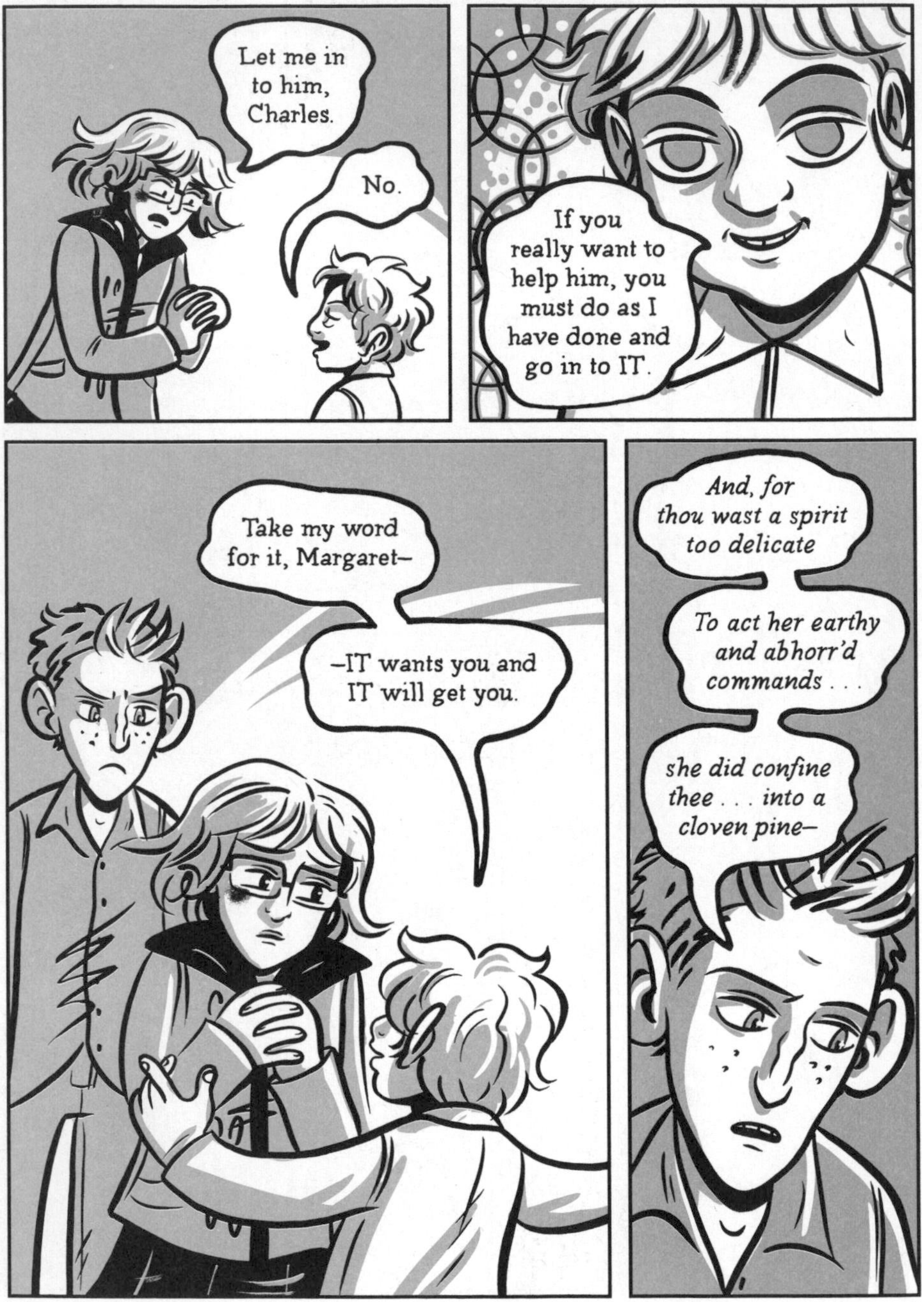
Let me in to him, Charles.
No.
If you really want to help him, you must do as I have done and go in to IT.
Take my word for it, Margaret–
–IT wants you and IT will get you.
And, for thou wast a spirit too delicate
To act her earthy and abhorr'd commands . . .
she did confine thee . . . into a cloven pine–

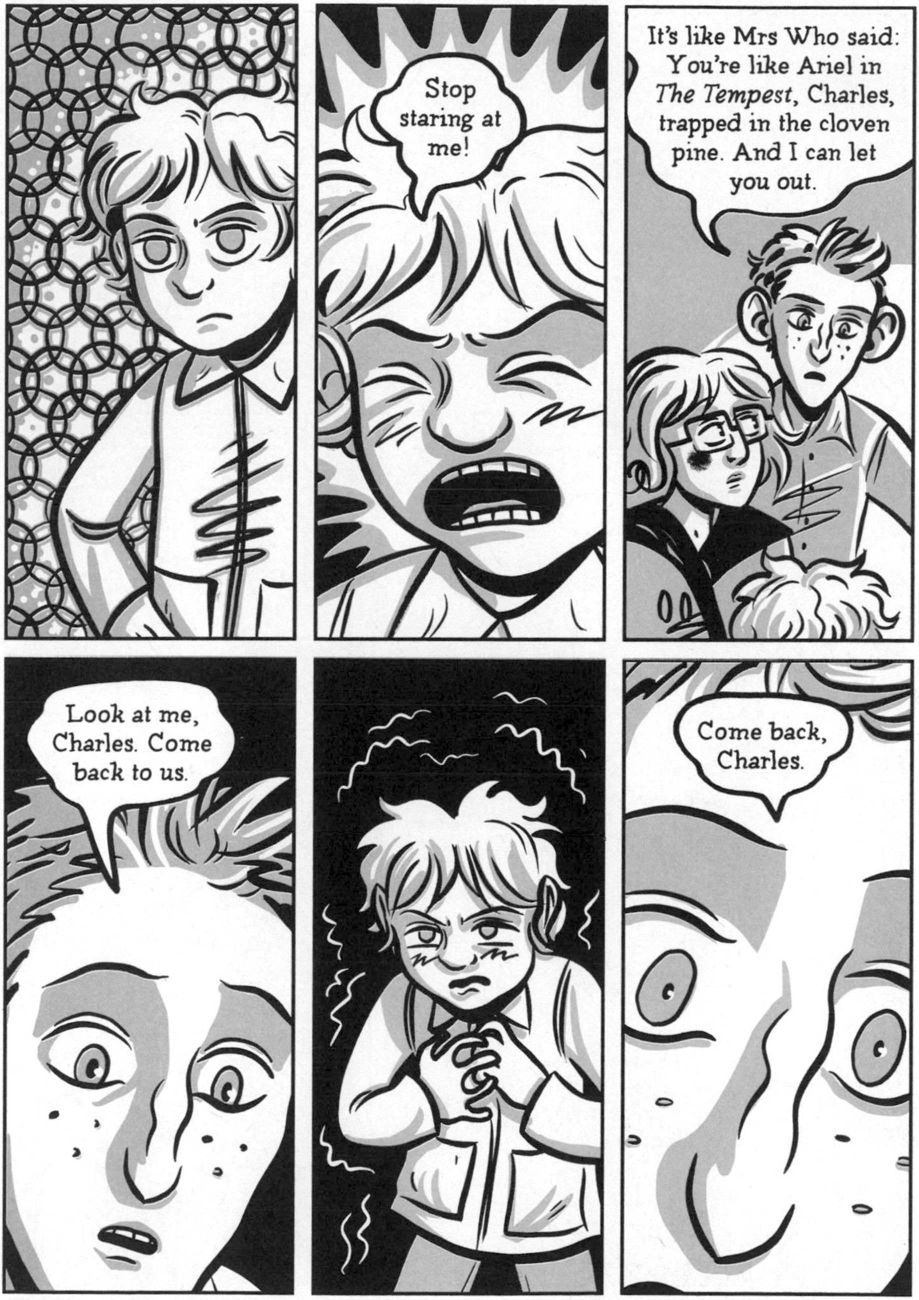
Stop staring at me!
It's like Mrs Who said: You're like Ariel in *The Tempest*, Charles, trapped in the cloven pine. And I can let you out.
Look at me, Charles. Come back to us.
Come back, Charles.

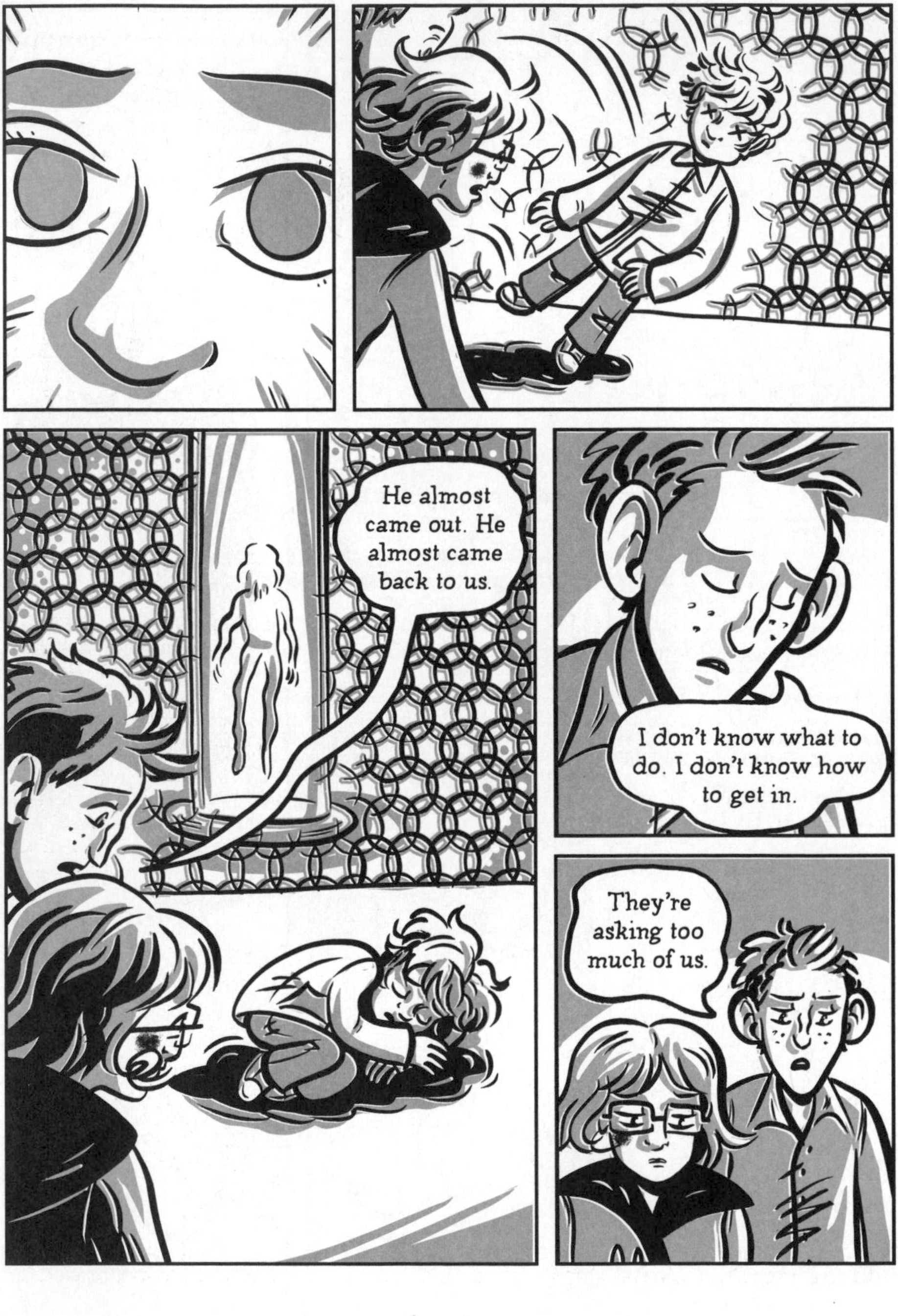
He almost came out. He almost came back to us.
I don't know what to do. I don't know how to get in.
They're asking too much of us.

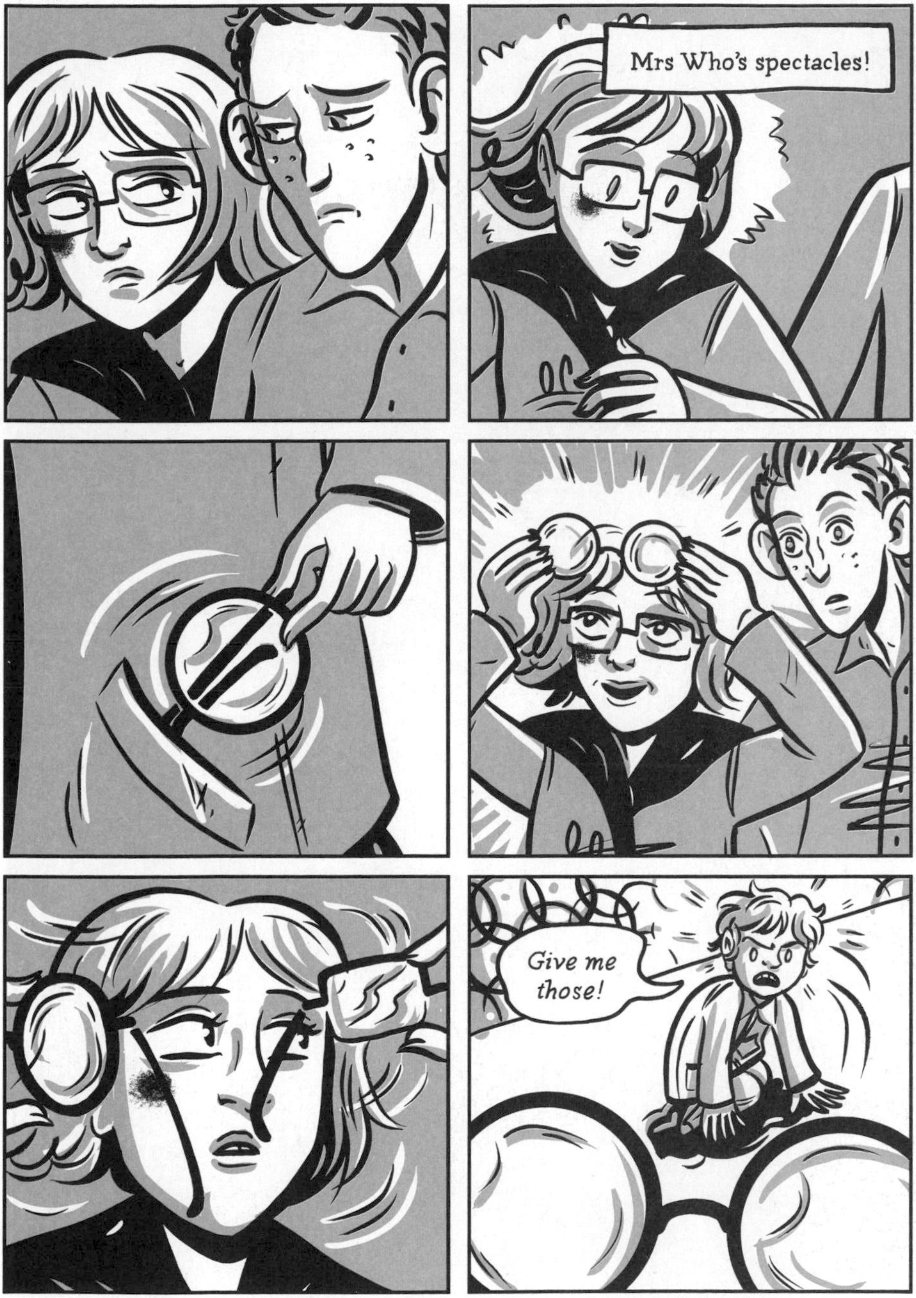
Mrs Who's spectacles!
Give me those!

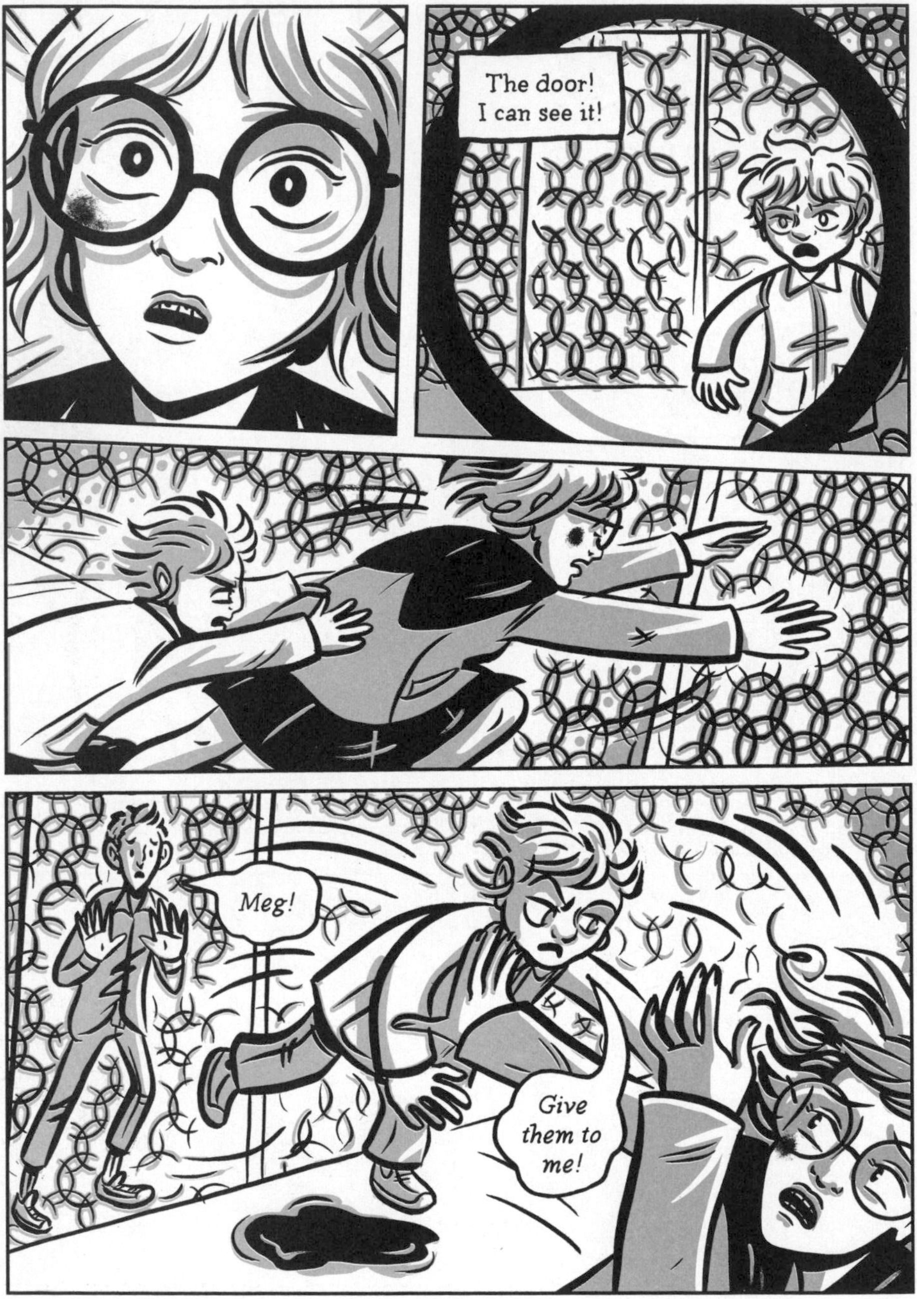
The door!
I can see it!
Meg!
Give them to me!

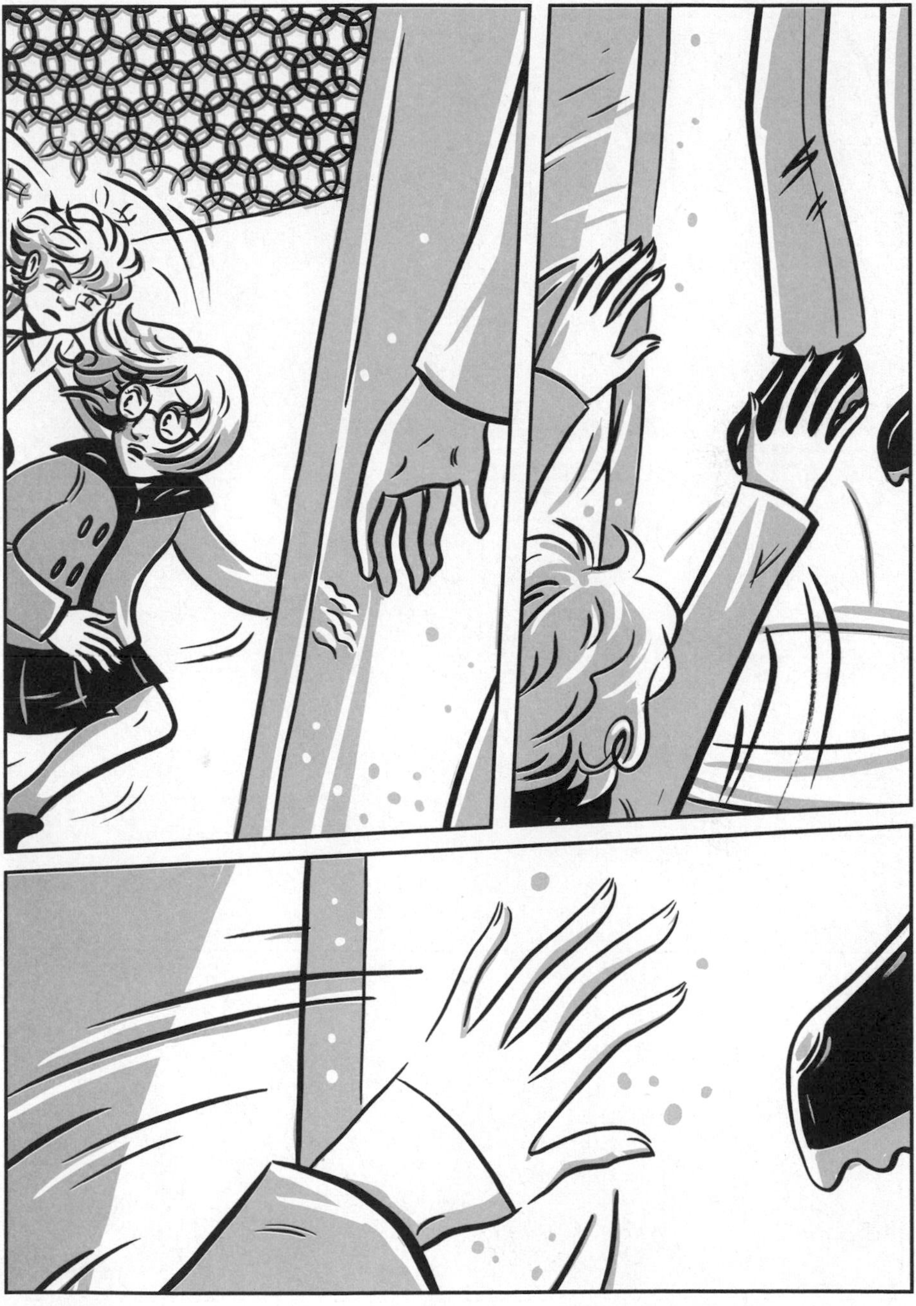

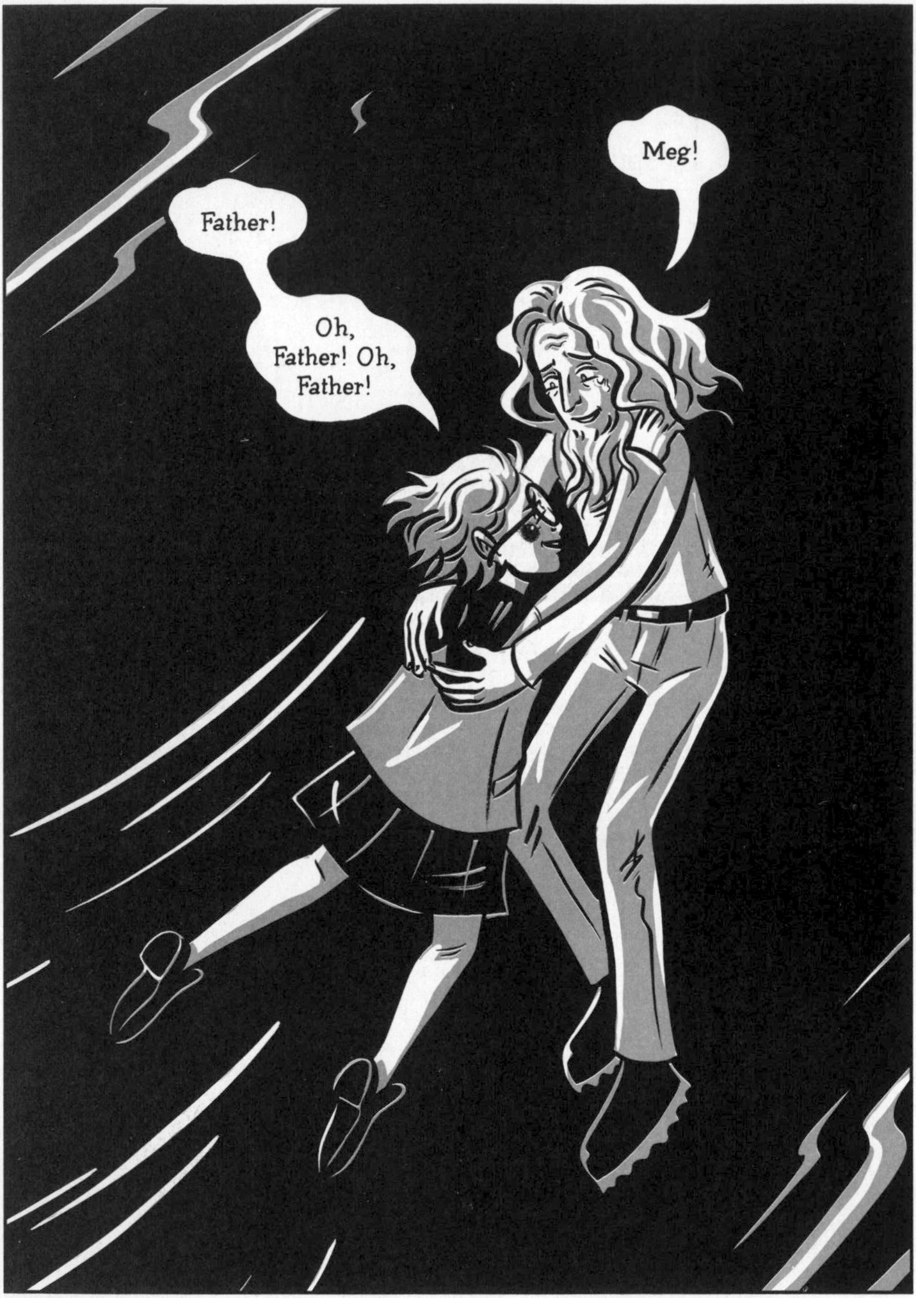
Meg!
Father!
Oh, Father! Oh, Father!

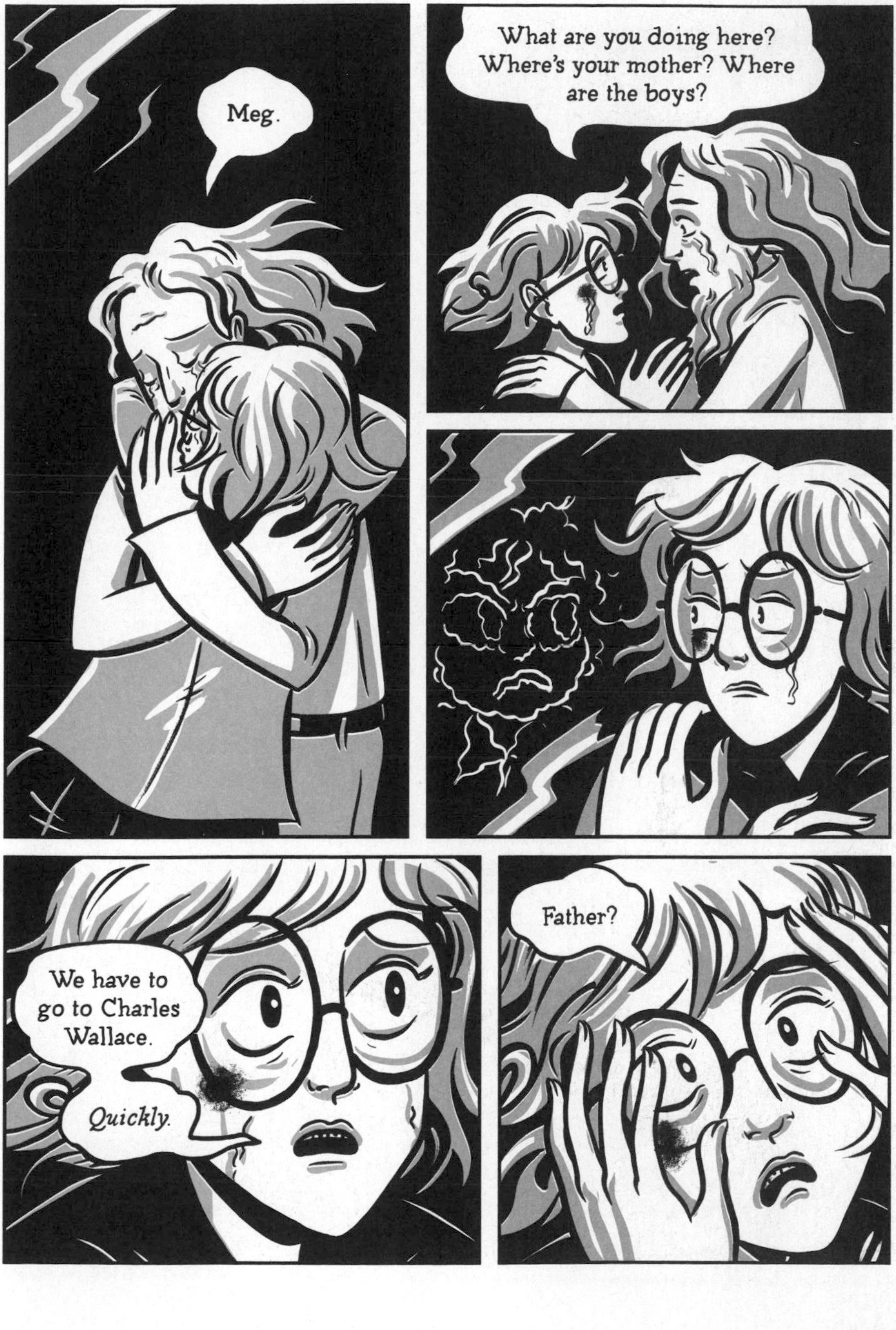
Meg.
What are you doing here? Where's your mother? Where are the boys?
We have to go to Charles Wallace.
Quickly.
Father?

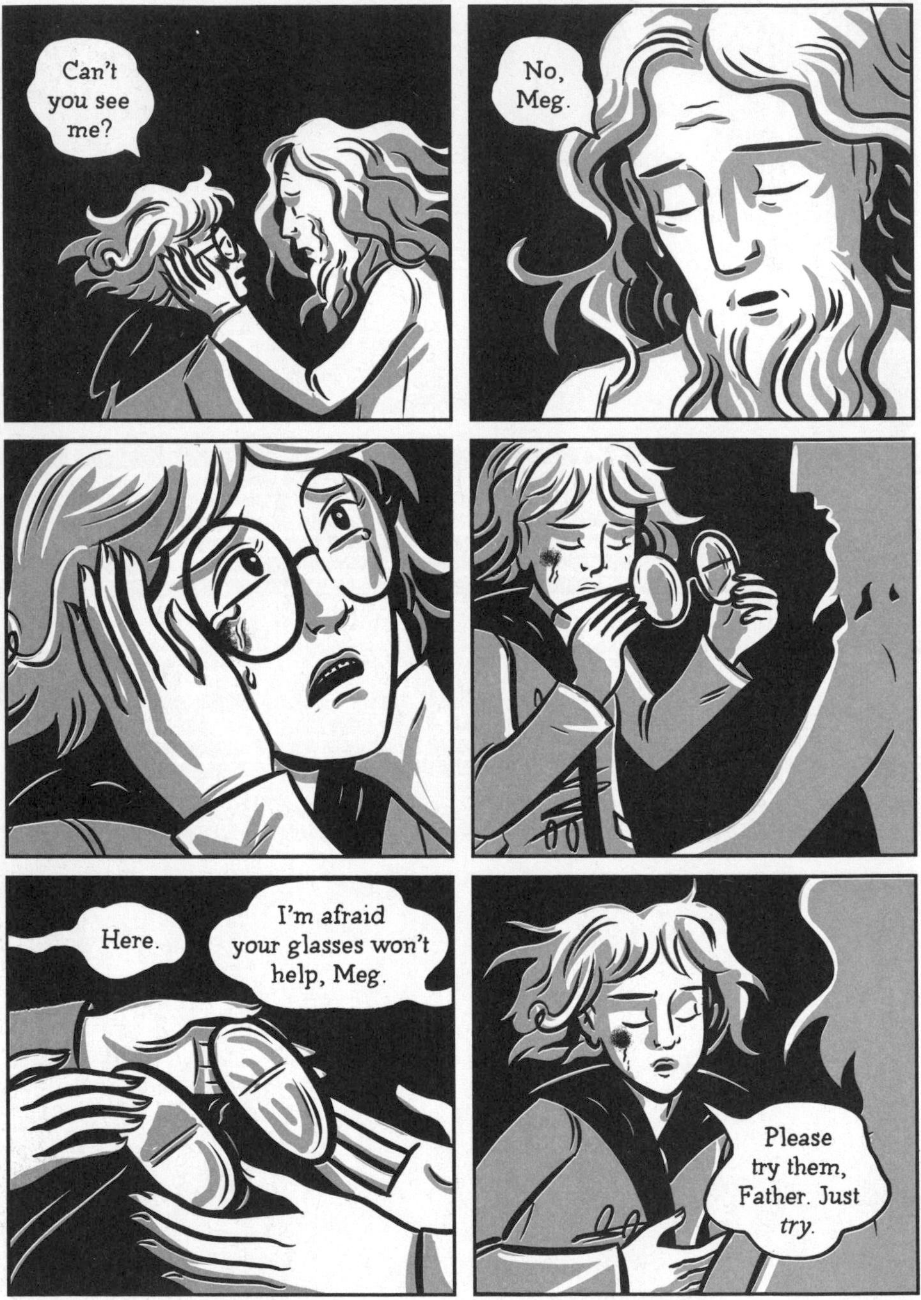
Can't you see me?
No, Meg.
Here.
I'm afraid your glasses won't help, Meg.
Please try them, Father. Just *try*.

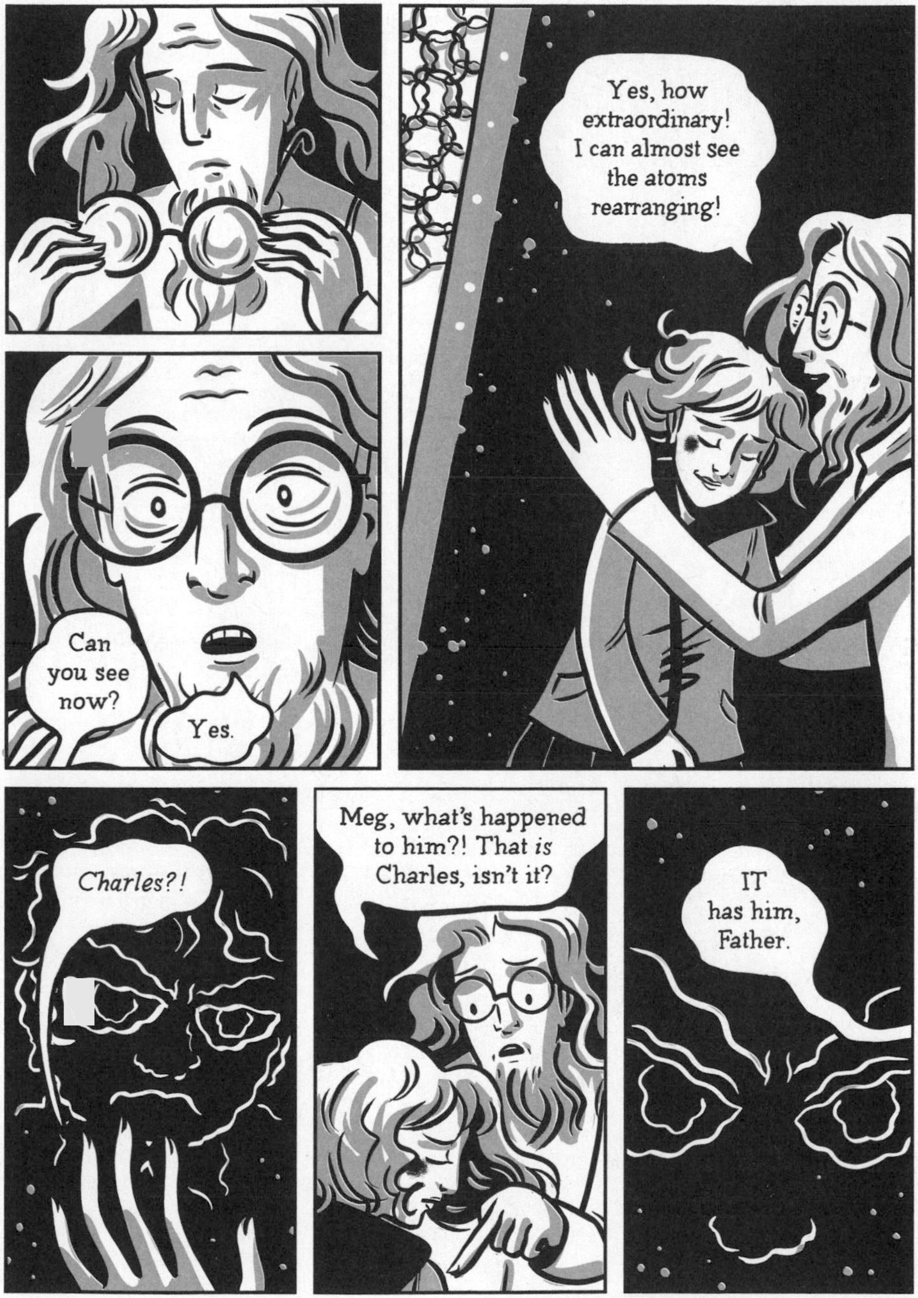
Can you see now?
Yes.
Yes, how extraordinary! I can almost see the atoms rearranging!
Charles?!
Meg, what's happened to him?! That *is* Charles, isn't it?
IT has him, Father.

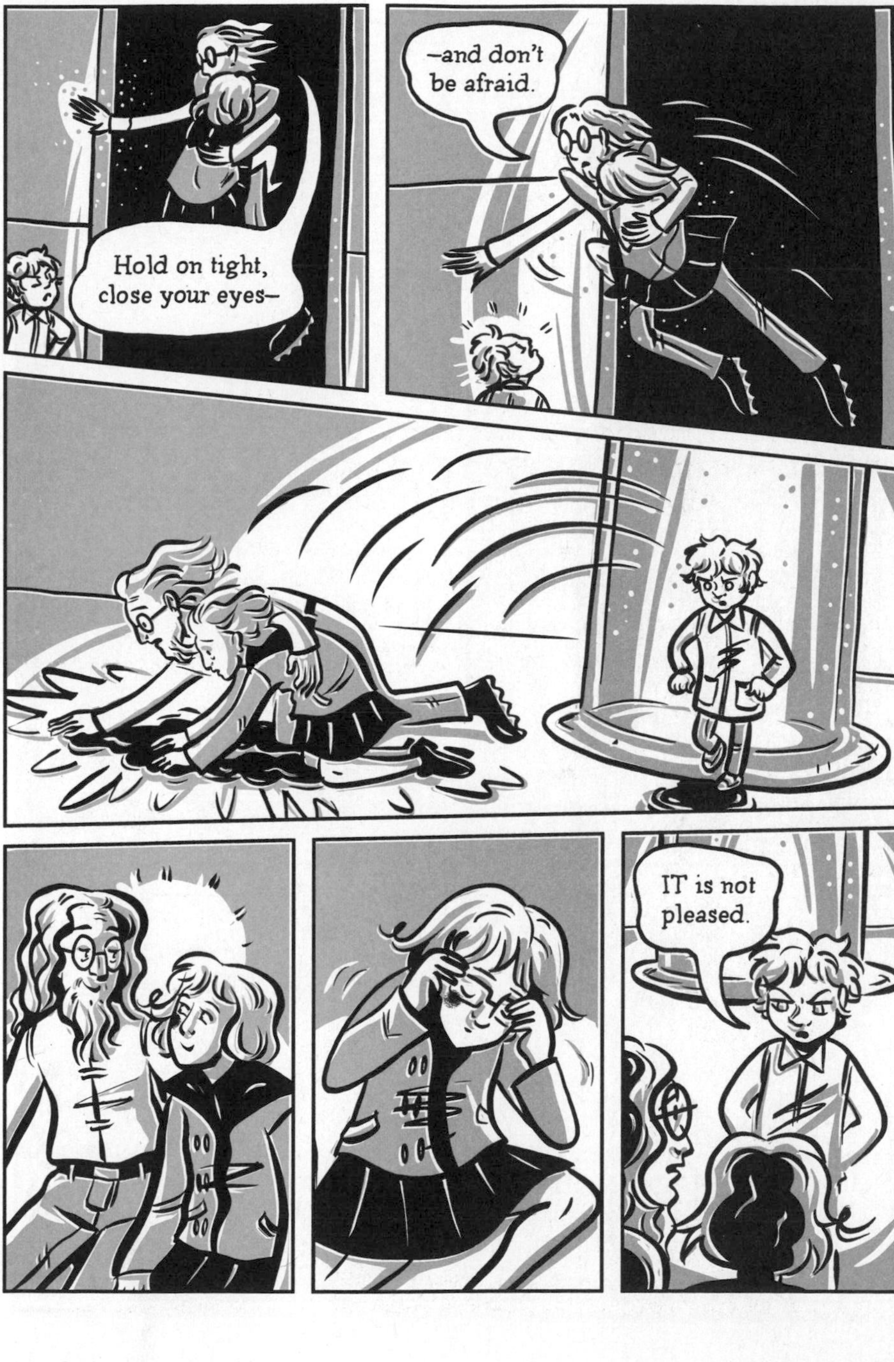
Hold on tight, close your eyes—
—and don't be afraid.
IT is not pleased.

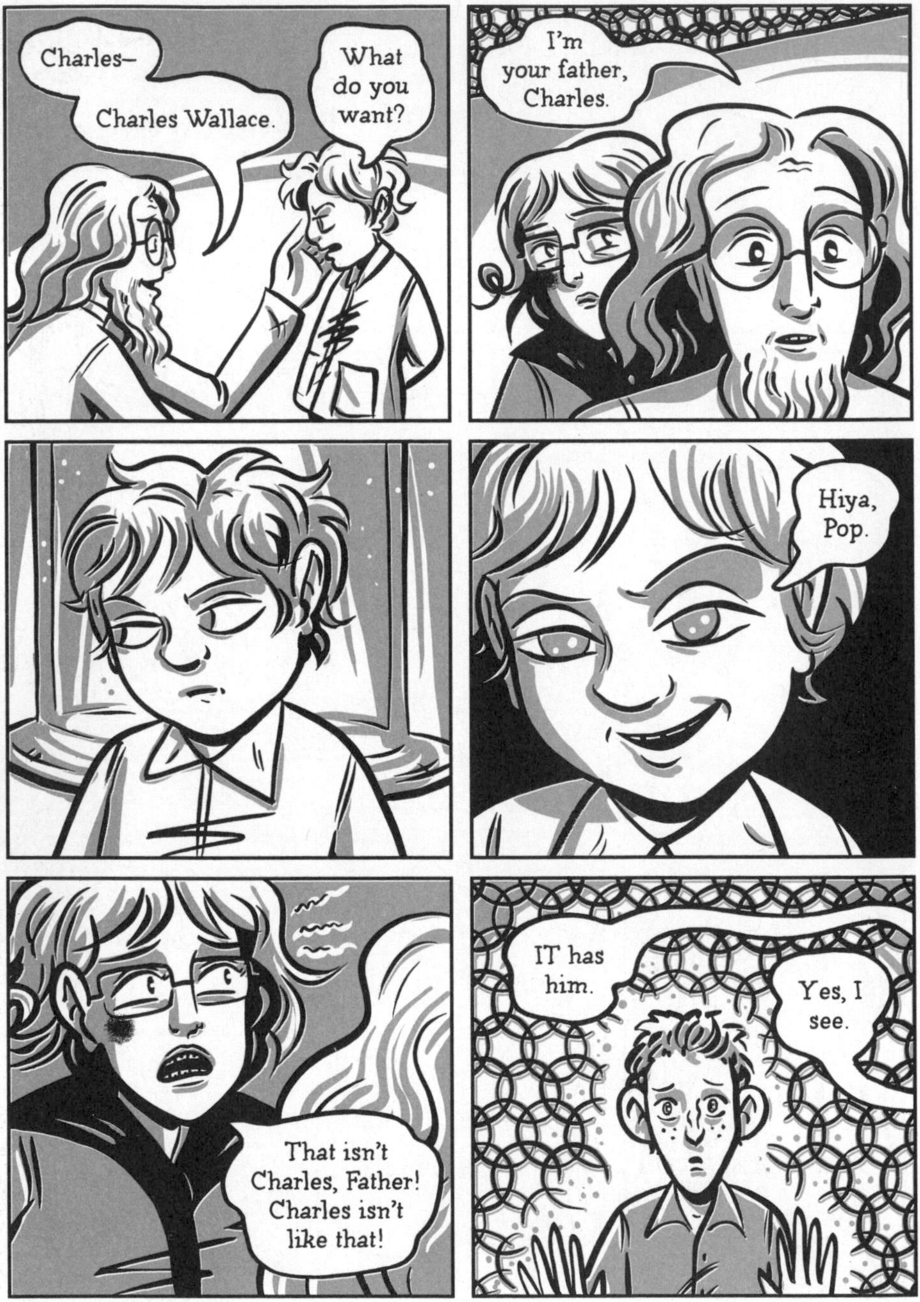
Charles–
Charles Wallace.
What do you want?
I'm your father, Charles.
Hiya, Pop.
That isn't Charles, Father! Charles isn't like that!
IT has him.
Yes, I see.

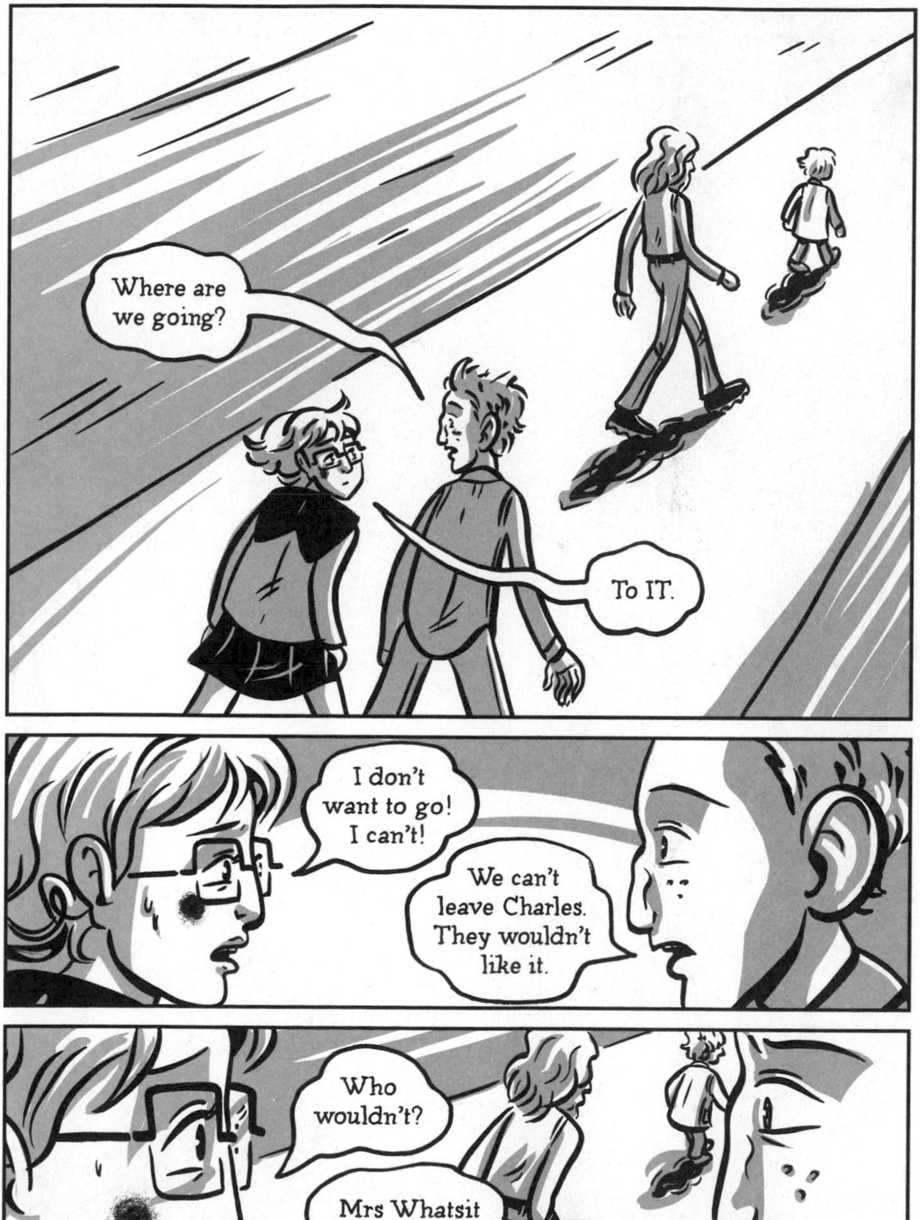

Where are we going?
To IT.
I don't want to go! I can't!
We can't leave Charles. They wouldn't like it.
Who wouldn't?
Mrs Whatsit & Co.

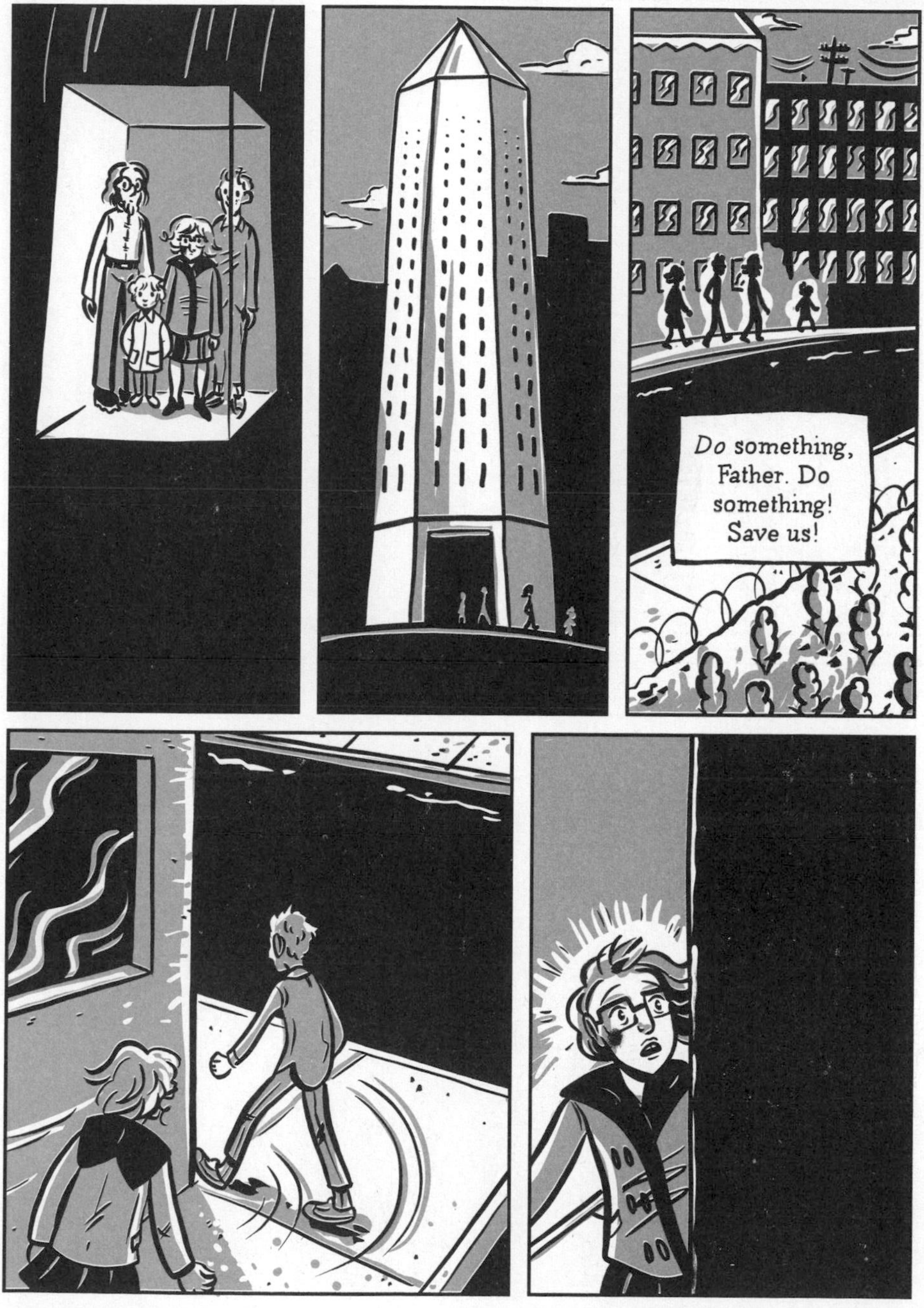
Do something, Father. Do something! Save us!

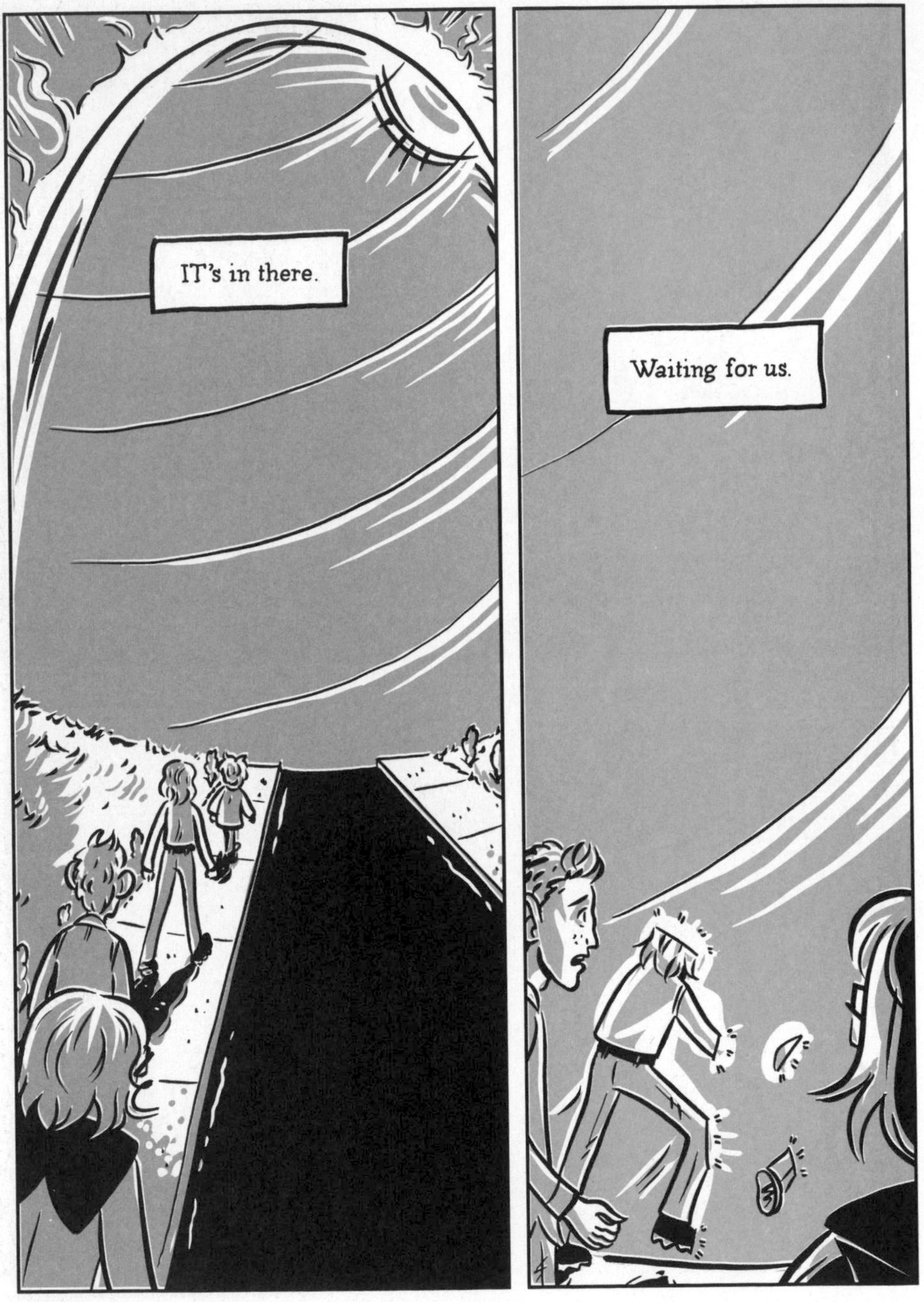
IT's in there.
Waiting for us.

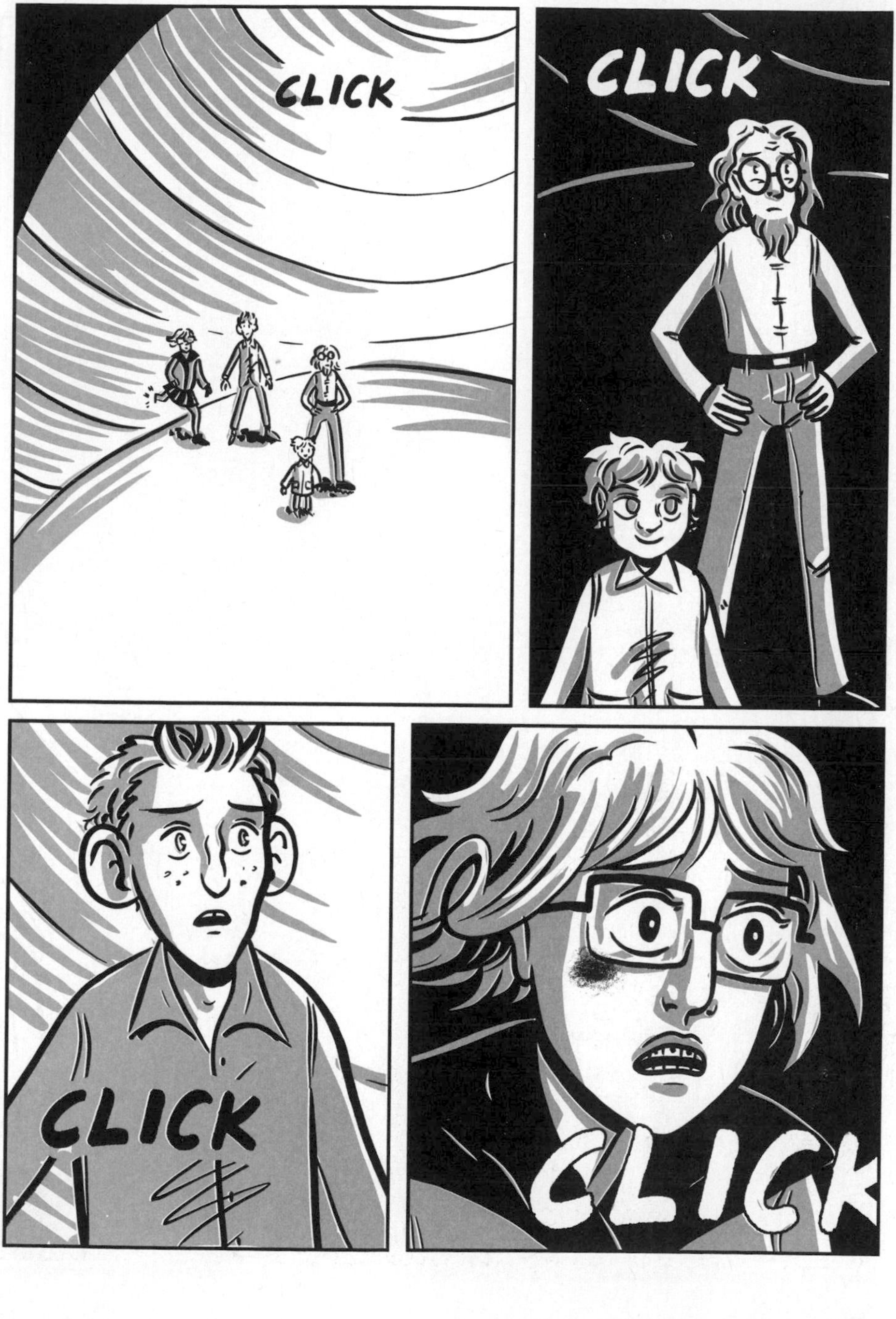
CLICK
CLICK
CLICK
CLICK

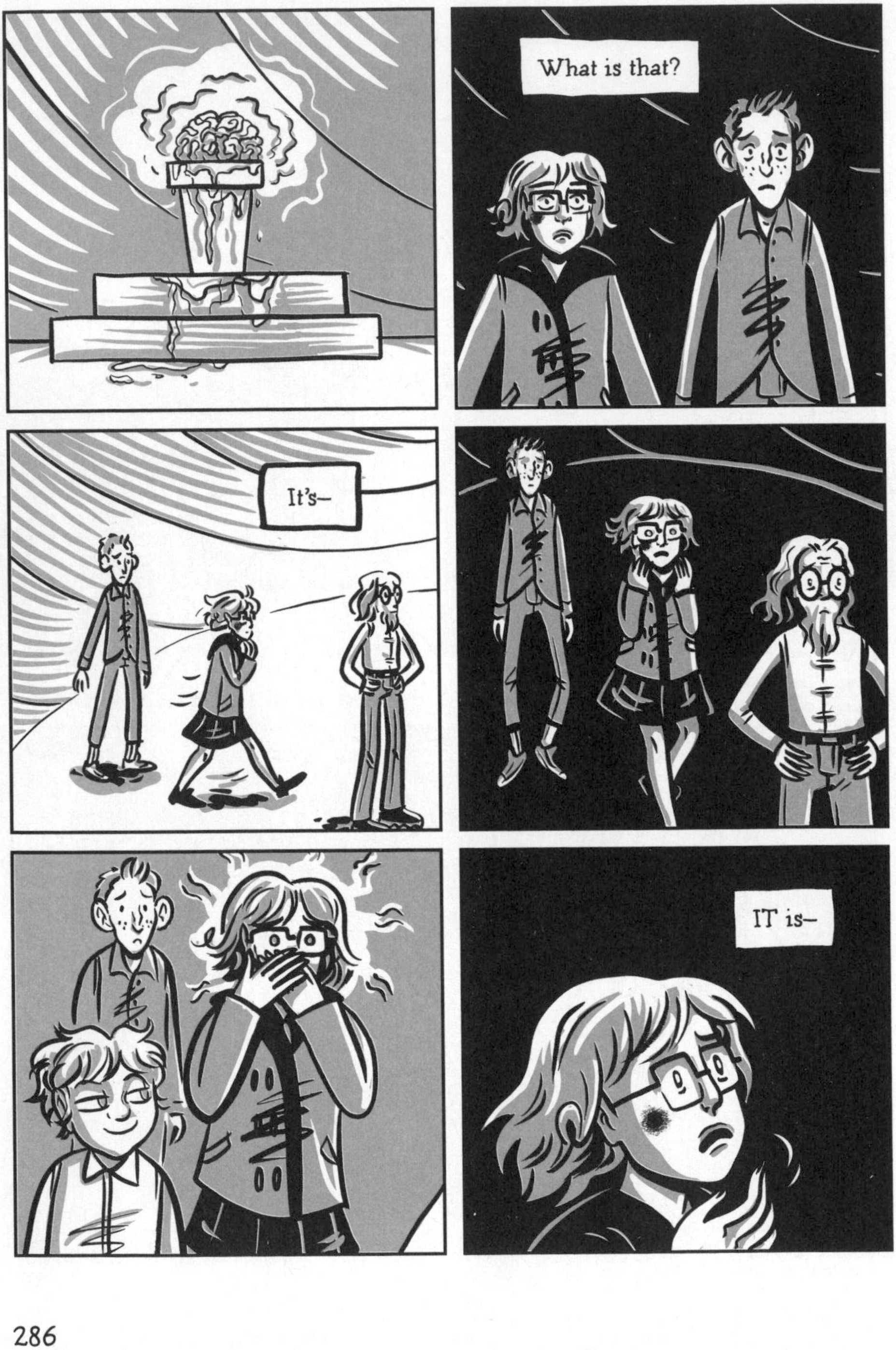
What is that?
It's–
IT is–

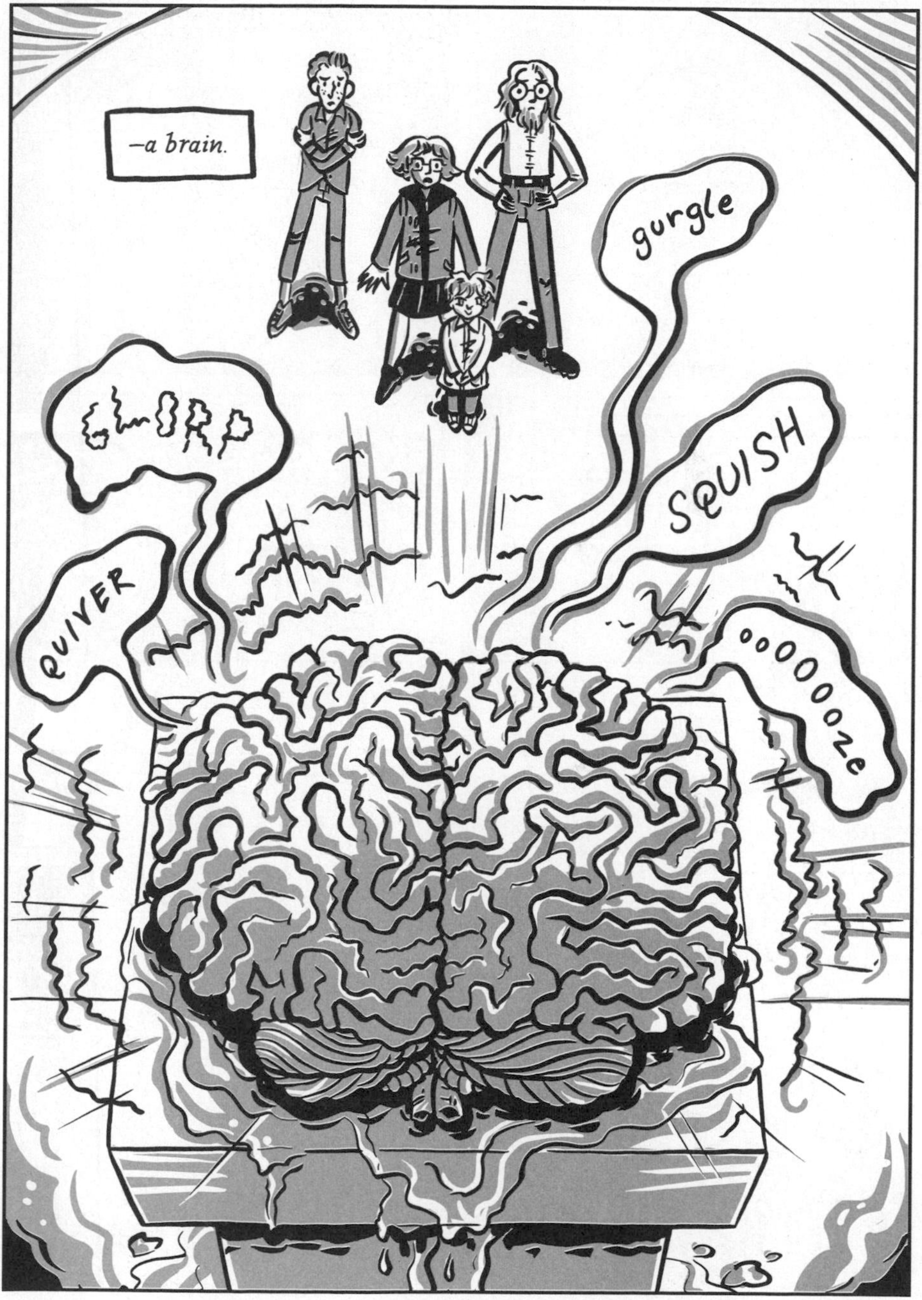
—a brain.
GLORP
gurgle
SQUISH
QUIVER
oooOOOooze

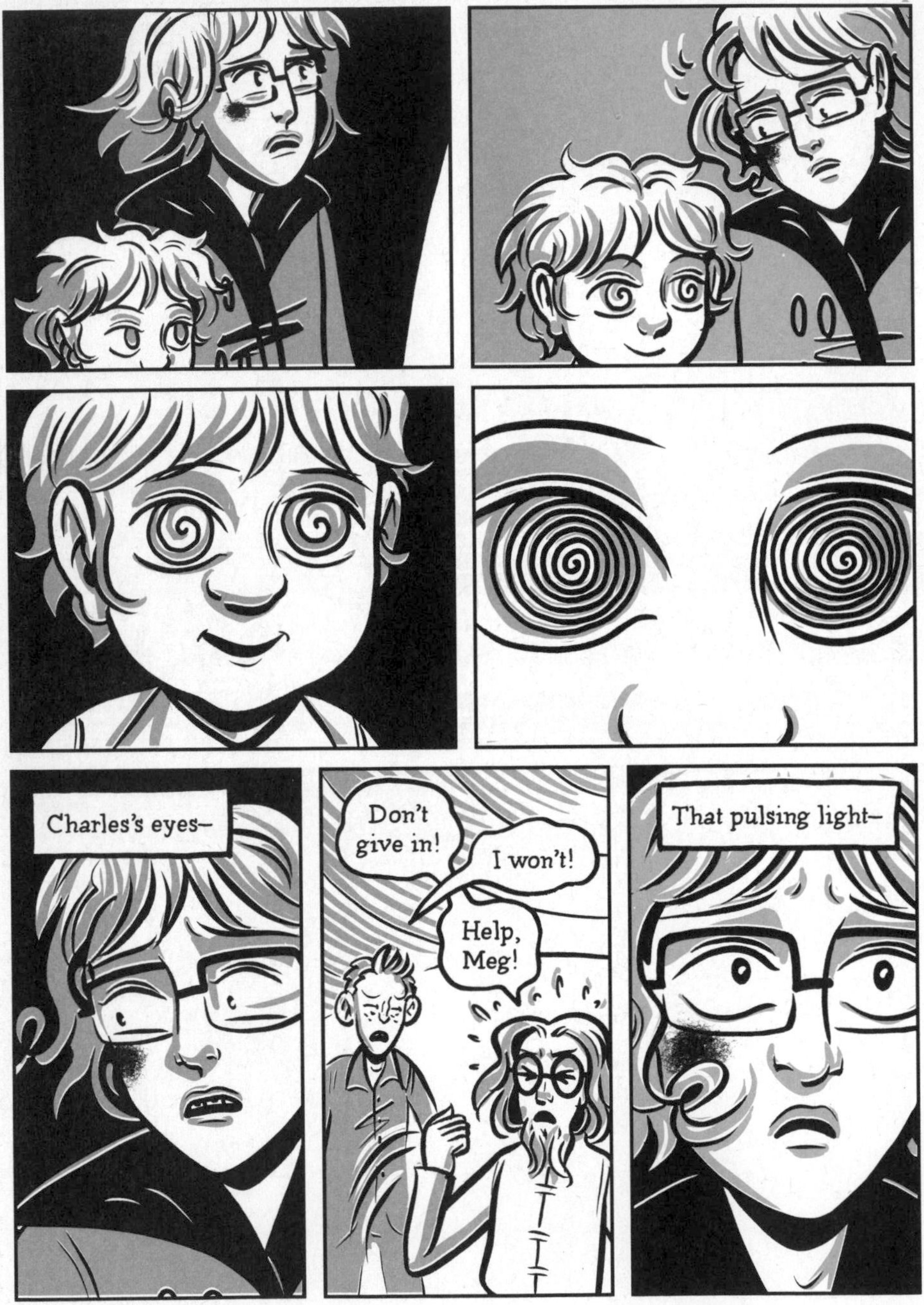
Charles's eyes—
Don't give in!
I won't!
Help, Meg!
That pulsing light—

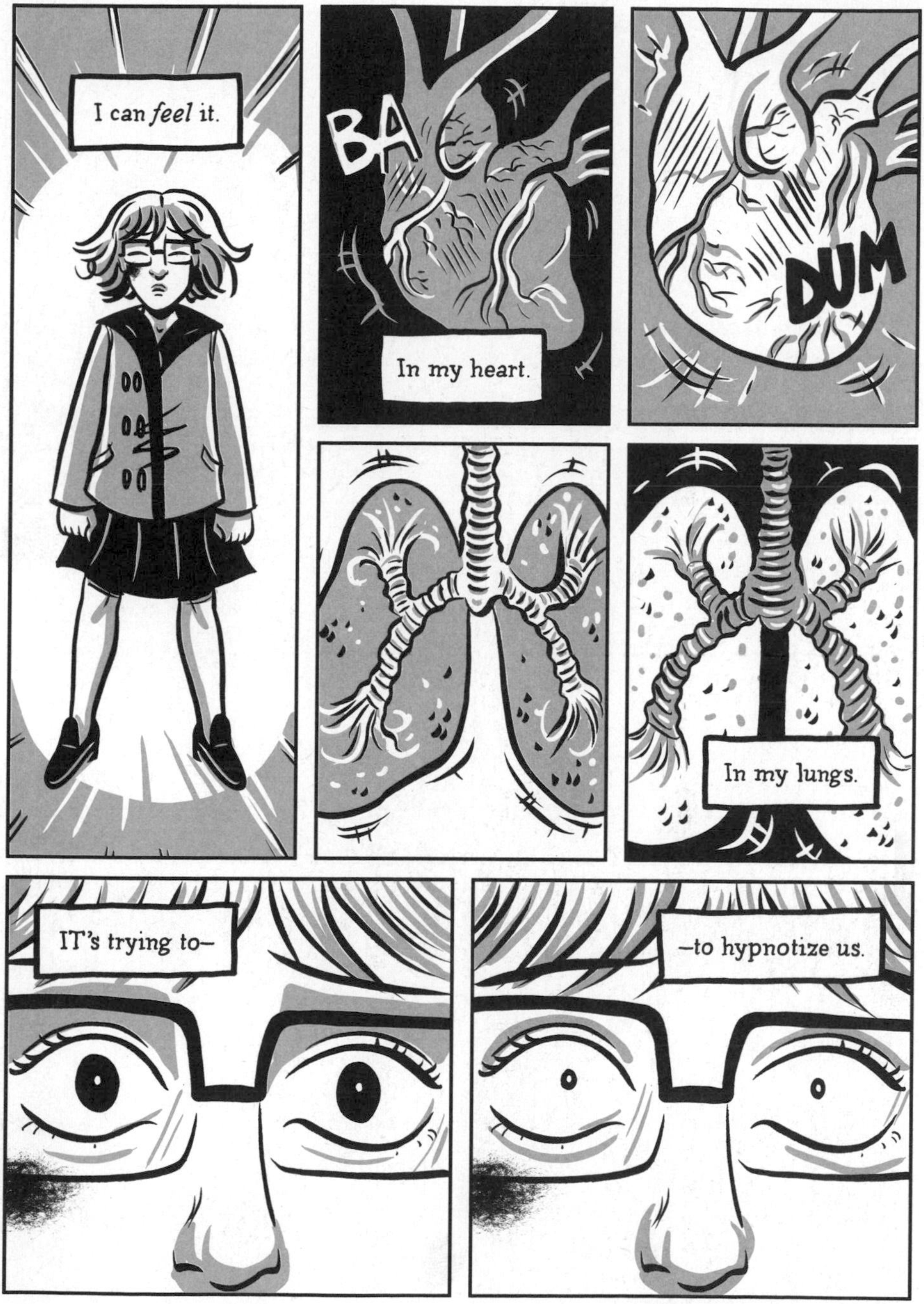
I can *feel* it.
BA
In my heart.
DUM
In my lungs.
IT's trying to—
—to hypnotize us.

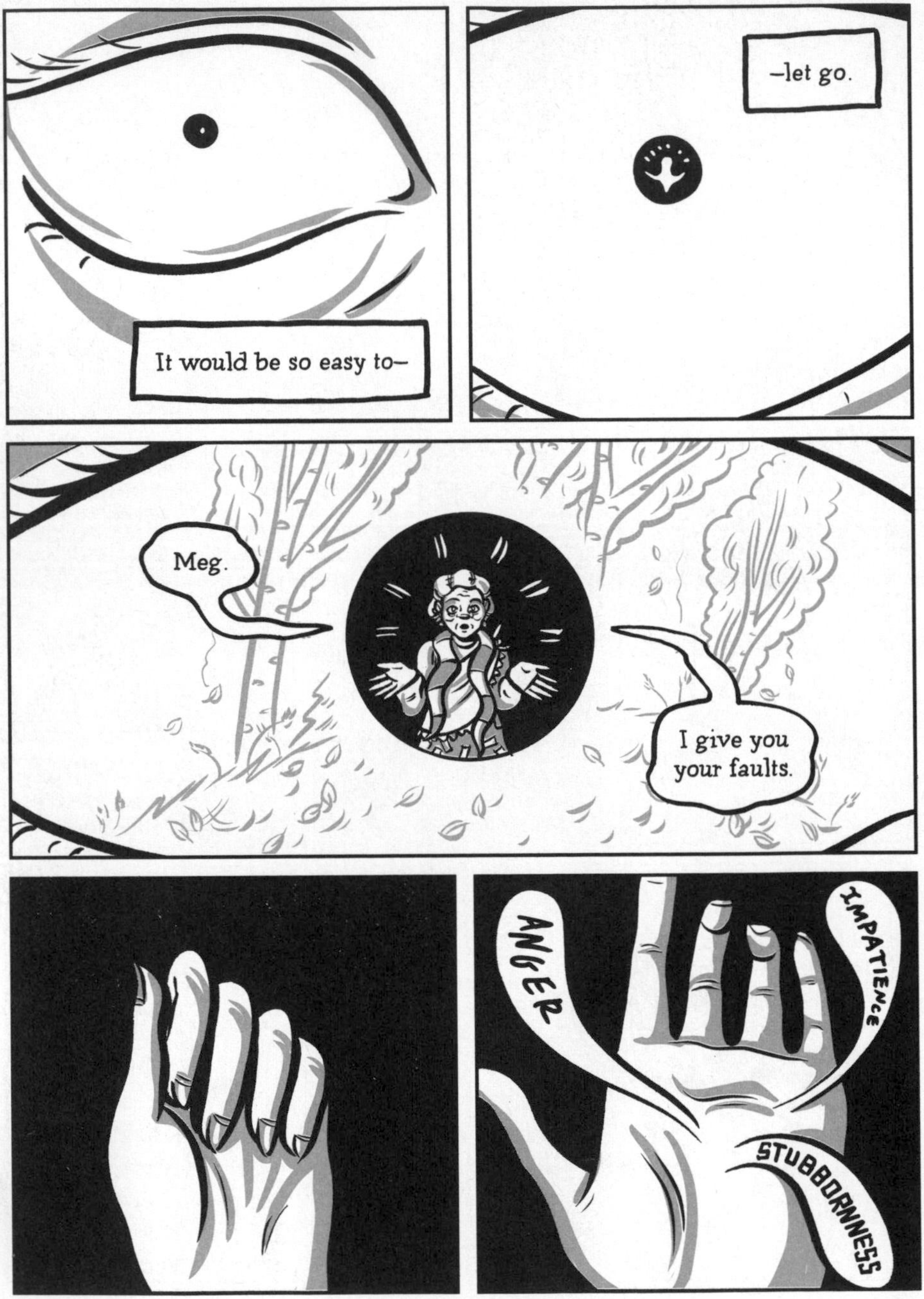
It would be so easy to–
–let go.
Meg.
I give you your faults.
ANGER
IMPATIENCE
STUBBORNNESS

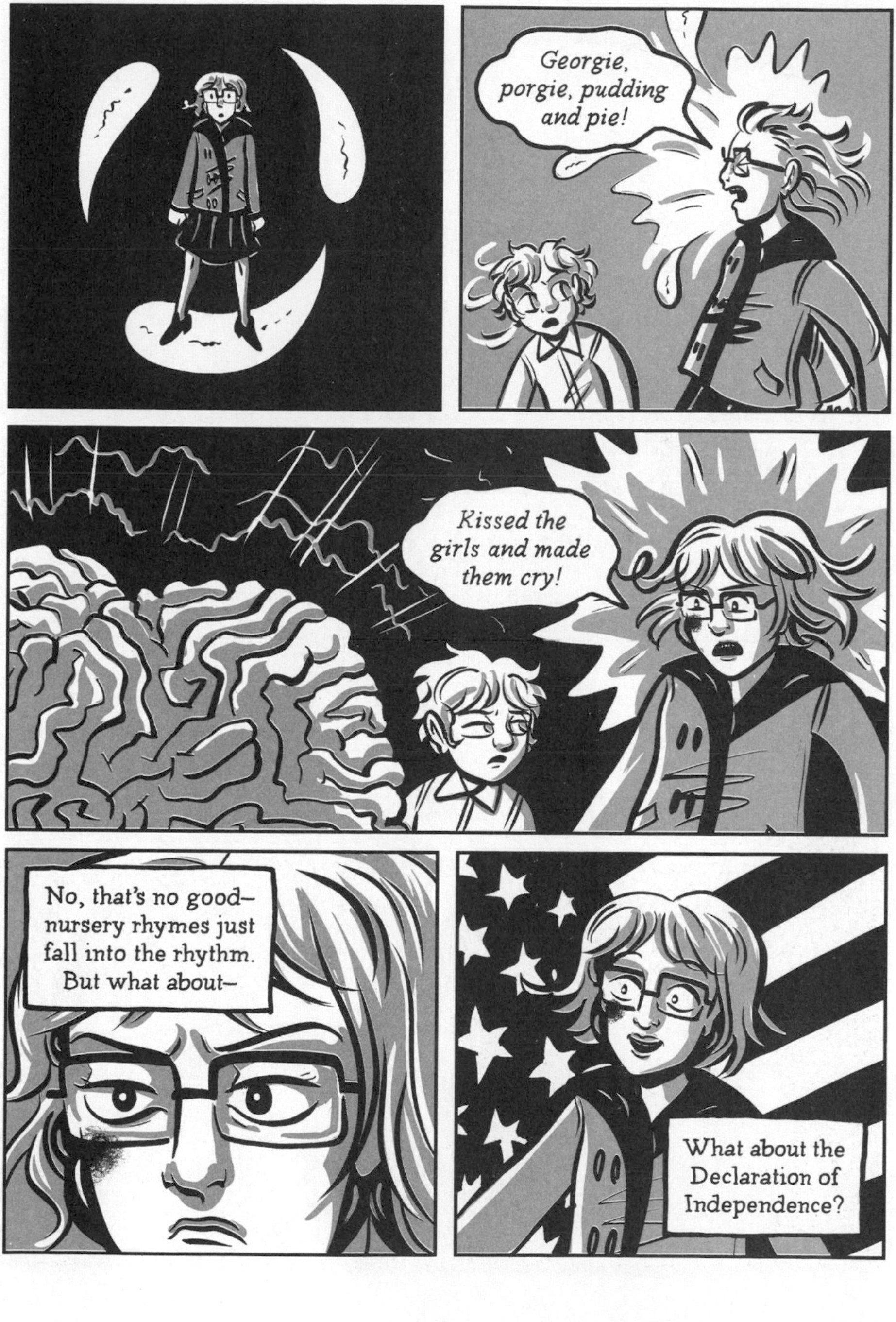
Georgie, porgie, pudding and pie!
Kissed the girls and made them cry!
No, that's no good– nursery rhymes just fall into the rhythm. But what about–
What about the Declaration of Independence?

292

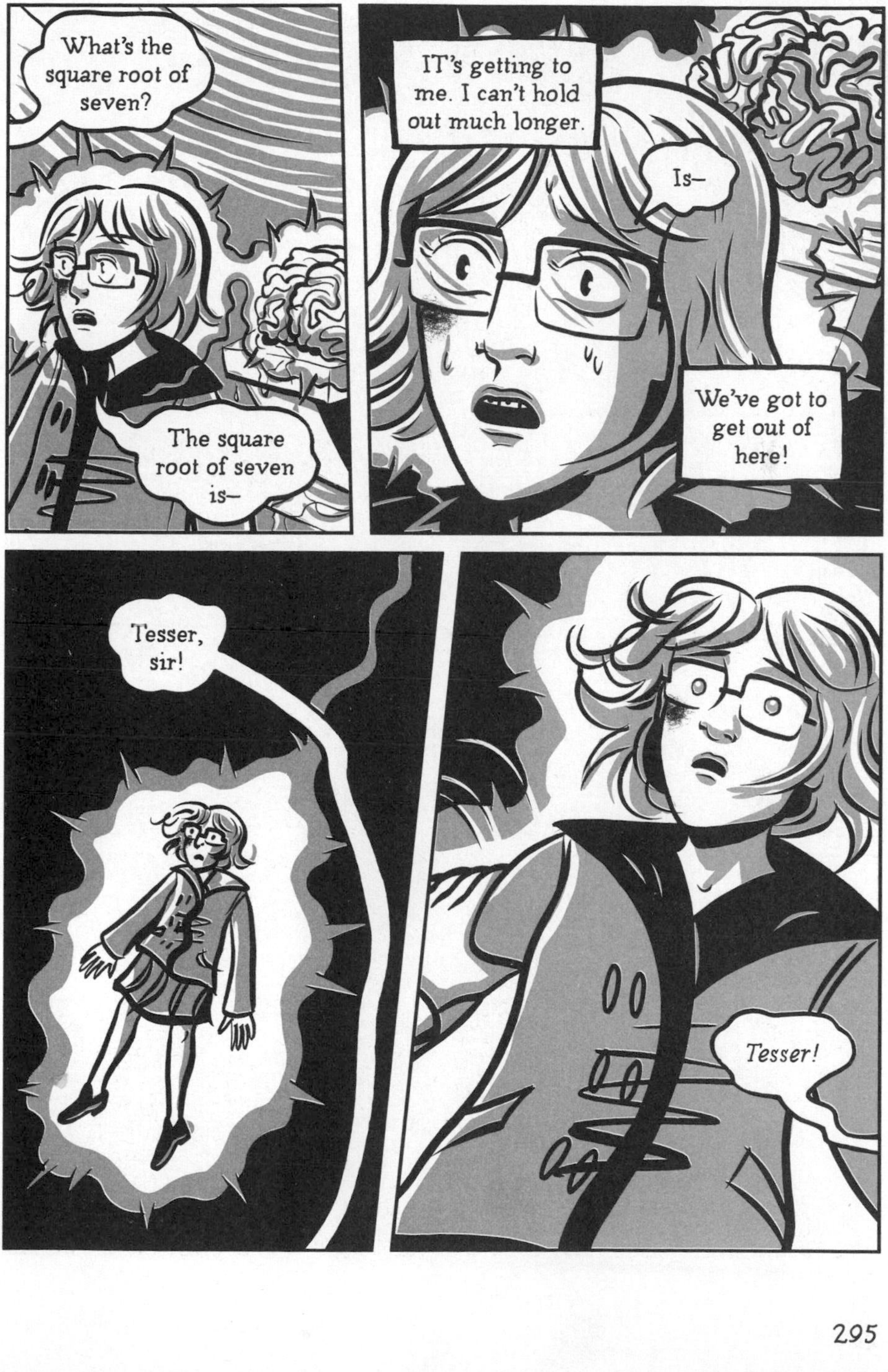
What's the square root of seven?
The square root of seven is–
IT's getting to me. I can't hold out much longer.
Is–
We've got to get out of here!
Tesser, sir!
Tesser!

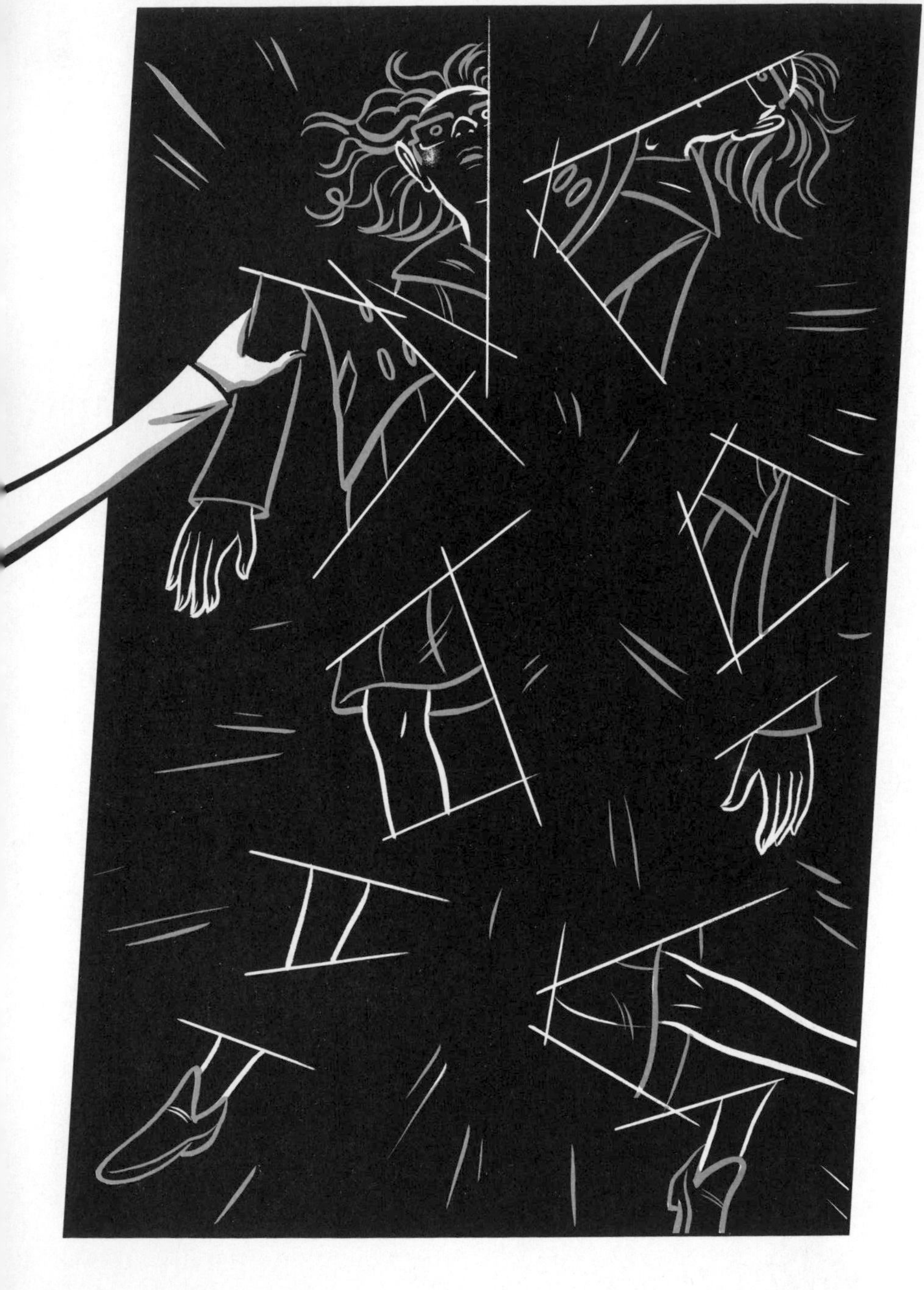

10
Absolute Zero

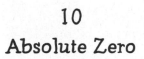

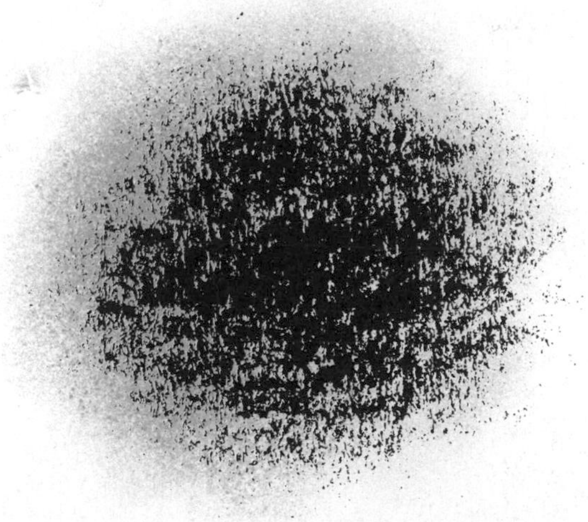

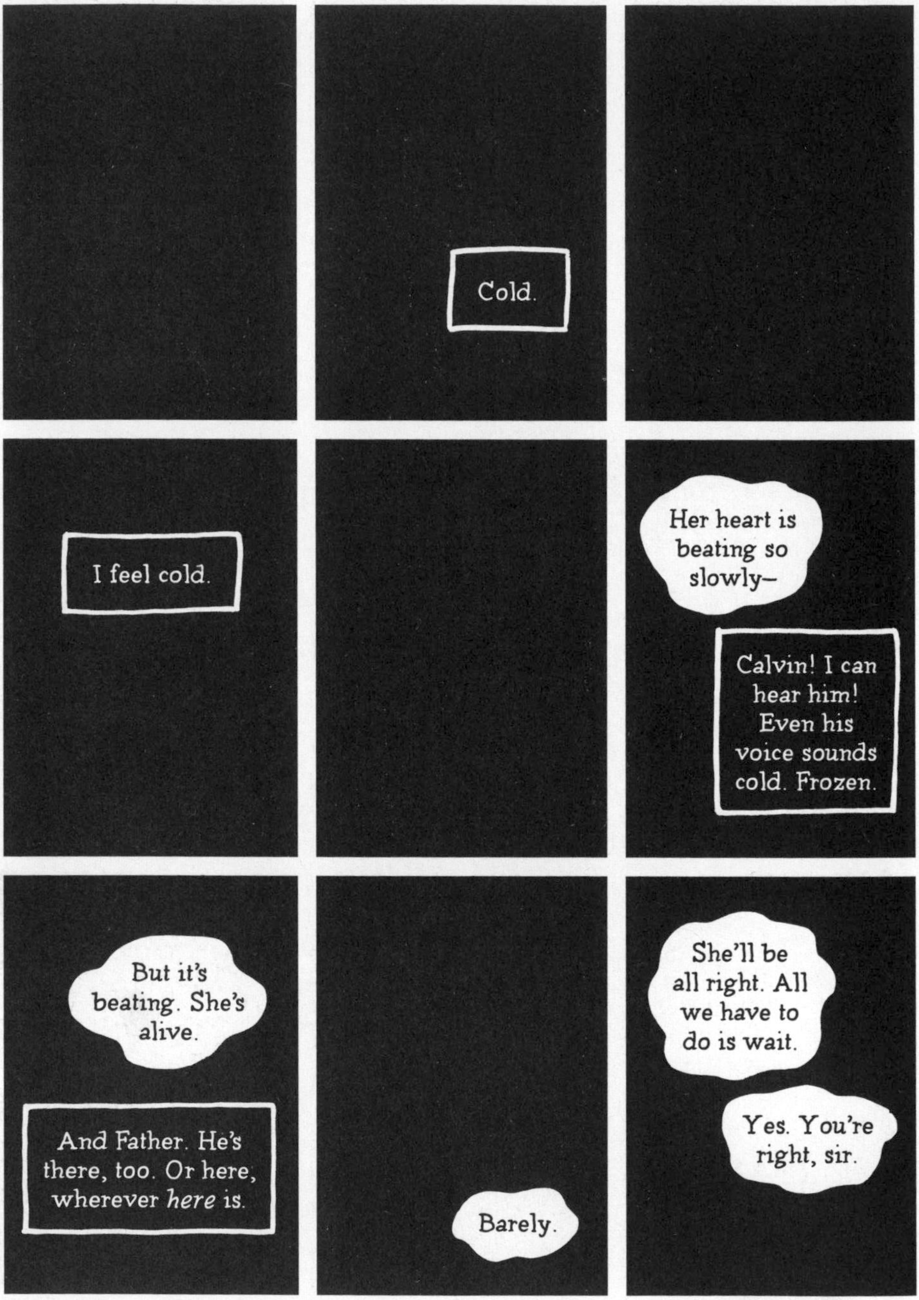
Cold.
I feel cold.
Her heart is beating so slowly–
Calvin! I can hear him! Even his voice sounds cold. Frozen.
But it's beating. She's alive.
And Father. He's there, too. Or here, wherever *here* is.
Barely.
She'll be all right. All we have to do is wait.
Yes. You're right, sir.

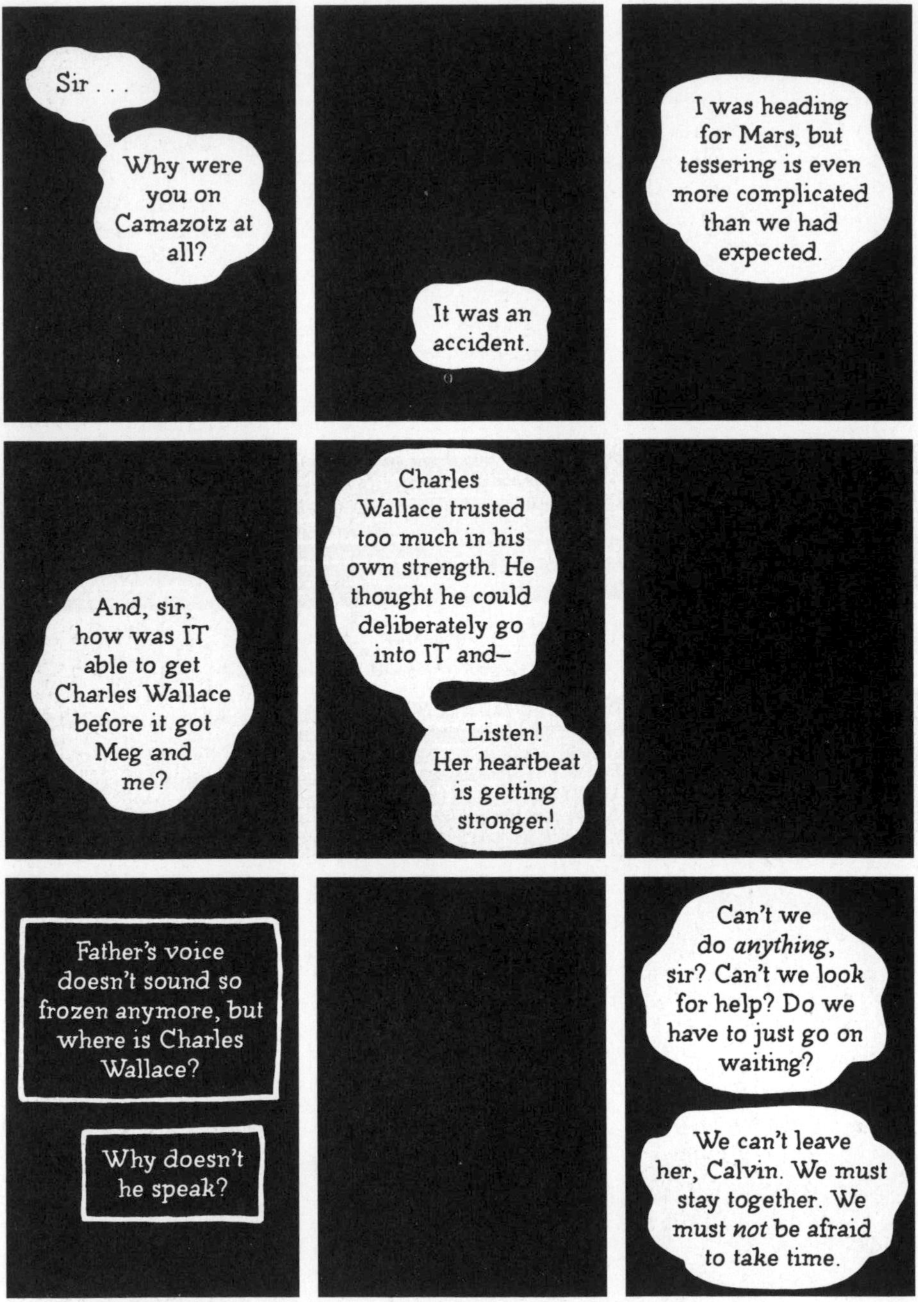
Sir . . .
Why were you on Camazotz at all?
It was an accident.
I was heading for Mars, but tessering is even more complicated than we had expected.
And, sir, how was IT able to get Charles Wallace before it got Meg and me?
Charles Wallace trusted too much in his own strength. He thought he could deliberately go into IT and–
Listen! Her heartbeat is getting stronger!
Father's voice doesn't sound so frozen anymore, but where is Charles Wallace?
Why doesn't he speak?
Can't we do *anything*, sir? Can't we look for help? Do we have to just go on waiting?
We can't leave her, Calvin. We must stay together. We must *not* be afraid to take time.

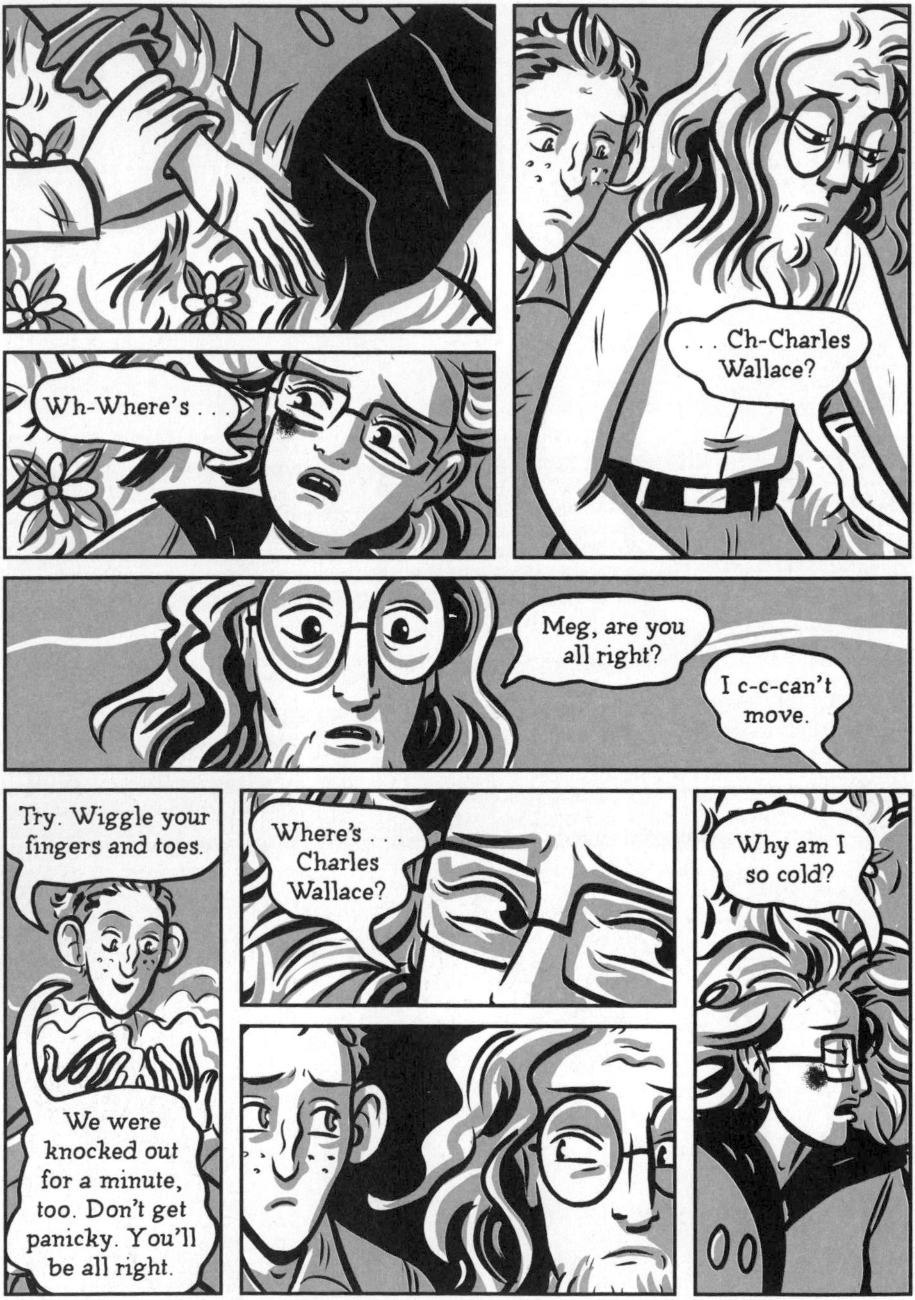
Wh-Where's . . .
. . . Ch-Charles Wallace?
Meg, are you all right?
I c-c-can't move.
Try. Wiggle your fingers and toes.
We were knocked out for a minute, too. Don't get panicky. You'll be all right.
Where's . . . Charles Wallace?
Why am I so cold?

If your father had tried to yank Charles away when he tessered us, and if IT had kept grabbing hold of Charles, it might have been too much for him— and we'd have lost him forever.

No, Meg, we didn't "just leave him."

And we had to do something right then.

Why?

IT was taking us. You and I were slipping, and if your father had gone on trying to help us, he wouldn't have been able to hold out, either.

You told him to tesser!

There isn't any question of blame!

Can you move yet?

No! And you'd better take me back to Camazotz and Charles Wallace *now*. You're supposed to be able to *help*!

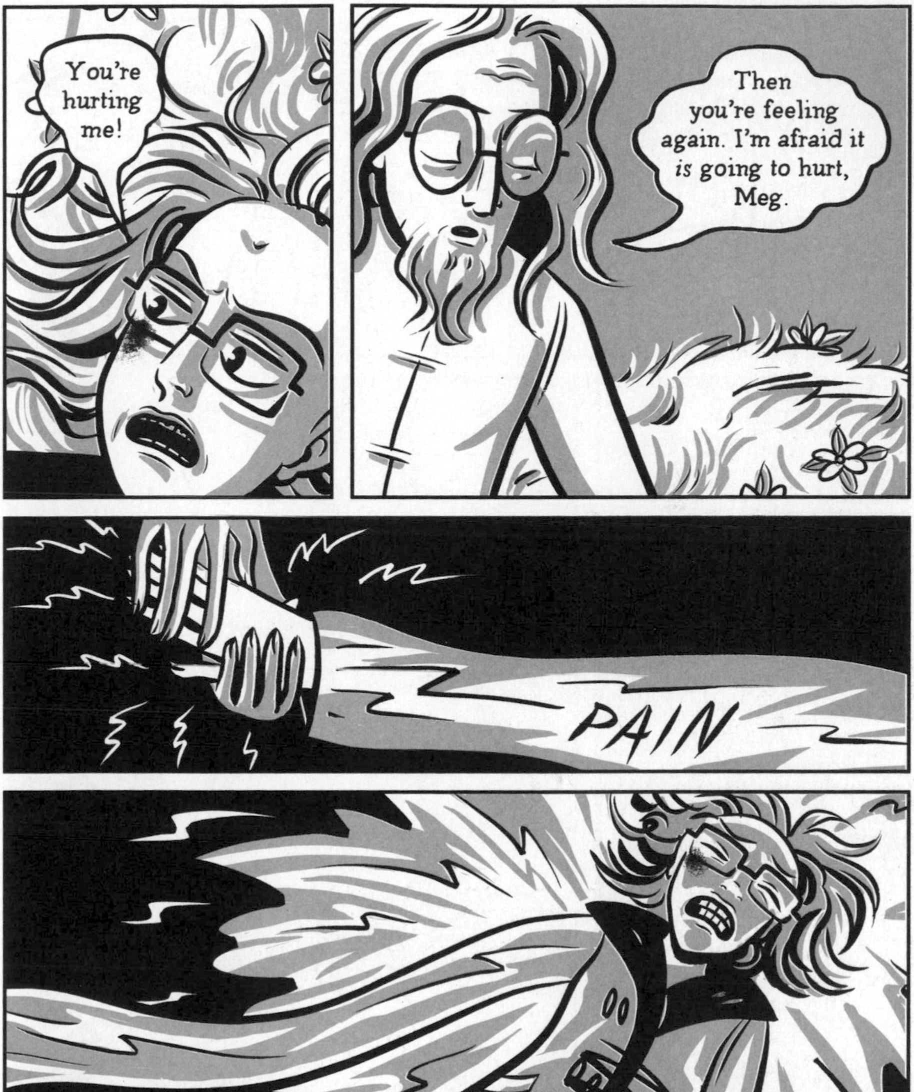
You're hurting me!
Then you're feeling again. I'm afraid it *is* going to hurt, Meg.
PAIN

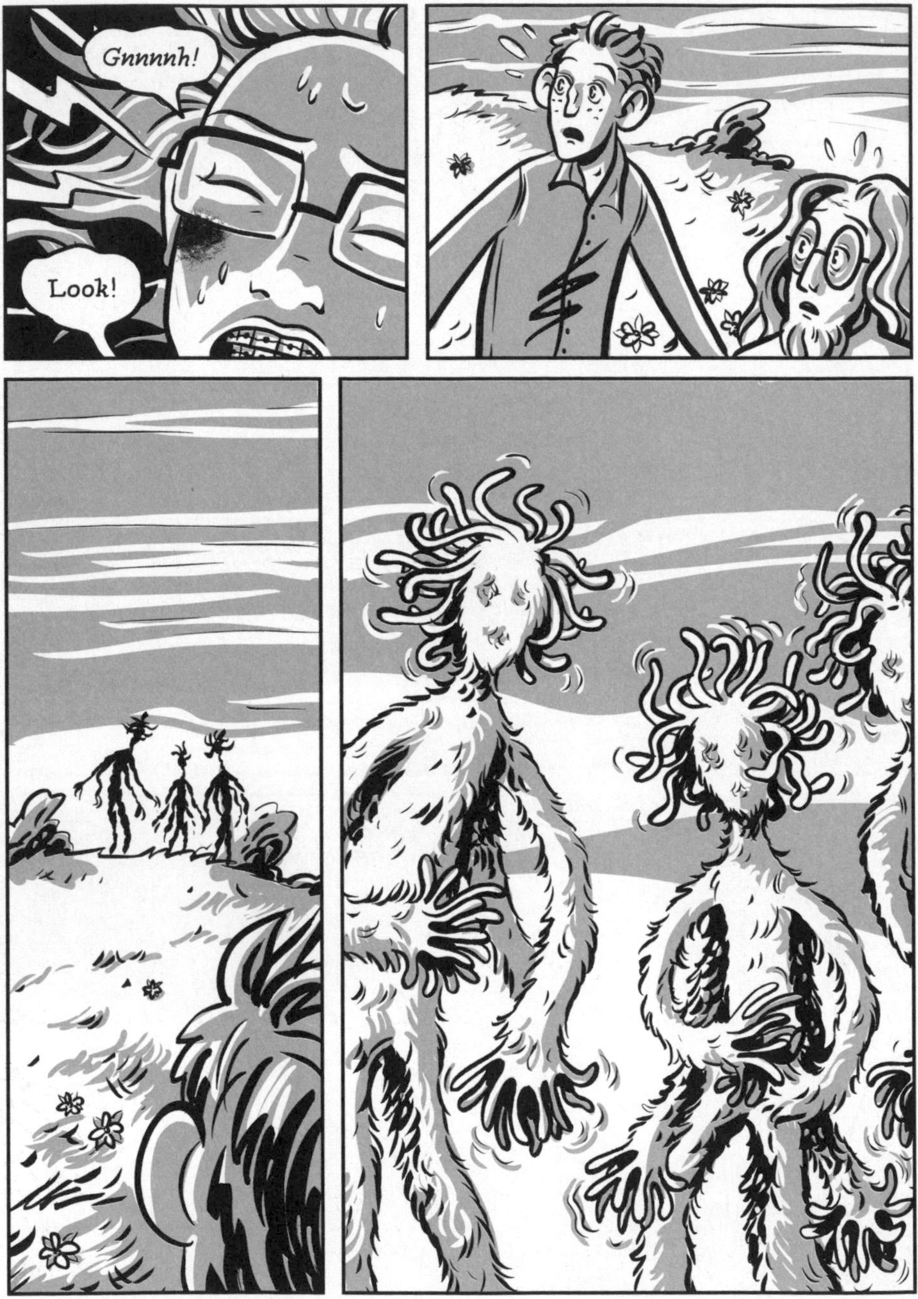
Gnnnnh!
Look!

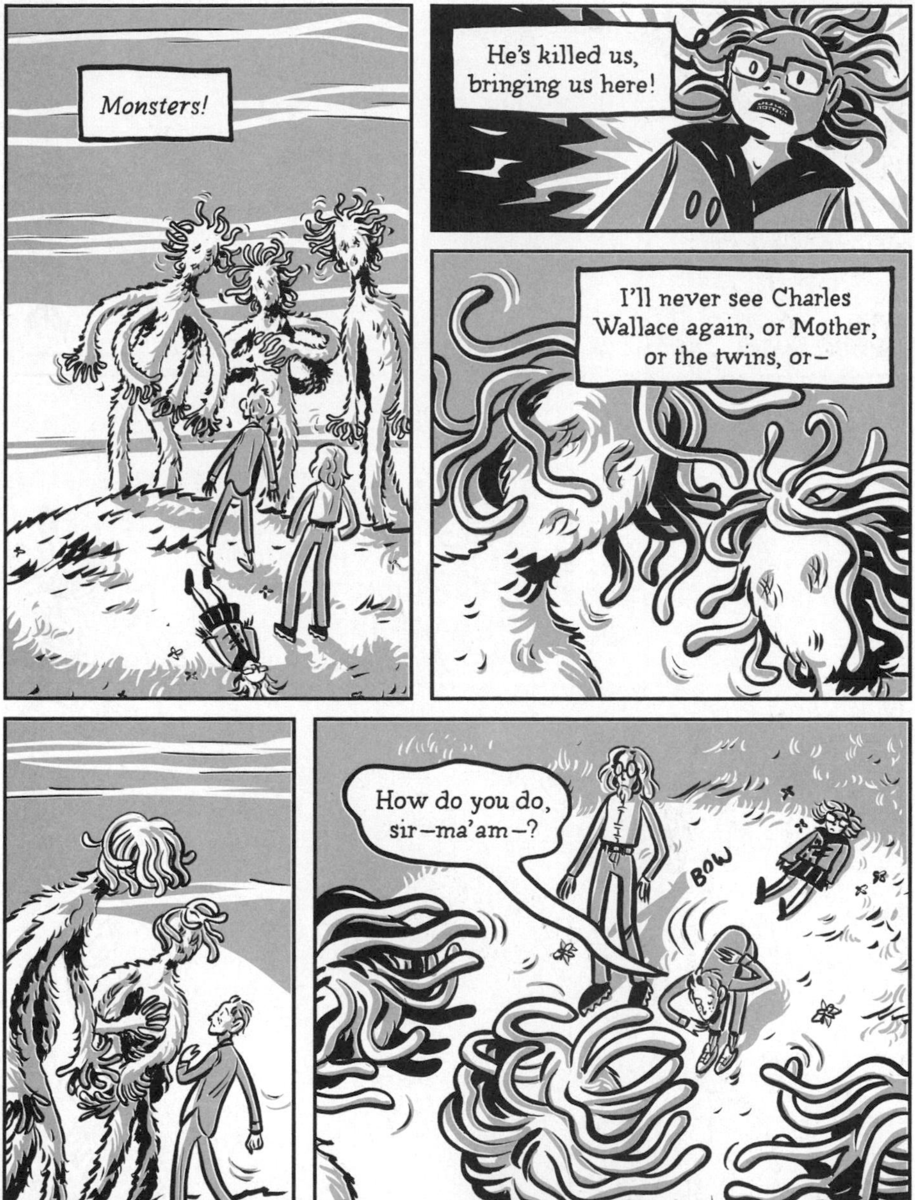
Monsters!
He's killed us, bringing us here!
I'll never see Charles Wallace again, or Mother, or the twins, or–
How do you do, sir–ma'am–?
BOW

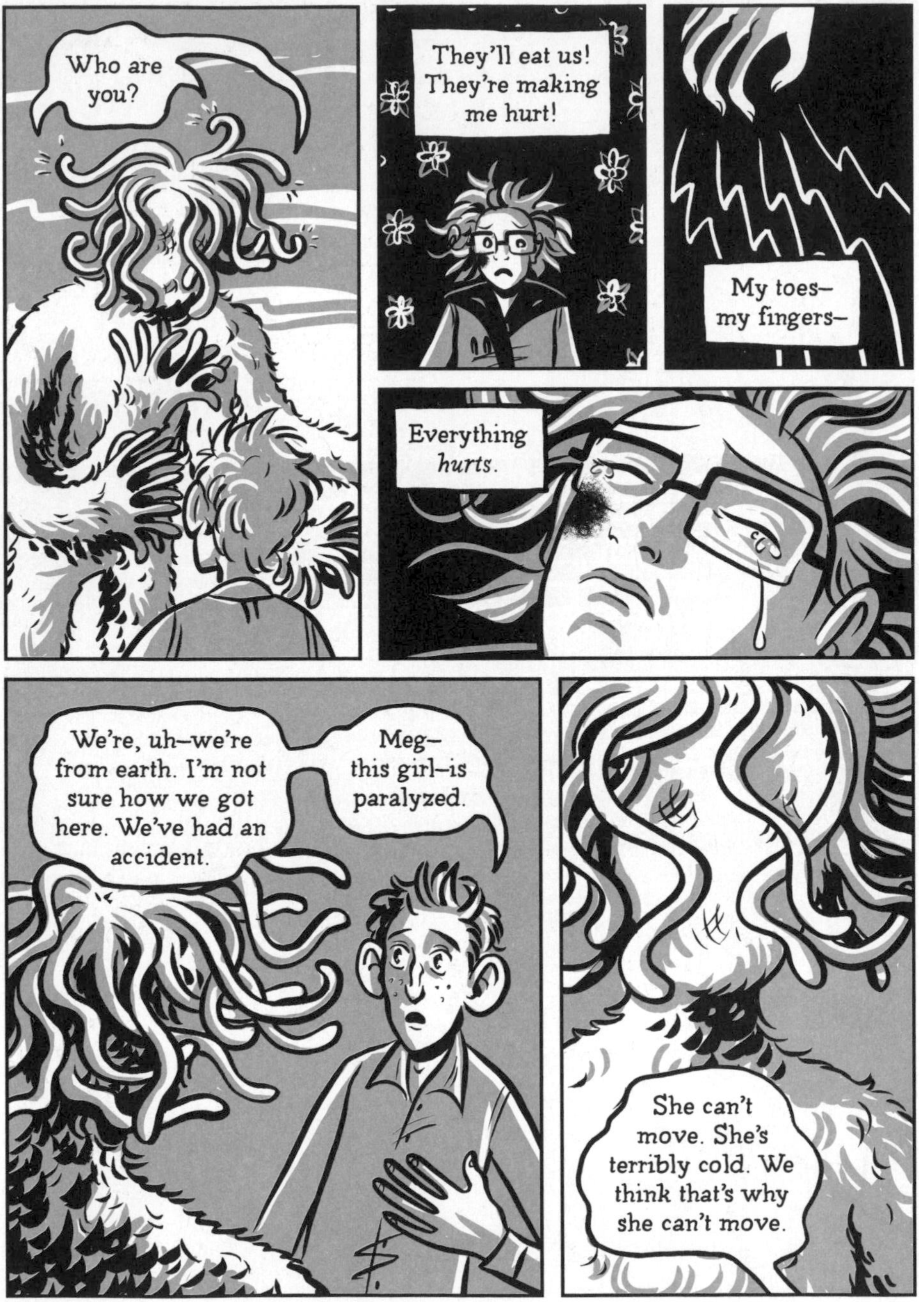
Who are you?
They'll eat us! They're making me hurt!
My toes—my fingers—
Everything *hurts*.
We're, uh—we're from earth. I'm not sure how we got here. We've had an accident.
Meg—this girl—is paralyzed.
She can't move. She's terribly cold. We think that's why she can't move.

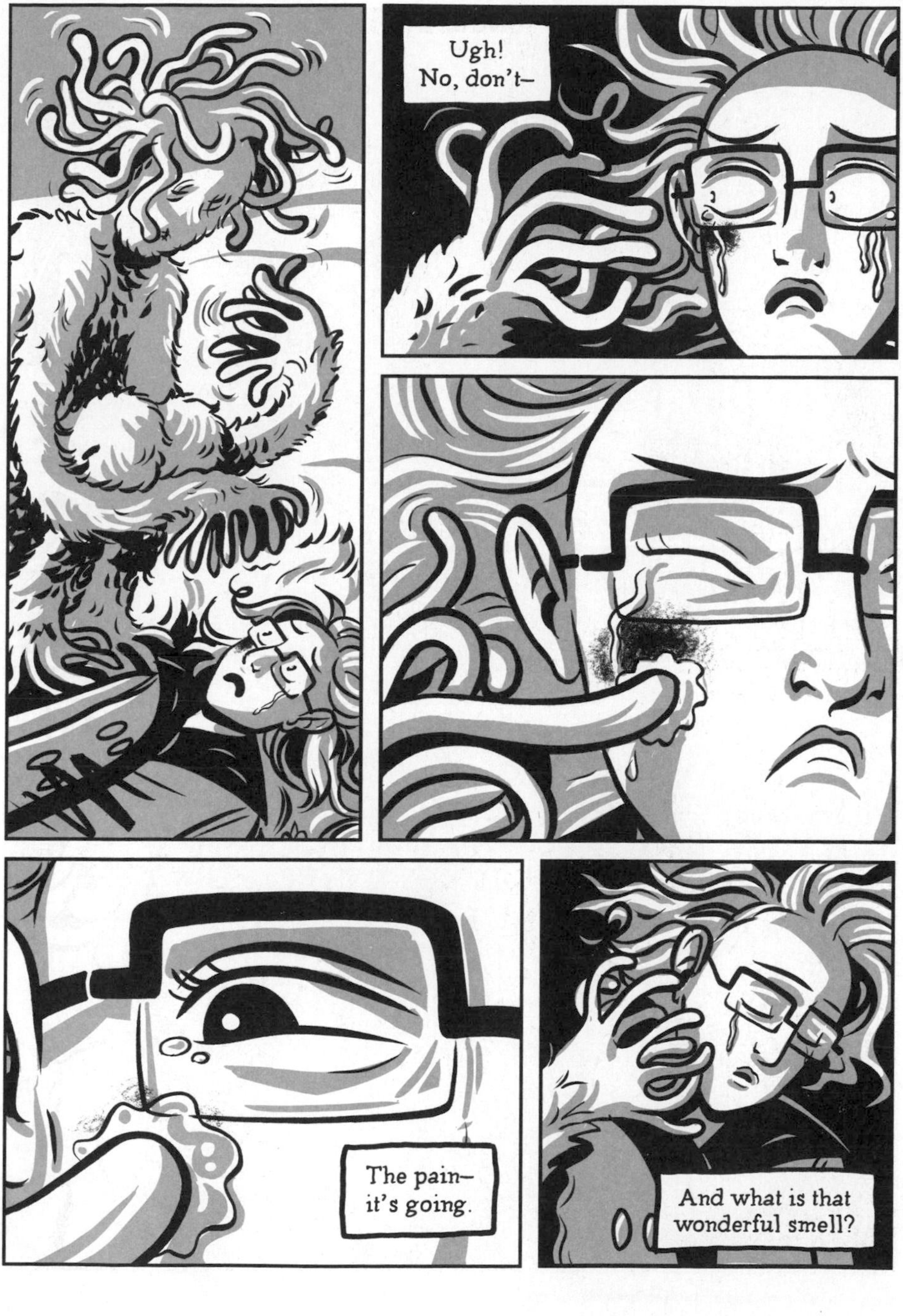
Ugh!
No, don't–
The pain–
it's going.
And what is that
wonderful smell?

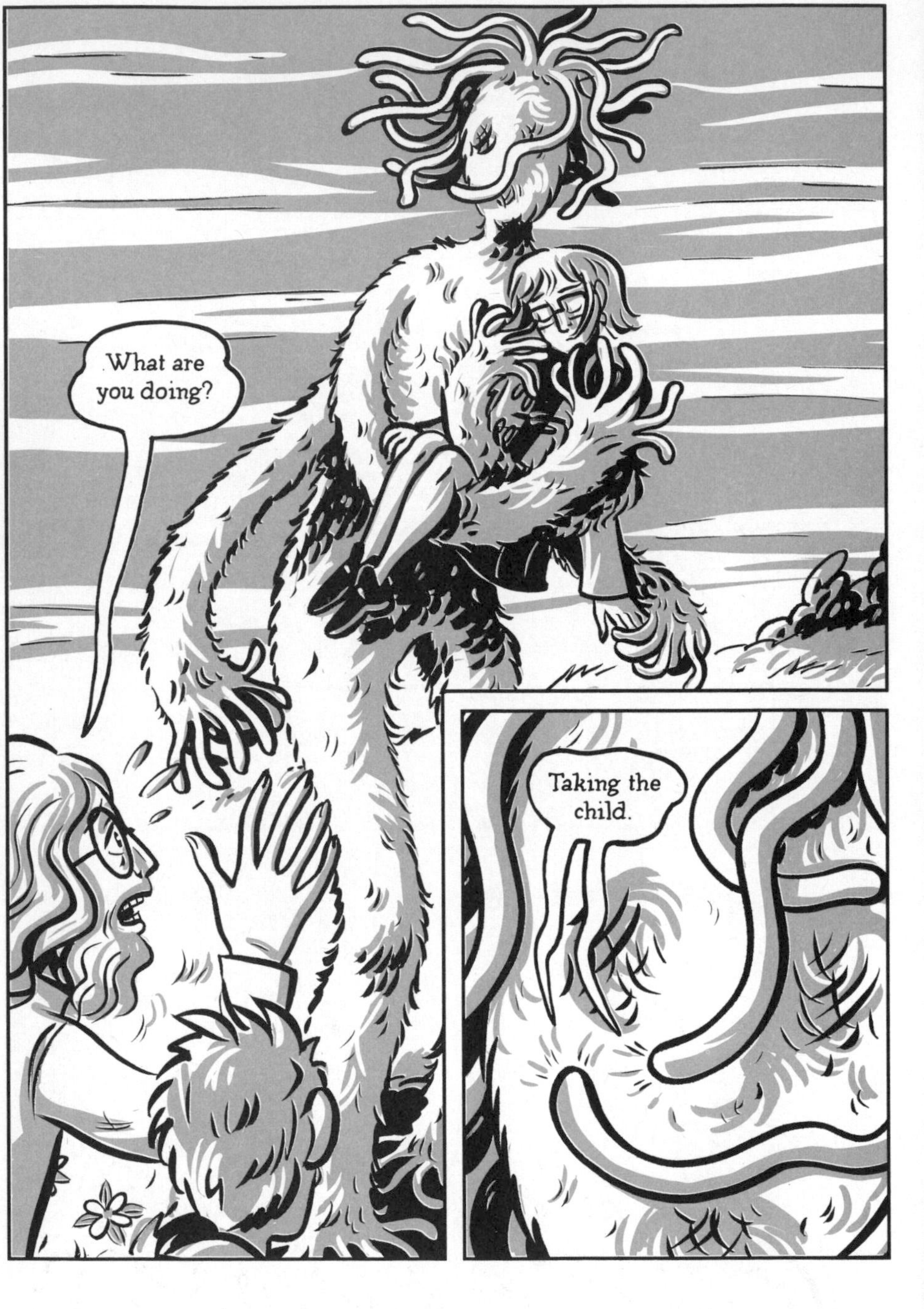
What are you doing?
Taking the child.

11
Aunt Beast

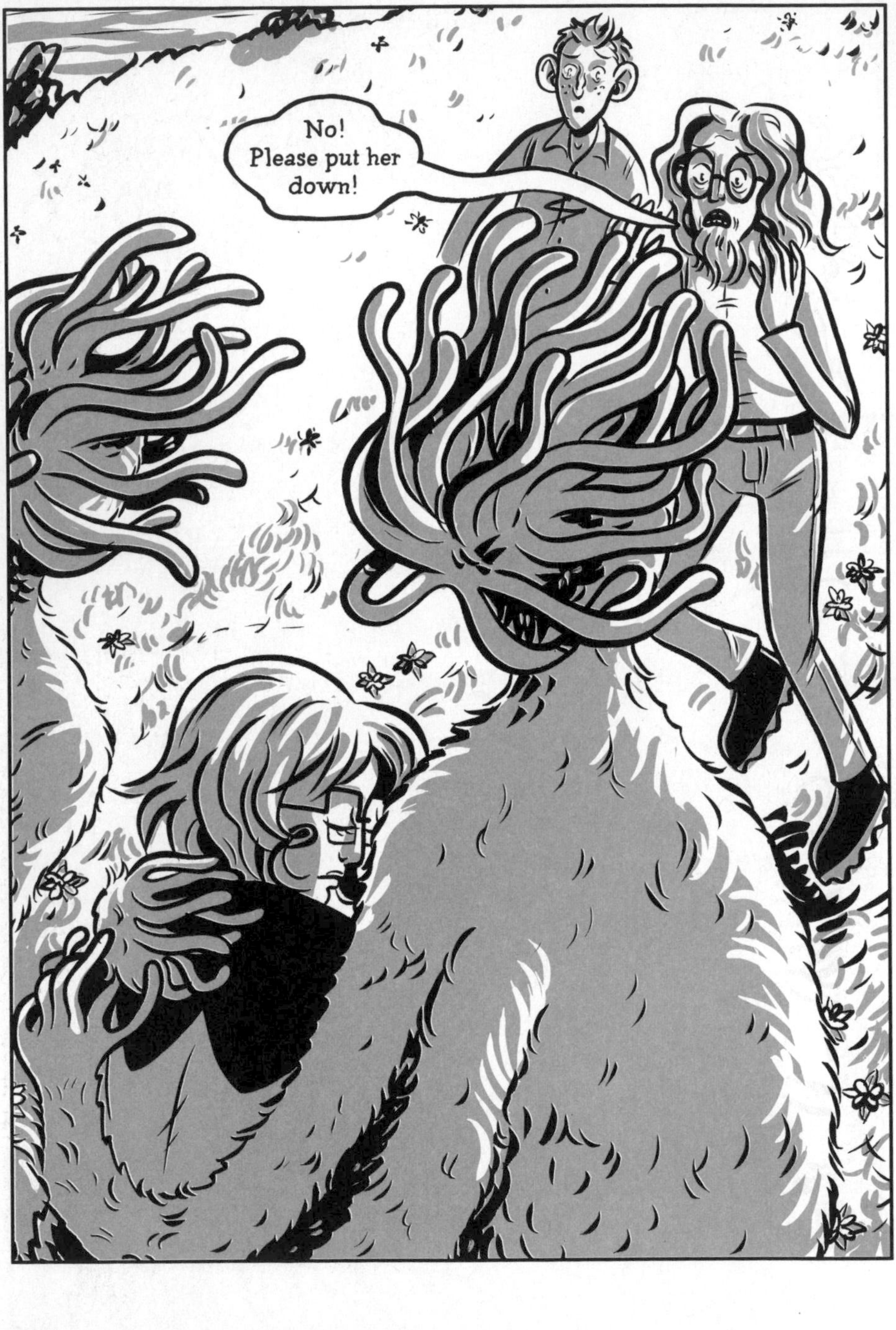
No! Please put her down!

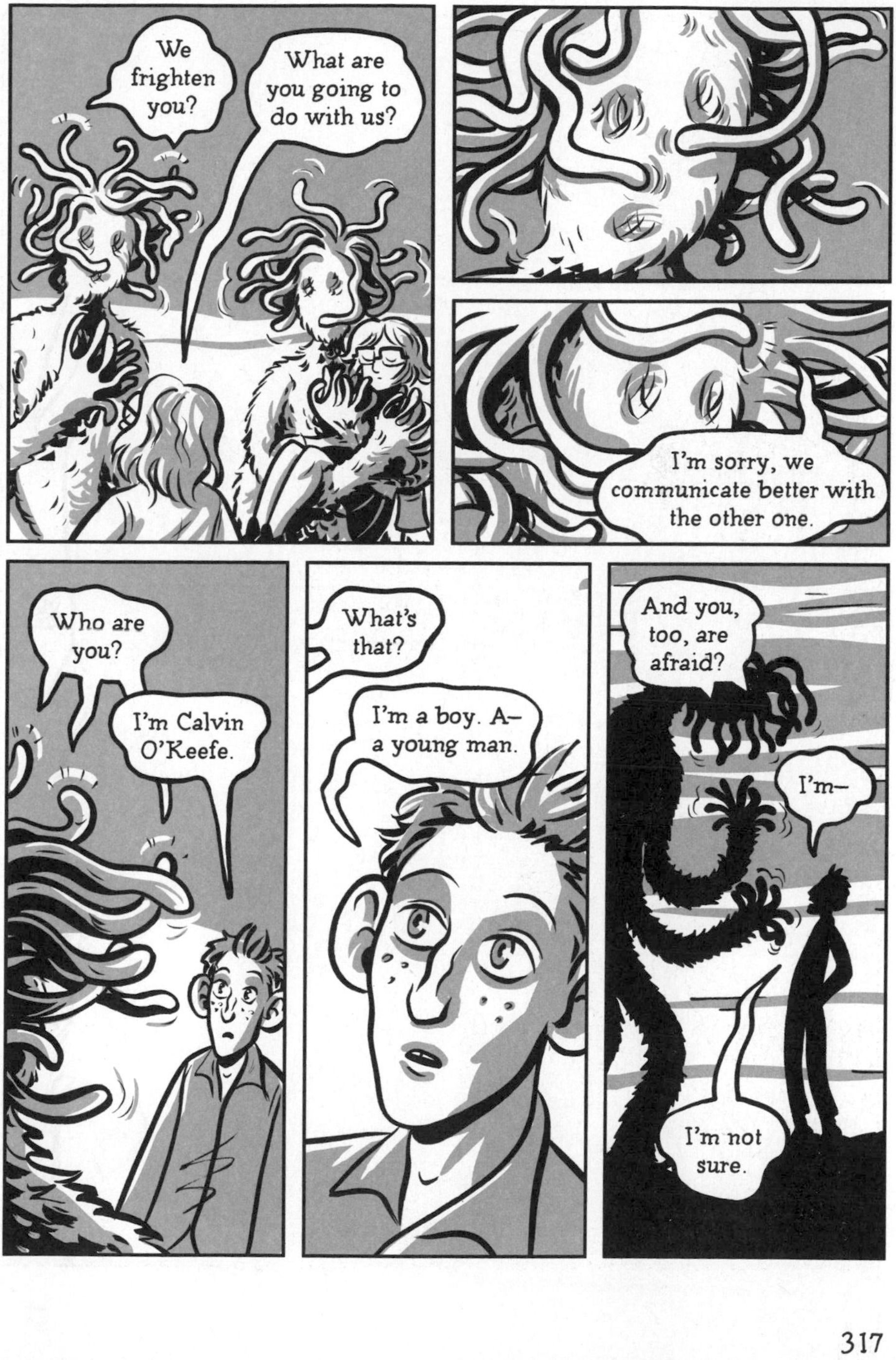
We frighten you?
What are you going to do with us?
I'm sorry, we communicate better with the other one.
Who are you?
I'm Calvin O'Keefe.
What's that?
I'm a boy. A— a young man.
And you, too, are afraid?
I'm—
I'm not sure.

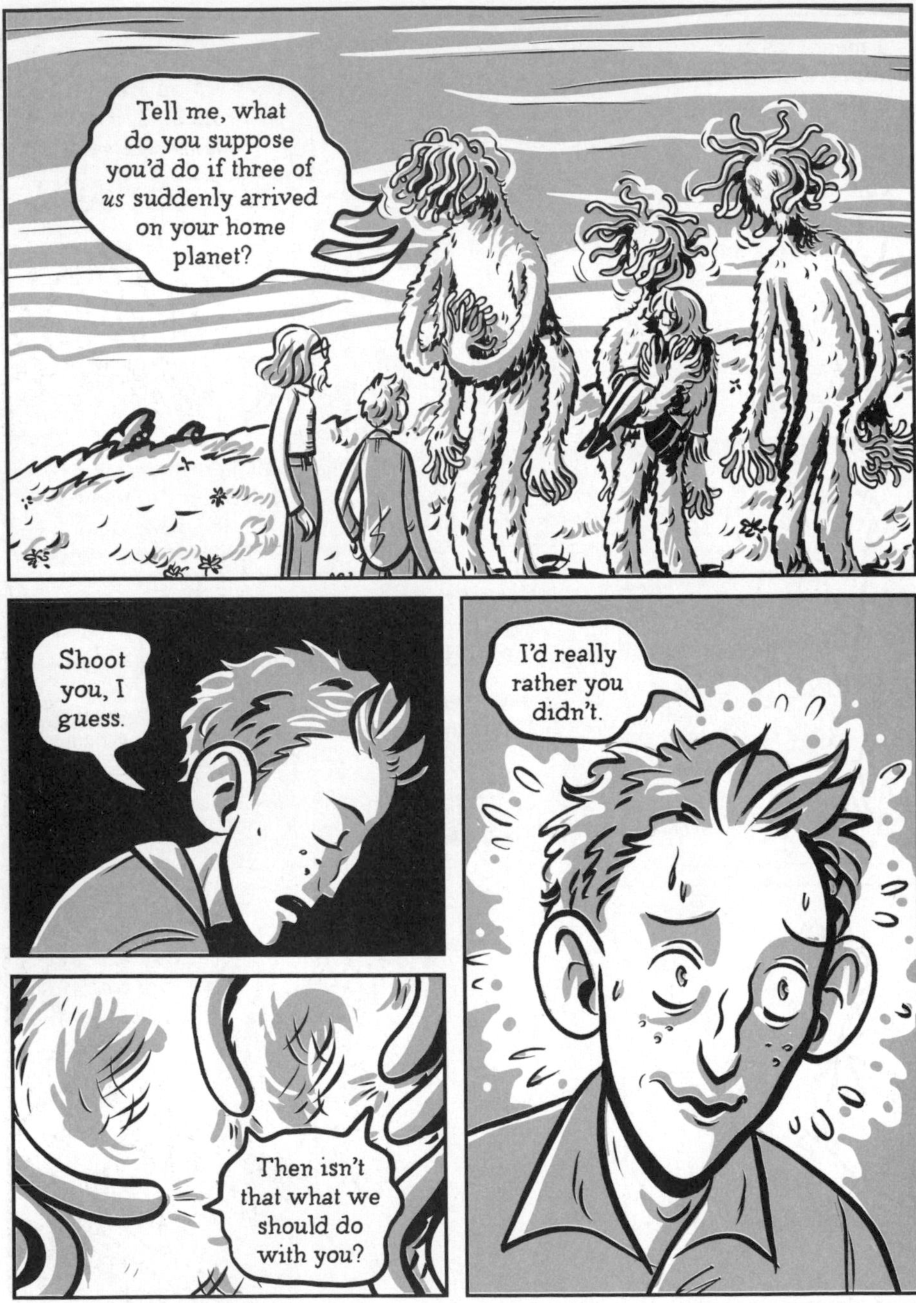
Tell me, what do you suppose you'd do if three of *us* suddenly arrived on your home planet?
Shoot you, I guess.
I'd really rather you didn't.
Then isn't that what we should do with you?

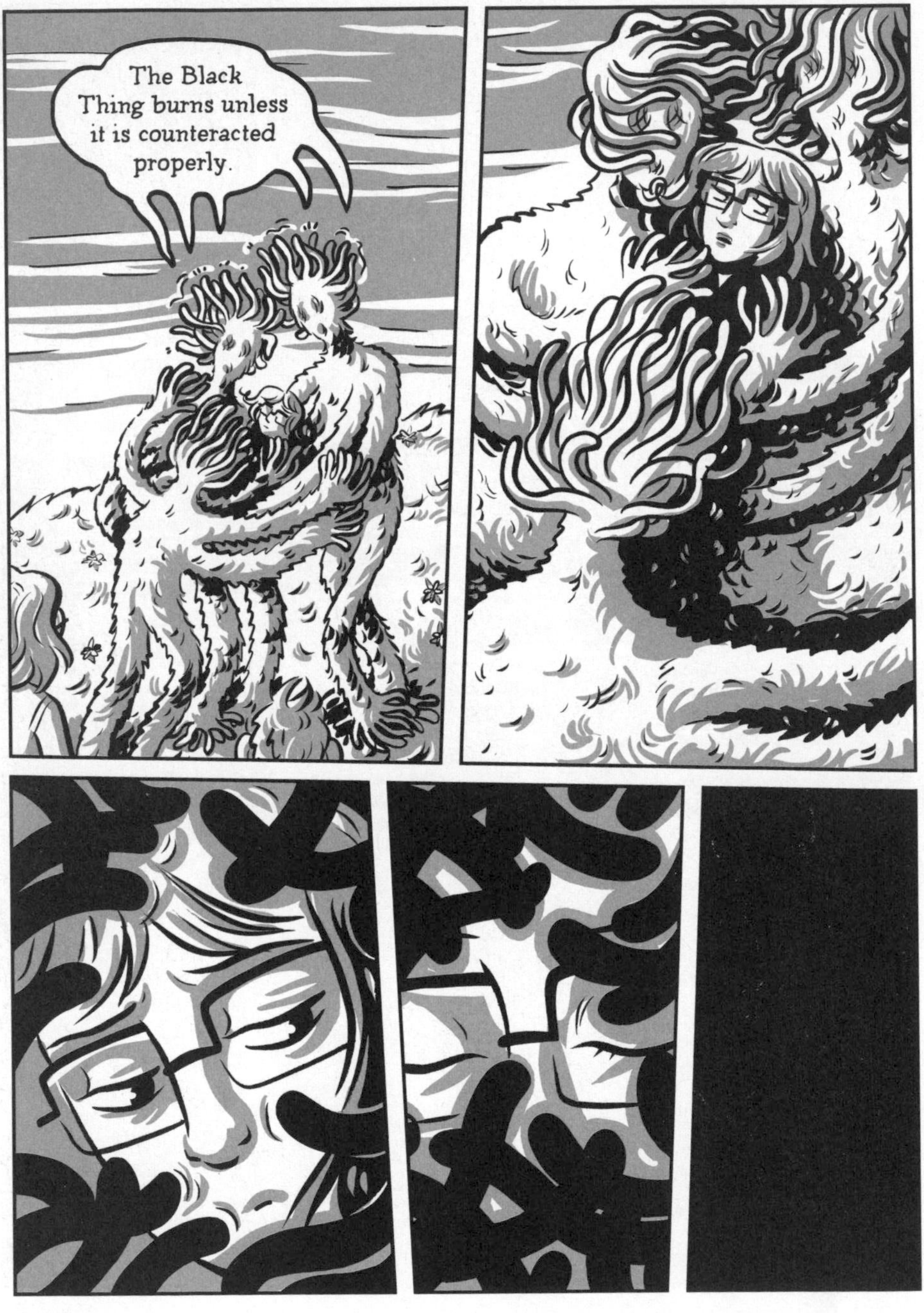
The Black Thing burns unless it is counteracted properly.

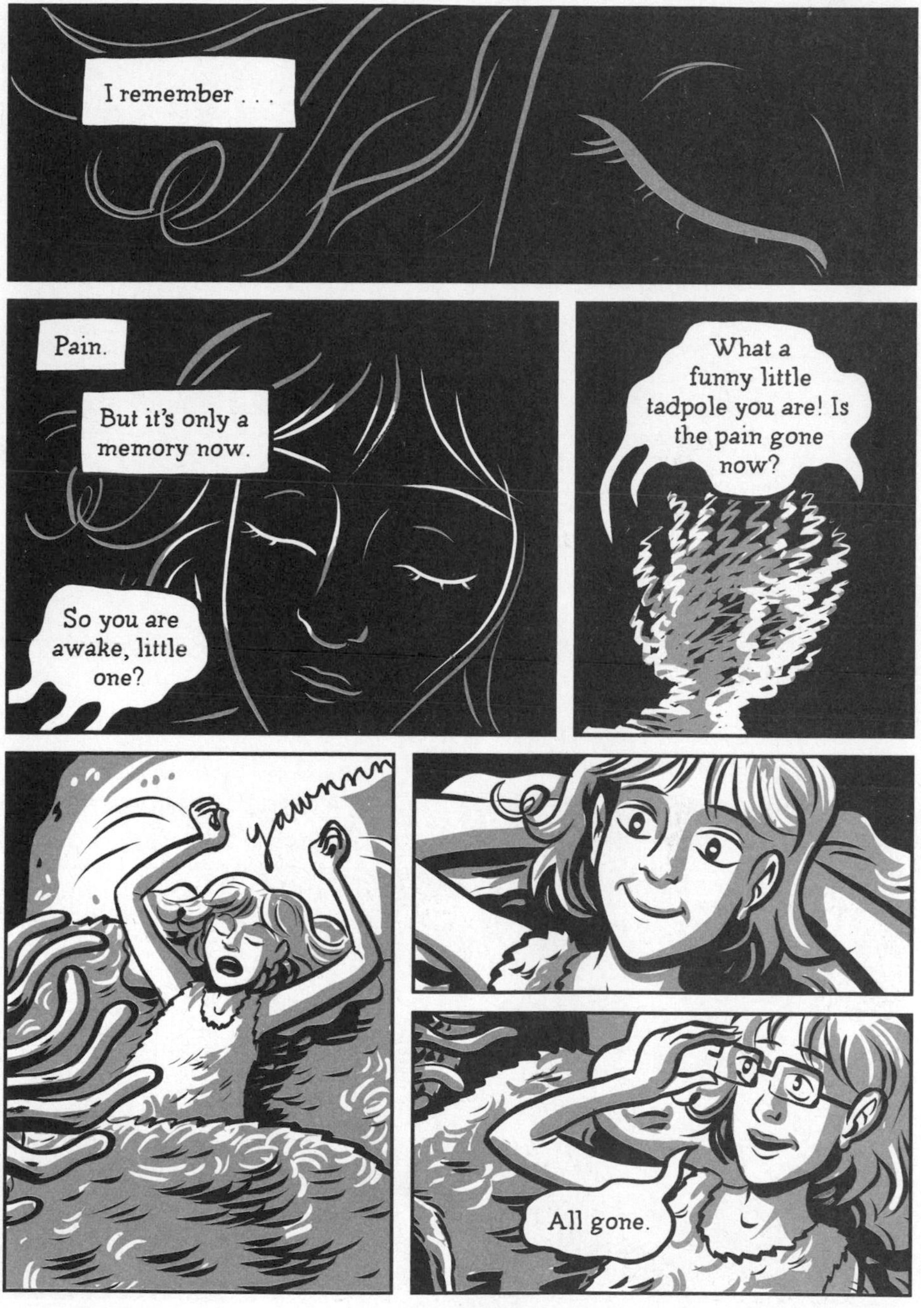
I remember . . .
Pain.
But it's only a memory now.
So you are awake, little one?
What a funny little tadpole you are! Is the pain gone now?
yawnnnn
All gone.

324

327

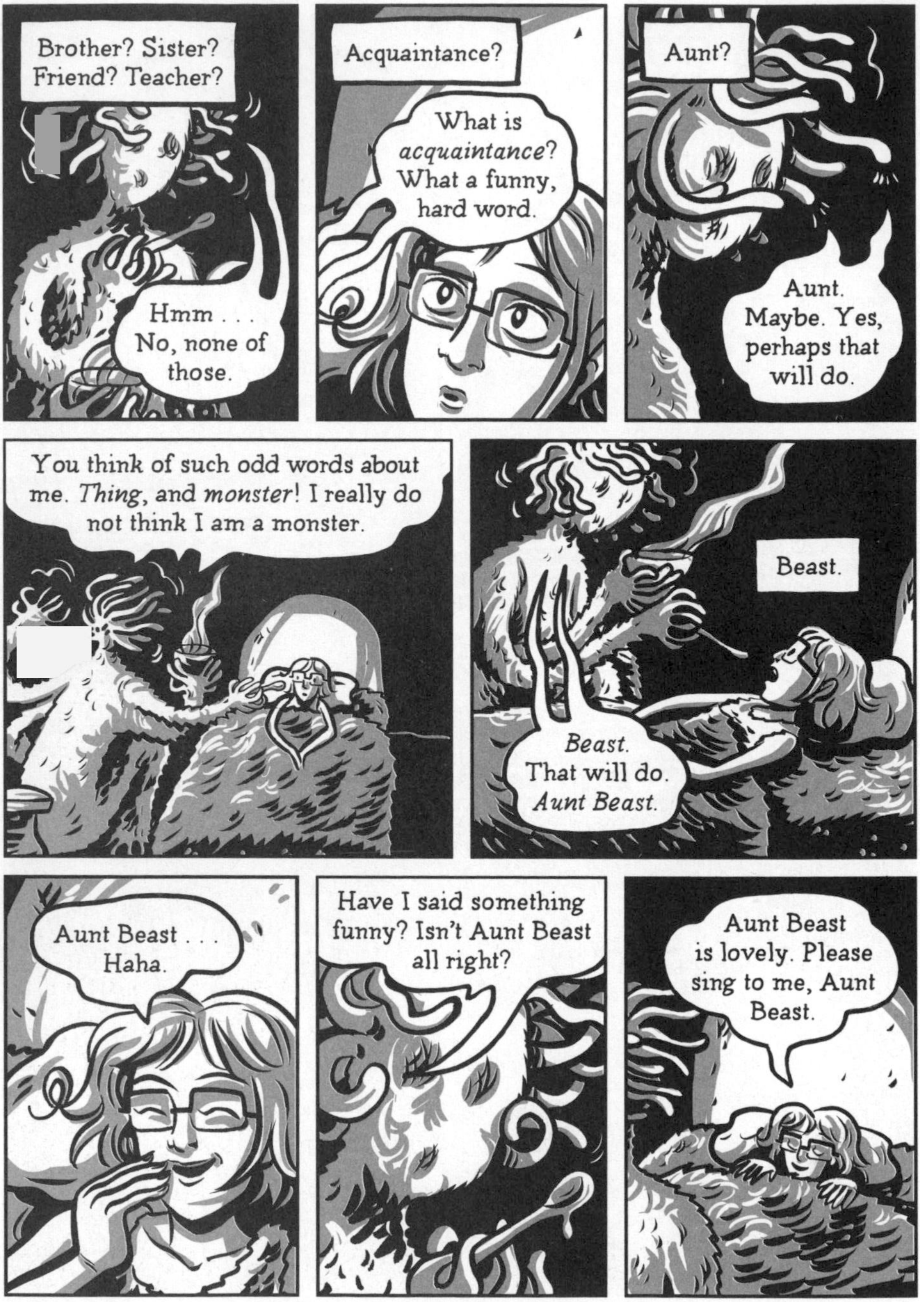
Brother? Sister? Friend? Teacher?
Hmm . . . No, none of those.
Acquaintance?
What is *acquaintance*? What a funny, hard word.
Aunt?
Aunt. Maybe. Yes, perhaps that will do.
You think of such odd words about me. *Thing*, and *monster*! I really do not think I am a monster.
Beast.
Beast. That will do. *Aunt Beast*.
Aunt Beast . . . Haha.
Have I said something funny? Isn't Aunt Beast all right?
Aunt Beast is lovely. Please sing to me, Aunt Beast.

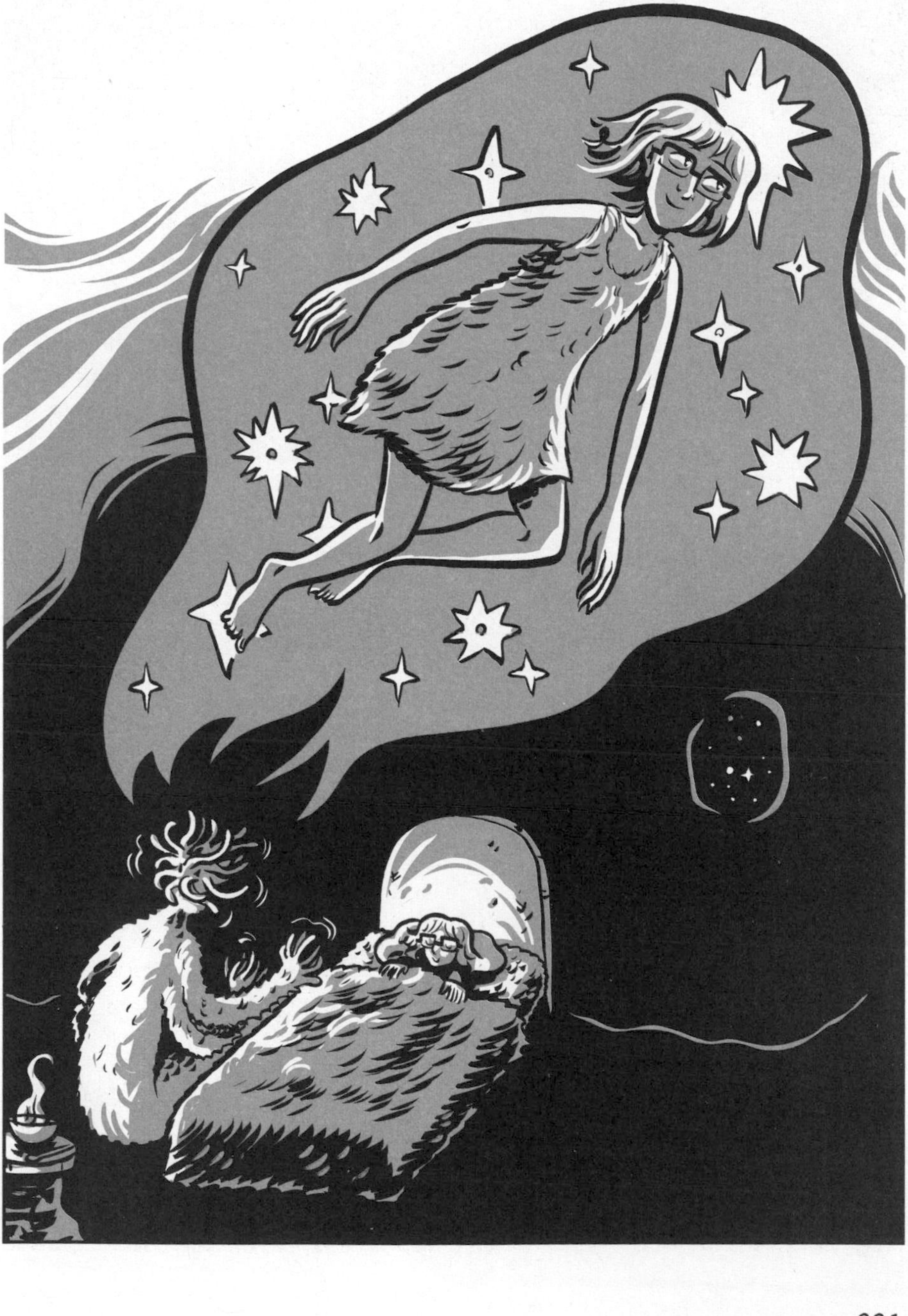

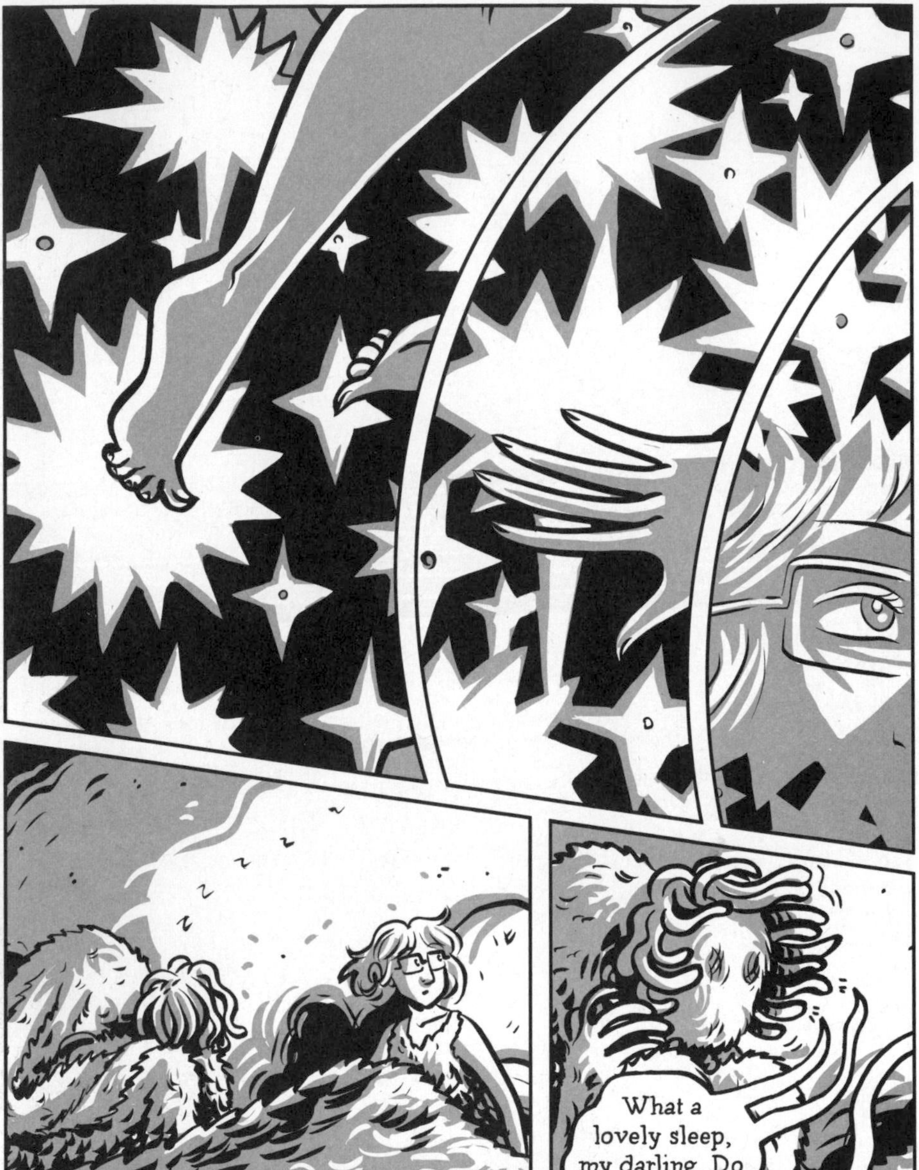
Morning?
How long was I . . . ?
What a lovely sleep, my darling. Do you feel all right?
I feel wonderful.

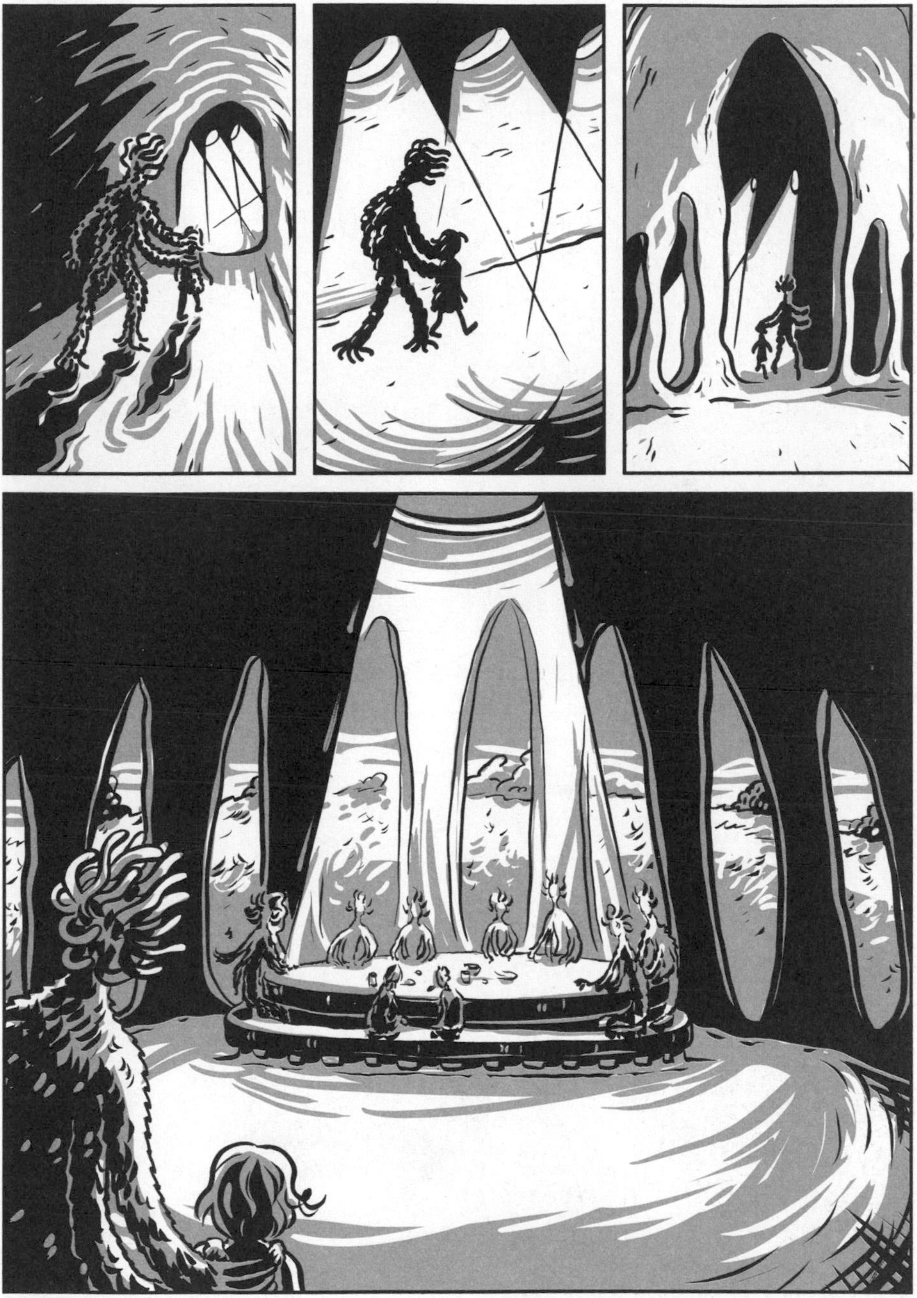

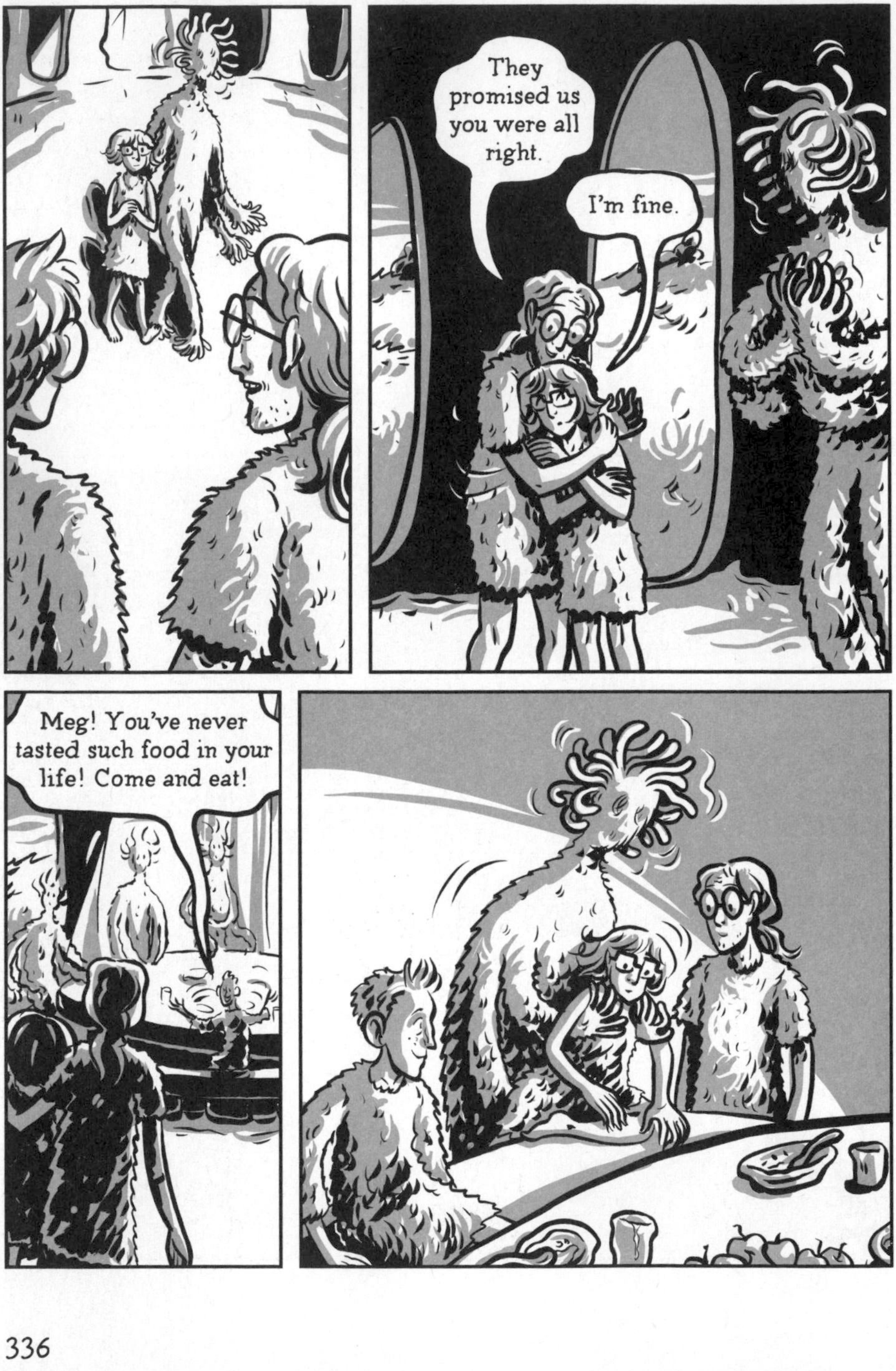
They promised us you were all right.
I'm fine.
Meg! You've never tasted such food in your life! Come and eat!

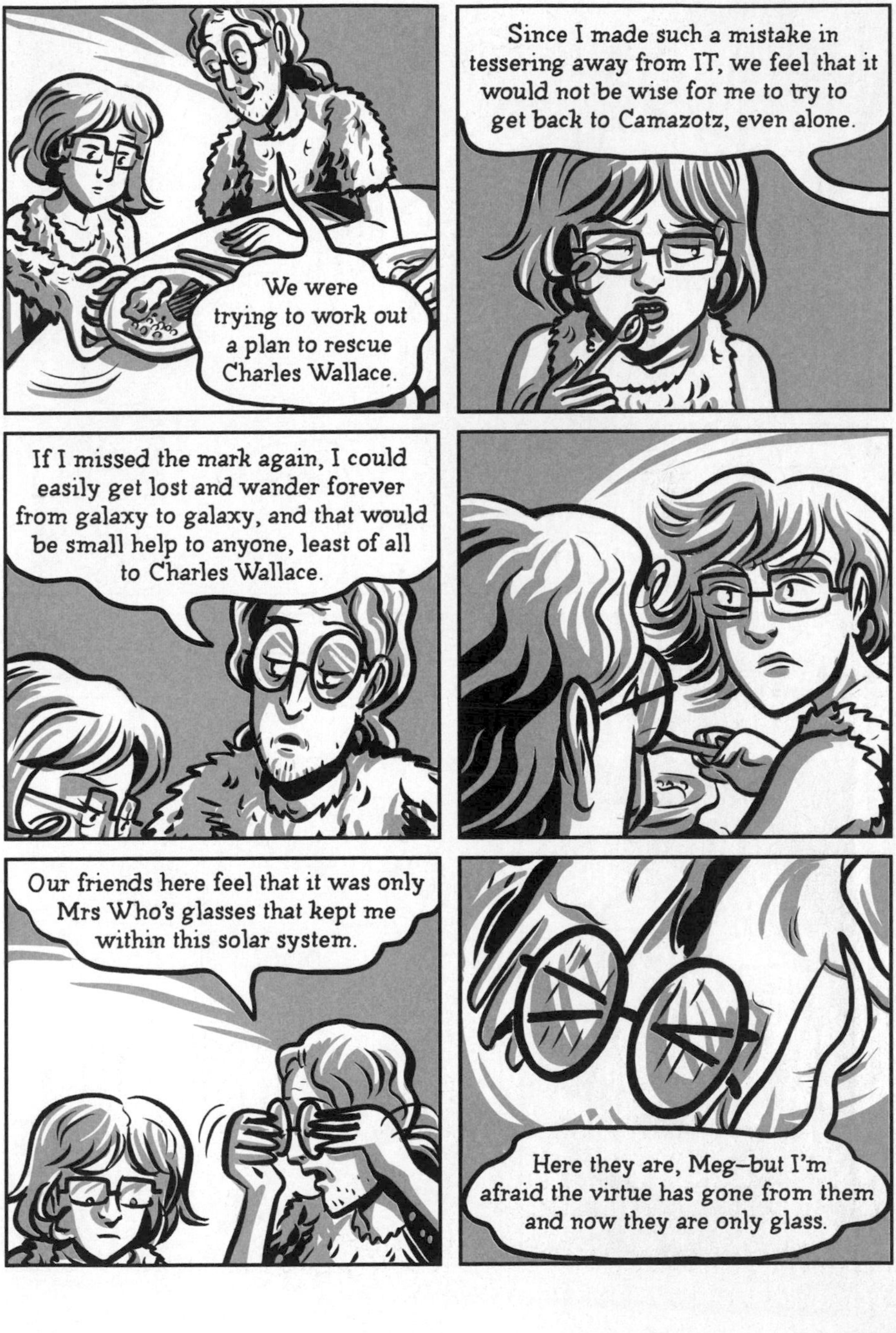
We were trying to work out a plan to rescue Charles Wallace.
Since I made such a mistake in tessering away from IT, we feel that it would not be wise for me to try to get back to Camazotz, even alone.
If I missed the mark again, I could easily get lost and wander forever from galaxy to galaxy, and that would be small help to anyone, least of all to Charles Wallace.
Our friends here feel that it was only Mrs Who's glasses that kept me within this solar system.
Here they are, Meg—but I'm afraid the virtue has gone from them and now they are only glass.

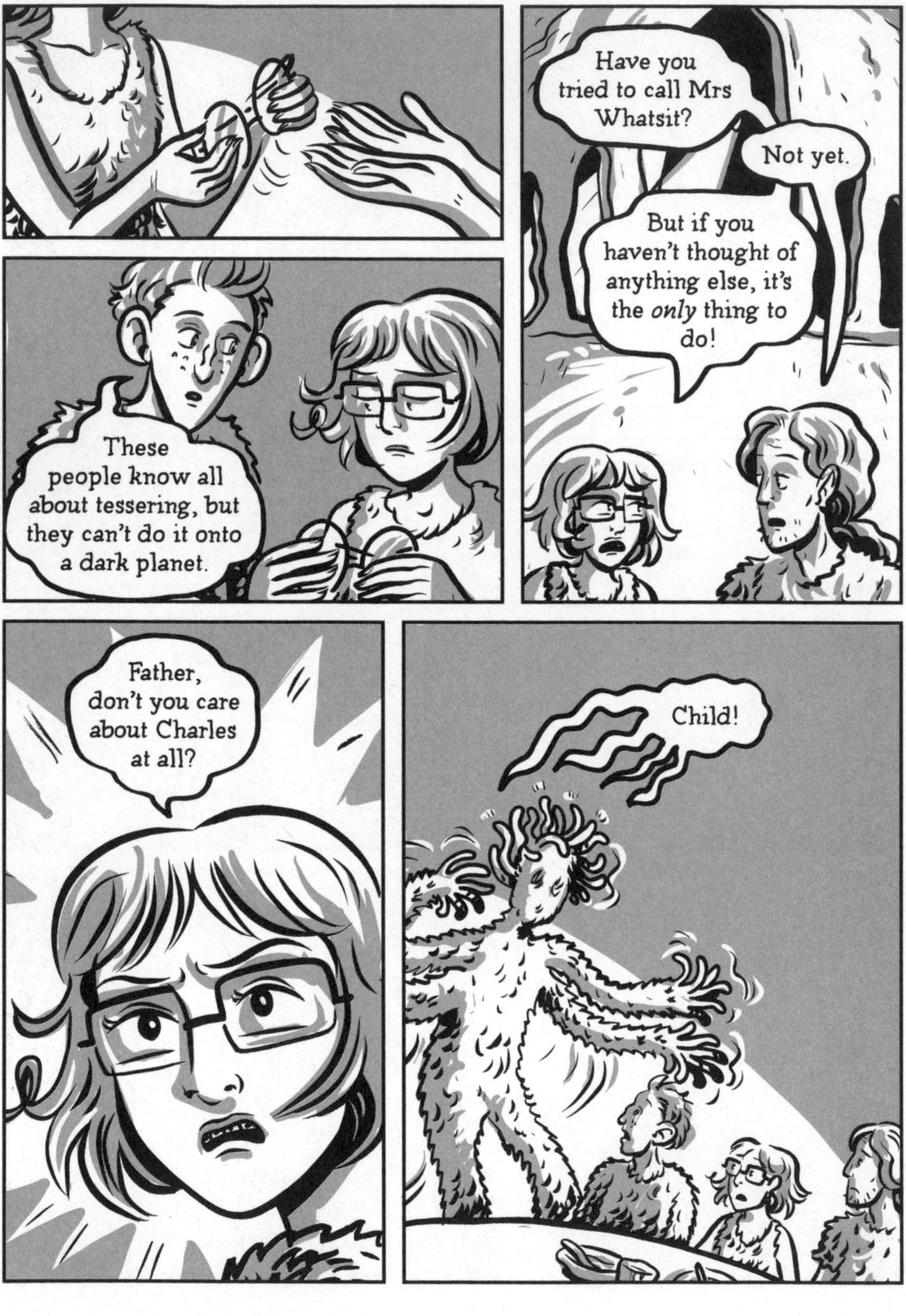
Have you tried to call Mrs Whatsit?
Not yet.
But if you haven't thought of anything else, it's the *only* thing to do!
These people know all about tessering, but they can't do it onto a dark planet.
Father, don't you care about Charles at all?
Child!

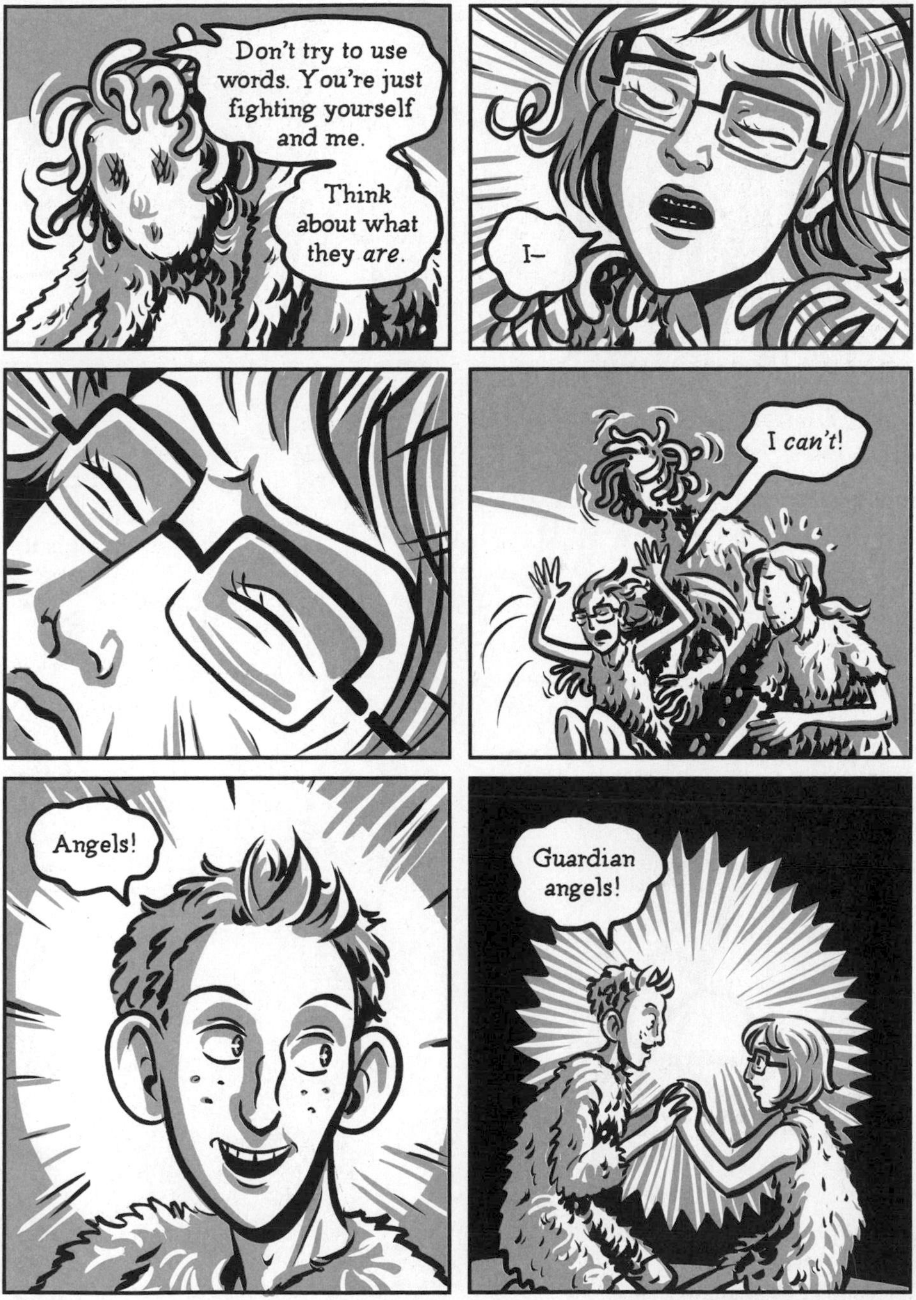
Don't try to use words. You're just fighting yourself and me.
Think about what they *are*.
I–
I *can't*!
Angels!
Guardian angels!

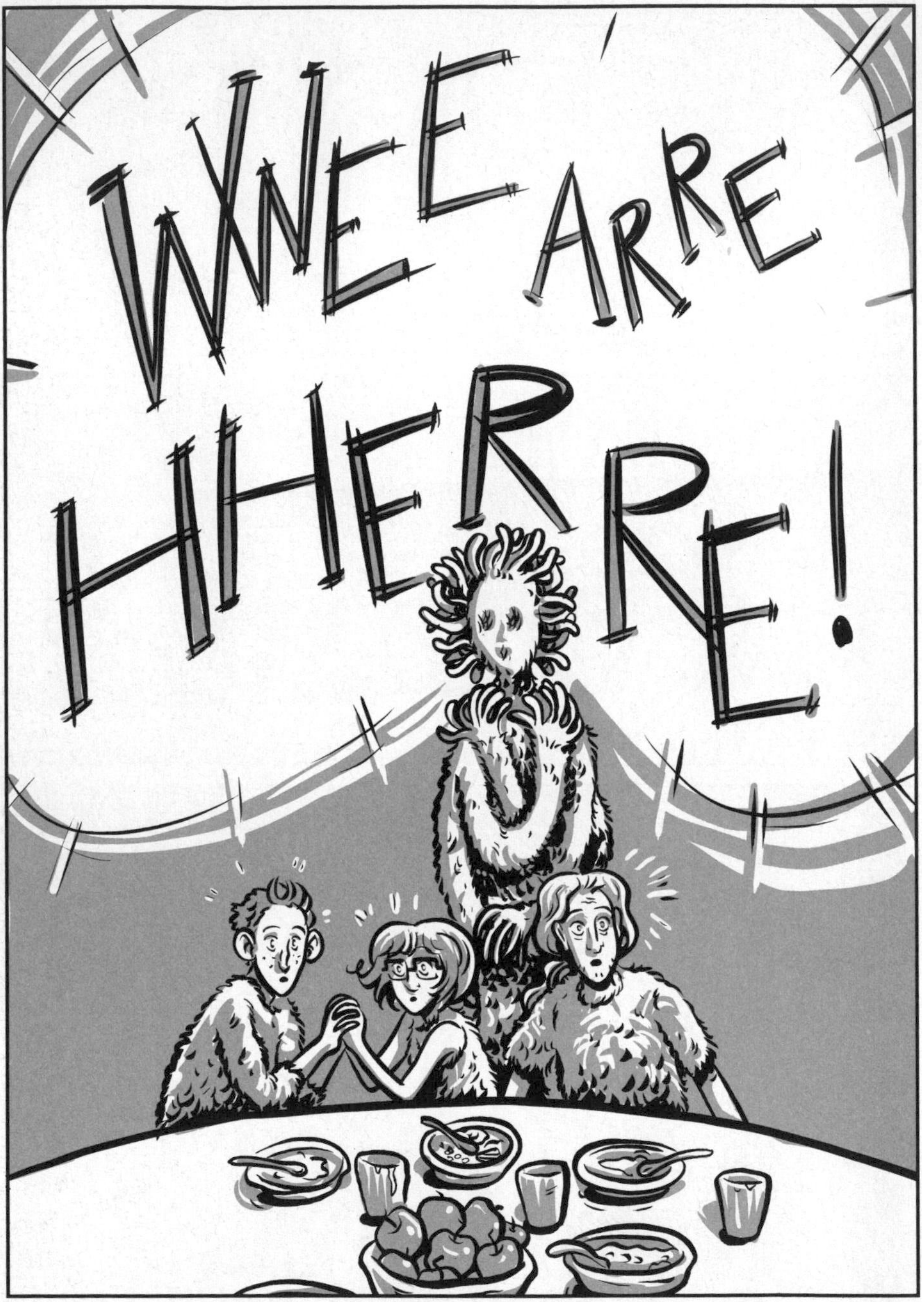
WWEE ARRE HHERRE!

12
The Foolish and the Weak

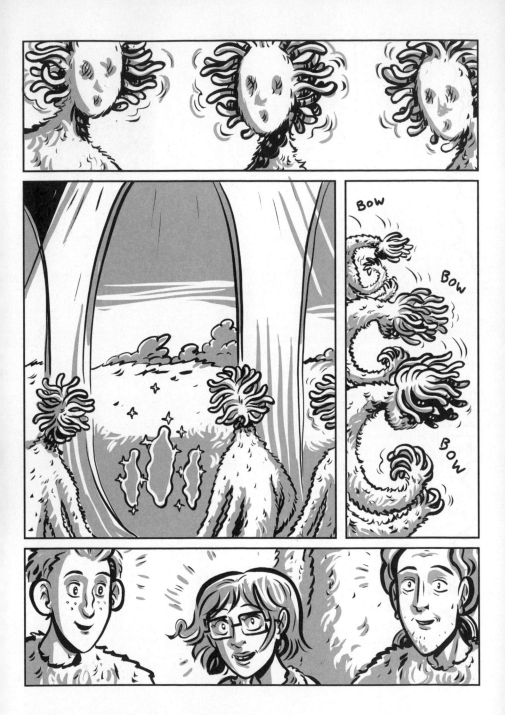

BOW
BOW
BOW
BOW

345

346

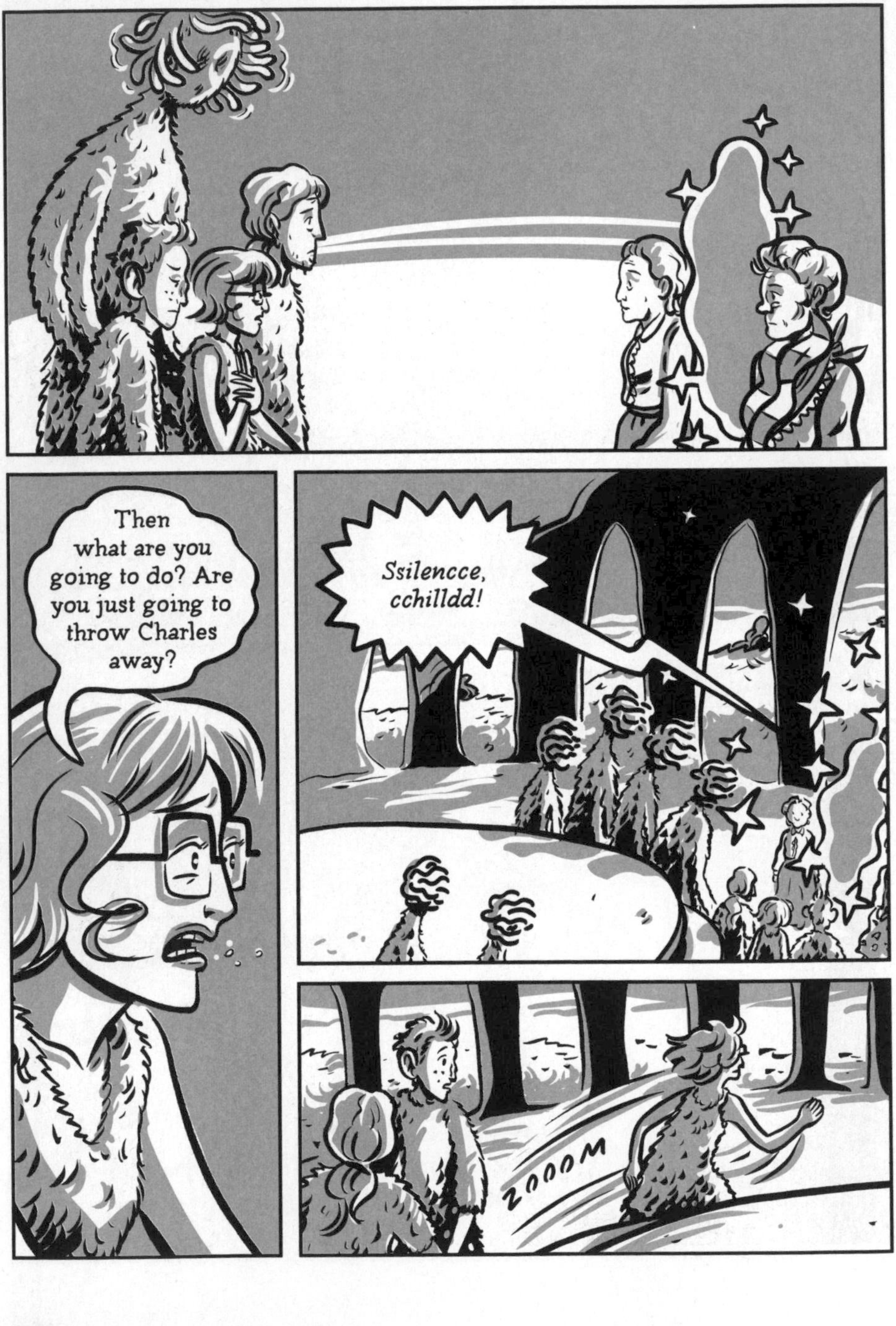
Then what are you going to do? Are you just going to throw Charles away?
Ssilencce, cchilldd!
ZOOOM

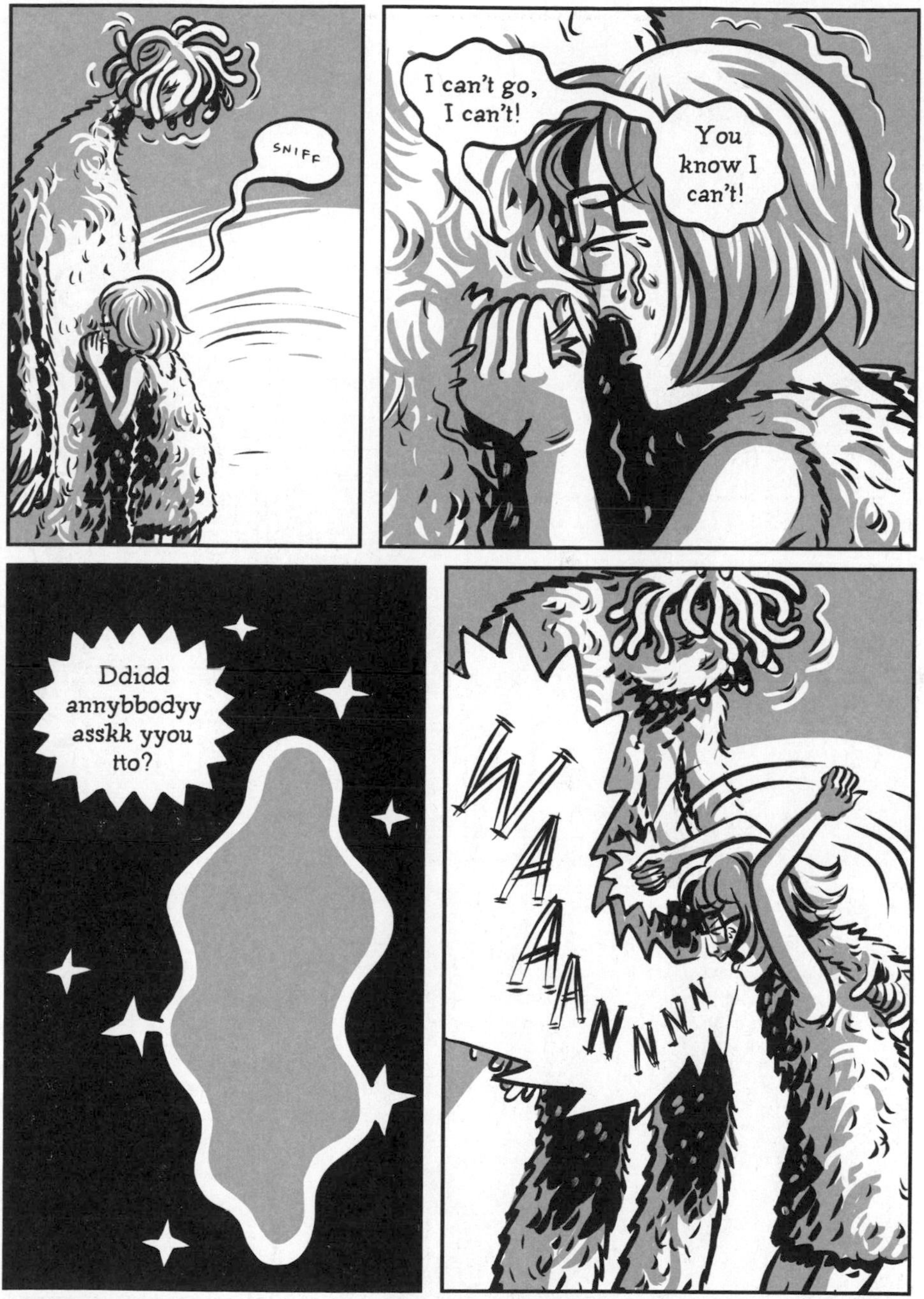
SNIFF
I can't go, I can't!
You know I can't!
Ddidd annybbodyy asskk yyou tto?
WAAAANNNN

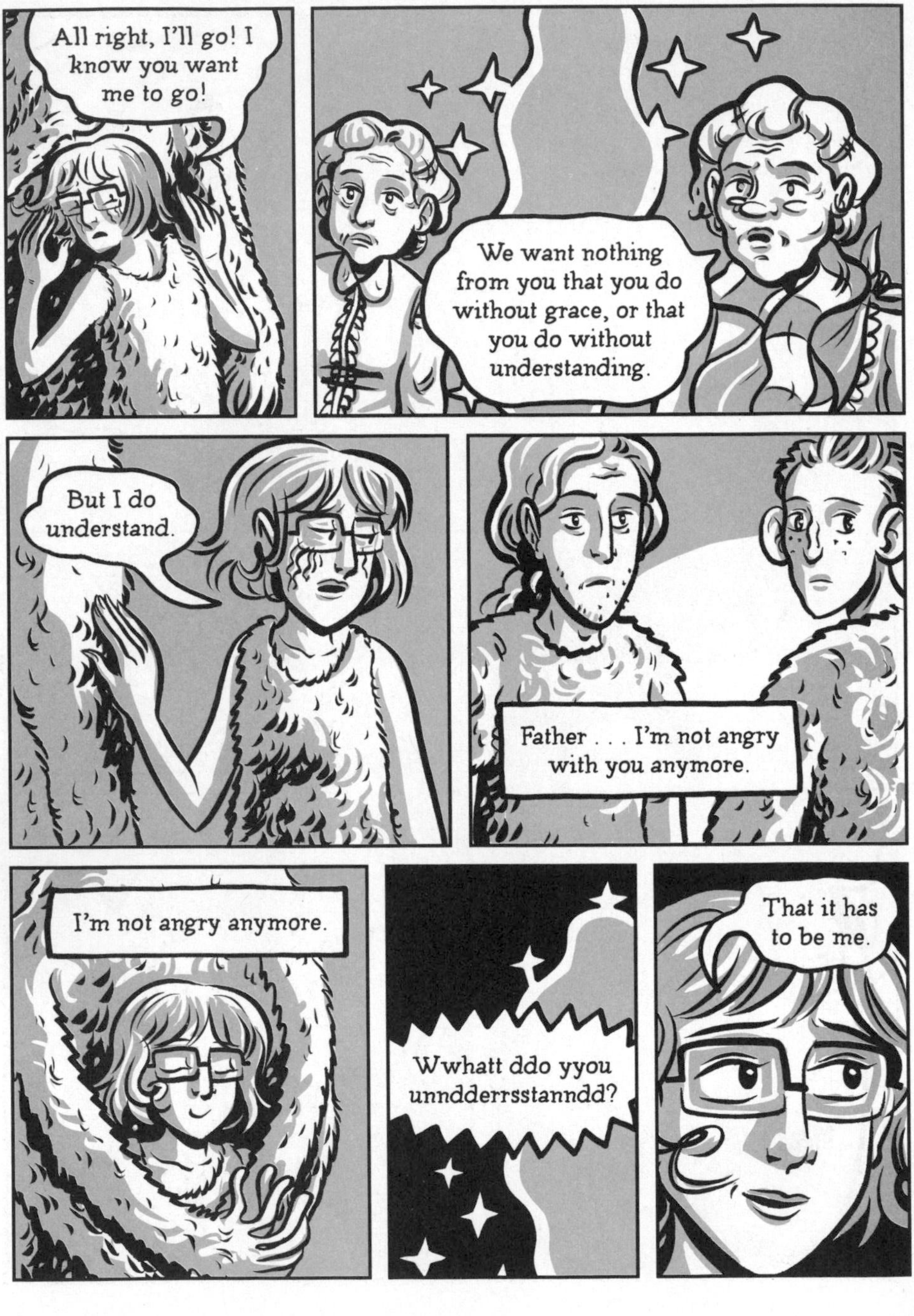
All right, I'll go! I know you want me to go!
We want nothing from you that you do without grace, or that you do without understanding.
But I do understand.
Father . . . I'm not angry with you anymore.
I'm not angry anymore.
Wwhatt ddo yyou unndderrsstanndd?
That it has to be me.

353

354

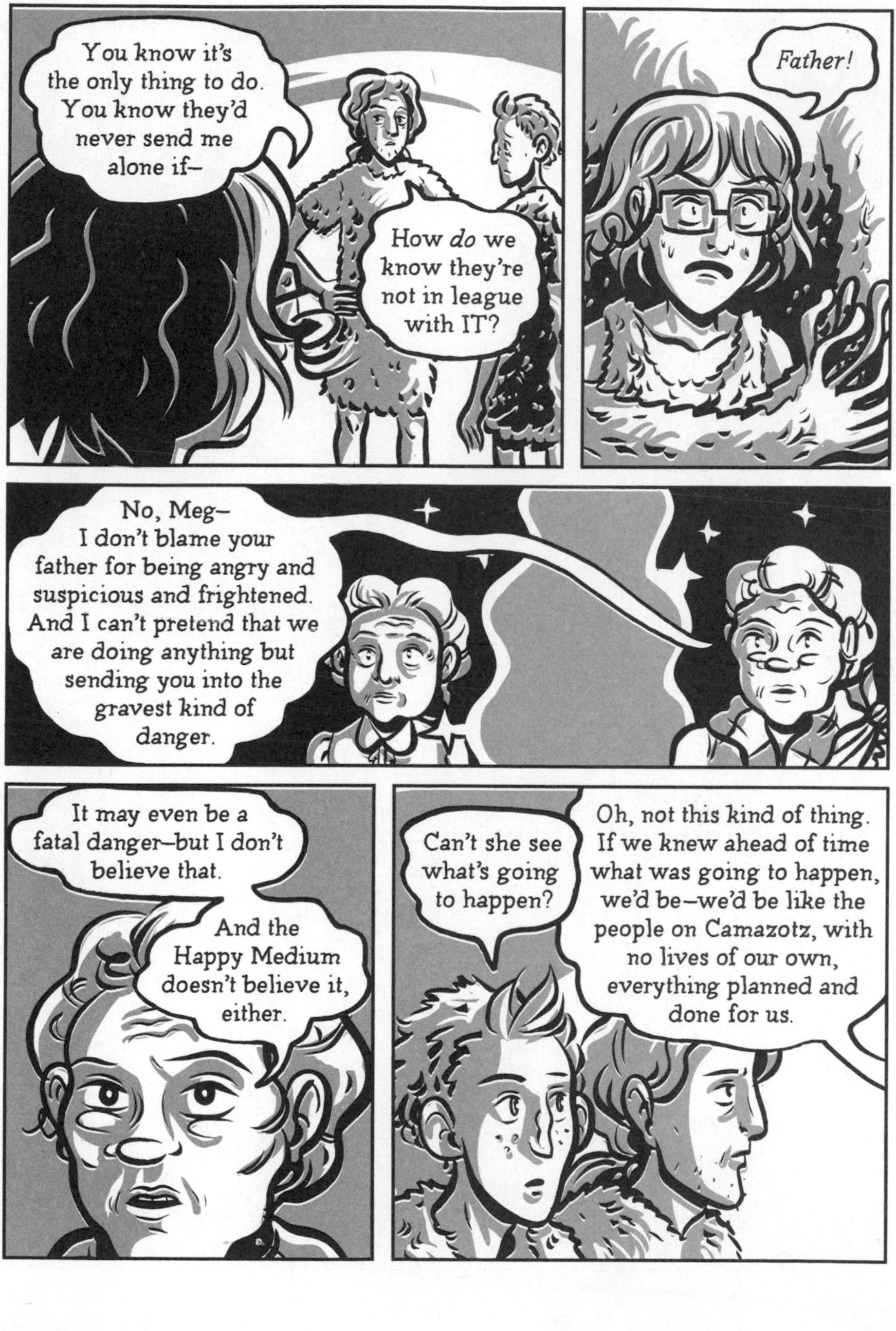
You know it's the only thing to do. You know they'd never send me alone if–
How *do* we know they're not in league with IT?
Father!
No, Meg– I don't blame your father for being angry and suspicious and frightened. And I can't pretend that we are doing anything but sending you into the gravest kind of danger.
It may even be a fatal danger–but I don't believe that.
And the Happy Medium doesn't believe it, either.
Can't she see what's going to happen?
Oh, not this kind of thing. If we knew ahead of time what was going to happen, we'd be–we'd be like the people on Camazotz, with no lives of our own, everything planned and done for us.

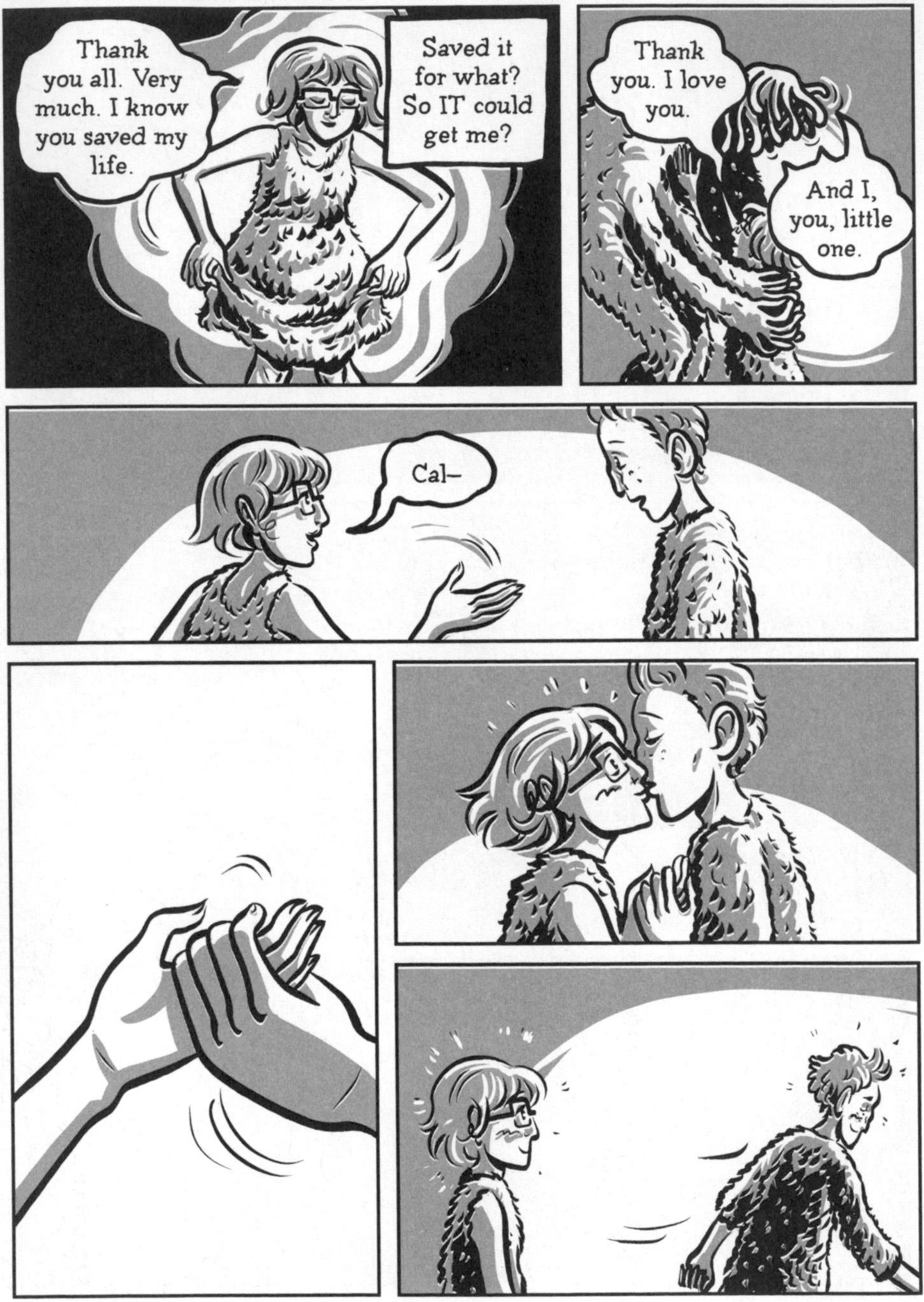
Thank you all. Very much. I know you saved my life.
Saved it for what? So IT could get me?
Thank you. I love you.
And I, you, little one.
Cal–

I give you my love, Meg.

Never forget that. My love always.

Your father is right. The virtue is gone from them.

The foolishness of God is wiser than men; and the weakness of God is stronger than men. For ye see your calling, brethren, how that not many wise men after the flesh, not many mighty, not many noble, are called, but God hath chosen the foolish things of the world to confound the wise; and God hath chosen the weak things of the world to confound the things which are mighty. And base things of the world, and things which are despised, hath God chosen, yea, and things which are not, to bring to nought things that are.

And what I have to give you this time you must try to understand not word by word, but in a flash, as you understand the tesseract.

Listen, Meg. Listen well:

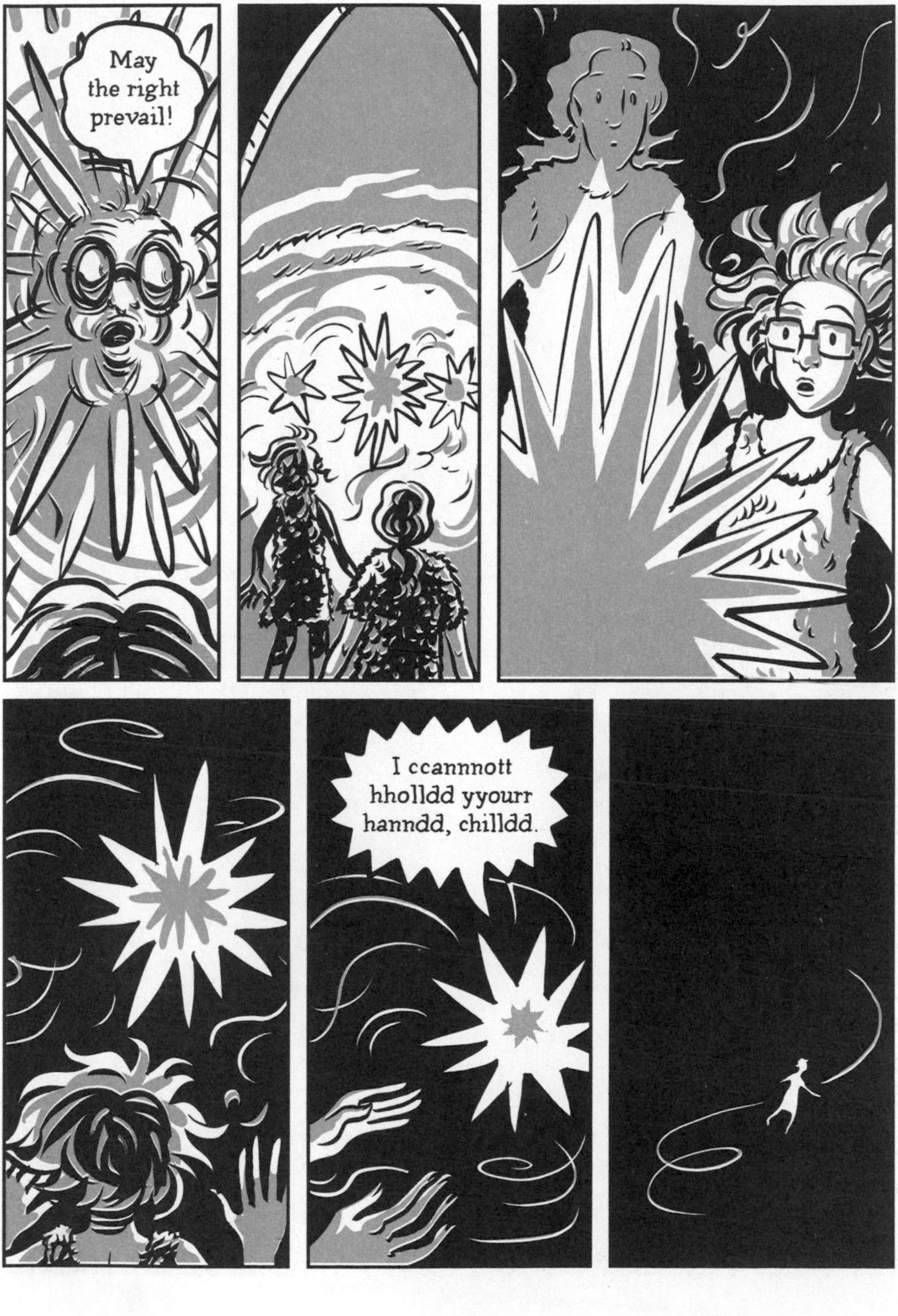
May the right prevail!
I ccannnott hhollldd yyourr hanndd, chillldd.

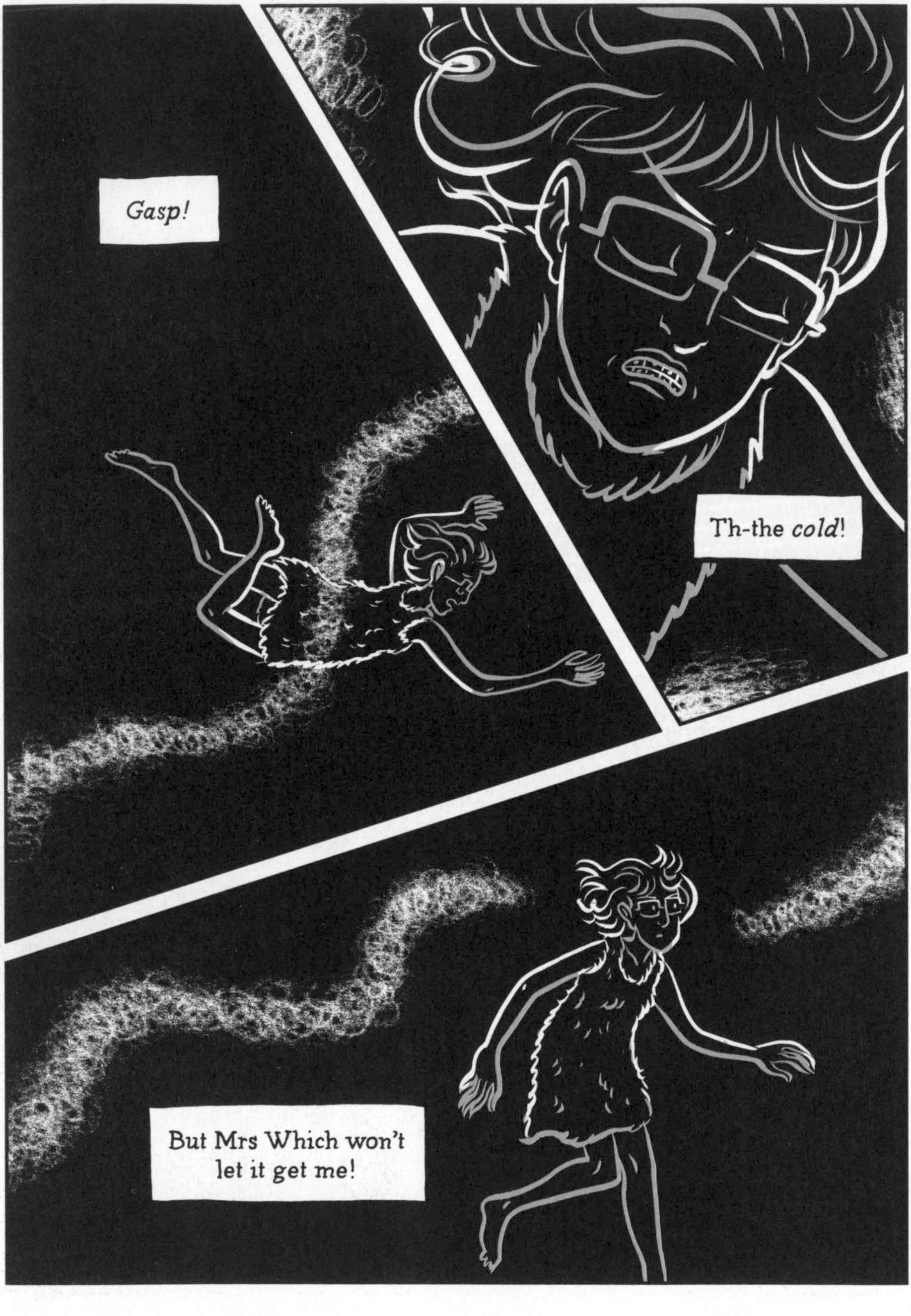
Gasp!
Th-the *cold*!
But Mrs Which won't let it get me!

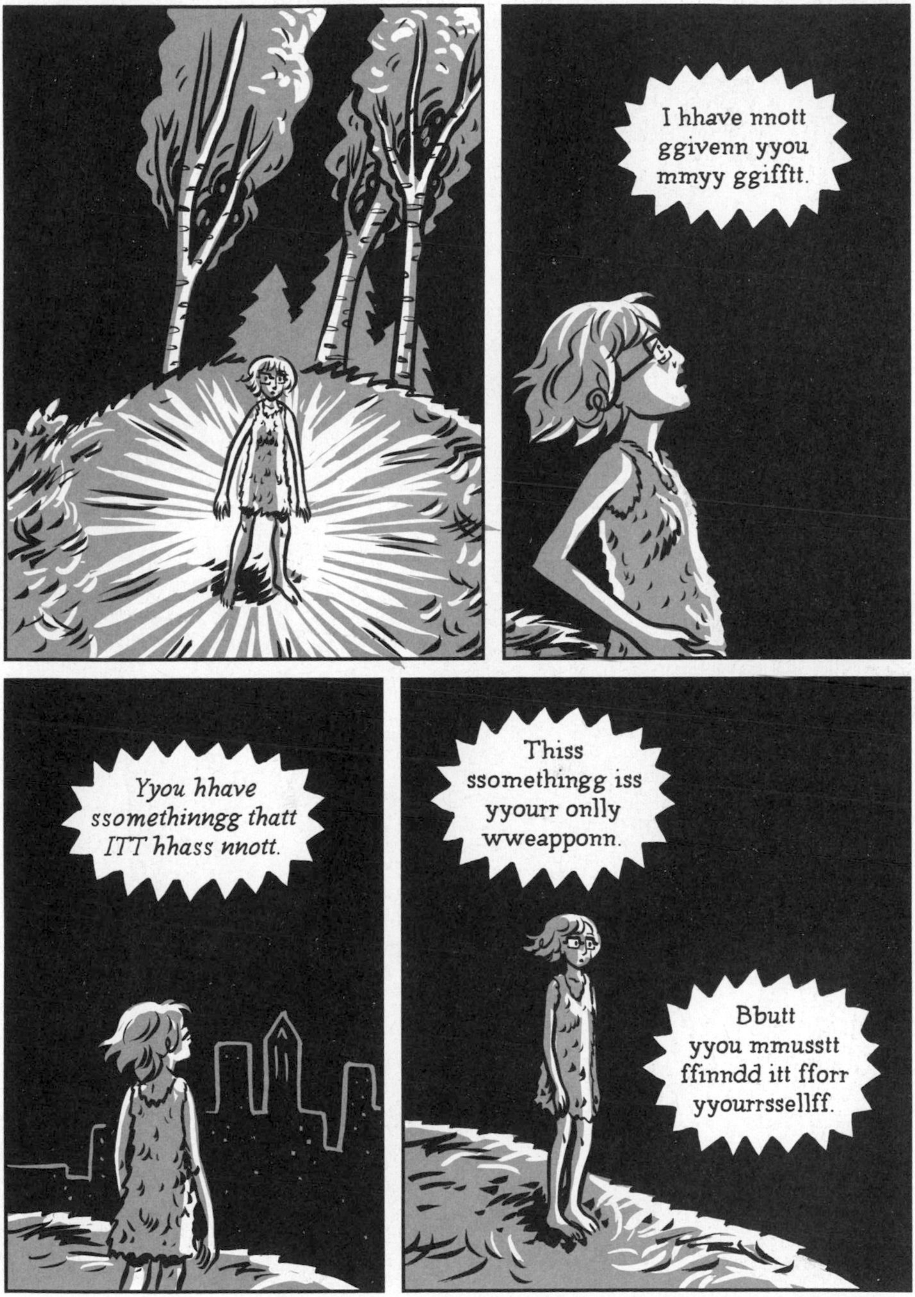
I hhave nnott ggivenn yyou mmyy ggifftt.
Yyou hhave ssomethinngg thatt ITT hhass nnott.
Thiss ssomethingg iss yyourr onlly wweapponn.
Bbutt yyou mmussttt ffinndd itt fforr yyourrssellff.

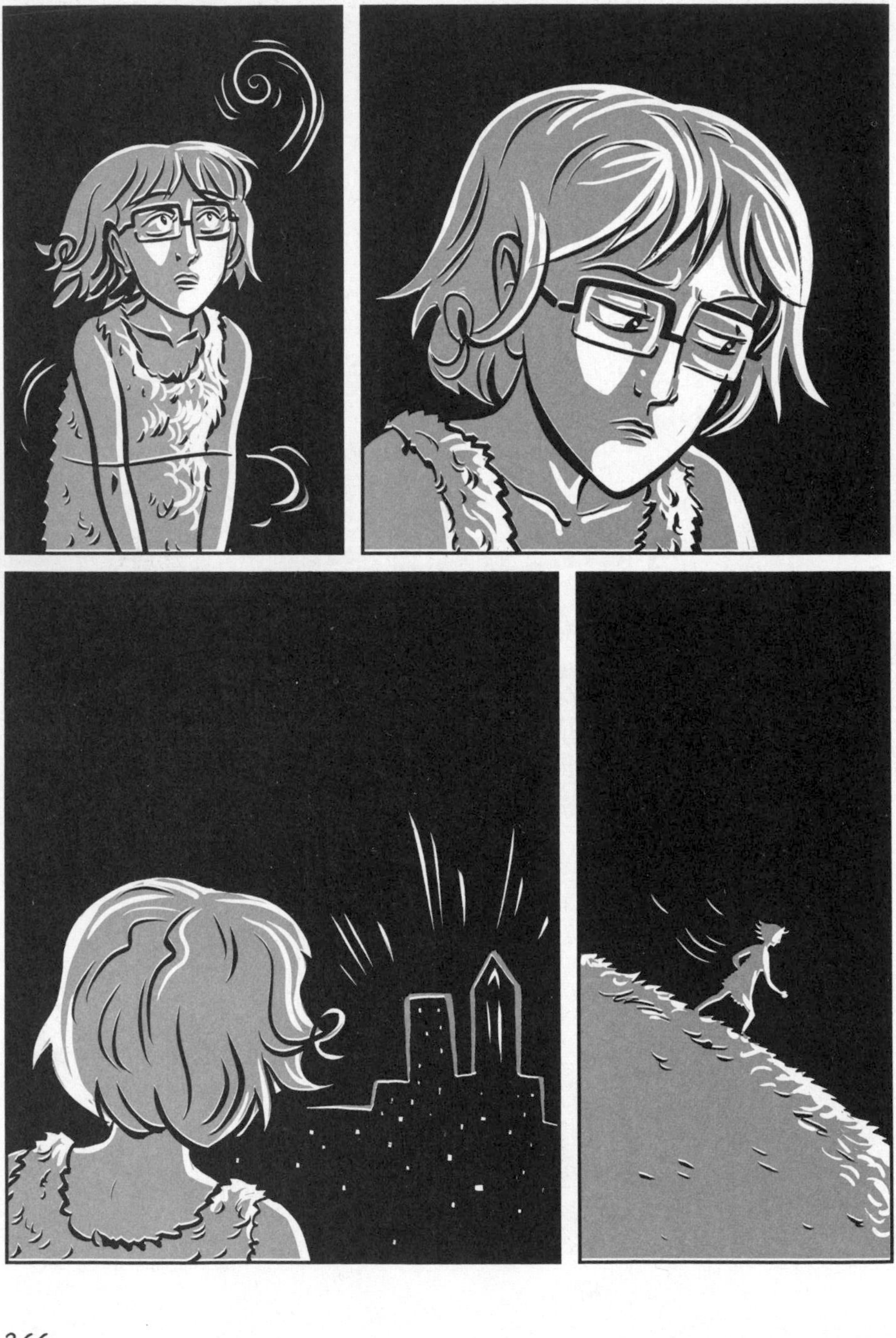

369

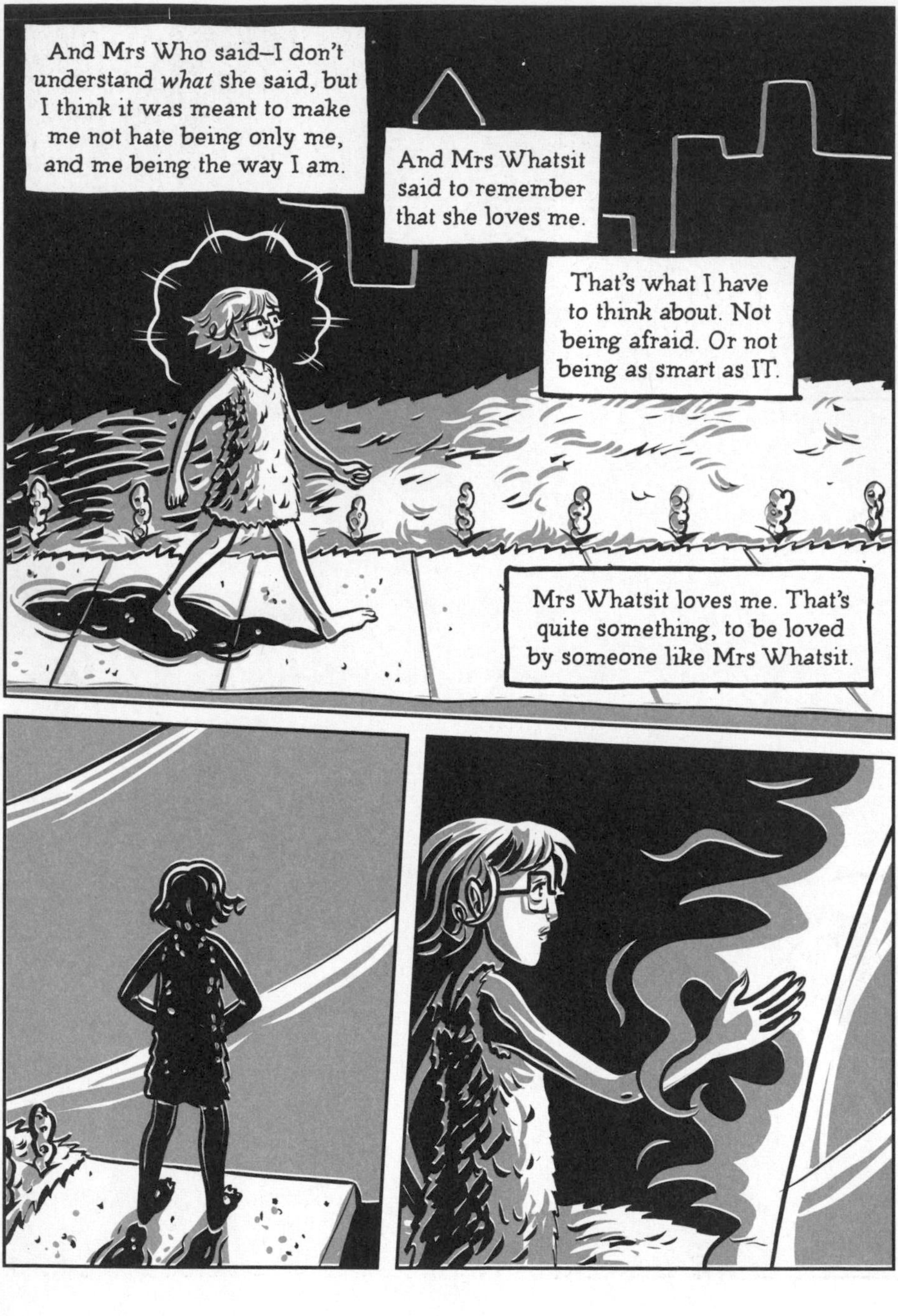
And Mrs Who said—I don't understand *what* she said, but I think it was meant to make me not hate being only me, and me being the way I am.
And Mrs Whatsit said to remember that she loves me.
That's what I have to think about. Not being afraid. Or not being as smart as IT.
Mrs Whatsit loves me. That's quite something, to be loved by someone like Mrs Whatsit.

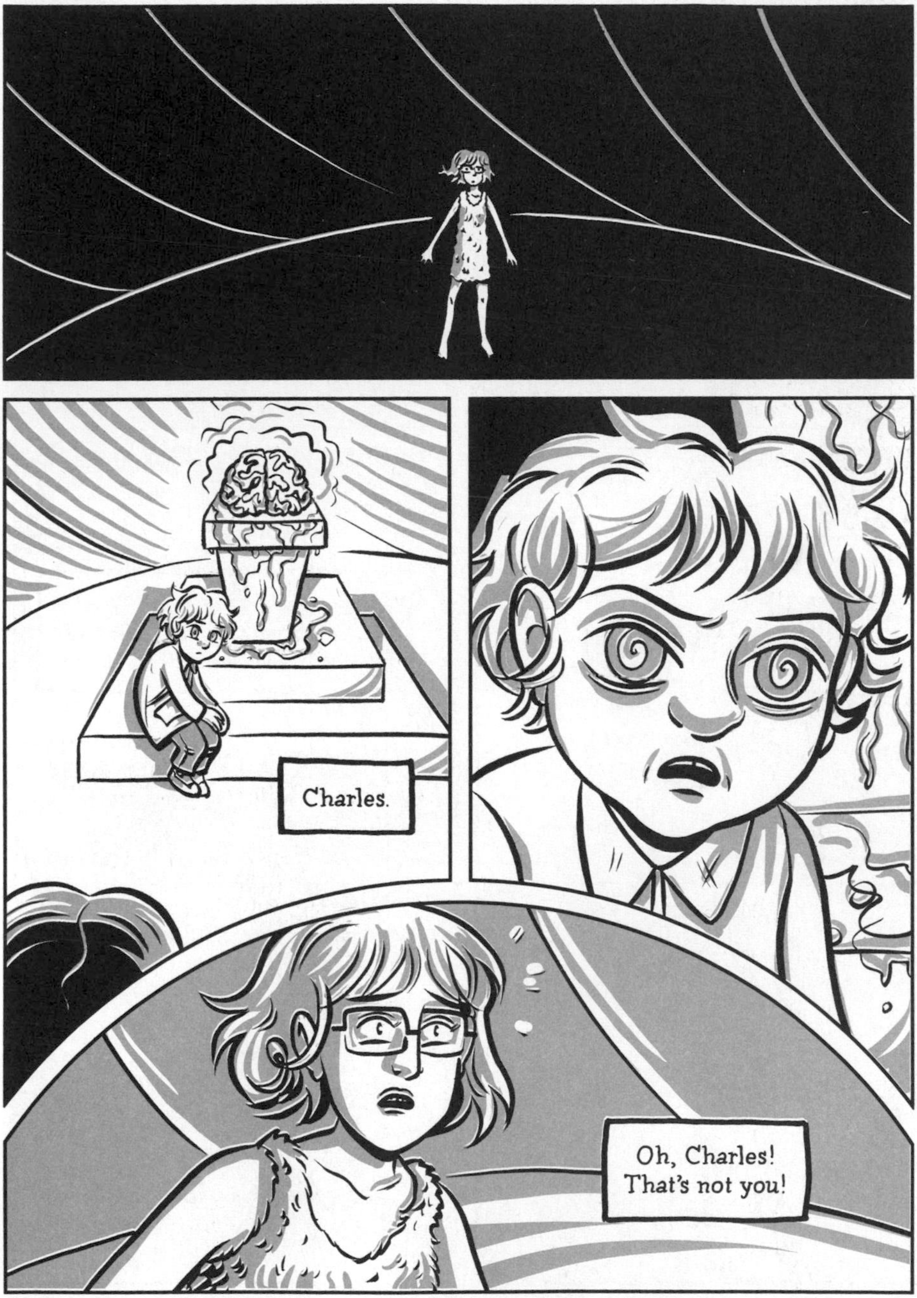
Charles.
Oh, Charles! That's not you!

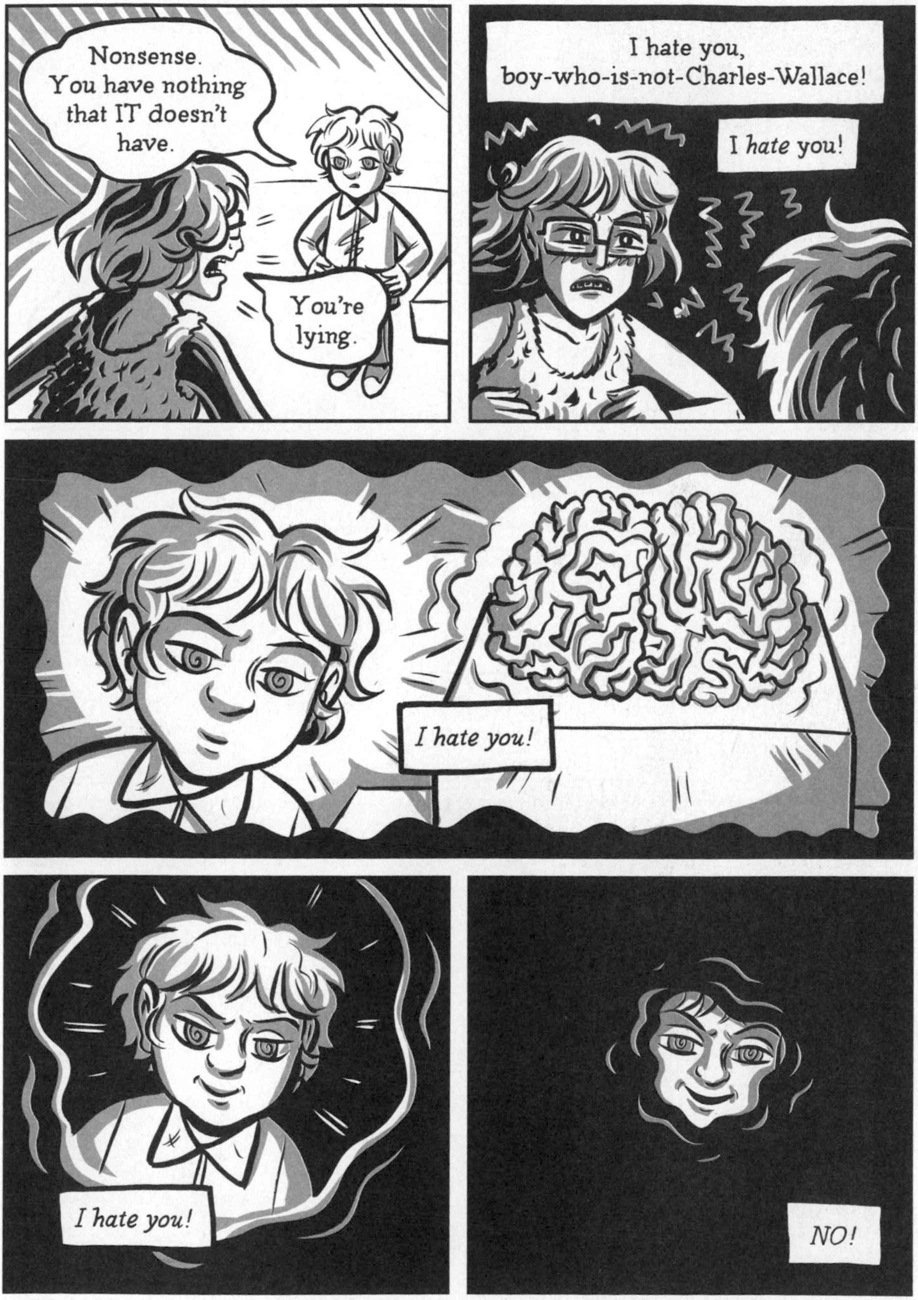
Nonsense. You have nothing that IT doesn't have.
You're lying.
I hate you, boy-who-is-not-Charles-Wallace!
I *hate* you!
I hate you!
I hate you!
NO!

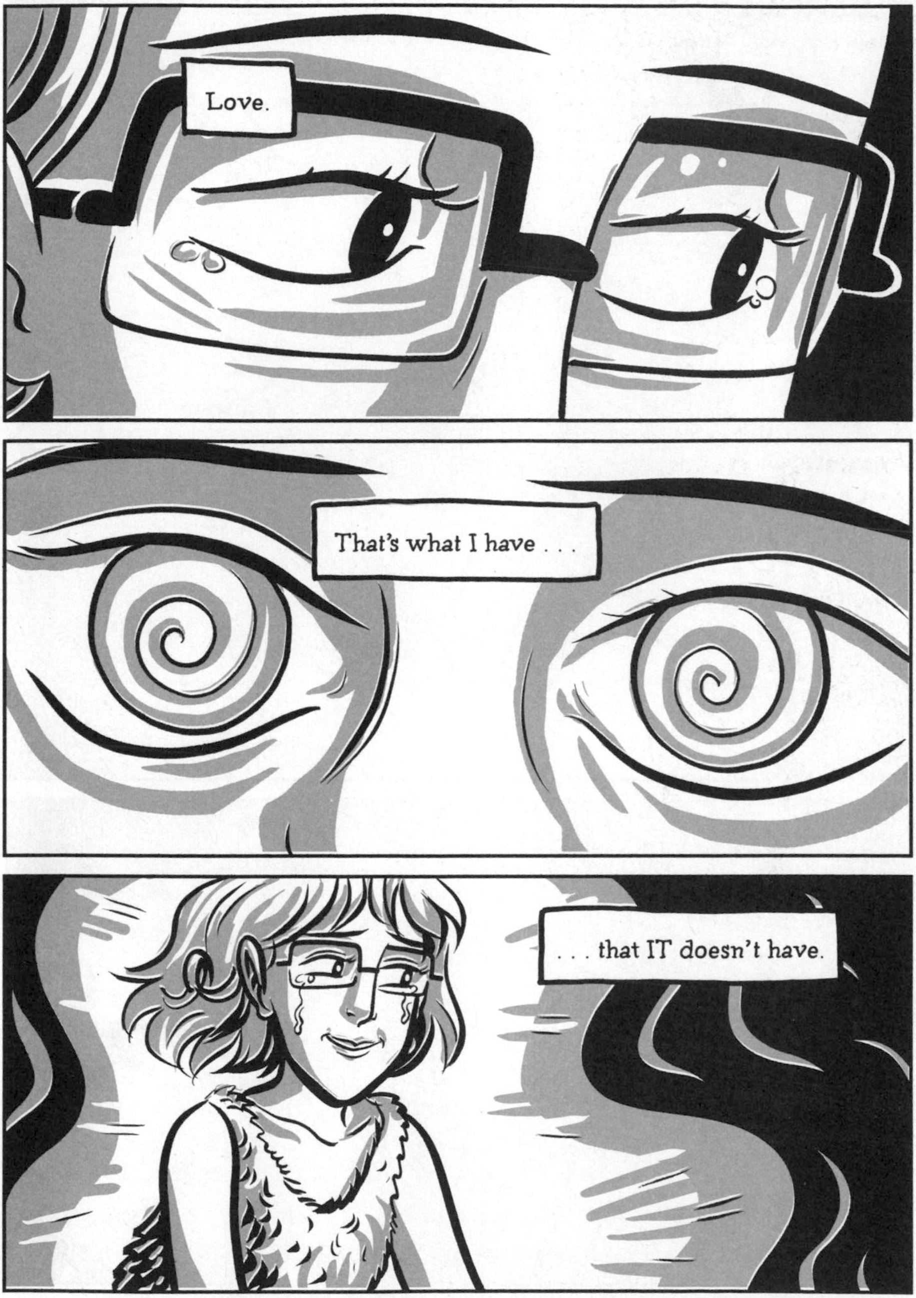
Love.
That's what I have . . .
. . . that IT doesn't have.

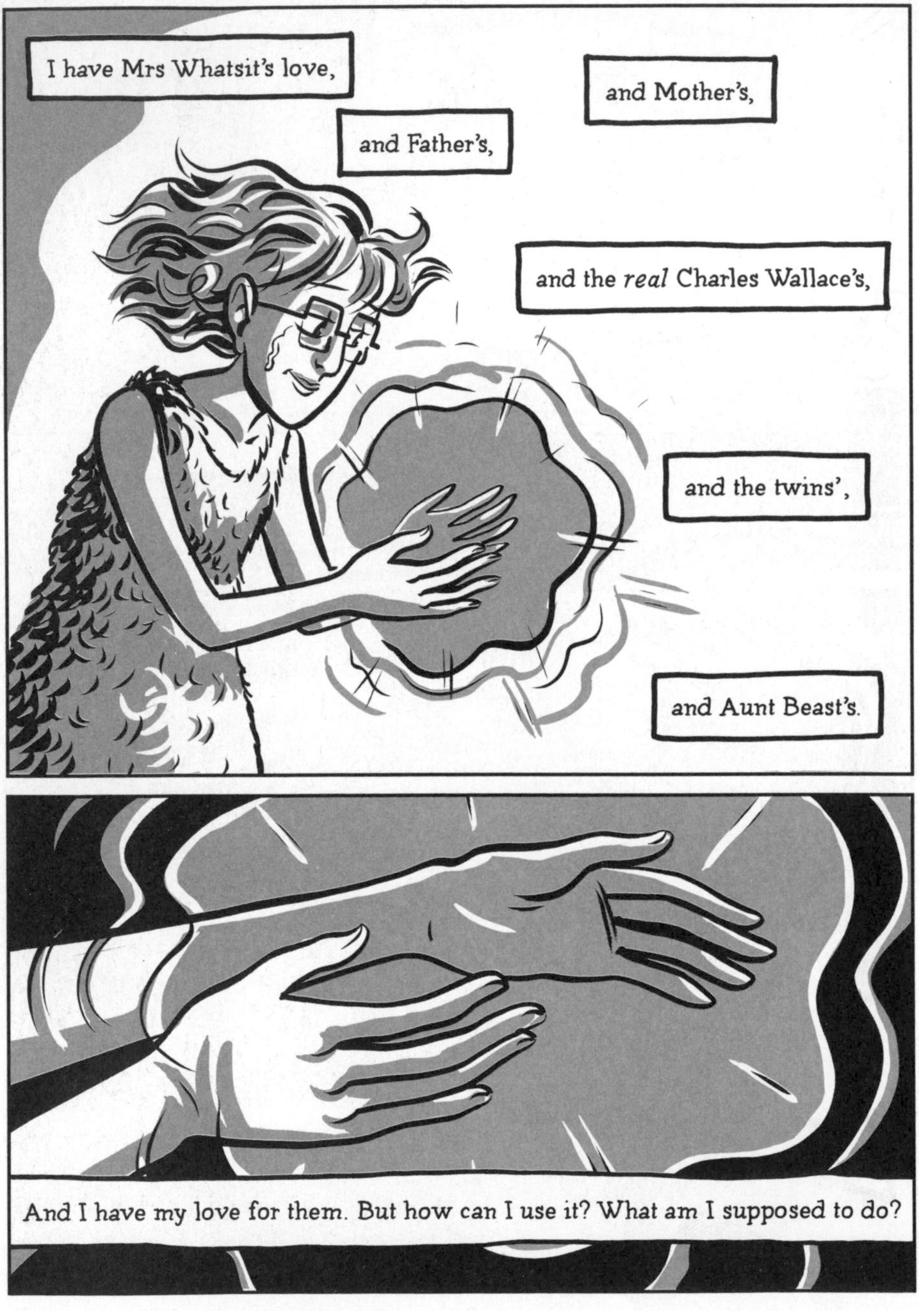
I have Mrs Whatsit's love,
and Father's,
and Mother's,
and the *real* Charles Wallace's,
and the twins',
and Aunt Beast's.
And I have my love for them. But how can I use it? What am I supposed to do?

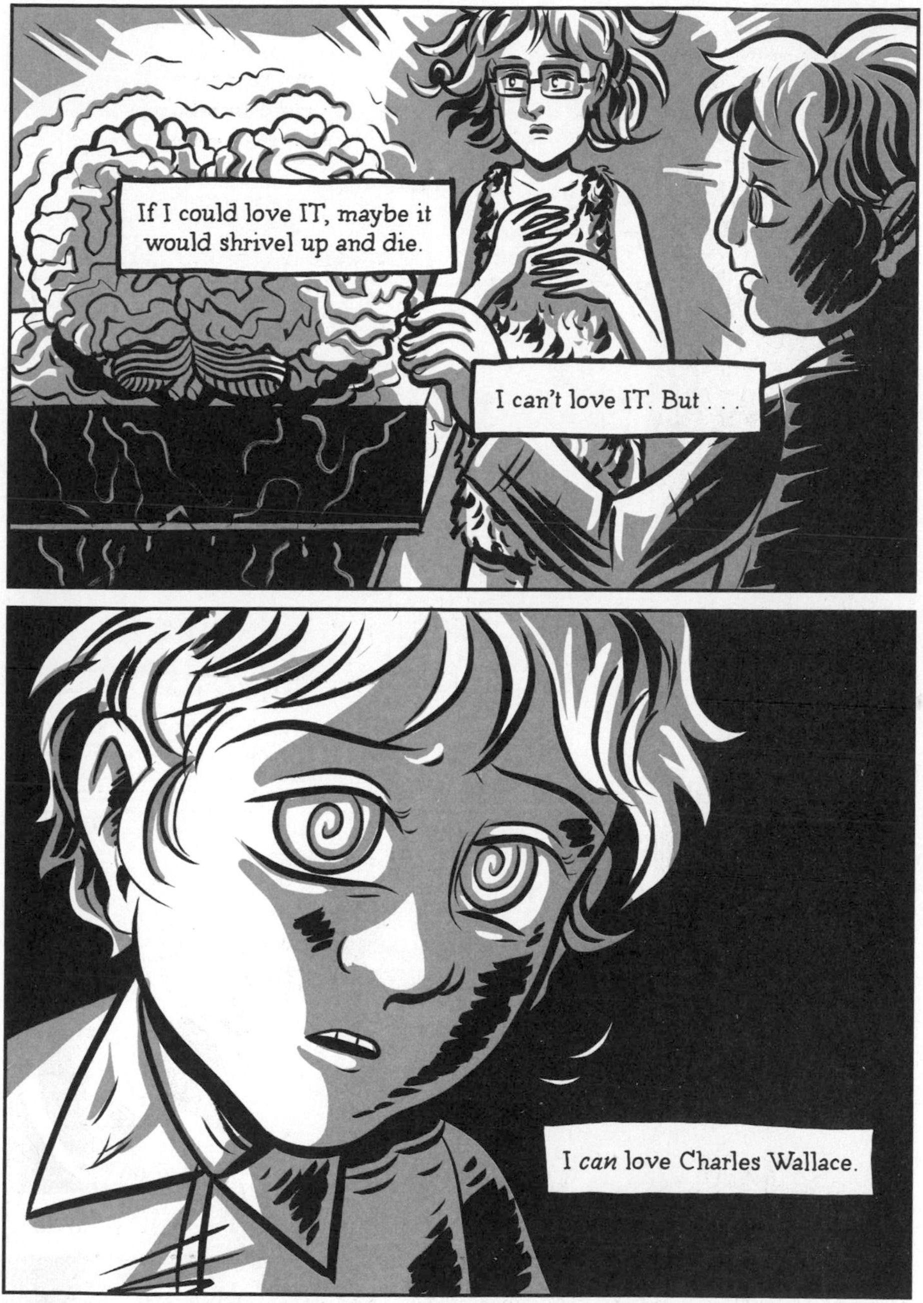
If I could love IT, maybe it would shrivel up and die.
I can't love IT. But . . .
I *can* love Charles Wallace.

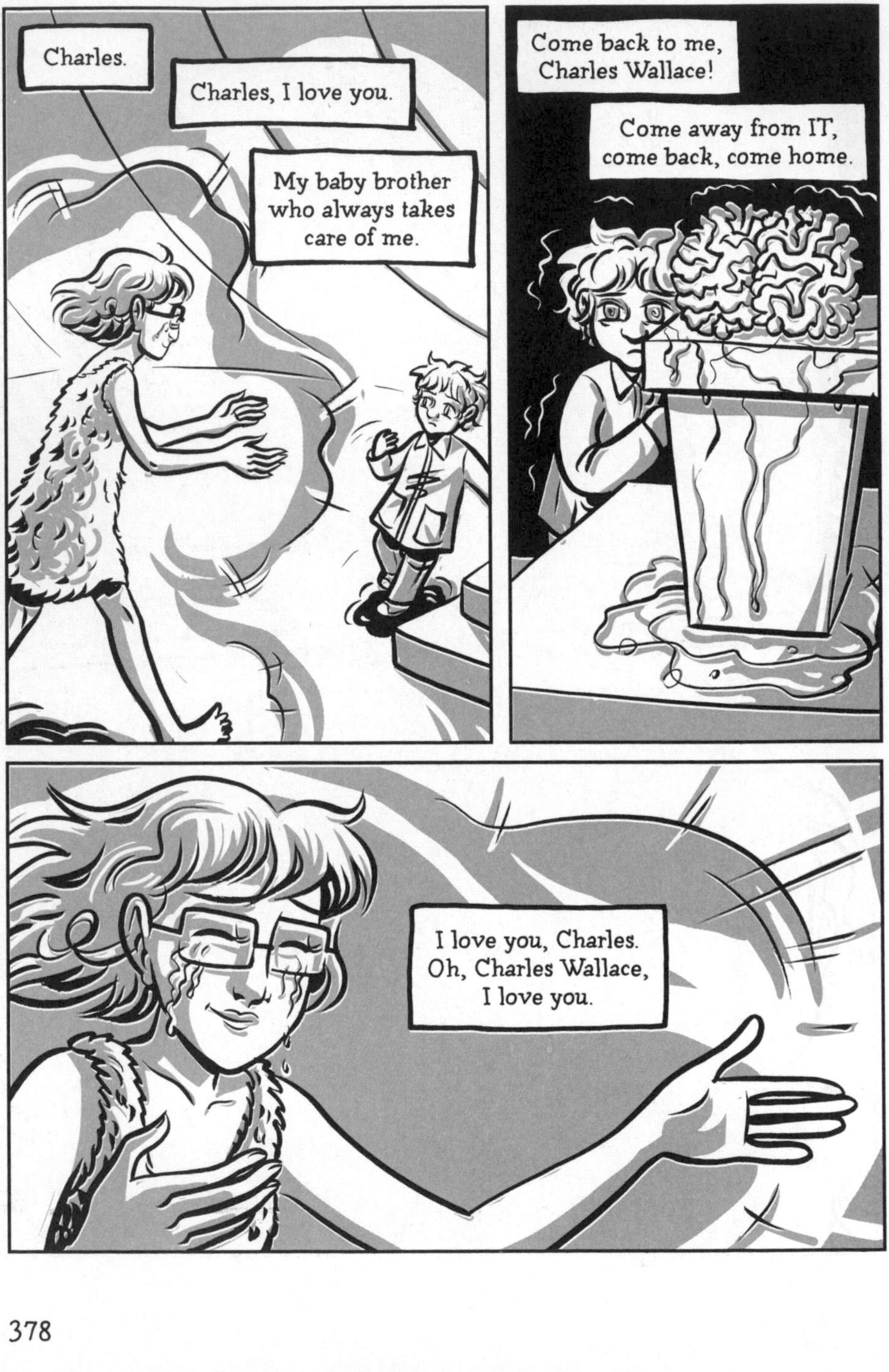
Charles.
Charles, I love you.
My baby brother who always takes care of me.
Come back to me, Charles Wallace!
Come away from IT, come back, come home.
I love you, Charles. Oh, Charles Wallace, I love you.

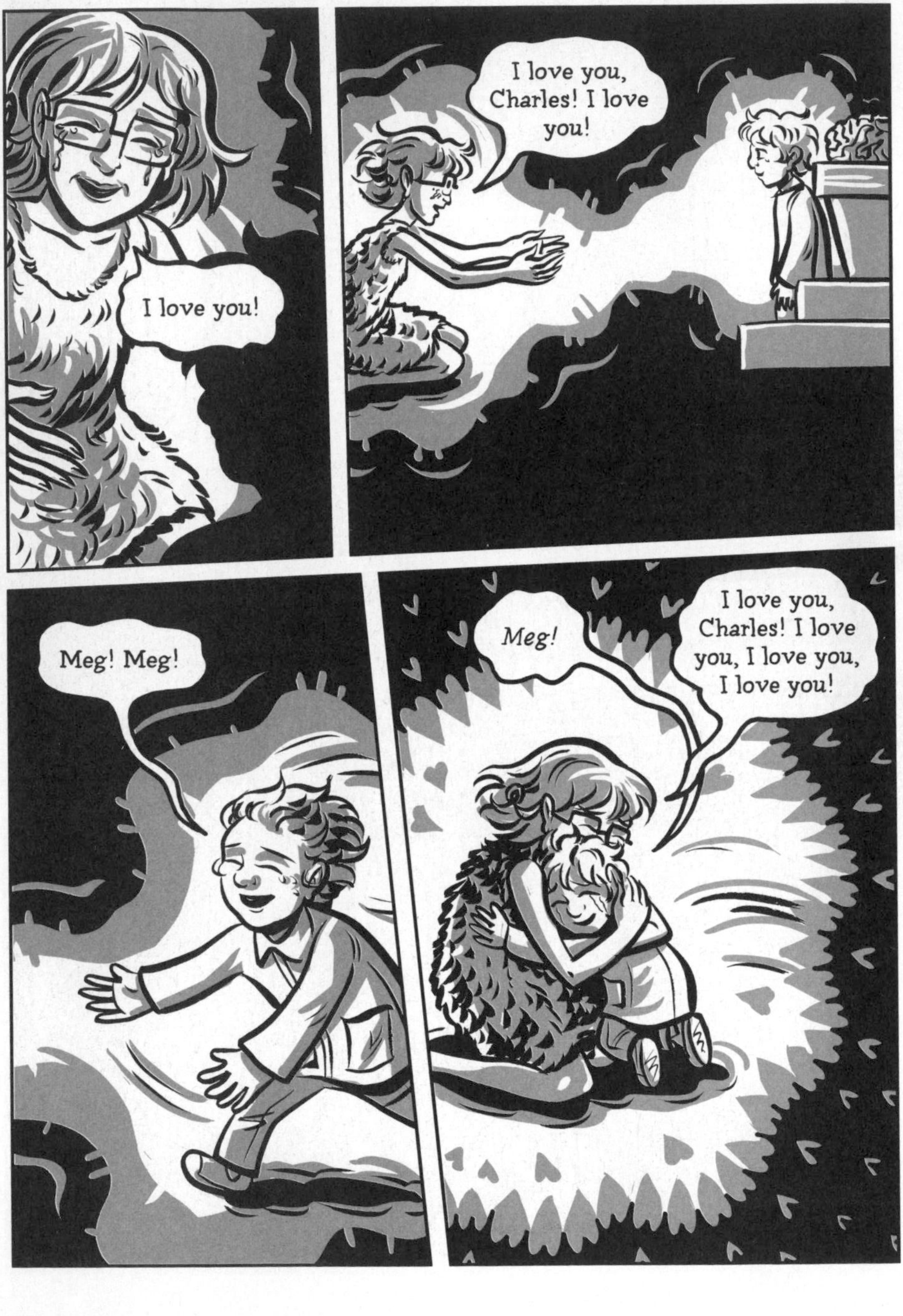
I love you!
I love you, Charles! I love you!
Meg! Meg!
Meg!
I love you, Charles! I love you, I love you, I love you!

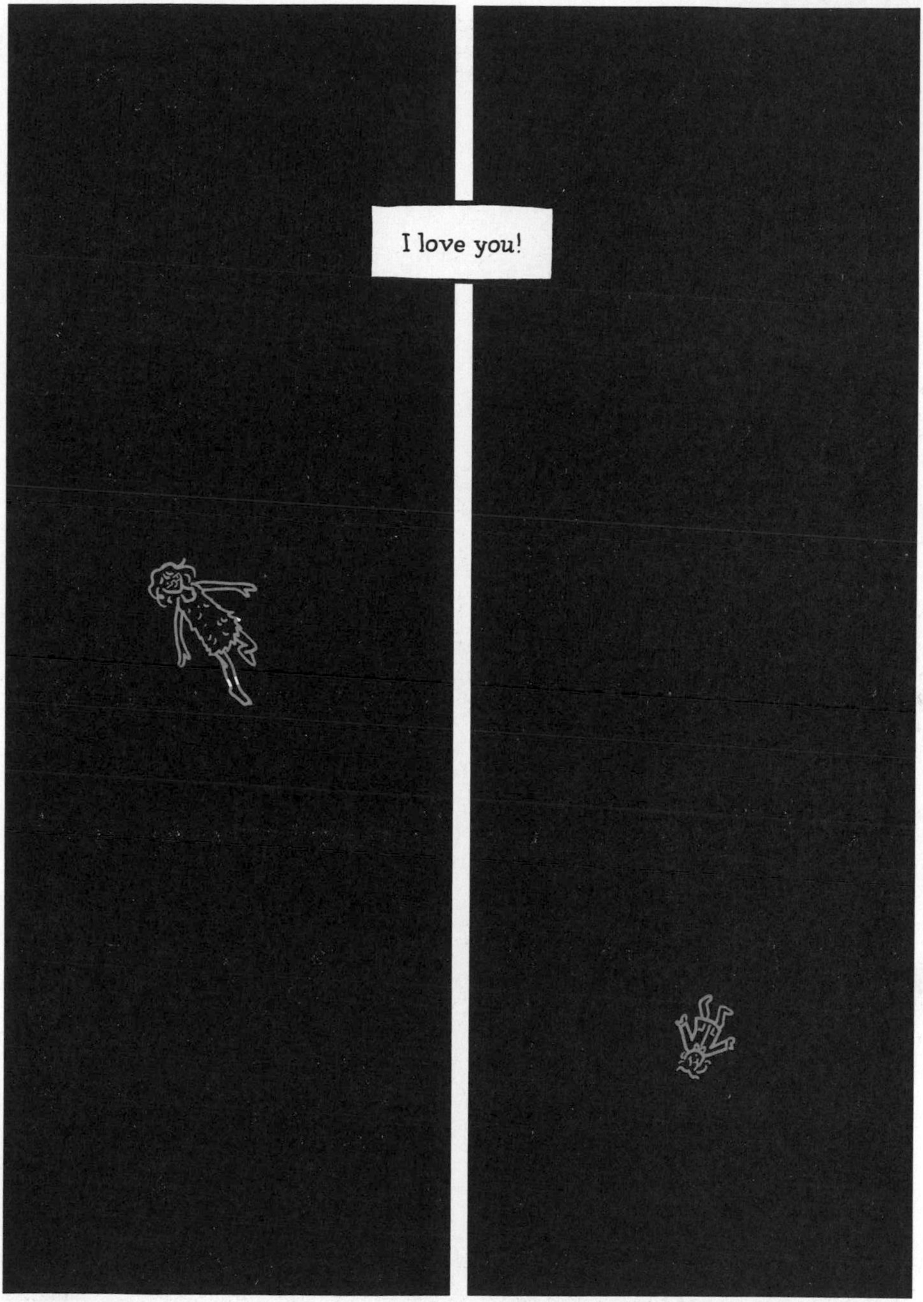
I love you!

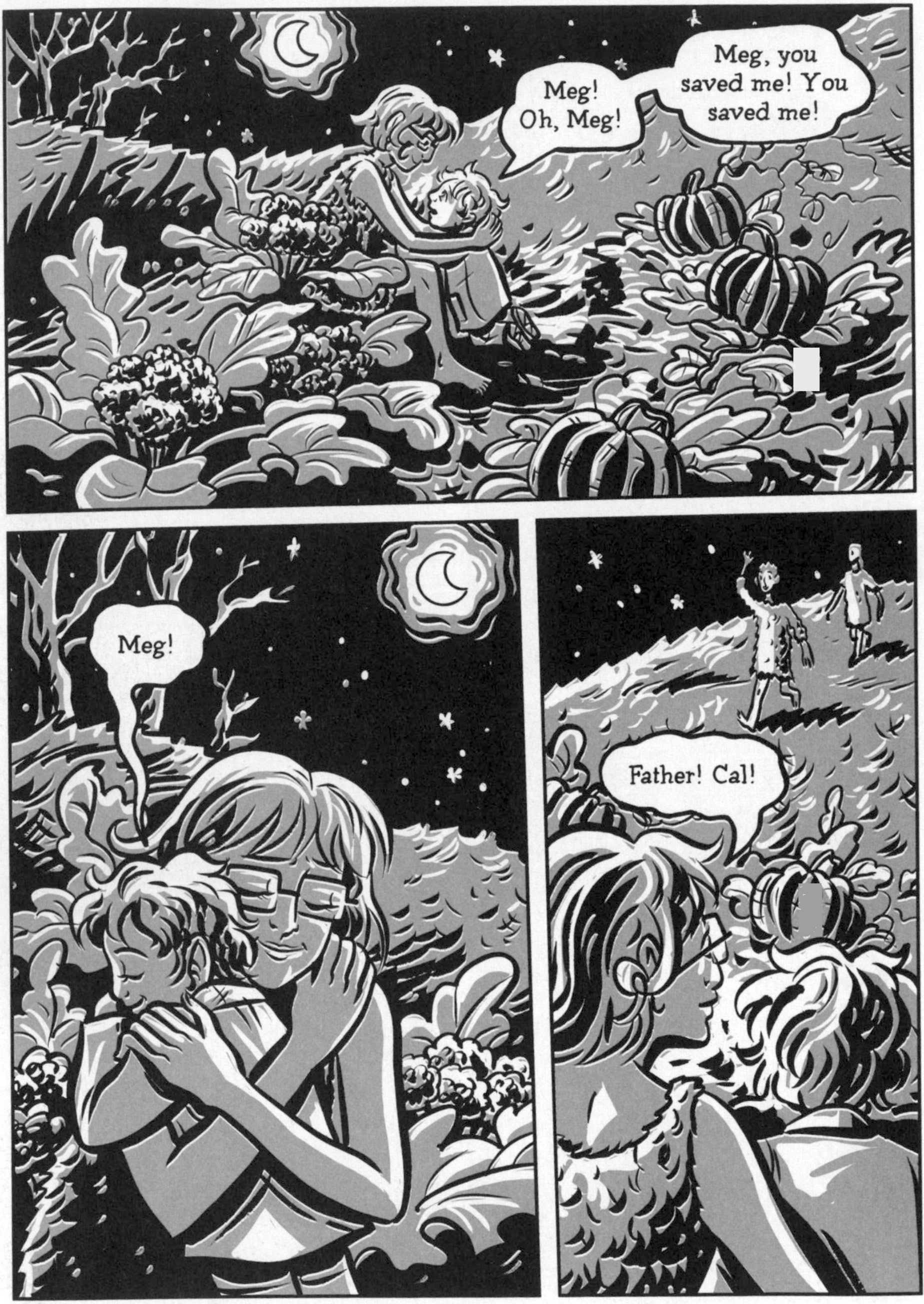
Meg! Oh, Meg!
Meg, you saved me! You saved me!
Meg!
Father! Cal!

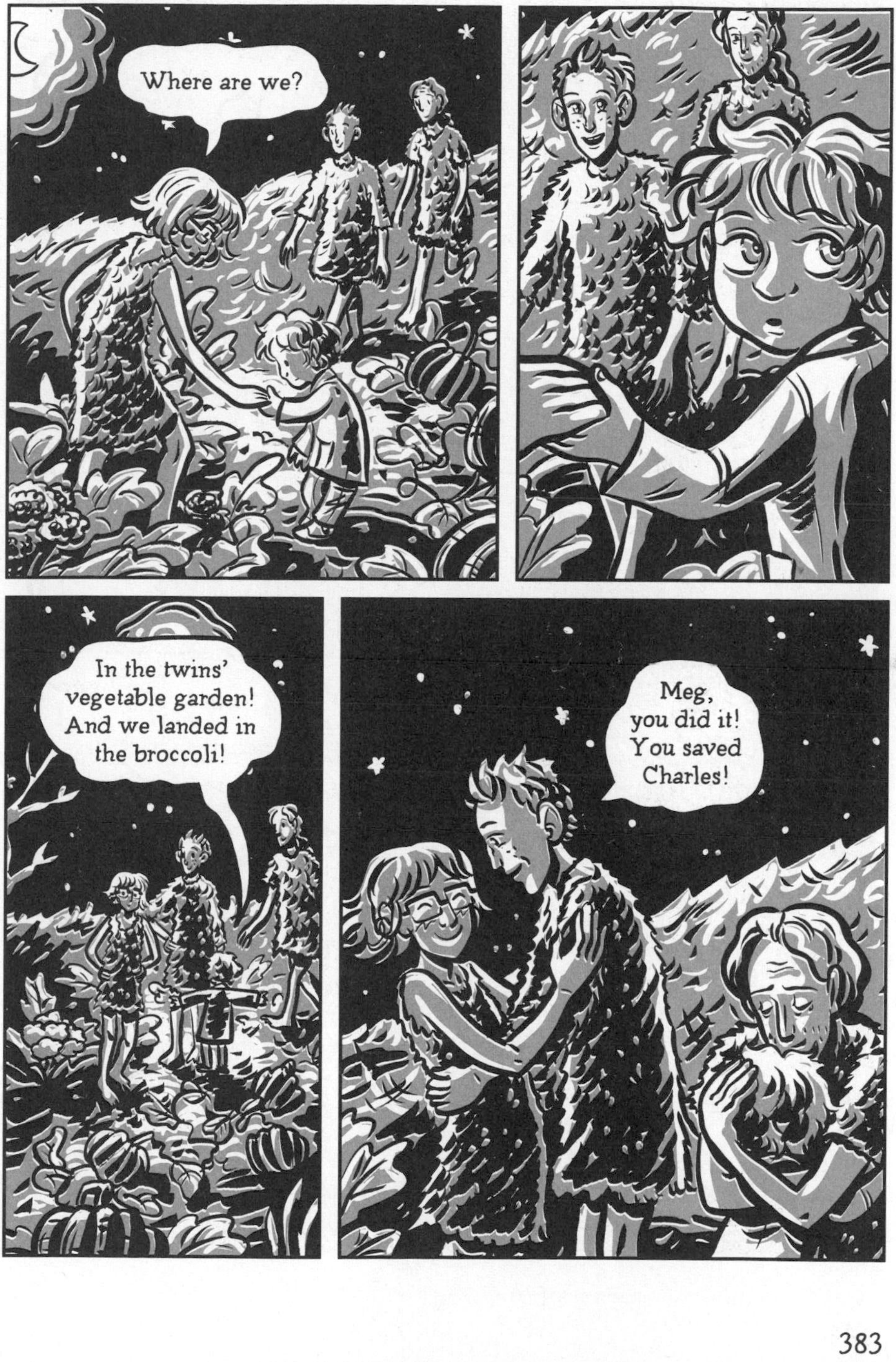
Where are we?
In the twins' vegetable garden! And we landed in the broccoli!
Meg, you did it! You saved Charles!

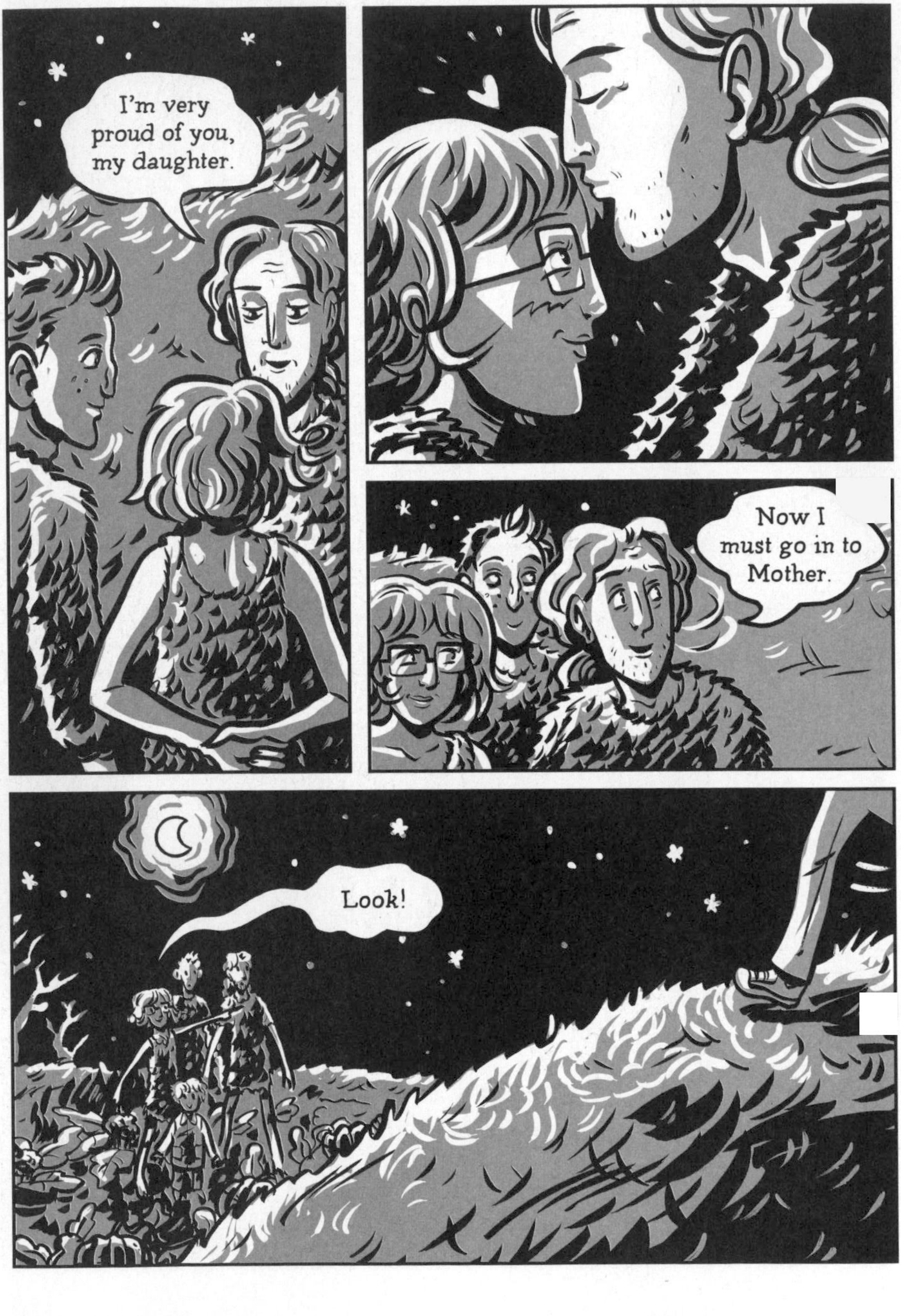
I'm very proud of you, my daughter.
Now I must go in to Mother.
Look!

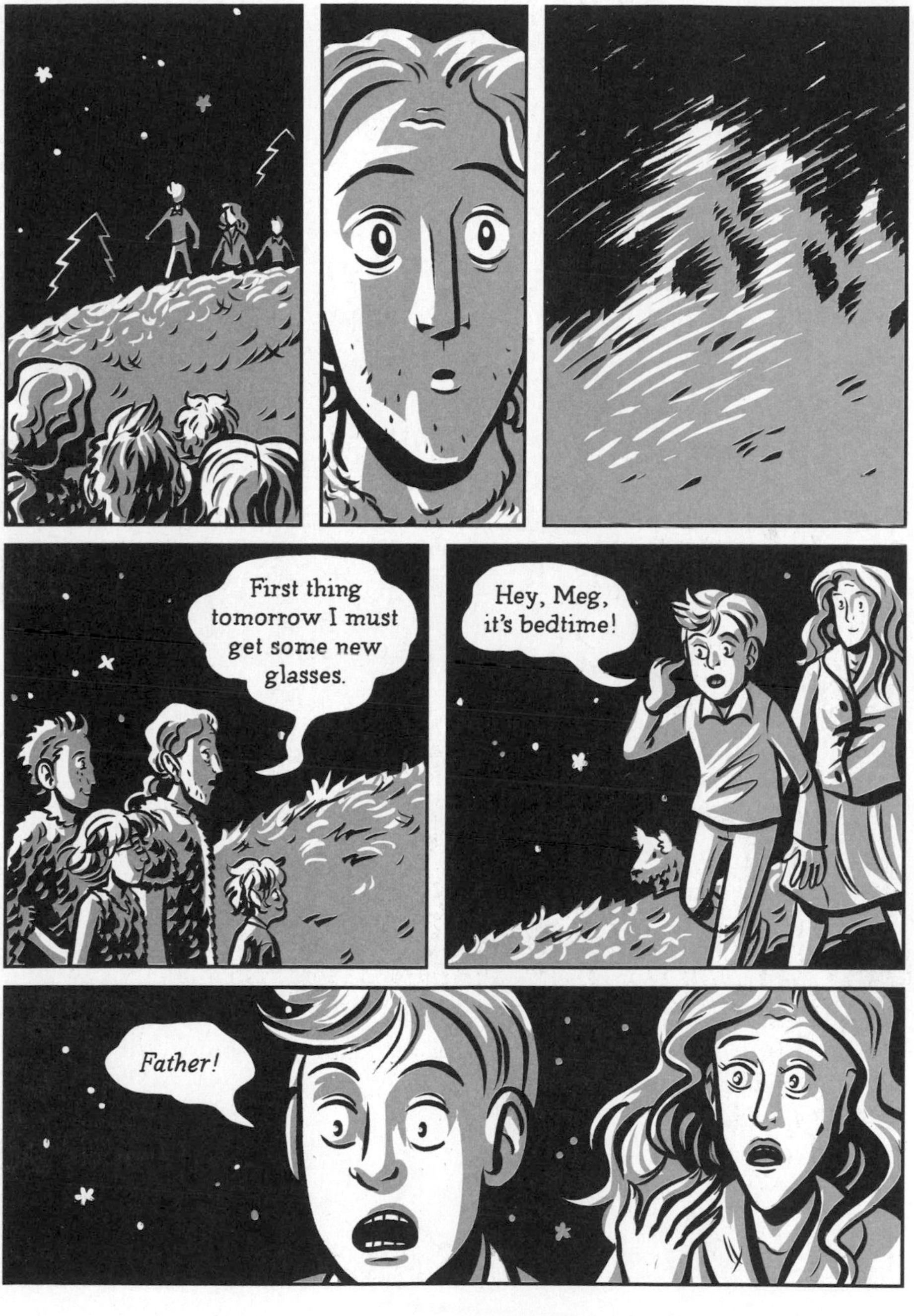
First thing tomorrow I must get some new glasses.
Hey, Meg, it's bedtime!
Father!

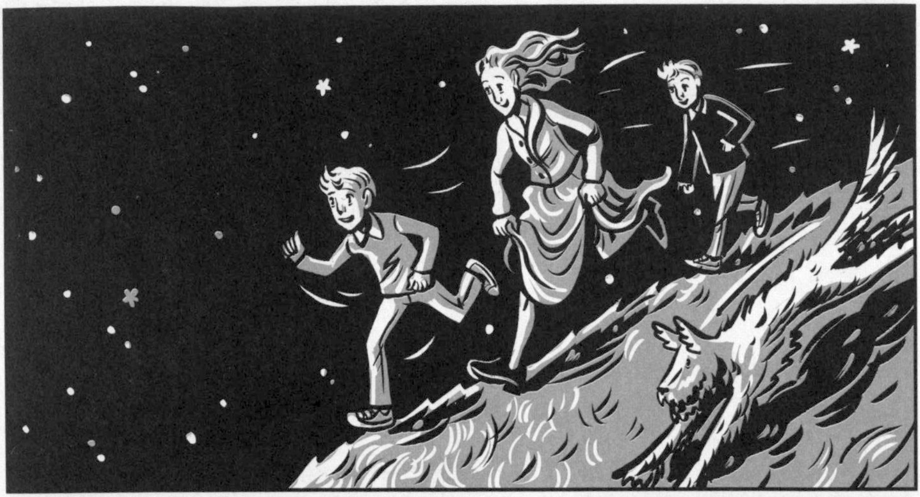

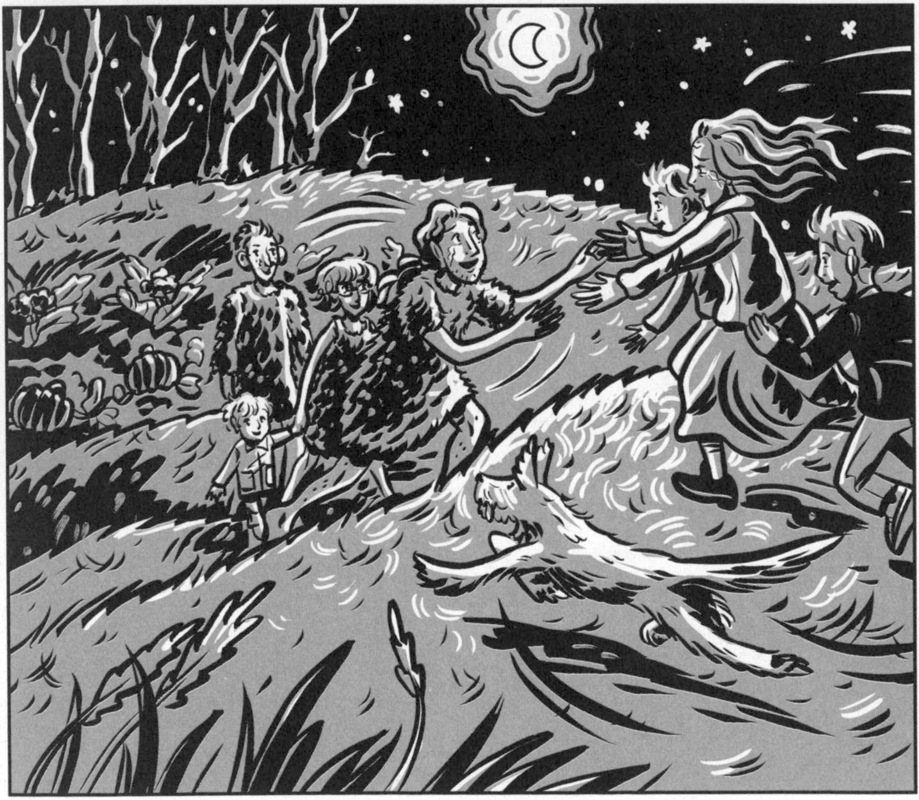

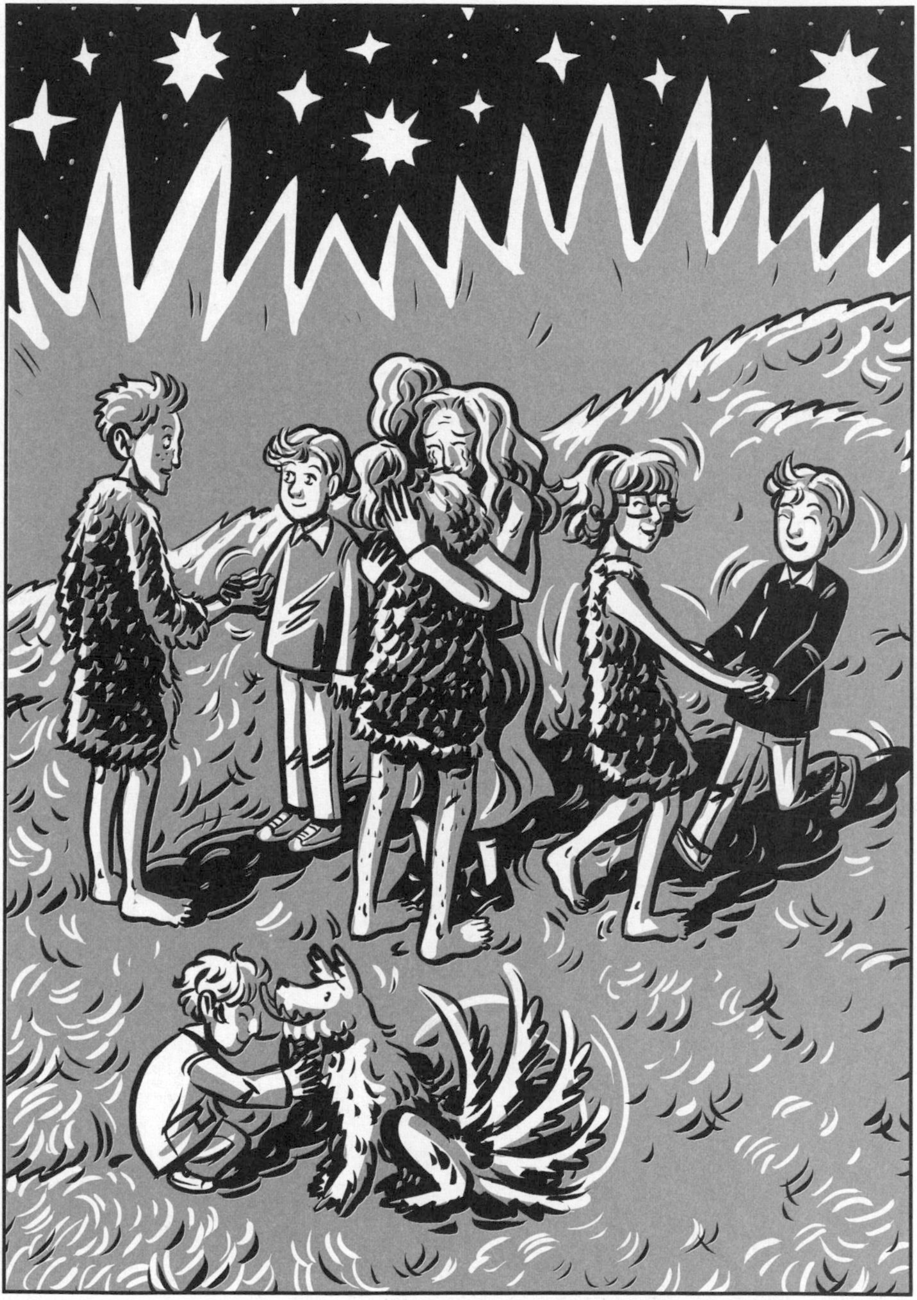

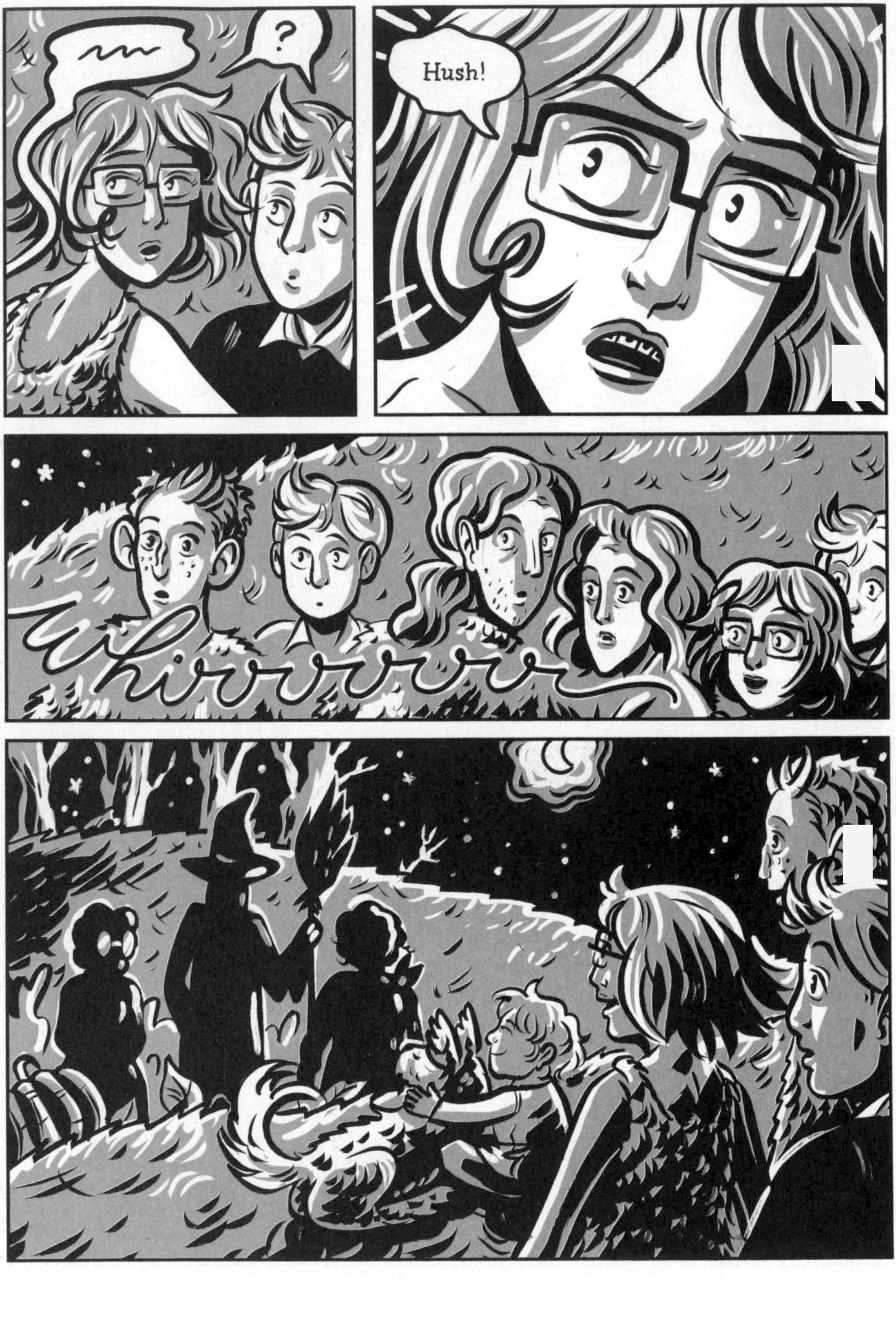
?
Hush!
whirrrrr

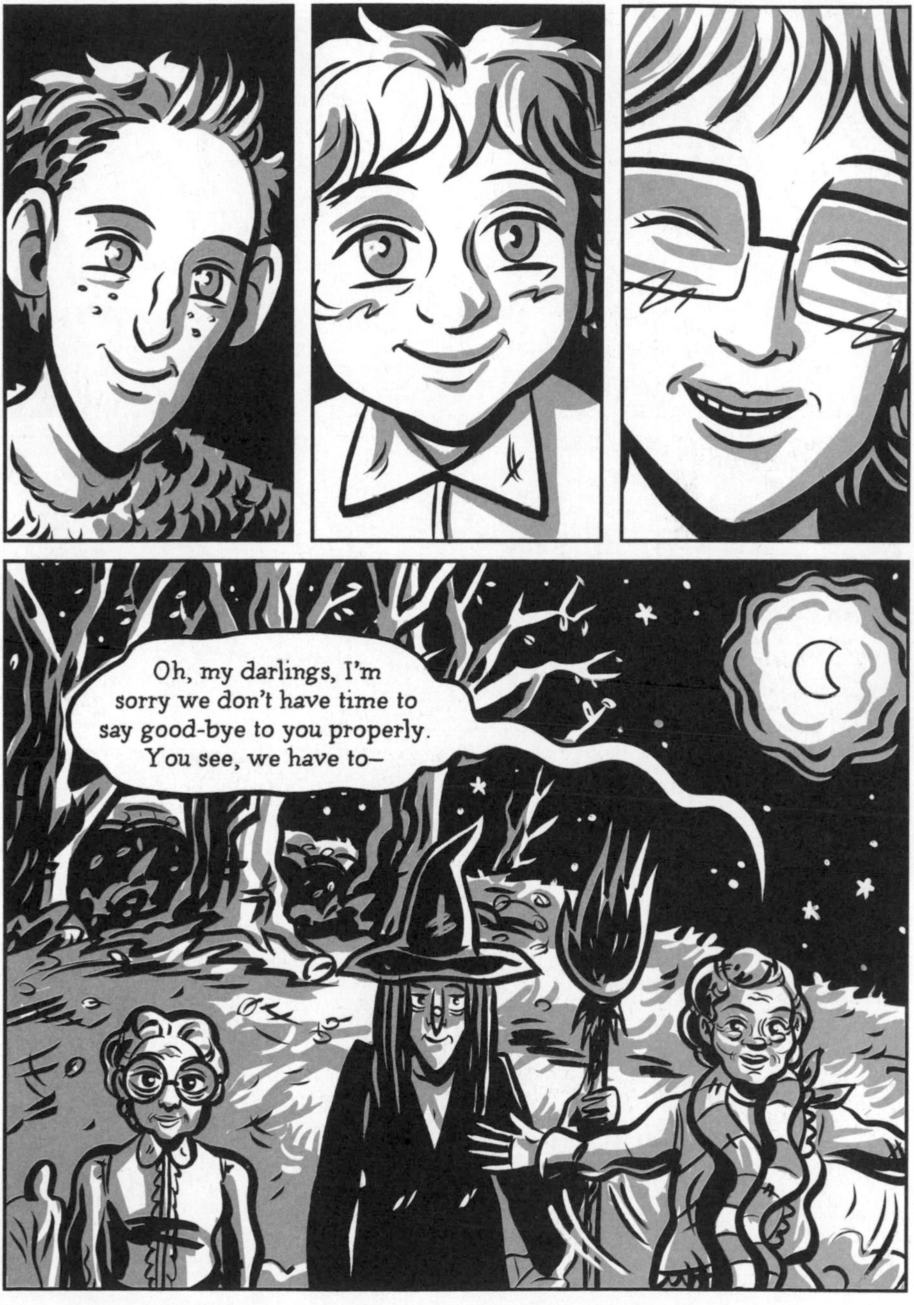
Oh, my darlings, I'm sorry we don't have time to say good-bye to you properly. You see, we have to–

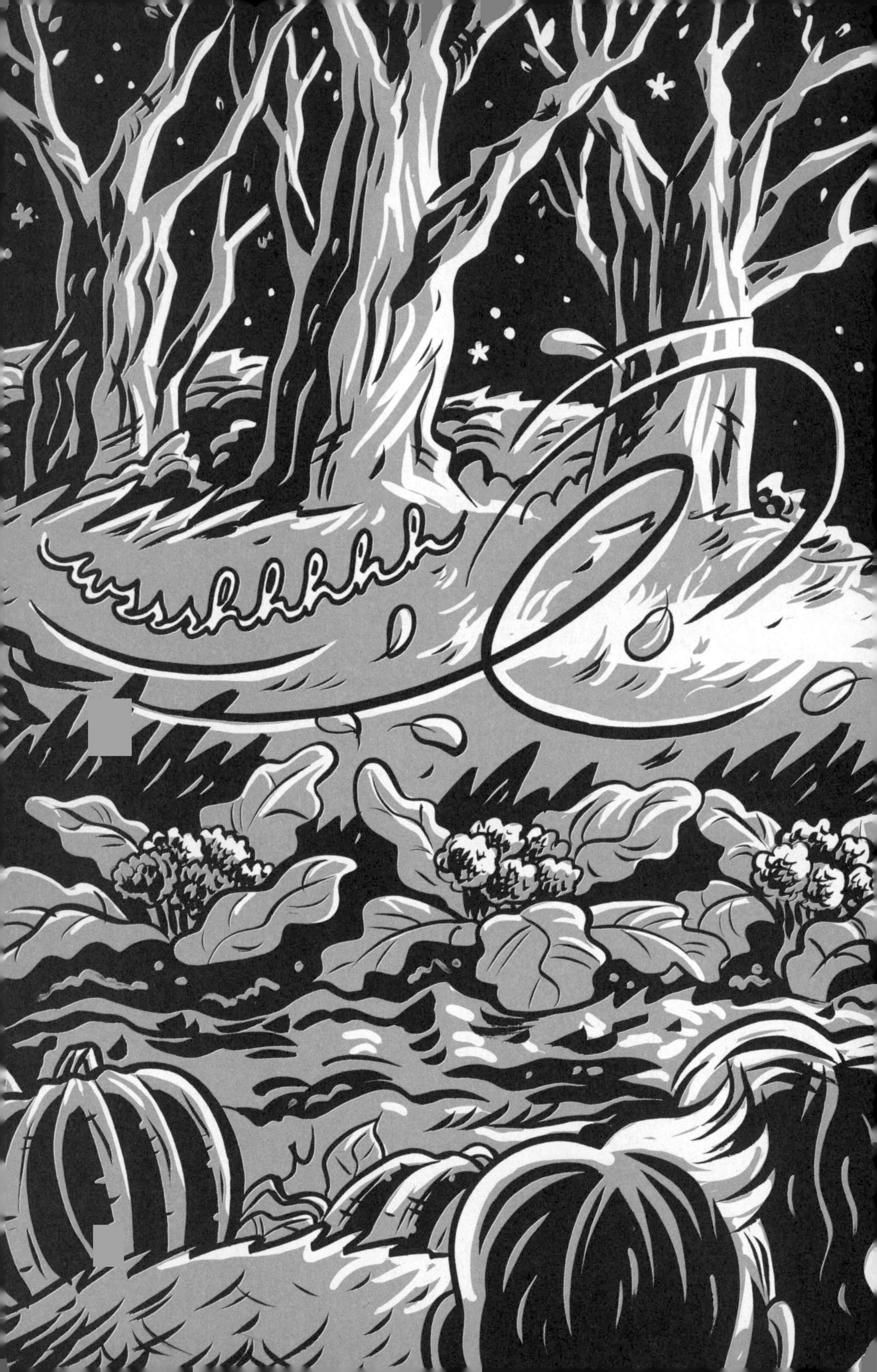
wsssshhhhhh

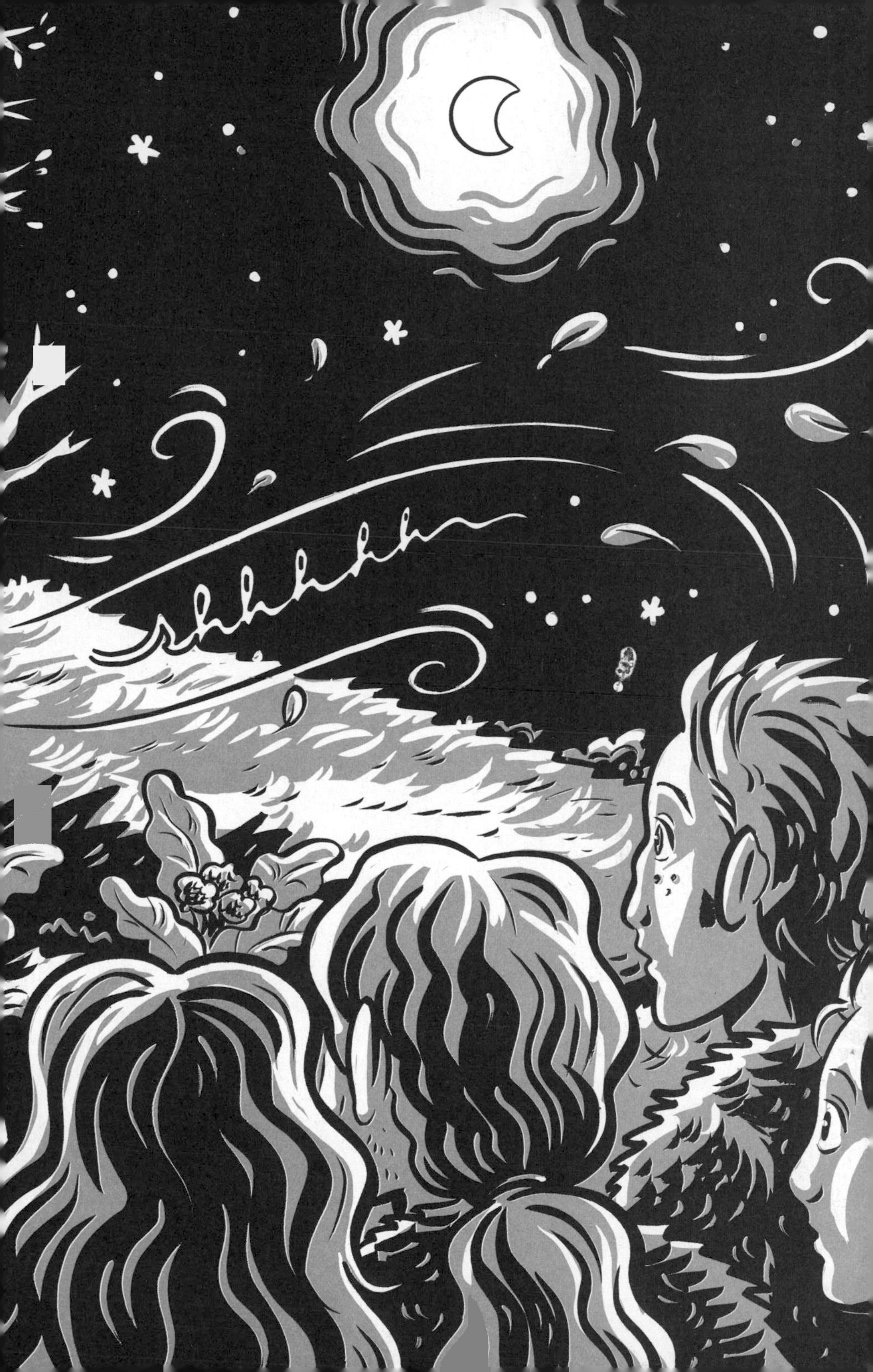
shhhhhh

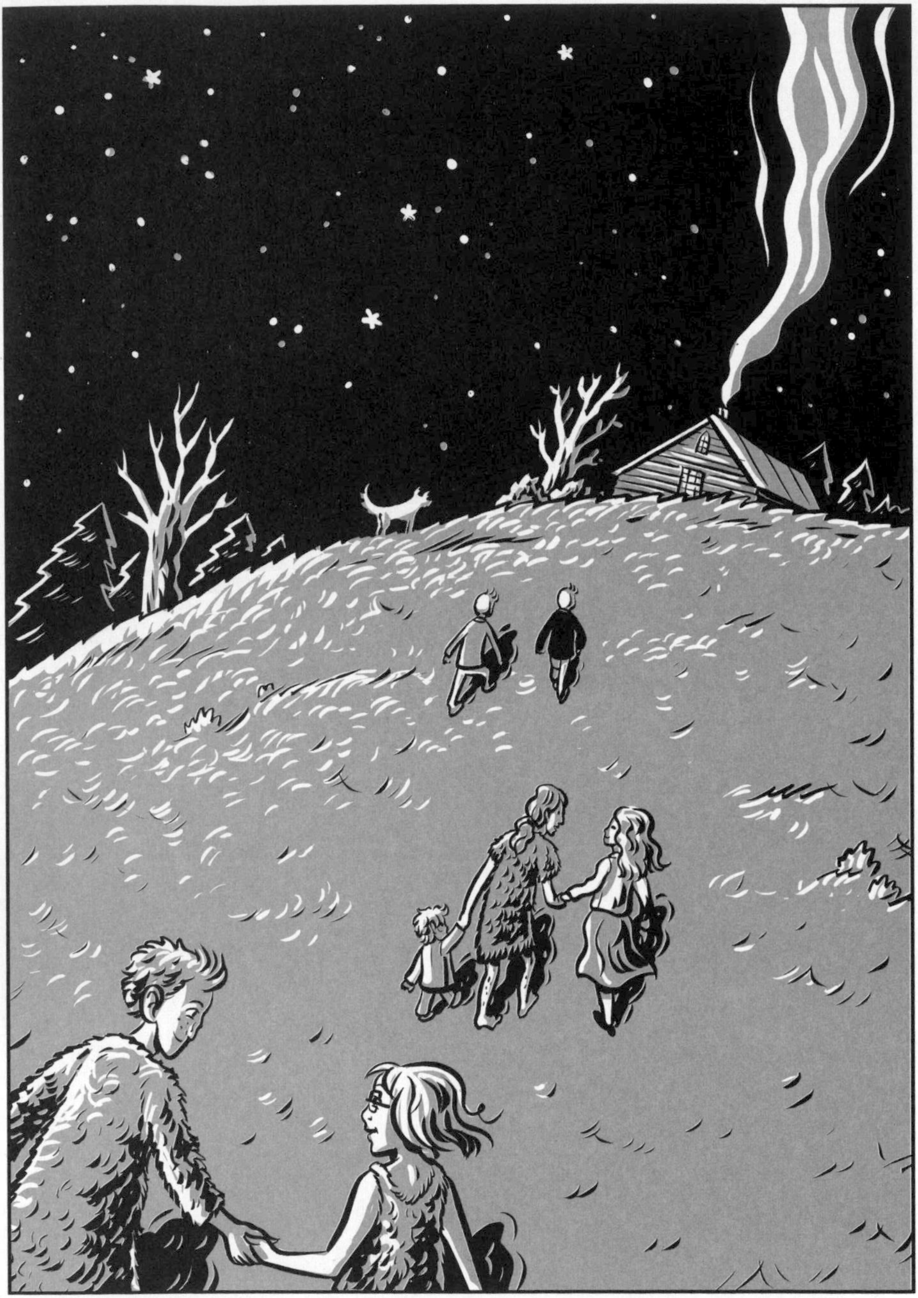

THE GRAPHIC NOVEL

BONUS MATERIALS

In 2007, Square Fish spoke with Madeleine L'Engle for what would become her last interview.

What did you want to be when you grew up?

A writer.

When did you realize you wanted to be a writer?

Right away. As soon as I was able to articulate, I knew I wanted to be a writer. And I read. I adored Emily of New Moon *and some of the other L. M. Montgomery books and they impelled me because I loved them.*

When did you start to write?

When I was five, I wrote a story about a little "gurl."

What was the first writing you had published?

When I was a child, a poem in Child Life. *It was all about a lonely house and was very sentimental.*

Where do you write your books?

Anywhere. I write in longhand first and then type it. My first typewriter was my father's pre–World War I machine. It was the one he took with him to the war. It had certainly been around the world.

What is the best advice you have ever received about writing?

To just write.

What's your first childhood memory?

One early memory I have is going down to Florida for a couple of weeks in the summertime to visit my grandmother. The house was in the middle of a swamp, surrounded by alligators. I don't like alligators, but there they were, and I was afraid of them.

What is your favorite childhood memory?
Being in my room.

As a young person, whom did you look up to most?
My mother. She was a storyteller, and I loved her stories. And she loved music and records. We played duets together on the piano.

What was your worst subject in school?
Math and Latin. I didn't like the Latin teacher.

What was your best subject in school?
English.

What activities did you participate in at school?
I was president of the student government in boarding school and editor of a literary magazine, and also belonged to the drama club.

Are you a morning person or a night owl?
Night owl.

What was your first job?
Working for the actress Eva La Gallienne right after college.

What is your idea of the best meal ever?
Cream of Wheat. I eat it with a spoon. I love it with butter and brown sugar.

Which do you like better: cats or dogs?
I like them both. I once had a wonderful dog named Touche. She was a silver, medium-sized poodle, and quite beautiful. I wasn't allowed to take her on the subway, and I couldn't afford to get a

taxi, so I put her around my neck, like a stole. And she pretended she was a stole. She was an actor.

What do you value most in your friends?

Love.

What is your favorite song?

"Drink to Me Only with Thine Eyes."

What time of the year do you like best?

I suppose autumn. I love the changing of the leaves. I love the autumn goldenrod, the Queen Anne's lace.

What was the original title of A Wrinkle in Time?

"Mrs Whatsit, Mrs Who and Mrs Which."

How did you get the idea for A Wrinkle in Time?

We were living in the country with our three kids on this dairy farm. I started reading what Einstein wrote about time. And I used a lot of those principles to make a universe that was creative and yet believable.

How hard was it to get A Wrinkle in Time published?

I was kept hanging for two years. Over and over again I received nothing more than the formal, printed rejection slip. Eventually, after twenty-six rejections, I called my agent and said, "Send it back. It's too different. Nobody's going to publish it." He sent it back, but a few days later a friend of my mother's insisted that I meet John Farrar, the publisher. He liked the manuscript, and eventually decided to publish it. My first editor was Hal Vursell.

Which of your characters is most like you?

None of them. They're all wiser than I am.

Newbery Medal Acceptance Speech

THE EXPANDING UNIVERSE
August 1963

FOR A WRITER OF FICTION to have to sit down and write a speech, especially a speech in which she must try to express her gratitude for one of the greatest honors of her life, is as difficult a task as she can face. She can no longer hide behind the printed page and let her characters speak for her; she must stand up in front of an illustrious group of librarians, editors, publishers, writers, feeling naked, the way one sometimes does in a dream. What, then, does she say? Should she merely tell a series of anecdotes about her life and how she happened to write this book? Or should she try to be profound and write a speech that will go down in the pages of history, comparable only to the Gettysburg Address? Should she stick to platitudes that will offend no one and say nothing? Perhaps she tries all of these several times and then tears them up, knowing that if she doesn't, her husband will do it for her, and decides simply to say some of the things she feels deeply about.

I can't tell you anything about children's books that you don't already know. I'm not teaching you; you're teaching me. All I can tell you is how Ruth Gagliardo's telephone call about the Newbery Medal has affected me over the past few months.

One of my greatest treasures is the letter Mr. Melcher wrote me, one of the last letters he wrote, talking about the medal and saying he had just read *A Wrinkle in Time* and had been excited about it. This was one of the qualities that made him what he was: the ability to be excited. Bertha Mahony Miller, in her article "Frederic G. Melcher—A Twentieth Century John Newbery," says that "the bookstore's stock trade is . . . explosive material, capable of stirring up fresh life endlessly." I like here to think of another Fred, the eminent British scientist Fred Hoyle, and his theory of the universe, in which matter is continuously being created, with the universe expanding but not dissipating. As island galaxies rush away from each other into eternity, new clouds of gas are condensing into new galaxies. As old stars die, new stars are being born. Mr. Melcher lived in this universe of continuous creation and expansion. It would be impossible to overestimate his influence on books, particularly children's books; impossible to overestimate his influence on the people who read books, write them, get enthusiastic about them. We are all here tonight because of his vision, and we would be less than fair to his memory if we didn't resolve to keep alive his excitement and his ability to grow, to change, to expand.

I am of the first generation to profit by Mr. Melcher's excite-ment, having been born shortly before he established the New-bery Award, and growing up with most of these books on my shelves. I learned about mankind from Hendrik Willem van Loon; I traveled with Dr. Dolittle, created by a man I called Hug Lofting; Will James taught me about the West with Smoky; in boarding school I grabbed *Invincible Louisa* the moment it came into the library because Louisa May Alcott had the same birth-day that I have, and the same ambitions. And now to be a very small link in the long chain of those writers, of the men and women who led me into the expanding universe, is both an honor and a responsibility. It is an honor for which I am deeply grateful to Mr. Melcher and to those of you who decided *A Wrin-kle in Time* was worthy of it.

The responsibility has caused me to think seriously during these past months on the subject of vocation, the responsibility added to the fact that I'm working now on a movie scenario about a Portuguese nun who lived in the mid-1600s, had no vocation, was seduced and then betrayed by a French soldier of fortune, and, in the end, through suffering, came into a true vocation. I believe that every one of us here tonight has as clear and vital a vocation as anyone in a religious order. We have the vocation of keeping alive Mr. Melcher's excitement in leading young people into an expanding imagination. Because of the very nature of the world as it is today, our children receive in school a heavy load of scientific and analytic subjects, so it is in their reading for fun, for pleasure, that they must be guided into creativity. There are forces working in the world as never before in the history of mankind for standardization, for the regimentation of us all, or what I like to call making muffins of us, muffins all like every other muffin in the muffin tin. This is the limited universe, the drying, dissipating universe, that we can help our children avoid by providing them with "explosive material capable of stirring up fresh life endlessly."

So how do we do it? We can't just sit down at our typewriters and turn out explosive material. I took a course in college on Chaucer, one of the most explosive, imaginative, and far-reaching in influence of all writers. And I'll never forget going to the final exam and being asked why Chaucer used certain verbal devices, certain adjectives, why he had certain characters behave in certain ways. And I wrote in a white heat of fury, "I don't think Chaucer had any idea why he did any of these things. That isn't the way people write."

I believe this as strongly now as I did then. Most of what is best in writing isn't done deliberately.

Do I mean, then, that an author should sit around like a phony Zen Buddhist in his pad, drinking endless cups of espresso coffee and waiting for inspiration to descend upon him? That isn't the way the writer works, either. I heard a famous author say once that the hardest part of writing a book was making yourself sit down at the typewriter. I know what he meant. Unless a writer works constantly to improve and refine the tools of his trade they will be useless instruments if and when the moment of inspiration, of revelation, does come. This is the moment when a writer is spoken through, the moment that a writer must accept with gratitude and humility, and then attempt, as best he can, to communicate to others.

A writer of fantasy, fairy tale, or myth must inevitably discover that he is not writing out of his own knowledge or experience, but out of something both deeper and wider. I think that fantasy must possess the author and simply use him. I know that this is true of *A Wrinkle in Time.* I can't possibly tell you how I came to write it. It was simply a book I had to write. I had no choice. And it was only *after* it was written that I realized what some of it meant.

Very few children have any problem with the world of the imagination; it's their own world, the world of their daily life, and it's our loss that so many of us grow out of it. Probably this group here tonight is the least grown-out-of-it group that could be gathered together in one place, simply by the nature of our work. We, too, can understand how Alice could walk through the mirror into the country on the other side; how often have our children almost done this themselves? And we all understand princesses, of course. Haven't we all been badly bruised by peas? And what about the princess who spat forth toads and snakes whenever she opened her mouth to speak, and the other whose lips issued forth pieces of pure gold? We all have had days when everything we've said has seemed to turn to toads. The days of gold, alas, don't come nearly as often.

What a child doesn't realize until he is grown is that in responding to fantasy, fairy tale, and myth he is responding to what Erich Fromm calls the one universal language, the one and only language in the world that cuts across all barriers of time, place, race, and culture. Many Newbery books are from this realm, beginning with Dr. Dolittle; books on Hindu myth, Chinese folklore, the life of Buddha, tales of American Indians, books that lead our children beyond all boundaries and into the one language of all mankind.

In the beginning God created the heaven and the earth... The extraordinary, the marvelous thing about Genesis is not how unscientific it is, but how amazingly accurate it is. How could the ancient Israelites have known the exact order of an evolution that wasn't to be formulated for thousands of years? Here is a truth that cuts across barriers of time and space.

But almost all of the best children's books do this, not only an *Alice in Wonderland*, a *Wind in the Willows*, a *Princess and the Goblin*. Even the most straightforward tales say far more than they seem to mean on the surface. *Little Women, The Secret Garden, Huckleberry Finn*—how much more there is in them than we realize at a first reading. They partake of the universal language, and this is why we turn to them again and again when we are children, and still again when we have grown up.

Up on the summit of Mohawk Mountain in northwest Connecticut is a large flat rock that holds the heat of the sun long after the last of the late sunset has left the sky. We take our picnic up there and then lie on the rock and watch the stars, one pulsing slowly into the deepening blue, and then another and another and another, until the sky is full of them.

A book, too, can be a star, "explosive material, capable of stirring up fresh life endlessly," a living fire to lighten the darkness, leading out into the expanding universe.

An Interview with Hope Larson

What did you want to be when you grew up?
*I always wanted to be an artist. Ever since I was a little kid, I'd
made little illustrated books, and what I do today is the grown-up
version of what I was doing at age five. I also had phases when I
wanted to be a geologist, a vet, and an animator, but none of that
stuck.*

What's your favorite childhood memory?
*I remember one night when I was little, my dad woke me up and
took me downstairs. It was very windy out—there was probably a
storm moving in—and he wanted me to see the trees blowing in
the backyard. It was magical.*

When did you realize you wanted to be an illustrator?
*I've been drawing for as long as I can remember. I was the always
the "art kid" at school. My mom's side of the family is artistic, so it's
in my blood!*

Who is your favorite artist?
*I couldn't pick one. There are so many artists I love, and they're all
so different: Dan Clowes, Rumiko Takahashi, Mitsuru Adachi,
Lynda Barry, Seth, Charles Burns, Kerascoët. I'm always finding
new artists to love and finding inspiration in new artistic voices.*

What is your favorite medium to work in?
Brush and ink on smooth Bristol board.

What was your favorite book or comic/graphic novel when you were a kid?

A Wrinkle in Time *and the rest of the Time Quintet were definitely on the list, along with the Chronicles of Prydain and the Chronicles of Narnia.*

When did you first read *A Wrinkle in Time*?

I read it for the first time after hearing some adults talk about how strange it was. That piqued my interest for sure! I was probably seven or eight.

What was it like to revisit *A Wrinkle in Time* as an adult?

I was surprised by how much I'd forgotten, and also that the way I pictured some of the characters—especially Meg—was the result of my own childhood imagination, not the descriptions actually in the book.

What was your experience like creating *A Wrinkle in Time: The Graphic Novel*? What was most difficult? What came easily?

Overall, working on this book was as painless as it possibly could have been. I had a wonderful editor and Ms. L'Engle's estate was incredibly supportive. The most difficult part was how long it took to complete: two years. It's by far the biggest project I've undertaken, and although it was rewarding, it was exhausting. As for what was easy, I was surprised by how, once I started drawing, it felt the same as drawing a book I'd written myself. In spite of my love for the novel, I was worried I wouldn't connect with it on an artistic level. In the end, though, I did.

When you think of Madeleine L'Engle, what comes to mind?
That I'm sorry I never got to meet her. I've met her family and they are absolutely delightful people.

Where did you find inspiration for your illustrations in the book?
I bought some old Sears catalogs for reference. Aside from that, it's all drawn from the descriptions in the book and from my imagination.

What challenges did you face in the artistic process, and how did you overcome them?
I couldn't figure out how to abridge the book—I didn't want to cut anything out, because every part of that book is precious to someone—and we resolved that issue by including every scene and almost every word of dialogue in the graphic novel. That's why the book is so long!

What's the best advice you have ever received about illustrating?
This applies mostly to comics, but you have to learn how not to be precious about the art. There's just too much of it to spend hours and hours making every panel perfect. Some of the greatest

cartoonists aren't technically proficient illustrators, but they are great storytellers. That's the important part.

What would your readers be most surprised to learn about you?
My hobby is making ice cream. I attended the Penn State Ice Cream Short Course and I write all my own recipes.

What do you want readers to remember about your books?
All I hope is that my books make readers feel something—happy or sad or even angry. That's the important thing.

Behind the Scenes

I drew the rough version of this book in black-colored pencil on regular printer paper. I worked quickly and loosely in an effort to maintain a firm grasp on Meg's inner journey, her feelings, and the whole sprawling story. Later, after making changes to the rough draft with my editor's help, I refined and redrew the pages in ink. They were then colored by Jenn Manley Lee. Lastly, I hand-drew and placed all of the speech balloons. The type is set in Times New Larson, a font I commissioned years ago for use in my comics. It was created by me and designer John Martz.

—Hope Larson

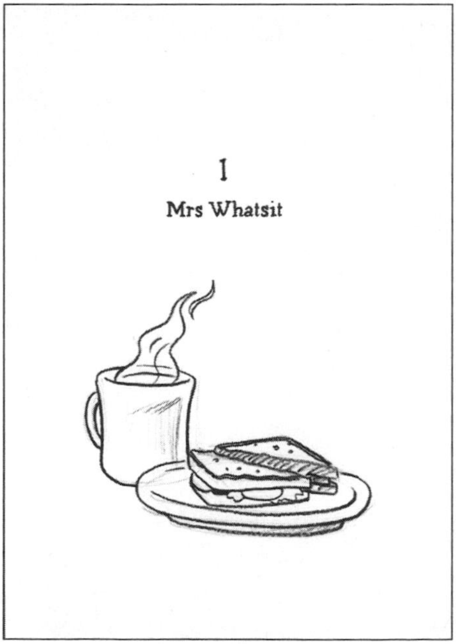
I
Mrs Whatsit

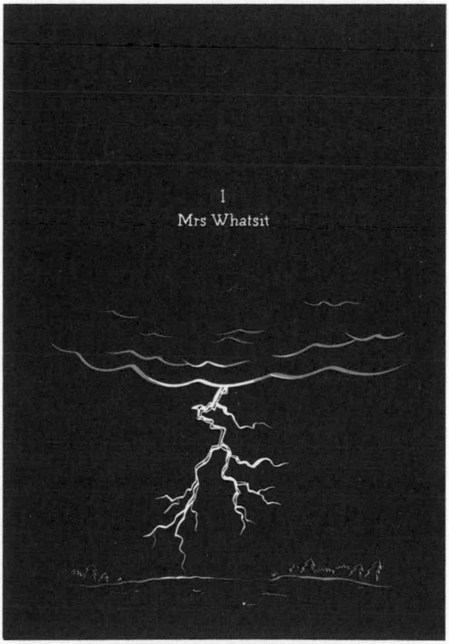
1
Mrs Whatsit

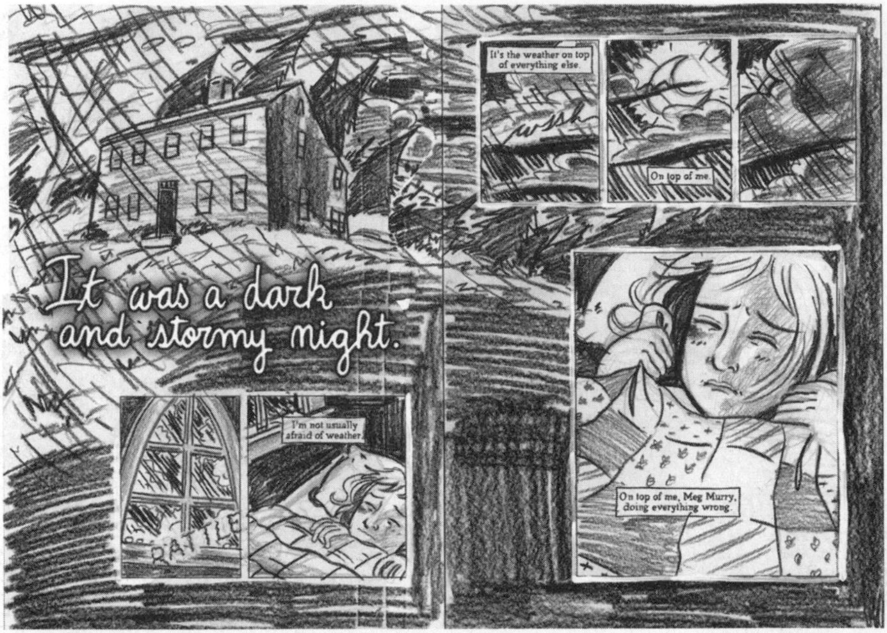
It was a dark and stormy night.
RATTLE
I'm not usually afraid of weather.
It's the weather on top of everything else.
wssh
On top of me.
On top of me, Meg Murry, doing everything wrong.

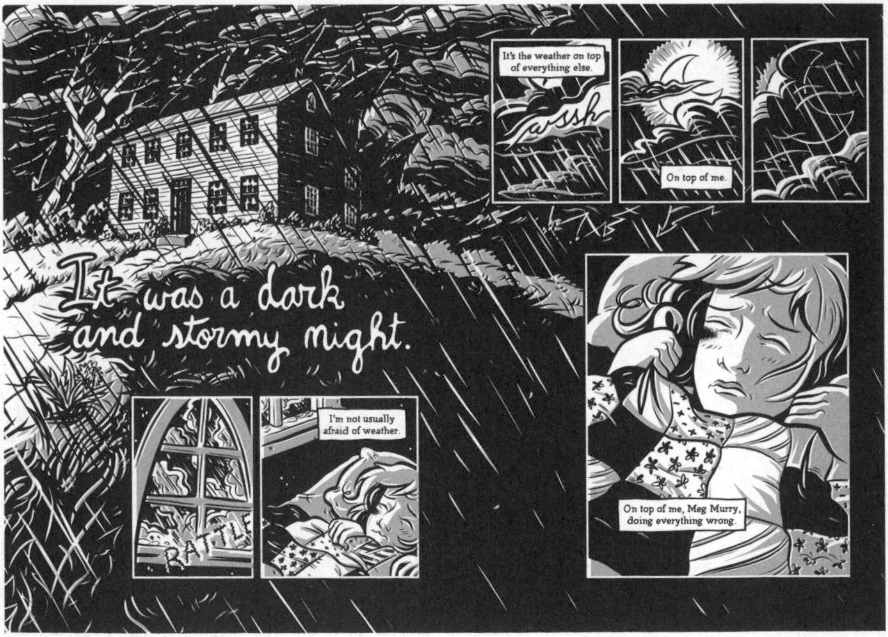
It was a dark and stormy night.
RATTLE
I'm not usually afraid of weather.
It's the weather on top of everything else.
wssh
On top of me.
On top of me, Meg Murry, doing everything wrong.

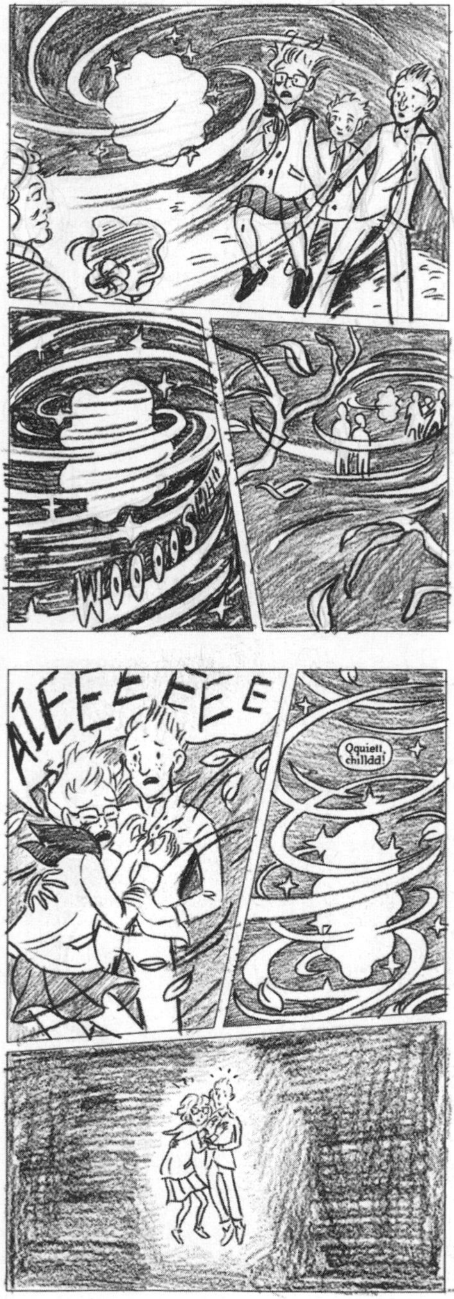
Qquiett, chilldd!

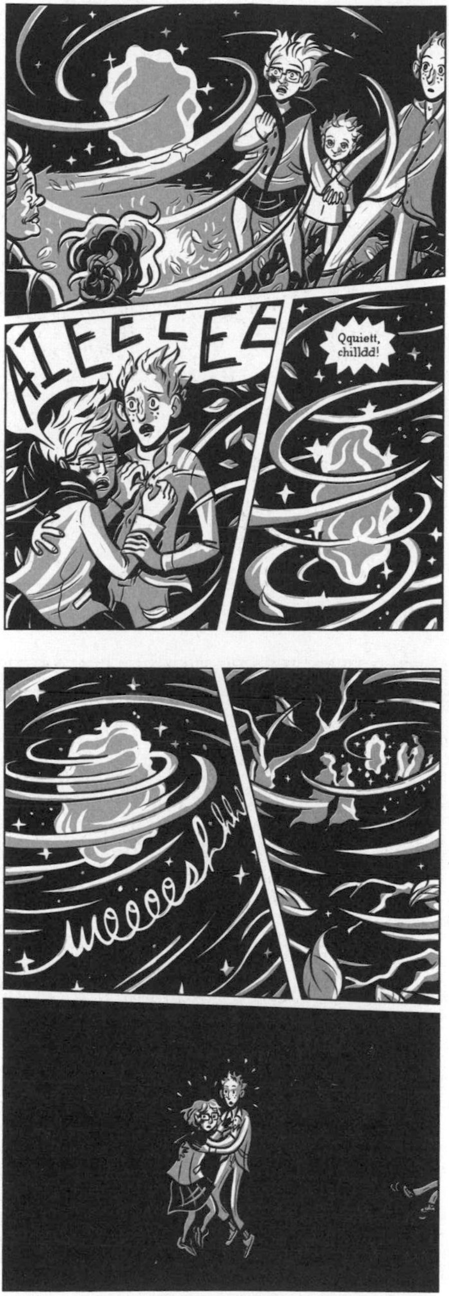
Qquiett, chilldd!

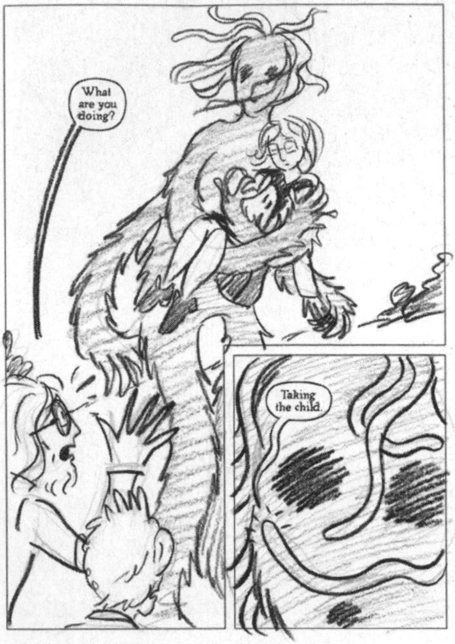
What are you doing?
Taking the child.

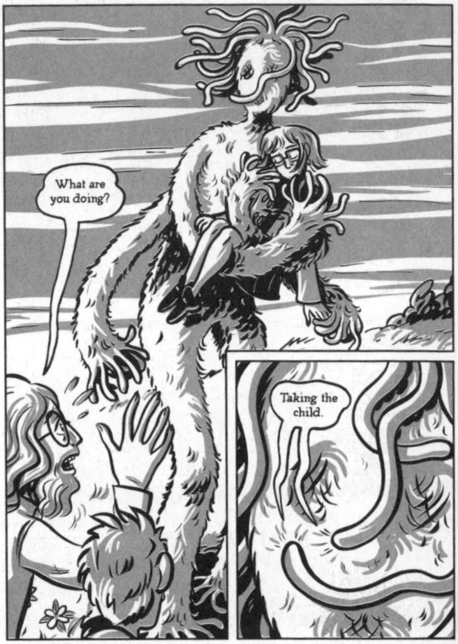
What are you doing?
Taking the child.

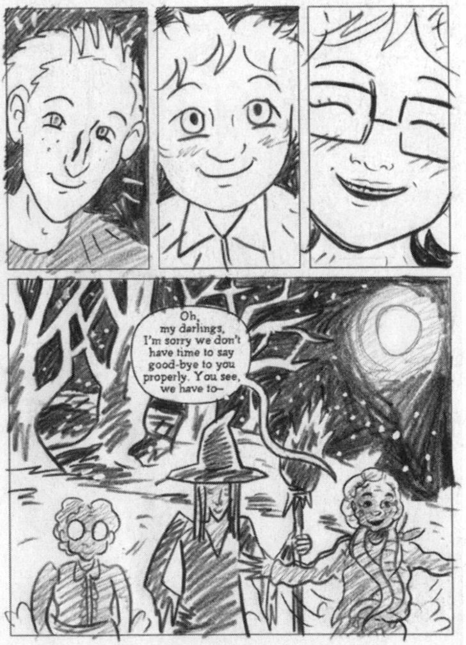
Oh, my darlings, I'm sorry we don't have time to say good-bye to you properly. You see, we have to–

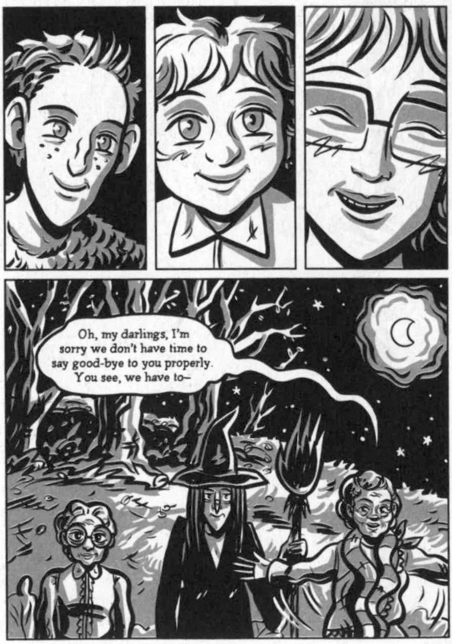
Oh, my darlings, I'm sorry we don't have time to say good-bye to you properly. You see, we have to–

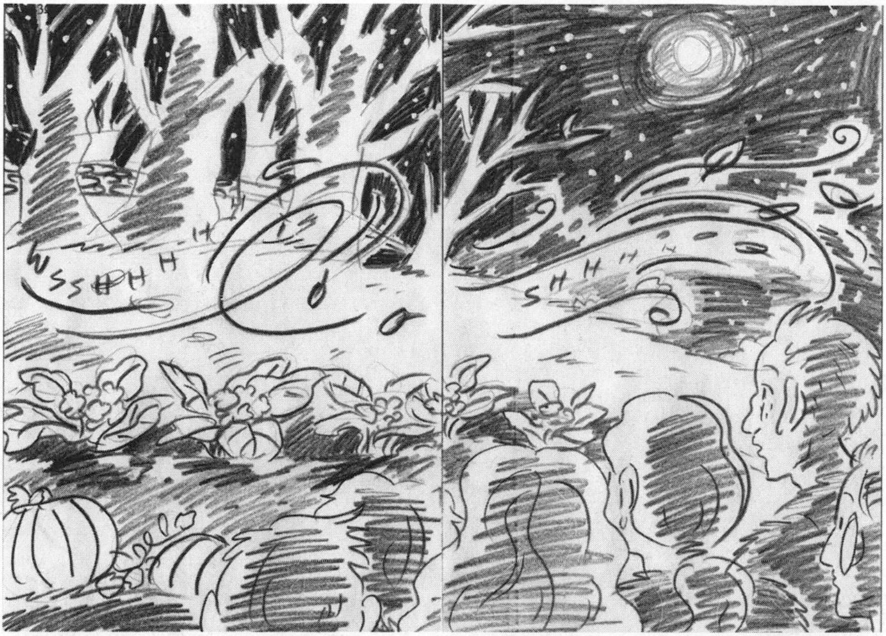

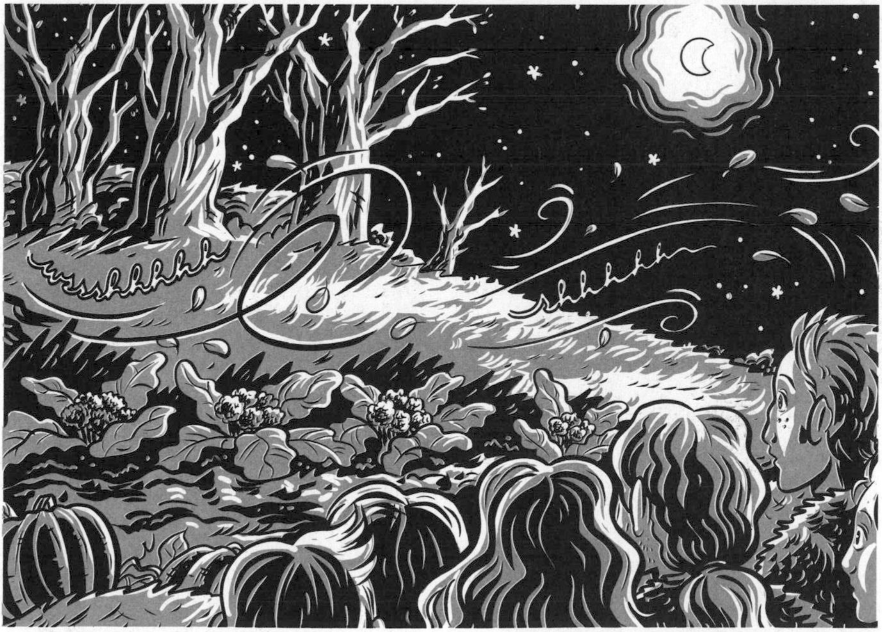
wsshhhhhh
shhhhhh

Discussion Questions

1. This graphic novel was adapted from a classic prose novel. Adaptations are very common—many movies and plays were originally books. What is unique about adapting a book into a graphic novel? How is it similar to adapting a book into a play or movie?

2. Before they confront IT, Meg, Calvin, and Charles Wallace are given gifts. Calvin's natural gift of communication is strengthened, Meg is given her faults, and Charles Wallace is given the resilience of his childhood. What gift do you think you would receive from Mrs Whatsit?

3. IT argues that everyone is safer and happier because IT controls them—but obviously Camazotz is a very scary place. What do you think is the right balance between freedom and playing by the rules?

4. Meg, Charles Wallace, and Calvin rely on instincts to make many of their decisions. What do you think of this strategy? Do you trust your own instincts?

5. Many graphic novels represent three dimensions on a piece of paper—but this one had to represent two, three, and more dimensions when the children traveled via tesseract.